AFTER THE RAIN

Anwer Dherma

New Generation Publishing

Published in 2009 by New Generation Publishing

After the Rain

First Edition

Published by New Generation Publishing

For more information regarding the author and his work go to

go to http://arbackyard.com

For all the people of Manchester and Salford...

ONE

What was that whistling noise? Fuck me, it was loud. What the hell was it? It was high pitched and it appeared to be growing louder and louder like that of a crazy banshee doing her best to break through my already restless sleep. Had Donna opened – or for that matter left the window open? All I knew for certain was the noise grew stronger and stronger as I shook my head and tried to open my eyes... but what the hell was going on? Now I couldn't seem to open my eyes. This was trippy as fuck I thought instantly reaching for my eyes – but what was this? Something was covering my eyes – was it the duvet? I didn't think it was. But what the hell was it if it wasn't the duvet?

As I started to panic I grabbed at whatever it was blinding me so and as I struggled with whatever the material was, I started to roll and I felt the hard, abrasive surface against my body. Now that surely couldn't be the bed could it? Jesus – this wasn't right was it I thought to myself as the noise grew louder and more piercing.

My fingers gripped at the material that was blinding my vision. It felt rough to my touch as I tore away at it – and shards of light started to break through as I pulled and pulled frantically at the material that I now noticed was bandage like as it shred away from my face and I sat up right with utter shock – staring in sheer bewilderment at my surrounding. For I wasn't in bed at all – in fact I wasn't even in my flat – *what the fuck!*

I was sat there all alone in the middle of the road. In fact it was the bridge that crossed from one side of Bonsall Street to other. I stared disbelievingly at my surroundings of the estate where I had always resided – yet something *wasn't* right. In

4

fact this entire scenario wasn't right – everything was in harsh blacks, greys and whites – and everywhere was deserted. There wasn't a living soul in sight. In fact there wasn't even a car or any kind of vehicle for that matter to be seen anywhere.

As I stared at the obvious dull spectrum of Manchester's skyline I suddenly realised that was where the high pitched squeal was deriving from. Staring back down at my hands they were covered in the bandages that had blinded me. They were also covered in blood. And that was the next weird thing that struck me, for the blood was the only thing in colour that I could see. The dark crimson streaks covered the material and my hands as I threw the bloodied material to the road and clambered unsteadily to my feet.

As I stood there I looked all around me as everything began to spin faster and faster as all the blacks and greys whipped around me. The bloodied material that had blinded me was now caught up within the vortex of where I stood grounded to the spot. It felt as though I was caught in the middle of a tornado as the screeching sound pierced my ears. I found myself unwittingly closing my eyes tight and covering my ears to block out what was happening – tighter and tighter until that damn squealing banshee who was caught up in the cyclone started to deafen me.

I felt my mouth drop open as I began to scream – *not in pain* – but to try and drown out the deafening sound that was engulfing me. As I dropped to my knees and felt what could have been tears flowing through the fingers that covered my eyes as I pulled them away and opened my eyes I realised that there was blood pouring from my eyes. In fact it wasn't just pouring – it was gushing – spraying widely and as I shook my head it sprayed extravagantly thrashing against the vortex that was closing in on me – closer – nearer – almost there.

I stayed rooted to the spot helplessly – the blood began to hit the spinning mayhem that imprisoned me in small and large splashes. And against the dull blacks, greys and whites they started to resemble a Jackson Pollack painting, which then reminded me of the Stone Roses album cover.

All I could hear was the sound of my screams and the screams of the crazy witch who was closing in on me along with the fortification of the hurricane that was a engulfing who I was – *closer* – nearer – *even closer* – fuck this I suddenly thought leaping from where I was knelt.

I stood defiantly toe to toe with the environment within where I felt imprisoned. And as I opened my eyes fully I allowed the blood to combat the fatality that was about to take me. I raised my arms and my screams suddenly turned into words.

'What the fuck do you want?' I yelled my defiance and started to bang my chest in almost a Neanderthal way whilst wiping the blood from my eyes and as I did so. The vortex suddenly without hesitation began to draw away from me slowly – then a little faster and then suddenly the noise that had started all of this mayhem to begin with, began to twist and turn almost as though it was caught up in whirlwind as it spun and twisted away from me faster and faster – *quicker and quicker* – as it then spun out of control.

The tornado was sent crashing into the balconies of decrepit squats and flats that surrounded Hulme and the estate – shattering all of its windows as it did so. I watched it disappear, continuing its path of mass destruction in both the direction of Manchester's city centre and the direction of Moss Side.

I noticed that my eyes had stopped bleeding, but that there was still blood everywhere – *covering me* – and the road where I was stood. It also looked as though the blood that has been caught in the twisting coil of deadliness had carried its way across all of the surrounding buildings creating those wild splashes of what I had earlier described as Pollack's artwork. In fact I realised instantaneously that in fact it was still the only thing that was in colour as everything – and I mean everything – was still in those dull shades of non existent colour.

I felt the silence overwhelm my surroundings once again as I stared at my estate. What had happened? What was happening? Where was everybody? I turned to face the block of flats where Donna and I – where in fact most of the crew lived and saw the near destruction of what had taken place. It looked as though Manchester had been hit with a nuclear bomb – Had it been? This just wasn't right. Had a bomb taken out everything and everyone I knew – or for that matter *everybody,* as nobody was in sight – *I mean nobody* – nothing – what the fuck was this shit?

As fear took hold of me – *not fear for myself* – but my first thoughts were for Donna, who when I had last seen her was lay beside me in bed. Without a second thought I ran towards the block of deserted flats – when I heard the screams high above me again, I stopped and stared at the skyline as I saw what couldn't have been, for they looked like vultures circling high above the Manchester skyline. And there wasn't just one or two of them, for there was so many that the skyline began to darken with their wings that spread out in what resembled that of a dark angel. Their squawks were high pitched as they waited patiently to come and take advantage and devour whatever was left from what had taken place.

Sprinting towards the stairs I leapt three steps at a time until I reached our floor and ran like a man possessed down the series of what now appeared to be never ending balconies. They were balconies that for some strange reason, I didn't appear to fully recognise. Despite the fact I spent my entire life here. I suddenly found myself at my flat door and without even trying the door handle, I kicked through it and ran up the stairs to the bedroom and crashed violently through the door as I did so... Only to discover the room had been vacated. No Donna – no bed – in fact there wasn't anything at all in the room that had been completely stripped of all its belongings.

I couldn't comprehend what was happening it was all so confusing. Hearing a noise outside I sprinted down the stairs and out onto the balcony as I stared down at Bonsall Street in disbelief – *absolute disbelief.* For there was a parade of Rhinoceros's traipsing down the street. In fact an entire herd was scrambling with panic written clearly all over their faces. It was almost as though they were running scared from something that was chasing them... But I mean – what the hell would Rhinoceros's be scared of?

Just then without any warning – as was usually the case in Manchester, the skies opened up as the very familiar, torrential downpour began to pound down against every possible surface. And as the rain pelted down with sheer ferocity the herd began to thin out I saw someone walking calmly behind them – it was Scotty – *Scotty was down there –* but this strange – even stranger than the herd of Rhinoceros's. For Scotty had his mouth bandaged and I could clearly see that he too had blood seeping through the bandaged mouth. His mouth was bandaged like my eyes had been and with the rain striking down upon him the water was staining the blood as the streaks of blood ran freely from his mouth area down the front of the white shirt he was wearing.

The other bizarre thing was that he was surrounded – surrounded I might add by what look like a herd of farm animals. An entire assortment of beasts from sheep to cows to chickens to pigs – in fact lots of pigs – there was an assortment of all kinds of pigs in various sizes and shapes and they were everywhere.

I called out his name, but it fell on deaf ears. Not only his but mine also as the noise from the farm animals grew louder and louder and louder along with the deafening screeches coming from high above in the form of the vultures. It so deafening in fact that I couldn't even hear my own voice – or for that matter the sound of someone approaching.

As I felt their presence at the last moment I turned to see only the sight of the glistening steel against the concrete backdrop slicing through the air as I felt the pain of the machete striking down into my face, forcing itself with complete ease down through the right side of my face as I gritted my teeth against the shocking pain of what had just been inflicted.

My head was spinning from the shock and confusion as it mingled into one, as I began to recover. But only to see the viscous, blood stained, lethal blade striking back down towards me once again, as I noticed my predator was undeniably Paddy from Salford. And behind Paddy, was Chris who was holding a baseball bat – smacking it menacingly against his hands. As I saw the blade within millimetres of the oncoming onslaught that was inevitable to me, I threw my fist back in vain at Paddy as I suddenly felt time shift – and with that I also felt myself violently shift with it – as I was bizarrely floating – floating away from where I had been like that of a spirit. But maybe that's what it was?

Had Paddy just killed me? Is this what happened at the time of death? Was it really like this I thought as I saw the two of them still stood there on the balcony with the rain drenching them as they stared in what appeared to be their own scepticism as they watched me float away in such a surreal manner.

Yet at the same time it appeared very clearly to me as though I could perceive my bloodied lifeless body still lay there motionlessly on the balcony before the two of them. The vultures were still circling above me and they seemed to call out to me in their strange voices, which in that very moment and time I felt I completely understood as I floated towards them. To join them in unison as I felt my arms spread wide – wider – *wider* – as my head dropped back and I allowed

8

whatever was about to happen take it's course as the rain that was beating down upon my face felt so good at that moment in time.

As I opened my eyes I saw Sean high above me and he was smiling like he always smiled. He held his arms open in a welcoming gesture and I realised that he was okay – *that he was in fact fine* – he was still here with me – with us for that matter. And that's when I saw him begin to drift away from me as I approached him faster and faster as the rain began to dissipate and then finally stop. And after the rain ceased, and the skies cleared, turning a dazzling blend of crystal blues, Sean was almost out of sight as he moved further and further away from me as I called out his name clear as day to me, 'Sean – Sean – Nooooo.'

'Chopper – *Chopper* – Wake up Chopper – *Chopper* – Come on you're sweating – *Wake up.*' The voice called to me as I struggled once again to open my eyes shaking my head as I did so and as light began to creep in and force them apart. Was it the vultures calling? Was it the voice of angels? Was it... before I could finish the thought I felt myself shoot up right shivering as I did so... I found myself sat there still in bed – sweating and breathing hard as I shook my head to try and bring myself round from the nightmare in which I just been so viciously trapped.

'You okay Chopper?' It was Donna sat next to me on the bed as I stared vacantly back at her. 'You've been restless all night. Are you alright?'

'Jesus,' I answered realising what had just happened. This was fucking weird – I mean I didn't have that many dreams – not that I could ever remember. And definitely not like that thing. Not like the nightmare that was still so vivid in my mind as I suddenly began to smile realising that's all it had been.

'That was fucking bizarre Donna. Jesus Christ what the fuck was that?'

'It's the funeral Chopper,' replied Donna ignoring my comment as she brought me crashing back down into the reality of what was about to take place. 'You sure you're okay?'

'Yeah,' I sighed. 'Just some trippy fuckin' dream is all.' I smiled as best as I could at her, as she stroked away the hair that was stuck to my forehead of sweat. 'I'll be alright.' I told her as I rolled away from her and stared at the wall before me

thinking about what had to be the creepiest fucking dream I'd
ever had.

TWO

They had finally released Sean's body almost two weeks later for burial. The funeral was held on a Thursday morning, eight limousines had been booked for family members and people from the crew close to Sean. Prey had made all of the arrangements for the service, informing his family that they need not worry about any of the costs. It was the least that could be done.

I was stood by myself, away from the rest of the group as I stared out onto the estate where the stretched dark vehicles awaited us. And in that very moment I realised that they were perceived in two very different lights.

'Are you alright Chopper?' Donna asked me as I stood under by the stairwell that led out to Bonsall Street. 'How are you feeling?'

'I'm just glad that we are finally laying Sean to rest y'know,' I told her, kissing her as I did. I glanced up at the darkening skyline that hung heavily Manchester's city centre and was instantaneously brought back the nightmare I'd had endured only hours before. It was weird though, for it fitted the sombre mood that was more than apparent on everyone's faces around us.

Looking back at the estate that surrounded us, once again feeling the aftermath of the dream that had taken hold of me, I felt a deep ache. Not for how we choose to live our lives – but for how Sean's had ended. I let out a deep sigh and I smiled as best as I could at Donna for the second time that morning, as she stood there before me with tears brimming beneath her blood shot eyes which suggested that she hadn't had the best of nights sleep either.

11

'I'm really glad we're finally able to do that at least Donna,' I finally replied.

'It's still so hard to believe,' she answered wiping at the tears that were starting to congregate at the base of her eyes.

I felt his presence as I always did for some strange reason before he was even close to me. As I looked from Donna to the direction of Prey as he approached, I watched – observing – as all the people around him, without trying to do so, yet failing so miserably in trying – stared admiringly at the character with whom they all either admired or feared. Prey was a formidable character and one that I was more than happy to be on the right side of.

'Alright Chopper? Are you ready for this?' he asked ignoring all of those around him and laying all of his concentration before me.

'In remembrance of Sean eh?' I replied nodding as I did so, as we both embraced one another in a rare moment of open emotion. 'May he never be forgotten Prey.'

As Donna watched us she began to cry, as did Helen whom was stood near by with Kathy. I couldn't help but feel more than a little overwhelmed by the events that were taking place in the aftermath of Sean's slaying at the hands of Paddy, after the Stone Roses gig at Spike Island in Widnes.

As the precession made its way down Bonsall Street, I remember looking out through the darkened windows at all the people that were watching from those series upon series of incessant balconies. Those that weren't attending the funeral itself that was. The sight only deepened my sorrow to a further level as Donna sat next to me squeezed my hand compassionately.

It was also impossible not to notice that the vast amount of police that were everywhere that day. And I mean *everywhere*. Armed police were openly wandering the streets of Hulme and they even had a police helicopter that was circling the area. I figured as I observed all this, that they were so paranoid of any trouble starting, as there was so many of Manchester's and its surrounding boroughs so called Gangsters... well as they police liked to think of them anyway.

They were all attending Sean's funeral out of respect. The sight of what they witnessed on the streets of Hulme that morning must have scared the hell out them. In fact thinking about it, there probably hadn't been such a congregation of so many of Manchester's main head's, as they were better known to us, in one place at one time in as many years.

There was near to three hundred people that had attended the funeral that day. Because of this, only those closest to Sean were able to fit inside the church itself for the service.

It had been a nice respectful service in honour of Sean and I was at peace knowing that he had finally been finally laid to rest. And that now that he had – we could get on with just what it was that we was about to do in order to seek vengeance for what had taken place.

As we were leaving the church to be taken the short distance over the road to The Parkway pub, where it didn't seem that long ago I'd been celebrating my eighteenth birthday. Only now we were there for a very much different reason. As I walked towards the vechile it was obvious that two plain clothed policemen were watching us with about as much discretion as a bull in a china shop. I stared coldly at them then glanced at Prey who shook his head at me.

'What the fuck!' I exclaimed spitting my words ignoring Prey. I was instantly infuriated by the mere sight of them. For it was obvious that they were not part of the patrol keeping an eye on the crowd. They were separate and they were here for different reasons. I was certain of it.

'That's them Chopper,' Donna stated as she nodded in their direction placing her arm on mine to try and calm my anger. 'That's the two that interviewed me at the station in Widnes.'

'You fuckin' what! They're 'ere today,' I was suddenly filled with even more cold rage towards them both.

'Chopper... Easy ar'kid...' Prey said with warning eyes that glared at me as he saw me head straight for them.

'What the fuck are you two doing 'ere?' I snarled at them, 'Couple of no good fuckin' pigs,' I added spitting the last words out at them furious at them being here.

'Alright Chorlton? Sorry – Chopper ain't it?' The shorter of the two said to me – who I have to admit looked familiar to me, but I couldn't quite place the face.

'Do I know you or something?' I asked. 'Or do you all just stink the same stink?' I was enraged at the mere sight of them.

'Damn shame what happened to Macreedy,' the taller one said totally ignoring my comment and whom at first glance I did not recognise, but who it has to said held a certain air of

13

authority about him. 'Pity you weren't there on the night itself Chopper. You could have possibly helped him eh?'

'You fuckin' what!' I snarled back at him. I'd known exactly what the comment had meant. 'You accusing me of something or what? You think maybe I should give my brief a call and we talk about harassment?'

'We were just wondering if you could shed any light onto what actually happened that night Chorlton.' The taller one calmly commented.

'Ain't you two got any respect or what?'

'Well we were just in the vicinity. That's all Chopper,' the shorter one said. 'Just thought we'd drop by and check you're all okay,' he added sarcastically.

'We just wanted to pay our respects to a dead crook. Maybe if you'd been there on the night it could have been two...' the taller one sneered at me with a knowing smile.

But all this did was completely enrage me, not only was it disrespectful towards Sean. But in not so many words he'd just wished me dead also. Without a second thought I flew at the two of them with wild anger coursing through my veins just as Prey suddenly reached out and yanked me back.

'Just back the fuck off....'

'Alright O'Prey? How's it going? Long time no see,' said the shorter one, who was still smiling at me, knowing what he was doing was working in winding me up at the same time.

Prey still had hold of me refusing to let me go. 'Alright Walshy. It's been a while ain't it,' Prey grinned back at him winking at me as he did so.

I suddenly remembered where I knew him from. It was from all those years ago when we were interviewed in Crumpsall after the fight with Paddy, Prey and both crews.

'Certainly has O'Prey,' Walsh then smirked knowingly at the two of us. 'How you lads been? Very active from what we've been hearing lately?'

'Why don't you two just go home and let Sean rest in peace,' Prey told them shaking his head as he did so. Then smiling at the two of them he began looking around and then up towards the sky. 'You seen how many heads are 'ere today Walshy? Even with all these coppers around you – and a police helicopter for that matter. Well – you see its funny how two people could merely disappear from sight.' He clicked his fingers and nodded knowingly at the two of them, before adding. 'Just like that.'

'You trying to threaten us Prey?' the second one snarled as he suddenly noticed, that as Prey had snapped his fingers, everybody surrounding us had turned their full attention to the situation that was taking place.

'I ain't trying,' he smirked knowingly at them as the scar that rolled down his face twitched. 'Stevenson ain't it?'

'There better be no fucking trouble following Macreedy's death you hear me,' said Stevenson who'd now been identified to us.

'How's trouble going to be caused?' said Donna stepping forward. 'If you pathetic wankers haven't even got a suspect yet?' she snapped.

'Hello Miss. Hayes,' Stevenson said sarcastically.

It was just then that the cars began to move toward the exit, rolling by us coming to a halt. The second car was closest to us and the doors opened on the opposite side to where the Detectives now stood as we walked away from the confrontation.

'You better catch the ones responsible for ar'kids slaying,' Prey said still holding eye contact with them before ducking down into the car.

I couldn't help but smile knowingly at the two of them still stood there, as they obviously felt more than a little uncomfortable by the large crowd that had started to close in on them menacingly.

'Who the fuck were they?' asked Steve, who had been keeping a low profile in the back of the limousine as we joined him there. The smell of the interior was one of detergent – I wasn't even sure why now noticed it at that moment in time but I did. As I made myself comfortable and looked out of the mirrored windows, as the car rolled past the two Detectives – they turned and walked away from the crowd pushing their way past everybody.

'That's who questioned me,' Donna told him.

'I can't believe those fucks turned up today of all fuckin' days.' I snapped. 'Sean's funeral. It's just so fuckin' disrespectful.'

'We all know Chopper,' Prey said looking at me. 'But you just got to calm that temper of yours down. You hear me?'

'I know – It's just...' I started to say but trailed off.

'Don't get me wrong Chopper,' Prey smiled. 'It's good to have sometimes. But you've just got to control it brother.'

'What's going to happen now Sean's buried?' Donna asked bluntly.

'Don't you worry about that,' I told her.

'Well don't you give me that sort of answer then,' Donna snapped back at me.

'Get them – get all of them. For what they did – you must get them. They must be punished,' Helen said weakly from beside where Donna sat as tears continued to tumble down her face.

'Just don't you worry about it,' Steve smiled at her, as he took her hands into his – then nodded at me and winked as he did so.

He knew that now Sean was laid to rest... That revenge would be taken.

'How fuckin' long Prey?' I protested. 'At least twelve months. C'mon, I know we said we'd wait. But they killed him for fucks sake.' The four of us were situated out of way in the back room that the landlord had let Prey use – Quite simply so that we were out of ears way.

'It does make sense Chopper,' Steve said.

'They'll be all over us if we do it too soon,' Prey told me.

'The chief's right brother,' Sleeper declared. 'You know you lads are going to have to watch out for any action that goes down after this. Sean was a connected lad, the old bill know this. They'll be itching for you to fuck up and do something stupid.'

'Yeah,' Prey added. 'And think about it this way. Paddy's going to think it's all forgotten about. That he's got away with it.'

'Look I know what you're all saying,' I sighed. 'It's just – y'know...'

'We know Chopper,' Steve was nodding at me. 'Look you lads know that even though it ain't my thing to go getting involved with this kind of thing. Well I just want you to count me in on whatever it is that you decide to do.'

'Cheers Steve, that's really appreciated mate,' Prey told him.

'What you've got to do is keep your mouths shut about who done this,' Sleeper declared. 'Play dumb on that score. Even to the rest of the crew,' he was shaking his head at us. 'Guaranteed, this Paddy ain't going to go shouting his mouth off about it. Not unless he wants the police involved.'

'No fucker knows anything,' I stated. 'Everybody concerned has kept stum about it. I think the crew knows we know. But even so, they must know why we're keeping ar' mouths shut about it.'

'Good. Now just one other thing,' Sleeper stared directly at me. 'You've got to keep your cool on this one Chopper.'

'That right,' Prey injected. 'We all know that Paddy is going to be about town and that we're going to run into him... What you got to promise though is that you won't pop him right there and then. You hear me?'

'It'll be hard.' I replied.

'The last thing we need is to go loosing you Chopper,' Steve said smiling at me.

'Alright then,' I nodded in agreement. 'But what I can't promise is that if he goes making the first move that I won't react back.'

'Just try,' Prey said sternly. 'For all of ar' sakes.'

'Sean's too brother,' Sleeper added.

THREE

Awakening from my extreme hangover Friday afternoon, it was safe to say that I felt like complete shite. We'd stayed after hours in The Parkway drinking until the early hours of the morning. We'd been talking, remembering all of the good times – and bad – which we'd had with Sean over the years. It was hard to imagine that he was gone forever – that he'd been killed.

I mean we weren't stupid… We all knew the dangers of the involvement within the world in which we lived. But the realities had been brought so close to home. Sean had been – *just as Prey had*

and still was – like a mentor to me. I'd loved the guy like he was family. And I suppose in a way that he was as close to family had been – proper family that is.

'You alright Chopper?' asked Donna who lay next to me and was already awake staring at me.

'Apart from the fact that I've got a mouth like a vulture's armpit – I suppose I'm alright girl,' I confirmed rubbing my head and sore eyes in unison.

'Don't ever leave me will you,' Donna suddenly said to me in a gust of what I imagine had built up, in whatever amount of time she'd been lay there awake.

I turned on my side to face her properly with a genuine look of shock upon my face.

'You what Donna?'

'I'm scared Chopper,' she clearly had tears rolling down her face, and I noticed immediately that she'd obviously been awake and crying for quite some time as both her hair and the

18

pillow were soaked. 'I know I try not to show it – but really deep down… I'm so scared.'

'Why?' I asked taking her in my arms. 'What's the matter?'

'You know what the matter is,' she began to sob uncontrollably. 'I know what you're going to do. You're going to kill Paddy – Aren't you?'

'Don't worry about it Donna,' I replied as that was about all that I could manage. I wanted to tell her that we wasn't going to do anything – it's just that I loved this girl and honestly didn't want to lie to her.

'What if he comes after you?'

'Look, why don't we head into town.'

She pulled away shoving me hard as she did so. 'See… See what you're doing,' she snapped at me. 'You're just changing the subject so not to deal with it.'

'No I'm not,' I was protesting holding my hands up defensively. 'The reason I ain't saying anything is 'cause it don't concern you.'

'How the fuck doesn't it concern me?' she snapped again 'The fact I might lose you – has nothing to do with me?'

'You ain't going to lose me.'

'What if that had been you fatally shot? Killed – Just like Sean was that night.' She was pushing me away again almost as if she couldn't stand to be near me.

'Well that's exactly the point… Ain't it Donna,' I sneered the words back at her. She didn't half pick her bleeding times. My head was wankered and she was giving me grief. I just didn't need this shit right now so I let her know it. 'Go on Donna. Just close your eyes and imagine that it had been me.'

This only made her cry even more – and for that matter make me feel like even more of a shit for dong so. But truth be told she had to hear this.

'No – No – I don't want to.' She sobbed clinging onto to me.

'Alright – well let's just say for arguments sake 'ere that it had been me buried yesterday. That it had been my funeral,' I said, taking her in my arms. 'What do you think? That it would have just been forgotten about? That Prey and Sean would have let it pass? Y'know – like nothing had happened?'

'I'm so sorry Chopper,' she suddenly began sobbing uncontrollably again, as she suddenly realised just what would have been done if it had in fact been me killed that night. 'I'm just scared that's all. I never want to lose you.'

19

'Just don't think about it,' I responded, kissing her wet face and as we began to kiss more passionately – then overcome with what had just passed and the feeling of loss – we began to grab at one another – tearing at each others underwear as we both collapsed onto the bed engulfed with a mix of passion and loss rolled into one.

'How's it going mate?' I asked Prey as he opened the front door, rubbing his weary eyes as he did so
'Alrighed Chopper – Shit my head is banging.'
I laughed at him as I made my way through the door. 'I know mate. I was exactly the same. Donna's gone to see how Helen is after yesterday. I thought I'd make breakfast for us.'
'Sounds like a top idea. What time is it anyway?' He yawned, stretching as he did so.
'Put it this way. It ain't breakfast time. How many for anyway Prey?' I enquired, stretching and yawning in unison as if it was contagious. 'Is Sleeper, Eazy and Lisa still 'ere?'
'Nah mate. They headed back first thing; Sleeper had shit to take care of down that way. And Eazy had to get back to the shop.'
'So it's three then? I take it Kathy's upstairs.'
'Nah fuck that,' he laughed. 'I sent her straight home after a nosh last night. Just wasn't in the mood.'
'That's a first ain't it?' I laughed closing the front door behind me.
'It's still for three though,' he continued laughing. 'Steve's on the settee in there,' he grinned pointing towards the living room.
'Sweet mate,' I said, smiling at him. 'Are we going to mention that thing to him today?'
'Reckon so,' he replied disappearing upstairs.

I ended up cooking shit loads for us to eat. Bacon, sausages, mushrooms, an assortment of egg dishes, black pudding, toast, French toast and freshly sliced breads with a lot of black coffee.
'You know something lads,' Steve said through a mouthful of sausage. 'You notice how much weight that Scotty kid has lost?'
'Yeah,' replied Prey glancing at me. 'I noticed that last night,' he added, passing me a smouldering spliff.

'I seen it,' I was nodding at the two of them. 'The thing is I reckon it's just the amount of Es he's been dropping, that's all.'

'You sure Chopper?' Steve asked. 'He's really drawn in the face for just that. Plus he was pissed up last night and kept asking me last night all sorts of questions. You know, shit like where I knew you lot from and what did I do. Crazy – nosey shit like that.'

'What you tell him?' Prey enquired.

'Just that me and you was old mates. That's all. I mean I don't tell anybody shit – you should know that by now,' he said throwing another sausage into his mouth.

'Keep it that way. Only those concerned know who you are,' Prey stated.

'What the fuck was he asking you questions for,' I said thinking out loud. 'Anyway, I checked with Diamond. You know to see if he was hammering the rocks or not.'

'What's he say?' Prey asked.

'Says no way,' I told them. 'Says that neither Scotty, nor his bird for that matter buys them.'

'What about smack?' Steve asked, now making himself a bacon and egg toastie.

'No way man,' Prey shook his head. 'Not Scotty – he'd never touch that shit.'

'Ain't that the truth? Y'know that me and him go way back to being little kids together,' I declared, smiling at the thought. 'We never went near the shit. Detested it. That's why I thought that it might have been the rocks.'

'Every cunt likes that shit,' Steve said. 'I could see how any fucker could get a nice little habit on that gear.'

'What do you think it is Chopper?' Prey enquired.

'I reckon he's just missing my cooking,' I laughed.

'I reckon you could be right there,' Steve grinned throwing his fourth sausage into his mouth.

I sat there as silence (apart from the noise of Steve eating of course) took over as we all were left there with our own thoughts. I thought about Scotty, I hadn't seen that much lately. It was funny how things – how life turned out. I mean that I was till close to him – yet it wasn't how it used to be anymore. Anyway – changing the subject I looked at Steve and smiled. 'We got a proposition for you.'

He swallowed his sausage. 'What's that then?' he enquired gong to work on the black pudding.

'Well me and Chopper have been talking about something Steve. Just wondered if you might be interested,' Prey smiled at the older man.

'Well... You going to tell me what the fuck it is or not?' he took a bite of his French toast with the black pudding that was also covered in egg yolk.

'How do you feel about becoming a full partner?' I asked him.

'Shit – Are you lads serious?' He almost choked as he said the words.

'Don't we look serious old man,' Prey laughed at the yellow yolk dribbling down his chin.

'So you want in or not?' I smiled at him.

'Shit! Of course I do,' he said gulping his coffee to wash down his food. 'I just can't believe you lad's have asked me.'

'Well we figured that you were already in on most of it with us anyways,' Prey smiled. 'So it just seems right to make you a full partner.'

'Only thing is, you'll just need to put in the purchasing capitol. Sean's money has been taken out and distributed to his family and we even made sure that Helen got her cut too. But then after that it's an even split between the three of us,' I told him. 'But as far as the crew knows, things stay the same as before. The last thing we need is to bring heat down on you... *or us for that matter.*'

'Sounds good to me lads,' he grinned sticking his fork into one of Prey's left over sausages. 'Sure sounds good to me,' he added, as the sausage disappeared through his open mouth.

We both laughed at him. 'You enjoy that Steve?'

'Course mate' he chuckled at me like a small child who just polished off a bag full of sweets. 'Any chance of doing some more, Chopper?'

Seven months had passed since Sean's slaying and it was a known fact that Paddy was back knocking around town, although I hadn't seen him myself. We'd taken much stricter measures concerning business matters since Sean's death. No risks could be taken and to be honest I'd spent pretty much the entire duration as quietly as possible. Despite the development of the clubbing scene which appeared to grow to greater heights more and more as each week past us by. I'd not felt like going out much, which had its plus side as this had pleased Donna immensely.

If truth be told, our week nights were spent mainly in front of the television watching videos or listening to music. Between the three of us we'd set things up so they almost ran themselves, whilst we sat back reaping the vast benefits brought back in from business.

It was the way it had to be for the time being. The additional police activity in the area was also growing, so we distanced ourselves from the business. It was as Sleeper had told us. Until Paddy was taken care of, this was the way things had to be.

It was early Wednesday evening when the phone rang. Donna and I were just settling in for yet another night in front of the box. Oh what joy eh?

'Chopper mate, it's Jonah.'

'Yes mate,' I answered pleased, yet also a little concerned to hear his voice on the other end of the line. 'What's up? Is everything alright?' I could hear a lot of commotion in the background.

'It's Scotty mate.' He replied.

'What's happened and where the fuck are you?'

'Dry Bar mate. Kezlo's sat with him now,' he told me. 'He's fucked up on gear mate. He's wasted big time Chopper. Jackie and him had some argument or some bullshit. He's gobbing off and shit. Look Chopper I ain't grassing or anything. But you two go back a long way and I just thought that you... Well y'know, you should know about it, kinda thing.'

'Sweet Jonah thanks a lot,' I honestly told him, after all I was still concerned about Scotty. 'Look I tell you what. You two stay with him. I'll come straight down there, alright.'

'Alright Chopper,' he said as the line just went dead.

I replaced the receiver and turned as Donna eyed me quizzically. 'Is everything alright?'

'I ain't sure y'know,' I replied, concerned as I always was for my best mate – Scotty.

'That was Jonah. He says that Scotty's fucked up in Dry Bar. I'm going to find out what the fucks the matter.'

'Wait a minute,' replied Donna as she rose from the settee. 'I'll come with you. In fact I'll drive.'

Donna eased her silver Mini Cooper behind Dry Bar. I really hated this car with a passion, with me being over six feet tall; it was way too fucking small for me to get comfortable in. I'd really wanted to buy her something else once she'd passed her driving test, but the moment she'd seen this little silver car she'd fallen in love with it,   Therefore I'd obviously purchased the bloody thing against my better judgement.

As soon as we entered Dry Bar we spotted the three of them seated at the back area, Kezlo was eagerly waving us over as we headed in that direction.

'Chopper, yes mate – and Donna, how you two doing?' Scotty asked whose milky looking eyes were completely screwed up. 'What are you two doing 'ere?'

'We're sweet Scotty,' I replied embracing him trying my best to ignore how messed up he was. 'How about you?' I enquired holding him at arms length, staring directly at into his eyes and telling him with all honesty. 'You're looking pretty fucked ar'kid.'

'I'm proper sound – Don't you worry about me,' he announced buoyantly, as he kissed Donna on the cheek.

'Where's Jackie?' Donna enquired staring at the state of him.

'Oh we had a major bust up,' he laughed. 'Nothing really. In fact I can't even remember what it was all over now. I'll call her later.'

He was definitely off his face on something for certain; I was trying to work out exactly what gear Jonah had been on about. 'You lads alright?' I asked the other two who were shaking their heads at Scotty who now had his back turned to them both.

Kezlo looked at me mouthing the words, 'he's rocked out of his fuckin' nut.'

'Scotty – what the fuck you been up to boy?' I asked him with a concerned look upon my face. 'Your eyes are wasted big time.'

'I'm double sweet mate,' he smirked back at me all lively and jumpy. 'Let me go get some drinks in – my round – alright?' And with that he disappeared to the bar.

'Shit!' Donna exclaimed. 'He looks absolutely hammered.'

'He's rocked out of his mind,' Kezlo stated, shrugging as he did so before swigging his bottle of Becks in a sigh of relief. 'He's been smoking them all day.' He then added.

'I couldn't say shit over the phone to you,' Jonah told me.

'He's what?' Donna gasped, surprised at what she'd just heard.

'I reckon he's just upset about Jackie,' Kezlo sighed. 'Y'know he ain't stuck with any bird for longer than a week before her. Well they had this massive barny this morning whilst I was on the phone with Eazy. Shit was getting smashed everywhere – Eazy was laughing his tits off on the phone – *but shit* – I had to actually be there for it.'

'Ah fuck it he'll be alright,' I declared so not too worry Donna. 'Just let him cane the rocks today if he wants to.'

'You what Chopper!' Donna snapped at me.

She had no idea that Scotty smoked rock, in fact... she didn't even know that I smoked them myself now and then for that matter, and I had no fucking intention of letting her know either.

'It's just his way of getting it out of his system,' I told her. 'He'll be alright. Besides we'll stay with him,' I smiled trying to reason with her.

Scotty suddenly appeared as he bounced back from the bar carrying a bucket filled with an iced bottle of Bollinger champagne. 'Let's celebrate.'

'What are we celebrating Scotty?' I asked.

'Freedom ar'kid,' he grinned at me. 'To freedom – No offence Donna,' he added smirking away, but you could see that beneath the surface something just wasn't right at all.

By ten o'clock we were all pretty fucked, more so Scotty who kept disappearing outside for a quick pipe of rock before returning back inside. Donna had already left by this time; she couldn't stand seeing Scotty in the state he was in. After all she had both known and liked Scotty for a long time now. And for years now the two of us were so close.

Scotty came bouncing back into Dry Bar. 'I've got a top idea,' he suddenly declared, his eyes held the appearance like he'd stuck his finger in a plug socket and he had an electric current running through him. 'Let's shoot off to The Hac, its Wednesday night, always a quality night in there,' he announced enthusiastically.

'Sounds alright,' I told him, determined to stick it out with him no matter what happened tonight.

Jonah smirked broadly at the thought. 'Sound idea lads.'

'In'it,' Kezlo added. 'I've proper had enough of this gaff. Jonah, you got any pills on you?'

He smirked even more so now. 'One or two I think.'

We all laughed, as we knew he would be carrying a bagful with him.

The Hacienda was still pretty quiet when we got in there, so I went to get the drinks in whilst the others plotted in our usual spot. Scotty was pure hyperactive this evening after caning the rocks all day. He kept repeating himself about how he didn't give a shit about Jackie.

The truth was though, that we'd never seen him like this before over a bird. It had always been easy come; easy go with Scotty. But Jackie seemed to have got to him like no other girl had. I kept thinking that it was a great night though, I hadn't been out with just the lads for pure time and it felt well top to be here.

We'd been inside for almost an hour now, when I suddenly noticed Jonah's face change. 'Chopper – you seen whose just walked in,' he was nodding towards the entrance.

It was Paddy, along with Chris and about three other lads from what I could see. It had been the first time since that day at Spike Island in Widnes since I'd seen him. I couldn't help but notice straight away the neat scar running below his left eye from where I'd managed to slice him that day, and I have to admit that without thinking about it I smiled to myself on that score.

'Fuck him Jonah,' I shrugged, 'I don't give a toss about that dickhead. We don't stay kids forever – do we eh?'

'You two looking at what I'm looking at?' asked Kezlo who was now stood beside us.

'Yes mate,' Jonah smiled. 'I know you don't give a fuck Chopper, it's just I heard he's been bad mouthing you and Prey lately. You in particular mate.'

I shook my head as if I didn't care; after all I'd promised not to do shit to him until the time had been decided. Besides which, because I'd rushed out of the flat earlier I wasn't carrying my Beretta 9mm semi-automatic pistol that I'd become so used to keeping on me at all times these days. And chances were odds on favourite that Paddy would be tooled up in some way.

As Paddy passed by us, he was smiling menacingly; he then stopped and glared directly at me. 'Alright Chopper, I see that you're still the same little scally twat you've always been. Some things will never change, will they eh?' He was stroking the scar below his eye glaring at the other two. 'Alright there kids? Bit late ain't it? Especially on a school night?' He grinned at his own humour.

'That's a nice little scar you got yourself there Paddy,' I responded all the while smiling back at him. 'Cut yourself whilst still practising to shave you dick.'

He just continued to stroke the scar without saying a word, before turning and disappearing with his entourage of follower's close behind him.

'Go get Scotty over 'ere Kezlo.' I said whilst keeping my focus on Paddy's back.

'So we're leaving... Are we?' he asked.

'Are we fuck like,' I told him. 'That cocksucker ain't running me from any gaff – *ever*. No I just want Scotty where we can keep an eye on him.'

As Kezlo disappeared Jonah turned to me. 'So what was all that about with Paddy?'

'Don't know what you're talking about mate,' I replied winking at him.

'Say no more, Chopper.' He shook his head laughing.

'It's shutting Chopper,' Kezlo said. 'We got to leave brother.'

'Where to now?' asked Scotty who'd been oblivious to any kind of friction coming from Paddy's group all night.

'Home pal,' I told him. 'That's where to. Let's get out of 'ere now.'

'They're right on us Chopper,' Jonah informed me as we set off towards the exit.

'Look, when we get outside just try and get Scotty out of 'ere,' I said shaking my head. 'I don't reckon he's in any state to start battling.'

As we closed in on the exit, Paddy's lads made a dash for the door, cutting off our path so to leave first. Although Paddy hung back, staying behind us.

I found myself dropping back slightly from the others as I knew what this was all over and it wasn't fair to drag them into it.

As we walked out into the cool night air Paddy was still behind me. Jonah turned back towards me shaking his head, mouthing to me, 'Can't see them anywhere,' I was nodding back at him.

'Head for the bridge.' I told him in hushed tones.

'What the fuck's going on?' Scotty asked baffled by our actions.

'Just walk,' Kezlo told him.

Paddy was right behind us as we made our way across Whitworth Street towards the Railway Bridge. Suddenly Chris appeared from behind the bridge, along with the three other lads, all of them waiting for us.

'Alright Chopper,' it was Paddy from behind me, 'ain't me and you got unfinished business to settle.'

Concentrating on Paddy, I left the other three to keep an eye on the others. No one was making a move; Paddy's right arm was hidden well out of sight behind his back. That was when it suddenly happened without any warning whatsoever as the next thing I knew, Scotty appeared from behind me, and ran straight at Paddy.

'C'mon then you fuckin muppet,' he screamed at him, suddenly aware for the first time that evening that there was any trouble brewing.

But in all fairness – Paddy was way too fast for Scotty, as he merely side stepped him with nothing but utter ease. His right arm appeared in quick succession with an empty beer bottle. 'You little fuckin' prick,' he screamed as he slammed the

28

bottle down onto Scotty's head, as it shattered into pieces, making clear contact as it did so.

I knew straight away that the bottle had been intended for me. And right there and then it all erupted into a mass of bloodshed. As Scotty was falling back towards the ground, stumbling as he did. You could hear the mayhem behind me as Jonah and Kezlo began battling with the rest of them as the screams and shouts from people standing by consumed the air.

I stood my ground, my eyes bore into Paddy's with a knowing glint. But he just laughed in a sinister way as he glanced back and forth like true predator. I merely nodded my understanding back to him as I knew what was to follow, and there wasn't going to be any kind of backing down from either corner.

'C'mon then Chopper,' he scowled at me, 'I think that I owe you something – Right?'

I looked back down at Scotty who was pulling himself from the road and grinning foolishly at me as he did so. As he steadied himself on shaky legs. Blood was pouring with ease down the front of his face, but he seemed oblivious to both that and the pain.

'Go on Chopper – I'll give the others a hand,' he told me as he smirked foolishly at me, stumbling passed as he went to give Jonah and Kezlo a hand fighting off the other four.

Paddy snaps open his lock knife nodding knowingly as he did so. 'Its payback time you little twat.'

Prey and Sleeper's words raced through my mind – but now faced without any other option bar running – and to be totally honest that just wasn't an option I willing to take I simply said. 'Lets go then Paddy – I ain't even carrying you prick.'

'Oh by the way Chopper,' he sneered at me. 'How's Sean Macreedy these days…? I ain't seen him about town lately.'

That was the last thing he should have said to me as he sent me into a complete rage, as I ran straight at him mindlessly without thinking of any consequences. The thing is no matter what I think of Paddy – he is without a doubt a trained psychopath who knows what he's doing. So as the blade swished through the night air with deadly speed and accuracy. The cold steel sliced open my shirt, piercing cleanly through the flesh on my stomach area.

I felt the rigorous pain hit me as I cringed, biting down on my teeth to draw out the pain. Although my only true feelings were those of complete anger that were growing into deep hatred. Paddy was slicing back towards me with a backhanded slice; I bobbed and weaved so to miss any contact. And as he forced himself off balance, I took advantage of the situation, kicking out with my right foot as hard as I possibly could.

My right foot crashing violently into his left knee socket as I observed it buckle and he lost balance. I witnessed his face incapacitate with vehement anguish as he fell to the ground grabbing onto his knee as he cried out in sheer agony into the night.

Cars skidded to a halt around us as I was already back on my feet again as Paddy lay there grabbing onto his dislocated knee socket. I ran at him, slamming my right foot down onto his right arm, crushing it so that the knife fell free from his grip.

I then kicked it away into the road. 'C'mon then big man,' I sneered menacingly at him. 'Let's see what you got without your blade then,' I said straightening upwards as the pain shot across my gaping wound, although I tried my best to ignore it.

I allowed him just enough time to struggle to his feet, as he did though; I flew straight at him again, vaulting through the air at him with his head the target against my own. Only this time, as I grabbed onto him we both crashed into the road, both of our bodies collapsing impenetrably into the tarmac. I brought my forehead crashing down into his nose and felt it shatter against the force as I heard him scream out in anguish.

Jonah screamed out from behind me. 'Chopper – quickly – c'mon – it's the police.'

You could hear the sirens growing louder and louder – closing in on us, clearer and more audible as they drew closer and closer. Glaring down at Paddy lay beneath me; I stared coldly at him.

'There's still payback you fuck,' I spat the words at him, dropping my head back down towards him, my mouth gaping wide open and snarling like a crazed animal. I began sinking my teeth into his right ear, biting down fiercely onto the rubbery flesh.

His screams were intense with the distress, as he struggled to break free from my hold on him; this only made his own pain more intense as I continued to bite down until I felt my own teeth strike against one another. I pulled away, tearing the flesh from around his ear and the side of his face free from its hold. I then spewed the bloodied rubbery piece of flesh to the floor.

Paddy broke free from me and was rolling around screaming and shrieking, holding the space where his ear once had been. I was merely staring at him, climbing up from where he laid rolling around, and sneering back at him with no feelings towards the damage I just inflicted upon him. Blood was streaming down my mouth across my chin as I wiped it with my sleeve. The disillusioned gapes upon people's faces told me just how fucking mad the scene must have appeared to them as it probably looked more like something you'd see in a horror movie than a normal Wednesday night out in Manchester.

I suddenly felt Jonah dragging me backwards. 'Let's get the fuck out of 'ere.'

As the four of us began to run back towards the bridge I noticed all of Paddy's lads including that prick, Chris Walker lay there, blood running from their wounds, all whimpering like hurt animals. I spat my disgust at them as we past, as we made our way back to Hulme.

FIVE

As we crashed into the flat, we were all filled with mixed feelings of panic and adrenaline running side by side as I collapsed helplessly onto the floor. For the first time I realised just how bad the knife wound was, the pain was so intense my head felt a little light.

'Chopper... Chopper, you're hurt badly,' Scotty was stood above me; the blood now dried in patches across his face, although watching it still seeping out from the wound itself.

'Look whose talking.'

Jonah tore the remains of my shirt away. 'Fuck! It looks bad Chopper.'

'Phone Prey,' I instructed as I winced with the sharp pain that tore through me.

'Just have,' it was Kezlo, 'he'll be over with a Doc as soon as poss' mate.'

'Get me the fuck out of these clothes,' I told them. 'Get them burnt or something. They're covered in Paddy's blood also – *Arahhhh* – stick me in the bath or I'm gonna bleed all over the fuckin' place.'

Jonah and Scotty undressed me tossing the clothes to Kezlo who was bundling them into a black plastic refuse sack. As they lifted my now naked body from the floor my head began to spin – In fact everything began to spin as I passed out.

'Chopper... Chopper... you hear me,' I could just about make out Prey's voice as I began to come round.

Everything around me was spinning as my eyes began to flutter open. 'Yeah... *Araggghhh*.'

'Chopper... We need to get you out the bath.'

As I fought to get my eyes fully open; I lay there in the bath naked. My own blood covering me and seeping through the towel draped over my stomach and groin area.

Dr. Hassid stood above me, smiling weakly at him I said. 'Alright Doc?'

'I need to get you out of there Chopper,' he told me. 'I need to examine that cut of yours properly.'

'How you feeling ar'kid?' Prey asked as he helped Dr. Hassid get me out of the bath.

'It's just stinging now, that's all,' I told him honestly. 'I tried Prey... but he smashed a fuckin' bottle against Scotty's head though.'

'I know all about it mate. Doc 'ere, needs to put a few stitches into him next. We'll talk after,' he was nodding at Hassid.

I nodded my understanding back to him, knowing exactly what he'd meant. As I perched on the toilet seat I leant back so that I could be examined.

'Jesus Chopper,' Dr. Hassid exclaimed, 'you're one lucky son of a bitch.'

'How bad is it?'

'Very clean slice – That's good. Probably why it hurts so much though,' he looked at me. 'Hasn't cut anything major. You're lucky – very lucky. You got to take more care though. I mean how long's it's been now since the last time I seen you eh? Five or six months,' he shook his head still examining the slash.

'Is it a hospital job Doc?' Prey asked.

'Fuck that,' I snapped as Prey grinned knowingly at me.

'No I should be able to stitch him up here alright,' he smiled. 'But you got to take it easy for a while son. No more playing football with your mates,' he informed me as his smile turning into a knowing smirk.

'Cheers Doc,' I replied, grinning knowingly back at him.

I'd needed forty-seven stitches and it hurt like hell once Doctor Hassid had put them in. 'Better go put a plaster on the other one then,' he said disappearing out of the bathroom.

'Thanks again,' I shouted after him.

Just then, Steve appeared through the door. 'You alright Chopper?' he asked concerned.

'What you doing 'ere?' I was surprised to see him.

'I called him.'

Steve bent down looking at my stitches then laughed. 'You're pure nutty boy.'

'Look it wasn't my fault,' I sighed out loud. 'I know I promised – *But* – Well...'

'It's alright mate,' Prey smiled. 'The others told me what happened. It's fair to say that you had no other choice in the matter. Not that I'm saying you had to bite his fuckin' ear off though,' he said, just then the two of them burst out laughing at me, I tried to laugh along, but couldn't do so from the pain that rocked through me.

'I tell you Chopper,' Steve said. 'I'm just so thankful that I got you on ar' side.'

'I spoke with Errol who was on the door tonight,' Prey was saying. 'He says that Paddy and Chris got away. But that the others all got nicked across the road. He also said that Jonah, Kezlo and Scotty had pretty much left them all fucked up. Actually Errol says that Jonah and Kezlo gave them a right kicking before Scotty even got near the action.'

'So hopefully he's not going to go running to the hospital. 'Cause they'll go informing the police about him,' Steve said.

'Hopefully.'

'He'll be pretty fuckin' dumb to go there after they've nicked his mates won't he,' Prey added. 'Plus if the police get wind of you two scrapping tonight it'll fuck our future plans up.'

'Does Donna know yet?'

'I ain't phoned her,' Prey shook his head at me. 'I didn't reckon you'd want her knowing it was with Paddy.'

'I don't,' I blurted out. 'But she's got to know – so give her a bell. Tell her it was some dodgy fuckin' Scouser's or something like that.'

'Alright – I've got to go pay Doc anyway,' Prey said walking out of the bathroom.

Steve stared at me. 'You scared the shit out of me Chopper,' he shook his head at me.   'You know I ain't told you this before. But I've always liked the thought of you as the son I always wanted to have. You know what I mean. My Michael ain't the brightest of lads and well – you...' he trailed off, not quite sure what else to say.

But if truth be told – nothing else needing say as I smiled back at him.

Six

As it happened, Paddy had ended up in Hope Hospital's emergency room that very night. He'd needed immediate attention to his ear... Well let's just say for arguments sake – where his ear had once been eh! Truth be told, it was probably still lay somewhere on Whitworth Street outside The Hacienda.

'How the hell has this happened Mr. McNally?' asked Dr. Richardson.

Paddy was chewing his lip to try and drive out the agony he felt. 'Just fell off my Motorbike Doc... How bad is it?' he enquired, although he wasn't too sure he wanted to hear the answer.

'Look son,' Dr. Richardson began to say sighing deeply as he did so, 'that isn't a fall off a bike. I can see teeth marks and your nose don't look much better. It isn't my business but...'

'That's right – it ain't your business is it doc?' Paddy snapped. 'Now can you sort it or not?' he added as the pain he felt intensified.

'Easy son... Look it needs to be cleaned properly before we can even consider doing anything with it. You've got a lot of dirt in there,' he told him. 'And I'm afraid to say that you'll be missing a large chunk from your ear. A very large chunk at that.'

'Whatever Doc – just patch it the fuck up so I can get the hell out of 'ere,' Paddy said, still biting his lip. 'Just do me a favour and give me something for the bastard pain will you – It hurts like hell.'

'Alright then,' he said shaking his head. 'The nurse will be here in a second. I've just got to go get some clean gloves and

35

I'll tell the nurse to give you a shot,' he added, disappearing behind the screen.

As soon as he was away from Paddy he glanced back through the curtain just to make sure he was out of earshot. 'You had better phone the police on this one,' Dr. Richardson said to the duty nurse who was heading towards reception. 'I just hope the other guy is still alive.'

'Sure thing Dr. Richardson,' the nurse replied, smiling and batting her eyelids at the same time as she did, hoping to raise some interest from the doctor that they all had crushes on.

'Oh one more thing – make sure you give his name first so they can check if he's got any priors,' he added before turning away – yet at the same time smiling at her. 'I wouldn't be at all surprised if he has.'

'No problem,' she eagerly answered, still batting those eyes at him.

'Just a few more stitches Patrick,' Dr. Richardson said. 'Are you feeling okay?'

'I'll feel a whole lot better once you've finished and I can get out of 'ere Doc.'

But as he said this, the screen keeping them away from the general public was drawn back; Walsh was stood there smiling knowingly at him. 'Evening Paddy. Not looking too healthy there son,' he laughed.

'What! What the fuck? *How?* You fuckin' bastard Doc – *You...*' he stopped himself realising the Doctor still held the needle being thread through the severed skin where he'd lost his ear.

'Just procedure Patrick,' Doctor Richardson said still working away.

'What the fuck do you want Walshy?' Paddy sneered. 'You working over time? I ain't seen you around in a long time.'

'Well there are three of your lads over in Saint Mary's Hospital, who have all been nicked,' he grinned knowingly at him. 'It looks like they got run over by a bulldozer outside that club on Whitworth Street. It also looks like you're the one who – how shall we put this? Oh yeah – almost got away,' he added still smiling at him all the while.

'Fuck you Walshy,' Paddy snapped again. 'I had an accident on my motorbike, that's all. Besides which, what the fuck you got on me? Nothing – That's what,' he absolutely loathed Walsh. He had nicked him more times than he cared to remember whilst he was stationed in Salford. That was before Walsh had been transferred into town, and he of all people hadn't been sad to see the back of him.

'That's kind of funny you know. Because you know how some crimes are like a jigsaw puzzle? You know – you've just got to fit the pieces together to get the full picture.'

'What the fuck are you going on about Walshy?'

Walsh suddenly produced a plastic evidence bag from his pocket and with that his smile extended. 'Looks like we found the missing piece to that jigsaw Paddy.'

'Is that what I think it is?' Dr. Richardson asked, snipping the thread free. 'Can I see that please?'

For inside the bag was the chewed bloodied, filthy missing piece from Paddy's ear.

'We couldn't have used it anyway – it's too badly damaged,' said Dr. Richardson without any remorse at all.

'So what now Walshy?' Paddy asked still sat there looking at the bag the Doctor was holding.

'Causing affray for starter's son,' he smiled. 'And how about telling me who done this to you tonight?'

'Fuck you. Charge me with the pocksy charge if you really want to,' Paddy yawned at him. 'My brief will laugh it out of court,' he smirked knowingly at Walsh. 'He's done better than that. Remember Walshy?' he added tauntingly at the detective.

'Well there'll be other charges later. Now – who done it?'

'Better take a look at your jigsaw puzzle hadn't you Walshy,' he said pushing himself down off the bed. 'How about some lads from out of town did it. Funny accents that I couldn't understand at all. Besides I ain't going to take it any further.'

'Funny that. I thought you might have said Chorlton. You know – Chopper?' he watched for Paddy's reaction, not receiving one.

'Now why the fuck would you think he could do something like this to me?' Paddy calmly asked.

'Just the investigation into Macreedy's death,' Walsh dropped his bombshell, he'd heard from one of their grasses that there had been a fight with Paddy inside that concert at Widnes, but the grass wasn't sure whether or not it was Chopper. He just thought it might have been, so if there was any truth in the matter, then this made Paddy a good suspect.

Truth was – they still hadn't come up with shit on the shooting yet, apart from someone else's blood type being there.

'What's Macreedy's death got to do with me?' he enquired with a little caution.

'The way I heard it,' Walsh started. 'That little scar below your eye was caused by Chopper at that concert.'

'Nah man,' Paddy sighed deeply, wondering where this was leading. 'Which budgie have you got chirping bullshit to you nowadays Walshy?'

'From what I hear you all had a bit of a scuffle inside.' He paused for a second. 'Who knows – maybe even outside also.'

'Well when you're sure – why don't you come back and talk to me then.'

'Oh we will son,' Walsh replied still watching for any response from him.

'Look Walshy if you had anything on me at all. Well we'd be having this conversation down at the nick, not sat next to the hospital bed. Wouldn't we now?' Paddy was being very cautious with what he said; it had been the first mention of Macreedy's shooting.

Everybody involved on his side had been more than severely threatened into keeping their mouths shut. Plus he'd not heard any rumours around town about it from anybody, which meant they'd kept their mouths shut also. But he couldn't be sure what they actually knew or whether Walshy was just trying to be a smart arse or not. He just had to keep his cool for now.

Walsh looked around the screen into the next cubicle where the Doctor was treating another patient. 'Is he ready to go Doc?'

'Yes he's alright to leave,' he replied not taking his eyes away from his new patient.

'Right come on then Paddy,' Walsh said taking his arm. 'I got a car waiting outside for you. Might as well go meet the rest of your mates hadn't you. They should be arriving at the cells about now also.' He was smiling again as he pulled back the certain to reveal two uniformed officers who stepped forward and handcuffed him.

They were all in court Thursday afternoon charged with causing affray, disturbing the peace, drunk and disorderly. Walsh knew that it was pretty pointless, especially with Paddy's brief being Samuel Neilson.

Neilson had had so many of Paddy's previous charges dropped or thrown out of court in the past. Through lack of evidence, entrapment, witnesses not testifying, in fact anything he possibly could do to twist the law to his client's advantage.

What Walsh had achieved though – was to drop his hunch concerning Macreedy's death. He was certain that Paddy had somehow been involved with it. They just had no evidence backing it.

The tyre marks found at the scene had been traced to a stolen black Ford Escort that had been totally burnt out once found. The car had been reported stolen that night by some students from North Cheshire College in Warrington who'd been at the concert also, and they definitely weren't the ones responsible for the shooting.

One of their grasses had told them about the fight that had happened but could only be sure that it was Paddy's lot involved. He'd mentioned Chopper – but then had quickly denied that he thought he'd been involved.

Walsh thought about the state of Paddy's ear the previous night and then thought that the grass was probably just scared shitless of giving Chopper's name even if he knew it had definitely had been him. After all, the state that Paddy had been left in was a right mess.

He was convinced that the description given of the other assailant last night was also Chopper who'd used his own method of amputating Paddy's ear.

What Walsh was afraid of though was what was going to happen next. All these fucking crews around Manchester and the surrounding boroughs battling with one another was getting well out of hand. Too much blood was being spilt on the streets of Manchester and Salford – and everybody knew it.

It had been the reason his old friend, Mike Stevenson had brought him in on it, to try and find a way through – a way to break them. He had to find that way – and the sooner the better he thought to himself.

SEVEN

'You'll both see when we get there,' Prey told us with an air of excitement about himself. 'It's just an idea I've got. Look we got to be there for two o'clock to meet someone else.'

'Be where exactly?' enquired Steve a little bemused at the way Prey was carrying on.

'You'll just have to wait and see won't you,' he grinned mischievously at the two of us. 'Look it's just gone twelve now. C'mon, we'll grab some scran at Chan's on the way.'

'Now that sounds like a sound idea,' I said as my stomach had begun to remind me that it was dinner time. 'Araggghhh… Shit,' I cried out through gritted teeth as I rose from the settee.

It had only been a week since the encounter with Paddy and my stomach was still in a lot of pain as the stitches were right at the crease of my stomach. Donna had gone ballistic over what had happened that night, although I think that it was more out of concern than anger. Also, I didn't reckon for one minute that she bought the story about the Scouser inflicting the damage.

'You alright Chopper?' Steve asked helping me up.

'Yeah mate,' I told him. 'It's 'cause I was sat down that's all.'

'How's it healing Chop?' Prey asked pulling on his black leather D&G jacket.

'Sweet considering y'know,' I replied as Steve helped me with my new Sprayway jacket. 'It's only been a week so I ain't too worried. At least the bleeding has stopped now. Hassid called by last night to check on it.'

40

'Has there been any comeback since Paddy got nicked?' Steve asked.

'Nah man,' I grinned, 'and after what Ant and Andie from Salford told me, he'll be way too steaming to want to let the coppers handle it.'

'What he saying then?' Steve asked as the three of us made our way out the front door onto the balcony as the cold wet weather sent a shiver through me.

Prey laughed. 'Both Andy and Anthony said that he's well messed up. Stayed out of sight, he's that fucked up. He said that it looks like a little piece of putty stuck to the side of his head. Both eyes are black and his nose looks like he ran into a brick wall.'

The both laughed; I also tried too laugh along with them, but the pain wouldn't allow me too.

After we'd eaten at Chan's and with still with no clues as to what Prey had in mind we all strolled down Market Street towards St. Ann's Square.

'What the fuck we doing in the Royal Exchange Prey?' I asked curiously.

'There he is now,' he answered, ignoring my question and taking off in front of us.

We both could see him heading in the direction of a well-suited middle aged man who was obviously stood there waiting for someone. 'Hello Mr. O'Prey. How are you this afternoon?' he asked politely, shaking Prey's hand.

I was staring bemused at Steve, the two of us shaking our heads in confusion.

'These must be your partners,' he said shaking our hands as Prey introduced the two of us.

'Now Mr. Wilson, could you be kind enough to show my partners what I have in mind,' Prey said in a very restrained Mancunian accent.

Mr. Wilson began to open the doors to a disused shop unit that had an estate agents sign in the window with To Let in large bold black letters written across is. 'Here you go then,' he declared as he hit the light switches, on his way into the large empty and very spacious store

'So then,' Prey turned to look at the two of us. 'What do you think?' he asked smiling away as he looked back around then back towards both Steve and I again still stood there, and still very much confused by it all. 'Well?' he asked us both again.

'Well what?' Steve shrugged.

'I want to take the lease over on the property,' he announced, 'and set up ar' own clothes shop.'

'What the fuck! Excuse my language mate,' I said, looking to Mr. Wilson who merely shook his head smiling. 'But what do we know about running a clothes shop?'

'Well between the three of us me and you know what all the lads are after Chopper,' he was almost bubbling over with excitement. 'As for Steve he obviously knows about the suit side of things. I mean after all that's just about all the old bugger ever wears,' he grinned at Steve.

'It still don't mean that we can run a shop,' Steve stated as a matter of fact.

'Well I already thought about that score,' he smiled as if he was really proud of himself. 'What about Donna? She's already Assistant Manager at that one she's at now. We'll just poach her,' he was full of exuberance and what he said about Donna was true.

She had soon been promoted to Assistant Manager shortly after her promotion to supervisor. And if truth be told, I'd seen Prey like this before and there was no stopping him.

'So then, are you gentleman interested?' Mr. Wilson asked who could obviously smell his percentage already.

'It sounds alright,' Steve nodded, 'but obviously we need to discuss it further.'

'As you can tell Mr. Wilson, it's kind of been sprung on us,' I added shaking my head at Prey.

'You make sure that you decide soon though. As I've got a lot of other people interested in it,' he was trying the hard sell, but hey, you can't blag a bunch of blaggers can you eh?

'Okay then Mr. Wilson we'll be in touch,' I told him with a touch of sarcasm in my voice.

'Is that the paperwork?' Steve enquired nodding at the file he was carrying.

'It sure is,' he said holding the folder towards Steve. 'I tell you what. Why don't you gentleman hold onto it for now.'

I coughed to get his attention, 'Just one more thing before we leave,' I said, 'I'd like to see out back and I'd like very much to see what kind of security system this property has installed.'

The comment merely made the other two laugh out loud.

'So what do you think then?' Prey asked enthusiastically, as the three of us were seated in Courtney's wine bar at the back of Kendal's drinking large brandy and cokes.

'I reckon that it's not too bad an idea,' Steve said.

'I've been thinking about it for a while,' he continued. 'You see I reckon between the three of us we've got a bundle of cash stashed away. Now, we're at a stage where we know the police are definitely onto ar' activities around town. So what I suggest is that we use this one to set up a legal venture.'

'What do you mean this one?' I was shaking my head at how far ahead of himself he was already getting.

'Well the way I figure it,' he said looking at the two of us. 'Is we set this one up just to see how well it would work. Then what we do is set another up down in London. Just think about it, do this one completely by the books. But the one we set up down there – well obviously with it being so busy down there, tourists and all,' he smirked at the two of us.

'Are you getting at what I think you are?' Steve asked smiling.

'Of course I am,' Prey laughed. 'Just think about how much dough we could launder down there,' he was nodding his head knowingly at us.

'Now that definitely makes sense,' I added, thinking about just how much cash of ours was floating about out there.

'If we're going to it though then we'll have to it properly,' I told them both. 'I mean get ar' selves some decent buyers for a start.'

'Don't be stupid Chopper,' Prey laughed. 'We know what all the lads are after... Steve can look after the suit side. I mean that's all the cunt ever wears.'

'Alright – I'm definitely in then,' I added thinking that is was a great idea after all.

'Me too,' Steve smiled at the thought of it. 'Do you reckon Donna will be interested Chopper?' Steve asked.

'I don't see why not,' I replied. 'We will need to sort things proper though,'

'Thought of a name for it yet?' Steve enquired.

Prey stared at us knowingly. 'What the fuck do you think we're going to call it?' he smiled at the two of us. 'Macreedy's of course.'

'Yes mate,' I nodded my approval.

'That's quality Prey,' Steve smiled. 'In memory of Sean.'

So in the usual fashion of celebrating things the three of us stayed in Courtney's until closing, and it was pretty safe to say that by the time of leaving the establishment the three of us were well and truly hammered.

'Are you serious Chopper?' Donna asked as I woke her to tell her the news. 'You know you're boozed out of your head.'

'Yes,' I was slurring my words and knew that I was bladdered, 'Adrian Black's coming down to the estate agents tomorrow to make sure the papers are all in check,' Adrian being the brief – or solicitor I should say – that we always used.

'So you are serious? Aren't you?' she said looking at me.

'Told you so.'

'And about me being the manageress?' she asked excitedly.

'Of course...' was about all I managed before collapsing fully dressed onto the bed, falling heavily into a drunken sleep.

'It's not some over night venture you can set up, you know,' Donna told us shaking her head as she did so.

We'd signed the papers that afternoon, putting the store in Steve's name. We'd figured as he wasn't supposed to have anything to do with the drug side of things, this was the best cover for him to have as he'd obviously be in town a lot more from now on.

'We know that Donna,' I told her tutting as I did so. 'What we need to know is whether or not you're interested?'

'Look Donna,' Prey said taking her hand. 'We don't know how to run a shop for fucks sake. But you do. So we want to employ your services.'

'Alright – first off. What is it you want to stock in there?'

'Gear like what all the lads are wearing,' he then grinned at Steve. 'Suits as well for the old gits out there.'

'Bastard,' answered Steve laughing.

'Why not divide it into two?' she suggested.

'What do you mean?' I asked. 'Bird's gear?'

'Of course that's what I mean,' she sighed at me. 'Do you realise just how much us girls like to spend on our shoes and clothes.'

We all nodded in agreement at her suggestion.

'Also the buyer for our store isn't at all happy with the stock they're asking her to buy. She's got some better ideas on what girls actually want.'

'We'll hire her,' I declared.

'It's not that's simple Chopper. These aren't your people from the street you know,' she said scowling at me. 'Also another thing you three were right about. You haven't got a clue about setting a shop up and that definitely includes the buying side of things.'

'Course we have,' Prey said defensively, 'we know exactly what the lads want.'

'That's not what I'm going on about,' she shook her head. 'You need to know how fashion changes with season stock. You need to know your accounting budgets. You need to know the suppliers. You need to know trade shows to attend. You... look am I getting through to you guys or what?'

'What you got in mind then Donna?' Steve asked laughing as he knew full well that she was exactly right.

'Well the same girl I was telling you about, Sam, her boyfriend Jason works for a large sports chain from Newcastle as a buyer. But I know the kind of gear he likes to wear, it's similar to you lot so he'd be ideal for the store.'

'Okay cool – you've sold me on that note. Now what about you?' Prey asked. 'Are you interested and if so when can you start?'

'I have to give two weeks notice and of course I'm definitely interested. But I already told you that it's not an over night job to set up.' She shook her once again.

'No, we now know that,' Steve said. 'But we'll pay you to start as soon as possible to get things set up properly.'

'Alright then,' she smiled, 'now that you've mentioned pay. How much are you offering?'

'I thought I'd just pay you in kind Donna,' I said kissing her cheek.

'Yeah right,' she laughed. 'No seriously?'

'Alright, I tell you what then,' Prey looked very thoughtful, then added. 'You hand in your notice tomorrow. Try and set a meeting up with these buyers of yours. It's obvious that you know your shit. So let's say we'll double whatever salary you're on now. How's that sound?'

Donna's jaw literally dropped. 'Double...' was about all that she managed.

EIGHT

Donna had handed in her notice the next day and then spent the entire two weeks of her spare time going over things that needed sorting out. She had been completely right about the three of us; we were totally clueless on the entire matter. She was a star for sure and I was really proud of her. You see to us, we merely thought that it was a sound idea to do. Also giving a means to account for some of the cash we had.

'Right then, we need to discuss a proposition for Sam and Jason,' Donna announced as she waltzed through our front door.

'So they're interested then. Are they?'

She returned my smile. 'I reckon so,' she told me. 'After I told them what your plans were to stock in there. The thing is we're meeting them on Friday night. So I suggest we book Chan's for then. Come to think of it you've not taken me there for a while – Have you Chopper?'

I grinned at her. 'I don't know what you mean – I always eat there.'

'Very funny,' she replied sarcastically. 'I meant the two of us.'

'Friday's sound anyway,' I informed her as she sat on my lap, giving me a kiss. ''Cause we can take them to The Hac afterwards. Have they been there?'

'Of course they have.' She then laughed at how dumb the question actually was. 'You've met Sam. But as I remember it you just kind of grunted like you normally do.'

I began laughing at this. 'Just being myself,' I told her. 'It'll be a double celebration anyway. It's your last day at the shop before you officially start working for us.'

'Oh is that it then,' She pulled her face at me. 'I'm one of your grafters now am I,' she giggled as I grabbed her waist pulling her towards me.

I tickled her, making her laugh hysterically. 'You'll always be my little grafter,' I told her as she giggled some more before our lips met and we began kissing passionately

'So what else you got in mind for Macreedy's Donna,' Prey asked, the four of us were sat in Chan's waiting for our guests to arrive.

'For the shop fitting itself I thought something a bit different,' she told us. 'Make us stand out from the usual high street stores. Kind of give the shop a club atmosphere. Fit it with a top sound system, pine wooden floors, flyers, all that kind of thing. It's that kind of crowd that you're wanting to attract so we'll appeal best by creating a atmosphere that they're used to in a club.'

'That sounds proper tidy,' I nodded, smiling proudly at her.

'In'it,' Prey added. 'What else?'

'Do you think the unit is big enough Donna?' Steve asked.

'Definitely,' she smiled. 'More than enough room for what we need. One other thing you'll definitely need though is a computer. Actually you'll need at least two systems. One for the store itself and one for the buyers to keep control of everything.'

'What about Kneildy's mate?' I smiled knowingly at Prey who knew straight away whom I was on about.

'What's the grin for?' Steve asked curiously.

Prey began laughing. 'Yes mate. I think that Steve might be very interested in meeting him.'

'Why's that then?' Steve asked looking puzzled.

'He's the guy that gave you up to us.'

'Oh is that right,' Steve looked all serious at the two of us. 'Then I think you're right, I think I would like to meet this guy for myself.'

The three of us then laughed out loud, Steve stared at the two of us knowingly. He knew we'd never give him up to anybody.

'So are you three going to let me in on this little joke of yours?' Donna asked all serious now, as she didn't have a clue as to what we were referring to.

'It's nothing,' I was still grinning. 'Personal joke

47

that's all.'

Donna cut in. 'Here they are now.'

I recognised the two of them immediately from The Hacienda. Donna made the formal introductions before Prey literally took over as the host. Being his usual self, he over did everything on the ordering side. He was making a real fuss over the two of them. But if truth be told we'd seen him like this too many times to mention.

We all discussed the style of garments we were looking to stock, although seeing the way Jason dressed he knew the style we were looking for anyway. Donna told them her ideas for the store itself, they both said that if they came on board they'd both like to be involved with the merchandising of the store itself. They said that too often, after they'd bought packages, the way the stores merchandised the clothes themselves, created poor sales themselves.

We discussed a package that would suit them both and you could tell that they were interested from the beginning. It was safe to say though that we were also interested as they both had good ideas and both were very clued up as to what we were looking for at the end of the day.

'So what do you both think then?' Prey finally asked as the last of the dishes were being removed from the table.

'It certainly sounds alright,' Jason smiled. 'I'll give you that much.'

'So you're interested then?' I asked a little too eagerly.

'Put it this way,' Sam said. 'I mean you'll give us the freedom we're looking for. Plus you'll open up a new area on the merchandising side of things. The only thing is that you're a new company starting out. Which basically means that this could be as much of a risk for the two of us quitting and coming to you as it is for you three? Job security wise that is.'

'That's true,' Steve agreed. 'But we're only new in this kind of business.'

'Why, what other businesses have you got?' Sam asked curiously.

'Nothing much of any real interest,' I said staring at Steve.

'Let's just say that the money side of things is covered,' Prey said in a casual demeanour. 'We've signed a two year lease on the property, with first option there after for a ten year contract.'

'Alright,' Jason nodded, 'I tell you what. Give us the weekend to think about it.'

'Is that okay?' Sam asked.

'That should be alright,' Donna said looking at the three of us, 'shouldn't it?'

'Of course,' Prey smiled.

'That's sweet,' I told them thinking that we really wanted the answer tonight. 'But tonight you are ar' guests for the night,' I was smiling holding up my glass of champagne.

The Hacienda was already rocking by the time we got in there. The music was pumping out and you could literally breathe in the heat omitted. But as always it was rocking atmosphere. In fact it was one that I felt at that moment in time that I would never grow tired of.

'So you into this kind of thing pal?' I asked Jason as we made our way over to our usual spot.

'It's well sound in here Chopper,' he smiled enthusiastically. 'Me and Sam did all the big old warehouse party's over in Blackburn. That's where I met her.'

'You want anything tonight?'

'You mean to drink?' he asked naively.

'Drinks or anything else you might want?'

'What!' he exclaimed all excited. 'Do you know someone for gear in here?'

'What do you want?'

I was hoping that he didn't have any idea who we were. This would be good for us. Although after Steve's comment earlier they probably suspected something.

'What about any Es or Charley?' he asked humbly.

'Oh I could certainly try my best for you,' I laughed, as both Prey and Steve began shaking their heads at me.

'Jonah,' I yelled over to side of the dance floor, 'come 'ere mate.'

I introduced Jason and Sam to him, I then whispered to him to go find Dougsy. 'Get a quarter of bugle off of him. Oh and you may as well get ten of the pills also.'

'You partying tonight Chopper?' he laughed.

'Nah mate,' I said, smirking slyly at him. 'Just an idea I got about something that I want to try, that's all.'

'Whatever,' he shrugged before disappearing to find Dougsy. I watched him vanish into the crowd, and then winked at Jason; I'll have my answer by tonight I thought smiling to myself.

Jonah returned a few minutes later with the gear. 'Ere'are mate,' he passed the bag swiftly to me as we shook hands.

'Sweet mate,' I was nodding my response. 'How's Scotty been lately? I've only seen him a couple of times since that trouble.'

'Alright – I suppose,' he didn't sound too convincing. 'He's back with Jackie. I checked around the estate to see whether or not he's buying a lot of rocks.'

'What you hear?'

'He's clean,' he sighed. 'I got them that day for him. But no one says he's buying. Especially Diamond.'

'Alright then mate, let's just make sure he's alright,' I replied, smiling at the thought of my oldest friend; glad he wasn't smoking the rocks too heavily because that wouldn't be good for business if he was.

'Laters Chopper,' Jonah said, 'I got some shit over 'ere I got to take care of.'

'Cheers for that mate,' I thanked him, then turning to Jason. 'C'mon mate. Let's have it to the downstairs bar.'

As we locked the cubicle door behind us, I began to chop out four large lines of charley for us. 'Ere'are mate, bang a couple these up your nose,' I said, handing him a rolled note.

'Cheers Chopper,' he grinned, wasting no time in shuffling the gear up his nose.

I quickly disposed of the rest of the gear without a second thought as I looked at the glazed look that had taken hold of Jason's features.

'Fuck me Chopper!' he said his eyes already spinning. 'I ain't had gear as good as that before. What do I owe you?'

'Fuck all mate,' I said passing him the bag full of Charley and E's. 'Like I said before the night's on us.'

'What this Chopper?' he asked looking at the bag.

'Just a few more grams of Bugle and some E's mate,' I told him, 'and make sure you share it with Sam – don't go getting the greed eh.'

'Are you serious?' he looked shocked as I opened the cubicle door. 'There's shit loads here mate,' he was trying to hold back his smile.

'You did what Chopper,' Steve asked starting to laugh at what I'd just told him.

'You're a crafty little bastard,' Prey laughed.

'Well look, the way I figure it is that they're both alright,' I said. 'Y'know the last thing we need is a couple of twats working for us.'

'That's the truth,' Prey agreed.

'I'll second that,' Steve said still laughing.

Jason's face looked hammered as he bounced around at the side of the dance floor. He'd obviously abused that bag I'd given him. 'You alright mate?'

'Sweet mate – swee – good – real – you...' he couldn't get his words out properly; I was merely laughing at the sight of him.

'Thanks for gear Chopper,' Sam said kissing me, who I have to say looked to be in a lot more control of herself than her boyfriend was. 'You sure you don't want any money?'

'Nah it's alright.'

Donna had obviously been at their bag also, as her eyes were glazed also. She began to dance all seductively towards me then kissed me. 'Come here,' she said kissing me hard.

'What was that for?' I asked, knowing a normal kiss and that wasn't one of them for sure.

'Thanks for everything Chopper,' she kissed me again. 'I really love you and I promise I'll make Macreedy's work for all of you.'

'So will we,' I heard Sam say.

'You're both in?' I asked smiling.

'Su... re... Sure am,' Jason managed to say as his mouth gurned uncontrollably.

'That's quality,' I responded, shaking Jason's hand and kissing Sam.

'We both reckon that you're going to do well with the shop,' Sam told me.

'You sure it's not just the gear talking?' I asked laughing.

'Not at all,' Sam smiled.

'That's really fantastic,' I announced, turning and winking at Prey and Steve.

They both knew from the look on my face that they'd agreed to Macreedy's. They both saluted me mockingly, laughing as they did so.

Macreedy's opened almost three months later with a lot of very hard work put into it.

Jason and Sam had to call in a lot of favours from their contacts in order to stock the store. Most of the clothing companies were only selling for the following seasons, although we managed to stock Macreedy's with some excellent garments.

But the one thing that the three of us loved more than anything was the wholesale prices of the stock. It really was unbelievably cheap at wholesale with a huge mark up into retail value. On some items almost three hundred percent mark-up could be made. And that, we liked immensely.

Donna had been involved from day one with everything from the interior of the shop itself. She'd worked closely with the design company on producing a great logo for Macreedy's, going for a quite simple but effective logo.

She was a true asset to us. The truth was that we'd still be sat in Courtney's wine bar now trying to figure out what the fuck to do with everything. Robert, Kneildy's mate had come over to help set up the computer side of things. I hit it off with lad straightaway, as he was clearly clued up in all aspects of computers.

Between the two of us we designed ourselves an unbelievable security system, with my previous knowledge of the systems and his vast knowledge of computers we wired one hell of a system that only he and I knew actually how it worked.

These computers really fascinated me; they were something else to play about with. You could achieve so much with them these days and each day that passed they advanced one step further.

Kezlo had wired us a top of the range Bose sound system in the store, along with a large selection of the tapes he'd put together. By the time opening day came around we were very proud of the way everything had turned out.

And obviously, we felt that Macreedy's was by far the best looking store in Manchester stocking without a doubt the best clothes were stocked in there... well it had to be it was ours – wasn't it!

For opening day we had spent a small fortune on advertising the day offering a fifty- percent discount with the advert for that day only. After all with the mark up on the clothes themselves it wouldn't dent our balance too much. And it has to be said that our crew took full advantage of it of course.

NINE

Alright mam,' said Chris smiling at as his mother who'd just opened the front door.

'Hi'ya son,' she looked surprised and yet still delighted to see her boy – as she still thought of him. 'What you doing here? Not that I'm not pleased to see you. Come in. We've got a visitor'

'How's things been mam?' he said kissing her as they made their way through to the living room. 'I got a little something for you,' he said as he produced an envelope from his jacket just as they entered through into the living room door.

'Hello Chris,' said the deep voice as they entered the living room, as Chris's jaw tensed as he stared the huge man that was sat on the settee with a knowing smirk upon his face.

'What the fuck...' Chris exclaimed shocked at the sight. 'What the fuck do you want?' he snapped viciously at the man before him.

'Chris...' his mother scolded him back. 'That's no way to talk to your Uncle Robert, is it?'

'Uncle... *Uncle*,' Chris snarled at the guy who he loathed. 'He's a piece of shit... Aren't you Anderson...? The best thing that mam ever did was marry the old man to get rid of your fuckin' name.'

'The old man eh. Steve's still banged up in Strangeways isn't he?' he winked as he said it. 'What you got there?' he asked nodding suspiciously at the envelope. 'Still up to your old tricks I see?'

'Don't you ever go mentioning my old man you twat,' he responded annoyed at being in the same room as his so called uncle – his mother's brother. 'And the envelope has got shit to

53

do with you. Alright? I see you're still a nosey no good wanker then,' he passed the envelope of money to his mother.

'Chris, stop talking to your uncle like that,' his mother tried her best. 'It was nothing to do with him why your dad was sent away. Look – I'm going to put the kettle on. Please you two try and get along,' his mother disappeared through the living room door shaking her head as she did.

'What with all the hostilities son?' Anderson suddenly sneered at Chris.

'Don't call me son... And what the fuck are you doing back around town anyway?' he asked a little more cautiously now. 'I thought they'd sent you down to London.'

'They had,' he nodded. 'It also looks like they brought me back though. Doesn't it? I got the same sort of area to run as I had down there though. So it's all good. Obviously they just can't handle their own manor so they sent for me didn't they,' he said lighting a cigarette, as he looked at Chris with nothing but pure contempt.

'Well we don't want your kind 'round 'ere.' Chris was becoming more wound up by the minute. 'No one knows you're my uncle – and that's the way it stays... You hear me?' he snarled the last bit at him as menacingly as he possibly could as shock instantly took over all the bravado he'd just shown.

Because before Chris knew what had happened he was pinned against the wall with the hot tip of the cigarette pressed near to his left eye.

'Now you listen to me *son*,' he spat the words so that his spittle hit Chris's face,   'Don't you *ever* – and I mean *ever* you little fuck... Talk to me like that again you little piece of fuckin' shite. Especially in front of my kid sister. The only reason I tolerate you is because you're my sister's kid. You fuckin' hear me or what you cocksucker?'

'Get off me,' Chris suddenly pleaded, fear controlling his eyes, for all his gobbing off, he'd been turned into a scared little child within mere moments from the man stood before him, holding him so tightly he was doing all he could to stop himself from screaming out loud.

'Now I'll be seeing you around you little son of a no good cunt,' he sniggered at his own humour.   'And you'd better keep yourself out of my way and my people or I might just have to come looking for you. Hadn't I now,' he was still taunting Chris with the burning cigarette, the smouldering red hot tip singing the minute hairs on Chris's face, and they crackled slightly as they did filling the air with the aroma of singed hair.

He stared menacingly at him, soaking up the fear that he regularly impregnated on all the people around him, as he suddenly freed Chris from his grip watching him slump to the floor as he did so.

'Fuck this... I'm getting off,' said Chris jumping to his feet, brushing himself down, trying to keep face, even though at that precise moment in time he was completely scared shitless. 'Just stay away from me. I don't want shit to do with you or any of your lot. You hear me,' he was still trying his best to appear undisturbed, but was almost certain that his fear was transparent to his uncle.

His uncle scared the shit out of him, he always had done. Chris had always hated him and had always blamed him for the fact his old man was serving sixteen years in prison for a series of armed robberies that Chris knew his old man hadn't been solely responsible for. Well at least not all of them, that is.

'Like I said,' Anderson said, casually taking his seat again, 'Stay the fuck out of my way.'

'Chris... Chris,' his mother shouted as she saw him head for the front door.

'I gotta go out mam,' he said not looking back at her.

'The kettles just boiled,' she shouted after him, but all she heard was the front door slam behind her only son.

'What wrong with you?' Paddy asked Chris who'd just called round and who was obviously more than a little pissed off about something.

'Nowt,' he snapped pacing about the room like a caged animal whilst Paddy prepared his crack-pipe. 'I'm just fucked off about some'ut that's all.'

'Business or personal?' Paddy casually asked, not really caring one way or the other.

Chris thought for a moment, he really didn't want Paddy to know about his uncle or the fact he was back around town. 'Both I guess,' Chris said sitting down. 'Look what are we going to do about Chopper?' he said to try and change the subject.

'Y'know what Chris,' Paddy said igniting the small pile of rocks that were sat upon the pipe. As the drug crackled away and filled air with its powerful aroma, Paddy took the smoke in as deeply into his lungs as he possibly could, and then exhaled the thick steam from his nostrils and mouth before passing it to Chris. 'We should have killed that fucker along with Macreedy y'know.' The smoke continued to drift aimlessly from his mouth as he sat there.

'Tell me about it mate,' Chris said relighting the pipe.

'Y'know that little cunt has scarred me twice now,' Paddy sighed, absentmindedly playing with the small piece of flesh at the side of his head.

'Fuck it then,' Chris sneered. 'Let's kill both of 'em. That Prey fucker too,' he added.

'Y'know that Prey has caused me some fuckin' headaches over the years. The thing is though; he's too well liked around town for his own good. He's got to way too many outside people who'd be willing to step in for revenge afterwards.'

'So what,' Chris snapped, 'we'll still do both of them.'

'Look Chris,' Paddy said reloading the pipe. 'Me and Prey never had any bother with one another before you decided to try and have over Macreedy. Don't get wrong we never liked each other and I'm not having a go at you mate. All I'm saying is that all the trouble we got with them stems from that one fuckin' incident.'

'I know – But – Well...' Chris didn't really have an excuse. 'Let me do Chopper then. I reckon I owe you that much mate.'

'Chopper's mine,' Paddy said lighting the pipe again before allowing the smoke to aimlessly drift from his gaping mouth and nose, with a transfixed glare upon his face. 'I reckon that I owe him big time after what he's left me looking like,' he was now stroking his ear again.

'Alright. If you say so. But I'm helping you, and I ain't taking no for an answer. I fuckin' hate all that crew from Hulme,' Chris said as he took the pipe and began to fill it with the potent mix of rocks again. 'Y'know that they've opened a clothes gaff.'

'I heard,' Paddy said sitting back letting the powerful rock take control of his body. 'Y'know Walshy was sniffing around Macreedy's death.'

'You never told me that.'

'I know. I've been trying to figure out if he's full of shit or not.'

'And is he?'

'I reckon so,' Paddy grinned. 'They'd have pulled us by now for sure.'

'I've also been thinking you know,' Chris announced. 'The way I figure it, with all that crew living right next door to Moss Side and all the publicity surrounding that place at the moment. Well if we kill Chopper, then that's where they're going to go looking first in'it mate.'

Paddy smirked knowingly at Chris nodding his head as he did. 'That's a fuckin' good point that is mate. A very good fuckin' point indeed,' he smiled at the mere thought of payback, still stroking the lump of flesh at the side of his head as he did so.

'So we do it soon then?'

'Too fuckin' right mate,' Paddy smirked. 'In fact – the sooner the better as far as I'm concerned.'

'You heard anything about Paddy lately?' I asked Prey as the two of us sat drinking in Dry Bar. We were sat in the back area and I could smell the food being cooked in the kitchen and it made me realise just how hungry I was.

'Fuck all mate,' he smiled at me. 'I think you pissed him off slightly after amputating his ear the way you did.'

'That's what I'm concerned about Prey.'

'You ain't worried about him, are you Chopper?' Prey looked at me surprised.

'Nah mate it's not that,' I told him shaking my head. 'But Paddy and Chris aren't a couple of kids just coming onto the scene. I reckon us not seeing him for all these months gives me more to worry about. D'ya know what I mean Prey?'

'Yeah, but I wouldn't fret about it Chopper,' he told me. 'He knows that if he fucks with you then he's fuckin' with me as well.'

'Alright – look with the shop and everything I've kept my mind off it. But y'know as well as I do mate...' I stared hard at him. 'It's been a long time. *Too* fuckin' long in fact.'

'Funny you should mention it Chopper,' he grinned at me slyly. 'I've been speaking to Sleeper about it as well.'

'No offence to Sleeper,' I replied. 'I know he knew Sean and all. But he wasn't close like me and you were. It should be sorted by us,' I stated the truth. But the fact of the matter was that I wanted in on it personally.

'We need Sleeper brother,' he said sipping his bottle of Budweiser. 'More so than you realise. Why do you think he landed himself a name like Sleeper mate?'

'Fuck knows. How do any of us end up with ar' names?'

'Well that's it you see,' he looked at me seriously. 'Let's just say that Sleeper's a true brother. But if you ever get on the wrong side of him – *then shit* – I wouldn't like to be that guy. That's for sure.'

I suddenly understood what he was getting at. 'As in, he'll be reading you your last bed-time story eh?'

'Exactly mate,' he smiled and nodded at me. 'Believe me Chopper he's more experienced in the disposal business than either of us is.'

'So is he going to help us?'

'Of course he is,' he laughed. 'Maybe a lot sooner than you think as well. We're just waiting to hear on something very soon. If it checks out then we may be in business.'

'Good.'

'What did Steve say he wants to meet for?' I asked Prey as we sat in Chan's a couple of nights later.

'Hopefully what we've been waiting for Chopper,' He smiled. 'Truth is I'm not entirely sure mate,' I suddenly observed Prey's eyes momentarily wander.

But before I even had chance to turn, I was suddenly grabbed from behind and lifted right out of my chair. 'What... What the fuc...' I exclaimed, as I could see Prey laughing.

As I twisted myself free of the grip, I turned to face Sleeper. 'Yes Sleeper. How's it going? What you doing in town?'

'You alright lads,' he stared at me. 'What do you mean what am I doing here? I'm not welcome in Manchester no more.'

'Fuck that,' I was laughing back at him. 'Y'know you're always more than welcome around ar' back yard.'

'Where's the old man?' Sleeper asked sitting down.

'He'll be 'ere soon enough,' Prey smiled at his old friend as he rose and the two of them embraced one another. 'How was the train journey?'

'What are you doing travelling by train?' I asked shocked, as he always drove.

'You'll find out Chopper,' he winked at me. 'It was alright you know. It was double quick. Milton Keynes – Stoke – Macclesfield, then straight here. I was quite surprised at how quick it was.'

''Ere's the old man now,' Prey said nodding towards the entrance. 'I'll order the food then – I'm starving.'

'Alright lads,' Steve said looking cheerful as he strolled over to where we were seated.

'You alright mate,' I smiled at him. 'You look proper sound.'

'What's the story then?' Sleeper asked as Steve sat down.

'We're on,' he smiled.

'You sure?' Prey asked.

I was confused as to the nature of their conversation so I asked. 'Is someone going to let me in on this or what?'

They completely ignored my question, as Steve proceeded to tell Sleeper. 'Well I reckon I've got us the perfect little spot.'

'How secluded is it?'

'Not been occupied for years now,' he said lighting a Benson and Hedges cigarette. 'It's an old farm house, that's probably more than beyond simple restoration without tearing the fucker down and starting all over again. It's also probably the reason that nobody has bought it. Also the real bonus is that it is right out in the middle of a valley in Gawsworth surrounded by shrubbery and old half-dead trees.'

'And you're sure it's empty?'

'I'd forgotten all about it,' he blew his smoke out in a thick stream. 'I first seen it a few years back when I first came to the area. I was walking the dogs and seen a couple of squatters there. I chatted with them for a while; they said they were just passing through the area'

'And they're definitely gone?'

'I've staked the place for the last three days and nights,' Steve grinned. 'Even camped inside the place last night.'

'How's the access to and from it?' Sleeper enquired, obviously liking what he was being informed.

'Fine... Small country road,' Steve smiled at him. 'Then a dirt track leading you there. I know the area though, we'll be alright,' he said nodding at the waiter who'd just brought drinks over.

'What about noise levels?' Prey asked.

'As long as we don't go having a massive party down there,' he laughed. 'No one can hear shit for at least the surrounding couple of miles or so.'

'Sounds perfect,' Sleeper declared. 'I need to see it tomorrow.'

'No problem,' Steve replied. 'You can come stay at mine tonight mate.'

'Let me get this straight as you're all talking in riddles,' I was smiling, as I realised just where the conversation was leading. 'I take it that it's finally time?'

The three of them just looked at me and smiled,
nodding as they did.

'Alright then,' I asked just as the last of the dishes were
cleared away, 'When is it going to be?'

'After we've checked out that this gaff is totally secure,'
Sleeper began, 'then we need to sort out two secure motors.
Nothing hot. Totally clean but with false papers to match.
Also licenses in the correct names.'

'It's already sorted mate,' Prey told him. 'Ar' computer guy
has himself a nice little racket going again. Papers are
available within twenty fours hours of notice.'

'And I've sorted the motors out over Stoke way,' Steve
added.

'What motors you got Steve?' Sleeper looked a little
concerned. 'Nothing flash I hope.'

'Don't worry mate,' Steve smiled. 'I've got two nice little
family Volvo's on standby.'

'That's good. The last thing I need is to get a pull on the way
back,' he said staring at the three of us.

'So how soon can we move on this?' I asked impatiently.

'Patience Chopper,' Prey told me laughing as he did.

'I just want to....'

'We all know what you want to do Chopper,' Steve told me.

'It'll be worth the wait Chopper,' Sleeper smiled at me
knowingly. 'I promise you that.'

'Look,' Chris pointed out of the car window down the street. 'There's the little shit now.'

It was early evening as the two of them were cruising through Manchester's city centre down Deansgate heading back towards Salford.

'Is that his bird?' Paddy asked smiling. 'What the fuck is she doing with that cunt?'

'Yeah that's her mate. Nice ain't she?' Chris smiled also. 'Let's do him now... C'mon you said as soon as possible mate,' he suddenly sneered.

'In the middle of fuckin' town though?' Paddy asked astonished, then. 'Where's he gone? Where is he?'

'Take your next left mate,' Chris said. 'He's headed behind Kendal's. I'm sure of it.'

Just as Paddy eased his red three series BMW into the small street he noticed Chopper and Donna again. 'There – there they go,' he was all excited.

'Into Henry's bar,' Chris smirked. 'Y'know its right that we pop the little fucker right now in the middle of town. It just feels so right Paddy... C'mon – let's do the little fuck,' he smiled knowingly at his friend who was beginning to nod at the idea.

'We can wait down that side road there,' Paddy said nodding to the right hand side, for the unexpected plan they had in mind. 'As he comes out I'll be waiting for him. You just have the car ready Chris.'

'What about his missus?'

'Fuck her!' Paddy snapped. 'He's gonna get popped in front of her,' he added staring at Chris knowingly.

'About fuckin' time,' Chris smiled.

We made our way to the back area of Henry's bar, finding ourselves a seat. 'It's alright in 'ere,' I said, as it wasn't the usual spot we drank in, but I liked it.

'I know we've come here from work sometimes,' Donna told me.

'How was the shop today?'

'It was alright considering it's only Wednesday,' she told me. 'Are we going to eat? I'm starving.'

'No problem,' I said picking up the menu. 'What do you fancy?'

'Can I ask you something first though Chopper?'

'Of course,' I replied, looking at her; she'd seemed a little distant since leaving Macreedy's. 'Since when do you have to ask?'

'How come Sleeper turned up the other day?'

'No reason,' I shrugged. 'Just come to visit – that's all. Why'd you even ask?' I asked her, wondering what was up.
She looked at me. 'I saw Paddy today.'

'Where?' I enquired as calmly as possible.

'In the Royal Exchange,' she replied. 'He walked past the shop staring in whilst I was sat outside on one of the benches.'

'Did he bother you?' I snapped, anger building just at the mere thought of him.

'No – not at all – I don't think he even knows who I am.'

'What's wrong then?' I was even more confused.

'You bit his ear off? Didn't you Chopper?'

I was not expecting that question and I took a little too long to answer her, 'I – erm – I – No. What the hell kind of question is that?'

'Don't lie to me Chopper,' she said staring straight at me.

'What makes you ask that?' I snapped back unfairly.

'I heard Scotty the other week in Dry Bar laughing about it with Jonah,' she shook her head at me. 'They never saw me behind them both and I left immediately.'

'Well – y'know…' I trailed off, turning away from her.

'I didn't believe it at first,' she sighed. 'But when I saw him today I knew it was true.'

'He's the one who sliced me though,' I told her defensively.

'So it wasn't some Scouser then?' she said angrily.

'No it wasn't,' I snapped back at her – then instantly felt the guilt of doing so. 'I told you in the beginning Donna – I am who I am and I'm proud of it. You can't change me to who you want me to be.'

She touched my face gently. 'I don't want to change you Chopper. I never have. I just worry, that's all,' she said as tear began to swell...

'I also told you before, not to do that girl.' I said kissing her.

'I know you have,' she smiled at me. 'Kinda hard when you're like you are though.'

'Just try then,' I smiled.

'Pass the shooter Chris,' Paddy instructed, they had been sat outside for almost an hour now playing the waiting game. 'They've been in there a while now.'

'I've fully checked it,' Chris stated handing the Smith and Wesson semi-automatic pistol to him.

'Good. It's better if they're in there a while anyway,' Paddy sneered. 'It'll be darker for us,'

'Best swap seats now,' Chris suggested.

'You're right,' Paddy answered as he watched Chris descend from the passenger seat with him climbing over to it. 'I want to see the fear in those eyes of his when I pull the trigger,' he laughed as Chris climbed back through the driver's door.

'I'll ease the car past you as you walk up to him,' Chris told him. 'I'll have the motor running so we can get the...' he suddenly squinted. 'There they are now,' he smiled nodding toward the entrance.

Paddy grinned as he pulled the black woollen balaclava over his face watching Chopper and Donna walk onto the pavement outside the bar. ''Ere we go.'

'Hang on Chopper,' Donna told me, 'I've left my bag in there.'

'Alright – I'll wait 'ere for you,' I said, watching her walk back inside leaving me stood there on the pavement as I pulled my jacket tighter around myself to fight off the evening's cold air.

As cold as it was though, the night air only felt cool against my face, as I gazed up towards the darkening sky. I was totally in a world of my own standing there all alone, I hadn't even noticed the red car slowing down across from me.

Then suddenly something seemed familiar to me. Was it the car? I wasn't sure. Then with lightening speed the passenger door flew open, a fully masked dark figure was before me, and before I knew what the hell was happening I was caught completely off guard by whoever it was.

All of a sudden I felt a chill run through me as I focused on the cold steel that was thrust into my face; the cold eyes beneath the mask had pure hatred in them and despite the mask, I immediately realised who it was hidden beneath there.

It's the strangest feeling in the world having a loaded gun pointed directly at you. It's like nothing you could possibly imagine. You were filled with an array of miscellaneous feelings, from fear to what I imagine alcoholics would refer to as *'a moment of clarity.'*

You became fully aware of your surroundings – yet at the same time you feel distant from them. I then suddenly – for no apparent reason – found myself smirking. I knew that my time had come – and don't ask me why – I just seemed to accept it.

'You've just fucked yourself Paddy,' I calmly responded as he began to squeeze the trigger back. 'Go fuck yourself you dick!'

'Nnnoooooo - Chhhhooopppperrrr,' it was Donna who was now stood in the doorway. I kept my eyes focused before me, although fully aware where Donna was – only now I was more worried for her well being than myself. I couldn't let anything happen to her. This wasn't her problem. I was suddenly engulfed with the fear I felt for her safety.

'Get back inside Donna – *Now.*' I shouted to her whilst remaining solely focused on Paddy before me.

Everything then fell into slow motion as Paddy began squeezing back the trigger. I clearly witnessed that the end had arrived as I stood there awaiting the evitable... I simply closed my eyes and began smiling.

That's when it happened... Well *nothing* that is... Then nothing again! No thundering clap, no bolts of lightening from the gun, absolutely *nothing!* I opened my eyes and I realised that I was still stood there. It was still the city centre – not heaven – nor hell.

Sheer panic began to take control of Paddy's eyes as I was still filled with uncertainty as to what had gone wrong. What had just happened? Then with one final squeeze I saw him pull on the trigger again and yet still nothing happened – *I mean absolutely nothing.*

Paddy just stood there as confused as I was at what had just taken place. The fact was that we both had expected me dead only two seconds before... So without a second thought or another moment's hesitation, I swung out wildly with no particular target area, except that that was before me

But as I was striking out, he did the same with his right hand holding the pistol, and with his advantage in reach of the pistol he made first contact as the cold steel struck my forehead with some serious force. I felt the flesh tear open – and Christ – it was one hell of clout to receive.

I heard a mass of screams from behind me as I fell uncontrollably back towards the steps behind me. I witnessed the apprehension in Paddy's masked eyes as he stood above me, looking from me to the crowd now gathered in the doorway.

I began to become dizzy from the heavy blow, and found myself fighting to retain consciousness. He'd hit me a lot harder than I'd originally thought. Although I observed through some serious blurred vision the back of Paddy running away back towards that red vehicle he had momentarily exited. Then all I heard was the screeching of tyres and the stench burning rubber as he made his getaway from the scene.

'Chopper – *oh my God* - Chopper,' Donna screamed, holding me right there on the pavement.

'Did anyone get that number plate?' asked the barman now stood there, 'Anybody?' he shouted to no response at all.

'Chopper,' Donna said, tears streaming down her face.

'Get me out of 'ere,' I managed to say.

'Are you okay mate?' the barman asked. 'Just stay where you are – I'll phone for an ambulance and the police mate,' he disappeared back inside Henry's bar before I could respond.

'I need to get the fuck out of 'ere,' I said struggling to my feet.

'Chopper... stay where you are,' Donna pleaded. 'Your head's a mess.'

I knew it was, as my vision was becoming distorted from the blood running into my eyes. 'Just get me back on my feet – now Donna – we need to get the hell away from 'ere now,' I snapped at her. 'I can't have the coppers on my fuckin' back. Alright.'

Struggling to my feet, I shook my head to try and clear it. 'Right let's get the fuck out of 'ere now,' I told her as we began to walk away from the scene.

Donna was crying but I could see her plainly scowling at me, as she did so. 'I can't handle this anymore,' she sobbed.

'Oi – mate – *Oi* – where you going?' It was the bar man who was stood watching the two of us disappear out of sight. 'I phoned the…' he trailed off knowing it to be pointless.

'Let's get to the shop quickly,' I said, as we headed for St. Anns Square.

I thought you said that you checked it,' Paddy snarled, as they arrived back at Chris's flat.

'I did do,' he answered feebly.

'So what the fuck went and fuckin' happened you cock?' he screamed whilst at the same time he unloaded the clip still filled fully with the bullets.

'I don't know,' Chris sighed. 'There must have been some kind of block,'

'Block... What kind of fuckin' block you idiot,' he snapped.

'I've read somewhere that sometimes with semi-automatic pistols when the gun hasn't been cleaned properly that it can block some how. I don't know – I...' he trailed off.

Paddy was examining the shooter. 'Something must have jammed or blocked you're saying.' He pointed the loaded gun at Chris and tried to fire it again with the exact same reaction as before. 'What the fuck are you doing?' Chris screamed in sheer terror – Paddy was fucking losing it for sure. What the hell was he just thinking?

'Just thought I'd try it again,' he replied casually.

'I couldn't exactly test fire it in the car could I,' Chris declared sombrely shaking his head at what his so called friend had just done.

'He knew it was me,' Paddy told him, looking directly at him as he did.

'You fuckin' what?' Chris blurted out shocked. 'Are you sure?'

'Fuck yes. I'm sure,' Paddy shook his head. 'He's got some fuckin' balls on him the little twat – I got to give him that.'

'What the fuck are you going on about?'

'Let's put it this way mate,' he was still shaking his head whilst staring at the failed pistol in his hands. 'I wanted to see the fear in his eyes – I mean really wanted to see him shit himself y'know. And there wasn't any fuckin' fear whatsoever. The little bastard even smirked at me at one fuckin' point.'

'Are you fuckin' serious?' Chris blurted out again. 'He's got a gun shoved into his face and you're telling me that he wasn't scared.'

'Pretty much. Told me to go fuck myself,' Paddy said shaking his head in disbelief.

'Never,' Chris gasped, now shaking his own head.

'We'll have to watch ar' backs now,' Paddy said as he began loading a rock pipe. 'He'll want payback.' He added as he lit the fresh pipe and inhaled all of its fumes eagerly sucking away allowing the drug to work its magic.

'That's a fuckin' understatement – ain't it!' Chris exclaimed as he watched the smoke drift from Paddy's mouth as his face then began to convulse into the familiar crimsoned angered impression that Chris was used to witnessing more and more recently these days, especially with the increased intake of crack that Paddy smoked more and more each and every day.

He then suddenly stared at Chris with crazed eyes of a mad man. 'Fuck these Hulme cunts. *Fuck 'em all,*' he screamed out loud, shaking extravagantly at Chris as face contorted into a venomous scowl – one of pure hatred towards anything and everything at that give moment.

'Whatever you say boss,' said Chris not sounding so sure to even himself.

As we entered the empty shop I fell to the floor. 'Phone Prey.'

'No,' she snapped back with sheer anger. 'I want to know what's going on. Do you know what just happened? Do you realise or not just how fucking close you were to getting killed back there? Chopper fucking listen to me will you – this is fucking insane – *Chopper* – Will you...,' she screamed the words at me.

'Just phone Prey now – *Will you* – Please,' I said, trying as best as possible to calm myself; of course I'd known what had just happened for fucks sake.

Donna fell to her knees beside me sobbing as she did. 'Please Chopper. I can't go on like this... please... I love you... he wanted to kill you... who was it? Please... this is a nightmare...'

I left her lay there as I climbed unsteadily to my feet, dialling Prey's mobile number, he answered immediately. 'Pick me up now – I'm at the shop,' I instructed sharply, watching Donna lay on the floor crying hysterically.

Prey laughed. 'What am I? A fuckin' taxi service you twat.'

'Now,' I snapped, this time he knew I'd been serious.

'What's happened?' he asked, changing the tone of his voice.

'Somebody just tried to pop me outside Henry's,' I said flatly, but to tell the truth, deep down my anger was raging like inferno.

'You fuckin' what,' his voice filled with panic. 'Are you hit?'

'No – I'm still not quite sure what happened,' I was unconsciously shaking my head. 'Donna was there though.'

70

'You're fuckin' joking,' he blurted out.

'Just get 'ere now.'

'I'm on the way out the door. Kathy's 'ere as well... for Donna mate,' he said as the line went dead.

Replacing the receiver, I went over to Donna crouching down. 'Donna – Donna – Listen to me,' I said holding her.

'I was just so scared. Scared – I know what you said – but...' she was sobbing uncontrollably.

'I know,' I said, holding her firmly.

'He had a gun pointing straight at you Chopper,' she held onto me tenaciously. 'I still can't believe it.'

'C'mon now,' I tried with her. 'I'm still 'ere ain't I,' I said, kissing the top of her head.

'Why – Why – Why Chopper? Why's he do that?' she suddenly screamed pushing me away.

As I descended backwards, I just sat there on the floor, blood was still pouring from where he'd whacked me and along with Donna's ranting my head was starting to thump. 'Because it's what I do Donna,' I declared defiantly, glaring at her as she stared down hard at me. 'It's what I've always done. You just can't change some things y'know.'

She looked at me then wiped the blood from my head with her sleeve. 'I just don't know if I can handle it anymore Chopper,' she wrapped her arms around my head.

'Prey will be 'ere soon.'

'I'm serious Chopper,' she said still tears were rolling.

'You're going dehydrate you keep crying like that girl,' I was smiling at her.

'Oh Chopper,' she looked at me. 'What am going to do with you. Look at you joking like nothing has even happened. I just don't know what I'd do without you.'

The truth was though; I'd known just how serious it had been. However, I was trying to do my best to hide the anger that raged from deep within me.

If she had any idea what we were planning at the moment she'd go ballistic. It would really be the end. And that was one thing I couldn't live with. It wasn't even worth thinking about.

I still wasn't able get my head round it; Paddy had actually tried to take me out right in the middle of fucking town. Not only that, but he'd tried it in front of Donna. Just what the fuck was he thinking? And more importantly – what the hell had gone wrong?

71

I knew from the way his hatred turned to panic when the pistol merely did nothing that he wasn't out just to scare me. Besides which – you could see clearly that the safety catch on his shooter was not clicked into the safety position - *No* – It was safe to say that he definitely had every intention of killing me outside Henry's bar. He'd had every intention of killing me right there in front of Donna. What the fuck had happened? Whatever the hell it was I was more than little pleased to fuck by it.

The more I thought of him, the deeper and darker my hatred towards him grew. But I knew that for now I had to control that anger whilst Donna was here.

She couldn't know anything.

Both Steve and Sleeper had been at the disused cottage for the last couple of nights, making sure it was fully secure and preparing it for our guest.

'That's definitely the best route Steve.'

'It's a lot of cross country though, are you sure mate?' Steve asked rubbing the back of his head.

'Look, it ain't visible from the roads,' Sleeper was saying, 'and it takes me almost to the other side of Congleton where I can skip straight onto the motorway heading south after that.'

'Alright, I suppose it makes sense,' Steve finally agreed. 'But we do a few dry runs first, and then on the night in question I do the driving. If you go getting yourself stuck out here in the dead of night; you'll be fucked for sure. Last thing you'll need is farmer fuckin' Giles coming to your rescue.'

'Okay then,' Sleeper nodded his agreement, 'let's do a few runs now in that old clapped out motor of yours then. You know it's a good job that you don't drive back and forth to town in it or I'd have got the train again.' He laughed looking at Steve's worse for wear Escort that he'd had for years.

'You taking the piss out of my motor or what?' Steve laughed along. 'It holds a lot of good memories that does.'

'C'mon then,' he smiled heading for the car.

'Sleeper,' Steve said, staying stood where he was. 'Can I ask you something mate?'

'Sure Steve – What's on your mind?'

'What's going to happen to his body afterwards?'

'Disposal service in London will take care of it.' He said flatly with no emotion whatsoever.

'How good of a service is it eh? You know this disposal service of yours,' Steve stared at Sleeper with a look of intensity.

'To be honest mate,' Sleeper said leaning casually against the car. 'It's why I have to take him back down there. You see I've got a good friend down that way who happens to run a crematorium. No trace whatsoever.'

'Crafty fucker,' Steve smiled, the lines of intensity dissolving from his forehead for he'd liked the answer.

'I've just got to make it back safely,' he told him. 'Which to be honest should be alright at the time that I'll be travelling at. These motors you're sorting are defiantly going to be sweet ain't they?'

'Double kosher mate. Guaranteed,' Steve told him walking around to the driver's door.

'When can we get our hands on them?' Sleeper asked climbing into the Escort.

'Just as soon as they're needed. I figured that until the actual day of the job it wasn't worth picking them up,' Steve told him. 'You know in case any nosy fucker happened to look twice at them.'

'No, that's good,' Sleeper nodded. 'Although I still wouldn't mind getting to have a look at them before hand though.'

'No problem. We'll shoot over there tomorrow afternoon,' Steve said firing up the engine.

'Excellent,' Sleeper smiled. 'I reckon we should be in business by Sunday night then. It's a good night to use with it being just before the week starts. Hopefully I'll just appear to be a salesman travelling down to London for my job.'

Steve smiled at his way of thinking. 'Right come on then,' he eased the car into gear, 'Let's do some dry runs on this route of yours then.'

They didn't arrive back at Steve's until late. They'd gone over the route over five times trying to figure out the best possible route, avoiding surrounding farmhouses or where they were at all visible from the road.

'You want a drink mate?' Steve asked Sleeper as they walked into the house.

'Cheers,' he replied, then. 'Looks like you got a few messages Steve,' Sleeper nodded at the answer machine.

'It's me – where the fuck are you? C'mon answer the bleedin' phone.' It had been Prey sounding more than a little

74

anxious on the answer machine. In fact he'd left six messages in total.

'Shit!' Steve exclaimed grabbing the phone punching in Prey's number. 'What the fuck could have got him so rattled?' he added looking at Sleeper still stood there.

Prey answered almost immediately. '*Yes.*'

'It's me,' Steve announced. 'What the fuck's up?'

'Where the fuck, have you two been?'

'Easy brother,' Steve told him. 'You know where the fuck we've been,' he said, although sensing the panic in Prey's voice.

'Yeah – yeah 'course I know where you've been,' Prey said taking a deep sigh. Before exhaling a little calmer now. 'Someone almost got to the kid tonight – and to make matters worse it was whilst his missus was also there.'

'You what?' Steve knew instantly whom Prey was referring to. 'Are they alright?' Sleeper looked straight at Steve sensing something wasn't right.

'Look – you two better come straight over,' Prey told him. 'The kid's alright. Just a bit ruffed up. Nothing too serious, but we need to talk.'

'Be there in about an hour,' Steve said replacing the headset.

'Is Donna alright?' Steve asked looking at my new addition of recent stitches.

'Yeah... Well no... Well not really y'know,' I kissed my teeth at the thought. 'That cunt shoved the shooter in my face whilst she was stood there. It's kinda freaked the shit out of her, y'know.'

'Where is she now?' Sleeper enquired.

'Kathy's with her upstairs,' Prey looked at him. 'Hassid gave her something that seems to have knocked her out.'

'He said it would calm her down,' I smirked. 'She looks like a baby sleeping. I might need to get a prescription off Hassid for any foreseeable arguments.'

'And the gun just clicked? And that was it?' Sleeper asked smiling at what I had said as he did so.

'Well sort of – I think so anyway – I think that was it. Either that or nothing happened. I know it sounds odd but the safety was definitely off and the fuckin' thing just seemed to do fuck all,' as I said this, I began smiling at them. 'I ain't got a clue what happened to be honest. But he pulled the bloody trigger three times with every intention of killing me.'

75

'You're the luckiest bastard alive,' Prey laughed. 'That could only happen to you.'

'Maybe it wasn't loaded. Maybe he just wanted to scare you,' Steve suggested.

'It sounds like stoppage,' Sleeper informed us. 'That's why it's important to keep your shooter cleaned on a regular basis. Whether you use it or not. Stoppage is what stops the bullet loading into the chamber. I've seen it happen before. That's why those old reliable revolvers are the best you know? The chamber merely rotates round to the next chamber,' Sleeper certainly knew his shit, I thought listening to him.

'I could see it in his eyes. I mean you must be right Sleeper,' I told him. 'If it wasn't loaded then he certainly didn't know about it. I can tell you that much. I reckon he almost crapped himself more than me when fuck all happened.'

Sleeper laughed. 'This goes down Sunday night then. Hopefully that higher grace of yours up there will watch over all of us until then Chopper,' as he said this, he looked up toward the ceiling.

'I've already got the paper work today,' Prey said pulling an A4 envelope from behind the settee. 'I got everything to cover us, including some credit cards. But for fuck's sake don't try using them will you. They're just for show, that's all.'

'The next step is snatching him. It needs to be so low-key, 'cause we don't want to raise any alarms for at least twenty four hours if at all possible,' said Sleeper who had now stepped forward and had my head in his hands as he examined the wound.

'Well I reckon the best thing to do, would be to snatch him from his gaff on Sunday night,' I suggested.

'What if someone else is there with him?' Steve asked.

'That's exactly why it also makes sense,' I told them. 'If he's got company then we tie them up and leave them there. No fucker will know shit for at least that amount of time.'

'He's right, you know,' Sleeper said letting releasing my head and looking and looking to the other two. 'Although I don't particularly want any other fucker involved.'

'So what's the next move then?' Prey asked.

'What time we got?' Sleeper then asked.

'Just gone one thirty,' Prey told him.

'Right let's take a look at his gaff now,' Sleeper announced.

'Right now?' Prey asked looking shocked.

'Why the fuck not?' Sleeper said smiling. 'It's as good a time as any. You've got his address haven't you?'

'As long as he hasn't moved,' Prey shrugged. 'Last time I was even near that place was years ago.'

'Well there's only one way to find out,' I told him already out of my chair and pulling my jacket on without a moment's hesitation.

We were plotted in Steve's Mercedes at the top end of Mayfield Avenue in Crumpsall, hidden in the darkness of the shadows produced from the trees.

'You sure that's it?' I asked.

'Used to be,' Prey simply replied.

'Alright – we've been here about an hour already,' Sleeper stated. 'No one's home or at least not the one we're looking for ain't.'

'So what do you suggest?' Steve asked.

'Let's take a look at the area itself,' Sleeper suggested.

'Wait – Look,' I suddenly said just as Steve was about to start the engine. 'There he is - with Chris as well.'

Paddy had just pulled up outside the two-floor block of flats; his being the first one as you reached the top of the steps.

'Was that the car Chopper?' Prey enquired.

'I don't know mate,' I told him honestly. 'I think so. All I remember about the motor was that it was red so it's more than fuckin' likely.'

We watched as the two of them disappeared through Paddy's front door, 'Alright now we know that's where he lives for sure. Let's get the fuck out of here,' Sleeper said.

'That's it?' I asked a little annoyed - but not quite sure at the same time what I was thinking we were going to do.

'For tonight,' he replied. 'I'll stake it out for the next couple of nights until Sunday.'

'What do we do?' I asked.

'Well for starters I noticed his gaff is belled up Chopper,' he grinned at me. 'So you'll need to get a look at it before hand. We need it disabling on the way in and engaging on the way out. It needs to quick – very quick.'

'That won't be any problem at all,' I was smiling confidently.

'As for Steve and me – well we've still a lot to cover anyway.'

'And me?' Prey looked to Sleeper.

'As for you chief,' he smiled at Prey. 'Just make sure you get that list of gear together for tomorrow night.'

Donna was still passed out on my return. I thanked and kissed Kathy goodnight as she left with Prey.

Sleeper headed back over to Steve's gaff in Congleton to finish off over that way.

Undressing quietly in the darkness of the bedroom, I watched Donna sleep. I'd been so scared that day for her safety. I loved her so much, even if I was pretty shit at showing it sometimes. I thought about how peaceful she looked as I climbed into bed.

She stirred, snuggling closer to me. 'I love you Chopper,' she said still half asleep.

'Me too Donna,' I said kissing her. 'Sorry.'

We both fell into deep sleeps holding one another close.

'Prey and me will just drop in on him whilst he's still jerking off to the TV,' I said as we were heading over to Paddy's, Steve and Prey were following in the other Volvo. It was just coming up for ten o'clock.

'What if that other lad is there?' Sleeper asked. 'It could be risky you know.'

'If we leave it like last night when we were watching his gaff and wait for Chris to leave – Well it'll be way too late,' I stated, knowing it made sense.

'That's true,' Sleeper agreed. 'You sweet on the alarm system Chopper.'

'That's a bit of a dumb question isn't it?'

'Alright then – you just make sure you act fast on this.'

'I'm fucked after last night Paddy,' Chris said rolling about the settee.

He'd only left around five that morning, after a night of caning crack-cocaine together. He'd been wasted by the time he had left the flat heading back to his own place of residence.

'I know what you mean,' Paddy said walking back in from the kitchen chucking a can of Stella Artois at his friend. 'I could do some more though.'

'It gets like that. Don't it mate?' Chris laughed as he opened the can.

'You heard anything from town? Y'know about what happened last week,' he asked swigging at the can.

'The lads say they haven't seen Chopper or Prey all weekend,' Chris grinned. 'I reckon they'll be shitting themselves by now.'

'I told you I didn't give a fuck – Didn't I,' he laughed. 'They're nothing but a bunch of scared spineless little pussies down at that estate.'

'I know,' Chris chuckled. 'I reckon we should make a move on their action, you know. They've ran the Es in town now for time – but things have changed. There's a lot more contacts out there for them now.'

'I know what you're saying mate,' he smiled. 'They've made top dollar from all the action they controlled. I think it's about time we showed them just who are the ones who are really running Manchester eh. Besides which I've got me some top contacts for the pills over in Liverpool,' he was starting to get all excited.

'Good – that's that then. Fuck the lot of 'em.' Chris shouted nodding his head whilst gulping his beer back.

'Tell you what. My treat mate,' Paddy said smirking at Chris with a knowing glint in his eye. 'I'll pay – but you go and get 'em.'

'How many you want?' he asked knowing exactly what Paddy was on about.

'Just get an eighth of stone,' he said throwing some money at Chris. 'Should be enough there.'

Chris was already pulling his jacket on. 'I'll go see Mikey,' he said heading for the door. 'I'll see you in a bit – I shouldn't be too long.'

'Don't be – I'll have the pipe waiting,' Paddy smiled as he followed his friend to the door, 'oh and don't forget the snouts for the ash. Last thing we want to do is run out again.' He added as Chris disappeared out the door, with Paddy automatically re-setting the alarm.

'Right here we go,' Sleeper said as we turned into Mayfield Avenue.

'Wahhhooo... stop,' I said spotting someone down the road, 'Take a look at that,' I added pointing in the direction of Paddy's flat.

It was Chris climbing into his Sierra outside of where we were heading. 'I wonder where he's off to.'

'Fuck knows – but now we got to act double quick in case he comes straight back.

'Fuck, he's heading this way,' Sleeper said. 'Get down Chopper.'

80

We just caught a glimpse of his headlights flashing past our car. 'I hope they ducked out of sight also,' I said, glancing behind me at Prey and Steve's Volvo.

'Damn that was close. Right you're clear what we're going to do?' Sleeper asked me as I nodded. 'Right – No time to waste then let's get moving,' he said as I was already out of the car heading in the direction of Paddy's flat with Prey already in tow.

'You've got your piece Chopper?' Prey whispered to me, just as we came upon Paddy's alarm box. Both of us were fully masked up in black ski masks.

I simply nodded acknowledgement to his question. 'You see who just left?'

He nodded back at me grinning beneath the mask. He then nodded at me silently that he was heading up the steps.

Unscrewing the small electrical box fixed to the wall, I went to work on the alarm – shit, these home alarm systems really were terrible. They were way too easy to bypass. Although to still be on the safe side I filled the outer box that was fitted with the actual alarm bell with insulation foam that hardened immediately – just a secondary caution to silence the sound of the bell in case by chance I had missed something.

'You done already?' Prey asked surprised as I was already working on the bedroom window.

'Piece of piss,' I shrugged, easing open the window that was luckily down the left side of the building, so not visible from the road.

'Shit, you are fast lad,' he said as I was already climbing through the window into the darkness of the bedroom. The room smelt of dirty linen and old smoke.

We could hear the television blaring from the other room. I nodded in that direction at Prey, who had just crawled behind me signalling where the sound was coming from.

Peering through the gap in the bedroom door towards where the light was descending from. Just then a large shadow walked straight past the door startling me a little. You could see the back of Paddy disappearing into what we presumed to be the living room.

The two of us crawled silently up to the living room door. You could clearly see Paddy clearly making himself a rock pipe from an old empty water bottle and biro as he was totally oblivious that he had any guests.

I signalled to Prey to take a look for himself. Prey did exactly that... then without any warning, he instantaneously crashed through the door sprinting straight for Paddy. He jumped out of his chair screaming in shock and panic.

'What... nooo... how... where the fuck...' Prey smashed his Glock 9mm into Paddy's face with all the force he could muster.

I observed Paddy spin round from the blow straight back into the leather settee, from the doorway. Prey pressed his foot down hard into Paddy's head to hold him. Casually walking through the door, I smiled through my mask at Paddy lay there helplessly. I observed the fear all over Paddy's face as he saw me, and it gave me nothing but pure pleasure to bare witness to.

'Please... no... it wasn't *me*,' he pleaded.

'I haven't accused you of anything,' I smiled, pulling the mask from my face, 'yet... that is,' I added casually.

Prey pressed his foot down harder into his face. 'I think we need to go and have a little chat – Don't we Paddy lad?'

'Nooooo,' he started to wail as I smashed the butt of my Beretta semi-automatic into his face tearing the flesh from his nose as I did so.

We could see he was still conscious though as Prey released his foot allowing Paddy to drop to the floor. As he began to struggle up, I grinned at Prey, and then smashed the gun into the back of his neck.

'Lights out Paddy,' Prey said smiling.

'Stick these on him Prey,' I said throwing the handcuffs to him.

Prey swiftly locked his hands behind his back as I wrapped the silver duct tape around his mouth and feet.

He began to stir, so I smashed him once again at the back of his ear to put him under again.

Prey hitched Paddy's body up onto his shoulder as I was doing my best to straighten things out, switching off all the lights and television. 'Let's get out of 'ere.'

'Found them,' I declared dangling Paddy's keys in front of myself. 'Let me check the front out first.'

Signalling that things were sweet to go, Prey shot passed me into the dead of night with Paddy's limp body slung effortlessly over his shoulder. Locking the front door behind us, I could see Prey was already at Sleeper's car dumping

Paddy's body into the boot, which we'd completely covered in plastic sheeting.

I signalled once again for them to ease the cars back down the street into the darkness of the trees, as I still had the alarm to take care of. I was not able to set it from inside, as I didn't have the code. Besides which, I was more familiar with them from the outside of the building.

'Everything go alright?' Steve asked Prey as he climbed into the back seat ducking down.

'Yes mate,' he half laughed.

'Where's Chopper?'

'Got to sort out the alarm. Re-wire it back on,' Prey informed him smiling proudly. 'He sure is good at that shit y'know.'

'Lights – we've got lights Prey,' Steve said ducking down and just about seeing Sleeper do same in the front car. 'Shit, I think it was him.'

'You what?' Prey said trying to peek out. 'You think it was Chris... shit... fuck,' Prey exclaimed. 'I can't see Chopper.'

'Is it him?'

'Yes,' Prey said as he caught a glimpse of Chris running towards Paddy's flat.   'Fuck... shit... fuck... where's Chopper?'

I'd just finished with the alarm as I heard the sound of an engine making its way down the road.

I quickly ducked down under the steps from where I'd only just descended, and clear as day I saw Chris's Sierra pull up to the curb. 'Shit!' I'd whispered out loud – we didn't need this – especially me. I was standing there as still as possible doing my best to conceal myself from view.

Chris was out of the car heading straight for me. I felt that I was concealed by the shadows enough – although how well was hard top tell from my position.

Chris darted up the steps, taking the first few steps two at a time. He then suddenly stopped.

Shit – Fuck – I really didn't need this. Had he seen me? Had I made a sound? Was he suspicious that there was no lighting on in the flat?

My breathing sounded as though it was echoing with the tranquillity of night, standing there, my mind raced as I wondered what move to make next.

'Arhhh... you bastard... shit... fuckin' snouts!'

I suddenly heard Chris say out loud – Was he addressing me?

As I stood my ground, I eased open my lock knife as quietly as possible – Just then Chris bounced back down the steps towards the car, mumbling something to himself as he did.

He was gone as quickly as he'd arrived – I finally let my breath out again, and then darted from the shadows, sprinting to Sleeper's Volvo.

'Shit – now that was close,' I stated, jumping into the passenger seat.

'Let's just get the fuck out here,' Sleeper declared as he started the engine up, easing out into the road.

'Steve's going to drive slightly ahead of us just in case anything goes wrong he can either bell us on my mobile or try and work his way back to help us.'

'I thought I was going to have to deal with him also,' I said, knowing that my breathing was both fast and uncontrolled as my adrenaline raced to new levels.

'Good work though.'

'Cheers,' I replied, 'it's far from over yet though.'

Not far now Prey,' Steve said as they were easing the Volvo's through the blackness of woodland, the car lights illuminating the trees were the only things that were visible to the naked eye.

'Fuck me!' Prey whistled. 'This is definitely out in the sticks Steve... Ain't it?'

'Here we go,' Steve said pulling the car over as both Sleeper and I pulled up along side of them.

'What the fuck are you going on about Steve?' Prey enquired, as he looked around bewildered. 'I can't see shit.'

'You alright Chopper?' Steve asked shaking his head.

'Yeah – I thought we were going to be disposing of two bodies instead of one,' laughed Prey as he walked over.

'In'it,' I added, popping open the boot of our car.

Paddy looked desperate as he lay there staring at the four of us merely smirking at him. 'Evening son,' I said, dragging him from the boot.

You could stench the aroma of his fear that had taken hold of what was once one of Manchester's most feared and notorious characters. Yet now here at this moment in time he looked nothing more than a scared little boy as I pulled him up to face me. Smiling menacingly at him, I then spat my hatred at him.

'Let's get him inside,' Sleeper instructed.

'Where exactly is... inside?' Prey asked, whose eyes still hadn't adjusted to the dark and who still couldn't focus on anything.

'Just follow us,' Sleeper said as he casually butted Paddy in the face to knock him out – then with total ease threw him over his shoulder. 'And don't forget the holdall mate.'

The three of us made our way into the bare, damp hollowness of the cottage as Steve snapped on the torches hanging in the two far corners of the room.

As the torches enlightened the room, they revealed the room to be covered wall to wall and ceiling to floor with industrial plastic sheeting. Even I have to admit that the sight alone, mixed with the cold damp air sent a slight shiver up my spine – God only knows what Paddy's true fears would be.

Sleeper dumped him into the wooden chair, which held centre stage to the room. I stepped forward taking out my cock and then started to piss all over his face as he started to regain consciousness. He instantly began panicking at the sight around him as he began to focus on his surroundings, all the while shaking his head to try and free the stench and dampness I'd just covered him with.

I then tied the ropes from the holdall around him to secure him firmly; I began grinning coldly at his now scared shitless face. 'Welcome to hell you fuck!' I sneered at him as I finished with the ropes.

Prey reached down into the duffel bag producing two baseball bats. He threw one to me. Then he began to nonchalantly swing to bat back and forth – Back and forth – Taunting Paddy, the room was deadly silent apart from the heavy breathing descending through Paddy's bloodied nose.

'What did you think Paddy…?' Prey began, whilst still swinging and pacing about as we stood there staring down at him. 'Did you honestly think that we'd just forget about Sean? Did you?' he snarled the last part at him.

'I mean that just wasn't enough, was it? Then you had to go after Chopper – didn't you?' Prey shook his head and kissed his teeth, producing a clicking sound giving the appearance of a school-teacher punishing their student for a mere spelling mistake. 'Just couldn't leave it alone could you Paddy? I mean I let it go after you did this,' he stroked the scar that ran the length of his face.

'Y'know why I left it,' he paused, glaring directly at Paddy. 'Because that was over business. It wasn't like some personal vendetta. Was it you fuck?' he screamed at him as Paddy struggled about frantically at the perception of Prey before him.

He then bent down so that his face was inches from Paddy's face. He then took a long dramatic sniff, and then shook his head at the stench that was a mixture of fear and urine. 'I can smell your fear Paddy,' he smirked, and then began playing with the small lump of flesh where Paddy's ear had once been. 'I mean even after you slayed ar'kid in cold blood... You went after Chopper? Didn't you Paddy? I mean just look at yourself. Why oh why? I have to ask...' he continued to play with the lump, and then began laughing at both Paddy himself and the mere sight of the clump of flesh.

'Chopper could whip your sorry arse in his sleep – but you not being the sharpest tool in the shed – somehow don't seem to realise this. I mean what was that all about – I mean really,' he stopped and stared at Paddy, his face was wall of stone.

Paddy was sat there shivering as the trepidation took control. You could see that he'd already wet himself, the warm yellow piss dribbling out from the bottom of his jeans onto the plastic, its stench replenishing the dense atmosphere.

Just then Steve and Sleeper lit a further two torches and shone them directly at Paddy who now had tears rolling down his face. His head was frantically shaking from side to the other, his muffled cries falling onto our deaf ears.

Prey crouched down in front of him holding his bat to the floor. 'Why did you try to kill Chopper in the middle of town?' Prey stepped away as I stepped forward without a moment's hesitation.

'In front of fuckin' Donna as well you cunt,' I was screaming as I suddenly slammed the bat full swing into his head knocking both him and the chair over, splitting the flesh from bone instantaneously.

A dark crimson tide of blood was pouring freely from his forehead as Prey lifted his fallen chair up again with Paddy still attached but barely conscious. He then whispered menacingly into Paddy's ear. 'Y'know what Paddy. This was always going to happen to you. We just wanted you to think you'd gotten away with it.'

Striding forward again, I slammed my bat forward for a second time, only this time making contact with his upper torso. 'Bastard,' I screamed as I started into his eyes that looked ready to pop, as his face darkened with the intense pain with which he was receiving.

'So as you can see Paddy. You needn't have ever worried about us forgetting about you. We never did do,' Prey said slamming the bat into the back of him.

Then between the two of us we began to simultaneously, repeatedly, slamming the bats into him. Each blow was filled with anger, hatred and sweet vengeance all in one sweet motion.

With each blow you could hear his bones snapping, crushing, breaking as blood began to ooze through his clothing. Stepping back and staring at him barely conscious, my hate was raging from deep within me as I strode forward again swinging the bat upwards into his dropped face sending him crashing backwards into the sheeting behind him.

My breathing was both fast and hard, as I tried my best to control it. 'Throw some petrol on his face,' I instructed. 'I want him awake for this next bit.'

'Wanker,' Prey screamed as he kicked him in the balls whilst he lay there.

Steve splashed the petrol onto his face. 'He's still with us – *barely*... But he'll know what's happening,' he smiled as he sat him up in the chair again.

'Here Steve,' Sleeper said passing to him one of the sawed-off double barrel shotguns from the holdall, as Prey took the other one.

Paddy's eyes were barely open as he sat there a broken man, bloodied and fighting against the petrol fumes... That was until Steve shoved the shotgun into his face hitting him as he did so; he soon opened his eyes fully as he stared down two barrels of a fully loaded shotgun.

'Y'know what's coming next – don't you?' I said grinning at him as Steve then pointed the sawn off at his balls.

He was becoming frantic, skirmishing as he did.

'This is for Sean Macreedy. May you remember his name you cunt,' Steve screamed the words whilst squeezing back the trigger, the blast exploding into his groin area. The pain he must have felt in that precise moment had expanded like stretched rubber across his face.

Next Sleeper took Prey's gun from him and stepped forward. 'And this is for going after Chopper,' he casually said, the second blast cutting into his stomach tearing it apart.

Steve lifted the chair up right once again and then splashed more petrol onto his face, he was barely alive as Prey and I stood before him.

His eyes flickered slightly as we both pointed out guns to his head. 'And this – this you cunt...well this is just being born you twat,' I spat the words at him as we both pulled the triggers simultaneously.

His head seemed to literally explode from the blasts of the two shotgun cartridges taking what little life was left in him, his body thrown back through the air from the force of the discharge.

Prey stood over him. 'Well then... one fuckin' ear – No fuckin' balls - Well you wasn't much fuckin' use to anybody in the end, was you Paddy?' Prey laughed, as I just grinned, staring at the sight of his motionless bloody corpse lay there whilst thinking to myself that it was finally over. Payback for everything he'd done had been taken sweetly.

Sleeper was the one who cleaned all the evidence away as we all changed into fresh clothing, placing everything into the boot of his Volvo that had also been fitted with the industrial plastic.

Prey and I met both him and Steve at the meeting point. 'You sure everything's going to be sweet?' I asked.

'Has been in past,' he laughed as he swapped seats with Steve, who had just exited the car.

'Sleeper...' Prey began to say.

'I know brother – don't mention it,' he smiled as he closed the car door. 'I still owed you anyway.'

'See you soon. Well I hope I see you soon mate. It's been a real pleasure working with you,' Steve said smiling as he shook his hand.

'Thanks again Sleeper,' I said winking at him with a little nod of the head 'It was as you promised mate – Well worth waiting for.'

'Alright, I'll give you lads a ring once everything's disposed of fully. Alright?' he fired up the engine.

'You sure you'll be sweet getting back?' Prey asked.

Sleeper casually took his handgun out placing it next to him on the passenger seat he then smiled at the three of us. 'Let's hope so – or I'll be disposing of more than just Paddy back there.'

Then without another word he took off into the night.

'He's still not shown up you know Mike,' Walsh was saying as the two of them sat in the office high above the streets of Manchester as they stared out at the city centre down below as people ducked for cover from the torrential downpour that was in full flow.

'Who's that – McNally?' asked Stevenson. 'What do you reckon Martin? How long has it been now anyway?'

'It'll be just over two months this weekend,' he stated glancing at his watch. 'My thoughts are that he has disappeared permanently.'

'You reckon so?'

'That's my guess anyway,' Walsh replied. 'Paddy's not likely to have disappeared for this amount of time if it wasn't for a very good reason.'

'Do you know if he any recent trouble with anyone?' Stevenson asked sipping his coffee.

'You kidding or what?' Walsh laughed. 'That little shit had grief with just about everybody in town. No one liked him – he just put fear into people around him, so to control them. A lot of the crews around Manchester... hell even the guys out of town wouldn't deal with him. It was just a few of the Salford lads. But from what I heard even they were becoming more and more pissed off with him.'

'What about anyone else besides those Salford lot?'

'It could be someone else,' he looked to be thoughtful on the matter. 'I remember him from years ago. I know he used to be one of the main lads around town back then also,' he told him. 'You know one possibility Mike? Years back now when he was still only nineteen or so we were looking into the possibility of him dealing with the IRA.'

'You're joking – aren't you?' Stevenson's mouth dropped with the news that was new to him. 'Are you serious, what the fuck was he doing with them lot?'

'We got wind of it through some guy we busted back then. Said he'd give us a big score to go after.'

'How's that relate to Paddy and the fucking IRA?'

'It turned out that Paddy was apparently trading guns for cannabis. Case fell through of course as we couldn't get enough evidence and the grass funnily enough, also disappeared. Plus we reckon the Irish somehow got wind of us being on to them and they just seized trading with each other. Well either that or they just got a hell of a lot more smarter on us eh?'

'Could be them then,' Stevenson said shaking his head at the story. 'I mean you don't go pissing them lot off and fuck knows what Paddy was up to.'

'I very much doubt it – But you never know,' Walsh took another sip of his coffee. 'I mean it's not even a case to be honest. He was due in court over that fracas outside of that club in town, only he never showed for it. That's the only reason he's on the missing list at all. His family actually seemed pleased he isn't around. Not that you could blame them of course.'

'I remember you saying,' Stevenson said putting his feet up. 'You sure it's not over that, you know shitting himself that this time it was jail time.'

'Not fucking likely with Paddy,' Walsh laughed. 'You know who his brief is?'

'Who?'

'Samuel Neilson.'

'Right – I see what you mean,' Stevenson said lighting a cigarette.

'You remember when I was over in Salford. Well we had him bang to fucking rights on a murder case. The fucker killed this young lad outside of Kentucky Fried Chicken in Cheetham Hill; poor lad was just buying food with his girlfriend. Paddy didn't like the way the kid looked at him so he jumped the kid, slashing his neck with a machete. The kid bled to death right there in the street.'

'I remember that case,' Stevenson sighed.

'I was on the original arrest. We were positive that we had finally nailed him,' Walsh said gulping his coffee shaking his head. 'Anyway, this Neilson character has been Paddy's brief that long. He twisted the law in every possible which way in favour of his client. Even the girlfriend ended up refusing to testify, as did any other witness's. In the end none of us could believe it when the judge threw it out on lack of substantial evidence.'

'Like I said, I remember it well,' Stevenson said blowing out his smoke.

'So anyway, as you can see Mike, I honestly don't believe that this charge would have bothered him in the slightest,' Walsh said grabbing for the pack of cigarettes.

'He did have shit loads of previous though,' Stevenson said. 'You checked his place out.'

'We got the warrants that afternoon once he failed to show up for court,' Walsh said throwing the lighter down. 'Nothing was out of place at all, even the alarm had been set liked he'd left to go out somewhere. About the only odd thing was his motor was still outside.'

'What about his lads, the ones on the street?'

'That's the other odd thing,' Walsh sighed again. 'A couple of the grasses that I know over that way are saying that he has still got a shit load of money on the street. They say that his right hand man Chris Walker is trying to collect at the moment, he's just not having much luck on his own though. Especially with no Paddy around to back him. Although word is that he's began to recruit some of the younger lads from over that way.'

'That is strange though,' Stevenson sat up looking at Walsh. 'If you was going to do the off somewhere, then surely you'd collect any outstanding debts first wouldn't you?'

'Well you'd think so, wouldn't you,' he replied. 'I just don't know.'

'What's the interest anyway?' Stevenson asked curiously

'Well he could have skipped town, I mean we've got warrants out for his immediate arrest on the basis of not attending court that day,' Walsh looked at Stevenson. 'The truth is I think somehow it's tied in with our lot from Hulme.'

'How's that then?'

'The reason I went to see him that night in hospital that night was to drop my hunch on him about Macreedy's death.'

'You never told me about that.'

92

'That's because he never let anything slip,' Walsh responded. 'But the word around town after Paddy had his ear bitten off, was that it was Chorlton. Only thing was though we didn't have shit to back it as usual.'

'So how do the two connect?' Stevenson asked a little baffled.

'They might not do.'

'So what the fuck are you interested for then?'

'Just a hunch that I've got over something that I heard about that concert in Widnes.'

'What the fuck was that then?' Stevenson wasn't quite following his partner.

'Because I heard that Paddy was at that concert that day.'

'Yeah – where's this leading though? Half of fucking Manchester was there that day for the Stone What-sits.'

'Yes – but they all didn't get kicked out over a fight. Did they now?'

'And the fight was with?'

'That's what we weren't entirely sure of,' Walsh sighed deeply again. 'Although it was a good possibility that it was Chorlton and Macreedy.'

'Why the fuck haven't we pulled Chorlton in on this then?'

'What the fuck are we going to pull him in on Mike?'

'Alright,' he nodded his understanding, 'carry on.'

'I've got a grass that is certain that Paddy's lot got kicked out for sure after a fight inside the concert itself,' Walsh looked at Stevenson. 'Also this same grass is the one that tells me that Chorlton was the one who used his own method of amputation on Paddy.'

'Well why didn't Paddy hit back after that one then?' Stevenson inquired.

'Now hear me out here Mike,' Walsh stared at him smiling. 'Because a report was put in a couple of months ago about an attempted shooting outside of Henry's bar. You know that wine bar behind Deansgate.'

'And...'

'And... only the bar itself reported the attempt after they called for an ambulance,' he told him. 'No one else reported that it had happened to themselves.'

'I'm still not following you Martin,' Stevenson shook his head at him.

'Well it was the week before our Paddy disappeared,' he smiled. 'And guess just whom the description matched of the so called victim of this attempt?'

'Don't tell me – Chorlton... fucking Chopper,' he sighed staring at Walsh.

'You got it in one,' Walsh smirked. 'Both were near perfect descriptions of him and the very delightful Miss. Hayes.'

'Don't tell me though Martin,' Stevenson sighed deeply. 'Once again we had nothing solid to back any of it and go after them on it,'

'That's the one,' Walsh shrugged. 'You know we're not getting anywhere, with this fucking Hulme lot Mike,' he stared at him hard. 'We're going to have to look for a different angle to break this lot. It's like you said before they're so fucking tight. I mean they've even got themselves a clothes fucking shop in the town centre now. From what I hear anyway.'

'That's why I brought you in Martin.'

'I know it is,' Walsh stared at him shaking his head. 'It's just conventional methods just don't seem to be working... Do they?'

'Well you know us boys,' Stevenson smirked. 'It's been known that we can get a little unconventional before now.'

'That's true. We've just need to find that angle that we've not tried yet.'

'You got any unconventional suggestions then suggest away mate,' Stevenson stared at him knowingly.

'Well this could be nothing really,' Walsh smiled knowingly, opening his draw. 'It's just Carter dropped these by this morning for us to take a look at,' he threw an A4 envelope at Stevenson.

'What are these then?' he asked opening the envelope. 'I thought Carter worked Moss Side area of Manchester,' he said pulling the black and white photos free.

'I know... he does,' Walsh grinned again. 'But he knew what we were working on so thought they may be of interest to us.'

'Is that who I think it is?' Stevenson asked staring at the photographs.

'Certainly is mate,' he replied.

'What the fuck is he doing in Moss Side?' Stevenson smiled knowingly. 'I mean if he is involved with them lot from Hulme. Why is he...' his smile transformed into a smirk.

'You having the same thought as me there?' Walsh asked

94

'This could be good you know Martin.'

'It could be the angle we need. But then again it could be nothing,' Walsh said stubbing out his cigarette. 'I've asked Carter to keep an eye out for him anyway. It could be fuck all... but it does seem a bit suss' though. Especially that he's putting money into their pockets instead of his own crew.'

'We need something on him – Something solid.'

'Easier said than done though eh mate.'

'Ain't that the fucking truth?'

They both shook their heads at one another and sighed before both reaching for the same pack of cigarettes sat between them on the desk.

New Years Eve 1991 had arrived. Months had passed since the passing of Paddy. We never spoke of either him or the night in question, in fact the last time it had been mentioned was when Sleeper had informed us of a couple of days later that everything had been taken care of. After that the three of us had agreed never to talk about it again, unless it was an absolute necessity.

Although everybody around Manchester had been talking about how Paddy had just disappeared. Chris hadn't shown his face around town since that night, keeping himself only to Salford. We just played along with anybody who ever mentioned it to us, like we were as surprised as the next person as to what could possibly have happened.

Donna had suspected what had taken place, especially after Paddy had tried to shoot me right in front of her. Although I never told her anything, she wasn't stupid; she'd worked it out for herself as to who had tried killing me outside Henry's bar that evening. So obviously when the rumours around town started about where and what had happened to Paddy, she held her suspicions, just preferring not to mention it at all to me though. Which I had to say... I definitely preferred.

Things had been harder between us since that event. It really had scared the shit out of her, so since then I'd done everything possible to try best to make things better between us.

Macreedy's was doing really well for us. It didn't generate anywhere near the same kind of money we made from our other activities. However – more importantly, it was legal. So for us, that was a good thing. Apart from anything else, it made things so much more difficult for the police to get near us.

We'd continued to use Robert, as Sharon and Janine had been successfully smuggling the gear from Amsterdam into the country for the last couple of years now. Robert had started to produce new identifications for them with each trip they made, everything from passports to driver's licenses.

An end to another year was upon us, so obviously everybody was looking forward to New Years Eve in The Hacienda that night. It would be a great night out as each and every year in there was always a great event to attend. They never failed to put on a quality night that would always be remembered.

'What time are we leaving Chopper?' Donna shouted to me, as I lay soaking in the bath thinking about the night ahead.

As I lay there without a care in the world enjoying a heavily loaded skunk spliff from a fresh batch we'd picked up that week I yawned. 'Whenever – why?' I enquired lazily.

'So that I know how long I've got to get ready,' she shouted back to me.

'What the hell have you got to do?' I asked, fully relaxed. 'You've only to put your clothes on for Christ sake.'

'I've got to do my hair – then I've got to do my make up – then I've got to make sure what I've picked out to wear is right – then I've...' She wasn't half going on with herself.

So I halted her in her tracks. 'I've just got to phone Prey that's all,' I called out to her.

It was the one thing that I'd never been fathom out. Birds and how long it took them to get the fuck ready. I wouldn't mind so much if Donna wore loads of make up, but the fact of the matter was that she hardly wore any at all. She never needed to, which was just *one* of the things that I'd liked so much about her.

'Is Steve coming tonight?' she shouted to me.

'What – What you say?' I hardly heard her – damn this skunk felt real good. 'Steve – oh yeah. He says that he'll meet us in there later on.'

'What time?' she called out.

'Will you stop worrying the fuck about how much time we've got,' I replied back to her. 'What about Jason and Sam. Are they coming tonight?'

We'd been out a few times with them and I really liked both of them.

'Everybody's coming tonight,' she told me. 'From Macreedy's that is. It's going to be a quality night. Ain't it Chopper?'

'Yeah – whatever,' I just about managed, lay there stoned out of my mind and loving every minute of it.

We finally arrived at The Hacienda for around ten thirty after hitting a few bars in town first. As we approached our usual corner in there, I noticed Steve was already there, and he was talking with Jonah and Kezlo.

It was just then that I noticed this gorgeous girl stood by Steve's side. A girl that I'd never seen before. I knew that for sure, as she stood out so much from anybody else, she was proper nice I kept thinking as we all approached.

'Yes lads,' Prey said cheerfully as he walked up grabbing Steve round the neck. 'How's it going old man?' He began play fighting with Steve.

Prey really was in good spirits tonight, besides the fact it was New Years Eve. He seemed to almost be alight tonight, on a natural high. Kathy was out with us also. Still none of the lads could believe that he was still with her. Don't get me wrong we loved the girl, she was a good laugh to be around and to be honest very pleasant on the eye. It was just none of them usually lasted with Prey... ever.

Steve struggled free from Prey facing Donna and myself. 'Donna – come here and give me a kiss,' He said grabbing her; I noticed that the unknown girl looked straight at him.

'You alright lads,' I asked, nodding to Jonah and Kezlo.

Steve then took Donna's hand. 'Donna I'd really like for you to meet Claire,' he announced proudly presenting the unknown girl.

I instantly noticed the way she dressed, very smart, almost business like. She really was very striking... and also very young looking. Thinking about it, she was maybe as young as seventeen or eighteen. But there was no denying it, she definitely was a stunner. You could see Jonah and Kezlo nodding with permanent grins on their faces looking at me as I also found myself staring at her.

'Hello Donna,' she said shaking her hand, smiling as she did. 'Steve's told me a lot about you.'

'And this is Prey and Kathy,' Steve stated, beaming away with utter pride written all over his face as he did so.

'Oh I've heard all about you Prey,' she grinned.

'Is that fuckin' right,' Prey laughed. 'Well you should hear the shit we've got to tell you about Steve then.'

'Donna you've already just met,' he laughed. 'But she's the one who's with this little scallywag here,' he said as he brought Claire before me like a man who'd just won the pools. 'I've always said that she was way too good for him.'

'So you must be the famous Chopper then,' she smiled at me... that gorgeous smile for that matter.

'Is it that obvious,' I laughed, smiling at her. 'I'd definitely leave that famous bit out of there for sure though.'

'Well seeing as your just about all Steve ever talks about. I thought you must have been famous or something,' she laughed as everybody else did. 'You had me worried for a while. I thought you and Steve had something going on the side quietly. But after meeting Donna, I know that that's impossible now,' she smiled again winking as she did.

I took an instant liking to this girl. She was something else to look at. 'I wouldn't be too sure,' I said smirking, then grabbing hold of Steve, and kissing him jokingly.

All the girls were soon acquainted with one another. It was like they were all old friends the way they were carrying on with each other.

You could see all the lads stood around were itching to ask Steve about Claire. Therefore I wandered over to Donna and pulling her to one side. 'Ere'are Donna,' I said, passing her a handful of cash. 'Why don't you and the girls go to the bar and get the champagne in,' I told her.

'And what is it you're going to do?' She smiled kissing me knowingly; she knew exactly what I was going to do. So I pinched her backside as she and the other girls all headed off towards the bar.

Almost simultaneously, we all started with pretty much the same question. 'Alright old man,' I laughed as the others quietened down. 'How the fuck, have you managed to pull that then? She's well nice you cunt.'

Everybody was laughing. 'Come on now,' Prey stared at Steve. 'You've got to be old enough to be her old man... easy. Fuck... Maybe even her grandfather you twat?' He sniggered.

'I know,' he roared. 'It's fantastic – ain't it,' he had everybody in stitches.

'Seriously Steve,' Jonah asked, 'Where the fuck did you meet her?'

He grinned broadly at all of us before giving Prey and I a knowing wink. 'Well this will really piss you lads off,' he roared with laughter again. 'But I was in Macreedy's a few weeks back now looking at the new stock. She just happened to be in there at the time,' he said, smiling at the memory.

'Never,' Prey blurted out. 'And just where the fuck was I?'

'Now this is really going to piss you off,' he laughed. 'But you and Chopper was in the back with Donna,' he roared with laughter once again.

'You bastard – I can't – you...' Prey trailed off smiling as he did.

'Honestly?' I asked. 'Alright then. Just how the fuck did you manage to pull her then?'

'Well ain't it obvious lads,' Steve smiled brushing himself down. 'Obvious style for starters. Then it was obvious charm. Then quite obviously...' he said stroking his face. 'The obvious good looks I've got,' he laughed as we all did.

'Fuck you Steve,' Jonah hit his shoulder.

'Alright then,' he calmed down a little. 'Well I told her that I was one of the owners of Macreedy's and guess what? That seemed to do the trick perfectly.'

'You are one hell of a crafty... or I think more like lucky fuckin' bastard,' I said as we then all fell about laughing.

We had all carried on enjoying ourselves and the evening ahead. I was having a great night before suddenly realising I was proper missing somebody. Therefore I set off looking for Jonah.

'Jonah, where's Scotty?' I asked, realising that I hadn't spotted him yet.

'I don't know mate,' he shook his head. 'He's been getting double lazy lately.'

I hadn't understood the *lazy* part properly. 'Yeah but it's new years eve,' I stated, looking around for him. 'All the crew is out for tonight. He can't miss this.'

'He said that him and Jackie will be down later on,' Kezlo shouted to us, overhearing our conversation.

'Look Chopper,' Jonah shook his head again. 'I need you to come see somebody with me,' his tone of voice had taken a serious edge to it. 'I'd been hoping to stay the fuck out of it... but... well...'

'Why?' I asked concerned at the look upon his face. 'What's up mate?'

'Just come with me for a minute,' he said as the two of us took off, leaving everybody else behind.

We headed downstairs into the basement bar. I immediately spotted Batty from Wythenshawe looking over to reach our attention.

'Yes mate,' I said, shaking his hand. 'I didn't know you were even in 'ere Batty.'

'Alright Chopper,' he smiled warmly at me. 'It's been a while ain't it.'

Batty had been one of our main contacts for years now on the weed side. I'd obviously become well acquainted with him whilst controlling the weed side of our business and had always liked him. I still often hooked up with him for a drink or to go watch Manchester United together on match days… which he proper screwed about, because he was a full on Manchester City fan.

But being one of the cities greatest ticket touts (aside all the other shit he was also involved in… but this is where he'd got his main lot of money from to become involved at the level he was today) meant he could always get me a ticket when I wanted one for the United match. And he came along purely for the simple fact we always made a day of it and had a proper crack. It was fair to say that Batty was a proper sound lad that I had… and always will have the utmost respect for.

'This is who I wanted you to meet Chopper,' Jonah informed me. 'You need to hear him out on something.'

Now I was a little confused as looking to Batty. 'What's up mate?'

'Chopper, we've always done good business together. Haven't we?' he asked shaking his head at me. 'Y'know that I'm double sweet when it comes to sorting things out with your crew.'

'Yeah,' I signalled and nodded for Jonah to go get some drinks in, wanting to be alone as possible with him. 'What the fuck is up pal?'

'Look I know it's new year's eve and all that,' as he said this, he dropped his head slightly. 'I got a problem – and y'know I definitely ain't one to go causing trouble. But – well it's Scotty mate,' he looked up at me.

'And…' I asked, 'What about Scotty?' I then shrugged, but at the same time concerned as to what he had meant.

'He's shorted me twice now on the bees,' he sniffed. 'Not that much… but at least a few hundred on each occasion.'

'You what!' I asked surprised, as either Prey or myself usually counted the money before it was distributed to which area of business it was to be used in.

'That's not all pal,' he sighed. 'He's constantly double late for meetings... even missing them twice now. Always phoning with some kind of pony excuse the next day.'

Jonah returned with the drinks. 'I told you he was getting lazy. Didn't I?' he said passing the drinks to us. 'It's ever since that bird of his showed up on the scene.'

'I've put the bees back in myself. But I can't keep doing it. The reason it seemed so strange, was that your crew has never shorted me,' Batty said swigging his beer.

'I don't believe this,' I said shaking my head in disbelief.

'The lateness and missing pick ups though,' Batty shook his head. 'Now that I can't be doing with... I mean it's not a fuckin' joke the business we're in.'

I shook my own head agreeing precisely with what he had just said, yet I was still confused. 'What the fuck is he playing at?' I asked out loud, probably more to myself than the other two before me. I was totally bemused about the situation at hand.

'Look Chopper,' Batty said sternly. 'I know you and the kid go way back now. That's why I sought out Jonah to approach you first. It only seemed fair... to ... well...'

'No... I know what you mean. Thanks mate,' I told him shaking his hand. 'I really appreciate it. I mean you not going to Prey on this. He'd have gone ballistic over it.'

'What are you going to do?' Jonah blatantly asked me.

'I tell you what Batty,' I sighed out loud. 'I'll be down myself personally, next week sometime. We'll all sit down and sort this lot out. Besides I've not been down to Wythenshawe for time... It'll be good to see the lads again.'

'Scotty looks more like stir fried shit every day Chopper,' Jonah then added.

I motioned my head in a kind of agreement then added myself. 'Alright then – whilst we're stood down 'ere,' I winked at them both. 'Anybody for a couple of liveners in the toilets?' Believe me when I say it wasn't something that needed asking twice when bugle was involved.

It was almost quarter to twelve when Prey began banging two empty champagne bottles together to get everybody's attention. 'I've got something to announce - Listen up will you.'

'Best get a move on – It's almost twelve,' I shouted to him, knowing how he could go on with himself sometimes.

'Kathy come 'ere,' he told her. 'Right is everybody 'ere. Listen to me...' Kathy was stood in front of him as he stood on the seat.

'What the fuck's up with his majesty now?' Steve laughed by my side.

'Right before we celebrate the New Year... I've first of all got an announcement to make,' he smiled at everybody.

'You're retiring,' I smiled at him.

'You fuckin' wish,' he laughed at me, as everybody else began laughing.

'No it's nothing like that...' he smiled broadly again. 'But I'm going to become a father... Kathy's pregnant,' he announced holding his glass high.

'What the fu...' I trailed off as that was about all I managed to get out as everybody began cheering and congratulating the two of them.

Prey made his way over to Steve and I. 'Are you serious mate?' I asked, still shocked at his news.

'Sure am,' he smiled proudly at the two of us. 'Maybe a son... to make me double proud eh? I'll make sure that he's not involved in any of this shit though eh lads,' he said and he appeared to be so contented with himself it made me smile.

'I don't know what to say...' I told him, at a loss for words.

'Come here man,' Steve said grabbing hold of him, giving him a hug, as all the girls made a fuss of Kathy.

'A little Prey eh,' I added, laughing as the two of us hugged each other.

He then looked at the two of us and smiled. 'So I take it you'll both be the Godfathers then?'

'Are you kidding?' I exclaimed.

'It would be a real honour mate,' Steve said shaking his hand.

I glanced at my watch and saw that there were only several minutes to go now I thought to myself. Everybody now seemed to be even more in high spirits than before after Prey's announcement. Just then, I spotted Scotty and Jackie as they both walked into the club. The two of them looked smashed already; he spotted me and waved over.

As soon as they were both upon me, I kissed Jackie's cheek quickly. 'The girls are over there,' I announced flatly, staring at her as she got the message and disappeared.

'Yes Chopper,' Scotty said, his eyes rolling and glazed over like icebergs. 'Fuck man – I almost missed it, eh,' he laughed a stupid sounding noise.

'Wouldn't be the first thing that you've missed lately would it,' I replied, staring coldly at him.

'What…' he looked at me, then quickly away.

'I know that you've been slacking big time lately,' I said sternly. 'We won't go there tonight… but we've got to sort it out.'

'What the fuck are going on about Chopper?' he suddenly snapped at me.

I continued to stare at him. 'You want to do this now? D'ya?' I sneered at him.

'You forget who you're speaking to Chopper,' he stared back at me. 'Mr. Fuckin' high and mighty now… You forget just how far back we go eh?'

'Don't you fuckin' insult me,' I snapped, holding his glare. 'Let's just say I ain't said shit to Prey about you… Although if you like, I could change that.'

He turned away not able to hold the stare as I glared at him with steel eyes. 'What've you heard?' he asked feebly.

'Y'know exactly what I've heard and where it came from,' I told him. 'Look… just have a good time tonight. We'll meet next week to sort this out. Alright?'

'Alright mate,' he said not able to look me in the face.

'You better go congratulate Prey Scotty,' I said, changing the subject. 'He's going to be a dad.'

'Really!' His face told me that he was as shocked as I'd been.

Just then the whole place erupted into a mass of cheers and indoor fireworks. Everybody shaking hands and hugging one another, kissing each other and looking like they had no troubles whatsoever.

Suddenly the three of us found ourselves facing each other. 'Into 1992,' Steve grinned holding his arms open, as the three of us began hugging one another cheering like crazed people.

''Ere's to even better times than we've already had up to now,' Prey smiled.

I held my glass in the air and looked around to check no one was within ears shot 'Happy new year Sean... We've finally laid you to rest proper pal.'

'Too fuckin' right,' Prey said raising his glass.

'Happy fuckin' new year.' Steve shouted raising his glass high looking up to the sky lights above.

We all did the same smiling as we did and remembered our lost friend that we had finally avenged and laid properly to rest.

'You're coming to see Batty with me and that's that alright,' I told Scotty as we sat round at the old flat.

'Me and you go way back Chopper,' he looked at me sorrowfully. 'And you're gonna believe fuckin' Batty over me. That's out of fuckin' order and y'know it is.'

'Listen Scotty,' I told him holding eye contact as his own eyes diverted mine. 'You're lucky that he came to me and not to Prey over this. All I know is what he's told me. Now I'll sort the bees out this time and we won't go there again you hear me. If you need any dough just come to me.'

'So I'm fuckin' thief as well now... Am I?' he snapped.

'Look Scotty – Batty says it was short,' I snarled back at him. 'We've never had any money troubles before and either Prey or me counted those bees. Now Batty says that it was short and I've got to respect what he says. Batty said that the only reason it had bothered him any was that he's never been shorted by our crew before.'

'Batty this... Batty fuckin' that,' he sneered back at me again. 'What you two best of mates now or something?'

'Fuckin' grow up will you,' I was losing my temper with him.

'So do you believe me or not?'

'Alright – on the money side,' I replied. But even I wasn't 100 percent as I shook my head at him. To be perfectly honest, it was the first time in my life that I was not entirely sure whether or not to actually believe what Scotty was saying to me... and to be perfectly honest, it really bothered me.

'That's more like it,' he said smugly, as though he'd scored himself a point.

'But what about the pick ups?' I added, looking at him to try and fathom out what the hell was going on, 'Turning up late. Not even turning up sometimes. I mean what the fuck is that all about?' I was staring him directly in the eyes, but couldn't tell what was going on with him.

'He's lying he is,' he said turning away from me. 'Why do you keeping believing him,' he was still not able to look at me.

'I've got a lot of respect for Batty,' I confirmed. 'He's been around some years now and has always been sweet with me. So don't fuckin' go lying to me,' I screamed the last words at him.

'Oh so that's it... Is it? You're the big man now,' he stared at me as his eye started to shake and he looked as though he was about to break down, then defiantly all of a sudden he snarled at me. 'And I'm just a little shit who've not got your respect,' he was spitting the words at me with real venom.

'Fuck you Scotty – go on fuck yourself you – fuckin' – fuckin' – you...' He was really beginning to piss me off now as he had really wound me up, breathing deeply to calm myself down a little I sighed deeply then held my hands up. 'You're right Scotty. We do go way back ar'kid. But you hear me now and you hear me fuckin' good,' I stared at him trying to control my anger as I shook my head. 'This ain't personal... This is business... This is what we do. And brother or no fuckin' brother... I will cut you the fuck off,' I sneered the words at him.

He could see how he'd got to me and appeared to physically slump against the wall behind him in defeat. 'I'm sorry mate. I shouldn't have insulted you like that,' he head was head dropped out of sight. 'I know that it's business.'

'Listen I don't want to be fuckin' arguing with you Scotty,' I sighed deeply for a second time. 'But if you start to fuck up. Well, it'll go straight over my head. Whether me and Prey are full partners or not. I'm just looking out for you man.'

'I know,' he said in barely a whisper.

'Things have got to be put right,' I declared tirelessly. 'No more of this turning up late or not turning up at all. Count the money whilst you're both together. This is a serious business you're involved in. It's not kids stuff anymore. And if you fuck up – Then the only way to go... is down mate,' I really was trying to be as reasonable as possible.

'Alright Chopper,' he looked up at me, his eyes full of what appeared to be anguish. 'I'm sorry mate. C'mon, we'll sort things out with Batty. Then I promise I'll make sure everything's alright after that mate.'

'That's more like it,' I said starting to feel a little better about the situation, shaking my head as I did so. 'That's all I needed to hear. Now get your jacket on. You're driving mate, we've got to meet him in half an hour,' I was smiling at him to show him things were alright. If truth be told I always worried about him – too fucking much sometimes.

'Shit!' Walsh exclaimed. The two had followed Scotty's car from Hulme to The Maple Tree in Wythenshawe 'You seen who the fuck is with him Mike?'

'Isn't that Chorlton?' Stevenson smiled knowingly. 'I don't believe it Martin. I never realised that it was him when we picked up their tail you know.'

'The question is,' Walsh said. 'What the fuck is Chorlton doing here? He no longer deals at street level. Not even for pick ups, so why the fuck…'

Stevenson stopped him. 'And take a look at that will you,' he grinned. 'Old Trevor Batley is coming out to welcome them both.'

'Is Batley still one of the main dealers in Wythenshawe for weed?' Walsh asked already snapping away with his Nikon zoom lens camera.

'From what I hear – Batley's got his fingers into just about everything these days from weed to Es… and let's not forget the ticket touting he's still known as the king of around town. You name something dodgy that can make money and he's definitely at it.'

'Shit they're going inside,' Walsh said still snapping away furiously with the camera.

'You got the pictures though. Right?' Stevenson asked looking at him.

'Yeah I got them,' he said almost dishearteningly. 'More for the fucking photo album eh?' Walsh knew that the all the surveillance shots weren't much use without something solid backing them.

'It was a colossal night in there the other night? Wasn't it Chopper?' Batty said as we walked through into the bar area.

'Yeah mate,' I smiled. 'You hear about Prey?'

'Yeah... Another little Preyster going to be running about eh,' he laughed out loud. 'So anyway... Are you lads here for business or pleasure?'

'We'll see,' I said, grinning at him. 'Ain't any reason why we can't do the two together if you've got something good on offer.'

'Always got something good Chopper,' he laughed turning to Scotty. 'And how are you today Scotty?'

'Sweet Batty,' he said not looking directly at him. 'Look – I'm sorry about...'

Batty cut him off. 'We'll get things sorted out today, alright. Then we'll get everything running smoothly again,' Batty was trying his best to as reasonable as he possibly could, given the situation.

'Alright lads,' I said, smiling as we approached the table where Tommy, Jason, Brian and Tony all sat smoking some potent smelling weed.

'Been a long time Chopper,' Tommy announced as the others nodded recognition. 'You ain't been down to the estate for time now.'

'I know I ain't. I've been pure busy all of last year.'

'How's the shop doing?' Tony asked. 'You got some don gear in there. I was in there the other day.'

'So how about some decent discount then Chopper?' Brian asked as he drew heavily on the loaded spliff hanging from his lips.

'You'll have to talk with the manageress on that score,' I laughed at them.

'You kidding or what Chopper?' Jason asked me.

'I tell you what. If you lads let me know when you're going to be going into town first, then I'll let Donna know so she'll sort you lads something out.'

'Sweet Chopper,' grinned Tommy.

'Just you lads though. I know what you lot are fuckin' like. You'll take half of fuckin' Wythenshawe down there,' I added as we all laughed knowing it to be the truth with this lot.

'What you two drinking?' Batty asked.

'I'll come with you mate,' I told him. 'So we can talk,' I added, leaving Scotty sitting with the others.

'So is everything sweet or what Chopper?' Batty asked as we waited for the drinks.

'Yes mate,' I nodded at him. 'I spoke with him just before we came down 'ere.'

'Good.'

'Ere'are – this is for you,' I smiled passing him an envelope.

'What's this?' he asked taking the envelope.

'The bees that was shorted for you. I put a bit extra in as well for the inconvenience. Also I'd like this to kept to ar' selves – alright.'

'Cheers Chopper. There was no need for that. I appreciate it though,' he said shaking my hand. 'Y'know I'm a fair man. That's why I come to you first off. Besides I want us to stay in business. Good business at that.'

'So what're you holding at the moment then?' I asked changing the subject.

''Ere check this out,' he passed me a bag of this sticky looking, purple and green in colour weed. I could smell the fumes through the plastic bag it was that strong. Yet it didn't just smell solely of weed it also smelled of something a little stronger – almost like chemical like.

'Jamaican yard weed – but the only thing is – It comes with a real kicker.' He was smiling at me.

'I ain't had any of this for pure time,' I informed him smelling the contents of the bag that smelt different from the usual weed we'd had from there before.

'You ain't had it like this before. I can tell you that much,' he was smiling deviously at me. 'It was brought over in coffins. The gear was caked in balming fluid from the corpses,' he roared with laughter.

'What the fuck is balming fluid?'

'It keeps the corpses fresher,' he was still laughing.

'And?' I shook my head confused.

'And – And… Well let's put it this way Chopper,' he winked at me. 'It makes the gear almost addictive mate. You seriously can't get enough of it.'

'Honestly,' I said inhaling the bag again and enjoying what I smelt.

'I tell you what mate. As it's you. I got me forty keys of this gear,' he informed me. 'I'll give your crew first option on twenty of them. The rest I'm keeping for the estate. It's way to good to let it all go.'

'Best give it a go then,' I replied.

We stayed in The Maple Tree all afternoon drinking and smoking this crazy weed. Batty had been right about how mad it was; I'd not been so smashed from weed alone for a long time.

'I'm going to make a call mate,' I announced pushing myself from my seat. 'Can you sort the gear out tonight?'

'No worries mate,' he replied smiling. 'All twenty keys?'

'Yes mate. I'll get Kezlo to bring the bees over,' I confirmed. 'That way he can take me back later. Scotty can drop the gear off back at the estate.'

'Go use the boozer's phone,' he winked at me. 'The lines safe back there.'

'You see who else just arrived to the party?' said Walsh still snapping away with his camera.

'Mark Kulshaw,' Stevenson simply said. 'Just who the fuck does that dreadlocked white boy think he is for Christ sake? You think someone forgot to tell him he was not born black.' He added with ignorance.

'You clock the bag he's carrying?'

'I noticed it,' Stevenson said lighting a cigarette. 'You thinking what I'm thinking?' he asked looking at Walsh.

'Something's got to be going down,' he said taking a cigarette for himself. 'I mean we've been sat here all day with our dicks in our hands and what've we got to show for it.'

'We've got no warrants though and they'll spot us before we even walk in there,' Stevenson said blowing out his smoke.

'Let's stick around,' Walsh said staring at Stevenson. 'We can always get the traffic boys to pull them on a routine check for something.'

'It's got to be worth a go,' he sighed. 'Just make sure you don't take your eyes from that boozer's door.'

'What do you reckon Kezlo?' Batty asked.

'It's colossal gear,' he laughed. 'Shit it's almost fuckin' trippy it's that strong.'

'You get everything sorted?' I asked my eyes were glazed to fuck from sitting there all day getting stoned.

'Sweet Chopper,' he said passing me the holdall full of money. 'It's all there.'

'Alright Batty,' I looked to him. 'How'd you want to do this?'

'Tommy will go with Scotty and sort it out,' he informed me. 'You two stay 'ere – with the bees of course, until Tommy gets back.'

'Ere'are Scotty go with Tommy,' I instructed him bluntly as he was already making his way out of his seat. 'Head straight back afterwards. Y'know what to do Scotty. What time you got?'

He looked at his watch. 'Nearly seven mate.'

'Alright, me and Kezlo are going to stay down this way for tonight. I'll see you tomorrow. Okay?' I said, whilst doing my best to focus through blurred vision.

'Should I put it to sleep Chopper?' Scotty asked.

'For tonight. Y'know the score,' I was shaking my head at him. He knew what we always did with the gear. We always put everything away for at least a night, just to be on the safe side before packaging it up ready to be distributed.

'Look Mike,' said Walsh suddenly pointing the front door of The Maple Tree. 'It's Scotty and some other lad coming out.'

'Where's Chopper?' asked Stevenson scanning the area to no avail.

'No sign of him. Just them two,' he added, looking at him for instructions whether they should follow Scotty and his acquaintance.

'I wanted Chorlton... shit... cunt... fuck... mother fuckin'... bastard.'

'He's not carrying the bag,' Walsh told him ignoring his outburst of sudden tourettes. 'They're getting in Scotty's car. What should I do?'

'I wanted Chorlton,' he snapped. 'Let me think a minute.'

'We ain't got a minute Mike. They're taking off now,' he informed him, still trying to get clear photo shots of them leaving.

'Fuck it – Get the fuck on there tail,' he responded back again. 'It's better we follow them than sit here all night. Fuck Chorlton for now.'

Walsh was already easing the car out into the street as the saw the car pull out of the car park, screeching its tires as it did so.

'Wait 'ere Scotty,' Tommy told him. 'I'll be a few minutes alright.'

They'd arrived at some disused garages on the other side of Wythenshawe hidden away behind a lot of undergrowth to

113

keep any inquisitive eyes at bay; Scotty made himself comfortable as he began the waiting game.

Fuck – I could do with some rock he thought as he sat there getting restless as his mind started to go into overtime. That weed was alright but just a bit of rock... Just to see him through the night. He had to start sorting things out business wise. Chopper had been more than fair with him, he knew that.

He'd also made it clear that he'd cut him off if he continued to fuck up. He could still do with some stones to see him through. Oh yes, that would be nice. No one knew just how much he'd been caning recently. But he sure as hell loved the shit. Maybe stop on the way back and pick some up. Yes that was it... there would be more than enough time.

Besides, he wasn't due to see Chopper until tomorrow now anyway. Oh that's going to be so sweet. A proper nice chunk of that glorious stone on top of that pipe – Oh yes... he was buzzing at the mere thought of it.

Fucking Batty he then started thinking to himself. He'd almost put him right in it with Chopper – fancy grassing him up like that.... after all, it had only been a few quid. Besides which, he didn't think he'd have missed it.

He'd just spent more than usual on the rocks that week he thought to himself. Nothing too serious – he usually had the money for it... right. Well he use to anyway.

It had been becoming more and more difficult recently. Still, he'd have to make sure things were alright now. Besides which, no one could get between him and his own time... as he liked to refer to it.

Not ever... It wasn't a habit was it? It was just something he enjoyed doing. Yes that was it wasn't it? It was purely recreational he convinced himself. No one could ever find out though. *No one*. He wasn't no junkie fuck head. No that wasn't it... he just enjoyed himself on them. That's all it was... right?

He suddenly jumped – startled and dazed all in one motion as he was rudely – *he thought* – brought out of his day dreaming by Tommy banging loudly on the window of the car.

'Open the boot Scotty,' Tommy instructed, carrying a large stereo box with him.

'Sorry mate,' he apologised. 'I was in a world of my own there,' he laughed as he got out of the car. 'Must be that fuckin' weed.'

'It's well mad gear ain't it?' Tommy added whilst struggling with the box.

'Is that all of it?' Scotty asked opening the boot of his car.

'Yeah all twenty keys mate.'

'You need a lift back?' Scotty asked placing the box into the boot.

'Nah mate,' he shook his head. 'I'll get a baxi back to The Maple. You take it easy Scotty,' Tommy shook his hand, and then quickly disappeared into the night.

'Looked at bit on the heavy side for a stereo. Didn't it?' Stevenson smirked as they both turned away from the bush they'd been hiding behind watching the scene before them take place. 'What do you reckon Martin?'

'I know what you're saying. Only thing is we ain't got a warrant,' Walsh confirmed putting the camera down as they headed back to the car.

'Fuck it. Let's just stay on him for now,' Stevenson told him. 'We can get traffic boys to give him a pull, like you suggested.'

Starting up the engine they then took off after Scotty's Escort; he seemed totally oblivious to the fact he was being followed at all as they wound their way round the estate that was Wythenshawe. And Christ – didn't all the roads round here look the same.

The kept their distance – but kept him in sight as he made his way back down The Parkway, heading straight back towards Hulme.

'You radioed the traffic boys to take him just before the estate?' Stevenson asked.

'There's a car ready and waiting Mike.'

'What the fuck...' Stevenson gasped. 'What's he doing now?' he asked as Scotty took a left turn at the traffic lights.

'Looks like he's heading into Moss side,' he said easing their car left to keep on him.

'Shit there's our car waiting back there also,' Walsh said nodding in the direction of the traffic police. 'Best radio through to them. Tell them he's changed direction and to sit tight until further instructions,' he said sharply as they watched Scotty pulling down into one of the side roads on the outskirts to the estate. His car eased its way over to the pavement beside a darkly lit alleyway.

Scotty eased over to the dimly lit pavement. 'Ere'are Dominic... Dom over 'ere mate, it's Scotty,' he was calling over to a group of young teenage black lads stood in the alleyway to the back of the houses.

'Scotty man,' he smirked as he appeared from the shadows. 'What's happening brethren? What can I do for you tonight Scotty man?' he said in deep Jamaican patois – that Scotty wasn't that convinced was genuine as the youth flashed his three gold teeth proudly at him.

'A Henry' of stone mate,' he told him impatiently.

'It'll 'ave to be in singles boss,' Dom said grinning away into the night.

'C'mon Dom... Y'know me man... Sort it out for me,' Scotty shook his head at the young lad of no more than fifteen before him. He knew better than anybody that buying in singles would cost a lot more than buying the whole weight in one single chunk.

'I tell you what man,' he nodded. 'I only got singles. So me give you 'ickle discount. How's about that eh?' he flashed that familiar grin again knowingly as he did. He had a bag stashed away in some waste ground filled with rocks of crack cocaine of all weights and sizes. But he could sense the eagerness in Scotty's eyes as he sat there. It was something he witnessed more and more these days.

'Alright – just hurry will you,' Scotty snapped.

Dom turned and whistled a signal into the night and within moments another teenager appeared on a mountain bike... And as quickly as that – the transaction took place.

'Can you believe this,' Stevenson smiled.

'I know,' Walsh grinned as he picked up the radio. 'Best still pull him for something else though. Speeding or whatever...'

'We've got the little bastard,' Stevenson smiled. 'Let's just keep our fingers crossed that it's something good that he's got in the box 'cause that packet he was just handed won't amount to much.'

Scotty eased his car back in the direction of Hulme and began drifting into a world of his own again. He smiled absentmindedly at the thought of getting home and getting the

116

pipe going. A slight buzz went through him at the mere thought of it.

Just then he noticed the flashing lights behind him. 'Arhhh shit... fuck... fuck... *fuck this shit*,' he was cursing to himself.

He knew better than to make a run for it. Besides it was only traffic cop's anyway. No worries there he thought to himself as he began pulling over to the side of the road to hear whatever bored little story they would make up for pulling him over. He watched as the officer left his motor walking towards his car. Fuck 'em, he thought to himself as the officer was now upon his car.

'Evening son,' the uniformed officer said, stood by Scotty's window. 'Do you know why we pulled you over?'

'Because you got fuckin' nothing better to do with your time,' Scotty replied sarcastically.

The officer ignored the sarcasm and replied. 'No actually it was for the red light you just ran through back there.'

'Y'what... What red light for fucks sake?' Scotty snapped, although he was racking his brain trying to think whether or not he had done.

'Back there at the crossroads,' he informed him, smiling as he did. 'Will you please step out of your vechile son?'

'What... what the fuck,' Scotty exclaimed, climbing from the driver's seat. 'You're trippin' right... This is nothing but fuckin' bullshit,' he snapped becoming irritable.

'Enough of the language,' he sneered back at Scotty. 'Now what's your name? Are you from around here?'

'You what? What? This is bollocks...' Scotty spat the words at him, he was becoming excitable. 'You're fuckin' with me right... That's it, ain't it? You're just fuckin' with me – winding me the fuck up copper,' he was beginning to forget about the drugs stashed in his jacket pocket... Never mind the twenty kilos of that fine Jamaican weed in the boot of his car.

'Right if you're going to be like this,' the officer responded angrily. 'Then you're gonna start making me all suspicious. You know there been a lot of burglaries in the area recently. Why don't we take a look in your boot?'

This suddenly brought Scotty round. 'No fuckin' way,' he snapped. 'I live not five minutes from 'ere... Beside which you've got no warrants or shit to go searching my car. Besides which you're just traffic coppers...'

'So what – that doesn't makes us real police officers does it?' he snarled his response as Scotty climbed from his seat onto the pavement. 'Now open the fucking boot son or I'm going to lose my rag with you, you little shit,' he yelled at Scotty now stood before him. 'I'm losing my temper here,' he was clearly becoming more irritable by Scotty's attitude.

Scotty suddenly panicking about the situation at hand – without a second thought he then lashed out at the officer before him as hard as he possibly could. But before Scotty had come close to even achieving contact with the officer – the officer had simply side stepped him as his partner who Scotty hadn't even realised had exited the car had smashed his truncheon into Scotty's right arm.

As he stumbled backwards, the officer caught him once again in his chin, this time knocking him cleanly to the floor.

'AAAArrrrggghhh – you fuckin' twat,' Scotty screamed hitting the ground with force as the first officer stepped forward over Scotty his truncheon held in a striking pose about to inflict more damage to him.

'That will be enough for now,' Stevenson said walking over.

'Come on – get up,' Walsh said helping Scotty to his feet.

'What... What the fuck!' Scotty gasped as broke free from Walsh. 'Where the fuck did you two co...' he stopped himself in his tracks as he suddenly realised what had just taken place.

'Right, are you going to open that boot of yours Scotty?' Walsh said grabbing hold of his arm again.

'Go fuck yourselves you couple of...' Scotty spat the words, seeing nothing but red now, before suddenly shutting his mouth as the reality of what was at stake dawned upon him.

Without warning, Walsh dipped his hand into Scotty's jacket pocket. 'What have we here Scotty?' he asking smiling whilst holding the small snappy bag filled with the crack he'd just moments before purchased. 'You having yourself a little party. Are you?'

'You planted that. You did,' Scotty said defensively. 'That's not mine – no fuckin' way are you pinning that on me,' he was really beginning to lose his nerve now.

'Shut the fuck up Scotty and open your boot for us,' Stevenson said tossing the car keys to him.

Scotty panicked and pathetically tried to make a dash for it.

'You're not going anywhere son,' Walsh casually said gripping tighter on his arm.

'Open the fucking boot son – now,' Stevenson screamed.

Scotty stepped forward and reluctantly opened the boot revealing the stereo box lay there, as he turned back towards the others he could clearly see Stevenson and Walsh both smiling broadly at him.

'Now what do we have here Scotty?' Stevenson asked looking into the boot of the car curiously.

'It's just a stereo that's all,' came the feeble reply from him.

'Really – is that so,' Walsh laughed at him. 'So I presume you've a receipt for it then.'

'Fuck you two…' Scotty sneered the words at them.

'I'd like to take a look at the stereo if you don't mind that is,' Stevenson smirked at him.

'Yes I do fuckin' mind you cocksucker,' he said to him.

Walsh quickly – without any warning punched Scotty directly into his solar plexus dropping him to his knees. 'You little shit.'

He dragged Scotty to his feet; but he was breathing fast and uncontrolled as Walsh dragged him roughly over to the boot of the car.

'Right. Now fucking open the box or I'll throw you into the boot of the car and take you down to the nick. Open it there if you like,' Walsh smirked at Scotty.

Scotty knew he was completely fucked, so did as he was told, slowly tearing back the tape from the box. 'There,' he announced turning away.

Stevenson looked into the box and smiled. 'Looks like little Scotty is trying to save the rainforest on his own or something.'

Walsh smiled and winked at Scotty as he dropped his head in disbelief at what had just taken place. 'Get him down to the nick,' Walsh said to the two uniformed officers as they cuffed him.

'I'll take his car,' Stevenson said shutting the boot.

They both looked at each other nodding then smiled knowingly at one another.

Scotty was aching so badly for a toot of the drug he so desired. He'd never had to go without it before, always finding a way to buy it somehow. How the fuck had they got him? Just how much did they know? Fuck – Shit – Fuck!

What was he going to do? *Not prison*. No fucking way. *Shit... Fuck... Shit... This was bad*. He wasn't a grass. But he needed to get out of here. Oh no – Shit – Maybe this was a bad dream.

I'll do... *No I won't...* Fuck... *This wasn't happening* – was it? *No – No – No – No – what the fuck was he going to do eh?* This was madness – totally fucking bizarre – there were voices ringing out through his demented mind as he struggled to calm himself.

It was killing him – fuck – shit – what was taking so long? This is unreal – Yes it is you dumb little fuck... The voice taunted him.

Scotty's head was completely in bits. He couldn't think straight at all. He just couldn't get it together whatsoever.

Hot and cold sweats had hit – shivers – itching – scratching of the skin... Stop – *please stop*. He was pleading with nobody and yet in his twisted mind... everybody as he fought to stay in control... Leave me alone – he pleaded with no one but himself as he lay there shivering away... All alone in the cell with only the horrendous fear that controlled the situation.

Suddenly the cell door banged open as Walsh stepped through the door and menacingly glared at the state of him after several hours left all alone in there – knowing that his mind must have been working over time.

120

'Come on Scotty it's time.'

They didn't take Scotty into an interview room like normal, instead taking him into an office where Stevenson was already waiting for them.

'Hello Scotty,' Stevenson smiled at him. 'Not looking to clever son. How do you feel?'

'Alright,' Scotty said weakly, his face buried out of sight.

'I sure bet you'd feel a whole lot better with a toot of this,' Walsh said as he examined the bag of crack in full view of Scotty.

Scotty ached even more when he saw the bag before him. He needed it so badly that tears began rolling down his face at the mere thought of smoking the contents of the bag... knowing full well what the effect would be.

'Have a look at these,' Stevenson said throwing the days surveillance photos to the table.

Scotty began looking through the photos shaking his head. He now knew they'd followed him... In fact as he stared at all of them, he realised that all day they'd followed him and he hadn't even noticed them.

'We've got you bang to rights here Scotty,' Walsh announced gleefully.

'Twenty kilos of pure skunk... a bag full of crack which is obviously already to sell as they're in separate weighted pieces,' Stevenson told him nodding as he did so.

'I think it's more than just a possession charge we're dealing with this time are we?' Walsh added.

Scotty desperately needed a way out of this. 'Can I call my brief?' he asked feebly.

'Have you not noticed yet Scotty,' Stevenson sniggered. 'We've not even read you your rights yet. You've not even been arrested yet!'

'What. *You fuckin' what*,' Scotty snapped, he hadn't even thought about it.

'Not that it matters with what we've got,' Walsh simply told him. 'You're looking to go down for at least a seven to ten stretch on this one son.'

'No more of this gear either,' Stevenson said, picking up the bag. 'Probably end up a smack head like the rest of them inside.'

'Maybe even catch AIDS off one of the dirty fuckers whilst sharing his needle. Well either that or when they rape your arse in the showers,' Walsh was doing his best to scare the shit out of him – and at this precise moment of his vulnerability, it was achieving its destined goal.

The terror had taken a hold. What was he going to do he kept thinking to himself as his mind raced at seemed like a million miles an hour to him. They had him by the balls and he damn well knew it. And all he wanted to do was get out and smoke some of the rocks they were teasing him with... right there in front of him. That would make things alright... *wouldn't it?* Make things clearer. Help him through all the madness before him.

'What is it you want then?' He feebly asked them.

'Its simple Scotty,' Stevenson informed him. 'You come work for us,' he stared straight into Scotty's eyes.

'What... *I can't do that...*' he stopped himself. 'They'll kill me,' he added in hushed tones as if Chopper and the crew were going to overhear their conversation.

'We'll give you everything back like nothing happened,' Walsh told him, playfully playing with the bag that Scotty was obsessively staring at... teasing his desires.

'Everything... Just like nothing happened at all,' Stevenson declared shaking his head smiling. 'No one will be any the wiser at all. But then you belong to us. What we need you will give us. And when they go down you'll be free of it all.'

'I can have it all back?' Scotty stared at the bag of crack cocaine instead of the two detectives.

'Plus we'll supply you with some rocks for any good information you give us,' Walsh smiled as he threw his bone at Scotty.

They had him... He knew that... He had no other choice he was thinking to himself... It was the only option he had – surely it was the right thing to do eh?

'Alright... *I'll do it*,' Scotty blurted out, finally giving in to them – But if the truth had been told... it was most of all giving in to the power the drug itself that had a grasp over him.

'That's more like it,' Stevenson smiled nodding at him. 'You know what Scotty. We're going to bring your crew down,' he let out a depraved sounding laugh as he said this.

'And you're going to help us do it Scotty,' Walsh licked his lips as he stared at Scotty stood there looking so pathetic.

What do you reckon Prey?' I asked, pausing between mouthfuls of Schzhuan Beef. 'You know about what Steve was saying?'

'Steve's been around the block Chopper,' Prey said scooping a mouthful of duck meat from the noodle soup onto his chopsticks; he then stopped looking at me, before it disappeared into his mouth. 'He must have spotted something. I don't reckon he was just being paranoid.'

'I just can't work it out though,' I told him. 'We've always kept Steve as far away as possible.'

'Think about all the increased activity within our world though Chopper,' he said staring hard at me, 'It's becoming bigger than it's ever been before due to the clubbing scene. I mean prior to the Es, people were still thinking that all drugs were just heroin and evil and shit like that... or it's only a smoke now and then... or he can afford it... y'know, the coke habit is only for the weekends. Or better still... ohhh the big C eh! Crack... but hey – that's only in America right? It's never on ar' streets is it?' He laughed.

'I know what you're getting at but...'

'But since this clubbing phenomenon, a whole new generation of people who previously would never have taken drugs. Never before considered it... are now bang into it.'

'I know what you're saying but how does this relate to Steve?'

He ignored the question, and appeared to be lost in his own deliberation. 'You see everything that's happening around us is like some kind of fairy tale, only it's our fairy tale Chopper.

123

Y'know, it's like *once-upon-a-time-in-Manchester* or some bullshit like that. You see, in years to follow, these times in particular will always be spoke of and remembered as some of the best times ever had by anyone. No matter what happens to the way the club scene will turn out. We were just there at the right time to exploit all of this to our advantage. And it's pretty fuckin 'safe to say that we've taken... and continue to take full advantage of it all.' he stopped what he was saying and looked directly at me. 'But like anything that is connected to our world. Ar' way of living. There comes another page to the fairy tale that we've been exploiting. It's all an illegal business that we run Chopper.'

'I know that...' I stared at him, shaking my head at such a comment as if I hadn't realised. 'Now how's this relate to Steve?'

'Well the media. Especially the press are having a field day with rise of all this so called drug culture. It's almost like it's never been around before the way they're going on about it. But more so than anything it's like I said... All classes of people are now starting to fuck about with them,' he looked at me smirking. 'So that's what all the extra police activity is about. Then they have to appear to the public's eye to be out there fighting against all this evil that's taking control of their next generation of children. So with that extra activity – they've obviously clocked Steve about town with us. Maybe even on the estate with us – so naturally if they're checking into us then they've tried to run a check on Steve also.'

'You reckon they've got anything on him?' I enquired. 'I'd hate for anything to happen to him y'know Prey.'

'I know what you're saying Chopper,' he smiled. 'Kinda grows on you – don't he... the old bastard.'

'So what do we do with him then?'

'Well I reckon Steve's got himself more than covered. Probably more so than we even realise,' he laughed. 'As long as they don't get onto the name change he should be sweet enough. I tell you what we'll do though. Just to be on the safe side. Keep it as it is for now, Steve out of town for the next few months... apart from the shop. We can concentrate on making things tighter on the estate. Jonah and Kezlo can work out a new schedule for sorting out the gear from over that way.'

I took another mouthful of food and began chewing thoughtfully then smiled. 'Sweet Prey I reckon he'll be happy with that himself... Especially since he's got Claire now.'

'I still can't get my head round that one,' Prey laughed shuffling more duck into his mouth.

'Ain't that Scotty?' Batty asked my as they drove his Range Rover back through Moss Side estate after sorting some business out with some of the lads they occasionally did some work with.

'It sure is,' Tommy grinned looking up from the spliff he was building. 'What's he up to there?'

'Looks like he's buying rocks,' Batty declared tutting as he did. 'See the little black kid there. His name's Dom... Jason has got it off him a few times before now.'

Scotty was oblivious to Batty and Tommy cruising by, observing what he was doing and not what was around him.

'Why's he buying them 'ere though?' Tommy asked. 'Ain't his lot already doing 'em?'

'They sure are,' added Batty looking back over his shoulder at Scotty as he eagerly took off after his purchase. 'So maybe Scotty don't want anybody knowing about the fact he's buying them.'

'What do you reckon we say then Batty?'

'We don't say fuck all,' he snapped at Tommy. 'It ain't ar' business... Besides we all cane a bit of that gear ourselves from time to time. Don't we Tommy?'

'Sweet boss,' he laughed, he knew Batty hated being called boss, only ever doing it to wind him up. 'Don't go sweating it.'

Batty gave him a scolding look. 'Look – Scotty's been alright since new year. Hasn't he?' Batty stared at Tommy with one eye on him and one eye on the road. 'We've had no more fuck ups. So let's not go rocking the boat eh? So to speak that is,' he laughed realising what he'd just said.

126

'Yes boss,' Tommy smirked, laughing along also as he now lighted the finished spliff.

'Between you and Jackie mate. You probably keep me in business,' Dom laughed taking Scotty's money signalling for the amount to be brought over.

'C'mon Dom man,' Scotty said as he watched his cash disappear. 'You got to start sorting me out better prices man. I'm a regular customer.'

'Fuck that Scotty,' said Dom flashing his gold teeth at him. 'You think I'm stupid or what boy?'

'What the fuck does that mean...' he snarled back at the arrogant teenager. 'And don't go calling me boy. *Eh boy.*'

'You pay top dollar or just go fuckin' find yourself someone else to sell you the shit. Someone, who won't go giving you up that is,' he smiled knowingly at him again.

'Listen up boy... you either come buy it from me or just maybe your crew finds out that you ain't putting bees into their pockets. I know your crew sells the shit. You just don't want them to find out how much your fucked up ass is smoking these days – isn't that right 'ickle boy?'

'Just give me the shit man...' Scotty was becoming irritable with the confrontation.

'No problem man,' he added shrugging, as the mountain bike appeared with one of Dom's lads riding it. 'And you be sure to come see me soon... *boy,*' he laughed as he disappeared out of sight down an alleyway.

'Where've you been Scotty?' Jackie impatiently said as he walked into her flat. 'I was worried. You've been so long.'

'Don't sweat it girl,' he said taking his jacket off. 'You got the pipe ready?' he asked as he sat down.

'Of course babe,' she said passing it to him as he was already loading it up. 'Are you staying over tonight babe?' She said playfully stroking the top of his thigh.

'We'll see,' he said lighting the pipe. 'I got to pop out in a bit to see somebody,' He passed the pipe to her he then watched her greedily suck on it, as he then instantly reloaded it.

'I'll make this next pipe real special babe,' she said whilst undoing the zipper belonging to his jeans. 'Just how you like it,' she groped for his semi-erect-semi-flaccid cock then crawled down onto her knees in front of him.

'That's it baby,' Scotty lay back and grinned to himself.

He absolutely loved this. He sucked on his pipe as Jackie sucked on his cock. Fantastic... he thought to himself as the pure 100 percent crack cocaine hit his blood stream.

'Look... That's all I've got *for you*,' Scotty snapped.

'You just keep telling us the same shit Scotty,' Stevenson snarled back at him. 'It's just on different street grafters... that's all.'

'That's all I've got,' he looked away.

'Just look at the state of you lad,' Walsh shook his head. 'You're already fucked up aren't you?' he was staring into Scotty's glazed over eyes.

'Fuck you Walsh...' he screamed. 'Just give me my shit.'

'No... not this time Scotty,' he said, smiling at Scotty, seeing the panic now in his eyes. 'This time you've got to earn it.'

Stevenson grinned at him knowing exactly what his partner was up to. 'That's right Scotty. We need more from you son.'

'That's all I know. Please,' Scotty pleaded.

'Tell you what Scotty,' Walsh added. 'You go home tonight and you have yourself a good think about things. Tomorrow morning at eleven we're going to show you pictures and you're going to tell us stories relating to those pictures. After all that's what you're good at. Ain't it Scotty?'

'Go fuck yourself Walsh,' he yelled at them. 'Just give me the gear will ya,' he was close to tears.

'We'll see you tomorrow morning Scotty,' Stevenson smiled at him.

'That's not fair,' he pleaded with them both. 'You've got to give it to me.'

'We don't have to do shit,' Walsh blatantly told him shaking his head. 'Now get the fuck out of the car you little cunt.' he screamed at him.

'Give me some money then.'

'Now,' Walsh screamed again.

Scotty climbed out of the back seat. 'You're both a couple of no good twats' he yelled as tears streamed down his face.

'See you at eleven in the morning,' Stevenson said as he wound his window back up and they took off.

'Bastards...' Scotty screamed after the green Sierra as it disappeared into the night.

Fuck... fuck... bastard... he couldn't believe it... he'd really needed that rock as he'd caned all of what he bought off Dom earlier on. Thinking he was going to be all right after he'd seen them two that night.

Fuck it... Jackie will have to go out and get some. No matter what she has to do to get it for them.

'On time Scotty,' Stevenson said as he climbed into the back seat. 'We like that. Good lad.' He added in a condescending way.

'Don't patronise me you twat,' he snapped back at him.

'Right have a good look at these Scotty,' Walsh said ignoring him and not wasting any time whilst throwing a stack of envelopes containing photos to him. 'We want to know everything there is to know about all of them.'

'I'll do my best... I promise,' Scotty said humbly – it had been a hell of a night – they'd not got any more rocks and it had left him desperate.

As he sat there he began to rearrange to stack of photos into some sort of order. He looked at the surveillance shots of all the people that he knew... and had known for years.

'What the fuck are you doing? What's taking you so long?' Stevenson asked irritably.

'Just give me a minute will you,' he sniffed. 'You've got a hell of a lot of photos 'ere to go through.'

After a few minutes of sorting through them he stared at the two of them and sniffed loudly again, then rolled down the window and spat of green venomous vile to the car park before rolling up the window again.

'Right then – let's begin,' he passed them photos back from each pile he'd set about neatly in stacks beside him – giving them the names of each person as he did so.

'Those are the street grafters for the weed mainly. But this one is Dougsy. He pretty much looks out for them at street level. It used to be Jonah's job before. That's Kezlo who makes sure that they're supplied as required and needed. He's above them. But he also works closely with Jonah, as do all of them lot,' as he said this he pointed to the pile of other shots.

'They run the weed – but they also knock out the Es, whizz and trips but none of the other gear,' he informed them both.

'Where do the Es and other shit come from?' Walsh asked.

'I honestly can't help you there. I tried to find out. But there was no chance and I didn't want to push too much,' he told them. 'All I know is that Jonah used to be completely in charge of that side with Chopper. But after Chopper was made into a full boss, Kezlo was also put into helping Jonah out. Jonah was promoted to lieutenant along with Kezlo and me. Although I moved into the purchasing side of only the weed. Which is a lot better a position than they've got? Although I'm still at the same level as theses two.'

'What the fuck are lieutenants?' Stevenson laughed.

'It means that they're in charge,' Scotty snapped back at him. 'What the fuck do you think it means Stevenson?' he sneered at him. 'Like I told you – I'm a lieutenant myself,' he then stated proudly.

'Yes sir,' Walsh saluted mockingly.

'Fuck you both,' he snarled, as he then passed them two more photos. 'Alright Sharon and Janine are still some how connected but I really don't know how anymore. They both used to be street grafters. But now I don't know exactly what it is they do.'

'What about the rest?' Stevenson asked.

Scotty passed another pile of photos to them telling them each name of the person in the photo as he did; 'Once again that's just the street grafters for the smack and the rocks only. You see if the want anything else it's only a phone call away and another trip down the road for the punter. That way it's a lot safer.'

'What else then?' Stevenson asked as Scotty stopped and stared at them.

'Alright before we go any further. Am I going to be sorted out proper for all this information or what?' he stared at the two of them with cold eyes.

Walsh produced a bag filled with at least a quarter ounce of pure crack cocaine in it.

'This do you?' he asked, then grinned at Scotty as his eyes lit up.

'Alright,' he said hurriedly. 'Now these are Johnny and Knieldy. Now they have complete control of the smack that's sold. And these are Parksey and Diamond who run the rocks, the two business's are combined but Knieldy seems to have a bit more control over all of them lieutenant's.'

'More fucking lieutenants,' Walsh laughed.

'That's fuckin' right, more lieutenants,' he snapped once again, becoming annoyed at their attitude. 'The operation is run military style,' he informed them shaking his head.

'And... there's a lot more photos yet Scotty,' Stevenson said as he tossed another pile to them.

'They're just lookouts,' he told them. 'You'll never get anything on these lot – total waste of your fuckin time... As they're never holding anything,' he told them smirking as he did.

'What do you mean lookouts?' Walsh asked.

'As in they keep watch all day,' he said looking at them like they were stupid. He thought that no wonder they'd never got close to the crew before... they were so naïve. It was unbelievable.

'And that's all they do watch the street?' Stevenson asked.

'They are the eyes and ears of the estate,' he told them bluntly. 'If somebody wants something usually they'll set it up with one of the street grafters.'

'Seriously? And they get paid for this?' Stevenson seemed surprised.

'No they do it for free,' he sneered at him. 'Why is it you think you've not been able to ever hold any of them for anything other than petty charges before? They're vital to the street.'

'With your testimony against them though... We'll be laughing,' Walsh was nodding more to himself than anybody else.

'Even I know that that won't hold up against the lookouts in a court of law,' he smiled back at how stupid what Walsh had just been. 'I mean it will literally be my word against theirs. Like I said they won't ever be carrying gear to sell and a pocksy possession charge ain't what you're looking for. Is it?'

'They really have got things set up tightly? Haven't they Scotty?' Walsh added, almost admiringly.

'Of course,' Scotty answered proudly. 'Why the fuck do you think that you've never really got at all close to them. It's a professional set up. Always has been,' he loved the thought of how they'd never got close to the crew before.

That was when the guilt suddenly hit him, as he was now handing it all over on a plate to them. Giving up his best friends and associates that he'd known practically all his life.

'Alright Scotty,' Stevenson asked. 'And the last three are?'

'First off... Y'know that I don't know shit about the old guy,' he shook his head as he handed the photos of Steve back to them. 'That's the truth. I mean if I'm giving you all this and I knew something on him then wouldn't it make sense that I'd give you him as well. All I know is that he's connected to Macreedy's clothes shop.'

'Alright,' Walsh nodded; he actually appeared to believe him. It was like he said if the old guy was involved it wouldn't make sense to leave someone out there to track him down after all this had gone down. 'The last two then?'

'These are all of Prey,' he sighed. 'That's Kieran O'Prey to you.'

'And...' Stevenson persisted.

'You know who this is...' he stared at the photos of Chopper filled with more guilt than he could possibly imagine as his closest and oldest friend – nah... he was more than that – *his brother* – was staring him back from the photos he held in his hands.

'We need to hear it from you,' Walsh injected.

'And what it is they both do?' Stevenson added.

'You really are a couple of bastards...' he sneered at them.

'Come on now Scotty,' Walsh winked waving the bag before him as bait.

'Alright it's Chopper... Billy Chorlton,' he spat the words out at them.

'And what is it they do?' Stevenson asked.

'As far I know they are both the bosses. But nothing ever comes directly from them though,' he said letting his eyes drift out of the window as the rain trickled like a real life game of snakes and ladders.

'Carry on...' pushed Walsh.

'How much more do you both need?' Scotty sighed.

'This is just the beginning Scotty,' Stevenson said. 'This... what you've give us today has been good. But if we're going to make sure that they go away for a very long time we need to build an airtight case against them. We need something more solid on O'Prey and Chorlton. We need to start coming up with dates and events that we can use against them.'

'You'll be working for us for a very long time yet Scotty whilst we build up enough evidence. By the time we take them to court there will be no way possible for it to get kicked out in any way,' Walsh added, throwing the bag to him in the back seat.

'Although if you keep coming up with good information like today... Then I'll make sure we look after you real special lad,' he smiled knowingly as Scotty grabbed the bag of crack.

'Right I'm off then,' he said opening the back door. 'I'll see you next week. Make sure you get me something like this again Walshy and I'll come up with some dates and shit for you to use.'

'See you soon Scotty,' Walsh said smiling at him. 'You stay out of trouble – you hear me son.'

'Do you know when I'm going back out there Jonah?' Sharon asked as Jonah eased his Black VW Golf GTI through traffic down Oxford Road.

'Not at the moment,' he said looking at her. 'Why?'

'I'm just a bit short of cash,' she smiled at him stroking his hand on the gear stick to try her best to win him over.

'You've spent your entire last take,' he said shaking his head. 'You make more money than me girl,' he laughed.

'That'll be the day,' she smiled seductively back at him.

'Where's it all gone this time?' he asked... yet already knowing the answer.

'Well – I had to buy new clothes so that I always look good for you Jonah,' she was trying it on big time now.

'You don't *always* have to go buying new clothes,' he laughed leaning over kissing her. 'You just *like* buying new clothes all the time,' he suddenly noticed her eyes come alight with panic.

'Jonah – *watch the fuck out*...' she suddenly screamed.

He slammed down on the break pedal as hard as he could – skidding to a halt at the pedestrian crossing, only just in time stopping to a full halt as all of the pedestrian's gave him long hard, cold stares, as he sat there mouthing the word sorry to them.

'Fuck me!' he sighed out loudly. 'I shit myself then. Sharon, are you alright?' he asked, quickly turning to her.

135

'Yeah – I'm sweet Jonah,' she said as he reached over to give her a kiss, just as he kissed her he could have sworn he just saw Scotty.

He looked again... had it him or not he thought to himself? It sure looked like him – Although he couldn't be too sure... It looked like he was climbing from the rear of that green Sierra hidden away at the side of the medical college.

Just then the lights changed to green as he was still trying to get a better look before the horns sounding irritably behind him brought him back round..

'What are you looking at?' Sharon asked looking out of the window, as he was still trying to see whether or not it had been Scotty or not.

'Fuck all Sharon,' he said smiling at her. 'I just thought I saw somebody. That's all girl.'

August had arrived and my birthday along with it... it was only days away now. It all seemed so mad, remembering back to my eighteenth birthday and how much had happened since then.

So much in fact it that it was hard to take it all in. I really was still quite young to have already achieved as much from life as I had done. I was one of the main heads in town and had a lot of respect from those around me, although I have to say that I never played on it. Or used it... or manipulated those around me like a lot of the other people I knew who were in the same situation as me. I think I was more than fair with those around me.

The money that the three of us controlled was colossal. I was only in my early twenty's and already amassing more money then I could ever have possibly imagined. We'd begun making investments into some legal assets, accounting for them through Macreedy's.

And yet in a funny kind of way, I still felt that this was merely the beginning of things. The future and whatever lay within its grasp still lay before me... Prey... and not forgetting Steve of course. Business that year had been more than good to date. In fact, both business's had grown from strength to strength.

Donna had continued to run Macreedy's for us, working closely with its continuing augmentation. The three of us had been so proud at how well she had run the store that we just left her to it. All we were concerned with was the accounting side of the business, as our initial plan was to expand into London with another store to launder a fraction of our money through. That was something that we'd put on hold for now though.

We'd kept Steve away from the estate until only the previous month. The extra heat seemed to have calmed down slightly from how it had been at the beginning of the year. Although they were still active, we knew that much. Prey and I had taken tighter security measures with all areas of the business to be on the safer side. We'd really mixed things up so we continue to keep those around us on their toes.

Despite all this though, we'd had none of the previous year's problems now that certain people were out of the way. This had made things so much better between Donna and I. Especially as we had not been arguing the way we had done before – and I felt proper sound about that. She was everything to me, and the mere thought of losing her wasn't imaginable.

Kathy was due to have her baby any day now also. Although Prey, still kept her at her own flat. He told us that she needed her space also, which was complete bullshit as the only space required was in his bed as he was shagging just about anything else he could get his hands on... Some things would never change though.

Steve was still with Claire. She genuinely seemed to truly love the old guy. It still put smiles on our faces though, when we thought about the two of them. Steve was a good man though, if anybody deserved to be happy, then it was him. Plus she'd only just turned eighteen. The lucky...*or* dirty bastard whichever way you wanted to look at it.

Suddenly the phone rang bringing me out of my thoughts. 'Chopper... It's Batty,' he said with real urgency in his voice before I'd even chance to say anything.

'What's up mate?' I asked, sensing that something wasn't right the way he'd come on the line.

'Stay where you are Chopper,' he simply said to me. 'I'll be there in half an hour mate,' he finished and the line went dead, with me left standing there confused staring into the headpiece of the phone.

'What's happened?' I asked immediately, opening the front door.

'Tommy and Scotty have been nicked,' Batty said as he walked through into the flat.

138

'You what!' I exclaimed shocked, shutting the door behind him. 'When?'

'This morning at Tommy's gaff,' he sat down rubbing the back of his head. 'The weed had only just arrived when Scotty turned up. Tommy was running about the house like a mad man trying his best to sort things out. When out of the blue, Scotty just turns up,' he stared at me. 'That's the odd fuckin' bit though Chopper.'

'What is?' I asked, not sure what he meant.

'It wasn't due until tomorrow,' he informed me. 'The full batch that is. I already told him that the other day. I said that we'd be getting a fraction of what the buy was this morning, but not the amount he'd need until tomorrow.'

'How'd you know all this?'

'Because Jason was in the kitchen as they busted through the front door. He was out of the back door quicker than a rabbit on acid,' he looked at me, shaking his head.

'They didn't get near him... he came straight round to mine to let me know what had gone down.'

'This is well mad.'

'Jason says that Scotty turned up for a buy. He brought ten gee's with him. Did you give him that?'

'Not personally,' I said looking carefully at him.

'Y'know what the fuck I mean Chopper,' he snapped at me.

'He said the money was needed for a small buy only,' I told him sitting down myself now. 'He said that you were collecting this morning and that he could only pick up a small amount from you lads. Besides I only arranged for the bees to be dropped off with him. I never even seen him Batty.'

'I spoke with him a few days ago and he said he was running low,' he told me lighting a cigarette to try and calm his nerves. 'But I told him that it wouldn't be today it would be tomorrow before he could collect himself.'

'Where are they both now and what did the copper's get?'

'This is where this all turns a little pear shaped Chopper,' he stared hard at me as he exhaled the smoke. 'You see they got picked up with ten keys of resin in the house. Now financially that won't hit hard and I'll look after Tommy – but...' he trailed off staring hard at me.

'But fuckin' what...' I snapped staring back at him. After all it was my guy... my best mate that had been nicked as well.

'But Chopper...' he sighed shaking his head in disbelief. 'How the fuck is it... that your guy is leaving the station after only one hour?'

'How long?' I asked in disbelief.

'Exactly Chopper,' he said, sitting back staring at me.

'So you're saying he's grassed then,' I snapped at him, after all I knew Scotty. He'd never do that.

'Well – it's certainly looking that way... Ain't it Chopper.'

'Never...' I protested. 'Scotty would never grass.'

'Look Chopper – there's something you need to know about your boy,' he was shaking his head at me. 'I've seen him down Moss Side enough times now.'

'So fuckin' what!' I replied angrily.

'So fuckin' what Chopper,' he snapped back at me. 'He was buying rocks down there. Didn't say anything before as it's not my business,' he watched for my reaction.

'Are you sure?' I stared back at him accusingly.

'Not 100 percent,' he sighed, unwittingly nodding his head at me. 'But c'mon Chopper. What the fuck else would he be doing down there with them lot? And whatever the fuck it was, he was paying for it.'

'I still can't believe he's a grass though Batty,' I told him. 'I mean we just go too far back.'

'Look Chopper - you're a top lad,' he told me. 'But Scotty man... we've been down one road with him this year already.'

'I know... but...' I was trying to think of a way to defend him.

'He turns up a day early for the pick up. Just after the delivery has been dropped off as well... and then we get busted. Then he's back on the streets only an hour later,' he sighed deeply. 'C'mon Chopper for fucks sake... It looks dodgy as fuck.'

Just then we were both startled, as the repeated frantic thundering of the front door broke us from our discussion. I cautiously peered through the peephole and shook my head, glancing briefly at Batty before opening the door.

'Scotty – just the man we were talking about,' I told him as he frantically barged past me into the hallway.

'Chopper... Cho... Chopper... you're not going to believe what... jus...' he was trying to get his words out as he was inhaling and exhaling, both hard and fast as though he'd run all the way from Wythenshawe.

I cut him off before he went any further. 'You got nicked in Wythenshawe this morning – right?'

'How the fuck do y'know?' he exclaimed, genuinely startled by my reaction.

'I think you'd better come through, hadn't you,' I told him walking back towards the living room.

As we walked through the door and revealed Batty sat there, Scotty flew straight into one. 'Batty – Batty man – y'know Tommy got nicked this morning... Me as well...' he was out of breath and excitable. 'Jason was there. Although he might have made it away – he wasn't in the van with us.'

'Just slow the fuck down – will you,' I told him, 'We need the full story.'

'Yeah... You stop off in Moss Side on the way back or something?' Batty sneered at him.

'What the fuck does that mean?'

'How'd you get out so soon Scotty?'

'I told them that I'd just gone to see an old mate over that way. That's why I was in the house.'

'Yeah right,' Batty began, 'and they said – *Okay son* – you run along and have a nice day now. Did they you lying little fuc...' he was seething; you could see it clearly written all over his face.

'No... not at all,' he blurted out. 'They questioned me solid for an hour about ten keys of weed they found upstairs in a bedroom. Apparently though... I wasn't a suspect as they were just about to bust the house as I turned up. That's what they said anyway.'

'Why the fuck did you turn up today anyway?' Batty asked.

'Er... well I er... well... I spoke with Tommy this morning,' he lied. 'He said that I was sweet to pick up five keys after eleven thirty... *Honest*.'

'Yeah right,' Batty said shaking his head at him. 'I already told you that it would be tomorrow before you could have your full load.'

'We needed some gear today though,' he snapped. 'We was low,' He looked at me for support.

'What about the bees Scotty?' I enquired.

'They never mentioned it,' he said a lot calmer now. 'I know they got it though. They questioned me about who else was in the house and I said fuck all,' he told us both, really controlled now.

'What about the cash?' I asked again.

'I told them that Tommy was an old mate of mine who I was just visiting – that was it. They fucked me off after that, saying that they'd maybe be in touch.' He'd totally blanked the question I'd just asked.

'Yeah right Scotty,' Batty snapped. 'You ain't nothing but a lying grassing fuckin' rock head.'

'You fuckin' what,' screamed Scotty. 'What did you just call me you fat fuckin twat?' He flew straight past me and straight for Batty who was already moving from his seat at him.

I leapt between the two of them, just as Batty swung hard at Scotty as I blocked the punch and got in between them both. 'Calm the fuck down – this ain't solving shit for any of us,' I yelled at the two of them.

'Who you calling a liar,' Scotty snarled the words at Batty who was now stood by the living room door. 'You're the lying grassing cunt round 'ere,' he was bouncing around hyperactive once again. 'You grassed me to Chopper... remember... liar... grasser.'

'You fuckin' little fuckin' piece of shit,' screamed Batty, swinging wildly at Scotty - only this time I was not able get between them and Batty whacked him so hard I thought that he was going to fly straight through my front door as he crashed into it. I just about managed to grab hold of Batty before he inflicted more damage to Scotty; as I then threw him back onto the settee.

Then turning back to Scotty lay there covering himself I screamed. 'Get the fuck out of 'ere Scotty,' I was seething at the way he'd just treated Batty. 'Go home – I'll see you later,' I was staring at him as he scurried to his feet and scrambled out of my front door within sheer terror at what had just taken place plastered upon his now swollen face.

'Batty mate,' I said sitting down sighing deeply. His face held a scornful appearance.

'I just don't know what to say mate – I don't what's got into him. I thought he'd been alright lately.'

'Fuckin rocks – that's what's got into him,' Batty snapped at me. 'Open your eyes mate,' he said sitting up.

'I just can't see it,' I told him shaking my head to try and convince myself.

'Chopper – mate – you're a good lad,' Batty told me exhaling noisily as he did so. 'You always have been mate. Look – don't let that little prick fuck you up. 'Cause that's what's going to happen, y'know.'

142

'We go way back,' I told him not able to look him in the eye.

'I know you do mate,' he paused and stared at me, concern frosting his eyes. 'But I'm through with him. I'll have someone talk to Tommy as soon as I can. Just to see what's been said. But I'm afraid no matter what the outcome Chopper I ain't dealing with him no more.'

'You what!'

'Look, put Jonah or Kezlo on it,' he told me. 'I trust both of them fully. They're both sound lads who I've known for time now.'

'Consider it already sorted Batty,' I replied looking at him sombrely.

'One other thing Chopper,' he said. 'After today I don't want him anywhere near the estate again. Also you let him think that we're no longer together anymore, business wise that is. Obviously we will be seeing each other around and I'm not falling out with you over that little shit – alright?' he nodded at me as he rose from the settee.

'Sweet mate,' I said shaking his hand, although not moving from my own seat as I sat there deflated. 'All I can do is offer my apologies to you mate.'

'It'll never be you,' he said smiling. 'Always remember that Chopper. I respect you with the same recognition that you give me mate.'

He smiled and then nodded as I watched him leave the flat.

As I walked straight round to Scotty and Kezlo's gaff, I could hear things being smashed as I advanced towards the front door, and still having my own key, I therefore let myself in.

'Scotty... Scotty man,' I pleaded immediately as I walked through the door, observing him grabbing hold of anything within range of him and launching it wildly. But it was as if he couldn't even hear me. 'Scotty man – for fucks sake – calm the fuck down will you - *now*,' I screamed at him.

Kezlo was already doing his best to try and calm him, but Scotty was in one hell of a wild rage. Just then he grabbed one of Kezlo's records from the turntable and threw it at the wall, as we all witnessed it shatter to pieces.

'You fuckin' twat,' Kezlo screamed at him... and who then rightly so, smashed his right fist into Scotty's head knocking him once again to the ground.

143

I was real glad, as it instantaneously calmed Scotty the fuck down. 'You dickhead Scotty,' Kezlo said spitting the words at him as he began picking up the pieces to his record. 'That was a classic Ice-T track you cocksucker,' he snapped at Scotty lay there. Kezlo seemed more concerned over his record than Scotty mumbling his apology to him.

As I reached down and grabbed him from the floor, I lifted him to the settee, and went straight for him. 'I want the truth Scotty...' I screamed at him. 'Have you been buying fuckin' rocks in Moss Side?'

'What... There you go again... I don't know what you're on about.' The question had startled him; you could see it in his panic stricken eyes.

'Tell him the truth,' Kezlo yelled at him in his own rage, still examining his broken record – looking well distressed by it.

'A few,' he sighed. 'Not that many though,' he added feebly to me.

'It's nothing extreme Chopper,' Kezlo then said defensively to me. 'Saying that though he's round at Jackie's most of the time anyway.' He added as an after thought.

'Have you got yourself a habit Scotty?' I sighed deeply, bending down to him looking up directly into his eyes, noticing just how bad they really looked for the first time. You could literally see the veins running their clouded mass, around their obscured deep surroundings. 'I need the truth brother?'

'No I haven't Chopper,' he looked me straight in the eye. 'No more than you have – or you Kezlo for that matter,' he glanced at him also.

He was right, both Kezlo and myself smoked them – just not that frequently. 'Alright listen up Scotty,' I said sitting next to him. 'I don't know what went down today for sure.'

'I've told you what went down Chopper,' he said turning to me.

'So it's right then?' Kezlo asked still looking at that broken record.

'All I know is what they've both told me,' I told Kezlo. 'I tell you what Scotty... After today Batty and me ain't doing business again. He's still alright though. I don't want you causing any fuckin' trouble with him.'

'Really,' Scotty smiled at me like he had earlier that year, almost smugly like he'd scored yet another point to himself.

'The thing is though Scotty,' I said staring at him. 'The other contact for the weed will only deal with Kezlo himself,' I said, nodding at Kezlo who immediately understood what I was getting at.

'That's out of order Chopper.' he snapped at me.

'Fuck out of order Scotty,' I responded harshly back at him. 'That's the way it's going to be from now on – *understand?*' I sneered the last word at him.

'What the fuck am I supposed to do then?'

'You'll move back into your old position at street level,' I informed him. 'You're still a lieutenant Scotty. Plus it'll do you some good to get back to the street. You was always a top grafter in the position. You'll still be in charge of the weed, just at distribution level now.'

'So do I do the Es now as well?' he asked a little over anxiously, as his eyes were momentarily alight.

'No,' I told him shaking my head. 'That has to stay the way it is for now anyway.'

'Why has it?'

'Because the same guy will supply the weed,' I said thinking quickly to throw him.

'Alright then Chopper,' he said dropping his head from me. 'Sorry for any trouble with Batty... Also about the money mate,' he muttered to me sitting back up sighing deeply.

'Don't worry,' I told him, 'you'll be paying us back every penny of it. It's not like you've got an insurance plan is it Scotty?'

What a fuckin' day I thought sat there staring at the two of them silently. I knew that Scotty knew that he'd fucked up – but we went to far back not to stick by him now. At least that's what I thought looking at the back of his head, which was still dropped as he sat there before me like a man defeated after only a few rounds.

'That was good work this morning son,' said Walsh as he passed the bag full of crack cocaine to Scotty.

They'd both been getting hassle from upstairs to show some results, to show that their contact was actually of some use. Scotty had told them to wait for a few weeks then, as he had promised he would do, he gave them the bust that morning in Wythenshawe. Even if it wasn't a major bust it had showed their bosses that Scotty was of use to them.

'The drug squad picked up 10 kilos of high quality cannabis resin from there this morning.' He added.

'I don't think that they bought the story though.'

'What are you on about lad?' Stevenson asked.

'Look... that fuckin' Batty twat saw me leaving the station. Didn't he,' he responded angrily at them. 'Plus he told Chopper that I was a fuckin' rock head.'

Walsh wanted to tell that he was one – but somehow managed to hold it back.

'Everything's all right though?' Stevenson asked a little worried. 'Ain't it Scotty?' He added as he saw his head drop.

'I got dropped from purchasing,' he sniffed loudly.

'What the fuck you on now though?' Walsh asked, panicking slightly that Scotty had been kicked off the firm all together.

'I'm back on the street,' he sighed deeply then exhaled shaking his head. 'I'm still a lieutenant though.'

'That's even better then,' declared Stevenson. 'Now what you have to be sure to do is make certain you start do excellent work for them so they won't think about dropping you all together,' he added. 'So do you have access to anything else?'

'No,' he told them shaking his head. 'Well... what I mean is that I still won't know where the other gear comes from. Only who it's to be distributed to at street level.'

'Well just make sure that you still discreetly gather as much information as you can and we'll still be laughing.' He glared at Scotty then smiled, 'Look Scotty... You needn't worry about today,' Walsh stared at him directly. 'We made sure that Tommy will be told that you said nothing whatsoever. Also his brief will be provided with the statements that we've put together to show that you said fuck all. It's going to be down to the fact that the bust was already in place to go down – you just happened to show up. Just don't stress it lad.'

'That's easy for you two to say,' Scotty told them.

'Just one other thing Scotty,' Stevenson shook his head as he then added. 'That bag you carried in there was full of old books... no money.'

'You think I'm going to put my neck on the line for the bees also,' he sneered at them both. 'You're both trippin'. I didn't take any money with me. Did I now?'

'So what the fuck were you going to buy the weed with then?' Walsh asked curiously.

'They arrange the pick ups don't they,' he said. 'That's when I receive the money for the buy. I never arrange it... I just made out that I'd just gone to see Tommy,' he said smiling as he did – his best blagging head fully in position.

'Alright then son,' Stevenson said as he smiled at him. 'Once again, you did good work for us today.'

'Laters,' Scotty grinned at them then climbed from the backseat.

It worked perfectly he thought to himself as he walked away from the car glancing back around at the two of them still sat there now talking with one another. He'd planned for this day after they had mithered for information on a bust that they could take the credit for.

He'd waited for the right opportunity. Not wanting anybody on either side to go getting burnt too badly from his scam. But they'd all bought it – he couldn't believe it. They all actually bought the story that there was no money there... All of them, including Chopper and Batty who would now just think that it was the coppers that nicked the cash. Especially when Tommy tells them that there was no money there either.

He was ten grand richer – And he had it all to blow completely on rocks. Yeah right he'd pay Chopper back as his friend had told him… but he'd lie and blag his way round that for as long as he possibly could. He began to grin to himself at the mere thought of it like the cat, who had just gotten the cream, as he now watched Stevenson's green Ford Sierra disappear around the corner.

What time is it for fuck's sake?' I asked sleepily answering the phone to Prey. As I glanced at the clock, I was sure that it only said something bizarre like 4:30am.

'It's just gone four o'clock,' he yelled excitedly at me, he was completely ecstatic on the other end of the line, 'and I've just become a dad.'

It certainly did the trick in bringing me round from my sleep. 'Are you serious? Yes mate,' I screamed back at him. 'On my birthday as well,' I added as Donna started to come round next to me.

'Who is it?' she asked sleepily.

'What is it?' I asked ignoring her.

'It's a lad mate – a little baby boy,' he sounded so full of joy.

'A – boy – yes pal. A proper lad for sure...' I was still screaming as Donna grabbed the phone from me.

'Congratulations Prey... how's Kathy?'

'She's fine,' he told her. 'She should be out on Thursday in time for Friday night.'

'How much does he weigh?' she enquired.

'Seven pound something,' he laughed. 'I'm not too sure – Kathy will tell you later. Put Chopper back on the line.'

'No problem.' She replied handing me the receiver.

'Happy Birthday Chopper,' he laughed joylessly down the line at me. 'Damn shame that my son was jinxed with the same birthday as yours eh.'

'Cheers Prey,' I smiled as I said this. 'See you later mate. All three of you for that matter,' I added, replacing the headset.

Steve and Claire were already there once we arrived that morning at Hope hospital over in Salford near to where Kathy lived in Walkden.

'I take it you received a similar call as me at four thirty this morning,' Steve laughed as we both approached.

Everybody wished me happy birthday. Prey was wearing this permanent grin across his face. In fact – it was a grin he'd wear for at least the next week.

After all the congratulations and so forth had past, I finally asked. 'Where is he then?'

I was oblivious to the fact that Donna was already sat there with the baby in her arms. Shite... was my immediate thought as I saw that look upon her face of utter joy. I didn't think I was quite ready to go down the road of having kids just yet.

'C'mon...give us a look then,' I said, acting all cool like I didn't really give a shit as I walked over. All that coolness just melted away as I looked down into this little baby's face.

'No way – look at him,' I genuinely smiled at the little baby 'A little Prey – ahhh,' he was so cute just lay there helpless in Donna's arms; I wasn't even able to blag myself.

'Have you decided on a name yet?' Donna asked Kathy.

'Sean O'Prey,' Prey stated proudly before Kathy had chance to say anything.

'That's excellent,' Steve said.

'Why Sean?' Claire enquired.

'He was a very good friend of ours who died,' Donna told her still rocking little Sean in her arms.

'How you doing Kathy?' I asked her.

'I'm fine Chopper,' Kathy smiled, although she looked exhausted. 'I still can't wait for Friday night though. It's been so long since I've even had a drink never mind anything else.'

Gazing at little Sean, I then suddenly said, 'Give us a hold then,' I hadn't given it a second thought and immediately thought – *whoa shit* – where the fuck did those words just come from. Then they all began staring at me with questioning glares.

'Are you serious?' Donna asked me.

'Err – yeah sure – why not eh,' I said suddenly nervous as hell about holding him in my arms.

'Here Chopper,' Donna said passing Sean to me. 'Make sure you support his head.'

'Ahhh look,' Steve teased. 'It looks like we've found Chopper's soft spot then,' he added, as they all laughed, but I was oblivious sat there with little Sean in my arms.

After the rest of the afternoon was spent drinking in Dry Bar celebrating – wetting the baby's head so to speak, we headed off to Chan's for some food.

'Ah Prey – Just the man I need to see,' Chan grinned broadly as we walked through the door. 'You must be psychic or something my boy. I was going to phone you later.'

'You'd better congratulate him first Chan,' I told him whilst shaking his hand.

'Ah why so?' Chan enquired.

'He's joined the fatherhood crew with us Chan,' Steve told him.

'Ah Prey my son. Congratulations. And what have you been blessed with?' Chan said hugging him affectionately.

'A little lad,' Prey announced proudly. 'We called him Sean,' he smiled at the old man.

'It's a double celebration Chan,' Donna then told him. 'It's Chopper's birthday also.'

'In that case – tonight you dine as my guests,' he smiled warmly. 'For my favourite customers it's on me. That is as long as I can have the pleasure of dining with you.'

'Of course Chan,' Prey said putting his arm around Chan. 'It's ar' honour mate.'

'Okay – but tonight you must let Chan order food instead,' he said as we made our way over to the table. 'Tonight we eat not from menu. But Chan have Cooks prepare special dishes instead for special occasion.'

'Now that sounds good,' I said, smiling at the mere thought of not eating the same thing that Prey always ordered.

'Damn right,' Steve added as Prey looked at him. 'Well – it make a change from you ordering your fuckin' banquet's all the time,' he added confirming he'd just had the very same thoughts.

'What you trying to say,' Prey shrugged.

Chan shouted one of his waiters over and began to order the food in his native tongue.

'What's he ordering Chopper?' Claire asked.

'Fucked if I know,' I laughed.

'Ah would you girls like to see?' he asked the two of them.

'Oh yes please – can we really?' Donna asked, all excited.

'Of course – you girls follow Chan to kitchen. You watch cook's prepare dishes,' he said leading them away.

Chan returned sitting back down shouting over for drinks then turning to us. 'Okay my boys. Now girls in kitchen, Chan have something very important to discuss with you. I know you have very important things on your mind with the baby but...'

'What's up Chan?' Prey asked cutting him off with a wave of the hand that said business was still business as usual.

'I have very important job needs sorting out,' he looked at us. 'I need outside of family help. You boys are like family. I trust you.'

'You've never asked for our help before Chan,' I stated fact. 'Why now?' I added curiously.

'Because this time if my people act,' he stopped whilst the bottle of Bollinger was brought over and the waiter left us be before continuing. 'This time it would go to an all out war in China town. It will split two important families apart and put China town in Manchester – back many years. It would be like nothing you see before. It would also create me problems that to be quite honest – I do without.'

'What's the actual problem?' Prey asked.

'My family has many old traditions,' he began to tell us. 'They are traditions that go back many generations and should always be respected. Only some of the new generation – the young generation – they no respect this,' he sneered the last few words.

'What are you getting at?' Steve asked lighting himself a cigarette.

'These younger people no like old traditions. They want everything now,' he sighed shaking his head. 'But they don't want to gain respect like we had to. They feel that money is power and they will try achieve this respect by any means necessary.'

'Money is power though Chan – That's just an unfortunate fact of life,' Prey told him.

'The ones you describe Chan – They could be us but just another race,' I added.

'You not understand,' he told us. 'You boys have already earned my respect. You Prey earned it the day you help my son from the hands of evil. For many years now I consider you all family.'

He then looked from Prey to Steve. 'Steve will understand – Yes?'

152

'What Chan means Prey is that in our world traditions are very different,' he said looking at Chan nodding. 'With our people we gained respect by our means that were necessary. Chan's younger generation has too earn respect within Chan's world by different means of gaining respect. Am I right Chan?'

'Yes – yes very much so Steve,' he smiled. 'Now you see.'

'So what is it that you need for us to do then?' I asked confused as to where any of this was actually leading.

'Last week my people lost very big shipment,' he finally announced. 'Shipment was hijacked by younger wannabe's as our lorry turned off motorway into Knutsford. They took lorry by armed force and they put my brother into hospital. He still there now.'

'How much?' Prey asked.

'They take fifty kilo of our heroin,' Chan shook his head at us. 'It does not sound a lot – but well – you see it hits my people very badly.'

Prey whistled. 'Shit, that's still one hell off a lot of gear Chan.'

'We know. The thing is – after what they do to brother,' he screwed his face. 'My main concern is that they pay. That they are left never forgetting what they did.'

'So I take it you do know who hijacked the shipment then,' I said staring at him.

'We know,' he nodded at me. 'I have instructed bosses that I deal with situation myself or they will intervene on problem. If that it is so – much blood will be spilt on streets of Manchester.'

'That won't be good for any of us,' Steve said as he shook his head at the thought of this.

'I know,' Chan added. 'It will attract more authorities to area. Create bigger problem in long run. You understand?'

'We understand Chan,' Prey informed him nodding as he did so. 'But you've not exactly been too clear as to what exactly you want for us to do for you.'

'We know when deal is set to go down for purchase of gear,' he smiled knowingly. 'What I need is for you boys to take it back for Chan,' he watched for our reactions.

'How do you know that this won't backfire on us though Chan?' I asked. 'I mean the last thing we need is to go to war with your people.'

'No one will ever know that you did job for Chan,' he told us. 'All my bosses will know is that Chan sort problem with outside help – that will be all they want to know.'

'Are you asking for us to take these guys out Chan?' Steve asked shocked at the request.

'No... no... not at all,' he said shaking his head. 'But I do want them punished very severely though. Example must be made of these kids... So that no other attempt to take from us will ever happen again.'

'Surely then they'll hit back though,' Prey declared.

'It is reason why outside help I feel is required,' he told us. 'This way they will be led to believe that our people were never involved. We will retain our goods back and my brother will be avenged. But most of all streets of Manchester will only shed blood spilt that night.'

'Alright then Chan,' I said staring at him. 'You've told us what you want doing. Now what would be our outcome Chan?' I asked, smiling at the old man. 'I mean would we be forever in you graces – or to put it bluntly what will we get out of the deal?'

'At the end of next week when this transaction will take place – It will involve some younger generation from London also. Four of them will be there. Also four from here in Manchester. We know where transaction will take place. It will happen at the old disused warehouses at old dock site in Salford,' he nodded then smirked knowingly at us. 'You do this job then you give us back our goods and you keep transaction money for yourselves.'

'This has just suddenly become very interesting indeed,' Prey was rubbing his chin.

'You know sort of money that we're talking about – Don't you Prey,' he grinned broadly. 'It won't be anywhere as near what the gear is worth to us. But still be a very substantial amount for you take from them.'

'What about the London lot?' Steve asked.

'Do to them as you do to others,' he told Steve with no emotion shown whatsoever. 'We have every reason to believe that they were also behind planning of hijack.'

'Alright Chan,' Prey said. 'How come you've already found so much out? How do you know this definitely going to go down?'

'One of younger boys from London mend his ways of error to family after they punish him severely,' Chan now rubbed

154

his long silver beard thoughtfully. 'Now he's a good boy – a very good boy who now tell us everything we need to know,' he smirked knowingly.

'It's very short notice,' I said. 'I mean for planning and more importantly for hardware.'

'No worries on the hardware,' Chan told me. 'You give Chan answer by end of weekend then I guarantee you'll have whatever you'll need for job.'

'Alright Chan – You need to give us chance to check this out,' Prey said. 'Obviously if we consider this then we can't do it by ourselves so we need to check out who we can bring in on it.'

'Of course,' he smiled. 'I wouldn't expect anything less.'

We all nodded at one another.

'Oh and one more thing,' Chan continued. 'If you decide to do this job for Chan. Then I will be in your debt. Maybe one day you will require Chan's help with a situation and Chan will happily resolve one of your problems for you. And my word counts for a lot in the world we live within.

Friday night had arrived, although my birthday had been earlier that week we were celebrating it tonight. Prey had managed to book basement bar, known bizarrely as The Gay Traitor located downstairs in The Hacienda for my birthday party.

'Eazy – It's been too long mate,' I said shaking the big mans huge hand.

'You're getting bigger Chopper man,' he grinned giving me a bear hug. 'You're looking good though. You working out or something?' he held me at arms length then grinned. 'You still cooking all that food I bet,' he laughed.

'Of course he is,' Donna smiled kissing his cheek. 'It's the one reason I keep him around,' she then laughed.

'I bet it is girl,' he replied hugging her also.

'Danny,' I shouted, suddenly seeing a good friend from the past. Danny had been one of the original lads from the early Breakin' days; with the start of it all of what has followed.

I hadn't seen him for about a year now as he'd gone away to University in Leeds to further his education within the graphic design industry. He'd been an excellent Bombin' artist back in the day. For him to continue with his education had always been something that we'd respected in him. It was something that none of us had ever been bothered about, but Danny had believed that it would be his making in life.

Both he and Kezlo were both superb DJs. Both had always stayed in touch and tonight Danny was going to be just one of the DJs for my birthday.

156

'You alright Chopper,' he said shaking my hand. 'You're looking good brother.'

'You too man,' I said smiling. 'How's university going?'

'Cool y'know,' he replied. 'Got my final year coming up – Still enjoying it though.'

'That's good,' I told him. 'It's good to see you man,' I added, smiling at my old mate. 'You remember Donna – Don't you,' I added.

'How could any man forget Donna,' he told me what I already knew whilst kissing her cheek 'Always said you were with the wrong man,' he grinned at her.

'You look well Danny,' she told him.

'Danny, this is Eazy mate,' I said, introducing the two of them. 'He owns BoomBasticSounds down in Brixton.'

'Alright Eazy,' he said shaking his hand. 'Kezlo's told me enough about you man.'

'Like wise Danny,' he voice boomed over the bass. 'He tells me that you're one mean son of a bitch on those decks and that we've got the pleasure of hearing you tonight.' That's all that needed saying between the two of them; they were very well acquainted after that.

'Yes Jonah,' I said walking up to him stood by the bar.

'Did you catch Scotty?'

'No – Why?' I asked, a little confused.

'He was 'ere earlier on then fucked off with Jackie,' Jonah told me. 'He looked fucked Chopper.'

'I can't believe he's laughed off my party off,' I said shaking my head in disbelief.

'Look Chopper,' Jonah sighed. 'I've known both of you for years now. You're both like brother's mate. But I heard what happened with Batty last week. Now you're going to put him on the street.'

'Well what am I supposed to do with him?'

'He just seems different these days Chopper.'

'Who seems different?' Donna asked who had suddenly appeared.

'Scotty,' Jonah told her before I had chance to say anything.

'Ain't that the truth,' she agreed nodding. 'That Jackie he sees as well.'

'Just keep an eye out for him mate,' I told Jonah who just nodded his response.

'Happy birthday Chopper,' said Batty and Jason in unison as I walked over.

'Alright lads. What's the word on Tommy?' I asked shaking their hands

'They shipped him off to Walton until the trial,' Batty said shaking his head as he did. 'I'll make sure he's looked after.'

'Has anybody spoken with him?' I asked.

'His bird did,' Jason said.

'And?' I asked.

'She says that they told him that his brief has seen Scotty's statement and he said nothing at all,' he told me. 'Although Tommy says that he told Scotty that what was arriving that morning he couldn't have any of. He said that he would have had to wait until the following day.'

'That was probably just miscommunication Batty,' I found myself defending my friend once again.

'Whatever Chopper.' Batty replied shaking his head.

'He didn't say anything though. You said it yourself Batty,' I told him defensively, although I suddenly felt that I was saying this more to convince myself of it.

'There's one other thing though Chopper,' Batty stared at me. 'They say that there was no money there.'

'What do you mean no bees,' I exclaimed.

'I know that Scotty brought the bag of bees with him. Well saying that, I seen the bag,' Jason said.

'Coppers,' I simply said tutting.

'That's exactly what we thought,' he said, 'I mean they said that they found only the weed – but no cash. Also that he said shit to them – and he wasn't part of their initial bust. But I still don't want him on the estate.'

'That's sorted now anyway ain't it? Kezlo been to see you this week hasn't he?' I asked as they both nodded. 'No money...' I added as an afterthought.

'We thought that you should know,' Jason informed me.

'They must have taxed it. That's got to be it. The coppers have taxed it,' I said nodding my head.

'Well yeah you could be right. Well either that or...' Jason began to say.

'Or fuckin' what,' I snapped at him.

'Or your boy took it,' he stated simply shrugging as he did so.

'Now how the fuck is he going to manage that then Jason?' I asked. 'He's not fuckin' Houdini, is he?' I snapped at him again.

'Easy Chopper,' Batty said. 'We just thought that you should know. That's all.'

'Yeah alright,' I sighed. 'Look what you lads drinking?' I added changing the subject.

'Alright Sleeper,' I shook his hand, 'and the lovely Lisa – It's been way too long,' I said kissing her.

'You alright birthday boy,' he asked embracing me. 'C'mon let's get the champagne. We've got shit to do upstairs. Prey and Steve are waiting,' he then told me then looked at Jonah. 'You too Jonah.'

We found the other two waiting in a dark corner out of the way.

'Easy lads,' I said smiling as the three of us sat down. 'What's the meeting for then?' I grinned at Prey.

'The favour asked the other day by our mutual friend is going to go ahead,' he said, pouring the champagne into the glasses.

'That's double sweet with me,' I told him raising my glass.

'So are you in Sleeper?' Prey asked.

'You know when we're talking the kind of cash we are that I'm always in brother,' he smiled.

'And you Jonah?' Steve asked.

Jonah had only been informed that quite possibly there was a big job coming off; something heavy was all he'd been told.

'I'm in,' he nodded not needing to know anything further at this moment in time.

'Right there isn't much time to plan this as it will go down next Friday night,' Prey said. 'All the lieutenant's are to be involved except for Knieldy who's in Spain for the next two weeks. Plus we will need three others beside you Sleeper – and they need to be professionals,' he added.

'No problem – I've got that covered,' he told us.

'Sweet,' I said rising from my chair. 'But tonight can we just celebrate my birthday,' I began grinning at the two of them as I was about to walk away.

'Chopper – sit down,' Steve instructed. 'We need to talk.'

Sitting back down looking at the other two as Jonah and Sleeper then disappeared back downstairs. 'What's wrong?' I enquired curiously.

'I heard what happened with Scotty the other day mate,' Prey said.

'I've sorted it out,' I said sipping my champagne.

'I know you have. And you were right to put Kezlo onto the purchasing side of things,' Prey told me nodding as he did so.

'But don't you think it was suss' what happened?' Steve asked.

'I got to admit that I did do,' I told them both. 'But I've just spoken with Batty before and he says that Tommy says that Scotty never talked according to his statement.'

'That's one thing I suppose,' Prey sighed.

'One more thing that you should know though,' I said staring at them both. 'They said that there wasn't any money there.'

'You what...' Steve exclaimed.

'Look – Jason said that Scotty definitely turned up with the bees,' I told them. 'But the coppers say there wasn't any money there. Obviously I don't suppose that Tommy will be arguing the point any.'

'Fuckin' coppers must have taxed it,' Prey snapped.

'My thoughts exactly,' I said.

'Fuckin' coppers – They're the most bent fuckin' criminals going. Aren't they?' laughed Prey.

'What about next Friday. Does Scotty know anything?' Steve asked, looking concerned.

'Not at all,' I shook my head.

'That's the way it stays then,' Prey stated firmly. 'I know that I said all the lieutenant's were to be involved but Scotty's not to be involved on this score. Nor is he to know about it.'

'So you don't trust him then?' I asked a little hurt at the prospect of Scotty being shut out like that.

'It's not so much that Chopper. We've all known him for years. He just doesn't look up to the job – that's all mate,' Prey said.

'Alright,' I said, knowing that there was no point in arguing the toss. 'Now can I get back to my party?'

'Have Jonah make sure that Scotty does the job properly on the street,' Prey added.

I was smiling at them both. 'Already taken care of.'

It brings me great pleasure that you have decided to do job for me,' said Chan beaming at us. 'You please an old man very much indeed. I have every faith in you boys to do good job.'

We'd gone to see Chan at the restaurant on the Sunday morning, before he was due to open the restaurant for lunch time trade.

'We need all the details Chan,' Prey told him. 'Don't miss anything out.'

'Of course not,' Chan said placing two envelopes in front of him. 'Right – first of all the transaction is due to go down on Friday evening. It is set to go down on the top floor of the old warehouse that once belonged to Marshall's Import and Export. It's not been used for at least the last ten years now and is totally deserted around that area.'

'I know the place,' I told them. 'I bombed it a few years back now with Scotty.'

'Bombed it Chopper!' Chan stared at me in disbelief.

'He means graffiti old man.' laughed Prey.

'Oh right,' he was still staring at me. 'Anyway inside the building there is access to the top floor by driving.'

'How?' Steve asked.

'From the ramps the fork lift trucks used to use,' said Chan.

'The boys from London will arrive on Thursday,' he told us. 'Only thing is we not know where they will stay.'

'What about the lads from town?' Prey asked.

'Everything you need to know about them is in this envelope,' he passed one of the envelopes over to Prey. 'That contains photos of Manchester boys. It also contains their address in Didsbury.'

'And the other envelope?' I asked nodding at it.

'This only contains photos of London boys so that you recognise them,' he told me as he past the envelope over.

'Alright Chan,' said Steve. 'Just how reliable is this source of information that you've got for us?'

'Very reliable indeed,' he told Steve smiling. 'The young family member I told you about who mend his ways is still fully involved on deal as far as they're concerned.'

'So is he going to be there?' I asked.

'No – He will fly to Hong Kong on Wednesday as his mother has indeed become very sick over there,' he grinned at us and winked.

'So they'll be none the wiser,' Prey nodded.

'Do y'know how much they're bringing in for the transaction Chan?' I asked.

'Half a mill',' he said casually, as if it was nothing more than mere pocket change. 'It's worth a hell of a lot more than that as this is pure uncut heroin. Especially to us it is. It is also reason why we believe the London boys are also to be involved with ripping us off,' he sipped his tea.

'How soon can you get the hardware Chan?' enquired Prey.

'What do you need Prey?'

'I need eight sawn-off shotguns. They need to be one hundred percent clean though,' he told the old man who was taking a mental note of the order.

'No problem,' Chan replied. 'What else?'

'This is a bit trickier,' Prey said looking at the old man. 'Four high powered hunting or military rifles with scopes and silencers.'

'Ah yes – A little trickier, but Chan will see what he can do for you Prey,' Chan nodded as he looked thoughtfully to Prey. 'I will have all of your requirements by Wednesday evening. Is that sufficient enough?'

'More than sufficient Chan,' Prey informed him.

'Have you any idea what they'll be packing Chan.?' I enquired.

'No Chopper,' he shook his head. 'But let's say their loyalties being some what distrustful, so to speak. Then I would expect them to be heavily armed.'

162

'Alright after today Chan we will not see each other until after this goes down,' Prey told him. 'Diamond will pick up the hardware on Wednesday night.'

'Okay then my boys you go now,' he took another sip of his tea as he said this.

'We've got a lot to sort out,' Steve sighed.

'You boys have my full respect,' Chan said smiling as he did. 'Now you make sure you take care of yourselves.'

'I'll get on the blower to Sleeper,' Prey said throwing a chunk of the fried dumpling from Sampson's into his mouth.

'Y'know who he's thinking of using?' I asked taking a bite of my chicken.

'He's got three ex-military guys that he use's now and then. Also he's pretty fuckin' handy with a rifle himself,' he told me as he dialled Sleeper's number.

'You reckon we can handle the ground patrol?' Steve asked.

'No problem,' I smiled. 'They'll be eight of them and eight of us.'

'That's what I mean Chopper,' he said. 'They're going to go thinking it's a Mexican stand-off or something and Chan says no death toll.'

'Well that's why we've got four rifle men ready to pop four sets of knee caps before hand,' I smiled at him. 'Then it's gonna bring it down from eight to four odds on favourite. Besides that's what we've got the sawn-off's for Steve. Sawn-off's have got themselves a ferocious reputation ain't they? Nobody wants to fuck about when they're confronted with a sawn-off shotgun shoved in their face. Do they?'

'How much damage after our guys take them out with the rifles?' he asked me.

'We need to be as quick as possible on this score,' I said just as Prey replaced the headset and nodded at the two of us. 'I say we leave them all with a little kneecap damage.'

'Just enough to scare them,' Steve shook his head.

'Sleeper will be 'ere on Thursday,' Prey said sitting down. 'So we'll need to be fully prepared by then.'

'No worries,' I winked at them. 'I think that I've come up with the perfect plan for the job,' I smiled knowingly at them both.

'Really Chopper,' said Prey throwing another piece of dumpling into his mouth. 'I think we'd better hear it then.'

'I want you to go with Chopper – Alright Sleeper,' Prey instructed Sleeper who'd just arrived. 'Take your lads with you to the disused warehouse. You can make sure it's fully secure and that you've got what you need.'

'So these are your men then?' I enquired staring at the three rugged looking lads stood behind Sleeper.

'These three are the best,' Sleeper confirmed. 'Although there's no need for any kind of formal introductions.'

'So it's just one, two and three?' I asked.

'That's the way it's got to be,' the one in the middle responded.

'That's sweet with me,' I smirked walking towards the car. 'Always was shit at remembering names.'

'When can we see the rifles Chopper?' Sleeper asked climbing into the passenger seat.

'Today,' I told him. 'As soon as we get back from the warehouse.'

'Are they definitely reliable?' number three asked from the backseat.

'You'll be able to tell me once you've seen them,' I said starting the car up. 'I seen them last night and they look the bollocks to me. But you lads know your shit better than I do. Apparently they're a little older than our guy wanted. But it's a short notice job this one. He say's that they are Rigby hunting rifles with .275 cartridges. I can't remember the scopes but they seem more than good enough. Plus they're brand spankers. He's had them adapted for the silencers. Also they are 100 percent untraceable,' I smiled at them.

'We've not discussed money yet,' the one by the left hand window said bluntly.

'Sleeper will discuss it with the three of you tonight at the hotel,' I looked at Sleeper.

'I already told you that,' Sleeper snapped.

'Just checking,' he replied now smiling.

'There – Look,' Steve said nudging Prey who was just beginning to doze off whilst they sat watching the address in Didsbury that Chan had given them.

'What...' he said sleepily stretching.

'That's them there Prey,' Steve told him.

'You sure,' he said rubbing his eyes yawning.

'They're climbing into that black Beamer Prey,' Steve nodded in the direction of the black 3 series BMW.

164

'Alright, let's stick with them,' Prey yawned again. 'Just make sure you stay way back Steve. Last thing we need is to be spotted today.'

'They're heading into Wilmslow,' Steve told him as they stayed on their tail for about half an hour now.

'I fuckin' hate this town,' Prey said ducking down slightly. 'Always seem to get a pull when coming through here.'

'You want me to fuck them off?' Steve asked.

'What the fuck for! We're half way through the town centre now anyway,' he said sighing deeply. 'Might as well check out where they're going now.'

They kept on their tail until Alderley Edge. Just then the BMW turned into The Edge hotel car park.

'Pull up over there,' Prey said pointing to the side of the road. 'Don't pull into the car park.'

'Just check this lot out,' Steve laughed as he observed the four Chinese men as they all climbed dramatically from the car.

All were dressed wearing nice dark suits. Each one walked with the look of pure arrogance.

Prey laughed. 'Shit – They're really going for the *gangstar* look. Fuck – they look like something out of a movie,' he sniggered.

'We got names on these cats Prey?' Steve enquired lighting a cigarette.

'No – And I don't want them either,' he told Steve. 'I imagine that Chan had the same thought as we never received that information.'

'Look Prey,' Steve said nodding his head in the direction of the doorway as four other Chinese dressed in similar fashion walked out into the parking lot. All eight men were joyously hugging each other.

Prey smirked broadly at the sight. 'They looked pleased to see one another... Well either that or they were just pleased their so called successful heist.' He laughed at the last bit as Steve chuckled also.

'That must be all of them then Prey,' Steve nodded.

Prey smiled. 'Yeah and it looks like the old maroon Merc is their motor. Alright let's get the fuck out of here then Steve. We've seen enough for today.'

'You reckon the kids plan will work?' Steve asked starting the engine up.

'Don't see why not. The devious little fucker sure has it down to a tee I reckon,' he replied with a smile. 'As long as everything goes to plan on the night that is.'

'This is a nice site they've picked,' Sleeper informed me whilst looking around the surrounding's of the disused warehouse. 'We couldn't have planned it better if we'd tried.'

'I reckon there are good advantage points for both ariel purposes and ground control also,' I confirmed whilst looking around at the abandoned top floor that was to be used for the transaction site the following night.

'Right you three,' he said looking at the others. 'I need for you to go and find the best points to cover the floor from.'

'It's obvious that they'll be entering from over there if they're driving like you say they are,' said number two as he'd now been named.

'But how the fuck are we going to know where they'll stop?' the one whom had be given number three asked sarcastically.

'Hang on a minute. I'll just give them a call and find out for you. Alright,' I answered with the same sarcasm.

Number three stared coldly at me as I just grinned and nodded knowingly at him.

'Just find the best advantage points. We're going to have to hope they go centre stage,' Sleeper said shaking his head at number three in way of a warning.

Number one then looked at the other two. 'You both know what to do,' he snapped at them like giving an order.

'Get a feel of the floor. Find the best area's that cover all the best possible ranges. Like you've just said we won't know exactly where there going to land,' I said and with that the three of them went off in separate directions.

'How good is the information we're receiving Chopper?' Sleeper asked as the other three went about their ways.

'Let's just say that's it been kept in the family,' I told him.

'Now these three have been fully trained Chopper. They are three of the best I've come across,' he glared at me. 'Just so you know though - the coppers will recognise that this a professional hit with the rifles we'll be using.'

'There's to be no death toll Sleeper. It ain't that kind of party,' I shook my head. 'They're to be punished only. We just fuck them up and leave them here until they're discovered,' I told him firmly.

'So what do you want us four to do then?' he asked, obviously thinking that we were going to kill the people involved on Friday night.

'Take out their legs, preferably the knee caps of four of them. They won't know what's hit them with the silencers on the rifles,' I looked at him. 'After that we go with my plan.'

'No problem Chopper.' he shrugged, 'I just presumed it was a different kind of thing you wanted when Prey asked for these guys,' he smiled folding his arms watching the other three climbing the roofing beams already.

'They're like fuckin' chimpanzees,' I laughed.

'They're fuckin' good mate,' he smiled proudly. 'I'll just have to inform them it's different than I'd originally told them. I thought that you wanted this lot taking out for the count full stop Chopper.'

'Chan says that it'll create too many problems if we kill them,' I sighed deeply thinking I didn't want to go killing some guys over business that to be fair, wasn't really our business at all. 'But he wants them fucked up real good. Besides which their money will be just as good as if they're taking them out, so they haven't to worry on that score,' I added staring at Sleeper who was nodding his approval.

'So Chopper,' Sleeper winked at me. 'Seeing as you just brought up the subject anyway. When do we talk money?' he flashed a grin at me.

'Tonight,' I simply told him watching the others climb around, totally at ease along the steel girders running high along the ceiling.

'So now that they're out of the way. Let's get down to the important bit,' said Sleeper as we sat in his hotel room at The Piccadilly Hotel that had been booked under false names.

The other three un-known soldiers, as I'd commenced naming them had all gone with Diamond to check out the rifles again. Number one had informed us that if they hadn't been used they would need sighting and cleaning before hand.

'What kind of figures are we talking here?'

Prey explained what the four of us would be splitting between us which I could see made Sleeper more than happy.

'Sounding good already,' he declared. 'Now what about the others?' He enquired.

'The rest will receive Twenty-five gee's each,' I told him.

'That's more than fair,' Steve stated. 'We know that your guys are fully trained and all that. But we feel it would be unfair to our lads if they didn't get the same as they're taking just as much risk here.'

'That's more than fair lads,' he informed us. 'So what time does it go down tomorrow?'

'Vans will pick us up at seven,' Prey told him. 'It'll give us time to get everybody into position.'

'We get this done swiftly and I'll be heading home by eleven that night,' Sleeper said nodding his head at us.

'Yeah — Won't be too bad for a nights work. Will it?' I smiled at him.

The two dark transit vans eased out of sight around the back of the disused warehouse in Salford. The night air was still warm as we arrived, although the tension in the air was somewhat cooler. Kezlo and Jonah each drove a van; each van contained six fully armed men.

Each man sat silently collecting their own thoughts as we came to a halt behind the old empty rusted stacked oil drums. As we all climbed from the rear of the vans, we all looked at each other wondering what the next man was thinking.

We all made our way to the top floor of the hollow shell of what was probably a thriving business years ago. But now it sat there abandoned with all the windows shattered by kids and their boredom. From what I could tell though no one had been here for a long time, the kids soon boring themselves once they'd smashed all of the glass. Soon finding themselves a new place to destroy.

Pigeons fled from the top floor at the mere sound of us approaching, our commotion as little as it was disturbing their peaceful evening. Their wings batted frantically as they tried to flee the scene as quickly as possible.

The warehouse felt cool in the summer's nightshade. We stopped in the centre of the warehouse floor and looked around, trying to imagine how in just a couple of hour's time this stillness would be turned completely upside down.

'Right, get your men into position,' Prey said turning to Sleeper.

'This is an excellent choice of artillery, if I may say so,' number three told me. 'As for being an older model, well

170

they're still an excellent choice of artillery. I couldn't have made a better choice myself,' he then turned without another word, smirking as he did and followed the other three.

I kept thinking that number three was different to the other two; he carried coldness in those lifeless eyes of his. I mean after all – I suppose this is what he'd been trained for. But somehow it seemed different for whatever reason with him. It was like he took personal pleasure in doing this kind of work.

With this thought in mind, 'Only the knee caps… Remember,' I called after him. But he never turned back to me, merely lifted his rifle, to acknowledge my words.

'Right, it's more than likely that they will be driving a maroon Merc and a black Beamer tonight,' Prey confirmed. 'We will not know the position that they will take once inside.'

'Be prepared to take them from any possible angle though,' I added. 'Now we've left the warehouse in exactly the same state it was in when we first checked it out. Obviously, unless these are complete dicks that we're dealing with, they will have already checked the place out themselves. I do not believe that these men are complete dickheads – So you must all be very cautious.'

'Now the next step that we are going to take, is to check the warehouse fully from top to bottom,' I added, glancing at my watch. 'We still have the better half of two hours left. Now we've already checked the place each time we've been here. But just to be on the safe side we do it again tonight. The last thing we need is for any tramps or kids to be hanging around 'ere when this goes down.'

'Right you lads come with me,' Steve said to Diamond, Parksey and Johnny. 'You two will split off with Prey and Chopper,' he told Jonah and Kezlo.

'Now you're all straight as to how this is going to go down – Right?' I asked looking at each of them one at a time. 'Just remember that Sleeper's crew will take out four of them at the kneecaps only. That's when we go straight in. Let me remind you once more though. There will be no death toll tonight. Is that understood?' I stated as they all nodded their response.

'Do we know what they're going to be packing?' Jonah asked checking his shotgun.

'Haven't got a clue mate,' I informed him.

'Oh right so it's kind of like a blind date I went on once,' he replied smiling that public school boy smile of his at me.

171

'Alright once you've finished checking the warehouse take your positions and keep your masks ready and gloves on at all times,' Prey said.

'One more thing,' I said, 'No smoking whatsoever.'

'You are kidding right Chopper,' Diamond blurted out, with a look of true disbelief on his face.

'Chopper's right,' Steve confirmed. 'The place is supposed to be disused. They'll stink the smoke as soon as they leave the vehicles. Don't worry mate – I'm in the same boat,' he added.

'Right let's get to work then,' I said as we all went our separate ways.

'Right you all know the score right,' Sleeper said to his men. 'This goes down as they want it too. No going getting itchy trigger fingers or anything. That is unless Prey... or more to the point – Chopper gives you the signal to do so.'

'That's alright with us boss,' said number two.

'Ain't it,' agreed number one looking to number three whom remained silent and continued checking his rifle. 'Bring on more work like this and we'll stay very loyal indeed.'

'Alright then men,' Sleeper said. 'Best take your positions and wait for this to go down.'

'You alright Kezlo?' I asked him as he sat next to me silent, yet his breathing was both fast and hard.

We'd taken cover behind a stack of disused crates and pallets, awaiting our guest's arrival. The other four had taken cover and were lay flat on their stomachs by the demolished wall to what looked like it had once belong to an office on the right hand far side from us.

Sleeper's men were already positioned high in the steel iron girders that ran the length of the ceiling, camouflaging themselves so well that I wasn't sure myself where they actually were.

'I'm alright Chopper,' Kezlo told me. 'I'm just thinking about the bees mate,' he smiled a nervous smile at me.

'Everything will be double sweet mate,' I smiled, trying to make him feel a little better. 'Jonah...'

'What's up mate?' he asked casually.

'You alright?' I asked.

'Course mate,' he grinned. 'For twenty-five gee's – believe me, there ain't no problems whatsoever.'

172

'Be careful,' I reminded him. 'We don't know what they're packing.'

'Chopper's right Jonah,' Prey added. 'The last thing we need is for one of you lads to go getting hurt.'

Jonah simply, yet slowly nodded his understanding.

'Scotty ask any questions?' I asked Kezlo.

'Nah mate,' Kezlo simply said. 'He don't know shit about tonight at all.'

'You both make sure that you keep it that way – Alright,' Prey said firmly, staring at the two of them.

Kezlo just looked to me with questioning eyes as I merely shrugged my response.

'What you got for us Scotty?' asked Stevenson as Scotty climbed into the back seat of their car.

'I haven't got anything new,' he snapped irritably. 'But they're onto me – I know they are.'

'You're just being paranoid – That's all son,' Walsh told him. 'They don't know shit about you.'

'We're building a nice little case against them now Scotty,' Stevenson told him. 'Maybe another six, possibly seven months and we'll have enough to bring them down.'

'How fuckin' long?' Scotty blurted out. 'You two must be the ones on drugs if you think I'm in for that long.'

'If we don't build the case over that amount of time then there is a chance that it will fold in court,' Walsh stated fact to him.

'That ain't my fuckin' problem,' he told them. 'Y'know they'll kill me if they find out – they will – it won't be the fir...' he stopped himself in his tracks.

'What was that?' Walsh responded quickly certain of what he was about to tell them. 'What was you about to say then Scotty?'

'Nothing.' Scotty thought how much of a fool he'd just been. Stevenson looked at Walsh. 'Come on Scotty...You was about to say wasn't the first time that they've killed somebody. Right son?' Stevenson said staring at Scotty.

'No I wasn't,' he replied.

'Don't lie to us,' Walsh yelled.

'Fuck you Walsh...' he screamed back at him.

174

'All right, both of you calm down,' Stevenson told them trying his best to diffuse the situation.

'Look Scotty,' Walsh said. 'Did Chopper or Prey have anything to do with Patrick – you know Patrick – Paddy – McNally disappearing?' he asked staring Scotty straight in the eye trying to gauge a reaction.

'I don't know,' he told them honestly. 'Why'd you even ask that?' he added, now confused, as he wasn't even talking about that.

'Because we think that it was McNally that shot Macreedy,' Stevenson told him.

'You serious?' he exclaimed. 'Well if he did and they did... Then that cocksucker got more than he deserved. I fuckin' hated that prick. I mean look at what he did to me,' he pointed to the scar on his head.

'Did he now?' Walsh smiled. 'And just when was that Scotty?'

Scotty realised he shouldn't of said anything about that. 'A long time back now,' he dropped his head.

'You sure it wasn't the night that Paddy had his ear bitten off by Chorlton?' Walsh asked him.

He grinned at the memory of when Chopper sunk his teeth into that cunts ear and he found himself chuckling. 'No – But I wish it had been.'

'So it was Chorlton then?' asked Stevenson.

'I never said that then,' he snapped at them. 'I said I wish that it had been the time that he got his ear bitten off. I'd have loved to have seen that,' he smirked.

Walsh pulled out the bag of crack to temp Scotty with. 'Now are you sure that you don't know anything Scotty? About that night or Paddy's disappearance?'

Scotty merely shook his head at them, he wasn't that concerned about the bag of rocks Walsh was showing him as he'd just picked himself a quarter up before meeting them. 'I don't and to be perfectly honest if it related to fuckin' Paddy then I wouldn't tell you shit.'

'You'll tell us whatever the fuck we want to hear son,' said Walsh annoyed with Scotty's arrogance.

'Enough,' Stevenson scolded Walsh.

Scotty dropped his head and sighed. 'Something just ain't right at the moment though,' he said looking at them. 'I tell you I ain't being paranoid. Things just seem different – Like tonight.'

175

'You're just smoking way too much of that shit Scotty,' Walsh told him bluntly.

'What do you mean tonight Scotty?' asked Stevenson curiously.

'Y'what?' he asked unsure what he was referring to.

'You said things seem different like tonight,' he told him.

'Oh that,' he sighed. 'It's nothing really – Just a bit weird that's all.'

'How – How was it weird?' Stevenson persisted.

'All the main heads just disappeared from the estate tonight,' he sniffed not seeing any relevance to anything.

'When you say the main heads you mean the lieutenant's right?' Walsh asked.

'Yeah the lieutenant's. It was just weird they all seemed to disappear at once and no one knew where they were,' he told them both. 'I mean it was early on, so they might have just gone for a few drinks before The Hac later on. But they weren't in Dry Bar though, 'cause I popped in there to see somebody.'

'You think that something might be going down tonight Scotty?' Stevenson asked looking at him through his mirror.

'Nah – of course not,' he smirked smugly at them kissing his teeth as he did so. 'If there was and everybody was involved then I'd be there. I already told you both before that I'm also a Lieutenant,' he smiled at them both proudly.

'Yeah – so you did,' Walsh replied shaking his head as he did.

'Listen – Shush,' said Prey, his face was strained as he listened carefully into the dead of night. It was already gone 9:30pm and we were all beginning to feel a little more than anxious at their late arrival.

'I hear it,' I confirmed, pulling my mask back down over my face. It was the sound of an engine drawing closer and louder as it did so, breaking through the silence in the night air as they approached.

'That's the Merc,' Prey whispered bobbing back down out of sight.

'I can see them,' I stated quietly. 'There are four of them. It's the London crew,' I ducked back down out of sight.

'Listen – There it is now,' Prey said as the sound of a second engine could be heard as the black BMW eased up beside the maroon Mercedes, its engine purring throughout the warehouse.

It was as we had expected they went centre stage of the warehouse, the four men from Manchester now exiting their black 3 series BMW.

I silently observed as they all greeted each other, all seemed in good spirits as they chatted quickly in what I presumed to be Chinese. I couldn't help but grin at them though as I perceived the way they swaggered about in those dark suits of theirs. Waltzing with a swagger we'd all seen way too many times in a movie.

I suddenly realised what Chan had meant about these lads who were not much older than myself. They believed in status only. They all wanted to be so called gangsters.

177

People like this, were always breaking through into the business and would always be about. Too many of these characters existed. To them it wasn't just about business – about making money – it was about how they were perceived.

To them it was almost a game that they thought they could play. Well we were here tonight to show just how we play games in our world.

Two of the men from each side were talking in their native tongue to one another. We didn't have a clue what was being said as we watched them. They were both the smallest of the both groups, yet both of them carried that air of authority about themselves that showed that they were the ones in charge.

The other six men were now facing one another; all of them had their hands in their jackets. Obviously they were carrying, so it made no sense whatsoever to me that they kept them in their jackets. I was following their every move like a panther watching its prey, waiting patiently, waiting for the right moment when our men hidden above us would make their moves.

The sky had started to darken, making visibility harder. Only the lights that shone from the cars created any real light. I was just hoping it was enough light for the men to get clean shots at them.

One of the stockier men from the London crew came over to the back of the BMW as commanded from one of the two men now stood there.

He carried with him two large holdalls, he was large in build and his suit fitted him terribly because of his bulk. Placing the two black leather bags down on the floor before them he then proceeded to unzip them both, pulling back the tops to reveal the contents of them.

From the smile received I'd say that the money most defiantly was there. Then the other man popped open the boot to the BMW revealing its contents also.

The remaining men stood there, playing their parts in all of this trying their best to look as menacingly as they possibly could. It was almost comical to see them stood there like that. They really had seen way too many American movies.

The second of the two men leaned into the boot of the car, and then came up smiling as he did. But as quickly as the smile appeared on his face – It turned into pure agony as shots merely whistled through the hollow shell of the warehouse.

Both the smaller guys – the ones I still presumed to be in charge – were the first too drop to the floor, as their legs appeared to literally explode from almost certainly two of the four angles... if not more.

I hadn't realised just how powerful the rifles had been. I'd thought that they would only take out their kneecaps. Only it looked to have taken their legs out completely. They were a mess.

Also the silencers were achieving their full potential by baffling the fuck out of the men who were struck by both filling them full of panic and fear as they had no idea as to what was happening all around them. Only the screams of the men targeted, broke through the cold silence that had hung heavily above us. We still lay there waiting to make our move.

'Go now,' yelled Prey, above more shots whistling by as we all began running towards our confused victims.

We ran with the speed of cheetahs towards the parked cars from both sides, our sawn-off shotguns aimed clearly at their heads. I saw another of the men spinning from the force of the deadly – silent bullets that tore cleanly through his legs.

The one next to him was already lay on the ground screaming as he did so. Blood was spurting from his legs wildly spraying their surroundings. I could see splintered bones had torn through the flesh and the material from his trousers.

Shots were still whistling by above us, cutting through the air with their deadly silenced precision, like snakes slithering through grass toward their unsuspecting victims. You could see two others also lay in the ground, their legs in similar state to the first I'd witnessed.

I still counted five of them standing though, the stockiest of the group was still stood at the rear of the car as we approached – he was screaming at us furiously in what we still presumed to be Chinese as we all approached.

'Only three down...' I screamed out loud. 'Four – it should be four...' I yelled above the commotion although not at all certain if I'd been heard above the screams and shots.

The remainder of the Chinese had now pulled their weapons, screaming both wildly and loudly at us as we surrounded them.

The one closest to me swiftly pulled a sawn-off shotgun from beneath his jacket and swung it in my direction. His gun exploded as everybody, including myself else hit the ground. Before he had chance to re-cock to gun again – a further three shots whistled silently by into the night.

As I looked up from the ground I witnessed with complete shock his chest explode like a watermelon that had crashed into the ground as though it had been thrown from to top of a high rise. His body flung one way then another as each shot tore through him like paper mache.

He died instantaneously. I knew it for sure as I quickly leapt back onto my feet and walked cautiously towards the remaining four who stood rooted to the spot. But they still had their handguns out and were screaming at us frantically in their native tongue as their friends lay there screaming in agony.

'Put your weapons down now.' I screamed at them as I still moved forward, the shotgun pressed against the right hand side of my head, pointing directly at them. I glanced at the dead one quickly, just to be certain he was no longer with us, kicking his shotgun away just to be sure.

I glared at him again – shit – that wasn't supposed have happened I thought to myself. The rest were now completely surrounded with eight shotguns aimed directly at their heads, but still they weren't giving up those handguns.

'You are in a no win situation 'ere' I yelled at them. 'If you refuse to put down your weapons then we'll have no choice but to shoot you.'

'Fuck you.' one of them screamed at me in clear English.

I calmly stepped forward and pointed my gun directly into his forehead. 'No fuck you,' I casually told him now stood toe to toe with him as our faces were only a matter of inches apart.

Just then I heard another whistle of that now unmistakable silencer from up high above, and almost as instantaneously as it rang out – his face exploded violently before me, spraying my ski mask and eyes with his warm viscous blood.

'What the fuck… What the fuck… What the fuck…' I kept repeating myself as the remaining three quickly threw their guns to the ground.

180

'Fuck – What the fuck – *Fuck* – *Fuck*,' I was yelling out loud, totally pissed off with what had occurred; this hadn't been part of the plan.

As I stared at the remaining three standing Chinese who had instantly thrown their weapons to the floor after they'd witnessed what had happened to their associate. Sheer terror had now taken control of their eyes as I stared coldly at them– filled with adrenaline – and also confusion as to what had just taken place as I glanced round at Prey who was also shaking his head.

But the truth of the matter was that we had come to do a job – yet Chan's words of no death toll – rang out loud and clear through my mind, as I witnessed the sight before me.

Two of the guys stood there were physically shaking as one of them began to wet himself with the sight of eight shot guns still aimed at them. The one closest stared back at me with pleading eyes, stepping forward I dropped my shot gun violently into his kneecaps, he then too wet himself as I squeezed the trigger into a deafening explosion taking away his kneecaps.

Prey stepped forward and unloaded his cartridges into the two that had remained standing. Both of them collapsed along with their tortured screams of pure anguish as they clutched to their bloodied legs.

The night became still once more, the smell of gunpowder and blood mingled and now filled the night's air. The only sound was of muffled cries from the Chinese who had been ordered to stay as quiet as possible under the circumstances. Their faces were contorted as they lay there holding their legs; wanting so much to scream out loud with the pain they felt. Only the shotguns pressed against their heads were stopping them from doing so.

As I breathed deeply I calmed myself down and turned to Kezlo and Jonah. 'Go get the transport,' I instructed them both.

'Check the damage,' Steve instructed Parksey.

Just then Sleeper arrived with his men shaking his head. 'No fuckin death toll – No one was supposed to get fuckin' killed – Just what the fuck was that?' I screamed at them.

'Look mate,' it was number three who had his palms held up in defence. 'What was I supposed to do? I thought he was going to kill you,' he added as he then smirked at me, enraging me further still.

181

'Do I fuckin' look stupid you twat,' I said, seething at him. 'You knew very well that I had my shot-gun against his head. You just were too itchy after that first kill. Weren't you? I knew it was you straight away you cunt. I can see it in your eyes you cold fuckin' prick.'

'What did you just call me?' he snapped at me, his face as hidden as it was, was deepening with a crimson rage building from within him.

'Go fuck yourself you cock,' I screamed back at him, ignoring his apparent rage before me.

He aimed the rifle straight at my head cocking a bullet into the chamber as he did. I glared my hatred towards him, and then began to smile at him.

'And,' was all I had to say as each sawn-off shotgun was cocked and pointed straight at him. 'So – you want to do this? Do you? Do you really want to do it you prick?' I smirked back at him shaking my head in sympathy for him.

'Alright mate – okay – no fuckin' problem,' he said lowering the rifle, although the shotguns remained firmly pointed at him.

'C'mon kid,' Sleeper said. 'Call the dogs off. He leaves with me tonight. You won't see him again.'

I nodded as the guns were lowered. 'Now aim them where they should be fuckin' aimed.'

'Both dead,' Parksey suddenly confirmed.

I shook my head then looked over to Prey who was checking the bags. 'Are we happy?' I asked as he simply nodded back to me. 'Alright then get it sorted so we can get the fuck out of 'ere.'

Prey signalled Sleeper over to where he was giving him instructions then nodded to Steve.

'Everybody is to leave now,' Steve instructed. 'Leave your weapons behind and be sure to take a bag on your way out,' he said as they all started running towards the exit.

'Ere'are, leave that lot,' Prey winked at Sleeper who looked at the remaining cash and kilo of heroin still in the boot.

'All part of the kids plan,' he confirmed. 'And don't worry about any shots that you might hear after this.'

Sleeper simply nodded that he understood. Only the three of us remained there with the injured and dead Chinese. 'We need to get the fuck out of 'ere,' I exclaimed, looking at the others. 'This went down way too fuckin' loudly. Even if it is fuckin' deserted round 'ere.'

'Yes boss,' replied Prey

Prey then planted the gear into each car along with the shot guns that hadn't been fired, it was all part of the plan I'd put together.

Steve stood over the remaining Chinese holding his shot gun to their heads to try his best to muffle their cries of pain.

I took the shotguns and the rifles that had been used, removing the scopes from the rifles then forced each remaining man lay there shoot all of the used guns again. I then removed the silencers.

As I stood over them and stared at them with cold eyes as they looked both panic stricken and in immense amounts of pain I said, 'Now you lads consider yourselves lucky tonight,' I sneered at them lay there. 'You lived through it. You see it's not a game you're involved with. It's a very serious business. So if we see any one of you. And I mean any one of you,' I sniffed my arrogance pausing for a moment. 'Then we will seek each and every one of you... and your family members out and finish what was started tonight. You will end up the same way as your friends did tonight. Do you fuckin' understand me?' I stood back and observed the fear that filled them as they all nodded frantically at me.

'Let's go,' I nodded, turning to the other two.

We swiftly left the scene heading for the exit. I shook my head at the events that had just taken place and sighed deeply 'Bad day – Fuck it.'

What do you reckon Mike?' Walsh asked as they walked underneath the crime scene tape leading towards the top floor of the disused warehouse.

'I don't know yet Martin,' he said shaking his head. 'All that I know is what I heard this morning just doesn't sound right. You know, anonymous tip off. Just all sounds a bit dodgy to me.'

'It's not our case though,' Walsh stated flatly as he continued following him.

'I know,' he answered without looking back.

'What have we got Lucy?' Walsh asked as he walked over to the forensic officer.

'On the surface it looks like we've got a drug deal gone very sore,' she smiled still examining the holes in the side of the BMW.

'Tell us what you know – Please?' Stevenson smiled at her.

'Well we've got twenty-five grand in one car and what appears to be one kilo of very, very high quality heroin in the other one,' she sighed looking at them. 'There were six shotguns. New ones that were un-fired in the boot of the BMW. That was the car with the money in it.'

'How many more firearms did you find Lucy?' Walsh enquired.

'But we also found a whole arsenal of guns here,' she continued. 'Eight handguns – Everything from Browning's to Heckler & Kosh's. Also – we found four Rigby hunting rifles rifles. Look like old models, but we're checking into them at the moment. All had been used. Plus we found a further three

184

shotguns all fired. Now eight of the shotguns are exactly the same but one is a lot older and on first looks it also appears to have been used several times before.'

'And the Chinks?' Stevenson asked.

'All of them had been shot through the legs, mainly aimed at their knee caps from what we could tell. Although saying that, at least two of them won't be walking around in the too near future. They were a right mess.' She shook her head as she said this. 'Two were already dead when our boys turned up. Now this is what looks dodgy beneath the surface. I mean for starters – all shot in the kneecaps. That suggests that either they were piss poor at shooting or that this was some kind of lesson that they were being taught.'

'What about the other two dead ones?' Walsh enquired.

'Who ever shot those men,' she pointed to where the two dead men had lay. Forensic markers were all that remained. 'Well those most definitely weren't piss poor shots at all. It looked to me like they'd both been shot with precise precession. Now that would suggest to me a professional hit.'

'And remind me again just how we heard about this?' Stevenson asked.

'Anonymous tip off. Just after ten thirty last night,' she told them.

'What are the Chinks saying?' Walsh asked.

'Nothing as usual,' she shook her head. 'They seemed scared shitless to be honest. Also I had the reports back just before I came back here this afternoon,' Lucy looked at them. 'This is what will fuck this case up. All of their prints matched those found on the guns found here at the scene. Plus they all had GSR – gun shot residue on their hands from firing the guns.'

'Why do I get the feeling that you're not that certain about all of this Lucy?' Stevenson asked her.

'Can I ask why you're so interested?' she looked at them quizzically. 'I mean it's not your case – Is it?'

'Yes – I think that I would very much like to know the answer to that?' asked the deep throaty voice that approached from behind them. 'Eh Mike? The lady just asked why you were so interested.'

Stevenson turned to face his old partner from year's back. The two of them had never really seen eye to eye on anything, especially after he tampered with evidence on an armed robbery charge. Then to top that he'd practically half killed the kid in the cell, beating a confession out of him whilst he stood by helplessly.

They sent the wrong kid away for six years. Stevenson had kept his mouth shut and been tormented with the guilt ever since, loathing Anderson ever since. 'Hello Bob, I heard they brought you back into Manchester,' he said, not offering his hand.

He just stared at Stevenson, his face a blank mask of all expression, he then grinned knowingly at him before turning to Walsh. 'Hello I'm Detective Inspector Robert Anderson,' He held his hand out whilst Walsh shook it. 'Me and Mike were partners once – A long time back now though,' he turned to look at Stevenson.

'Martin Walsh,' he said feeling both the tension and the strength of the man before him, merely in his hand shake alone. He'd heard of Anderson – everybody in the police force had heard of Anderson.

'Well they had to bring me back – Didn't they?' Anderson cockily stated. 'The streets of Manchester were just turning to shit without me. Weren't they?' he laughed gruffly. 'So then – What's the interest in my case then Mike?' he said flatly.

'You know how it is,' Stevenson told him. 'Just interested. Remember, I like to get all the facts,' he stared coldly at him.

Anderson smiled at him. 'Ain't that the truth Mike? Always fuckin' interested, aren't you.'

'I just thought that it all seemed a bit odd,' Stevenson sighed. 'That's all.'

'Odd – Fucking odd,' he laughed. 'Listen Mike – We've got six Chinks all in hospital under armed guard, who've all been shot to shit. They're not saying jack as per usual. But just open your eyes man,' he said twirling around dramatically, looking about the warehouse.

'Car full of drugs – Car full of money and guns – A shit load of artillery at the scene where they just happened to have shot the shit out of each other with them. Now it doesn't take a fucking genius to work it out. Doe's it Mike?' He growled, grinning smugly at him.

'Something's funny though…' Stevenson was about to continue as Anderson started laughing loudly.

'You're right Mike I never thought of it that way,' he continued laughing wickedly. 'Two dead Chinks – Six badly shot up Chinks in hospital – A key of smack kept from hitting the streets. A whole arsenal of guns also kept from reaching

186

the street. You were right,' he continued smiling, and then suddenly turned serious. 'It's a fuckin' hoot ain't it Mike,' he stared at him coldly.

'Look I just...' Stevenson began to say.

Anderson cut him off. 'Well just don't anything Mike. This is my case,' he snapped viciously. 'Now why don't you run along back to whatever case you're working on.'

Stevenson stood his ground and Anderson's menacing stare for about all of two seconds before he and Walsh turned away leaving the scene.

'Just what the fuck was that all about?' Walsh asked as they headed towards the exit. 'I thought the two of you went way back – Partners and all.'

'We were,' Stevenson sighed. 'Doesn't mean that I like the prick though,' he pulled his packet of cigarettes from his pocket taking one out.

'So what's the interest anyway Mike?' Walsh took the packet from him. 'I mean it's like Anderson said this ain't our case. Besides you know Anderson works China town. That's why they brought him back from London.'

'Is it?' Stevenson said lighting his cigarette looking at his partner. 'From what I heard. Anderson the evil bastard that he is – near killed someone down there during interrogation. That's why they shipped him back to us lot. The guy's dangerous – very fucking dangerous Martin.'

'Yeah – You serious about what he did?' Walsh asked.

'That's just what I over heard. But it wouldn't surprise me with him though. He still scares the shit out of me now. Even after all these years.' Stevenson blew his smoke out.

'So what have these Chinks got to do with us anyway?' Walsh asked changing back to the original subject.

'Maybe fuck all Martin,' he told him. 'It was just something Scotty said last night... That's all mate.' Just then he stopped looking up towards the sky. 'Come on Martin we've got somewhere we need to go.'

'You read this Steve?' asked Prey as Steve walked back into his the living room with two beers. They were both at Steve's house in Congleton as Prey had travelled back over this way with Steve the previous evening.

'I know,' replied Steve looking down at the front page of The Manchester Evening News. 'Didn't take long for the media to get onto it, did it,' he said sitting down.

'This reporter has slapped it all over the front page and it's been all over the TV today,' Prey said sipping his beer. 'You checked the headline Steve? St. Valentines Day Massacre hits Manchester.'

'I know it does sound way over the top. Don't it Prey?' Steve smiled knowingly at his friend. 'I mean they weren't all massacred for starters,' he then laughed.

'I know,' Prey laughed also. 'It's hard hitting though. I'll give them that much.'

'That Anderson – That detective they've got working the case. The one I saw on TV. The one in charge of the case,' Steve said. 'He looked familiar you know.'

'He used to be one of the main coppers around town years back,' Prey sniffed. 'Just before my time to be honest. But what I do remember was that he brought down enough crews back then. Some of the major players from all the boroughs. He had a reputation for being one hell of a ruthless son of bitch. I remember stories from some of the older heads; nobody wanted to get nicked by this fucker, as he was pure evil. Just about everybody he nicked did time. Also he used to try his best to get you alone in the interview rooms, switching the tape off then getting pure nasty, both physically and mentally with you.' Prey seemed to shiver at the mere thought

188

of all this, then continued. 'Then he just kind of disappeared from round town. I think they promoted him and he moved down south or something.'

'You reckon he'll be a problem for us?' he enquired.

'I couldn't honestly say Steve,' he smiled. 'What I do know though is we are one hell of a lot richer after last night.'

'I know,' he laughed. 'Chopper's plan was sweet. At least that should throw them for a while on what actually took place.'

'In'it,' Prey said nodding his head. 'It was just a shame that that trigger happy cunt went and wasted those two. I figured when he done that we may as well have killed all of them – I mean shit – If we're going to banged up for two murders we may as well have made it all eight of them. Least that way there would have been no witnesses left. But we promised Chan I suppose.'

'Has everything been sorted with Chan?' asked Steve.

'Yeah – Diamond dropped off the gear this morning,' he nodded. 'And as y'know all the money is stashed nicely at your little safe house mate.'

'I meant about the two that were…'

'He'll understand,' said Prey cutting him off. 'I know that he will.'

'I still think it's best that no one touches the money for at least six months,' Steve stated.

'They were all sweet with that anyway,' Prey said swigging his bottle. 'I mean Sleeper's lot won't make any difference as they're out the fuck out of dodge.'

'It was a well good night afterwards – Wasn't it?'

'I know. All of the crew was buzzing in The Hac,' Prey responded with as he lifted his beer bottle to Steve. ''Ere's to more good times brother,'

'That you Chopper?' Donna called from the living room as I walked through the front door.

'Who the fuck else would it be?' I laughed walking into the living room. Both Kathy and little Sean were sat there. 'You alright,' I said kissing Kathy and looking at little Sean tickling his cheeks making him gurgle some incoherent noise.

'You knew what I meant Chopper,' Donna said as I kissed her.

189

'I thought that you might be expecting your bit on the side round. That's all,' I grinned at her as she threw a cushion at me as I sat down next to her.

'It's a bit late for Sean to be out. Ain't it Kathy?'

'He was restless Chopper,' she told me not taking her eyes from him. 'Wouldn't get his head down at all.'

'Give him 'ere then,' I said pushing myself out of my chair going to her.

'Be careful Chopper,' Donna said sternly to me. 'You look pissed.'

'I am,' I grinned taking Sean into my arms and sat down again rocking him in my arms.

'You know where Prey is?' Donna asked.

'Why?' I asked looking at her.

'Because the police came round earlier on,' Kathy added. 'That why.'

This suddenly brought me round. 'You fuckin' what?' I snapped, after all it was only the night after the warehouse job had gone down and the damn job had made it onto the television and the newspapers – both locally and nationally. 'Did they say what they wanted? Did they say anything?'

'No – Just that they needed to speak with Prey,' Kathy told me. 'It was those two that were at Sean's funeral Chopper though. The ones you were arguing with.'

'What time was this? Did they come round 'ere Donna?' I asked still rocking Sean in my arms.

'They were at mine about five thirty'ish.'

'I don't know Chopper,' Donna told me. 'I was still at the shop at that time.'

'Have you tried his mobile or Steve's?' I asked them.

'Every half hour,' Kathy confirmed. 'Steve's just rang. Prey's mobile was switched off.'

'Shit – Shit!' I said aloud trying to think what would I should do. 'You sure that they didn't say anything at all Kathy?'

'No Chopper. Like I said they just wanted to speak with Prey. That's all they said to me,' she said shaking her head at me.

'Alright – pass me that phone Donna.'

'You what!' she snapped. 'Since when were you incapable of doing it yourself,' she frowned at me.

'Since little Sean 'ere fell asleep in my arms,' I smiled smugly at her.

'Really!' Kathy smiled looking over at her son fast asleep.

'And you're positive that they were at Prey's flat last night Scotty?' Walsh asked irritably, after calling round to Prey's flat they had arranged a meeting with Scotty.

'I told you last night that they all disappeared early on,' Scotty said oblivious to why they were questioning him about last night, as he'd been in bed all day until they'd woke him so therefore he had not seen any television or newspapers.

'But you also said last night that you didn't know where they had gone,' Stevenson said.

'That was then,' he said sighing as he did.

'So how do you know they were there?' Walsh wanted to know.

'They all came into The Hac about eleven, eleven thirty'ish. That's how.'

'All of them?' Stevenson asked shaking his head at the information.

'The lieutenant's, I'm on about,' he added nodding his head.

'Doesn't it seem strange that they were all there? At his flat?' asked Walsh.

'What the fuck seems strange about it?' he asked confused. 'They were playing cards. I've known card games to go on for twenty four hours sometimes.'

'And then they all appeared in the club,' Stevenson shook his head again, not liking what he was hearing.

'How many times have we got to go over this for fucks sake? You boys called me this time.'

They both looked at each other and shook their heads. They knew Scotty was no use to them on this score. He was oblivious to anything that had taken place.

'Alright Scotty,' Walsh said. 'Just keep your ears and eyes open then.'

Scotty then grinned at them. 'I got something that might just be of use to you lot,' he smiled from the backseat. 'But it's going to cost you big this time.'

'What you got for us then Scotty?' Walsh now smiled at him hungrily.

'Another bust in Wythenshawe,' he announced proudly. 'All I know is that I heard Kezlo on the phone today whilst I was lay in bed, he didn't know I was there. But he was talking with Batty and he arranged for a deal to go down.'

'When? When for Scotty?' Stevenson asked eagerly.

'Well that bits going to cost you more than usual,' he smirked at them both.

'How fucking much?' Walsh snapped.

'I want an ounce of rock,' he told them both flatly.

'Alright - now tell us everything you know,' Walsh agreed without hesitation.

'I don't know quantities. But I heard Kezlo ask if Batty was sure it'll be there and you'll have it with you at the boozer. Then he said that would be double sweet and that he would personally meet Batty there. Then he said that he'd see Batty at The Maple Tree at nine o'clock on Wednesday night.'

'You sure it'll be good?' Stevenson asked. 'It could be anything.'

'Of course it will lads,' he smirked. 'If Batty's dealing with it personally, it's because he wants no fuck ups, which more than likely means it'll be a big deal that is going down. Also Chopper told me that they weren't to do anymore fuckin' business with that fucker. Obviously Batty just didn't want to deal with me anymore the cunt.'

'And why would that be eh, Scotty?' smirked Walsh.

'Alright you've got yourself a deal then Scotty,' Stevenson told him. 'We'll see you on Thursday night after this has gone down.'

'Are you serious Chopper?' Prey asked sitting down shocked to see me sat round at his flat waiting in his living room for his return.

'That's why I came back with Kathy,' I told him. 'Just in case they decided to call back again.'

'And it was Stevenson and Walsh?'

'That's what she said,' I told him looking around to check Kathy was still asleep upstairs. 'You think that they're onto us Prey? Y'know after last night.'

He sighed heavily. 'Y'know that would obviously be the first thought,' he appeared thoughtful. 'But they're not even on the case Chopper. That Anderson guy is on the case.'

'It'd be way too soon also,' I added. 'There would no way of connecting us to it so soon. Unless there were any witness's or the Chinese talked.'

'I can't see either one of those happening,' Prey told me. 'I think they were scared shitless by the time we'd left them there. Besides they never even seen our faces. Did they?'

'Best watch ar' selves now though,'

'In'it,' he smiled. 'Probably a good idea that we stashed the money over at his safe house today then.'

'Where've you been anyway?' I asked.

'Just to Steve's then we went on the piss over his way. Ended up in some pocksy Chinese gaff,' he grinned at me. 'I think Chan has spoilt us to much. It wasn't a patch on his scran.'

'I bet it wasn't,' I laughed.

What's all that fuckin' banging,' Prey grumbled burying his head under the pillow.

'What time is it Prey?' Kathy asked sleepily just as Sean began crying.

'I don't fuckin' know. All I know is that's it fuckin' Sunday morning,' he snapped. 'Go answer the door then.'

'Jesus Prey…' she moaned loudly, climbing out of bed. 'It's only seven o'clock in the morning.'

'Just go see who the fuck it is and tell them I said to go fuck themselves,' he screamed at her burying his head deeper under the pillow.

'You really are a twat at times,' she said picking Sean up out of his cot as he'd now awoken fully. 'Here – go to Daddy Sean,' she placed him down next to Prey in the bed.

Prey peeked out at his son and smiled. 'Thanks a lot Kathy,' he said as she disappeared out of the bedroom and ran downstairs grabbing at the front door.

'What's all the bleedin' banging for?' she yelled as she opened the door.

'Good morning miss,' Stevenson cheerfully said ignoring her ranting as he stepped through the open door way. 'Did we wake you?'

'What the hell do you want?' she snapped at them. 'And what do you think you're doing?'

'Is Kieran at home?' Walsh asked moving towards the door also.

'He's still in bed,' she told them with her hands held up defensively as if to stop them entering.

194

'Don't worry love,' Stevenson said as he simply walked past her totally ignoring her. 'We'll see him in there.'

'You can't just bowl in 'ere like that,' she yelled at him protesting, as he headed for the stairs.

'We just did do,' Walsh added as he followed Stevenson up the stairs.

Prey could hear the commotion downstairs. Then he heard the clear sound of feet clattering there way upstairs towards the bedroom. He knew it wasn't a bust though, as they wouldn't have knocked first so he lay back and relaxed.

'What the fuck do you two think you're doing?' Prey asked sitting up putting Sean into his lap as he did. 'You got warrants?' he then snapped at them.

'Just thought we'd save you the time and trouble of getting up O'Prey,' Walsh informed him sarcastically.

'Yeah, sure you did. Fuck you and your mother,' Prey said to him, he played with Sean trying his best to ignore them.

'We've just got a couple of questions for you,' Stevenson stated.

'Are you arresting me for something?' he snapped at them. 'Should we be?' Stevenson asked smiling.

'What is this bullshit?' he then casually asked – staring at them as Kathy walked back into the bedroom taking Sean off him and then immediately leaving the three of them alone.

'Either you two arrest me or get the fuck out of my gaff,' he told them, becoming irritable.

'Where were you on Friday night O'Prey?' enquired Stevenson.

'Well not that it's any of your fuckin' business,' he sighed. 'But I was in The Hac on Whitworth Street.'

'What time was that?' Walsh asked.

'Way past your bedtime Walshy.'

'Cut out the wise cracks son,' Stevenson said staring hard at him.

'Look – Are we going somewhere on this or are you here just to harass me filth?' He shook his head at the two of them. 'C'mon – just spit it the fuck out will you.'

'What can you tell us about what happened on Friday night Prey?' Stevenson asked trying to trip him up.

'What is supposed to have happened on Friday night then?' he asked nonchalantly.

'You know exactly what happened on Friday night,' Walsh was glaring at him.

195

'No I don't know,' he yawned stretching as he did. 'Why don't you boys go a head and refresh my memory for me.'

'The warehouse down by the old docks in Salford,' Stevenson said watching for his reaction.

Prey yawned again, as if bored by the entire matter. 'What about them?' he asked. 'Oh shit – Don't tell me that I missed one of those Acid House Parties… Did I?' he looked at them with mock astonishment upon his face.

'You little shit. You're a…' Walsh was beginning to lose it.

Stevenson cut him off. 'We're onto you fucking O'Prey. Mark my fucking words we are onto you,' he said viciously signalling for Walsh to leave.

'Now – now Mr. Stevenson,' Prey grinned at them both. 'Watch your language. There are children present… And my kids in the next room,' he laughed as the two of them disappeared down the stairs.

'What do you think Mike?' Walsh asked as they opened the car doors.

'I don't fucking know Martin,' he sighed climbing into the car. 'You know when you've just got that feeling that you know something.'

'I know what you mean. Unfortunately we can't prove shit on feelings these days Mike,' he told him what he already knew.

'I know that,' he started the engine up. 'They whole lot of them just wind me up so fucking much though.'

'Come on. You can drop me off at home. I can't remember the last time that I've been up at this time on a Sunday,' Walsh yawned and stretched before climbing into the car.

'Yeah no problem,' he replied.

'First thing tomorrow, we can go over the details for Wednesday night,' he added.

'Are we all set with the team in Wythenshawe?'

'Yeah I spoke with them yesterday,' he replied. 'They can't wait. They've had Batty on their radar for quite some time now.'

'Hopefully that's going to be a very nice bust,' he smirked as he said it, easing the car into gear. 'Should make a nice little dent to their business and score us a few brownie points at the same time.'

'What the fuck have you got me up at this time for Sharon?'
Jonah grumbled as they made their way to the shops on the
estate.

'We've been up all night anyway Jonah,' she laughed. 'So I
haven't got you up have I? You were already up lad,' she
poked his ribs.

'Alright then Sharon,' he laughed at her. 'Why you dragging
me to the shops at this time then.'

'I told you already. I need some munchies for breakfast.' She
kissed his cheek, as they walked. 'You don't want me walking
the streets by myself at this time do you?'

'Wait a minute,' he suddenly said, looking over the balcony
as they both stopped walking.

'What is it?' she asked looking over the balcony too.

'It coppers,' he said and pointed. 'Look in the green Sierra.'

'Looks they're leaving anyway Jonah,' she said tugging at
his arm.

'Yeah,' he said with a thoughtful look on his face.

'What's with that look?' she asked staring straight at him.

'I just know that car from somewhere,' he told her. 'I just
can't think where though,' He added with a look of
bewilderment.

'You'll have seen it around the estate Jonah,' she smiled at
him. 'That's all it is. Now come on. I'm starving.'

'Yeah you're probably right,' he told her smiling as he did.
'Damn it girl you're always hungry. You got to stop smoking
so much weed,' he laughed as they continued towards the
shops.

We're on,' Stevenson said, turning to face the rest of the police officers sat in the back of the removal van that was disguised for police use, situated only fifty feet from The Maple Tree in Wythenshawe.

'The white kid – the one that that figures himself for being black with all those things sprouting from his head. He's Mark Kulshaw and he's one of the main dealers from Hulme. Trevor Batley and his unknown associate have already arrived as pointed out to you. Now they arrived in the silver Range Rover as you all observed. Our officer inside checked the vehicle on his way in and says that the back of Range Rover appears to store boxes of varying sizes crudely covered with a blanket to try and hide the boxes. This most likely will be what Kulshaw is here to purchase as we've been informed that he's here the buy and it will take place at the premises.'

'Kulshaw is the one who's just entered the boozer car park in his black VW Golf. He appears to be carrying the bag – That must be the purchasing money,' Walsh told them observing through his binoculars, through the two way mirrored slit in the wood panel. 'You make sure that you've got those photos Nickleson.'

'Yes sir,' the young officer answered snapping away next to him.

'Now this is the way that this has to go down,' Stevenson said looking at the eight officers waiting for their command. 'Officer Newton is already positioned inside the premises fully fitted with a radio in his jacket collar. He has eye contact with Batley and the unknown. Now we know for sure that this

198

is going down tonight – Only we're not certain whether it will take place here at the boozer itself or that they will travel elsewhere for the transaction to go down.'

'We've got conformation on that registration guv',' one of the officers said who'd just finished on the radio. 'The Range Rover is registered to a Simon Hartley from Altrincham – Seems clean enough guv'.'

'Alright thanks a lot son,' Goodman said nodding at his young officer. 'You know this guy?' he looked at Stevenson.

'No – but he's obviously involved in this,' Stevenson simply told him smiling. 'All part of the bust,' he then smirked.

Walsh turned looking at Goodman, who was head of the Drug Squad for that area. 'We know that you're eager for Batley – but this our bust, as it was our information.'

'I know that,' he grinned at him. 'But if we can get Batley at the same time it's going to be so good. We've been after that wanker for so long now.'

'Well it looks like tonight's your lucky night then,' Stevenson patted his back. 'Now Goodman, as soon as your man inside gives the word we wait for them to come out to the Range Rover. We need to pick Kulshaw up as he's buying the gear.'

'My men know exactly what to do when it goes down, whether it's inside or outside. Or whether they decide to go to another spot for the transaction,' he stared at Stevenson, 'Remember we do actually do this for a living also Mike,' he said shaking his head at him.

'I know – I'm sorry,' Stevenson told him. 'But from what we've been told this should be a big one for both of us.'

Suddenly Goodman's radio came to life. 'Have eye contact on other suspect – He has just entered premises and has made contact with other two suspects – Over.' It had been Newton inside the boozer.

Both Stevenson and Goodman nodded at each.

'Alright Kezlo,' Batty said as he approached the table. 'How's it going mate? This is Simon, the guy I was telling you about.'

'Alright Batty,' he said and shook his hand turning to the tall smartly dressed, business looking man rising from his table. He wore casual clothing, yet had the look of a young executive on the way up. 'You alright Simon?'

'Not bad mate,' he said sitting down, then shaking his head rising again. 'Sorry mate – What are you drinking?'

'Cheers – I'll just have a beer mate,' Kezlo said as Simon disappeared to the bar.

'So how's it going Batty?' Kezlo enquired.

'Sweet mate. As always,' he nodded. 'How's Chopper and Prey?'

'They're alright,' he replied. 'I still can't believe that Prey's a dad though,' he said smiling.

'Why not,' laughed Batty. 'I got four kids running around this estate.'

'Never – honestly?' Kezlo looked astonished at Batty.

'All of them to different birds of course.'

'Shit – I never knew that man,' Kezlo shook his head then looked over at Simon at the bar. 'You sure this guys safe Batty?'

'Of course he is,' Batty declared. 'I've known Simon for years now. He's just not from the estate. Naturally... I mean just look at the way he dresses.'

'And he's got the gear with him?'

Batty nodded outside to the car park so that Kezlo would look. 'In the back of the Range Rover mate.'

'Sound,' he smiled. 'I really appreciate this Batty.'

'It's alright mate. If you hear of anything good then you let me know also,' Batty said. 'This Simon character knows a lot of those rich fuckers from Wilmslow and Prestbury. He can always off load gear as well as supplying it y'know.'

Just then Simon returned with the drinks. 'Here we go then lads,' he smiled as he sat down.

'Cheers,' Kezlo said, as they all raised their bottles to one another.

'So you've got all the money with you Kezlo?' Simon enquired.

'Right 'ere mate,' he grinned patting the record bag next to him.

'Alright, we'll stay and have a few drinks first then,' Simon smiled.

'That's sweet with me,' Batty said taking a swig of his beer.

'What's taking them so long?' Stevenson said becoming irritated as the three of them had been inside for over an hour by then.

'Newton says that they're just sat there drinking,' Goodman informed him, shaking his head at Stevenson's impatience.

'We've got to sit tight until this goes down Mike,' Walsh said to him.

Suddenly Goodman's radio sprang to life again. 'Subjects are on the move – Repeat subjects are leaving the premises – Will pursuit.' The radio cut dead once again.

'Right we're on,' Goodman informed his men. 'Now you all know what to do... Wait for my signal.'

'Here we go,' Stevenson smiled as he saw all three of them head towards the Range Rover.

'They're opening the boot of the vehicle – Move the van slowly down into the car park,' Goodman instructed.

Newton sprang to life again on the radio. 'Suspects are now observing boxes in the back of suspect's vehicle.'

'You still getting the shots Nickleson?' Walsh asked as they descended through into the car park.

'Wait for the money to be passed over first,' Stevenson instructed.

'They all look happy enough,' Goodman smiled as he observed the three men smiling and shaking hands.'

'They're removing the boxes guv' – Do we go in now?' one of the officers at the back of van asked just as they parked up with the back doors facing Kezlo's Golf.

'No – not yet. Wait for the money to exchange hands first,' Goodman told them. 'Nickleson tell Banks to get out of the van and walk into the boozer. Tell him not to even look in the direction of the suspects,' he said instructing for the driver of the removal van to leave the vehicle whilst they observed the boxes now being loaded into Kezlo's car.

'They've just seen Banks,' Walsh said watching the three of them stop a second to observe the officer as unknown to them head inside of the boozer.

'They're blatant as fuck – Aren't they!' Stevenson said smiling as he did. 'It's a lot of boxes there,' he nodded his head as he said it.

'Right they're loaded up Mike...' Goodman looked at him.

'Wait... Wait... Here it comes now... He's going for the money,' Stevenson said as Kezlo reached down into his bag and pulled out a large wadded envelope.

'GO... GO... GO...' Goodman screamed as the back doors of the van flew open, all of its occupants screaming as they leapt down from the back of the removal van. 'Police – Stop where you fuckin' are – Stop right there – All of you.'

Kezlo, Batty and Simon all stopped what they were doing – all in shock at the arrival of the now surrounding officers grabbing hold of them.

'What the fuck...' Batty exclaimed. 'What the fuck do you lot think you're doing... Fuckin' pigs... Get off me,' he was struggling with them.

'What is this all about officers?' Simon casually asked allowing himself to be cuffed with no hassle at all.

Kezlo looked at Batty confused. 'What's this bollocks?'

Batty shrugged at him then was cuffed. 'Fuck 'em – You're right this is bollocks,' he spat.

Just then Stevenson and Walsh along with Goodman, who Batty recognised immediately, walked through the crowd. 'Evening lads... Nice night ain't it,' Stevenson smirked at them as Walsh and Goodman walked past them all of them to Kezlo's boot and the boxes.

'How are you Kulshaw?' Stevenson smirked again.

'What the fuck do you want?' Kezlo spat the words at him.

'Oh just come to see you boys – That's all,' he smiled knowingly at him then turned to Simon. 'And what have we here,' he said bending down to pick up the envelope from the floor that he'd dropped with the surprise of being suddenly surrounded by police officers.

'It's my money officer,' he casually told him making no resist whatsoever.

'Really – and I wonder just what it was for? Oh and it's Detective Inspector to you son,' Stevenson sneered, as he began pealing open the envelope thinking that it wasn't quite as heavy as he thought it would be.

Just then Walsh called out. 'Er... Mike – You better come see this lot.'

Stevenson winked at the three of them. 'I think I'd better go see what we have in the boot of the car – Hadn't I boys,' he said, loving every minute of this.

'Yes I think you should do that... Officer,' Simon sarcastically called out to him.

'What we got then?' Stevenson smiled triumphantly as he walked over to Walsh and Goodman who weren't smiling back at him. 'What the fucks up?' he whispered.

'Take a look for yourself,' Goodman sneered at him.

202

'What...' he asked quizzically heading for the boot of the car.

'You won't be smiling Mike,' Walsh said as Stevenson started tearing at the boxes.

'No... no... no... This can't be right,' he sighed in disbelief as he stared at all the stereo equipment staring back at him.

'Be careful with my gear,' Kezlo shouted out to him.

'What the fuck is this lot?' Stevenson was absolutely steaming as he turned back to them.

'Told you that you weren't going to happy,' Walsh stated.

'This is bollocks... This is fucking bollocks... This... This...' Stevenson was fuming.

'You're fucking right this is bollocks Mike,' Goodman snapped, his back turned to the three stood there. 'Do you fucking realise just how you've made me and my men look tonight... You... You... Fuck it,' he snapped again.

'Excuse me officer – If I may,' Simon said putting on a rather posh accent. 'But may I ask exactly what the problem is here?'

Stevenson in a complete rage flew at him. 'Listen sonny... I tell you what we're going to arrest you on... I tell you,' he stood there before him shaking with rage, as Simon just smiled back at him. 'How about the selling of stolen goods – And,' he turned back towards Kezlo and Batty grinning at them. 'And receiving them – What do you all think of that?'

Batty started laughing. 'I tell you what I think you fuckin' idiot – I think you've gone to one hell of a lot of trouble for handling stolen goods 'ere.'

'Oh that's it – Laugh it up,' he smirked.

'Excuse me – Officer,' Simon said sarcastically again.

'I've told you it's not officer you little prick,' Stevenson yelled.

'Whatever – May I have a word... Officer,' he smiled as Kezlo and Batty began laughing.

'My name is...' Stevenson began to say.

Simon cut him off. 'Oh don't worry about your name just yet officer – I'll be taking all of names a little later on to present to my solicitor first thing in the morning,' he smiled.

'What... What did you just say you little prick...?' Stevenson was seeing nothing but red as he stood there, completely losing all objectivity from this bust not going the way it was supposed to have.

'Excuse me officer – but if you would please calm the fuck down for just one minute I will explain,' Simon smiled smugly.

'Just shut the fuck up – Will you,' Stevenson sneered the words at him.

'Now I've had just about enough of your negative bleeding attitude. Now my name is Simon Hartley of Hartley's in Altrincham,' he sighed as Stevenson stared at him. 'As in Hartley's the electrical store – As in we buy and sell electrical equipment officer. The stereo equipment in the boot of this young gentleman's car is fully above board. I have receipts here for all the equipment sold. I was just going to present them to my good client here. Just before you over eagerly began to arrest us all,' he stopped what he was saying and smiled knowingly at Stevenson as all the officers stood around dropped their heads.

Walsh stepped forward past Stevenson who he could see was losing it big time and went into Simon's jacket pocket removing the piece of paper unfolding it. 'Un-cuff them,' he instructed realising instantly he was defeated.

'What?' Stevenson gasped in disbelief, absolutely seething.

'Read it for yourself Mike - It's kosher,' Walsh confirmed. 'He's just sold him the gear at wholesale price instead of full retail price,' he shook his head then walked past Stevenson.

'You'll be hearing from my solicitors about this… Officer,' Simon said, as he was un-cuffed and set free.

'Just fuck off,' Stevenson told them, taking off after Walsh.

'Nighty night officers,' Batty laughed as they all started to disappear.

The three of them just stood there, looked at each other then began laughing hysterically.

Scotty was shitting himself as he headed towards the meeting point behind Oxford Road. He'd almost dropped dead when Kezlo had walked into the flat the night before carrying all the stereo equipment.

He had fallen about laughing, whilst relaying the story to Scotty of the night's events. Scotty had tried to laugh along, but knew that he was now in deep shit with Stevenson and Walsh. He clearly observed Stevenson still ranting and raving in the passenger seat as he approached the car.

He climbed sombrely into the back seat. 'Alright there,' came feebly from him.

'Just what the fuck was that bollocks you little fucking cunt – what the hell...' Stevenson was in a complete rage, he still hadn't calmed down any from the previous night.

'Look I honestly thou...' he started to say.

'Do you realise just how fuckin' dumb we looked out there last night Scotty? Do you know the amount of shite I've had to wade through today because of what you did to us – You – You fucking *little*...,' he screamed again.

'Calm down Mike...' Walsh tried with him. 'This won't solve anything.'

'I honestly didn't know until Kezlo came home last night,' Scotty said still not able to make eye contact with either of them.

'No, you just thought – I know... I'll have a little laugh with them,' Stevenson said, now a little calmer, his voice was still croaky from all the shouting. 'Make them look like a couple of cunts eh? Was that it?'

205

'I didn't – I swear,' Scotty pleaded.

'Look Scotty,' Walsh said. 'We've got you by the balls son. You know and we know it. There is no turning back for you now. We need results and that last night just made us lose a lot of trust that we've put into you.'

'I'll try and make things right,' he said quietly.

'Not try,' Stevenson snapped at him. 'Will – I *will* make things right,' He said mockingly.

'I'll see what I can do for next week,' he told them.

'No – Not after last night,' Walsh sighed. 'Suspicions may have been raised by us two being there. We're gong to only meet once a month from now on.'

'What – but what about my gea…'

'I suggest that you get the fuck out of the car now,' Walsh suddenly sneered at him with enraged eyes as he became the insane looking one. 'And work out what the fuck you're gonna do to make this all good again Scotty.'

That's his flight number there Prey,' I said pointing to the arrivals screen above our heads at Manchester Airport.

Steve and Claire had been in Portugal for the last couple of weeks. The two of us had recommended that he go away after Stevenson and Walsh paid Prey a visit, questioning him about the Salford warehouse job. He became so paranoid that they were definitely onto us that we thought it best that he left the country for a while.

'Look, there he is now. Both of them,' Prey began to smile. 'Shit Chopper... Check out Claire with a tan.'

I whistled at the sight, 'Jesus! She's looking good – in'it?' I said staring at her as they both approached.

'Alright lads,' Steve said as he came upon us with his trolley filled with suitcases and what looked like way too much duty free.

The two of us managed to break free our stare from Claire turning our attention to Steve. 'Bloody hell – look at you,' I laughed; we'd been so busy staring at Claire we hadn't even noticed Steve's tan. 'You're looking well old man,' I told him shaking his hand.

'Alright Claire,' Prey said taking her hands. 'Now you're a picture to look at,' he smiled then kissed her.

'Oi – enough of that,' Steve laughed. 'You forgetting that I know what you're really like.'

'Ahhh c'mon Steve. What do you take me for... you're way too old for me,' Prey replied as he wrapped his arm around his neck and kissed Steve playfully.

'Fuck you – you little runt,' he laughed pushing Prey away.

'How's little Sean? We've got some great presents for him.' Claire asked Prey as we all made our way outside.

'He's started to get big already,' he smiled at the thought of his son.

'Cheers for picking us up,' Steve said.

'It's alright Steve,' I told him. 'It's business also.'

'You what?' he asked surprised.

'We got a meeting. Very important,' Prey told him. 'We'll drop Claire off then we've got to shoot straight into town.'

'You what...' he repeated again.

'What's up old man,' I said, winking at Claire. 'Surely you've had enough sex for two weeks... Now enough is enough,' I smirked at him.

'One bleedin' track mind you lads have got,' he was smiling knowingly at the two of us.

'Ah – my favourite boys,' Chan greeted us cheerfully as we walked into his restaurant and he appeared from the kitchen smiling.

It had the first time since before the job we'd done for him that we'd been in there. Parties on both sides had felt it a necessity to not raise any suspicions, although the old man had told us not to worry. He called Prey earlier that day to arrange the meeting that night, he said that it been important that we go and see him.

'Ah Steve,' he took his hand and looked at him. 'You're looking fantastic.'

'Not half as fantastic as his missus looks though,' Prey informed Chan.

'Yeah – Some people get to go on holiday,' I smiled at him. 'Whilst the rest of us have to put up with rainy old Manchester.'

'Come – come with Chan,' the old man said and led us to a secluded table at the back of the restaurant instructing one of his waiters not to let anybody near this end of the restaurant.

The four of us were just about to sit down as a young Chinese lad around Prey's age, although more my size and build, which was very big for the Chinese, came over towards us. I'd never seen him before. 'Lee – how the fuck are you lad?' Prey greeted him warmly, grabbing hold and hugging him affectionately.

'Alright Prey. It's been a while hasn't it,' he smiled warmly – they obviously knew each other.

'You're looking good,' Prey confirmed holding him at arms length staring at him.

'Lee is back from college in America,' Chan stated proudly. 'Ah so sorry. Lee you must meet others,' he said taking Steve and I by our arms lifting us.

'This is my youngest son – this is Lee,' he proudly informed us. 'This Chopper and Steve,' he introduced us and we all became aquatinted.

'Keeping out of trouble over in the states Lee?' Prey asked smiling, obviously delighted to see him.

'Yes mate,' he nodded. 'Although I don't think I'd even be here today if you hadn't stepped in that day and saved me Prey.'

'I told you back then mate that it was no bother,' Prey said.

I suddenly realised who Lee was. It had been Lee who Prey had saved from a severe kicking all those years before – he was the reason that Prey and Chan were as tight as they were.

'So Chan says that you're studying law over there,' Prey smirked. 'How's it going?'

'Good... very good in fact,' Lee said smiling at his old man. 'Pop's said that to study law in America would be wiser than studying it here.'

'Of course it is. And with one other brother in America it so possible that you study there Lee,' Chan said to his son with a look of sheer pride upon his face.

'No Pop,' he replied smiling at his father. 'The reason you want me to study there is you know just how much money lawyers can make over there compared to England.'

'Ah – Maybe so son,' he smiled.

'How long have you got left to go Lee?' I asked.

'I go back next week to start my final semester,' he told me.

'Lawyer eh,' Steve smiled. 'Man, that must be one hell of a job to do in America.'

'It's been good to study over there,' he told us all. 'Although the Yanks are about as cultured as the dead turkeys they stuff themselves with at their thanks giving dinners as they call them,' he laughed.

'I can't believe how big you've got,' Prey said looking at him.

'It's those American size portions they give you,' he said.

'Well I think if you were in trouble again or should I say... if I was in trouble,' Prey grinned. 'I think that it'd be you stepping in and helping me Lee.'

209

'I very much doubt that Prey,' he replied. 'So, are you still up to your old tricks Prey?'

'Am I under oath 'ere councillor,' Prey laughed, using a terrible American accent.

'Fuck you Prey,' Lee joked.

'Well let's put it this way Lee,' he winked at him. 'If you get bored with being a lawyer over there. I'm pretty sure that I could find you plenty of clients over 'ere.'

'I bet you could – I *really* bet you could Prey,' he laughed as did us all.

Chan looked at Lee. 'Son. Why you not go and order food for all of us,' he said nodding at his youngest. 'I have things to discuss with my other boys. Then you come join us again'

'Okay Pops,' he smiled. 'You still just ordering the banquets Prey.'

We all laughed looking at Prey.

'I see some things will never change,' he said leaving us sat there.

'He's looking so good Chan,' Prey announced as he watched his old friend disappear into the kitchen. 'But I have a feeling that Lee being home wasn't the only reason for inviting us down here tonight.'

Chan smiled at us. 'I wish to thank you boys for most excellent work,' he declared, nodding at us. 'My bosses were most pleased indeed with your services. They complement you very much with many thanks.'

'For the kickback Chan… It was a real pleasure,' Prey told him.

'Sorry about the two that got wasted Chan,' I stated shaking my head. 'It was – well kind of unavoidable y'know.'

'Do not worry about it Chopper. Your work was outstanding,' he grinned and stroked his silver beard. 'The plan was most excellent,' he looked at all of us. 'In doing what you did at the scene made things much easier in the aftermath of it all.'

'It was the kid's idea,' Steve smiled at me.

Chan merely looked over proudly at me. 'Very good… very good plan indeed Chopper.'

'How do you mean? It made things easier afterwards?' I asked him.

'Well that is why I call you boys here tonight,' he sipped his tea then looked at us. 'I hear that you had two detectives come see you Prey.'

210

'Yeah,' he answered shrugging, 'but they weren't working the case Chan. Them two have just got hard-on's for our crew. That Stevenson seems to have had one for years now.'

'It's all okay anyway. You needn't worry about those two,' he confirmed. 'Mr. Anderson work case anyway. You will be first to know that case is now closed.'

'You serious,' Prey exclaimed.

'How?' I asked curiously.

'You see Mr. Anderson,' he pulled his face almost like he'd just swallowed something he didn't like. 'He is very well known in China town – Both in Manchester and London.'

'So?' Steve shrugged.

'So Mr. Anderson deals with lots of China town problems,' he said shaking his head, 'He very dirty police man indeed. But he can be very useful shall we say at times when we require his services,' Chan sighed at the thought if the detective he'd just mentioned.

'What are you getting at Chan?' Prey asked. 'Are you saying that Anderson works for you guys?'

'Not exactly,' he said. 'But we pay Mr. Anderson much money each month to keep at peace with him. So it was time for Mr. Anderson to repay us – shall we say... a little favour.'

'Why didn't you tell us any us this in the first place Chan?'

'Because Chopper... we did not know whether he would be put on case or not,' he told me.

'Fair enough.'

'Why'd it taken so long for us to hear?' Steve asked.

'Forensic results – Autopsy reports – General police bullshit,' he sighed. 'But now case is solved in Mr. Anderson's eyes. Now he sees things the same way that we see things. Which is good.... No? That is why the way you did things made it so much easier in the end,' he grinned knowingly at us.

'So we're in the clear?' Steve asked.

'Who've they charged with it?' I enquired.

'Tomorrow my boys – tomorrow,' he smiled.

'What about tomorrow?' Prey asked him.

'You read tomorrow's newspaper like everybody else and you find out,' he smiled. 'But tonight we just kick back and relax as you youngsters like to put it,' he laughed again as we all did.

FORTY
ONE

'You read this Martin?' Stevenson asked throwing The Manchester Evening newspaper onto the desk where he sat.

'I know,' replied Walsh glancing up.

'Have you read that fucking headline for Christ sake? Anderson Solves Chinese Massacre Case.' He looked more than a little pissed off. 'I spoke with forensics as soon as I heard.'

'I know Mike. I heard,' he said shaking his head. 'What did that forensic girl say? What's-her-name... Lucy?' he asked pouring himself a coffee.

'She says that Anderson has been on her case since this whole thing went down,' Stevenson said sipping his coffee. 'She says that he kept on at her so that he could charge them.'

'I mean just how the fuck did he get fucking confessions out of all of them last night?' asked Walsh.

'Well that's what Lucy says was still a little odd in her mind,' he said putting his feet up onto the desk. 'She says that in a court of law when asked on forensics values alone that she will have to say that everything said is justifiable and these men were responsible for the deaths of the two Chinks there. Also that it is justifiable that they all shot each other with the weapons fired at the scene of the crime.'

'But is she certain?'

'Not in the slightest,' he said now lighting a cigarette and throwing the pack to Walsh 'She says that it was all too clean for it all too just have been an accident. She reckons if they all plead guilty she might not even be called for. But even if she is, she will have to only give evidence as a forensic officer

212

and that the facts presented are justifiable. Her personal thoughts to the matter will not be questioned.'

'Really? You serious?' asked Walsh looking a little bemused.

'I tell you Martin,' Stevenson said blowing smoke out. 'I still say that those Hulme lot were involved with it somehow.'

'I agree that something wasn't right,' he replied, although he was far from convinced as his partner was as to their involvement. 'But...'

'Especially when Lucy also says that she heard that at least one of the Chinks said that they were ambushed for definite,' he said cutting him short.

'You what? Seriously?' he spat the words out.

'Yes,' he half laughed. 'But apparently he was also the one who Anderson got to confess first. You know like seeing the error of his ways or some bullshit like that.'

'Error of ways my arse,' responded Walsh.

'I tell you, that fucking Anderson is dirty as fuck. He's got a pure evil, nasty, twisted streak in him.'

'I know what you mean. But after this though, he's gonna be the golden boy around here,' Walsh smirked. 'So I'd be very careful what we say about him.'

'Do we know which ones they have charged with the killings?' Stevenson suddenly asked.

'They've all claimed self defence from what I hear. They all say that they pulled guns and pointed them at each other then shot the guns.'

'But surely they know who shot which fucking gun.'

'Like both you and Lucy said,' Walsh informed him. 'They all had residue on their hands along with prints that suggested that they'd all handled the guns at some point.'

'I still say it's bullshit though. All that I can say is, if that lot had something to do with this incident,' he sighed deeply. 'Then these sons of bitches are a clever bunch of little fucks.... God knows!' he sighed out loud. 'I just wish that I could...'

Walsh cut him off. 'Whatever you're thinking – Stop it now,' he said firmly. 'I'm telling you as a friend Mike. Anderson warned us off in the beginning from this case. Besides we've got fuck all that really suggests that our lot had any involvement in it. I mean they don't deal with the Chinks. Business wise that is. And as for going off something that Scotty said – And I mean *said* – not *told* us. Then we can't do shit about it. Like it or fucking lump it mate,' he finished and stubbed out his cigarette.

'I really do hate that fucking prick. Robert fucking Anderson,' he said angrily, thinking back to all them years ago when they'd been partners.

'You want to tell me why Mike?' asked Walsh.

'I just wish that I could mate,' he sighed even more deeply like a man defeated in only the very first round – then began to stare out of the window. 'I only wish that I could,' he repeated again shaking his head as he did so.

Dry Bar was busy as usual for a Friday afternoon. Weekends had become almost like rituals to clubbers, so people were always buzzing about town trying to score their gear for that night out or the weekend in general.

Kezlo, Jonah and I been sat in there all afternoon drinking, just for a change. Jonah had Dougsy running around the vicinity of town sorting business out whilst we were just getting more and more wasted that afternoon.

'What time is it Jonah?' I enquired as I'd forgotten my watch.

'Just gone five... Why?'

'I told Donna I'd meet her at Macreedy's, that's all.'

'What? Why? You're not getting off are you?' Kezlo said looking all concerned.

'What's with you?'

'Nowt,' he grinned. 'I'm just having a proper sound time in 'ere. That's all. Just thought we might as well just make a night of it now.'

'That sounds sweet to me,' Jonah smiled. 'Sharon's meeting me in 'ere later anyway.'

'Ah fuck it then,' I laughed. 'Might as well get Donna to just come meet us 'ere then. Especially if your missus is turning up Jonah,' I said, rising up from my seat.

'Where the fuck are you going now?' Kezlo asked.

'To the phone – if that's alright with you.'

Jonah started laughing as he pulled out his mobile phone. 'Ere'are, just use this Chopper. I don't know why you ain't got one. Everybody's got them these days.'

'I know they fuckin' have. But I've got this,' I said pulling my pager out. 'And this thing does my head in. All fuckin' day long you fuckers are paging me on it. Beep – Beep – Fuckin' beep,' I laughed punching the number for Macreedy's into the phone.

'You alright?' I asked smiling as I then kissed Donna. We all noticed this young girl trailing behind her, kind of funny looking, and almost hippie looking in her dress sense. With her hair all done in little bunches all over her scalp. Although despite this, she was quite attractive.
'You look pissed already,' she smiled at me then turned to the girl. 'This is Michelle everybody. That's Chopper and Jonah,' Michelle smiled at us both.
We both said alright to her as we watched Kezlo's reaction. 'And this is Kezlo,' she smiled as we all looked at him staring at this girl before him.
'Snap out of it,' I laughed at him.
'What – oh yeah,' he said almost gormlessly. 'You alright Michelle,' he smiled at her, although he was still staring.
'Chopper's you're real boss Michelle,' Donna smiled. 'Well one of them anyway.'
'You what?' I asked confused.
'Macreedy's is yours?' Michelle asked.
'Michelle has just started working for us this week. Top little sales girl as well,' Donna said nodding at me.
'That's good… For us anyway,' I smiled.
'What do you want to drink?' Jonah asked grinning as he shook his head at Kezlo.
'It's alright – I'll get them,' Kezlo blurted out.
'I'll just have a bottle of beer,' Donna said looking at Michelle.
'Me too,' Michelle smiled at Kezlo. 'I'll come with you,' she added.
'Top one,' Kezlo said a little too enthusiastically.
Donna sat next to me as we all laughed watching the two of them disappear to the bar,
'You see the state of him then?' I laughed.
The truth was none of us had ever seen Kezlo act that way before with a girl. All he usually gave a shit about was buying records or spunking more dough on stereo equipment.
'I know,' Jonah smirked. 'He's well smitten with that bird – Ain't he?'

216

'I thought they'd both like each other,' Donna smiled. 'That's what I brought her with me for.'

Both Jonah and I laughed out loud looking at Donna. 'Cilla fuckin' Black now is it,' Jonah said.

'You're a sly little sod Donna,' I grinned at her.

'Well – I thought it was about time that Kezlo found himself a girl,' she stated. 'I can't even remember the last time he was even with anybody.'

We suddenly saw Jonah's eyes move towards the doorway frowning. 'Shit – Just look at this.'

We both turned to see Sharon walking through the door carrying what looked to be at least ten shopping bags with her. 'Jesus – That girl certainly knows how to fuckin' shop Jonah,' I stated.

'Hi'ya hon,' she said as she bounced over and kissed Jonah. 'Everybody alright,' she enquired all bubbly.

Just then Kezlo returned from the bar with Michelle. 'For fucks sake Jonah,' he grumbled. 'Why didn't you remind me to get Sharon a drink if she was coming in?'

Jonah laughed at him. 'You'll just have to go back again – Won't you?'

'What do you want Sharon?' he asked shaking his head.

'Brandy and coke... Cheers,' she said as Kezlo then disappeared again.

'How much dough have you blown today then Sharon?' Jonah asked, scowling at her.

'Don't worry about it hon,' she told him batting her eyelids as she did; Sharon always knew how to get around him.

'He's nice isn't he,' Michelle said to Donna as she sat down next to her.

'Told you that you'd like him,' Donna smiled.

'Hi'ya – I'm Sharon,' she declared loudly. 'Seeing as none of these ignorant bastards have bothered introducing us.'

'Sorry,' Donna laughed at Sharon. 'Sharon – Michelle – Michelle – Sharon,' she said looking back and forth from the two of them.

'Ere'are Sharon. What the fuck?' Kezlo exclaimed, looking at all of Sharon's bags. 'How many fuckin' shopping bags have you got there girl. I wouldn't mind girl but every time I see you you're wearing something new.'

'Just 'cause you shop at Oxfam Kezlo,' she laughed as we all did.

217

He didn't shop at Oxfam, but he very rarely bought any new clothes as he was always blowing his money on those other things he felt were more important.

'What have you bought anyway Sharon?' Donna asked enthusiastically.

'Oh just wait till you see some of these tops,' she said excitedly as the three of them were then fully engrossed in the contents of Sharon's bags.

'Women,' I laughed at the other two.

'She's alright, ain't she,' Kezlo said quietly out of ears reach.

'Yes mate,' Jonah agreed. 'Just up your street mate.'

'I know,' I confirmed smiling. 'And for some unknown reason she actually seems keen on you too. Fuck knows why though you ugly twat,' we both laughed at him.

Eventually tiring of Dry Bar, we made our way down to The Hacienda, and as usual it was already kicking when we got in there.

'You like this kind of music Michelle?' Kezlo asked her. He'd been stuck to her all night, not letting her be. Although she seemed to be loving the attention.

'It's well top,' she smiled. 'I've heard your tapes in the shop. I really like them.'

'Honestly?' he replied startled. 'I suppose that they're alright,' he added sheepishly.

'Fuck that Kezlo,' I said handing them both their drinks. 'You're a quality DJ and y'know it. You just haven't really pushed yourself like the others. Y'know that you're as good if not better than even them lot in 'ere.'

'I love to see you play sometime,' Michelle told him.

'He's got a really good set up at his flat,' Donna said.

'Have you?' she asked smiling. 'Can I come and see it some time?'

'Of course – Anytime you want,' he blurted out at her.

I chuckled at the way he was carrying on then turning to Donna. 'They seem to getting along alright,' I said kissing her.

'I know,' she smiled knowingly at me.

We could see Jonah going on with himself with Sharon as he approached us. 'It's a fuckin' joke Sharon,' he snapped at her as she just shook her head at him smiling. 'Well it fuckin' is,' he added.

'What's with you?' I laughed at the way he was going on with himself.

'He's pissed off because of the cloak room charge,' Sharon giggled looking at Donna.

'You what?'

'Just cost me over twenty fuckin' quid to put all her bags in the bleedin' cloak room then,' he was obviously wound up by it.

'I'm sorry mate,' I apologised first before not being able to stop myself from a fit of laughter.

Dougsy came over shaking his head at us. 'Fuckin' kids,' he said which made me laugh, as he was only eighteen himself.

'What's up mate?' I asked him smiling.

'Some young Salford lads are in 'ere selling,' he informed us.

'Y'what?' Jonah snapped.

'I'm not sure who's backing them,' he shook his head at us. 'But I tell you. They don't give a fuck about ar' crew.'

'You know who they are?' Jonah asked.

'Seen them about town,' he shrugged. 'They're only young, but they're right up for it. I've had 'em in my face all night.'

I suddenly observed Jonah look behind me. 'You seen who else is in 'ere Chopper?'

Glancing over my shoulder, Chris Walker was staring straight at me grinning. He'd stayed out of town for quite a while after we had disposed of Paddy, but his name had been mentioned more than a few times recently, only I just hadn't paid much attention. 'Fuck him – He's a dick anyway.'

'Those two lads with him are a couple of them I was on about Chopper,' Dougsy informed us. 'Y'know I'm up for a bit of a rumble Chop. But them Salford lads are well mad these days. You never know whether they're going to pull a blade or even a shooter on you.'

'Don't worry about it Dougsy,' I told him. 'Just stick with your regular customers for tonight mate.'

'Alright Chopper,' he said disappearing again.

'You reckon Chris's trying to move in on our action?' Jonah asked me.

'Could never happen,' I grinned. 'But Dougsy's right though – y'know... about them Salford lads. They're getting one hell of a reputation for themselves now. Don't let anybody fuck about with them these days.'

219

'I know what you're saying mate,' Jonah shook his head at me. 'But no trouble tonight Chopper eh? Y'know, we've got the girls with us.'

'Sweet mate,' I smiled then nodded my head. 'I've been having a sound day Jonah, and the last that I want is trouble mate,' I told him truthfully.

Jonah then laughed looking in Kezlo's direction. 'You reckon he's in with a chance?'

'Don't see why not,' Donna said as she suddenly appeared with Sharon.

'They haven't left one another alone all night,' Sharon added.

'Must be love,' I laughed out.

Just then somebody grabbed hold of my shoulder from behind, as I turned, I was stood facing Chris and the two younger lads stood there. I immediately eased Donna back into the crowd. 'What do you want?' I asked staring coldly at him.

'You think that you're so fuckin' big time – Don't you Chopper?' he snarled at me.

'Fuck off you dick,' I replied nonchalantly. 'Go play with your school mates Chris.'

'I want to know where Paddy is Chopper?' he stared hard at me and I could tell he'd been drinking heavily – but then again so had I.

I began laughing directly in his face. 'How the fuck am I supposed to know where your girlfriend is?' I could feel Jonah's presence by my side.

'He disappeared Chopper. I know that you had something to do with it. So C'mon tell me the fuck he is?' he screamed at me.

'What's wrong Chris?' I smirked knowingly at him. 'You missing your girlfriend? No one to suck your dick these days? Or fight your battles for that matter.'

'Times change Chopper. I've taken over Paddy's business whilst he's away,' he put his face into mine, so close that you could stench the booze on his breath at such close proximity. 'I got a whole new bunch of eager lads. All just itching to fuck you up on my word.'

I drove him back out of my face with the palms of my hands. 'Best give the fuckin' word then Walker – 'cause you ain't ever gonna manage it on your own are you?' I sneered the

220

words at him as I saw the two lads stood by his side were becoming irritable.

He stepped forward into my face once again. 'Now I'm going to ask you one more time Chopper – And you better give me the right answer,' he was right in my space once again. 'I want to know what you did with Paddy – *Now.*'

Without any warning whatsoever, I slammed my forehead straight into his face, knocking him backwards. But just as quickly as I had hit him I hadn't noticed one of the younger lads moving towards me at deadly speed and accuracy.

The bottle sliced through the air with deadly precision aimed straight for my face. 'You fucker...' was the only thing I heard as the bottle shattered against the right hand side of my face with some serious force.

I immediately felt the skin surrounding the right cheek and eye tearing with the splintered glass as I cringed, my hand automatically responding to it... Then came the screams surrounding me. I began to stagger backwards trying to find my balance as I just about focused on the young lad running straight towards me for a second attack. I have to admit that this kid was very fast as he shot forward directly at me, totally fearless after his first successful onslaught. I also noticed that he held something that caught the light flashing... it was a blade.

Just as he swiped for me, I rescued my balance and focused properly. I had to react without any hesitation, as my mind raced, playing on pure instincts rather than anything else.

I stooped back down low to the ground, giving the appearance that I had lost my balance again as I saw the kid as he swung out wildly, swinging directly over me, catching the sight of the blade swinging recklessly through the air.

I threw an upper cut with my right arm, the punch swung almost from the floor, cut swiftly upwards catching him from behind in his kidneys. He squealed out loudly, jumping backwards from the powerful blow he'd received, as I managed to grab hold of him, then in one motion throwing him into the crowd now stood there.

The blade fell free from his grip as panic struck those once confident eyes. He could clearly see me descending towards him. I suddenly caught a glimpse of the backs of Jonah and Kezlo dragging Chris away.

The young lad lay there helpless as I towered above him sneering menacingly. As I both witnessed and soaked up his fear, I reached down to pick up his knife, smiling at him as I descended down, gathering him up I then used my head instead... butted him heavily on the bridge of his nose, feeling the bone crush with ease as he shrieked like a little girl.

As I held him close to my face I then did nothing – I merely released him half laughing whilst telling him, 'Go on – just fuck off.' His panic turned almost to shock as I watched him run for the doors.

I took off after Kezlo and Jonah who'd dragged Chris through the plastic sheeting where the loading bay was located out of sight of snooping eyes and CCTV.

'Chopper – your face,' Donna sighed as she saw where I was heading for. Sharon had her arms around Michelle who obviously wasn't used to this kind of thing at all.

Lifting my hand to my face feeling the warmth of the sticky blood, I looked at my hand then to Donna. 'Just get me a cloth,' I instructed, waltzing through the plastic sheeting to where the others were to be found.

Kezlo and Jonah were already kicking and punching Chris frantically, shouting obscenities at him as they did.

'Wait... Stop,' I commanded as they both dropped Chris's bloodied body to the floor heavily.

As they both looked at me I was touching the wound on my face as they began smirking at Chris. Reaching down to the floor I began staring coldly at Chris lay there panting, trying his best to catch his breath.

As my hand reached out I found what I had been searching for, a bottle that had already been smashed. As I lifted the broken bottle from the floor, we observed Chris's eyes suddenly open wildly staring at me.

Stepping forward past the other two, I witnessed the appeal written all over his face, but it was way too late for that now, 'Nnnoooooo – Please Nnnooooo – Chopper – Please don't...,' he pleaded as I stuck the serrated edges into his face, I felt the sharpened edges grind through his skin with ease as I then began, without any emotion on my behalf felt towards his anguish, twisting the shards of glass into his face

His screams were that of sheer agony and pain as the glass literally tore open the flesh holding his face together. I felt the blood beginning to over flow the bottle itself and begin to run through my fingers as his screams were merely drowned out by the thumping bass of the music pumping through the sound system.

222

'Chopper... We got to get out of 'ere mate,' Kezlo said grabbing my arm, freeing the bottle from Chris's mangled face, leaving him squirming around screaming holding onto his face.

All three of us exited the plastic sheeting finding the girls stood there. 'Here.' Donna said as she passed me the damp dishcloth.

'Cheers – We'd better go,' I said then looked at her. 'Sorry,' I added apologetically.

'I think I'm used to it by now,' she said shaking her head at me.

Just as we got to the door we turned witnessing both security and a group of young lads including the other lad who'd been stood beside Chris rushing through the plastic sheeting.

'What happened to you Chopper?' Errol asked as we walked outside quickly.

I was merely grinning at him.

'Where's the other one Chopper?' he shook his head back to me.

'Loading area,' I smiled at him. 'Your lads and his lads have just rushed in there Errol. Can you hold them off for me?'

He smiled at me knowingly. 'Go on mate. You've got a ten-minute head start on them. I'll do what I can for you,' he informed me, as he then began to pull down the steel shutters. 'Goodnight Chopper,' was the last thing I heard along with sound of the shutters making contact with its base.

'Just look at the state of you,' Steve sighed, staring at my face the following morning perched on the edge of my bed. 'Doctor Hassid has stitched you up yet again Chopper. Done a good job though,' he looked at the stitches on my right cheek and just above the eye.

'It was nowhere near as bad as it first appeared to be,' I told him stroking the stitches. 'Even I thought that my face was fucked – but it ain't too bad really.'

'Can't we leave you the fuck alone for just one night,' Prey laughed.

'What did I need you two for anyway,' I laughed at them both. 'We proper gave it to them anyway.'

'We're sure you did Chopper,' Steve smiled. 'Any idea who the kid was?'

'I've seen both of them in the shop,' Donna said, just as she was finishing brushing her hair.

'Only young lads,' I laughed. 'He kinda reminded me of what I was like back then. That's why I just let him go. Well after a couple of digs and a little scare that is.'

'And Chris says that he's taken over Paddy's business?' Prey enquired inquisitively.

'So he fuckin' says,' I told him. 'Looks like he's using the younger lads to back him. They all probably look up to him. I mean after all, he was with Paddy wasn't he? Plus those younger lads will be eager to make an impression.'

'I know,' Prey stated. 'We'll have to keep an eye out for them. Young lads these days aren't interested in just fighting with you. These, lot prefer to use tools to fight their battles with,' Prey said looking at my face.

'They're no different to what we were like Prey.'

'I suppose so,' he agreed with a small smile upon his face. 'Maybe I'm just getting old or something.'

'Maybe Steve's just rubbing off on you,' I smirked at him.

'Cheeky bleedin' runt...' Steve smirked. 'What do you want to do about Chris?'

'Reckon I done enough last night,' I said staring back at him. 'Y'know I'd hate to be him this morning.'

Donna stared at me shaking her head. 'I'm off Chopper – I've got to get to the shop. Matthew opened this morning and I promised I'd be there by twelve,' she smiled bending to kiss me. 'Besides you've got your two nurse maids here now anyway,' she winked cheekily at the other two.

'Cheeky cow,' Steve laughed at her.

'You're going away again,' I said to Steve.

We had made our way down to Henry's to eat, as I was ravenous. They had wanted to go to Chan's as usual, but I'd blagged it, saying that I'd eaten there the previous night.

'Only for the weekend Chopper,' he told me smiling.

'Dirty weekend more like it,' Prey added.

'You lads really have got one track minds,' he smirked at us.

'Look who's talking with that devious bleedin' grin. You're the one shagging an eighteen year old and you're the one whose more than old enough the be her old man,' Prey roared with laughter.

'So you telling me that you wouldn't,' he shrugged his response.

'Where you going to?' I asked as our food was brought over. 'Thanks,' I said smiling to the waitress.

'Just to the Lake District next weekend,' he said smiling knowingly at me.

'You're a lucky bastard,' I told him.

'Just for the weekend though,' Prey scowled at him. 'You're taking too much time off lately old man. I think that we're going to have to have another look at the holiday allowance in your contract,' we all laughed at this.

'Yes pops,' Steve said smiling at Prey.

'They can't keep their eyes off you Claire,' Steve nodded at the group of lads by the bar, as he sat across from her eating his meal. They were dining in the restaurant area of The Windmill that was situated down a secluded country lane in the Lake District. They'd already spent the previous evening at The Valley Guesthouse.

'Oh stop that Steve,' she giggled at him.

'They are though,' he stated. 'They're blatantly staring at you,' he said observing the group of young teenage lads still stood around the bar, who couldn't keep their eyes off Claire and were obviously talking about her.

'Come on Steve,' Claire prompted. 'Just eat your food and stop being silly,' she leaned over the table in full view of the group stood staring at them and kissed Steve passionately. As she was about to sit down again she gave them a little look, then tutted at them pathetically.

'You're right Claire,' he smiled broadly after the kiss. 'Guess I just get paranoid sometimes. I mean you know how I feel about you. Don't you? I'm just pretty shit at saying it sometimes.'

'I love you Steve,' she simply told him smiling as she did. 'You know that. So you're just being stupid. Aren't you?'

'If you say so,' he shrugged, and then glanced at the lads stood there and smiled knowingly at them.

'What do you want to drink Claire?' Steve asked as they both wandered through to the bar area after they'd finished their meal.

226

'Just a dry white wine please,' she answered making her way over to free table, the young group of lads already in keen pursuit of her.

'Hello love,' the larger lad of the group said as she sat down.

He looked to be around the same age, maybe a little older than Claire herself. He was well over six-foot tall with slicked back dark brown hair, and he appeared to hold an unspoken air of authority over the group of other lads.

'How are you tonight then?' he smirked at Claire whilst the group of lads were all egging him on.

'We are both fine. Thank you for asking,' Claire replied taking a seat.

By now the group of seven lads had surrounded the table, the same lad spoke again.

'Now what's a lovely young girl like yourself doing with an old timer like that?' he nodded towards Steve at the bar.

'Perhaps because I like to be with a real man,' she smiled pleasantly at him, and then glanced at the rest of them shaking her head whilst holding her smile at them.

Steve was observing all of this from the bar whilst he ordered the drinks. The lad looked and then sniggered at Steve before staring straight at Claire again.

'I'm just trying to work it out,' he rubbed his chin as all of his mates began to giggle like adolescent children at their leader's antics. 'Now is he some kind of a sex case or is he just your fuckin' pimp darlin'.'

'Fuck off,' Claire suddenly snapped viciously just as Steve arrived with the drinks.

'Is everything alright here?' he smiled at Claire then turned staring straight at the one who'd been doing all of the talking. 'You're not bothering the lady are you?'

'What the fuck is it to you old man,' the lad snapped getting right in Steve's face, his spittle making contact with his right cheek.

Steve casually wiped the vile spit away, and then looked at all the lads knowing that he was clearly out numbered so went for the calm approach with the lad. 'Look we don't want no trouble alright,' he smiled. 'We're just here to have a good time. Let's just let things be son.'

'Fuck you old timer. Just who the fuck do you think you are calling me your son,' he was still in Steve's face not budging.

'Just do all yourselves a favour and let it be eh,' Steve glanced towards the bar for support from the landlord who

227

merely smirked back at him, then casually looked away polishing his glasses as if to not to bare witness to anything that was happening.

'Do ourselves a favour? Is that what you just said to me?' the lad snapped back at him.

'That's what I just told you,' Steve sneered, standing his ground with him.

'Let's say that I'm going to take your little girlfriend away from you old timer,' he smirked staring coldly at Steve. 'Now what you got to say about that?'

'Please just...' Claire started.

'Shut the fuck up you little whore. You'll be shown what a real man is soon enough you little fucking slut,' he sneered, glancing briefly over at her, whilst all of the other lads began laughing hysterically.

Steve had heard more than enough by now. So without thinking about any consequences, he butted the lad as hard as he possibly could. 'Never call her that again you little fuck,' he spat the words out at him.

The lad stepped back shocked at what Steve had just done. All of his mates were now forming a circle around Steve whilst the kid he'd just butted put his hand to his nose touching the blood around his nose.

'Please... please... somebody stop this...' Claire cried out looking around as everybody looked away from the scene, ignoring the confrontation.

'You just made one hell of a bad mistake old man,' the kid grinned at him, then tasted the blood.

Steve couldn't help himself and let out a little laugh. 'You've been watching way too many Bruce Lee movies son.'

'You fucking what...' he snapped then went at Steve enraged swinging like a wild man as he did.

Steve casually stepped back then dodging three of the kid's attempts at him, swung a right upper cut that made clean contact with his solar plexus knocking the kid to the floor. 'Now just let it be – C'mon Claire,' he said putting his hand out for her.

The next thing he heard was glass shattering. Turning – he saw the kid stood there grinning holding a smashed pint glass. All of his friends began to jeer him on with taunts towards doing Steve damage. 'You're dead for sure now you old fucker,' he scowled menacingly, as he threw himself at Steve.

Steve kicked out as quickly as he could, knocking the kid back once again before he could even get close to him... That was the last clear thing he remembered as suddenly all of his associates rushed Steve from every direction.

He was doing his best to fend off his attackers and the imminent onslaught, but there were way too many of them all punching and kicking frantically at him. They just kept coming at him from all angles. He was trying to see Claire through the mass of arms and legs brutally attacking him.

Steve caught a glimpse of her screaming with one of the lads held onto her. He began to lose his balance under the swarm of abuse brought down forcibly upon him.

As he hit the floor hard... The flurry of kicks and punches were becoming unbearable under the progressing onslaught – Each blow taking more and more out of him as they continued to kick the crap out of him.

Then just as suddenly as it had all began, it suddenly stopped and there was a clearing above him – But Claire's screams only intensified as he suddenly saw the kid he'd smacked stood above him with a heavy wooden oak table high above his own head – Steve closed his then weary eyes and pictured his girl – Claire – Beautiful Claire – Then came the darkness.

'What his name love? Please come on?' the attendant in the back of the speeding ambulance enquired. 'It's important...' he tried again as Claire was in clearly also in shock.

'They wouldn't stop – They just wouldn't stop,' she sobbed uncontrollably.

Steve lay fully unconscious before her on a stretcher. Blood seemed to be seeping through every inch of his clothing and his face was beaten to a pulp. His face was so battered and the bruising and swelling had already consumed his flesh.

'Please miss...' he tried once again.

'Steve... Steve Griffin...' she sobbed dropping to her knees beside him. 'Is he going to be alright? Will he die? Please save him,' she pleaded frantically with him.

'We'll do everything we can for him,' he said checking his vital signs. 'What the hell happened?' he then asked looking at her.

'They all jumped him,' she cried out. 'So many of them – seven of them. Seven lads all beating and kicking and then,' she cried out even louder. 'The table – They...' She wasn't making much sense to him, although it was more than clear

229

that whatever had happened had endangered the life of the badly wounded man lay before him. He looked as if a high speed train had practically run over him.

'I promise they'll do everything possible,' he told her sympathetically putting his hand on her shoulder just as the ambulance skidded to a halt outside the hospital's emergency entrance.

The doors flew open as the driver helped to get Steve out of the back. 'We got to get him straight into surgery.' The one who had been speaking to her said to the nurse's waiting on standby.

They rushed through the hospital with Steve lay stretched out unconscious on the steel trolley, his clothing soaked with his own blood. Doctor's and nurse's seemed to be appearing out from everywhere at the mere sight of his condition.

'Is he going to be alright?' Claire sobbed following them just as a nurse took her arm.

'Please miss – Please miss,' she said smiling at her. 'You have to let them see to him now,' she told Claire looking sympathetically at her.

'Please – Please look after him for me,' she pleaded, watching him disappear through the doors surrounded by the doctor's and nurse's all shouting instructions to one another.

She stood there with the nurse who had her arm around her. 'Come on love. We need his details for the computer,' she smiled warmly at Claire.

'I need to make a phone call first,' Claire said breaking free from her embrace.

'Please miss,' the nurse called after her. 'It's important,' she cried out as she watched Claire walk away.

Only the words fell on deaf ears as Claire ran down the corridor making her way to the public telephone.

'Prey...' she sobbed down the phone line. 'Oh – Prey – It's Steve...'

'What happened?' he snapped sensing all was not right.

'They beat him... They...' she sobbed hysterically once again 'They beat him badly... He's in hospital Prey.'

'Who beat him? Claire talk to me,' he asked concerned.

'What's wrong?' Kathy asked from behind Prey as she sat there rocking little Sean.

Prey shook his head at her then continued to listen to Claire's crying. 'Claire speak to me.'

'There were seven of them Prey... It was horrible,' she bawled uncontrollably down the phone line.

'Just give us the address of the hospital Claire, we'll be there within the next couple of hours,' he said grabbing a piece of paper and a pen.

Prey was scribbling down the information that Claire was giving to him. She wasn't making much sense to him, but the one thing he clearly understood, was that one of his closest friends was lay in hospital from a beating he'd received.

'We'll be there as soon as possible Claire,' he informed her, when he was just about to put the receiver down. 'One more thing Claire – When the police arrive tell them as little as possible. We'll deal with it,' he added gravely.

'Please come – Soon,' she cried as she replaced the receiver still in tears.

'Excuse me miss,' came a voice from behind her. 'Hello miss, I'm Dr. Greenwood,' he smiled at her holding his hand out as she weakly took it.

231

'Hello,' she looked blankly at him, not sure that was ready for the worst.

'Sorry I don't know your name,' he smiled again.

'Claire,' she told him. 'Claire Russell – Is he going to be alright doctor?' she asked desperately, not letting go of his hand.

'It's way too early to tell Miss. Russell,' he said shaking his head. 'He's still unconscious and he's lost a lot of blood. We have no idea just yet how bad his internal injuries are until we do the scan. He gone in for x-rays now to give us a better understanding of the situation concerning broken bones and just how bad they actually are,' he sighed. 'He's in a really bad way. That's why it's important Miss. Russell that why you go through to reception and give us as much information on your father as poss…'

She cut him off, staring coldly at him. 'He's not my father,' she suddenly snapped. 'His name is Steve Griffin – he's my…' she stopped herself and just looked at the doctor.

'I'm so sorry Miss. Russell,' he looked away as he said this realising their relationship. 'Please forgive me – I didn't know.'

'It's alright,' she smiled at him weakly. 'Please doctor, help him. Bring him back to me,' she began crying again. 'I love him so much doctor,' she sniffed, trying her best to control the tears.

'Was that his family that you just phoned?' he enquired.

'As good as,' she told him. 'They are as good as his family.'

'Alright then,' he smiled. 'We'll keep you informed miss,' he said before turning taking off down the corridor.

'Claire – How is he?' I asked rushing into the waiting room, ignoring the two police officers stood there.

'Oh Chopper,' she ran straight into my arms as I began hugging her, suddenly dreading the worst.

'Where is he?' I asked frantically, holding her at arms length.

'Still in surgery,' she cried tearfully as Donna and Kathy took hold of her holding her tightly comforting her.

'C'mon,' I said turning to Prey.

'Who are you?' one of the officers asked. 'If you don't mind us asking?'

'Yes I do fuckin' mind,' I sneered at him, before heading off with Prey to find the reception.

'Excuse me?' he snapped at me as we completely ignored him, walking away. 'Oi – Come back here you,' he called after me in vain.

'Excuse me miss,' I said politely. 'Could you please tell me how my old man is? He was brought in earlier – Steve Griffin.'

She looked at me and smiled kindly. 'He's still in surgery.'

'Just how bad is he?' Prey enquired.

'I'm sorry love – But from what I've heard he's in a critical condition,' she smiled to try and reassure us. 'I'm sorry – But Dr. Greenwood should be along soon. I'll send him straight in to see you.'

'Thank you,' I nodded at her, heading back to the waiting room.

'Claire – Claire – Listen to me...' Prey said taking hold of her. 'What has the doc already told to you?'

'He said that his collar bone was crushed. His right arm snapped in two places. His left leg is smashed in three different places with his left knee is fractured,' she sobbed as he took her into his arms.

'Is he still unconscious?' he asked shaking his head in disbelief.

'Yes.' she cried. 'They say that he's suffered internal bleeding and they still need to do another brain scan. His whole body and face is battered and bruised. He was bleeding so badly... They were so bad to him – they – *they*...' he held her tightly.

I was holding Donna as Claire explained what she knew about Steve's injuries, as Kathy sat on one of the plastic waiting room chair's, also crying badly.

'Come here Claire,' Donna said breaking away from me and taking hold of her.

Glaring at Prey, I shook my head in disbelief at what had happened.

'Miss. Russell,' Dr. Greenwood said.

'How is he?' I asked anxiously.

'Sorry...' he looked at me quizzically. 'You are?'

'His son,' I said a little too anxiously – then immediately apologised. 'I'm sorry – But how is he? Please doctor?'

'He's still unconscious but we seem to have stabilised him,' he told us. 'He was hurt very badly. He has suffered a lot of internal damage as well as his surface wounds.'

'Is he going to make it doc?' Prey enquired.

Doctor Greenwood smiled. 'Put it this way – I don't know him personally but I can tell that he is strong willed. I just know he is.'

'He's definitely that,' I added trying my best to smile. 'But seriously doc... What do you think?'

'The next twenty fours are critical to him,' he sighed.

'Will he come back to us?' Claire asked wiping away tears on the arm of her sleeve.

'Like I said – The next...' he began.

'Thank you doctor,' I said cutting him off, knowing that he'd already told us everything that he possibly knew for now. 'Please, we'll be 'ere. Just let us know about anything. Anything at all.'

Just as Dr. Greenwood left the two uniformed police officers waltzed casually back into the waiting room.

'Right Miss Russell,' said the same officer who'd spoken to me previously. 'Now are you going to tell us what actually happened?'

'What's your name?' I asked annoyed with his attitude.

'P.C. Pemberton,' he stated proudly to me, 'and this is Officer Daikin.'

'Well Mr. Pemberton,' I replied, glaring at him. 'I hardly think that she's in any state to go answering any questions – Is she now?'

'I think that I've had just about enough of your cockiness son,' he glared back at me.

'Fuck off you prick.'

'What... What did you just say to m...' he scowled at me.

'I've already told you what I know,' Claire sobbed.

'Can't this please wait?' Kathy asked politely, her arms around Claire.

'Well we have waited for hours already as it is now,' he snapped, still Daiken hadn't said a word.

'Well you'll just have to wait a little longer. Won't you,' Prey told them as they both stared hard at him, although you could feel they were more than a little apprehensive about his entire presence. 'Have you been to the place where this happened?'

'Yes we have,' he told Prey shaking his head, 'and I really don't think that I appreciate your tone of voice with me at all.'

'You fuckin' what,' Prey said viciously, as he flew straight at Pemberton. 'What did you just fuckin' say to me?'

I leapt forward grabbing hold of him. 'Easy mate,' I told him. 'This ain't the time or the place.'

'Just what have you found out already?' I asked them both, whilst keeping a grip on to Prey's more than tense shoulder.

'Just that they were picked up outside The Windmill late last night,' Daikin informed us. 'We don't know who called the ambulance,' he added.

'Yeah the landlord says that Mr. Griffin was in quite a state when he left last night,' Pemberton smirked. 'You know kind of had way too much to drink. Must have stumbled over or something like that.'

'You *what*,' Claire was seething, as we all looked at Pemberton in utter disbelief at what he'd just said.

'Well that's what we've heard and you've haven't exactly been much help to us. Have you now?' he snapped back at her.

'Sorry,' Daikin said, looking at his partner. 'Could you please tell us what you know miss?' he tried to ease the obvious tension occupying the air between us.

'Look, just give her time alright,' I told him. 'It's been a long night and she needs to rest. We ain't going anywhere; we'll be right 'ere.'

'And you are?' Daikin asked smiling.

'Billy Chorlton,' I told him.

'I thought you said that you were his son,' Pemberton stated.

'I kept my mothers name afterwards… Fuck you dick head – what the fuc…' I suddenly stopped myself from explaining anything further. 'It's got fuck all to do with you,' I confirmed.

'Come on… We'll come back later,' Daikin said seeing that both patience and tempers were beginning to wear thin.

As they left Pemberton and Prey stared coldly at each other. But as soon as they were out of sight, I turned to Claire.

'Right Claire. Tell us everything that happened?' I said, crouching before her, and then adding. 'And I mean everything.'

'They're fuckin' dead. All of them Chopper,' Prey was in a rage outside of the hospital after Claire had relayed the story to us.

'I know Prey,' I was agreeing with him. 'But let's just concentrate on Steve for now – yes?' I suggested, trying to calm him down some.

'We're going to check this place out – the boozer that is,' he said pacing around like a caged animal. 'Then – then – then I'm going to.'

I cut him off. 'I couldn't agree with you more mate,' I nodded my head. 'But it can be dealt with afterwards – Not now,' I was shaking my head at him firmly. 'Besides which, if we're going to do anything then we're going to plan it properly. Not go in there like a couple of fuckin' cowboys alright.'

'Alright Chopper,' he agreed nodding as he did so, a little calmer now. 'But they are going to pay.'

'Ain't that the truth brother,' I told him half-smiling. 'Come on Prey. I bet Claire never thought to phone Michael, his lad.'

Even though Michael had moved out a couple of years back now and rarely kept in contact with his father, it was only right that he was informed of his father's critical condition.

'Alright. I'll give him ring now. He might as well stay put for now until we hear any more,' Prey stated. 'I'll give Jonah a ring also. It's only right that he should know also.'

Morning had arrived and the five of us still sat lounging around the waiting room. I looked over to Claire, who had her head lay on Donna's lap asleep. 'Is she alright?'

'She'll be alright,' Donna smiled at me. 'Let's just hope that Steve is alright.'

'I just wish that I could see him,' I told her shaking my head.

Just then Dr. Greenwood walked into the waiting room along with another doctor trailing behind. 'I'm just about to clock off my shift,' he told us yawning, as Claire awoke at the mere sound of his voice. 'This is Dr. Moore. He'll keep you all informed as to how Steve's condition is throughout the day,' he smiled.

'Can't we see him now?' I asked pleadingly.

'You shouldn't really,' he sighed shaking his head. 'I'll tell you what though; you and Miss Russell can have five minutes with him.'

'Thanks a lot,' I said smiling over at Claire who was already on her feet.

We were both led through to intensive care and through into a private secluded room where they had Steve.

'Oh my God,' I gasped, stood there shocked at the sight before me. 'Just what have they gone and done...'

Claire instantly burst into tears as Steve simply lay there still, unconsciously, oblivious to his surrounding's. He seemed to have tubes and pipes coming from just about everywhere. His face was unrecognisable with all the stitches and swelling, not to mention the deep purple and black bruising that seemed to swell endlessly around his matted hairline.

237

His right arm and legs had been plastered hanging above him. He looked in such a state that I found it hard to comprehend that it was actually Steve lay there. Although thinking about it, I was just trying my best to convince myself that it wasn't. I placed my arm around Claire as we both approached the bed towards him.

'Oh Chopper – Just look at what they did to him,' she sobbed heavily, as she gently placed her hand around his swollen one.

'I just can't believe it... I just can't...' I kept repeating.

'Chopper... You've got to promise me something,' Claire said staring coldly at me. It almost changed her angelic appearance, as she glanced briefly back at Steve.

'Anything Claire,' I told her honestly.

'Promise me that you'll make them pay for this,' she said as the tears began uncontrollably rolling down her face.

'They will,' I nodded, as cold punishable images flowed through my mind. 'Believe me they will.'

Pemberton and Daikin were waiting as we returned back to the waiting room.

I glanced at Prey and shook my head at him. 'It's bad mate – very bad.'

'How he is doing?' Daikin asked warmly.

'He's a fuckin' mess – That's how he is,' I said, ignoring his kindness.

'Alright – Now are you going to tell us what happened? Or at least what you seem to think happened miss,' Pemberton said staring at her.

'It all happened so quickly that it's hard to remember exactly,' she said as Donna and Kathy put their arms around her. 'I know that there were seven of them beating him. All of them were trying to kill him – then... Then came the main one again,' she stared at the two officers. 'Then he threw the table on top of Steve.'

'Is that so?' sighed Pemberton.

'Yes it is. And no one did anything to help him,' she screamed the last part at him, shaking her head frantically. 'Even the landlord turned away laughing.'

'Well from what we hear, is that your boyfriend was quite abusive on his way out of the establishment towards everybody – shouting and swearing at them. Really was in a drunken state.'

238

'You fuckin' what – You *fuckin'*...' Claire looked like she about to lose it.

'They also say that they could hear a lot of noise outside – banging about. Plant pots were smashing and so forth. The first anybody knew anything was when the ambulance arrived,' Pemberon smirked. 'Oh and he should consider himself lucky as the landlord isn't going to press charges against for the damage outside of his pub.'

'You fuckin' pigs...' she yelled breaking free from the two girls stomping right up into Pemberton's face. 'Just how the fuck did it happen then? You saying that he fell over for fucks sake,' she snapped at him.

'More than likely,' he responded by smiling at her. 'The landlord says that the two of you were both drinking very heavily.'

'Are you being fuckin' serious,' I snapped back at him. 'Don't talk crap for fucks sake.'

'Could you identify the men miss?' Daikin asked calmly.

'Go and fuck yourselves,' she screamed at them, I'd never seen her like this before.

'I don't appreciate your tone or manners miss...' Pemberton said sarcastically.

'I don't give a flying fuck what you appreciate you couple of pathetic wankers. Now why don't you get the fuck out of my sight – I can't help a couple of fuckin' no good tossers like you,' she had completely lost it.

'You heard her boys,' Prey grinned. 'I think it's time that you left now.'

Pemberton merely grunted turning to leave, as Daikin shook his head apologetically at us, glancing at his partner. 'We'll ignore those comments for now as we realise that you're upset,' Pemberton added looking back over his shoulder as he stormed off towards the exit.

'Fuck off,' she screamed after them.

'Come on Claire,' said Donna taking her arm.

'You heard her boys,' added Prey smiling as he did.

'Hello there,' it was Dr. Greenwood returning on his shift.

'Any change doc?' I asked, Claire by my side.

'A little,' he smiled. 'Now he's still in a coma, but he seems to have stabilised a hell of a lot more and appears to be reacting to the medication.'

'Can we go in and see him?' Prey asked eagerly.

'That's the reason why I've come to see you,' he smiled. 'I think as he has started to react to the medication, I think that if he hears familiar voices it may also help him.'

'Really,' Claire returned the doctor's smile.

We all took off down the corridor following Dr. Greenwood. 'I'll speak with the sister to allow you extra time in there. Although if you're planning on staying around I would suggest a bed and breakfast,' he told us. 'I mean we can't be at all certain just how long Steve will be in this state.'

'We were staying at The Valley Guesthouse,' Claire told him. 'Although I haven't called them since we were brought here.'

'I know the place,' he said smiling. 'I know the family that runs it. I tell you what I'll give them a ring now and explain the situation to them. Hopefully I may be able to sort something out for you.'

'Thanks a lot doc,' I said gratefully to him.

'No problem,' he smiled. 'Right there you go,' he added as we arrived at intensive care.

You could see their reactions as we walked into Steve's room, as I'd experienced the same thing that very morning.

'Oh Steve,' Donna cried out falling to his bedside holding his hand.

'What have they done to him Chopper?' Prey asked dumbfounded, standing next to me.

'Hi'ya Steve – How are you my love?' Claire said, kissing his swollen lips slightly.

'Alright mate – Y'know who this is,' I called out.

'Hi'ya Steve it's Kathy here,' she said placing her hand to his bruised face.

'It's me old man,' Prey said, a little uneasily. 'I told you before that you were having too much holiday time. So you better come back to us soon mate,' he smiled looking at him. 'He's just so still,' Prey stared at me.

I merely nodded back at him whilst the girls all began talking away with him lay there deep in his coma.

In the main entrance as we were leaving the hospital to head for the guesthouse, stood clear as day, two plain clothed officers waiting for us.

'Excuse me – Are you Miss Russell?' the smaller of the two enquired.

'Yes,' she answered.

'Good evening,' he said politely. 'I'm Detective Harlow and this is my partner Detective Bowe. How is Mr. Griffin?'

'He's still unconscious,' Claire shook her head at them. 'I thought that you lot didn't give a shit,' she snapped at them both.

'Well it's only just been brought to our attention,' Bowe stated.

'I told the other two everything that I knew,' she confirmed.

'Not that they give a shit though,' Donna snapped. 'They reckon he fell over.'

'That's what we were told also,' Harlow added. 'We heard that you were both heavily drinking.'

'Then what,' I sneered at them both. 'He fell in front of a bull dozer in the car park.'

'We don't take kindly to that sort of attitude son,' Bowe said flatly, staring at me.

'I don't give a shit what you take kindly too,' I snarled back again holding his glare.

'Could you spot any of the people you have accused from a line up?' Harlow asked Claire.

'Why? Have you arrested someone?' Prey asked smiling knowingly at them.

'No – Why?' he looked at Prey returning the smile as he did so in a knowing way. 'And just who are you two anyway?'

'That's not important who we are boys,' he told him firmly.

'What's the sudden interest?' I asked them both. 'You boys aren't interested in catching anybody for this.'

'Sorry miss could you...' Harlow tried his best to ignore both Prey and myself.

'No I couldn't help you,' she said coldly. 'Like you said – he probably fell over.'

'Do you lot know who done this?' I asked curious to why they'd showed up.

'No – But we don't want any...' Bowe began to say.

'Any what?' I asked.

'Any fucking trouble from you Chorlton,' Harlow snarled back at me. 'This is a peaceful area. We don't want any kind of your trouble around here.'

'So I imagine that y'know all of our names then. Funny how you just made out that you didn't,' Prey grinned.

'Yes we do O'Prey,' Bowe scowled at Prey. 'And we know all about you lot. Got yourselves quite a record between the two of you, haven't you.'

'Is that so?' I said smiling.

'And what has any of this got to do with Steve?' Claire injected, seething at the two of them.

'Hopefully nothing Miss,' Bowe said, looking at her then turning to the two of us. 'We're warning you two now. Do not go getting yourselves any idea's about trying to take the law into your own hands here lads.'

'Listen you two,' Prey growled menacingly. 'We are 'ere for ar' mate whose lay unconscious back there. Now I think I've heard just about enough bullshit from the two of you for one night. So if you're finished we're leaving.'

'Go right ahead,' Harlow smiled. 'But you have been warned.'

Just as we all walked through the doors feeling the glares of the two detectives as we passed. 'Oh by the way – Chopper ain't it?' Bowe grinned at me as I stared at him shaking my head.

'And Prey,' Harlow added, 'Stevenson and Walsh said to say hello. They say they'll be seeing you when you get back to Manchester.'

'Tell them we both said hello too,' I smiled back at them, realising where they'd been able to find out so much information on us.

A week had passed since Steve had been admitted to the hospital; he still remained in a coma. We'd all spent each day sitting around his bed all talking to him and trying our best to reach him. The week had been exhausting for all of us.

'I don't know. I just don't know,' I sighed deeply, sat in the waiting room that had become such familiar surroundings to us.

'He's just got to be alright... Daft old bugger that he is,' Prey smiled, trying to reassure me.

'Y'know Prey,' I said looking at him. 'We're going to have to watch how we handle this.'

'We know what we're going to do,' he said staring back coldly at me.

'Look Prey – We just can't walk in there and pop these fuckers,' I sighed, even though that's exactly what we wanted to do. 'I mean them two turning up like that the other night. And just how the fuck did Stevenson and Walsh know about Steve being in 'ere?'

'They're probably shitting themselves,' Prey laughed. 'Country fuckin' bumpkin coppers. Stevenson probably fed them all kinds of shit on us.'

'Probably... But that wasn't really my point,' I told him.

'What is then?'

'The point about just how did Stevenson know that we was 'ere in the first place,' I said looking straight into his eyes.

'What are you getting at Chopper?' he asked, shaking his head at me.

'I'm not exactly sure mate,' I sighed. 'It's been bothering me all week though… Those guys back there, really have got it in for us, haven't they?'

'People back at the estate would have heard about it Chopper,' he shook his head at me. 'They'll have just over heard about it. Y'know how it is.'

'Probably,' I said, although not that convinced. 'Anyway – How are things back at the estate?' I then asked to try and change the subject.

'Fine – I spoke with Jonah earlier. He was the only one that I could get hold of,' he smiled at me. 'He says not to worry about a thing… that everything is running sweet mate. Y'know that Jonah really is a sound lad isn't he? He's dependable as fuck.'

'I know he is,' I replied. 'Remember if it hadn't been for him then we wouldn't have even met Steve,' I stated, smiling at the thought of Jonah, as we'd become really close over the last couple of years.

'Yeah that's so fuckin' true. He's certainly is a true asset to the crew,' Prey smiled knowingly.

As I sat there completely awake beside the bed, I watched as Donna peacefully slept breathing in the night's calm air. We'd all returned back to The Valley Guesthouse late Saturday night, but I found myself over-tired and not able to settle down.

Although exhausted, my mind was racing. Thoughts of Steve – Thoughts of the business – Thoughts of life in general…

I began pacing the bedroom, staring out into the night's darkened sky then my eyes fell upon my clothes just thrown over the back of the chair.

Without thinking I began to dress. I kissed Donna's forehead before walking to the door, pausing to look at her once more… I then smiled before leaving.

The night's air was cool against my skin. You could see my breath as I began to walk in no particular direction.

I began walking and walking and continuing to walk with no destination in mind. I didn't even know the area were I was wandering so aimlessly through its deserted streets.

The night air was of complete calm and the air felt so clear to breathe. My thoughts were with Steve as I watched the shimmering stars flickering high above in the vast sheet of blackness. Memories began flashing through my mind as I continued to wander the streets.

I had no idea how long I'd been out there walking the streets, but I suddenly found myself stopping for no apparent reason. All that I knew was that something felt familiar as I found myself staring at the building before me. It was the hospital. I waltzed straight through the main entrance, I headed for intensive care.

'Mr. Chorlton – Billy – Excuse me,' it was the night sister.

Her words fell on deaf ears as I was gazing through the window into Steve's room. 'Sorry...' I said coming round.

'Can I help you?' she asked warmly smiling at me. 'It's very late you know.'

'I'm sorry. I know it is,' I said turning back, looking at Steve.

She could read the sadness written clearly over my face. 'Would you like to go and sit with him?'

'Really... Could I?'

'It's not really allowed – But...' she smiled at me.

'Thanks – Really, thanks a lot,' I told her smiling; thinking just how fantastic all the staff had been that week.

'You alright mate?' I asked walking through the door to his room. 'It's me,' I said pulling up a chair to his bed.

'It's late y'know. But I just couldn't get my head down at all. The sister said it was alright to come and sit with you. I hope that you don't mind mate.' I told him placing my hand on top of his.

'Y'know I was just wandering the streets thinking about all of the mad shit that we've got up to since meeting you,' I was smiling at him lay there so still.

'Y'know what mate? It really has been mad the last few years hasn't it? I know that I haven't known you that long really. But you mean so much to me. To all of us.'

'Y'know some of the shit that we've done together has been so crazy. Y'know like with Paddy and shit,' I said, grinning at the mere thought of that night. 'But only true friends could do that sort of things y'know.'

'I mean – That's why you can't go leaving us now Steve. You just got to come back to us. We've still got the rest of our lives together yet mate. Y'know we always take the piss – Calling you an old bastard. But you're not that old – Not yet anyway,' I observed his stillness then dropped my head again.

I looked up again, expecting to see that usual grin of his when we took the piss out of each other – But nothing came. I wondered just what was going through his mind as I sat there... Could he hear me? Was he able to even think?

'So anyway mate,' I began to stroke the recent scar on my face. 'You remember what you said recently that you couldn't leave me alone for just one night. Well just look at you now, eh? It looks like when you come back to us we'll have to stick by each other's side – Won't we?'

I held onto his hand as I dropped my head again, finding it uneasy to look at him in the condition that he was. 'You remember how once you told me that you considered me like your son. Well I've never told you – But I've always thought of you as my old man,' I began smiling at him.

'Y'know my old man never gave a shit about me or what I got up to... I don't even see him anymore. All he ever gave a shit about was whether or not I was out of the way,' I sniffed.

'But with you Steve, it was different,' I held his hand tighter. 'You took an interest in me. I know I've done bad things in life. But it don't make me a bad lad. I've just always had my own game plan in life and you understood that in me. That's why you can't leave me. Not now,' I pleaded, staring directly at him.

'You mean more to me than my old man ever meant to me. I need you to be around for me Steve. You just can't give up now – please – please Steve – please,' as I dropped my head, I saw a tear bounce from the floor.

I then began staring aimlessly at the polished hospital floor shaking my head. Feeling the tears swelling as trying my best to sniff them back

I held onto Steve's hand and continued to stare at the floor feeling myself beginning to drift off... The weight around my eyes felt like lead... All was becoming a blur as I began to drift away into the dead of night. That's when I was sure that I felt something... Did I? I wasn't sure if I was asleep or not.

I forced open my eyes, and found myself still facing the floor. As I tried my best to focus through the blur... I must have been dreaming... Then again... I felt it again... A twitch... I was certain of it.

This time though I felt it for certain – it was Steve's left hand... And again. I shot up and stared at him.

'Steve... Can you hear me? Steve...' My voice was in fluster as his hand twitched again.

246

I pinched my arm stupidly just to make sure I was actually awake and this wasn't merely a dream.

'Nurse – nurse – somebody – anybody please,' I called out, only it didn't seem like my voice leaving my mouth.

Just then the sister rushed into the room, as I was looking frantically from her to Steve. She rushed over to him and began checking him.

'Mr. Griffin... Can you hear me...? Mr. Griffin...' she called to him.

Then came a flutter from his eyes as I held his hand tighter still... Praying properly for probably the first time in my entire life as I closed my eyes and listened to the nurse call his name then opening my eyes I stared at Steve. His eyes fluttered again as they struggled to open... Then a weak smile came from his swollen bruised lips.

Steve had under gone the past three months of intensive physiotherapy since coming out of his coma. He'd sent Prey and myself straight home once he'd come round fully, telling us that it was more important to see that things back in Manchester didn't skip a beat. Claire had remained by his side throughout his road to recovery. We'd all continued to visit him whenever possible and he looked better with each visit.

All the doctor's and nurse's had been more than pleased with the speed of his recovery. It was like Dr. Greenwood had said in the beginning, Steve was strong willed in both character and strength.

Although Steve had told us that the food alone in the hospital gave him the strength and will he needed to get the fuck out of there as soon as possible.

We'd all missed having the old man around, although we were more than thankful that he was at least with us. I don't know how people, who have to go years with a loved or cared one in a coma... actually manage. The week that Steve had remained unconscious had drained me fully.

But it was December the twenty first as Prey and I both headed through the corridors of the hospital towards Steve's ward. Only this time the visit was of a different nature – As Steve had been given the all clear to come home.

'We're heading straight for Chan's right?' Steve enquired cheerfully from the backseat; Claire sat cuddled up next to him.

248

'Why?' I laughed. 'Didn't you like the food back there or something? I heard that hospital food was supposed to be good these days,' I was grinning at him as Prey laughed.

'That's 'cause you never go to fuckin' hospital Chopper,' he smiled. 'I think that old Hassid works full time for you back at the estate.'

'Ain't that the truth,' Prey agreed.

'Who's Hassid?' Claire asked.

'Let's just say that he's like Chopper's personal doctor,' Steve told her. 'I think Chopper's got some kind of phobia about hospital, as he never goes himself to be treated.'

'No – it's not that – it's – I just...' I trailed off as everybody began laughing at my pathetic attempt to defend myself.

'See,' Steve grinned at me.

'Ah Steve – My good man,' Chan greeted us warmly as we walked through into his restaurant. 'You look very good – Very well. How you feel?' he smiled at Steve holding him self steady with his walking stick.

'I'm feeling good Chan. A hell of a lot better than I did a few months back now,' He smiled joyously at the old man. 'I can't wait for some of your food though Chan. I'm craving for a decent bit of scran as these little scallywags put it,' he winked at the older man.

'Looks like everybody's 'ere Steve,' I said nodding to the tables that Chan had put together to form one huge table overlooking China Town itself.

All of the main crew was there... all but Scotty that was. I couldn't see him for some reason.

'Come 'ere Steve,' it was Jonah who walked up and hugged him.

'Jonah my good lad,' he smiled warmly at him then smirked. 'Are you keeping yourself out of trouble?' he laughed.

'No more than you are,' he replied, as just then all girls surrounded Steve and began making a fuss of him and kissing him.

'Easy... Easy girls,' Steve laughed joylessly. 'Damn – I should be put in hospital more often.'

'Don't go saying things like that Steve,' Donna said taking his arm leading him to the table.

'So how are you feeling then?' Kathy asked at his other side.

'I'm fine – Honestly. You've all got to stop making a fuss of me,' he smiled, although I knew that he loved every minute of it really.

'Here we go,' Chan said popping open the first bottle of champagne. 'Welcome home Steve.'

'Where the fuck is Scotty?' I asked Jonah quietly.

'He said that he didn't really know Steve and that he had something he had to sort out,' he informed me.

'You fuckin' what!'

'He reckons that Steve is just your partner with Macreedy's,' he whispered back to me.

'It makes no difference whatsoever what he thinks Steve is,' I snapped. 'Fact of the matter is that he was invited and he should have come along. I just don't know what the fuck to do with him these days.'

'Don't worry about it tonight Chopper,' he shook his head at me. 'We've got the old man back with us, so let's just have a good time. Oh and Chop, when you decide on what you're going to do about what happened. You be sure to invite me to that party – You hear?' he smirked knowingly at me.

'No problem mate,' I told him. 'You're right as well – Fuck Scotty for tonight,'

Although deep down I'd been disappointed that he hadn't come along tonight. No matter what he thought Steve was to us he should have shown some respect as he'd been invited.

'You alright Steve,' I asked as the first of the dishes were brought over.

'Much better now the food's arrived mate,' he smiled winking at me.

'My cooks prepare many good dishes for you all tonight,' Chan smiled as the waiters began placing the food onto the table.

'Fantastic,' Steve declared smiling as he did.

'So tell us Steve,' Kezlo asked, 'just what was it that brought you out of the coma?'

'Well you see mate,' he laughed glancing in my direction then looked at everybody. 'I just had to get Chopper to shut the fuck up babbling pure and utter shite next to my bed.'

Everybody roared with laughter as I glared at him. 'Bastard.'

'I mean it was the middle of the fuckin' night and he just wouldn't shut the fuck up... I mean a man has got to get his sleep – Right,' he was laughing along with everybody else.

250

'You're a bastard,' I told him smiling as he just winked at me.

Things carried on like this for a few hours as we all sat there. We were all eating and drinking – and generally enjoying each others company. I looked around and smiled at the situation in hand – it was a good night – and it was even better to have Steve home with us I thought to myself as I pushed my chair back.

'Chopper wait up,' It was Steve hobbling along on his walking stick, as I was making my way through into the toilet.

'You havin' a good time pal?' I smiled as we both disappeared into the toilet.

'Course – I'm having a quality night,' he confirmed, as we both unzipped.

'Ahhh - Shit that feels good,' he sighed, as the hot stream of piss glided down towards the porcelain basin.

'I bet it does mate,' I laughed at him. 'You've been clean in hospital; I bet that champer's tastes well sweet... Don't it?'

'Tell me about it,' he smirked. 'You sort that thing out for me that I asked for mate?'

'Oh shit mate,' I appeared startled.

'What... What... You didn't forget... Did you?' he had panic in his voice as I began smiling at him.

'You little twat,' he laughed; now seeing the funny side of it.

'Of course I didn't forget,psl,' I sniggered at him. 'Are you sure that you still want to go ahead with this though?'

'Why not,' he smiled at me as we both washed our hands and dried them on the towel before walking back out into the restaurant.

As the two of us approached the table, Prey rose clinking his glass to get everybody's attention. All fell silent as we sat down leaving Prey stood there. 'Alright everybody, time for a bit of a speech,' he smiled looking at Steve.

'Here we go again,' Steve laughed.

'Welcome home from everybody,' he said and then sat back down as everybody began cheering.

Rising from my seat and looking at Prey shaking my head laughing. 'Well – Either you can't shut Prey the fuck up or he's certainly knows how to keep it short and sweet, eh?'

'You got something to add?' Prey grinned.

'Well it'll be hard after your huge effort,' I informed him. 'Look – I ain't too good at this sort of shit, but I'll give it a go.

251

Right, we are here tonight to celebrate the return of our good friend. And it sure feels good to see you 'ere mate rather than lay in that hospital bed,' I announced as everybody clapped. 'But I just want you to know that you are more than a mere friend,' I said, raising my glass to him. 'You are family... That's the way it will always be – I thank you Steve.'

Everybody began clapping, cheering and whistling as Steve hugged me. I began clinking my glass again.

'Alright Chopper you've done your bit,' Prey laughed. 'Don't go kissing his arse anymore than you have to.'

'No listen – This is important,' I told them all. 'There's one more thing that needs saying. Only I'll leave this part to Steve,' I added, sitting back down as Steve rose from his seat.

'What is it Steve?' Claire asked as he smiled at her.

'I just want to thank you all for this – For everything really,' he smiled nodding to us all. 'We've only really known each other for a short while but it really does feel like I've known you all for way too many years now. I've been accepted by all of you as a friend and as family,' he smiled at Prey and me. 'With recent events of what happened to me... It made me realise just how important life really is. I had a hell of a lot of time in these last few months holed up eating all that crap hospital food,' he laughed turning and grinning at Chan.

'Anyway, if it hadn't been for the support that I had whilst in hospital,' he looked at everybody. 'Also filled with the knowledge that I'd return home to the same kind of support. Well to honest with you...' he sighed deeply then smiled. 'I honestly don't think that I would have made it.'

He raised his glass to us. 'That's the truth you know – So I'd just like to take this opportunity to thank you all for this.'

We all began clapping and cheering for him. 'Wait – Please wait one minute,' he continued. 'I know you're probably thinking – Alright, enough is enough old man. You've said your bit,' he laughed as we all did.

'But there really is one more thing that I need to do. For the whole duration of my stay in hospital there was one person. One very special person that is. She stayed by my side throughout out it all,' he took Claire's hand and looked at her smiling.

'I owe so much to this girl, who I love so much,' he looked at Claire who had a tear rolling down her face. 'I know I'm just an old bastard that really doesn't deserve to have her by my side,' he smiled then removed something from his pocket.

252

'But it would be a great honour if...' he snapped open the small silk box revealing the diamond ring that he'd asked for me to purchase a couple of days ago now.

'Claire – Would you do me the honour of becoming my wife?' he asked as the whole table fell into complete silence.

Tears began to roll down Claire's face. 'Oh Steve... I... I Just...' she couldn't find her words.

'It's alright Claire if you don't wa...' Steve was saying.

She cut him off throwing herself at him. 'Of course I will – Of course I'll marry you Steve,' she kissed him passionately as the whole table erupted into a frenzy of celebrations.

'Into yet another year eh,' Prey said to the two of us as he returned from the kitchen. 'They sure seem to come round quickly these days – Don't they?' he added throwing a couple of beers at us.

Christmas and New Year had passed us in similar fashion as always. Although we'd spent a lot more time with each other. It had been little Sean's first Christmas although he obviously didn't have a clue what it was all about. He'd been spoilt rotten by all of us and bought way too many presents.

We'd spent the morning round at Prey's going over our current affairs, what plans lay ahead of us for that year. Also, we'd covered our current financial situation which was extremely fucking good. In fact so good that it was just one of the things that needed addressing today.

'Y'know with all the money we've got stashed away we're going to have to consider the London shop y'know,' I confirmed.

'Chopper's right,' Steve nodded. 'Because unless we plan to move abroad to sunnier climates and open ourselves a bar or something like that, you know, just kick back and enjoy life.' He shook his head now, 'Then having all the cash stashed away like we have just ain't no good over here unless we start laundering it.'

'I agree with both of you,' Prey laughed. 'Although I do like the sound of that kicking back abroad bit,' he grinned at the two of us.

'In'it mate,' I agreed smiling. 'I'd never thought of us doing something like that.'

'It was meant as a hypothetical joke,' Steve said seriously.

'Still sounds alright to me though,' I laughed back at his serious nature.

'Alright we're agreed though. About the London store?' Steve said looking at the two of now both lost in thought on setting something up abroad. 'Snap out of it you will you.'

'Sorry mate,' Prey smiled at him. 'Yeah we're agreed. We'll look into it next month, alright. Besides we got to concentrate on this weekend first.'

'I know. Are you lads still sure about doing it this weekend?' Steve enquired shaking his head with an air of uncertainty.

'Definitely,' I told him. 'Look I got it all planned out.'

'But it's Sean's christening on Sunday though,' Steve announced.

'I know it is, but we booked it for January 7th a while back now,' Prey said. 'When Chopper came up with how we was going to do this then it just made even more sense to do it Saturday night.'

'And Chan's agreed also?' Steve asked sipping his beer.

'Of course he has,' I smiled. 'Once he knew what we had planned, he was only too pleased that he could help in some way.'

'What if something goes wrong over that way?' Steve asked. 'Y'know… with it being the christening.'

'Look, will you stop worrying old man,' I laughed at the way he was carrying on. 'Those fuckers deserve everything we're going to give 'em after what they done to you.'

'I know they do,' Steve sighed. 'I still don't want either of you two or anyone else for that matter to go shooting them though,' he added staring at the two of us.

'We promised you – Didn't we,' Prey said tutting, as that was what we'd originally wanted to do them. 'Besides you're right it would attract way too much heat.'

'It's not that I don't want them dead… I mean I fuckin' do,' he sneered. 'But the last thing I need is to lose you two. They'll be all over this one in the aftermath.'

'Don't worry… with my little plan they'll be kicking themselves afterwards,' I told him.

'Yeah we'll just fuck them up real good for you Steve,' Prey smiled at Steve.

'And you're sure that you know who they are?' he asked.

'We've been over this old man,' I said, shaking my head at him. 'Claire took me and Prey to the boozer. She pointed 'em out to us from the car park.'

'In'it,' Prey smirked knowingly.

'I had a hard fuckin' job trying to keep Prey in the car,' I laughed again. 'He wanted to pop them all there and then.'

'I just wish that I could come along with you,' Steve sighed.

'Fuck that old man,' I stared at him. 'You're not in any shape to go doing shit like that yet.'

'Alright pops,' he smiled warmly at me. 'Who's in then?'

'Well to be honest only Sleeper and Eazy know about it,' Prey told him.

'You're kidding right?' Steve said startled.

'No,' I smiled. 'It's all part of the plan. You see them two are bringing the vans with them for the job.'

'How the fuck do you know everybody's going to be up for it then?' he asked all bemused.

'Oh they will be,' I grinned at him.

'Do you reckon that this is going to work Chopper?' he then asked.

'Child's play mate,' I smirked as all three of us began laughing.

FIFTY

'I've got to get some more money Jackie,' Scotty declared, staring coldly at her. 'We need more money,' he then snapped at her, as he was just about to finish tooting the rest of his speedball mix of both crack cocaine and heroin that they'd now moved onto. This was a lethal mixture of the ultimate uppers and downers all in one hit – but it meant that the rocks lasted longer.

'I know Scotty,' she sighed. 'Since you've had me working the street for you... I'm bringing in what extra I can.'

Scotty had Jackie working Chorlton Street area as a prostitute for the last few months now. The money he made as a lieutenant for the crew just wasn't lasting anymore. The weekly bonus he used to receive from Stevenson and Walsh had turned monthly which just wasn't any fucking use to him at all. But he couldn't stop with them as they well and truly had him by the balls now. He couldn't run, as they'd use their resources to track him down.

He'd broken down one night telling Jackie about what he had been doing. He told her how he felt so ashamed that he was giving up information on his friends. He just couldn't win. All that he wanted was for it all to disappear.

Things had been going from bad to worse with his habit. He was hardly at the flat with Kezlo anymore as his intake of drugs had become so bad.

He was only just managing to keep up with his work as a lieutenant. Although saying that, he hadn't received any complaints from either Chopper or Prey. He was just so tired these days from all the gear they were doing.

The last thing he'd wanted to do was put Jackie on the street. But she was caning way too much gear for her not to be making any money also. They just needed the money so badly nowadays.

'But what the fuck can we do about it?' he suddenly yelled at her making her jump.

'You'll think of something Scotty, you always do,' she said smiling weakly at him. 'I can't work street side during the day as well... y'know that I'll be seen.'

'I know that,' he sneered back at her.

'Can't you give them some more information?' she asked feebly of him.

'No... no... no I can't do that,' he called out shaking his head frantically. 'They'll kill me... They'll fuckin' kill me... Oh my God. Just what was I thinking back then,' he had his face buried in his hands.

'You only did what you had to Scotty,' she tried reassuring him.

'Fuck that – we can – *you can*...' he screamed at her again as he she butted in stopping him in his tracks.

'You could always work the street with me,' said Jackie as she dropped her head. 'Y'know... like a rent boy.' She was looking up at him and immediately regretting what she'd just suggested.

Scotty eyes had turned to pure rage, shaking with the sheer madness that was about to explode. 'You fuckin' whore – What did you just fuckin say? You fuckin' piece of no good trash – *you fuckin'*...' he was screaming at her.

'I'm sorry... I'm *so*...' she began to plead as he stepped across the room and threw the back of his right hand across her left cheek, throwing her across the back of the settee with ease.

'Scotty please... *no*...' she appealed as he began stamping violently with his personal hatred towards himself – that was now being inflicted upon her, his eyes filled with the insanity domineering them.

'Fuckin' slag – You fuckin' no good whore... Smoke all my fuckin' gear you *no good cunt*,' he was screaming at her like a deranged mad man as he kicked and punched her, in the violent onslaught he brought down upon her as she scrunched into a ball to try and protect herself.

258

'Scotty... Please... *Please stop*,' she was whimpering her plea's with him as he just continued as though not hearing her cries for help.

She caught a glimpse of his face... He was already at breaking point. She knew it as she saw his rage... Then he crossed that final point.

'Call me a fuckin' rent boy – me – *me* - Scotty *O'Conner* a fuckin' *rent boy* you fuckin' little *slut*,' he screamed as he pulled his handgun from his jacket thrown over the settee still screaming.

'No... No... *You can't*... *No*...' Jackie was crying hysterically as she saw him go at her with the gun.

'Well why don't you suck on this you fuckin' *cock sucking slag*,' he yelled at her as he then shoved the gun into her mouth staring at her with demented eyes – sneering as he did so.

He glared at her with nothing but pure hatred... Then he stared at the gun... Then back to her... Then suddenly something changed in those eyes of his as he pulled the gun from her mouth and stared at it for what seemed like a very long time.

'I've got it – I've got it,' he said almost gleefully with himself. 'I know what I'll do Jackie,' he now seemed oblivious to his beaten girlfriend lay below him.

'I sorry Scotty... *I'm so sorry*...' she sobbed uncontrollably still tightly scrunched up in a ball.

'It's alright – Everything will be alright,' he said staring at her as the reality of what he'd just finished inflicting upon her finally hit him. He began pulling her to him dropping the gun to the floor. He held her tightly as he could as he could not bare to witness to the brutal damage he'd just inflicted so viscously. 'Don't you worry about a thing girl... Everything's going to be alright.'

This Saturday Chopper?' Jonah asked looking at me as the two of us were sat drinking in Henry's bar out of the way.

'Y'know mate,' I smiled at him, 'kind of like a pre-christening party for little Sean.'

'You sure that's all it is?' he asked staring at me.

'What's that supposed to mean then?'

'C'mon Chopper. Steve's been out of hospital a few weeks now,' he smiled knowingly at me. 'Is it payback time or what?'

'Alright... listen up,' I said staring straight at him. 'None of the crew knows anything about this at all. None of them mate... so it stays that way you hear me.'

'Sweet mate.'

'Right, this is how we're going to do it,' I looked around to ensure we were out of ear shot. 'As far as the crew will know we're meeting at Chan's for a private party at six thirty. All the birds are invited also. Only thing is we're not dining just then,' I said, smiling at him. 'We've booked Chan's for the entire night.'

'Let me get this right then. Chan is closing down for the private party we're having.' 'That's the one,' I laughed. 'We go through the front door then out of the back door into the waiting vans. All being well we'll get the job done and be back in town for twelve. Then we'll eat at Chan's.'

'I like it... I like it a lot Chopper.'

'Steve's not coming along and none of the lieutenant's will know about it until the actual night in question. Payback for Steve on Saturday night is going to be sweet – Ain't it?'

260

'What's going to be sweet on Saturday night?' Scotty asked who seemed to have appeared from nowhere staring at the two of us.

'What – er... oh nothing mate,' I said as he'd caught me off guard.

'What is it,' he snapped at me. 'Can't you trust me now?'

'What are you doing 'ere Scotty?' Jonah asked trying to change the subject.

'What? Am I not allowed to come for a drink now,' he then sneered back at Jonah.

'Course you are mate. Stop being a moody twat,' I laughed.

'So what's happening Saturday night?' he asked again.

'Just a meal at Chan's pal,' I replied smiling. 'Both you and Jackie are invited along. I was going to call you today. It's just a pre-party for little Sean.'

'Sounds good,' he then smiled. 'I'll look forward to it. Although – I don't know whether or not Jackie will be able to make it on Saturday night.'

'Why not?' Jonah asked him.

'She's got a job as a waitress in some Indian gaff in Rushulme,' he lied.

'What you drinking Scotty?' Jonah asked rising from the table.

'Just a beer mate,' he said as Jonah disappeared. 'Now Jonah's gone mate – I got a favour to ask you?' he looked at me.

'Sure – What is it?'

'Just a bit of cash Chopper,' he dropped his head slightly. 'Just until Saturday that's all mate. I'll be double sweet after that.'

'No problem,' I shrugged. 'How much do you need?'

'Five hundred,' he said watching for my reaction.

'How fuckin' much?' I gasped, expecting something more like fifty quid. 'What do you want that much for?' I enquired curiously.

'The cars fucked up again,' he sighed. 'I got some dough, but the garage says it's going to cost more than I've got Chopper.'

'Sweet mate,' I said shaking my head. 'I don't know why you don't get yourself a new motor mate. You make enough money for fucks sake. When do you need it?'

'Now,' he said a little too eagerly.

'What's with the rush pal?' I asked.

'I just need it sorted before the weekend, Chopper.'

I reached into my jacket pocket pulled out a wad of cash. ''Ere – It's just short of a monkey mate,' I said tossing it to him. 'It's all I got on me though.'

'Cheers mate,' he seemed too relax a little. 'It's only until Saturday, like I said after that I'll be double sweet,' he smiled at me and now appeared to relax completely.

'It's going to be a good night tonight, isn't it Chopper,' Donna said as we both lay in bed.

'Yeah it'll be alright,' I grinned to myself. The girls had no idea whatsoever what was really going down... or the crew for that matter. Steve was to explain everything to the girls once we left that night. As for the crew, well they'd be sweet with it anyway.

'I'm glad Lisa's going to be there,' Donna smiled. 'She's a really nice girl; I really get along well with her.'

'I know you do,' I said kissing her. 'We're thinking of opening a Macreedy's in London so we're going to talk with Lisa whilst she's 'ere about possible sites and so forth.'

'I didn't know about that,' she scowled at me.

'That's 'cause we only spoke about it the other day,' I told her. 'Apparently Lisa used to manage some clothes shop in Covent Garden a few years back. So she knows the area.'

'That should be alright you know,' Donna said sitting herself up on my chest.

'I know it should,' I laughed at her. 'That's why were going to it.'

'You fancy Lisa... Don't you Chopper?'

'Where the fuck did that suddenly come from?'

'I've seen the way you look at her.'

'What's that mean?'

'Nothing,' she pouted at me as she began to climb out of bed. 'I've got to get ready for work.'

'Oh no you don't – Come 'ere,' I said grabbing her waist and pulling her back in bed as she wriggled.

'What,' she giggled.

'Just what did you mean,' I said pinning her to the bed.

'I've seen the way the way you stare at her sometimes. I know you like her.' She squealed as I tickled her whilst she tried to break free.

'Not like that though you daft sod.'

'Are you sure Chopper?' she said playfully kissing me as I held her there.

'Why would I,' I said, pulling her nightshirt away leaving her lay beneath me naked.

'Chopper... Stop it,' she said playfully as she bit my nipples. 'I've got to get ready for work,' she said half heartily.

'Come on,' I began kissing her erect nipples.

'Stop it,' she moaned as she began to ease my boxer shorts off. 'I've got to get read...'

'Not for at least an hour,' I grinned easing myself into her. 'And that's coming from the boss remember.'

'That one there Jackie,' Scotty said as the two of them sat in his old Ford Escort on Stretford Road in Sale. The two had been up the entire night before smoking Chopper's loan.

'Are you sure about this Scotty?' Jackie asked lowering the sunglasses from her swollen and bruised eyes.

'What choice have we got?' he said looking at her, then immediately turning away so not to look at what he'd done to her.

'A post office though Scotty,' she stated.

'It's perfect Jackie,' he grinned pulling his handgun out. 'All you have to do is keep the engine running. I'll hold them up – take the money and then we'll take off.'

'I don't know though,' she said shaking her head. 'I just don't know.'

He swiped his hand at her making her flinch and jump nervously. 'You fuckin' what,' he screamed at her. 'You want to tell Chopper that you ain't got his dough tonight? Do you fuckin'...'

'Please – Don't hit me,' she began to cry.

'Look, I'm sorry,' he apologised, as he eased the car down the side road adjacent to the post office.

'Right just do as we've planned and everything will be alright,' he said kissing her swollen cheek.

'Alright Scotty – Let's do it,' she announced as bravely as she possibly could not wanting to let her man down. Although she was as scared as she'd ever been before in her life. But they were just so addicted to the gear now. And they needed the money so badly.

'Right I've been in 'ere before,' he told her. 'It's only a small one but they've got a bundle in there – I know it.'

'You just be careful Scotty – I love you.'

'Right let's do the last of this… Then we'll be set,' he smiled as he took out the bag containing the last tiny rock of crack cocaine concealed within it. 'It'll calm us both down a little.' He smirked as he loaded the pipe.

'Yeah you're right… That'll do it,' she replied eagerly, as she watched him lighting the pipe.

'We'll get some more straight after the job,' he coughed as the smoke left his nostrils and mouth.

'Give it to me,' she snapped at him as he blew the last of the smoke out.

'Ere'are finish it,' he said handing her the pipe climbing out of the car. 'Just be ready,' he added smiling dreamily from the hit of the potent drug.

She lit the remainder of the pipe as she watched him disappear round the corner. The pipe was practically dead.

'*Bastard*,' she screamed out as she saw him disappear around the corner of the post office.

Scotty's adrenaline was now racing along with that last hit he'd just taken as he stood outside the post office. The bell rang out as the door opened and he entered the small post office. The bell attracted no ones attention.

He looked around, only two customers. An elderly couple stood with their backs turned at the counter where a middle aged man, more than likely the manager, served them from behind the glass.

To his right was a young teenage girl behind the counter stacking cigarettes onto the shelves.

He glanced at the man behind the post office counter. He was a lot bigger in build to Scotty albeit he wasn't anticipating any foreseen problems.

No one took any notice of him as he pulled the ski mask over his face from beneath the navy baseball cap he was wearing. Now his face hidden completely as he pulled one of Smith and Wesson's finest's from the back of his jeans.

'Everybody stop whatever the fuck you're doing and put your arms in the air,' he suddenly yelled out startling everybody.

Everybody did as they were told, all with scared expressions on their faces at the prospect of being shot by this crazed lunatic pointing his gun in all directions.

'You... Behind the counter – *Oi girl,* are you listening to me? Move out of there. Now,' he said not taking his eyes from the post office counter.

'Please don't hurt me,' she sobbed as he pushed her into the old couple.

'What is it you want?' the manager asked.

'Well I ain't giving you three guess's am I mastermind,' he smirked.

'Please... Please,' the elderly gentleman said who was holding his wife tightly.

Scotty pointed his gun at them and suddenly was filled with guilt at doing so. 'Just keep quiet and nobody will get hurt.'

'Please my wife has a weak heart,' the elderly gentleman said as tears rolled down his wife's face.

'Alright then... You two sit on the floor with your backs to the wall,' he told the elderly couple, suddenly over-whelmed with the feeling of regret for putting them in this position.

As he watched them lower to the floor, the manager began to lower his right arm to the counter. He fumbled below the counter to find the silent alarm button. His index finger found it when...

'You behind the counter,' Scotty suddenly pointed the gun underneath the glass at the manager. 'What the fuck were you just doing you dickhead? Did you trip an alarm? Put those fuckin' arms where I can fuckin' see them you cunt,' he screamed at him.

'I wasn't doing anything – Please – Just take the money – Don't hurt anyone – Just leave us be,' he said full of panic at the gun pointed directly at him, and not at all sure whether or not he'd raised the alarm.

'Ere'are – Put it all in 'ere,' Scotty ordered pushing a black plastic bag under the glass.

The young girl was crying. 'Shut the fuck up will you,' he screamed at her as he watched the bag fill with the money.

'Hurry the fuck up – Now – Hurry – C'mon man I ain't got all fuckin day you cunt – Now – *C'mon...*' he yelled whilst at the same time he was thinking of all that glorious cash and just how many rocks he was going to be able to buy with it.

'Hurry up,' he repeated becoming irritable at how long it was taking. 'I ain't gonna tell you again you slow fuck.'

'Come on,' Jackie said looking at the clock in the car. 'What's taking so long... Come on Scotty.' She was tapping her fingers nervously on the steering wheel.

What the fuck is taking him so long she was thinking. Where is he? What's wrong? For fucks sake Scotty – Her head was beginning to ache.

'Fuck – Fuck – Shit – Hurry the fuck up...' she shouted out loud.

'What's that?' she suddenly said out loud to herself, forcing herself to listen. She could hear the police sirens drawing closer and louder as they did.

'Oh shit... Oh shit... *Fuck*... What am I doing here... *Oh no*. What was I thinking,' she was cursing herself as the sirens rang out louder and louder.

'I've got to get out of here... Oh no, he'll kill me... Fuck... Shit... What am I going to do... Scotty will kill me... *Fuck this*...' she said opening the driver's door.

The sirens were becoming deafening, as they surely must be upon them now.

'Fuck this,' she screamed again, slamming the door shut and easing the car into gear.

Jackie slowly eased out into the main road. She could see the blue lights flashing down the road heading towards her as she changed gear. She glanced once more over her shoulder... He still wasn't out yet.

'Fuck you Scotty O'Conner,' she screamed as loud as she possibly could as she drove away, abandoning him.

'What's that? – Shush – Shut the fuck up with that crying you stupid little whore,' he yelled at the young girl.

Everybody had heard the sirens drawing closer... everyone but Scotty that was, who'd been too occupied watching the bag bring filled with the money.

'Open the side door,' he shouted at the manager, 'just give me the bag or I'll shoot you and the fuckin' girl,' he said grabbing the bag.

He stopped and listened again. 'It was you – Wasn't it?' he stared at the manager as he now clearly heard the sirens becoming louder.

'I'll be back for you. You hear me you twat – Why'd do that? You've fucked up – I'll be back... I swear you're a *dead man*,' he screamed before slamming the gun into the manager's head watching him fall backwards.

With that Scotty turned and ran for the door, grabbing the handle and almost yanking the door from its hinges. As he ran into the street he found it already deserted and two police cars parked either side of him. Just then two more police cars skidded to a halt as four armed police exited the vechiles with accurate speed.

'Fuck off – All of you fuck off – *Leave me be...,*' he screamed out pointing his gun wildly as he eased himself backward to the side street and his car.

'Stop where you are son. There is no where to go,' one of the officers shouted out to him.

People at both ends were screaming as other officers were trying to calm the situation.

As he eased to the corner of the building he glanced smiling to where he thought Jackie and the car were. 'Bitch – Whore – *Fuckin conniving bitch,*' he screamed out loud as he realised that she had deserted him.

'Come on son. Put down your weapon down now,' one of the officers called out again, the one who aiming what looked to be a very serious semi-automatic rifle of some sort straight at his head.

Scotty looked around and could see four fully trained, armed officers pointing their guns at him.

His mind raced, as he stood there alone on the pavement. What the fuck had gone wrong? Why was all this happening to him he thought – It felt as though he wasn't even stood there but at the same time he was as everything around him began to spin uncontrollably as he didn't what he was going to do.

'Put down your weapon or we will be forced to shoot you,' another officer called out.

'Just leave me alone – Just go away – *Leave me alone,*' he cried out pathetically, as he started to break down... this wasn't happening.

What had gone so wrong for him?

'I will tell you once more then we will be forced to fire,' he called out again.

Scotty's sense's momentarily returned. 'Alright... Alright... *Don't shoot.* I'm putting it down,' he called out to them defeated.

'Put the gun on the floor and kick it away,' the armed officer called out. 'Then lay face down on the floor with your arms behind your head.'

268

Scotty did exactly as he was told to. He'd lost the battle and he knew it only too well as he lay there waiting for whatever was going to happen to him now.

'Come on son, give us your name,' the duty Sergeant said. 'You're doing yourself no favours here, are you? You little prick,' he snapped at Scotty.

They'd taken him to Sale police station. But he wasn't saying anything at all to them he couldn't just yet. He still needed to work things out before he opened his mouth.

'Come on… Give us you fucking name,' he shouted.

Scotty merely stood there, handcuffed, grinning at them all. His sniffed his arrogance at the duty Sergeant.

'You want it like then? Do you?' he smirked. 'Right, get his prints and get him checked out. Then throw him in the cells until we find out just who the fuck he is. It's obviously what he wants,' he sniffed back at Scotty mockingly.

'Fuck all you pigs,' he screamed defiantly as they dragged him away.

'Stop fuckin' struggling,' said the officer trying to get Scotty's prints.

'Fuck you,' Scotty spat only his second lot of words since his arrest.

Just as he spat the words a second officer stepped forward and slammed Scotty with his truncheon in his stomach as hard as possible.

He collapsed to the floor from the force of the blow taking the wind out of him.

'Right – You little shit,' the first officer said. 'Now we'll get your prints – you little fuck.'

'There you go,' the detention officer said throwing Scotty through the cell door.

Scotty pulled himself from the floor and sat himself onto the cold blue plastic mattress. The cell was just like any other he'd visited. So he made himself as comfortable as he possibly could do.

He sighed deeply then. 'Fuck – what a fuckin' nightmare this is,' he let the words fly from him, angered at being put into this situation.

Just what the fuck were you thinking? You daft twat he thought to himself. Well you're up the creek with no fucking paddle this time – Aren't you? Oh well, just tell them fuck all for now, they'll just have to find out the hard way who the fuck he was. He sighed again as he sat there thinking to himself.

What the fuck had gone so wrong in his life? His life was just so fucked up nowadays, compared to what it been in those early days. Just look at how things had turned out for fuck sake.

Chopper was one of the main lads around town. Full partner with Prey – he even had his own clothes shop for fucks sake. He'd achieved so much since they were just a couple of little scally's running about Manchester pulling down scores and bombin' the estate together.

He had to find a way out... But what could he do? There must be something – then it dawned on him... In fact two things had suddenly dawned on him. Now he sat back and relaxed from that point onwards, grinning knowingly as he did so.

Where's Scotty Jonah?' I asked looking at him as he shrugged. 'What about you Kezlo... You seen him?' I then asked looking to him as we arrived at Chan's.

'Been missing from the estate all day Chopper,' Jonah confirmed.

'He hasn't been home for time now Chopper,' Kezlo told me. 'Did he know about the meal Chopper?'

'Fuck yes,' I stated shaking my head. 'Both me and Jonah seen him the other day when he showed up at Henry's.'

'So he definitely knew,' Kezlo said, as his eye wandered over to Prey who was instructing the lieutenant's to follow him.

'Whatever... fuck him for now. I'll deal with him tomorrow. C'mon Kezlo,' I said nodding at Jonah. 'We ain't dining with the birds. Well not until later on that is.' I grinned.

'What? Where's Prey leading everyone Chopper?' he asked confused.

'It's payback time tonight,' I smirked taking off after the others towards the kitchen doors.

'Chopper – Chopper – Where are you going?' Donna called after me. 'What's going on?' She asked, now stood before me.

'I've got to go out for a while.'

'I'll explain everything Donna,' Steve told her taking her arm.

'Chopper,' she said as I turned and looked at her just before I was about to disapear through the kitchen door. 'Just be careful.' She added smiling at me.

'Aren't I always,' I grinned mischievously at her before taking off after the others.

Two Toyota Space Cruisers were waiting around for us at the rear of Chan's restaurant. The ten of us split off into to two groups of five into each cruiser.

'I like the vans Sleeper,' I nodded at him. 'I thought that you were just bringing transits with you.'

'Well, it's a bit of a journey,' he laughed back at me. 'I figured we may as well be comfortable.'

'Is Eazy going to be sweet in that one?'

'No problem mate,' he told me. 'Prey's in there also. He's going to go over the plan with Parksey, Kneildy and Johnny.'

'So I take it you're going to go over it with us then?' Diamond grinned at me.

'Yeah lads,' I said, 'I'm sorry about all the cloak and dagger shit. We just felt it would be a lot safer this way.'

'No worry's – Just tell us what's going down,' Kezlo smiled.

'Alright – 'Ere we go then,' I smirked as Sleeper fired up the engine.

It took just over two hours before we finally arrived in the Lake District for just before nine, parking the two cruisers out of sight about three minutes walk from The Windmill itself.

'So you're all straight just how this will go down then?' I enquired.

'Sweet as mate. Let's just do this one for Steve,' Jonah said smiling away.

'Alright then. Kezlo you come with me,' I said to him as we climbed from the back of the cruisers into the cold night air.

I nodded at Prey as he walked over. 'They all sorted.'

'Clear as a bell mate.'

'Alright then, me and Kezlo are going to sort the phonelines out then,' I informed him. 'That way we should get at least an hour head start on them.'

'Alright mate,' he replied. 'We'll meet you as planned.'

Kezlo and I returned ten minutes later to the scheduled meeting point just on the edge of the wooded car park to the boozer. Each man stood holding a single baseball bat smiling knowingly as to what was about to happen.

'Where's Scotty?' Prey asked as we returned.

'No fucker knows mate... He's on the missing list,' I told him as he just shook his head at me.

'Right, y'know what's going to go down,' I said taking a bat from Prey swinging it absentmindedly. 'You've just taken care of the cars, so they can't go anywhere real fast. Jonah and me are going in first. If a window breaks from the inside out – Then y'know it's a signal for you lot to enter,' I smiled. 'If these twats aren't in there, then we wait for your signal to go whilst in there.'

'This ones for the old man,' Prey winked at me as I nodded.

'Let's go,' I said looking at Jonah.

'Chopper,' Prey said.

'What?'

'You going in there with that now,' he smirked, looking at the baseball bat still swinging about in my hand.

'Shit – I forgot about that,' I laughed throwing it to him.

'Daft twat,' he laughed catching the bat from me.

'Evening Scotty,' Stevenson sighed walking through into his cell, Walsh closely in pursuit.

'I wondered just how long it would be before you two got 'ere,' Scotty smirked at them. 'What time is it anyway?'

'Late,' Walsh said sighing deeply whilst looking at his watch then back to Scotty. 'Just what the fuck have you gone and done now Scotty?'

'I don't know...' he shook his head dropping it. 'I needed the cash, didn't I? You weren't fuckin' helping me anymore and I just wasn't making enough money these days,' he held his head in his hands.

'You're a dumb little prick... Aren't you?' Stevenson said as he sat on the bed next to him.

'I needed money,' he replied feebly.

'Just what the fuck are we supposed to do now?' Stevenson sighed deeply, leaning back against the wall.

'Can't you get my off with it?' Scotty asked his head still buried.

'What the fuck are you thinking?' Walsh snapped. 'That you can go pointing guns at innocent people. Then after stealing the money you can go pointing that same gun at police officers and get the fuck away with it.'

'What if I can give you something big – Really *big*,' he said looking at them.

'Oh... What's that then Scotty,' Stevenson smirked. 'Another drug bust in Wythenshawe lad.'

'Alright, listen,' Scotty told them. 'If we do this then you'll have to use what you've already got on the crew.'

275

'We've not got enough on Chorlton or O'Prey though,' Walsh confirmed as Scotty grinned.

''Ere is a little taster then,' he nodded. 'I'll give you the whole crew tonight. There something going down right now with the entire lieutenant's involved in it.'

'That's it?' Stevenson asked shaking his head.

'Alright… not only that but there is an ace card for you also,' he smiled confidently at them knowingly. 'I'm not saying what this is just yet until I know that we've got ar' selves a deal for sure. I need to get off of all of what happened today. No charges. I want them all dropped. Then I want to be placed somewhere safe tonight. I want putting in protective custody where I'll be safe y'know. I'll give you some information to allow you to pick up all of them in the same place tomorrow. But until all of this is brought before the courts and I have to testify… You gotta keep me in rocks until then or I swear I'll lose my mind.'

'You what!' Walsh snapped shaking his head. 'Just what the fuck are you going on about son? You think that we're a local fucking chemist,' he laughed his disgust at Scotty's suggestion.

'Not quite – But you're pretty fuckin' close to one Walshy,' Scotty sniffed.

'But what could we possibly bring the entire crew in on what you're going to give us,' Stevenson added.

'Something big,' Scotty smiled. 'It'll be enough for you to hold onto them. Whilst you then go about charging them with the evidence I've already given you,' he stared straight at the both of them.

'I still don't think it's enough Scotty,' Stevenson told him shaking his head. 'We need something real good. What's the ace card son?' he needed more information.

'An unsolved murder that one of the main crew members committed. It's a good few year's back now. But they never did solve it… That's got to be worth more than a few brownie points to you two.' He then sat back down and leaned back against the wall and smiled at the two of them.

'Are you serious Scotty?' Stevenson looked at him.

'I sure am – I was there when it happened.'

'You what!' Walsh exclaimed. 'Why the fuck haven't we heard about this before?'

'He threatened to kill me also,' Scotty lied. 'So are you interested or what?' he stared directly at the two of them.

'We need to talk now,' Stevenson sighed staring at Walsh as he rose from the plastic mattress and they walked out into the corridor slamming the cell door shut behind them.

'What do you reckon Martin?' Stevenson asked as they both stood outside Scotty's cell. 'I mean he's holding all the cards here. Everything we've done with him for the past year will go down the tubes. And we've been after bringing this lot down for years now Martin.'

'I know what it will do Mike,' he shook his head. 'But we just can't go getting him off an armed blag for fucks sake. This ain't fuckin supergrass. Besides how do we know he's even being on the level with us? He must have been pretty fucked in the head to have gone and done what he did.'

'I know,' Stevenson said staring at Walsh. 'We're going to lose him otherwise Martin. Besides you didn't help with the crack situation …Did you?'

'That's below the belt Mike,' Walsh snarled at him. 'You knew what the fuck we were doing... *Unconventional...* remember.'

'Yeah – I'm sorry Martin,' he apologised. 'Look we ain't got that much apart from his word on things. Even with whatever he's going on about tonight, whatever they're up to. Unless Scotty takes the stand against them we're fucked.'

'What about this murder he's on about as well,' Walsh said lighting a cigarette. 'You reckon he's on about Paddy? You reckon that he's testifying against Chorlton.'

'I'd say it's got to be Chorlton, with the two of them going back so far,' Stevenson nodded at him. 'Although he said a good few years back now. So I'm not sure whether he means Paddy or not.'

'I'd love to see that little prick do life on top of everything else we could throw at him,' Walsh smirked. 'I still don't know what the fuck we can do though Mike. I mean he's pulled a fucking an armed robbery for Christ sake.'

'If we don't get him off, then we lose everything we've worked on,' Stevenson declared staring straight at him. 'We can't afford to lose this investigation now – We've got to do it Martin.'

Walsh sighed deeply. He'd worked his arse off on this case also and the last thing he wanted was to lose it all now. But at the same time getting Scotty off with an armed blag was probably the dumbest thing he'd heard on force... Although at the same time, he also knew that it was more than possible if what Scotty had was on the level.

'Let's give it a shot then,' he finally said pushing himself off the wall as Stevenson smiled at him.

As Jonah and myself entered through large solid oak doors to The Windmill, its sudden warmth and brightness engulfed both of us.

The pub was old in architecture but not décor. It had the appearance of something from the nineteenth century mixed with the late twentieth century. It was quite empty considering it was Saturday night. You could only see around fifteen, possibly twenty people sat in the bar area all chatting to one another.

Glancing through into the restaurant, you could only see a further eight people or so sat there eating.

We both looked around as we made our way to the bar. Our guys weren't even in there yet.

'Evening boys,' the landlord greeted us warmly. 'And what can I get you?'

'Just two bottles of Bud', my good sir,' Jonah said in a mocking accent.

'Are you boys new in town?' he asked as he opened the bottles.

'Oh no,' I said with similar mock to my voice. 'Although it is out first time to this establishment. You've got a nice place here my good sir. Don't know why we haven't been to this establishment before. Do you Henry?' I said to Jonah who you could see, was holding back his grin.

'No Charles,' he let out through a wide grin. 'I don't honestly know. But we'll certainly have to let our friends know about this place. Won't we Charles.'

'We have a fantastic restaurant also,' the landlord smiled.

279

'Superb my good man,' I said still in that take the piss voice.

'Tell me,' Jonah began. 'Does this establishment become busier later on?'

'Oh yeah boys,' he smiled to us. 'You stick around. This place can become quite lively. You never can tell what will happen sometimes.'

'Thank you, once again. Come along Henry, let's find ourselves a table,' I grinned at Jonah as we walked over to a free table and I noticed that the movie *Crocodile Dundee* with Paul Hogan as the hilarious *Mick Dundee* was on the TV set playing with the volume muted. I smiled at the movie I hadn't seen in years before we both took our seat.

We'd been sat in there literally only ten minutes when. 'Chopper – Look... Is that them?' Jonah nodded towards the entrance as seven lads all walked through into The Windmill, obviously all of them together as they laughed and joked with one another. Almost immediately people sat around the pub began greeting them. Even the landlord called out to them smiling as he did.

I nodded at Jonah then returning my attention to the tall stocky lad with slicked back brown hair, who I recognised immediately as the one who'd caused the trouble with Steve in the first place.

He was the one that I wanted. I observed him stroll about with pure arrogance, as my anger began to boil.

'Fuckin' twat.'

Jonah grabbed my arm sensing my resentment towards the lad in question. 'Easy Chopper... Just wait for the signal.'

'Where is it then?' I asked looking to him; just then an all mighty crash deafened the interior of the pub startling everybody.

I turned smirking; as we saw a picnic bench half lay over the back of the seat and half still hanging through the broken window itself. Appearances of pure disbelief and shock hung on all of the faces gawping at their surrounding of the pub.

'Your mask Jonah,' I said as we both stood pulling them over our faces.

Before anybody had chance to do anything Prey walked through the door with the eight others all fully masked up and carrying the baseball bats.

The next thing that happened was that Jonah launched his bottle of Budweiser straight into the group of lads who were merely stood there in shock at what to do next.

As the bottle smashed into the one of them I was already sprinting across the length of the room, running straight at the stocky lad. He just stood there totally unaware just staring at Prey's lot with pure confusion as they just stood there looking menacing. He didn't even notice me as I leapt through the air at him.

Turning from instinct at the faces around him he merely caught a glimpse of my head crashing into his face as I crushed his left cheekbone when I made contact with him, blood spraying recklessly as we both crashed into the floor.

'C'mon then you bunch of lying no good fuckers,' Prey screamed as he ran into the group of lads swinging his bat at everything that moved. As did the others as they began to totally trash the boozer and everybody else inside.

I repeatedly butted the lad over and over again who I'd locked beneath me with my weight; I screamed obscenities as my head crushed into his face.

Hearing somebody whistle, I looked up seeing Eazy guarding the door to prevent anybody from leaving by smacking those that tried with his bat, not that he needed really needed it, the huge fuck.

He nodded and grinned as he threw a bat to me. Catching it in mid flight, I then climbed up off the bloodied lad beneath me.

I glanced around at the damage being caused and took it all in. People were being knocked all over the place, windows and bottles were smashing everywhere. Prey was batting the landlord around behind the bar, pure rage racing through his eyes. Kezlo smashed the bar itself up leaving no bottle full or standing. The place was pure mayhem as the mass destruction took control.

'Please... No more... *Please*,' pleaded the lad lay bleeding badly below me.

'You fuckin' what? You're asking me to *stop* – you fuckin *cocksucking-motherfucking-cunt-of-a-whore*,' I screamed at him.

'What have I done to you? I don't even know you... Please stop now... Don't hurt me anymore,' he begged as I continued to smash the bat violently into him.

I looked around at the pandemonium and the deafening noises crashing all around me, as I glared back at the lad and smiled coldly at him.

Placing my hand to my ear I simply said. 'Sorry pal – It's a bit fuckin' loud in 'ere – I can't seem to hear a word you're fuckin' saying,' I was smirking at him as I began the onslaught once again upon him with my bat.

Each blow was filled with hate for what he'd done to Steve. Each blow crushing and snapping his bones as he screamed out with the anguish from the bat crashing violently into him from every possible angle.

I stopped and stared down at him lay there, barely conscious. My breathing was fast and uncontrolled as I witnessed the rest of the crew bringing the place to a stand still; all of them were screaming abuse to their victims lay beaten before them. A mass of bodies was lay bruised – battered – and defeated around the entire establishment.

I smiled at Sleeper who merely grinned back to me. Just then Prey appeared carrying a large wooden table above his head.

'This is what happens' when you go and fuck with one of ar' crew,' he screamed as he dumped the table sadistically into the lad below me.

Eazy whistled again looking at his watch, to signal it was time to leave. As we all ran for the doors both Prey and I stopped at the doorway turning and nodding approvingly at the sight before us.

'I don't think they'll be open in the too near future,' I declared as we both smiled knowingly at one another.

'Prey – Come on Prey – *Get up*,' Kathy called to him once again. 'We've got to be at church in an hour.'

She was rushing around the bedroom in a real panic. They hadn't got home until the early hours of the morning. They'd stayed in Chan's, as did all of them, until almost four o'clock before finally leaving.

'I'll be ready woman. Stop nagging for fucks sake! My head is wankered,' he called out, his head buried beneath the pillow trying his best to drown out her voice.

'We've got to get a move on Prey,' she told him again.

'Where's Sean?' he asked, suddenly remembering his son.

'Mum's got him,' she said. 'You know that Prey. She'll meet us at St. Patrick's church.'

'That's alright then,' he laughed. 'I got plenty of time then,' he grinned to himself out of her view.

'You've got to get ready,' she persisted, rushing around in a fluster.

'You'll have a bleedin' heart attack girl,' he laughed. 'Running about like that – I tell you what. Get me some pain killers and I'll get up,' he peeked from beneath the pillow at her.

'Alright… But then you get up after that. You hear me,' she called to him as she left the bedroom.

He stuck his head out from the pillow. 'Might as well make me a cup of black coffee whilst you're down there.'

'Bastard,' she yelled out.

'I heard that,' he smiled burying his head again.

283

'You alright Chopper?' Donna asked lay there stroking my chest.

'Double sweet,' I smiled at her.

'You know – I know what you did last night,' she looked at me. 'I know you say not to worry Chopper… But I do – it's just…' she trailed off.

'Just what,' I asked looking at her.

'I just worry so much about you all the time.'

'I've told you,' I grinned. 'There's nothing to worry about with me,' I kissed her.

'Look Chopper,' she smiled at me shaking her head. 'I hate to shatter your obvious illusions that you carry around with you. But you're not made of steel. You're not some kind of superhero, who can't get hurt,' she said poking my solar plexus.

'Oi - stop that,' I flinched.

'See,' she giggled.

'Anyway – I always kind of considered myself the Silver Surfer – well either that or Bat Man,' I smiled at her, thinking back to the comics that I used read as a kid. 'It was a top night though. Wasn't it?'

'Which part are you on about Chopper,' she raised her eyebrows at me. 'Earlier or later on in the evening?'

'Well seeing as you put it that way… Both were good fun,' I laughed.

'Steve was so anxious until you all finally arrived back.'

'It was for him last night. For what they did to him,' I said as my thoughts returned to Steve and I found myself smiling. 'Y'know…' It was my turn to trail off.

'I know Chopper,' she kissed me. 'I know what he means to you.'

'Anyway, you better get up hadn't you,' I told her. 'I know just how long it takes you birds to get ready,' I was laughing as she poked me again.

'Cheeky sod,' she giggled. 'It's going to be unusual seeing you in a suit Chopper. I've only ever seen you in one once before you know.'

'And you won't do normally,' I replied laughing as I did. 'Unless it's something like this – or they've got me in the dock for that matter. The old man hasn't rubbed off on me that much.'

'We'll be on time Claire,' Steve said as they were heading over from Congleton towards Manchester. They only got home at five that morning and were already heading back into town. 'Stop fretting girl,' he shook his head looking at her.

'We can't be late though.'

'I'm one of the godfather's Claire,' he smiled proudly. 'They can't start without me.'

'We should have left earlier last night,' she said looking at herself in the sunshields mirror. 'I'm so tired.'

'We could hardly have done that though,' he said looking at her. 'They'd gone and done what they done for me,' he then looked at her and then smiled to himself at the thought of what they had done.

'I know it was,' she smiled then leaned over and kissed him.

'I really wish I'd been there,' he smirked. 'It sounded like they fucked up everybody and everything in the place up,' he laughed cheerfully.

'Good – I'm glad they did it after what they did to you.'

'You know Claire you don't find...' he just smiled stopping himself.

'Too many friends like you've got,' she completed what he going to say. 'I know what you mean Steve. It's kind of strange at times. Feels like we're all family or something.'

'In a good sort of strange way though,' he said looking at her.

'That's for sure,' she smiled. 'Anyway how do I look Steve?'

'What, you mean since fifteen minutes ago when I told you how good you looked,' he laughed out loudly.

'Well,' she frowned.

'See woman – On time,' Prey smirked as they pulled into the parking lot of St. Patrick's church.

'Only just though,' she scowled at him. 'Your timing was just pure luck,' she laughed as she climbed out of the car.

'Luck had nothing to do with it,' he informed her as he climbed out of the driver's side. 'You alright lads?'

He started laughing as he looked at me. 'Look at you – All suited up Chopper,' he grinned.

'Look who's talking,' I told him.

'I look good though,' he smirked taking an admiring glance at himself. 'Don't I?'

'Just take a look around Prey,' Steve told him.

285

Prey smiled proudly as he looked around at all of the crew stood around suited up. 'Shit... It looks like something out of *Goodfellas*.'

'Where's the photographer?' Steve said looking around spotting him.

'Alright Sleeper, Eazy,' Prey smiled as they both walked up. 'How you lads feeling this morning?' he asked cheerfully.

'I'll feel a whole lot better once we get to the reception,' Eazy grinned.

'Looking good chief,' Sleeper said admiring Prey.

'Like wise mate,' he nodded.

'Donna says that suit sales went up by almost five hundred percent in the last couple of weeks after all the crew went in there buying them,' I laughed.

'Right c'mon then,' Steve said returning with the photographer. 'We got to get some pictures of this.'

We all formed into three rows on the photographer's instructions whilst he started snapping away.

'Have you seen them lot,' Kathy said as she rocked little Sean in her arms.

'I know,' said Claire smiling. 'Just who do they think they are?'

'They look good though – Don't they,' Donna smiled.

'I know, have you seen Kezlo,' Michelle said. 'I helped him pick the suit the other day. I tell you, for someone who doesn't seem to give a fuck about clothes, he sure was hard to please.'

'Fussy as hell,' Donna agreed. 'Wasn't he?'

'Ahhh – Look at little Sean,' Lisa said making a fuss of him.

'I know he's so cute – Ain't he,' Kathy smiled cooing at him. 'Nothing like his old man is he?' she said as they all laughed.

'Where's Jackie?' Sharon asked.

'God knows,' Kathy said shaking her head. 'Although I can't say I'll be too fussed if she doesn't turn up today.'

'I know what you mean,' Donna added. 'She's really changed a lot since I first met her.'

'Where's Scotty for that matter?' Sharon added looking about.

'I think he's lost the plot recently,' Donna sighed. 'If he wasn't Chopper's mate, I'd probably have fuck all to do with him.'

'Ain't that the truth,' Kathy said. 'He just looks so fucked up recently – Doesn't he?'

'They'll be top photos them,' Jonah grinned.

'We'll have to get a few copies of them for all the crew,' I confirmed.

'A day to remember,' Kezlo added as we both looked at him.

'Hang on a minute,' I said. ''Ere'are mate,' I was shouting over to the photographer.

'Yes,' he answered as everybody turned.

'We need just one more picture over 'ere.'

'Sure… What of?'

'Kezlo on his own wearing a suit,' I laughed. ''Cause no fucker will believe that we ever got him into one.'

Everybody began laughing as he scowled at me. 'Bastard,' he said, and then smiled proudly as the photographer took his picture.

'It's going to be a proper sound day Prey,' I said smiling warmly at him.

'I know – I know. All the crews 'ere. It's my sons christening and you two are to become the godfathers,' he mimicked Marlon Brando from *The Godfather* as he said this.

'It really is an honour mate,' Steve told him.

'Yeah mate,' I confirmed. 'It really is.'

'Well you're both like brothers so who the fuck else would I have asked,' he laughed putting his arms around us both.

Sean began to cry as the priest poured the holy water onto his head.

'Easy there – You'll drown him,' Prey announced, making us all laugh, the priest included.

We all made our way back outside after the service had finished. Everybody was in good spirits as we left the church to head for the reception.

'What the fuck?' Prey exclaimed.

'Morning O'Prey – Chorlton,' It was Stevenson stood there with Walsh beside him. Also stood there were the two coppers from the hospital in the Lake District, Harlow and Bowe.

The whole parking lot was filled with police vans, police cars, untold amounts of uniformed officers with dogs. You could even see armed police over at the edge of the car park as the helicopter circled above high in the sky.

'What the fuck is going on?' Prey snapped. 'This is my kids christening for fucks sake.'

'Well, you lads are hard to keep track of and seeing as for our initial arrest we wanted you all,' Stevenson smirked at us. 'We figured we'd pick you all up this morning, whilst you were together.'

'Pick us up for what?' I asked, angered at the position we'd been put in.

'Just about everything Chorlton,' Walsh smiled knowingly at me. 'But for now you're all under arrest for last night – Assault and battery - GBH – ABH – Affray – Damage to property. All that damage you lads caused last night – *I don't know*,' he shook his head.

'Oh and that's just for starters you hear,' Stevenson told us.

'So would you mind telling just what the fuck has supposed to have happened last night?' Prey said shaking his head.

'You caused some serious damage at The Windmill last night,' Harlow stated.

'At the Whatmill?' I asked.

'You fucking know what we're on about Chorlton,' Bowe snarled. 'We warned you.'

'I suppose with all these coppers 'ere Stevenson,' Prey grinned at him, 'that you've got warrants for all this shit you're accusing us of.'

'Oh we've got warrants O'Prey,' he smiled knowingly. 'Special ones at that. Got them drawn up especially for you lot this morning. Including the search warrants for certain flat that you both own. The very same flat that you and Chorlton are going to come with us to. Sound familiar lads?'

'No – Not at all,' Prey responded nonchalantly shrugging casually as he did so.

'Let's see,' Walsh said looking through the warrants. 'Parks, Knieldson, Walker, Davidson, Jones, Kulshaw – Oh and course not forgetting O'Prey or Chorlton.'

'Okay – Let's go then,' Prey yawned his response.

'I wouldn't be so fucking cocky son,' Stevenson suddenly snapped.

'I ain't saying shit until I see my brief,' he responded. 'I know where I was last night. All fuckin'night for that matter,' he held his hands out to be cuffed.

Just then all the uniformed officers began striding forward grabbing us then cuffing us all, reading us our rights as they did so.

I looked at Steve who put his arms around Donna and Kathy. 'Call Adrian,' I told him smiling as I did, as they dragged me away.

We were thrown into the back of the police vans. They threw Prey, Kezlo, Jonah and I into one van and the others into another. We could see all the girls stood outside of the church trying to comfort Kathy who was crying hysterically.

'On the day of the fuckin' christening for fucks sake,' Prey snarled watching Kathy stood there. 'They really don't have any respect... Do they?' he sighed.

'Fuck 'em,' I exclaimed. 'They've got fuck all on us.'

Jonah was sat there; staring out of the window at Stevenson, Walsh and the other two as they all climbed into the green Sierra. All of them were laughing with one another at what they'd just achieved. Something seemed strange though – Not quite right – But what the fuck was it, he kept thinking to himself.

It was the car... That green Sierra that he's seen before but couldn't place where he knew it from.

Suddenly it hit him – he knew exactly where he knew it from. 'Oh fuck me!' he groaned and gasped at the same time whilst still staring out of the window.

'What?' I asked, sensing his apprehension.

'That car,' he nodded out of the window. 'The green Sierra,' he whispered to all of us.

'Yeah – what about it Jonah?' Prey asked staring at him.

'I seen it before lads,' he said shaking his head.

'Probably Jonah,' Prey sighed. 'It's Stevenson's and Walsh's motor ain't it?'

'No listen... This is bad,' he said still staring at the car. 'I seen it a couple of times and couldn't work out why it seemed so familiar. But it was from the first time that I'd seen it – I just couldn't place it,' he looked at us shaking his head almost in disbelief.

'What are you going on about Jonah?' I asked confused.

'Scotty,' he said quietly.

'What about Scotty?' I asked, now really confused.

'I saw him getting out of it once last year,' he watched for our reaction.

'You fuckin' what,' Prey sneered; you could hear the loathing as he said it.

'Are you sure Jonah?' I asked.

'I am now. He was in it parked up the side of the medical college on Oxford Road,' he informed us. 'It's been bugging the shit out of me for time now. Although I'm positive about it now,' he sat back against the window shaking his head.

'And just where the fuck he is today or last fuckin' night for that matter?' Prey snapped.

'Notice that they didn't have a warrant for his arrest either,' Kezlo said dropping his head.

'I never even noticed at the time,' I said shaking my head not wanting to believe any of this.

'Fuck... *Fuck* this ain't good y'know,' confirmed Prey fearing the worst. 'When did you see him Jonah, getting out of the car?'

'About a year or so ago,' he declared.

'He could have given the whole operation up y'know,' Prey was shaking his head. 'Did he know anything about last night? He couldn't have done... Nah no one knew about it,' he whispered so the officers in the front couldn't hear us.

I glanced briefly at Jonah, as I suddenly realised that he might have over heard us in Henry's bar the other day, as we hadn't noticed him before he was stood before us. 'No way,' I said quickly wondering whether or not he had known.

'We invited him to the meal,' Jonah sighed. 'That was all we did.'

'Alright, we're going to have to wait and see what they've got on us first. If Scotty has given us up, then they'll going after the street next. But first they're going to see what they can get from us,' Prey sighed deeply. 'You all know the drill. Tell them where you were last night so they can check it out. Then strictly no fuckin' comment all the way.'

'Scotty though... For fucks sake,' Kezlo said letting out a deep sigh as though it had only just hit him.

I sensed Prey's anger building next to me. 'Fuck... *Fuck*... Fuck. This is *bad*. This is very fuckin' *bad*,' he said still shaking his head.

'I know,' was about all I could manage.

How had we been so blind to it... especially me, he'd been like my brother for so long. Even if we hadn't been as close recently I still thought of him as my brother. But he'd looked so fucked for so long now and I'd done my best to ignore it, not wanting to believe that he was so screwed up on gear.

They must have got him on something... That had to be it. He had to be fucked on gear to have given us all up though – I still couldn't quite believe that he was a fucking grassing wanker.

Not wanting to believe it... But deep down I think that I knew that it was true.

'I'm going to kill him,' Prey said coldly next to me. 'He's one dead mother fucker.'

'I know he is Prey,' was about all that I could manage as I dropped my head shaking it in utter disbelief.

The large dark figure was hidden within the confines of the dark shadows of the disused warehouse, located on the abandoned industrial estate in Sale. He waited both patiently and silently, on this usual wet dreary – not forgetting cold, Saturday night in January. He smiled to himself as he thought about how stupid these people could be at times.

They had definitely watched way too many Hollywood movies with their perceptions of shady deals in disused warehouses – which in their minds, was obviously one of the safest places to carry out such deals.

But he knew better than anybody that was complete crap. That was especially so, if there was someone like him waiting in the wings. As he waited he thought about the night before. That was when he to pay someone a little visit. This is where this information had been gained. He thought about just what it was that he'd had to do to finally divulge that information from that certain party...

Mark Hughes – or Hughsey as he was more commonly known, was one of their crew members. He was one of the older lads, whose own father had also been involved with the head of this crew.

You see, he'd needed information to carry out the start of his plans. There were things he couldn't allow to happen or they would cause him more problems in the long run. And they were the kind of problems he wanted to avoid.

Therefore he'd followed him to his home in Didsbury the night before. He watched as Hughsey had entered his house.

He knew that the lad had a girlfriend, but there had been no lights on when he had returned home – therefore he was presuming she wasn't home for the night. He waited patiently, just as he was right here – right now.

He waited until the guy in question had settled down for the night... A few hours had passed by and then finally, the lights had gone out. He waited further time to allow the man in question to settle down for the night.

And that is when he made his move. Picking the lock to the back door with the precession and ease of doing so many times over the years, he had then entered the house. He felt the warmth of the house take hold of him as he allowed his eyes to adjust to the dark, he then made a move for the stairs, moving silently to what he already knew was the bedroom door and he eased it open. Smiling to himself as he watched the man sound asleep with a little light from the gap in his curtains revealing his figure beneath the duvet where he slept soundly.

Moving with lighting speed, using the element of surprise, he grabbed the man viciously from his slumber, throwing him with serious force against the bedroom wall as both shock and then panic took control.

'What the fu...'

Before Hughsey could even finish he was grabbed from the floor, with his head slammed into the wall behind him, as he screamed in agony, the figure before him started repeatedly beating him, not allowing him chance to work out what was going on. Lifting Hughsey, by his now swollen face, he held him menacingly against the wall.

'I have some questions,' he sneered.

'Fuck you,' spat Hughsey defiantly. 'Who the fuck, are you anyw...'

'Shut the fuck up son,' he had responded as he carried him by his face as Hughsey struggled grabbing at the guys' arms, that felt like they were the size of tree trunks. And he wasn't a small lad in stature himself. Jesus, how big was this guy?

Throwing Hughsey into the office chair that was beside the desk that was covered with the variety of computer equipment. He punched the lad's face before him so hard that teeth came free, hitting the wall beside him, blood spraying freely, as his nose crumbled and the lights went out.

He had begun pouring water over the lads face as he watched with a dark humour, that he had started to come

around. But with the water being poured over his face he was
panicking, unsure what was going on.
'What the hell...'
'Like I said,' said the figure before him smirking as he did
so, as Hughsey blinked frantically trying his best to focus, 'I
have some questions.'
'What fuckin' questi...'
'We'll get to that,' he laughed, as he ripped the silver duct
tape and sealed it over the lad's mouth. 'But you see, I know
what you lads are like. So to save us wasting each other's
time. I figure what I will do is show you something first,' he
smiled in a sadistic way, as he suddenly lit a blow torch and
played with the control at the back of the device, as the
orange and blue flame blazed violently and he watched the
lads eyes before him almost pop from their sockets. 'Just to
show you I ain't fucking around – so that when I am done, you
will answer the questions I have to ask without wasting
anymore of my time.' He moved in towards his victim.

As he thought about that previous night, he realised now that
he had gone too far. Sometimes he overestimated people's
pain thresholds. But so be it. The body had now been dealt
with. However, he'd only gained part of the information that
he had required. Hopefully though – with a little persuasion –
he'd discover the rest of what he needed to know tonight.

As he waited he craved for a cigarette. To taste that nicotine
– his only drug of choice – well that and obviously the odd
tipple of whiskey. But neither of these came close to what
really fulfilled his desires.

These monkeys (as he liked to refer to them) whom were
meeting here tonight had other desires. They were the very
same desires like so many of this God forsaken town (albeit it
was his hometown that he had grown up in) was now into.
And that was Class A drugs.

He couldn't get his head round what or why the population
of not only Manchester – but it now appeared the rest of the
country saw in these drugs. But he wasn't a hypocrite. He had
worked within the industry (so to speak) for a number of years
now – only his agenda had always been somewhat different.

He could hear vehicles approaching. Could this be them
arriving. It had to be really. Therefore, he moved back further
within the confines of the shadows to ensure that he was
concealed from view. The sound of the engines became

louder, as he now, clear as day, saw the lights as they illuminated the interior of the warehouse, the beams of light bouncing from the filthy walls covered in an array of graffiti left there from over the years.

The first car was a dark (he wasn't sure whether it was black or navy in the limited light) Mercedes Benz, as it pulled over to the right hand side of the empty space with the second car (or was it a jeep of some sort?) followed closely behind – as it's lights revealed the first vehicle to actually be black in colour. The second vehicle was a dark green Range Rover. As they both pulled into the disused warehouse, they used the lights from their cars to keep the warehouse illuminated.

He watched silently as all the doors opened and eight men in total clambered down from their perch – each appeared to be squinting at the serious lack of light.

'Who the fuck, choose this location Vinnie?' said the large figure from the passenger seat of the Range Rover. He was well over six foot tall, with short dark brown wavy hair that was already starting to grey. He was a lot older than any of the men here tonight. He was smartly dressed in a dark suit, as were his other men stood around him. He had to be in his mid fifties at least. Although it had to be said, that he looked as though he knew how to handle himself. But seeing as the other three that had exited the vehicle with him were even bigger than he was he didn't think that really mattered.

'What's wrong with it, Alex?' replied Vincent (or Vinnie as he preferred) O'Leary from the driver's side of the Mercedes Benz. This guy was a lot younger in his mid twenties. He was dressed casually, however even he could tell that it was all designer gear that not only he, but also his lads wore. He was also the one who more than represented the one he was looking for. In fact it was his son. He was a small-wiry character – yet as small in stature as he was he carried a real air of authority with him. The three that had exited the Range Rover were all taking in their surroundings.

'Apart from the fact I can't see shit,' Alex sighed, then smiled, 'nothing.'

'Stop whinging like a little girl then,' replied Vinnie, whose features reminded him of a little weasel. 'You got the gear the old man ordered?'

'I take you've got the cash?' he replied walking to the rear of the vehicle and popping open the boot as Vinnie – followed closely by two of his men approached.

295

'Don't know what the fuck these kids see in this shit myself. Fucking ecstasy pills... well that is, if they are actually fucking ecstasy pills that you're selling us.' said Vinnie as he glanced into the rear of the Range Rover at the large stuffed bags containing the pills. 'Not that I give a fuck though. They sure are bringing in bucket loads of cash at the moment.'

'They're the same batch that you took off us last time Vinnie,' he replied shrugging his shoulders. 'There was no problems with them was there?'

'Apart from the fact they shrunk my cock to the size of a mouse's tail... Nah there was no problem,' he laughed as he waggled his little finger at the old man.

'So, no different to usual then eh, Vinnie?' said one of the men stood by Alex.

'You fucking what?' screamed Vinnie flying at the man as one of his men pulled him back.

'Easy now Vinnie,' said Alex placing his hand on his chest. 'Mickey was only havin' a laugh with you. Calm the fuck down,' he glanced back over his shoulder at the man in question. 'And you get the fuck back in the car and wait for me there.'

'You better watch that cunt, Alex,' Vinnie sneered.

'Okay son,' sighed Alex. 'Now let's just get this shit over with. You sure want this many. Not that's it's a problem. It's just four times the amount you usually take.'

'Yeah,' he smiled. 'We got some lad from Salford who can't seem to get enough of these things at the moment. You remember Paddy right?' He watched Alex nod his answer, whilst also shaking his head at the way he obviously felt about Paddy, the man in question. 'Well anyway, it's the lad that used to follow him round all the time. Not too sure how he's managing it to be honest. Especially with O'Prey's lot from Hulme controlling so much of the action. But all the same he always has the bees so fuck it right?'

'Ain't that the truth,' he replied, opening the holdalls in the back of the Range Rover revealing the bright yellow pills. 'So, Prey's still running shit then? What happened to that lad that used to knock about with him? Sean Macreedy? He was a sound lad. I used to do a lot of business with him back in the day – on behalf of Prey of course.'

'Shit – he got killed a couple of years back now old man. You seriously didn't know about that?'

'Nah,' he replied as he zipped the bags back up. 'Must have been out of the country back then.'

'Anyway, fuck it. Them Hulme lads have had the drugs side of things wired for so long now. Especially with the Es that we was just glad you showed back up when you did do Alex. We seriously needed a good connection back in town. You got those other samples the old man asked for? If they're right, we're gonna look at a way to start taking over some of the business for ourselves. It's about time the O'Leary's started to get in on the action again right? The old man is starting to see sense as to the kind of cash that we can make. He knows it's the right thing to do to get in on the business for ourselves,' Vinnie smiled. 'Paul, grab that case from the car for me will you?' He glanced round at the guy near the car still who just nodded his understanding.

'Yeah I got those...' began Alex as his body, suddenly, without any warning whatsoever, shot violently round to his right as though he'd been hit from some unknown force.

Vinnie stood there shocked as Alex's men suddenly produced an array of armoury as did Vinnie's own men. Alex screamed out in agony (albeit no one was entirely sure why at that moment in time)

'Alex,' called Vinnie, holding his hands up defensively, 'What the fuck just happened? Are you oka...'

'Fuck you Vinnie,' snarled Alex, who was struggling back to his feet as they all stood there baffled by what had just taken place. That's when Vinnie heard the slightest of what can only be described an empty crisp packet being popped as he watched Alex's face literally explode before him.

'You fucking cunt Vinnie,' screamed one of Alex's men as he aimed the pistol directly at him... But as he did so – his head suddenly jerked off to the left, as they watched in horror, as his face as blown cleaning away.

'What the fuck!' exclaimed Vinnie totally baffled as he looked in every direction to try and fathom what had happened in seemed like minutes (yet was merely a matter of seconds) when he suddenly saw more ferocious white flashes from the darkness of the warehouse – almost like bolts of lightning.

He watched in a state of complete shock as all the men who remained standing were brought down around him as the what was now obviously bullets tearing through them. Each and every one of them killed violently – yet very quickly, before his eyes.

'All right there son?' said the large dark figure who now appeared from the confines of the darkness where he had lay in wait for this very moment.

'What the fuck have you just...'

'Shut the fuck up, you little prick,' sneered the figure. 'I think me and you, Vincent need to go and have a little chat don't we eh?'

They had taken us from St. Patrick's Church where baby Sean had just been christened – and we'd all been arrested, straight back to Hulme estate, just outside of the city centre, where we all resided. They had search warrants for all of our homes, although they'd only find personal amounts of any sort of gear there so we wasn't really that worried about what they would find there.

But then they had walked Prey and I straight round to flat 464 – and confirmed our worst nightmares. They had really known about the flat. For it was the one main location that we'd used to stash all the gear we sold over the years. They had never known about it. They had never even had a visual on the place... yet somehow they had found out about. And I think, that not even deep down – we blatantly knew how they'd discovered its existence.

Of course it had to have been Scotty that must have informed them about it, although he'd of had no idea what was kept there nowadays. Because after he'd fucked up with Batty last year, he'd not had any access whatsoever to the flat.

The police tore the place apart and you could clearly see the gleeful looks as they did so. The walls that they ripped out, were all false. And they came apart with the kind of ease that reminded me of a wet Manchester Evening News coming apart in the hands of someone persistent enough to keep reading it, whilst the rain continued to pour.

I had no idea why I had that particular thought, as the two of us stood there observing silently. And to make matters worse still – they couldn't have picked themselves a better time for them to be here and do this. This was the worse time it possibly could have been for us, as the place had just been stocked up with all of the drugs purchased or produced from the last week.

As the walls were torn away like the wet papier-mâché, as that's pretty much all they were anyway. Behind them they found themselves over 1000 kilos of cannabis resin, 6 kilo's of heroin, 8 kilo's of cocaine, almost half of which was already cooked into its pure form of crack-cocaine. Then there was all the gear from the factory that was at least twenty thousand E's and 16 kilo's of pure 100% amphetamine, along with 100,000 tabs of acid that we'd just produced ourselves, through our guy who worked with Steve in Congleton.

Stevenson and Walsh couldn't stop smiling at one another, and then smirking at the two of us just stood there whilst we acted oblivious as possible to what they'd found at the flat. As far as we'd always been concerned, the place was just a disused squat, if this day ever arrived there was no way of proving that it had anything to do with us... well, that was until Scotty came into the picture.

'Guv',' shouted one of the officers from the bathroom, 'you'd best check these out.'

Both Prey and I glanced at one another, as we blatantly knew what was beneath the bathroom floorboards. There was a whole array of different handguns. Luckily all of them were clean; none had been used for any job as we always disposed of those ones afterwards.

'And what do we have here?' Walsh asked grinning like a Cheshire cat, as he walked over to us with the holdall full of the artillery. 'Are you lads thinking of starting a revolution or something?'

But still we merely stood there saying nothing to them. We both appeared to be bored by the entire matter. But if truth be told – *with Scotty* – if Scotty was indeed the one who'd given us up... then, God only knew how much they were already aware of.

'Right... Get the two of them down to the station now,' Stevenson instructed.

'Fuck the both of you,' I snapped defiantly as they began to drag us away.

Stevenson smirked at me. 'One more thing you should know Chorlton,' he smiled knowingly at my more than bored expression. 'We've got some questions to ask you about a certain dead security guard from Cheetham Hill a few years back now... I'm sure you remember what I'm talking about don't you son?'

I hadn't expected that one – the blow catching me slightly as I struggled with the officer detaining me, as my expression broke momentarily. 'What... What the...'

'Thought that might shock you,' Walsh smiled at me.

'Go fuck yourself Walshy. We ain't got shit to say to you boys until we get ar'brief down 'ere,' Prey casually said, then looked at me, nodding for me to turn away.

Shit – Fuck me... I hadn't even considered the prospect of that one. Scotty knew everything that had gone down that night. But he'd been involved... So why would he give me up for that one.

No way – No fucking way was that shit coming back to haunt me now. They weren't really going to try and fuck me over on that score... Were they? It had been years ago now. Shit... This was becoming worse and worse by the minute.

They then took us all down to the main Police Station in the centre of town where we were all immediately thrown into separate cells, so not to communicate with one another. The holding cells were buried in the basement of the building so there was no sunlight whatsoever – but that was the least of our worries at this moment in time.

'We got them,' Stevenson laughed joyously. 'We finally got them Martin.'

'It feels good... Don't it?' Walsh declared happily.

'I take it that you've been after this lot for a while then?' asked Harlow.

'Fuck yes,' Walsh said, pouring more whiskey into their plastic coffee cups. 'It finally all came together for us last night.'

'As soon as we got the information from our informant last night we put the call through. And as soon as they told us what had happened at the boozer – we put one through to your lot who contacted you two straight away,' Stevenson smiled at them both. 'It would have been nice to get them actually at the scene. But what the fuck eh! Our guy will testify that they were all going to do it anyway.'

'They caused some serious damage,' Bowe, Harlow's partner said shaking his head. 'There were twenty seven victims in all. All of them were beaten very badly with baseball bats. Plus they fucked up one of the Sarg's kids; they found him with the table still on top of him unconscious. That's why, when Griffin got the shit kicked out of him we didn't push to catch anybody for it. The kids a bit of a tearaway... but, he's still the Sarg's kid.'

'The damage to the boozer itself is so bad, that I'll be surprised if they open again before summer,' Harlow added.

'Are you sure, that your guy will be able to testify?' Bowe asked. 'There was no witness's from the boozer itself as they were all masked up. Well apart from the two that walked in first of all. But we are still waiting on confirmation on that score.'

'Don't worry about it,' Stevenson smirked. 'We've had one of their main guys working with us for the last year or so, building a case against them. He's going to testify against them for what we've found this morning and for all the evidence he's supplied over the last year now.'

'Also for what went down last night,' Walsh added. 'We worked all through last night to get the warrants on them. Prosecution is in later on to sort out the charges for last night so that we can detain them for the week. They are going to do it through special circumstances. The judge is going to allow us the time we need to build a case that will at least get them remanded whilst we put everything together for the Crown Prosecution.'

'Then... after that?' Harlow enquired.

'Then once we get them detained here for the next week,' he grinned. 'After that we're bringing down their street grafters. We just want them to feel that they're safe for the time being.'

'Then it's off to Walton on remand until the trial,' Walsh said rubbing his hands together. 'Then good-fucking-bye for a good few years.'

'Why didn't you bring the old guy in?' Bowe asked curiously. 'Steve Griffin.'

'Because we've got shit on him,' Stevenson sighed. 'Not even last night as our guy says that he wasn't going along. As far as we can tell he's just involved with the clothes shop they own.'

'They own a fucking shop?' Harlow asked shocked.

'Oh yeah,' Walsh said. 'You saw it all for yourselves this morning. These lads have been controlling drugs on that estate, along with the rest of town for years now. They've been making themselves a bundle of money. Although we've checked the shop and it's all fully above board in this Griffin's name. But they were just so fucking tight though, that we could never break them.'

'That was until we got our guy working with us,' Stevenson smiled nodding as he did. 'He's given us everything on them.'

'The only thing though... is,' Walsh sighed. 'We were actually hoping for at least another six months on the investigation before we brought them in. Especially, with the main two who run the crew, that being O'Prey and Chorlton. Just so we knew that it would be airtight against them. They have been untouchable for years now. We've never even got close to them before.'

'Don't worry about it,' Stevenson added looking at him. 'When Scotty testifies against them. They won't have a hope in hell of getting away with anything.'

'Let's fucking hope so,' Walsh confirmed, as they all raised their cups.

'Here's to catching the bad guys,' Harlow laughed.

'So O'Prey... Formalities are out of the way,' Stevenson smiled. 'Your brief is here. Not that'll do you much fucking good with what we've got against you. So why don't we start with last night then. Where were you and what did you get up to?'

'I can tell you everything about last night,' Prey yawned.

'Good... very good,' Stevenson smiled again. 'Go on then.'

'We... And by *we*, I mean all the lads and me, girlfriends included that is,' he began grinning as he stared at them all. 'Well we all went to Chan's Chinese Restaurant around six thirty, sevenish. Left around four this morning. Kind of, a little private party for my sons christening y'know. You remember the christening where you nicked all of us?'

'That's bollocks and you know it,' Walsh snapped.

'Is that so Walshy,' he said glancing at the clock behind him on the wall. 'Well it's five thirty now. Chan's should be open soon enough,' he told them casually.

'That's bullshit O'Prey,' Harlow snarled. 'We know that it was you lot that fucked up all those people at The Windmill last night. Not forgetting the state you left the pub in as well.'

'You keep going on about this Windmill or whatever you call it,' he yawned again and stretched. 'Would you mind telling just what the fuck it is?'

'You fucking well know what it is O'Prey,' Bowe yelled at him. 'We warned you a while back that we didn't want any trouble around our way.'

'What you being so hostile for?' Prey snapped back. 'I'm helping you 'ere. I'm telling you exactly where we were all last night,' he then casually sat back in his seat.

'Don't look so fucking smug O'Prey,' Stevenson sneered at him. 'We've got shit going way back on you and the rest of your fuckin' crew. Along with someone who's going to testify that it all true. This is merely the beginning of it. So if you want to play games. Then we'll play games,' he grinned.

'Look I think that my client is being more than helpful with you, detectives.' Adrian Black, Prey and Chopper's solicitor told them as he merely sat there observing just how they were tackling this.

'Well we'll see in the morning once we detain them for further questioning towards our complete investigation,' Walsh said ignoring Adrian Black, staring at Prey.

'On what grounds are you going to be holding my client?' Adrian enquired. 'What charges are you going to charge them with?'

'They'll all be formally charged with last night, so to be held for the week whilst there is an on going investigation. Let's put it this way Mr. Black,' Stevenson smiled. 'With everything that we've got on him and his crew, it'll take a lot longer than a day to cover it.'

'Alright get him out of here for now,' Walsh said. 'We'll interview the rest of them first and see what they've got to say.'

'What do you reckon Adrian?' asked Prey as the two of them sat there with a young trainee officer stood there silently observing them.

Adrian Black had known and represented Prey and his crew for years now, going back to when Prey was still only a teenager.

'I don't know yet, Kieran,' he shook his head. 'If Chan confirms that you were all at his last night, then they'll be hard pushed to convict you with it. But they're going to push it anyway so to hold you all for the week, especially with those other couple of detectives travelling all the way down here for this.'

304

'What about all the other shit?' Prey asked glancing at the uniformed officer stood there watching and trying listen in on their conversation.

'They seem confident that they've got themselves an airtight case against all of you,' he said. 'Can you tell me just why they're so confident?'

Prey shook his head. 'Maybe they've got themselves a little budgie that once belonged to us.' He was making reference to the sound of chirping that a budgie would make when trying to talk.

'Are you serious!' he asked looking above the rim of his glasses at Prey. 'That's not at all good Kieran.'

'Tell me about it,' he sighed, turning away from the officer.

'Alright. We need to find out more first. They'll charge you all with last night and they will get their extension to hold you all here for the time being,' he told Prey straight shaking his head. 'I won't lie to you Kieran.'

'How long?' he asked.

'Depends on what they produce in the morning,' Adrian told him.

'Alright then, we'll just play it by ear for now then,' Prey sighed sitting back in his chair. 'Thanks a lot, Adrian.'

'No problem,' he smiled. 'I'm off to see Billy now. I reckon it'll be pretty much the same as you though. I've got my other representatives already down here to start work with the rest of the lads.'

'Thanks again,' Prey said rising from his seat.

SIXTY

So you're telling us that they were here all night Mr. Yung?'
Stevenson asked the old man, again in utter disbelief at what
he was hearing, whilst the four of them stood at the rear of
Chan's Restaurant in China town located just near Piccadilly
in the city centre.

'Yes sir. And please call me Chan,' he replied politely as he
nodded, thinking that he hadn't expected all this to happen so
soon, despite knowing they'd been arrested that morning.
He'd known as both he and his wife had still been in the
church when they were outside being cuffed whilst making
their arrests. However, it hadn't made the least bit of
difference to him when they had decided to show up.

'I say it can't be so,' Walsh snarled the words at Chan.
'We've got them all somewhere else last night.'

'I don't see how so,' Chan shook his head at them. 'Mr.
O'Prey booked restaurant for entire evening. All those men in
pictures you show me, here from seven o'clock last night until
early hours of this morning. Not sure time – but maybe four-
five O'clockish in the morning.'

'You're telling us that on a Saturday night you closed your
restaurant for a private party?' Harlow shook his head; he
didn't like what he was hearing. 'And that they did not leave
the restaurant at all?'

'Mr O'Prey booked whole restaurant out,' Chan smiled at
them. 'If customer wants to do so... Then customer can do so.
He is one who pay, right?'

'But you're certain it is the men in the pictures?' Bowe
asked.

306

'Yes,' Chan sighed becoming irritated by of all of this, 'How many times Chan have to tell you all. Just which part of... them *here* and *all night*, you not understand?'

'But we've got them...' Walsh began to say.

'Lui,' Chan cut him off shouting to one of his waiters. 'Come here.'

'Yes boss... How may I help?' Lui asked as he approached.

'Lui, these gentlemen are Police Officers,' Chan shook his head at them as he said it. 'They obviously feel that Chan's eye sight is so old and poor that I don't recognise men in pictures. You please look with young fresh eyes at photos for gentleman.'

Walsh thrust the photos out at Lui and they all scrutinised him as he merely glanced at the photos then returned them smiling.

'Yes – I know these men. They were our guests from last night,' Lui said nodding to them all.

'You see,' Chan snapped. 'Chan's eyes don't lie.'

'You're positive now?' Harlow added, as they could all feel this one slipping away from them.

'What must I do? You are beginning to make old man angry,' Chan said obviously becoming more than a little irritated at being put in this situation. 'You want me to come to station with you? Identify men in person,' he then sighed deeply, showing his frustration.

'That's a good ide...' Bowe started to say as Stevenson cut him off.

'No... Thank you for your time Chan,' Stevenson stared at the others. 'We were just about to leave.'

The four of them walked back through the restaurant and past the prying eyes of the customers as they did so, and through the front door out into the cold open air.

'This is bollocks,' Harlow said as they stood outside Chan's restaurant.

They didn't appear to notice Chan was now upstairs on the first floor, by the front oval window, and he was observing the men stood there from the second floor shaking his head at them grinning as he did so.

'What the fuck can we do now?' Bowe snapped, staring to the other two.

'They've fucked us,' Walsh stated. 'I don't believe this.'

'What about your guy's testimony?' Harlow asked.

'He wasn't there though,' Stevenson said shaking his head in disbelief. 'I mean if we go to trial with this one, and old fucking Chink fuck and his Chink cunt waiters turn up, all saying that they were in there all night.'

'They'll laugh it out of court,' Walsh added.

'We know that it's bollocks though. We know it was them that did it,' Stevenson sighed deeply. 'Look, we'll interview the girls that were supposed to be there last night. Maybe one of them will fuck up, especially if we lean on one of them hard enough.'

'So what are we supposed to do?' Bowe asked him.

'You two head back to the Lake District,' Stevenson told them. 'Get these pictures shown to the landlord or anybody else in that area, who might just have seen them. See if you can get a positive ID on the two who first went into the boozer. Or for that matter any of them.'

'Are you still going to be able to hold them?' Harlow enquired still shaking his head in disbelief.

'Of course,' Walsh told them. 'We've still got years of evidence that we've built against them.'

'This is a major blow though,' Stevenson declared. 'We won't mention talking with the Chink... For now anyway. We'll interview the girls first and still hold them tomorrow morning on this charge anyway. After we get our extension to hold them, we'll push for everything we possibly can.'

'We're going to head back then,' Harlow sighed, as he shook their hands.

'Alright, we'll speak to you both tomorrow,' Stevenson said nodding at them. 'Make sure you get us those photos of what damage they've caused.'

'We'll courier them over to you in the morning,' Bowe told them. 'See you later. It's been one hell of a long day.'

'Tell me about it. See you both soon. Thanks for everything so far,' Steven said as he nodded at him then looked across at his partner. 'Come on Martin, we've got shit loads to do for tomorrow morning yet.' The two of them took off towards the car.

Stevenson and Walsh both walked in silence – each deep in thoughts of their own as they made their way through the deserted streets of Manchester to where they had parked their car.

'What do you reckon Mike?' Walsh finally asked as they were upon the vehicle.

'I reckon that they are without a doubt...' he sighed deeply whilst shaking his head. 'They are the fucking best and without a doubt, the fucking worse crew that I've ever had to work,' he half smirked at the mere thought of them. 'I mean you've got to give this crew credit here. They planned this like you wouldn't believe, Martin. It's like they knew all along. I mean *we* know it was them. But just what proof have we got Martin apart from our little rock head of a witness say so... Scotty eh? Great.' He blew the air out as he continued to shake his head.

'We'll just have to hope they come up with a positive ID on the two inside,' Walsh responded as they both climbed into the car.

'Even so... They've got an alibi for the whole fucking night,' Stevenson shook his head.

'We better hope that this other thing that Scotty's given us is above board,' Walsh said looking at Stevenson.

'I know,' Stevenson said turning the key. 'Although the death of that security guard checks out and it was never solved Martin.'

'I know it wasn't,' Walsh replied smiling, whilst he thought silently to himself of Chorlton.

SIXTY ONE

'Fuck me; look at how good this cunt looks eh, Jason.' Batty said jokingly as he laughed. The two of them had just walked through the doors into Dry Bar. He was staring at the huge figure that was Tony Henessy. He was a large imposing figure at well over six feet tall and built like a brick shit house, even compared to Batty who a large lad himself. Tony had certain style about him. He always had. He reminded Batty of someone who ran an accounting firm (which he supposed in a way he did – just not a legal one) well apart the fact his nose had been busted more times than one could ever imagine.

It was a known to almost everybody involved within the world they lived that he ran most of the security in town itself (not forgetting all of the timeshare activities he was allegedly involved with out in Spain somewhere.) He was one of the main heads from Ordsall in Salford. His father, Tommy Henessy had been in the game until the day they killed him. But it was safe to say that Batty had always admired the guy, even if he was from the wrong side of town from himself.

'How's it going Tony?' asked Batty as he walked up to his old friend who he hadn't seen for a few years now. 'You're looking good, pal. Seriously – I think I need to get out of the fucking rain and catch some of those rays you been getting in Spain eh?'

'Y'know that you're always more than welcome Batty,' smiled Tony shaking his hand. 'You all right Jason? Jeez – you've grown up haven't you? Still remember that little scally running round Wythenshawe. How's it going?'

'Good Tony,' replied Jason standing in Batty's shadow.

310

'Yeah well you know how it is Tony,' said Batty glancing round. 'Kinda hard for the likes of us to take holidays these days. It's gone mental in town over the last few years.'

'So I heard,' he smiled sipping his whiskey. 'Anyway, thanks for making the effort for coming down 'ere tonight. Hadn't really planned on staying in town. But it's too late to get on the road to where I've got to go to. Besides which, I figured I would have seen you today at the christening and I was going to have a chat with you there. What you lads drinking anyway?'

'Just a beer Tony,' replied Jason eagerly as Batty grinned at him.

'And I'll have the same as you, Tony,' added Batty.

'No worries,' replied Tony as he ordered the drinks.

'Anyway – how long you around?' asked Batty.

'Gonna pop up to Nottingham to see ar'kid. You remember Rachel don't you?'

'Who'd forget her,' he smiled as he saw Tony frown. 'Eh, only joking Tony. Y'know that would never happen.'

'Thin ice son,' laughed Tony. 'You're skating on very thin ice y'hear me?'

'What she doing in Nottingham?' asked Batty genuinely interested. 'Didn't she go to college or something?'

'She studying psychology, pal,' he smiled proudly. 'She's at uni' up there. Doing really well. Albeit I ain't too sure what she will end up doing once she graduates.'

'Sound,' replied Batty.

'Gonna spend a few days up there as I ain't seen her for pure time now,' he told as he turned to the bar, and collected the drinks, and then he slipped very discretely the sealed bag to Batty.

'Is that what I think it is?' asked Batty as Tony smiled at him.

They three of them were in the toilets in the basement of Dry Bar snorting the coke Jason had very eagerly just chalked up.

'So what you happened to you this morning?' asked Batty snorting loudly as he cringed at the Charlie he'd just banged. 'I didn't see you at the church.'

'Fucking flight was delayed. By the time I turned up the police was hauling them all off. What the fuck happened?'

'No idea,' shrugged Batty. 'All I know is they nicked all those lads as we was all leaving the church. I mean c'mon for fucks sake – of all the places to go nicking them.'

'They get all of them?' asked Tony as they exited the cubicle and made their way over to the sink.

'They took down the main lads from the crew from what I can tell.' He snorted loudly rubbing his nose, as he pinched at it with finger and thumb smiling. 'Prey, Chopper and the rest of the lads who deal at top level with them two.'

'Y'know how bad it is yet?'

'Nah... nobodies knows anything yet.'

'Was probably that fucking crack head Scotty,' added Jason as he checked his nose in the mirror.

'Who's that then?' asked Tony.

'Y'know Chopper right?' asked Batty snorting loudly, once again as they all left the toilets and made their way back upstairs.

'Yeah, quality lad,' smiled Tony. 'Met him a few times with Prey. Always liked that lad.'

'Everybody does. He's solid. No bullshit about him – and more than sound to do business with.' Batty smiled as he said this, and then made his way up the stairs. 'Anyway – did y'know him way back when? He used to always knock around with this other lad called Scotty?'

'Vaguely,' shrugged Tony as they arrived back at the bar. 'Only really dealt with Prey – and obviously Sean before... Well y'know. And Chopper was always there with Prey before I left for Spain. What about him anyway?'

'He's a fuckin' crack head,' Jason spat the words out in total disgust.

'And?' shrugged Tony. 'Was he part of the crew?'

'Certainly was,' said Batty. 'Although, I didn't see the little cunt there this morning y'know. Chopper used to deal with all the weed side of the business from Hulme. From an early age as well. Must have been around sixteen when Sean introduced him to me. I was a bit dubious at first, y'know... him being a kid really. But to be honest after the first time I done business with the lad, I knew straight off the bat that he was gonna be a sound lad to deal with. And all was good until Chopper moved up in the world. Which was more than fair play to the lad. I mean if anybody deserved it, then it was Chopper. But then he put Scotty in charge of that side of things. There was always something about the lad I never liked. But to be fair – he done

312

okay for the first year or so. But then it all started to go wrong.'

'How so?' asked Tony as he paid the bar man, once again and handed out the drinks to the other two.

'He just used to take the piss. Y'know – not show up for drops. Short the bees. All that kind of crap.'

'Why'd you keep dealing with them then?'

'Because of Prey... Well to be honest – more 'cause of Chopper. Like I said I really like the lad. Anyway – he fucked up more than once and in the end we all came to blows over it. Tommy got nicked after one of these episodes. So I told Chopper I would only deal with Jonah and Kezlo.'

'Jonah – he's that handy fucker from over that way right?'

'Yeah that's him,' smiled Batty thinking of some of some the fights he'd witnessed Jonah involved in.

'I seen him take on these six lads from the estate once,' said Tony nodding his approval. 'He took them apart like they weren't there. And these were handy fuckers that I am talking about. Lad's that I had used myself in the past.'

'That's the one,' replied Batty. 'Proper sound lad though. He's done well with Chopper and the rest of them lads from Hulme.'

'And Kezlo,' Tony snorted wiping his nose as he did so. 'Correct me if I am wrong. But ain't he the white lad with all the dreads right? The one that DJ's around town? Quality from what I remember.'

'Yeah that's him,' said Jason nodding frantically without realising it.

'Both are quality lads,' nodded Batty sipping his Jameson's whiskey and dry. 'Anyway – we only dealt with those lads after the Scotty debacle.'

'So what the fuck did this kid do then?'

'He was a fuckin' crack head like Jason says.'

'And?'

'And...' sighed Batty, 'I wouldn't be fuckin' surprised if it was his grassing arse that has got them all nicked. I mean I tried to warn Chopper. But y'know how it is. Especially with them growing up together and shit. We blatantly saw him buying the shit in Moss Side. And then one of my lads, Tommy like I mentioned, got nicked with him walking straight after – full of excuses. That's when we cut ties with the little cunt.'

'And they didn't see this coming?' asked Tony.

'Like I say – him and Chopper... and I suppose Kezlo as well all grew up together on that estate.' He shook his head. 'Suppose sometimes you just don't want to face reality at times like that eh Tony?'

'That's the truth brother.'

'So what's with Prey?' asked Tony. 'I hear he still controls the estate and most of the wholesale gear that's going through town.'

'Sure is,' agreed Batty. 'Not so much the weed, but all the best gear like the pills – that nobody seems to be able to touch them on, the speed they do is always 100 percent pure. In fact... truth be told I haven't ever had any bad gear from them.'

'Well,' smiled Tony, 'y'know that my money isn't involved in that side of things anymore right?'

'I know,' replied Batty. 'But I say from that smile you may have something to offer eh.'

'Possibly,' he told him. 'I have a source that runs through Gibraltar and he's looking to hook up with someone on this end for the weed. I have some finance interests so I want someone I can trust involved.'

'Serious?'

'Serious,' he replied. 'I was gonna talk to you about it when I seen you today. But obviously...'

'Why you not going to just use your crew over 'ere?'

'I want it to come through you rather than me,' he said. 'Basically... things on that side almost got me pinched last time round. Hence why I left town and set up business in Spain.'

'Fair play,' replied Batty. 'So what you saying though? You want Wythenshawe dealing with Salford?' He didn't look too sure about that side of things. It was a known fact that the two areas didn't get along with one another.

'Look... I'll ensure you only deal with lads who are sound to do business with. They will know that you are connected to me. So you won't have hassles.'

'Yeah but...'

'Hear me out Batty,' he stopped him in his tracks. 'I know I can trust you and I know that you can most definitely handle the weight that will be coming through. What do y'think? I am going go using the fucking O'Leary's for this. Behave son. Y'know how is. Every fucker is on my back to get back in the game. But like I say, I like the cash side of things, but can't be

314

seen to be personally involved. This way I can keep people happy and you'll be laughing at the same time.'

'Alright, tell me more...' smiled Batty.

We'd been remanded into police custody for a further week after being formally charged with an array of different elaborate charges relating to Saturday night and not forgetting the evidence that they produced on us towards their case against the entire crew. They were certainly going full out with this investigation – there was no doubting that with what they had come up with so far. However – they still hadn't mentioned the murder of the guard since the day of the arrest. But I knew that it was far from forgotten.

We'd all stood side by side in court and were all still wearing the suits worn from the previous days christening. It really must have been one hell of sight to look at as we stood there. The Magistrates had done enough (I imagined with the help of the Crown Prosecution) and what was necessary to hold us, although I was left with the distinct impression that they hadn't been given anywhere near enough time to prepare for it.

But no matter, they still got their week. After that they'd be looking to remand us indefinitely to H.M. Walton Remand Centre located in Liverpool until the actual date of the trial itself. We all knew now for certain that the backbone to their case lay with Scotty.

If Scotty was to take the stand and testify against us all – then we were all fucked and we knew it. He knew enough about how the whole operation worked to put us all away for a very long time. Especially me, with that murder charge they'd be looking to throw at me.

The real interviews and interrogations began Tuesday. As once they'd got their extension they'd have been putting together all of their evidence to bring into the interviews with them.

So as Tuesday morning arrived I knew what to expect as my cell door banged open, Walsh filling the void. 'Alright Chorlton... come on,' he smirked.

'My brief 'ere?'

'Yes son, we've just finished with O'Prey and you're next,' he said cuffing me.

As he lead me back to the same interview room as Sunday when we'd been questioned to our whereabouts on Saturday evening I immediately saw Stevenson was already sat there waiting along with Adrian as I arrived.

'Morning Adrian,' I smiled. 'How are you?'

'I'm fine Billy,' he responded back whilst still stacking papers before putting them down and shaking my cuffed hands. 'Are you alright this morning? You being treated alright?' he asked, as I hadn't seen him since the previous morning.

I sat down in the plastic chair that had been bolted to the floor. 'Can I get some water?'

'Later,' Walsh snapped as Adrian silently stared at him.

Walsh sighed and mumbled something that was incoherent as he shook his head then disappeared from the room whilst we covered the usual run of the mill merry go round for the beginning of the tape. Just as we'd completed the beginning, Walsh returned, gruffly putting the water down in front of me.

'Alright Chorlton – Back to Saturday night,' Stevenson began.

I sighed deeply then began glaring at him. 'I've already told you where we all were.'

'Well, we've got a positive ID on you and Jones, from the landlord,' Walsh grinned.

'No comment.'

'Look Billy,' Stevenson tried. 'You're not doing yourself any favours are you son. The landlord has given positive ID's on you two last night.'

'And...' I asked shrugging at him.

'And he's says that it was definitely you two first in there,' Walsh said.

'I already told that I was at the restaurant all night.'

'That's crap and we all know it Chorlton,' Walsh replied.

317

'Excuse me,' Adrian interrupted. 'But haven't you been to visit Chan himself.'

'Yes... But that's not...' Stevenson began.

'That's not what?' Adrian said cutting him off. 'You boys were there on Sunday night, weren't you? However – you found it more than a little convenient to leave that out yesterday morning. Didn't you?' he smiled knowingly at them both.

'But we know it was you Billy,' Walsh barked at me. 'We know that you're lying to us.'

'Now that's enough of that,' Adrian tutted his dislike at Walsh. 'My client has been more than helpful with you both about Saturday night. How you've got him all them miles away from Manchester when he's got a solid alibi that he was right here in town. I don't exactly know.'

'Oh our information is good Mr. Black,' Stevenson gloated.

'Yes right,' Adrian snapped. 'I suggest that until you have something more solid than what some informant has merely told you. And God knows what you lot let him off with to be receiving such scandalous accusations – Then I suggest we move on.'

'What are accusing us of Mr Black,' Walsh yelled, suddenly panicking that Adrian knew more than he was letting on.

'Probably no more than you're accusing my client of Mr. Walsh,' Adrian said sarcastically.

'Alright then Billy,' Stevenson said throwing a stack of photos to the table. 'Take a look at those for us. Will you?'

I began picking up the photos before me, I couldn't help but smile at the sight of all the damage we'd caused. Not only to The Windmill itself, but there was photos of the victims in hospital, all of whom got what they deserved in my mind. 'So what are these? Why are you showing me these?'

'What the hell are you grinning at Chorlton?' Walsh snarled at me.

'Sorry... Was I grinning?'

'You think that this is funny?' Stevenson sighed.

'No I don't think that these are funny at all,' I replied throwing the photos back onto the table. 'What I think is funny is that you two really haven't got anything solid on me except what some fucked up rock head has filled you with.'

'Alright then Billy, what about these photos?' he tossed another pile down onto the table. As I lifted them up observing all the shots they had of the crew on the estate I nodded then added.

'No comment.'

'What the hell do mean no comment Chorlton?' Stevenson snapped.

'What? Do I have to explain what no comment means to you,' I sniggered. 'Fuck me. They really do let all kinds join the force these days... Don't they?' I was laughing at them both, as I sipped my water.

'Are those men in the photographs your Lieutenant's Chorlton?' Walsh asked me.

I laughed out loudly at them shaking my head. 'My what?'

'Lieutenant's...' Walsh told me. 'That's what you call them isn't it?'

'No comment,' I was still laughing.

'You won't be laughing by the time we've finished with your lot Chorlton,' Stevenson told me.

'So what've you got to say about all the drugs that we found at the flat on Sunday?' Walsh asked.

'Also, the small arsenal of handguns that we retrieved from there also?' Stevenson added.

'My client has stated that the flat in question did not belong to him or anybody else that he knew for that matter,' Adrian cut in. 'Also, that when you actually did kick in the door to his flat – Which by the way, seeing as Mr. Chorlton was actually there with you and had his keys was completely unnecessary. But you didn't find anything that even associated him with the flat in question or with any of your so called evidence against him.'

'So is it true then,' Stevenson said, ignoring Adrian. 'That you and O'Prey control all of the drugs trade on Hulme estate along with a good area of Manchester city centre itself.'

'No comment,' I sighed.

'You are heavily involved and command those around you to purchase and distribute Cannabis resin, marijuana, heroin, you produce and distribute crack-cocaine, cocaine in powder form and also amphetamine,' Walsh stated smirking away.

'Also the distribution of pretty much all the Ecstasy tablets throughout Manchester... Oh and not forgetting that mind fuck of a drug LSD,' Stevenson added.

'No comment,' I yawned to show my boredom.

'But we've got somebody to testify that you are indeed one of two bosses who are behind it all,' Walsh added.

319

'Really.' I acted surprised. 'No fuckin' comment.'

'Alright take a look through these photos Billy and tell us what you know about them,' Stevenson threw yet another stack to me, only this was a much larger stack of photos.

They had shots of everyone I'd possibly known from the crew and more. They had shots of the street grafters, the watch command; the Lieutenant's with Scotty included were there vastly among them. There were multitudinous amounts of shots with Prey and myself in them. They had shots of us doing business in Wythenshawe. They had shots of us drinking in Dry Bar with some of the main heads from around town. They had stacks and stacks of these surveillance shots.

But I wasn't stupid, I knew that without Scotty to back these photos they meant absolutely nothing whatsoever in a court of law. The problem was though, that they did have Scotty and it threw a different light on the matter.

'Nice photos you've got,' I stated. 'You think that if I pick some out you could get me some copies for the album.'

'Don't get wise with us son,' Walsh snarled at me. 'Just what can you tell us about them?'

'How about no comment, just for a change,' I sighed at them, observing that their irritation was beginning to display.

'What you are saying then Billy,' Stevenson stretched staring at me. 'Is that you don't know anything about anything at all? Do we really look so stupid Billy that we'd be sat here wasting our time?'

I smirked broadly at them. 'Well, I think I better definitely go with no comment there or I might just really offend the two of you,' Adrian smiled to the side of me.

'Alright then Billy – What can you tell us about the dead security guard at Rasheed's warehouse in Salford back in 1986?' Stevenson suddenly sprung on me.

He brought that one on a little too quickly catching me slightly off guard. I thought that possibly I may have taken a couple of seconds too long in answering. 'No comment,' I said without it sounding quite as confident... even to myself.

'Well, that's not what we hear Chorlton,' Walsh informed me. 'The way we heard it was that the robbery turned sour once you killed the guard and you then threatened to kill Kulshaw and O'Conner if they said anything.'

'No comment. I don't even know what the fuck you're going on about,' I snapped back at them.

'So why are you becoming so irritable all of a sudden then Chorlton?' Walsh smirked.

'Fuck you... This is complete bullshit and y'know it is.'

'Take a look at these then,' Stevenson produced another pile of photos, only these were of the crime scene at Rasheed's from all those years ago. The dead security guard included in the shots both before and after they'd dragged him from the steel bins.

'These mean nothing to me,' I sighed.

'But we think that they do Billy,' Stevenson said staring straight at me.

'We know all about how you did the robbery and how the guard appeared afterwards as you was about to leave,' Walsh informed me proudly. 'We know that you stabbed the security guard then tried to dispose of the body. Then you made the other two try and cover up the evidence with the grease.'

'Then you drove to London in the stolen removal van and sold the stolen goods to somebody that *you* already knew down there,' Stevenson smirked knowingly at me.

'Then all three of you burnt out the van and travelled straight back to Manchester on the train,' Walsh added.

'At that point you then threatened to kill the other two if they said anything at all about any of the previous night's events,' Stevenson told me smiling.

'Have you got any forensic evidence to back what you are accusing my client of here gentleman? As you are fully aware, these are serious allegations you're bringing about here,' Adrian said.

'We don't really need it,' Stevenson smiled knowingly at me. 'Do we Billy?'

'No fuckin' comment,' I snapped thinking that their story, although for a good part to be true, Scotty for some reason had changed the last part around. And as for that fucking bit, about threatening to kill them... For fucks sake, he'd definitely lost the plot now.

'I really do suggest that you come up with something more solid if you wish to continue with this line of questioning,' Adrian told them.

Stevenson stretched. 'Alright then Billy... Let's go back to the beginning again.'

We continued down pretty much the same path all afternoon – whilst they constantly tried to trip me up with one thing or the other. They kept at me for almost five hours solid trying to wear me down and confuse me with their line of questioning. Eventually, the two of them tiring of the repeated routine, before finally requesting that I be returned to my cell.

Adrian had told them that it was necessary that he speak alone with me before they returned me to my cell.

'Just how bad do you think that this all is?' I asked as we were sat in the print room, a uniformed officer stood there.

'You tell me Billy?' he sighed. 'Just how much does this informant know?' he asked turning his back to the officer speaking quietly.

'Enough...' I said staring at him as he shook his head.

'What about this boozer that they keep going on about?' I asked. 'I mean they're saying that they got someone that will positively ID both me and Jonah.'

'But you've got Chan's word along with all of his waiters word that you were there that night,' he winked at me knowingly nodding.

'So we have,' I smirked.

'I think that they're still trying so hard with that one as it was all part of their initial arrest.'

Looking him straight in the eye. 'Look Adrian, what about this murder charge they're trying to stick on me?'

'I tell you what Billy,' he stared at me. 'If they've got only his word against yours on this it will be very thin indeed. What about Kulshaw, will he say anything?'

'He won't know what they're going on about,' I said, although being left with the feeling that I was trying to convince myself more than him.

'Are you sure?'

'He won't say anything conflicting if that's what you're getting at.'

'Good,' he simply said.

'Can I see Donna?' I then asked looking at him.

'You could do,' he shook his head. 'But it's like I told Kieran. I don't think it'd too good an idea for any of you to have any contact with the girls.'

'Alright... Whatever you think is best to do,' I sighed. 'Just tell her I'm alright though.'

'Already have been,' he smiled to me.

'Right then, what's the next step?' I asked stretching.

'They'll keep pumping you all week Billy... All of you that is,' he smiled at me. 'Just remain strong and don't worry just yet. I'll be in there with you anyway.'

'Thanks again for everything Adrian,' I said rising shaking · his hand with my cuffed wrists.

As Adrian left the room the uniformed officer took hold of my cuffs and lifted me out of the chair as we headed for the same door. Walsh had hold of Jonah as they were leading me back to my cell. Both of us were grinning and nodding to one another.

'Why... Afternoon my good sir,' Jonah said in that mocking voice we'd used at The Windmill.

'Why, good afternoon to you also my jolly good fella,' I said in similar ridicule fashion as we passed one another.

'Just get a move on Jones,' Walsh said angrily pushing him forward.

I laughed out loudly as I could hear Jonah doing the same as Walsh led him through to the interview room. They couldn't break us now, even if they did have us all down here.

All they really had was Scotty, as none of us would tell them shit... ever. Scotty had betrayed all of us and it hurt like hell that it been him to do it. The more I thought about it, the deeper the hurt cut its way into me. I was overflowing with miscellaneous feelings towards him. After all we'd grown up together from little scally's to where we were now.

'How are they?' Steve asked sitting down accompanied by Donna and Kathy.

The three of them had just arrived at Adrian Black's office. The office contained an old Victorian look that had been integrated along with a contemporary warm feeling to it.

Along the walls hung both paintings along with photographs of yachting boats, obviously something of keen interest to Adrian. A large oval window positioned itself behind Adrian's large leather chair and overlooked Manchester town centre.

'How's Chopper?' Donna asked eagerly as she shook her head. 'Sorry I mean Billy.'

Adrian smiled reassuringly. 'They're alright for the time being.'

'For the time being,' Kathy snapped. 'Well that doesn't sound too promising does it?'

Steve stared at both of them. 'Look Adrian, it's Wednesday already... Just what do you think the outcome is going to be?'

'Well, the problem we've got is their witness,' he shook his head. 'If this Scotty O'Conner testifies against them it's going to create all kinds of problems for us.'

'So they've definitely got him then?' Donna asked.

'Not that they've come straight out with it, no,' he smiled knowingly. 'But it's pretty obvious that they have. Apparently Jones unsuspectingly witnessed him leaving their car about a year ago now. For the moment they're just trying to do their best to find out what information they can to collaborate with the evidence he's given them.'

'So if they've got Scotty then they know pretty much everything?' asked Steve.

'From the questions they have been asking I'd say that they know a hell of a lot more than we could have ever anticipated.' He began to smile at the three of them.

'What's with the grin?' Kathy asked.

'I think at this precise moment both Stevenson and Walsh are pulling their hair out,' he nodded.

'Why's that then?' Steve enquired.

'Because each and every one of them is using their right to no comment and it's irritating the fuck out of them both, excuse my French,' he smiled once again.

'So what have they been charged with up to now?' Steve asked.

'Well for now, they're just holding them all on the charges relating to Saturday night and to the goods that they retrieved from the estate. This is whilst they continue to use this week to further their investigation,' he told them.

'And just what other charges are they looking for?' Donna asked.

'I'm going to be totally honest with all of you now, as it concerns Billy and Kieran more so,' he sat back in his chair and sighed deeply. 'With the two of them they're going to be going for one hell of a lot of conspiracy charges.'

'Shit,' sighed Steve deeply shaking his head, 'Honestly?' he added realising just how bad those charges could be. If the police managed to convict on those charges it could sometimes be a lot worse than them actually having you bang to rights on a charge.

'That's not all either. Apart from the conspiracy charges against them running this so called drug empire they seem intent on charging one of them with,' he looked directly at Donna.

'What... What is it?' she asked with concern as she realised it must be something relating to Chopper.

'They're going for a murder in the first degree charge against Billy,' he looked at all their astonished looks.

'You what!' Donna gasped her mouth wide open.

'Murdered who?' Steve asked panicking slightly that Paddy had come back to haunt them.

'A security guard from back in 1986,' he sighed again. 'Although the forensic evidence is pretty poor at the moment - but...'

325

'But what? This can't be true,' Donna blurted out. 'Not Chopper... No... He wouldn't,' she was shaking her head unconsciously.

'Well, apparently this witness is going to testify that he has all the details relating to the night in question, also Kulshaw was somehow involved. But for now they're only interested in charging Billy with it. Now I've had some research done into it and there was a murder back then. Whether or not they were somehow involved we don't know just how reliable this lads going to be to them.'

'This isn't good,' Steve said holding his head in his hands. 'Not fuckin' good at all.'

'Chopper's a bit on the wild side,' Kathy said stroking Donna's hair to comfort her. 'But he's no murderer. He'd never kill anybody. Would he?'

'It's not looking at all good with this Scotty going to testify. Does it Adrian?' Steve asked looking directly at him as he shook his head in answer.

'We need to get them through this week and see just what the final charges are actually going to be,' he told all.

'Then what?' Kathy asked.

'The prosecution will look to remand them to Walton in Liverpool, although we'll fight against that,' he told her.

'But do you honestly think they'll bail them after this?' Steve asked. 'I mean this is as serious as we're imagining, isn't it.'

'Yes it is Steve. I won't lie to you,' he smiled to try a little reassurance. 'Let's just see what they intend to do next.'

Steve nodded then turned to the two girls. 'Alright girls could you please give me a moment alone with Adrian please. I'll meet you both in Henry's afterwards,' he smiled at them as the two of them had tears rolling down their faces.

As they both left the office Steve turned and nodded at Adrian. 'Alright then Adrian, I need to know everything that they've got on them,' he lit a cigarette totally ignoring Adrian's No Smoking sign, exhaling the smoke dramatically whilst Adrian stared back at him and shook his head, then opened the office draw and took out a pack of Silk Cut cigarettes taking one from the pack and lighting it. 'And I mean everything Adrian.'

'Okay where do we start Steve?'

Steve had left the two girls sat in Henry's Bar once he'd finally returned from being with Adrian and made his way

326

across Manchester towards China town. He listened to everything that Adrian had told him carefully. He knew that they were all completely fucked with Scotty working against them. And as much as he hated it, he could only think of one option as he walked through the cold deserted streets of Manchester.

So Vincent,' said the voice, as he ripped the woollen balaclava from his face that had been placed around his head the wrong way round. The sweaty, due to the extreme heat, wool stank so bad it had been making him delirious. In fact, this entire nightmare was making him sick to his very core. He still didn't have a clue what was going on – or who his tormentor was. It felt as though he had been held captive for days – however it could have been weeks for all he knew. This freak didn't even question him. Just put him through as much pain as he could take before he passed out. And then he was brought round for further inflictions. He ankles were killing him and yet he wasn't sure why.

The punishment this guy kept inflicting whilst Vinnie was conscious was unbearable. And he still as yet, still hadn't told him what it was he wanted. As Vinnie gasped at the air, almost as if he was going to be his last, he tried get as much as he possibly could, before he knew the mask would be put back in its place. The figure was now stood before him. Only something wasn't right with this picture...

He realised that he was now hanging upside down, in what looked like a disused large commercial garage that had been closed down, but he couldn't be certain. All the windows were boarded up and the eerie silence from outside suggested that it was in the middle of nowhere. Also the lack of light made everything even more disorientating. He could see the two vehicles from the other night that had obviously been moved and were now stashed here along with him.

He'd been unconscious after the figure before him (albeit the other way round now) had struck him violently with the gun. The very same gun that was fitted with a silencer, hence why they hadn't heard anything that night they were ambushed when he... no actually – *they* – had all realised, albeit too late, what was happening. He now held that very same gun in a very casual manner.

This was the worrying factor thought Vinnie as he flinched as he bent low and began tapping Vinnie's forehead with the gun, was that the guy didn't appear to be all bothered by the fact that he was making no effort whatsoever to conceal who he was. Not that he knew who he was. He just knew that by him doing so he was obviously going to kill him. He just couldn't work out why he'd been kept alive as long as he had been. It just didn't make sense. But then again none of this did.

'What can you tell me about these photos I have of you?' asked the figure producing a brown A4 envelope and tipping its contents out onto the floor.

'Who the fuck, are you?' screamed Vinnie as he took in his surroundings once again ignoring the photos. What the hell was going on? He wasn't sure of anything anymore. 'Where the fuck am I now? What day is it?'

He honestly didn't recognise the guy. Seriously – who the fuck was he? And just what the fuck was going on here. 'I asked you, just who the fuck you are you cunt? Do y'know just who it is that you are...'

The gun slammed him hard once again. Only this time he didn't submit to slipping unconscious once again, and fought to stay alert. 'What the fuck...' he screamed.   'What is this shit you fuck?'

'The photos,' he casually answered as he dropped the array of different shots he had of Vinnie to the floor. Vinnie automatically recognised where the shots had been taken and he dropped his head in disbelief.

'What is it you want?' he asked feebly.

'Your father and I go back a long way,' he replied casually. 'Only thing is I've been out of town for a while.'

'I don't even know who the fuck you are.' He said struggling to focus through not only his concussion, but also his precarious position. 'What do know of my father?'

'I know for a fact that if finds out about these photos he won't be happy. Will he now Vinnie?' he smiled sadistically.

'Especially, after the incident that took place all those years ago, when you was still only a child yourself.'

'What the fuck is it you want?' he screamed, although more through fear than bravado. He didn't even know how this guy had got hold of the photos... but one thing was for certain and that was that if they came to light and his father was made aware of them... well he just knew that his old man would hit the roof. He had the first time round. But what was it this freak wanted? He couldn't give up his old man now... could he?

'I just told you,' he replied as he knocked Vinnie's head with the gun.

'You told me shit you freak,' he sneered as he took in the figure before him. He had never seen this guy before in his life. And how the hell had he gotten hold of those photos he asked himself once again?

This guy, despite the size (which let's face it, was very large) was such an imposing figure. It was his casual demeanour with along with his menacing aura that scared the shit out him. And he was Vinnie O'Leary for fucks sake. He didn't scare at all that easily. After all he had his old man to always back him. But this guy didn't even seemed scared of his old man, and the only other person he'd ever met who wasn't scared of his old man was Tony Henessy.

Was that it? Did this guy know Henessy? Was this Henessy at work here? Surely not. Tony hadn't even been in town for the last few years. Yeah fair enough, he had a lot of money working the streets and pretty much all the doors around town were covered by his crew of doormen that were assembled from all over the United Kingdom and even Northern Ireland. But even this shit wasn't Tony's style of play... was it? Besides which, he was certain that Henessy and his old man had sorted out their differences a long time ago.

So it couldn't be. Could it?

'There is two things that I need from you son,' he smirked.

'What the fuck is it?' he was still struggling with the ropes. 'And why the fuck did you kill everybody?'

'Didn't want to make this episode a party did I?' he responded nonchalantly. 'Beside which – figured it was best that I get to spend some quality time with you lad. You needn't worry about those lads anymore anyway. You will see what I mean by that soon enough, son. They are still to be

330

dealt with. Then they will be disposed of very easily,' he smirked. 'Especially with the contacts that I have.'

'What the fuck is it you need?'

'I think I already know this part. But amuse me all the same,' he smiled casually as though this was all some kind of normal everyday occurrence, 'I need the name of the lad in Salford buying all the pills from your firm. And you will give me the information.'

'Fuck you,' he sneered. After all he was no fucking grass, never had been, and never would be.

The figure before him casually started tapping his forehead with the gun. 'Now – now son – that's not the answer I was looking for.'

'I said fuc...' he didn't get to finish the words as the tapping turned into a full on slam – only this time he couldn't find the strength to fight it as he was knocked unconscious once again.

He wasn't sure what it was that brought him round. The stench of something so foul, it smelt like rotting burning flesh or the stench of petrol fumes? It fucking was petrol fumes! And it was being poured all over him. That was what brought him round as he struggled to focus. And to breathe as he watched in horror as the petrol from the canister from the rear of his very car was being poured over him.

'What are doing?' he screamed with everything he could muster.

'Answers,' was the simple reply he heard.

'Fuck you I ain't no grass,' he responded defiantly as he suddenly noticed that the figure was wearing rubber gloves and held something weird looking that he couldn't make out, in his hands. 'Go fuck...'

Only this time before he could finish he body shook violently and it felt as though a lightning bolt itself had struck him.

Jesus Christ – what the hell was that? His body was jerking one way then the other as the bright lights that seemed really close now shone brightly in his face. What the hell were they? Fuck me – he's moved both cars closer. What the hell is that? He saw the both cars had been moved to within a few feet to where he was imprisoned. And both head lights were blatantly pointed at him. But then there was something else. What the...

'You want to end up like your friends do you?' said the voice – although he wasn't sure where the voice was coming from. There was that smell again. And that's when he saw it. He

331

struggled to focus on what it was that he looking at. And then it became apparent as he watched the blazing pile between the two vehicles. It was the others... it was them piled into one heap – and not only that but they were on fire. They were ablaze with the sheer intensity of the flames that had engulfed their now bodies.

'You what you've got coming now don't you?' sneered the voice – but with both the flames and the lights Vinnie couldn't see where that voice was coming from.

He suddenly saw the spark from the left hand side. It was at that very moment he knew what he just sent that shock through him as the sadistic bastard before tapped the spark wires together, laughing as he did so.

'No don't,' begged Vinnie,' please – I beg you. Please don...' His words were engulfed with the intensity of the screams as the shocks from the jump leads exploded around his body as though at any moment he was going to burst into a ball of flames like the bodies that were blazing away only a matter of feet away from him.

Again this sadistic fucker hit him – again and again – and again as he shrieked and squealed like a pig. He had no idea how long this went on for. The pain he felt seemed like it been hours. Yet it could have just as easily been a matter of seconds.

He heard the laughing once again. Then he saw the sparks and the intensity of those alone scared the living daylights out of him. He couldn't take this.

'Please...'

'Name,' the casual response replied once again, as the sparks continued.

'Fuckin' Walker,' he screamed – thinking there was no way he was going to take this abuse for a prick like that. Grass or no grass. There was no way. 'Chris fuckin' Walker.'

'Okay,' said the guy. 'Now question number two...'

'What the fuck...'

'You honestly didn't think I came here just for that did you,' he laughed. 'I knew that answer already. I just wanted confirmation.'

'But you said...'

'I said that I had two things I wanted answering.' He paused and then threw the spark leads to the floor as Vinnie let out a sigh of relief. 'What was that?' he suddenly screamed at

Vinnie making his already nervous situation rise to another level.

'I thought...'

'You don't think you little prick,' he sneered as he then produced a mask. But it wasn't any kind of normal mask. What the hell was that?

'C'mon,' pleaded Vinnie, 'just tell me what the fuck it is that you want to know?'

'Information,' he replied as he suddenly started twisted something he couldn't se. All he heard was the wild hiss of gas being released. The figure turned and clicked the device in his hand. 'Amazing what you can find lying around these old garages eh son.'

Vinnie's face dropped as his watched the blurred figure pull what appeared to be a welder's mask over his face – in fact it didn't *appear to be* – it fucking was a welder's mask. And the clicking suddenly turned into a blaze that blinded Vinnie with its intensity.

Squeezing his eyes shut to prevent them from blinding he literally screamed out into the night as the flame tore away his shirt and burnt through the skin on his chest almost as if it wasn't there to begin with.

'Stop it,' he screamed and pleaded with everything he could muster.

'I need to get at your father,' said the figure as he turned off the flame and removed the mask. 'Only he seems to have gone straight these days. Well apart from obviously all the shit you to have going on in the side lines with crap like Saturday tonight. That and the fact I hear you're all looking to start getting in on the action around town for yourselves that is.'

'What do you want with my old man?' he asked whilst his body shock violently from both the pain and the shock his body felt.

'He's the reason I've been gone for so long,' he said. 'He had what was coming to him, and he only caught a break was 'cause I had to leave town when I did.'

'What the hell are you...?'

'Just listen you little prick,' he snarled. 'I want everything on him that you've got. I know what it is the O'Leary's have got planned. And I just can't have you lads getting yourselves involved at this moment in time. That's why I have to get at the old man, Vinnie.'

'But I can't give you the old man,' he sighed as he watched the mask drop once again. 'Please no...' He trailed off as the flame ignited and he felt it instantly hit his groin area... but it was too much as he gave way to consciousness.

Vinnie started to come round once again. His mind was filled with an assortment of deranged images and sounds as everything blurred into one. What had just taken place? He didn't know what he had done. He wasn't sure of anything anymore. All he knew was that he wanted it all to stop. He had begged. He had pleaded. But the sadistic fucker had just continued with the inflicted damnation of what he it was he appeared to gain great gratification from.

Struggling to open his eyes, heard the voice talking – only it wasn't to him. 'What was that, Chan?' said the voice. 'I'm kinda of busy here.'

There was a pause as Vinnie tried to focus. He saw the guy was talking on a mobile phone as Vinnie shook his head and the blood that dripped into eyes stung... not to mention the way his entire body felt as though it was literally on fire.

'Okay fine,' he heard him sigh, almost as though he was irritated. 'Give me a couple of hours though.' There was another pause. 'I'll see you then old timer.'

Vinnie wasn't quite sure what was reality and what wasn't at this point as he suddenly, very abruptly, felt his body hit the cold hard concrete. And the pain that he felt that very moment in time was like nothing he had ever felt before. He didn't know where he was or what exactly had just taken place. The confusion of everything was what was really screwing with his mind.

'You're a good lad son,' he heard the voice but he could barely focus. 'A deal is a deal right,' he added.

'What the fuc...' he coughed violently. 'What fuckin' deal?? And how'd you know my old man?'

'Ask him.'

'What...'

'You can ask him all about me when you see him,' he replied as he took Vinnie in his arms. 'That fucker owes me and I've come to collect my debt.'

'Why?'

'Don't you worry about that son,' he laughed. 'All you need to know is that you gave me what I needed and because of that... I'll see you right,' said the figure, as Vinnie felt himself being lifted from the floor. 'Besides which you'll be of use to me in time. Just remember my face, son.'

'What – I don't kno...'

'Shush now kid,' said the almost sympathetic voice. 'Let's get you out of here.'

'But...' was about all Vinnie managed as he felt the darkness came once again.

'You got my gear Walsh?' Scotty asked anxiously as the detective walked through the bedroom door late Wednesday night.

It had been the first time since the early hours of Sunday morning and they had moved Scotty to the safe house that anybody had been to seen him. They'd given him enough of the drug to see him through, although that had been no where enough to feed his habit and therefore had run out a long time ago.

They'd moved Scotty to a safe house or flat as that's what it was in Altrincham, situated beside a ruck of woodland secluding the property from public view.

Also all of it's the residents residing there were elderly couples retired. The location was perfect. Only one man at a time guarded Scotty as they felt that his main threat from the estate – as in Chopper, Prey and the rest of them were all locked deep inside head quarters.

'Hello Scotty,' Walsh smirked. 'How are you tonight?'

'Look, stop fuckin' about with me,' he snapped back impatiently. 'Just give me my fuckin' gear.'

'Keep it quiet Scotty... Will you,' Walsh sneered in return. 'Remember, there is only three of us that know about this and that the way it'd got to stay. All right? So you make sure that you stay in here or better still the bathroom in there whilst smoking the shit.'

'Yeah, yeah Walshy whatever you say,' he replied. 'Just give me the gear.'

'We need to talk first Scotty,'

336

'I certainly talk a whole lot better on it,' Scotty told him producing his hands that were shaking uncontrollably for Walsh to see.

'Alright then,' Walsh sighed producing the small plastic bag. 'Go and do it in the bedroom's bathroom over there though. The last thing I want is to be inhaling that shite.'

Scotty quickly disappeared out of sight into the bathroom slamming the door behind as he went.

Walsh put his feet up onto the bed and began to relax. The last few days were taking their toll on him, but he needed to persevere with it. He began recollecting thoughts on all the interviews that they'd covered over the last few days.

Not one of them was giving in to anything though. They had both exhausted themselves with the laborious task of the continued and repeated questioning. They were trying their best to collaborate things that Scotty had given them to somehow retain answers that corresponded with each other.

Only – up until now they'd been unsuccessful in any given attempts. Stevenson had wanted to continue in similar fashion through the remainder of the week. He was convinced that they'd finally break.

However as he was lay there thinking that he didn't hold out much hope with that technique. He saw the way the literally blanked answers. Acted clueless to any questions thrown at them, no matter how many times repeated over and over.

He saw how they just weren't going to break in the slightest for them. In a strange sort of way he'd even admired their arrogance towards them both.

He had admired their professionalism to just how they'd organised their activities, giving credit where credit was due. They were fully prepared, as if almost trained for the day in which their demise would fall upon them.

He truly believed that if they hadn't got Scotty to work for them at the beginning of last year, then they would never have been able to break them.

And as for Saturday night, well he had to give full credit to them. They hadn't even been aware of Scotty, yet had taken every possible precaution to ensure that if any heat was brought upon them, that they were once again in the clear from the authorities.

Walsh knew that Saturday night was already beginning to slip away them, but what their main concern was their entire operation against bringing them down. Just then the bathroom door opened as Scotty stood there with an appearance of calmness about him.

'Feeling better Scotty?'

'Yes – Cheers for asking,' he sniggered. 'Now what is it you want to ask me Walsh?' he asked as he sat himself into the bedside chair and began flicking through stations on the television set.

'We questioned the entire lieutenant's over the last few days Scotty,' Walsh told him. 'Also O'Prey and Chorlton and we got shit from them.'

'Well what did you expect Walsh,' Scotty laughed. 'That they were just to admit everything to you for fucks sake,' he sneered the last bit at him.

'Of course not. But we do have one problem in our hands,' he said, staring at Scotty. 'Saturday night.'

'What about it?' Scotty asked, looking to Walsh. 'I told you where they were. What, didn't they do the boozer in?' He asked shocked, as he was certain that's what he heard from that day in Henry's Bar.

'Oh the boozer was completely trashed,' he said throwing the A4 envelope to Scotty. 'Just take a look for yourself.'

As Scotty glanced through the photos he found himself smiling at the damage that they'd caused. 'Shit... They really fucked this gaff and everybody in it up,' he sniggered again. 'Didn't they Walshy?'

'Trouble is they've got Chan backing them that they were in the restaurant all night,' Walsh said. 'The old man says that Prey hired it out for the night.'

'He's done that before now,' Scotty said, still looking at the photos.

'To use as an alibi for themselves?'

'Nah nothing like that... Just for private parties and shit y'know,' Scotty told him. 'That's all.'

'Well, that's the problem then,' Walsh sighed. 'We've only got your word against theirs.'

'Fuck it then,' Scotty said tossing the photos back to him. 'What can I say? They sure are a bunch of clever fuckers.' Then a look of concern fell upon his face.

'What?' Walsh asked.

'Or maybe they were onto me,' he said looking at Walsh. 'Maybe they were going to do me in that night at the restaurant.' His paranoia began to kick in.

'I think they were as shocked as the next person when we nicked them Scotty.'

'So they know it's me then?' he asked looking astonished once again.

'Well, your names not been mentioned outright,' Walsh sighed. 'But we both know that they're not stupid.'

'What about the street grafters? Have you nicked them yet?' Scotty asked shaking his head at what the rest of them would now be thinking of him.

'Not yet,' Walsh told him lighting a cigarette.

'Why the fuck not?' Scotty snapped.

'Once we get these lot remanded to Walton then we'll take down the street next week,'

'That doesn't make any fuckin' sense,' he snapped again.

'Of course it does,' Walsh said blowing out his smoke. 'This way they'll think that were not onto them and continue trading.'

'Do not under estimate them,' Scotty said looking directly at Walsh.

'We're on them right now as we speak,' Walsh smiled. 'Are you sure that you can't give us more on Saturday night Scotty?'

'No,' he said shaking his head, in a way he was kind of glad that they'd done what they had done. 'I didn't know they'd use a front for fucks sake. Hasn't any fucker ID'd them,' he added to try and show he was a little bothered.

'We've got positive ID's on Chorlton and Jones from the landlord, but they've still got Chan,' he sighed letting the smoke drift from his mouth.

'You must have more than enough from what I've given you though,' Scotty said. 'To bring them down that is.'

'We were just hoping for more though. On them two at least.'

'What about the murder of the security guard I've given you though?'

'We're still waiting to see whether or not we can match any of the forensic evidence from way back then,' Walsh sighed deeply and shook his head. 'The original case got somewhat fucked up as the murder wasn't discovered immediately. Therefore a lot of the forensic evidence was screwed up before the initial investigation began. I mean we've only got your word as to how it all happened.'

'What's that supposed to fuckin' mean.'

'Nothing,' Walsh went quiet for a moment. 'Look Scotty, when you finally gave us that information you had your back against the wall.'

'So what?'

'So, you hadn't told us about it before,' Walsh stared at him. 'Had you now?'

'Always got to keep one or two secrets Walshy. You never know just when you might need to use one of them.'

'Yeah well you better just hope that when you testify against him, you do a good job,' Walsh told him. ''Cause at the moment, one piece of information you gave us on Saturday night doesn't look like it's going to pay off.'

'Ah fuck it,' Scotty sniffed. 'I'll be a star for you boys. After all, theres no turning back for me now,' he waved the bag at Walsh. 'You just make sure that you keep me in stock Walshy so that I can keep my head straight.'

'Whatever Scotty, I'm knackered,' Walsh began to push himself from the bed. 'Just keep thinking if you've got any more secrets hidden away son. The more we can get the better it'll be for you,' he smirked knowingly. 'After all son, the last thing you'll be needing is for them all to get off it and you be out on the street again. Is it now?'

'Fuck you Walshy,' he snarled.

'Whatever kid,' smiled Walsh

He watched as Walsh opened the bedroom door to exit. 'Walsh,' he said more quietly with his head dropped.

'Yeah,' Walsh asked pulling his jacket on in the doorway.

'So they definitely know it's me, right?' he asked feebly.

Walsh grinned broadly. 'Just what do you think son,' he said and with that he was gone.

We're just going over and over the same questions Billy,'
Stevenson said shaking his head at me.

Thursday had arrived, five days of this including Sunday had
past us all by. I'd been sat in the interview room all afternoon
whilst they spent the entire time covering their tracks on every
aspect of our business and the death of the security guard over
and over again with all of us. They were trying to wear us
down into submission... But none of us would break now.

Saying that though, they still seemed confident enough with
what they had to have a good enough case against all of us.
Everything that we'd been questioned about all had some
relevance to our business although we weren't just going to
hand it to them on a plate, were we now.

The truth was though, although none of us had spoken to one
another, apart from shouting nonsense to one another at night
through the darkness of the thick steel cell doors, which held
no relation to anything that they were investigating anyway.
But we all knew that if Scotty were to testify against us then
we'd be fucked for real and looking to go down for a very
long time, especially me with the first-degree murder charge
they were going for.

Adrian and his partners had spent all of their time with us
throughout the interviews. But even he wasn't entirely sure
which way they were going to play it with us. All he kept
saying was that the prosecution case against was weighted
heavily against us because of Scotty.

I kept thinking that once he took the stand before all of us,
looking directly at us that he wouldn't be able to go through

341

with it. But I knew deep down that I was just trying to blag myself. He'd do it alright. After all he'd been doing it all along... Hadn't he? Things weren't looking good and we knew it – Still we might as well make it as annoying as possible for them whilst we were at it.

'If you say so Stevenson,' I yawned.

'So all of the dates, all of the times, all of the places that we've covered,' Walsh shook his head at me. 'And you're still saying that you don't know anything about them at all.'

'For fucks sake... No bastard comment,' I snapped.

'You can't hide behind no comment all the time Billy,' Stevenson told me.

'And why's that then?'

'Well, just how do you think it's going to look in court Billy,' Walsh smiled knowingly.

'That's right Billy,' Stevenson sneered at me. 'It'll look like you're hiding something from us.'

'Oh alright then, you're both right,' I smiled. 'How stupid of me – I mean just what was I thinking, eh.'

'Exactly,' Stevenson smiled nodding.

'Exactly,' I mocked Stevenson's voice. 'I'll sit 'ere and tell you just what I know, so that then you couple of lying conniving twats can then go away and twist my words into further charges against me,' I was smirking at the two of them. 'Somehow – I don't think so boys.'

'Fuck you then,' Stevenson told me.

'That's right,' Walsh added. 'You all know that we've got more than enough to send all of you lads away for a very long time.'

'Er... No comment,' I smiled at the two of them.

'Interview terminated at five past six,' Stevenson said hitting the stop button. 'Now get him the fuck out of here.'

'We'll be charging you all very soon Billy,' Walsh said.

'Well, it won't be before time,' Adrian added sighing as he did so. 'That's for sure.'

Walsh stepped out of his chair and took me by the arm and led me through the door into the corridor and as he led me back towards my cell he whispered into my ear. 'Scotty says hello,' he said smirking as he did.

'Did he now,' I smiled back at him gleefully. 'Just how is the lying crack head of a witness Walshy? In good health I hope.'

'He gave us everything that we needed to send all of lads away for a very long stretch,' he stopped and looked at me as we reached my cell door. 'Also we'll be shutting down all of your operations on the estate and around town. We're closing you down and there's shit all that you can do about it.'

'Now are you completely sure that Scotty didn't just fill you full of more shit than you're already full of Walsh,'

'Fuck you Chorlton!' he snapped as all the others began banging on the cell doors shouting abuse as they could hear Walsh and I talking. 'Just get back in there. It's where you all belong anyway,' he pushed me as hard as he could through the open doorway.

'You're all full of shit,' I laughed turning just in time to see the cell door bang shut into the shadows once again.

I'd been lay there on the hard cold blue plastic mattress all evening thinking about what Scotty had done to all of us... me especially.

Just why had he done it for Christ sake? We'd both been through so much together growing up on the estate together as kids into adults. As I thought about all of the crazy shit that we always used to do, I couldn't help the joy that I'd once felt was now darkened by his betrayal.

Me, of all people should have opened my eyes to it for fuck sake. He'd been fucked up for so long now; I had merely not wanted to accept it as reality. Even Batty had blatantly told me that he'd seen him. Jonah had kept telling me – yet foolishly I'd just convinced myself that it couldn't possibly be so bad, after all I'd known him like a brother.

Maybe not for the last few years, but that was just the way the dice had rolled for us. I'd never expected partnership or for things to escalate to heights which had been peaked. It was just the way things had turned out and I'd been in the right place at the right time to take advantage of it.

Just what had gone drastically wrong? Fucking rocks, that's what. I mean we all smoked them and we all enjoyed smoking them – occasionally that is – not all the time. But you just had to be strong willed with them and control them – After all it wasn't a physical addiction like smack; it was a mental addiction.

I always considered him to be my brother, someone close to me. But not now, now he'd sold all of us down the river. We knew from the questions that we were being asked that he'd well and truly told them everything that he knew about our operation on the estate and around town itself.

As I lay there thinking about all of this, I heard that one of the cell doors across from mine was being opened – it was Prey's cell... or at least that is what I presumed. You could hear muffled voices but thought no more of it. It was probably just Stevenson or Walsh continuing with their entirety of hassle

'You know who I am?' the huge darkened figure blocking Prey's open cell door asked.

'What do you want?' Prey enquired quizzically, nodding his answer to the large figure.

The large figure walked into the cell, pushing the heavily steeled door closed to suppress any sounds that could be over heard.

'Looks like you lads have got yourselves a bit of a problem,' he said smirking at Prey knowingly.

'It's got fuck all to do with you,' Prey stated fact, not taking his eyes from the figure. 'So what's the interest?'

'Don't mind if I sit down Prey,' he asked doing so anyway. 'Do you now?'

'Be my guest,' Prey said shrugging as he was already seated beside him. 'It's not like I got a choice in the matter – is it?'

'You want one?' the figure asked offering Prey a cigarette ignoring the comment.

'No thanks,' Prey shook his head. 'Just how the fuck did you get in 'ere?'

'I know the detention officer,' he replied casually as he lit his cigarette. 'The night shift one anyway.'

'And? What is it you want?' Prey asked curiously.

'Just thought that I'd stop by and say hello,' he let a little laugh, although there was no humour in it whatsoever.

'Yeah right,' Prey sighed. 'Like I said before, this ain't anything to do with you, so what's the interest in it?'

'Steve sent me,' he said calmly looking at Prey as he blew smoke rings out.

'You what!' Prey exclaimed, fully startled. 'How the fuck do y'know...' Prey trailed off.

'We both know how,' he smiled knowingly, the smile making his feature appear even more sinister. 'Maybe I can help with your problem. All of your problems that is.'

'And just how could you do that then?' Prey asked staring at him.

The figure didn't even look at him. 'The address to the safe house of the one person in protective custody that is set to fuck all of you big time.'

Prey nodded, staring coldly at the figure. 'How much?'

'That's why Steve sent me to see you,' he said turning his head towards Prey, his face full of no emotion. 'He said he couldn't authorise it alone. Said that I had to come see one of you two. And, seeing as I remembered you, from way back when, just before I had to leave town. I thought I'd come check with you Prey.'

'So what are we talking then?' Prey sniffed.

'Let's just get one thing straight first,' he said staring hard at Prey. 'Only the address right. After that you'll have to make your own arrangements.'

'But are you sure that you've got the right information?' Prey asked staring at the figure.

'One hundred percent,' he smile full of confidence and contentment. 'I followed Walsh there last night after I'd spoken with Steve.'

'So what's the damage we're talking then?' Prey asked as he watched the smoke trail from his open mouth and nostrils. 'And is there going to be any comeback after this?'

'Of course they'll be comeback Prey,' he smiled knowingly. 'After this little venture together I'll be on your books... So to speak.'

'I ain't grassing anybody to you,' Prey said firmly.

'I was going to suggest that...' he paused, looking almost thoughtful then added, 'But now after meeting you in person I know you wouldn't Prey. It's just not your style,' he drew deeply on his cigarette holding eye contact with Prey as the cigarette crackled in the silence hanging between them. 'But let's just say that I'll keep you informed as the any relevant information that might be of interest to your crew.'

'So spit it out then. Just how much is this going to cost us?' Prey asked once again.

'Fifty gee's cash,' he watched for Prey's reaction not receiving one.

'That's sounds alright,' Prey told him nodding holding his eye contact. 'But where's the catch.'

'A further three grand a week there after,' he grinned.

'You're trippin' right,' Prey blurted out. 'That's well over the top and y'know it is.'

345

'Take it or leave it Prey,' he said rising from the mattress. 'I know it's shit mate. But hey, you lot live shit lives that make good, good money. You know it's not that much really. Not with the figures that you lads are bringing in.'

Prey held his head in his hands shaking it. 'Alright... But what time do we get the address? They're looking to charge us soon.'

'I know they are and from what I hear they've got themselves a solid case,' the figure smiled leaning back against the cell wall. 'Alright here it is then. As soon as you give your brief, the word tomorrow, then we're on.'

'Give him what word exactly?'

'Just stress to him that s he's to call Steve immediately to tell him to go and see the accountant that morning,' he threw his butt to the floor stamping viciously on it. 'As soon as Steve receives the call you'll have the address within the hour.'

'Then it's all down to us,' Prey asked looking directly at the figure.

'That's the one,' he grinned knowingly, opening the door slightly. 'If everything goes alright Steve will have further instructions for you lads after that. Understood Prey?'

'Sweet... You got yourself a deal then,' Prey said holding his hand out to be shaken.

'It'll be nice working with you Prey,' the figure replied as he took Prey's hand firmly. 'All three of you for that matter,' he smiled winking at him as he headed for the steel door.

'I just wish that I could say the same, Anderson,' Prey sighed as he watched the corrupt detective disappear through the cell door, turning over darkness once again to his confines.

What do you reckon Martin?' asked Stevenson as the two of them walked back into the office.

'I reckon that we'll be okay as long as Scotty sticks to the story and we build upon that.'

'You think they stand a chance of getting bail?'

'Nah,' smiled Walsh. 'They haven't got a chance in hell. Look based on what we've got there is no way in hell they would have give the extension they have done if they were even considering giving these cunts bail – is there?'

'I suppose not,' sighed Stevenson as he opened just one of the many files on the desk in front of him as Walsh walked to the window and stared out to the usual dismal evening that hung so heavily in the Manchester skyline.

'So what's the problem?' asked Walsh looking back over his shoulder.

'Nowt,' he replied apprehensively. 'It's just I can't believe after all this time we've only got what we have.'

'It's more than enough.'

'You think we'll get the conviction against Chorlton on the murder of that security guard?'

'He did that 100 percent Mike,' stated Walsh as he reached to desk and grabbed the packet of Silk Cut, taking one for himself, lighting it and then tossing the packet to his partner as his did the same. 'You can see it written all over his face every time the subject comes up.'

'I know what you're saying.'

'Chorlton is one of the most blasé characters I have ever come across when you've got him in a interrogation room – but from that very first moment we hit him with the knowledge we had of this...'

'I know,' smiled Mike.

347

'He shit himself,' laughed Walsh. 'You saw the way it hit him. So fuckin' what if we haven't got a shit load of forensics to back this up. With Scotty's word and the evidence of the details that were never released, we'll nail this fucker for good. On top of all the drug charges we'll bring against them, Chopper... Sorry, Chorlton – will never see the light of day. '

'Good,' replied Stevenson inhaling deeply on his cigarette. 'Out of all them – there is something about Billy that really gets under my skin.'

'I know what you mean there,' nodded Walsh. 'Like I said ever since that day all those years ago – I don't think I have ever come across anybody that has wound me the fuck up as much as him.'

take it that that is mine Steve?' asked Anderson staring at the black holdall that Steve was carrying into the kitchen at Chan's restaurant.

The meeting had been set for Friday lunch time one hour after Steve had received his call from a very baffled Adrian. Chan had allowed for the meet to take place at his, as he knew both party's concerned, although he was carrying a complete look of displeasure as he stayed in the background.

'You got what we require?' Steve asked as he lifted the black bag onto the stainless steel work surface.

'Of course Steve,' he sneered, looking the man before him up and down. 'But you don't mind just pat you down first?'

'Pat away Anderson,' he held his arms up as he began to search Steve. 'But in that case, you wouldn't mind if I at least see that you have the information with you... Would you?' Steve stood his ground as the large bulk of a man stood before him.

Anderson stopped patting Steve down then half grinned as he reached into his jacket pocket producing a manila envelope. 'It's alright Steve,' he winked. 'Here you go,' he passed the envelope to him as the holdall was lifted over to his eager grip.

Anderson tore open the zip to reveal the bundles of used bank notes grinning knowingly as he stared at the sight before him. 'Nice – Very nice indeed,' he smiled then looked to Steve. 'Right... this one's for free.'

'You what?' Steve looked at him confused.

'Don't worry Steve,' he smirked. 'I mean this little bit of extra privileged information I'm about to give you.'

'What's that then?' Steve asked as he began to tear at the envelope not taking his eyes from Anderson.

'Okay, let's just say first off, don't ask me just how I know this, but apparently a young lad over in Sale was arrested last Saturday whilst committing an armed robbery. The suspect was collected before being charged with the crime by the two investigating detectives involved with your case. Funnily enough the kid disappeared soon after,' he raised his eyebrows in a knowing manner at Steve.

'Scotty,' Steve sighed as Chan looked up.

'That's not all Steve,' he added, staring obstinately at Steve. 'I have a friend who also says that one of the very same detectives' trips down to the disposal furnace lately has become a lot more frequent.'

'They've been keeping him rocked up?' Steve shook his head. 'If the defence got onto this it'd get thrown out of court.'

'But the defence isn't going to get onto it? Are they now Steve?' He snapped viciously, his glare turned icy cold. 'Like I said, that was privileged information that remains that way. Besides I like my friend a lot who runs the furnace.'

'You sure this information is on the level?' Steve asked changing the subject as he read the contents to the envelope.

'You can trust me Steve,' he told him. 'Ask Channy boy here, he'll tell you so,' he gave Chan a cold look who was acting oblivious to the transaction-taking place before him in his very own establishment.

'Whatever you say detective,' Chan said examining one of his meat cleavers with a small glint in his eye.

'See,' Anderson announced smugly.

'So what happens after this?' Steve asked.

'First off I want to make something very clear to you now,' he began to zip the holdall up again. 'There will be one officer guarding this kid. I don't mind him taking a knock, but nothing else,' he said firmly, then as an afterthought added. 'Well, that is unless you'd like to discuss other financial arrangements to allow for that Steve.'

'I don't think so Anderson,' Steve shook his head. 'This thing will attract more than enough heat afterwards. The last thing we need is for over anxious coppers running about looking for the killer of some dead officer now. Isn't it?'

'Okay,' he shrugged and shook his head. 'That's also the reason why when this has gone down I don't want any contact with any of for at least one to two months, unless an absolute necessity that is.'

'What about your dough then?'

'You lads can act as a bank for me,' he replied as he began to stroke the holdall. 'After all I think I'll be alright for a couple of months.'

Steve shook his head. 'You certain that there is only one guard on duty with him?'

'That's all there was the other night anyway,' he nodded. 'But then again it's not my problem is it.'

'So that concludes business then,' Chan injected still not looking at Anderson.

'Reckon so,' he answered flatly, heading for the exit. 'Oh and just remember I don't want any comebacks from these events or I could make things extremely difficult for all of you lads. Always better to keep on the friendly side of me. Isn't it Chan?' he stared at Chan until the old man returned his glare.

'Yes Mr. Anderson,' he said shaking his head. 'I believe it is so.'

'I'll be seeing you both,' he winked and then with that he was gone out of the back door leading through to the alleyway.

Steve turned to Chan. 'He a slimy bastard ain't he Chan?'

'He nothing but trouble Steve,' Chan's face was twisted with the dislike that he felt towards him. 'Mr. Anderson has taken from my people for a very long time now.'

'Why have they never done anything about it?'

'Once they did try to do something about it. They shot him three times, leaving him for dead. That was a long time ago now. Left him to die in the gutter like the dog he is,' Chan sighed. 'But he lived and now makes things even more difficult for us. One day though... One day, his day will eventually arrive when the timing is just about right,' he added almost absentmindedly to Steve.

Steve shook his head. 'Thanks anyway Chan,' he said stuffing the envelope into his pocket.

'No thank me Steve,' Chan said firmly. 'Just remember that I warned you about him already.'

'We had no other choice in the matter Chan,' Steve said shaking the old mans hand.

'Just remember that this is not to be considered as a favour,' Chan held Steve's grip. 'I believe he will only bring new troubles for you all.'

'Thanks anyway Chan,' Steve smiled then disappeared through the door that Anderson just had gone through.

As he stepped into the alleyway he looked around then spotted what he was looking for as he walked in the direction of the silver Mercedes.

'Was that him?' Sleeper asked as Steve climbed into the back seat and nodded at Eazy in the passenger seat. 'The big geezer that came out a couple of minutes ago?'

'That was him,' Steve shook his head. 'I can see why Chan has a dislike for him you know.'

'Why's that then?' Eazy asked Steve.

'I've only met with him twice now and already I'm left with that bad taste in my mouth. He has this habit of constantly using your name as though you're good pals with one another.' Steve looked deep in thought as the other two looked at him. 'Not only that, but, he sure looks like a pure evil twat when you get face to face with him. If truth be known then I have to admit that he scares the shit out of me more than anybody else that I can think of.'

'You got the information though?' Sleeper enquired taking in the information carefully.

'Yeah – cost enough fuckin' dough though,' Steve said, producing the envelope from his pocket removing the small slip of paper containing the information. 'Plus that's not the end of it either.'

'Prey approved it though, didn't he?' Sleeper asked glancing from the envelope to Steve.

'Yeah, what other choice did we have,' Steve sighed.

'None mate,' Eazy answered simply patting Steve on the shoulder.

'Alright then, do you know where this place is then?' Sleeper asked.

'I know the town – just not the place, although that shouldn't be too much bother after we get there,' Steve smiled.

'Yeah,' laughed Eazy, 'plus we could always just ask a copper for directions.'

352

As Anderson sat in his car outside Hope Hospital where Vinnie had been dumped, he was thinking about the information that O'Leary's son had given him. The stupid kid didn't even realise what he was telling him. By that time he was feeling so much pain and anguish he would have revealed all the details to the photos that had scared the shit of him in the first place.

But despite the photos, they were not really his concern or his area. In fact it was better that he kept hold of those to keep Vinnie in check for the time being. Especially, seeing as he was worth more to him alive than dead at this moment in time. Anderson had dealt with the bodies of the others after he'd dumped Vinnie at the hospital. It had been easy enough – well most things were with the contacts that he held in his pocket.

Vinnie had undergone so much from his little torture session. So much so, that it had taken all this time for them to find out where he was. The information that he had revealed him had been more than enough.

He'd been so pleased when they had pulled him back into Manchester from London. After all this was his town wasn't it. Not only that but he many old scores – and many new ventures he wanted to both settle and set up.

He saw the two cars come screeching into the car park. Old Dominic O'Leary was the first to jump out of the vehicle as he was closely followed by five men – men whom he knew. All of them were old school just like he was. But he didn't have anything against these guys. They were merely foot soldiers for the O'Leary's. He watched as they all ran through the front doors to the emergency room at the hospital.

As he thought about the plans he had in mind as he thought about the other – in fact it was probably the only other with whom he would have considered as someone whom would need dealing with – dealing with – not controlling which is what he wanted to do.

Only he knew there were certain characters in town that he couldn't do that with. Dominic O'Leary, the old man, being one of them. The other would have been Henessy – Tony Henessy – son of Tommy, whom was shot dead many years ago. In fact, it was that shooting that had wet his beak so to speak as it was through the information he had supplied – that being the first time that he realised the perks that came with the job. Oh and how he had exploited those perks over the years. It was through people like the O'Leary's and Henessy's he had discovered ways and means to make the job more useful to his own advantage of course. But Tony wasn't going to be a problem as he was no longer in town – in fact he wasn't even in the country any more.

He smiled once again to himself as he turned the key in the ignition. He had to be somewhere. Especially now that he knew he had a few hours on his hands as Dominic O'Leary would be with O'Leary junior for at least a few hours. And a few hours would be all he would need.

SEVENTY

The three of them arrived at the block of flats in Altrincham later that afternoon in the Ford Granada that Steve had arranged. The place had taken a lot longer to locate than they'd previously thought.

'Damn,' Eazy exclaimed as the three of them were ducked out of sight in the ruck of woodland, just beyond the boundaries of the flats. 'They sure have got him hidden away, haven't they?'

'It should work in our favour that, anyway,' Sleeper confirmed, staring through his miniature binoculars.

'It's the far block on the right,' Steve said pointing towards the flats.

'Just how the fuck do you figure that?' Eazy asked whilst opening his third bottle of Guinness punch from Sampson's where he'd made them stop on the way to pick up some Jerk fried chicken and dumplings.

'Because its number 53 and they have five blocks,' he informed him. 'It makes sense that's block one and two – and well – eventually figure that's the fifth.'

'Oh yeah,' Eazy shrugged as he gulped away at the drink. 'It sure feels out in the sticks here compared to London.'

'From the flat number that we've got I'd say it's got to be that one there,' Sleeper said ignoring Eazy's comment as he pointed and handed the binoculars to Steve.

'Second floor eh,' Steve focused the binoculars into sight. 'I see it... Not much sign of life though.'

'We'll just have to be patient on that score,' Sleeper replied.

355

'You sure that the information is good Steve?' Eazy asked leaning back against a tree trunk that seemed instantly under duress due to the size of him.

'Chan wouldn't have let us use Anderson, if it wasn't,' he said not taking his eyes from the flat.

'Alright then,' Sleeper announced tapping Steve's shoulder. 'We'll come back tonight and check this plot out. For now though, I want to get a feel of the area itself whilst there's still a little day light left.'

'Alright then,' Steve said pushing himself from the ground.

'Good,' Eazy suddenly smiled. 'You know of any decent food gaffs around here – I'm starving Steve.'

They both merely laughed at him.

'Come on Chorlton it's time to see your brief again,' said the detention officer as he stood in my open cell doorway with the hand cuffs at the ready.

'Are we being charged today?'

'No idea son,' he answered shaking his head. 'All I know is that they've sent me to collect you.'

As the two of us made our way through the outer steel doors that were surrounded with bars, Prey was being escorted back through to his cell. It had been the first time that I'd seen him since we'd been nicked, although we shouted over to one another late at night.

He was smiling away like he didn't have a care in the world. 'You alright Chopper?' he said cheerfully.

'What you smiling about?' I couldn't help but grin to myself at his contented nature.

'They can't break us,' he laughed out loudly. 'Just keep smiling ar'kid.'

'They charged you yet?' I asked, as the detention officer pushed me past him.

'No talking Chorlton,' he said gripping my left arm.

Prey just shook his head grinning as he did so. 'Nah – Fuck 'em – Let them go fuck themselves – They ain't got shit the halfwits.'

'You're off your head,' I shouted after him, smiling as I did so, just as he disappeared.

'They can't charge me with it though...' he continued to laugh as his voice began to trail away. 'Can they mate?'

'Don't bank on it Prey,' I called after him.

I really loved Prey's nonchalant attitude at times. At this precise moment in time we were all looking to go down for a very long time and he was laughing like he didn't give a fuck about it.

'Here you go Chorlton,' the detention officer said as he led me through into the small room where Adrian was waiting for me.

'Alright Adrian,' I said shaking his hand with both of my cuffed ones. 'You just seen Prey?'

'Yes I have,' he shook his head half-laughing.

'So did you put that smile on his face?'

'I wish I had Billy,' he smiled. 'I was expecting for all of you to be charged today but they've arranged your court hearing for Monday afternoon to have you all remanded to Walton in Liverpool.'

'Nice,' I replied thinking of that cesspool of a prison. 'Surely they've got to give you lot some time though.'

'Monday morning is what they're giving us,' he sighed. 'You see it's only to have you all remanded on the charges that they'll produce that day, added to ones they'll either stick to or drop from this Monday just gone. Realistically they should have released you all by now – but they've had some serious backing from upstairs hence why they've managed to drag it out all week.'

'What do you reckon then?' I asked still smiling to myself at the thought of Prey.

'We're putting Macreedy's up against your bail that they'll set for the two of you,' he sighed once again.

'But you don't honestly think we'll get it – D'ya pal?' I smiled. By now, I was more than prepared for that part of this nightmare.

'I won't lie to you Billy,' he nodded. 'I honestly believe with the charges that they're going to throw at you two – especially *you* – then they'll get it.'

'By especially me? I presume that you're referring to this security guard that they've been hammering me with all week in questioning?'

'I know that Kulshaw has denied all knowledge also. But...' he stopped himself.

'But what?' I asked. 'You reckon that they'll get a conviction from the word of a crack head or any of the forensic evidence that they've got?'

358

'The forensic evidence isn't my main concern at this moment in time. But what is... It is some of this information that they've questioned you on. The stolen removal van and some of the information that he's given,' he looked at me. 'My firms done some checking into it and they say that some of the information was never published to the public.'

I calmly looked at him and smiled. 'So we'll throw it back onto the one with all of the information,' I said as my smile twisted into a grin. 'I mean obviously if both me and Mark know shit all about it. Then it must have been the informant.'

'Just so you that you know though,' he told me. 'I reckon that they will most definitely go for the murder in the first-degree charge.'

'So be it,' I sighed. 'What else?'

'They'll charge both of you then on similar charges,' he bent his neck from side to side making it crack. 'Drug supplying on all accounts from class A to B, possession with intent charges, firearms charges. Then they'll go for a lot of conspiracy charges against the two of you on organised crime charges relating to the control of this so called drug empire.'

'And when it finally reaches crown court?'

'Then it could go off in all sorts of directions.'

'What's that mean then?'

'Well you could, if convicted you all could be facing anything from five years to life,' he stared at me.

'Shit... really?' I sighed shaking my head.

'That's looking at the worst case scenario. But I just want for you all to prepared for the worst,' he smiled trying his beat to reassure me.

'What's the chances though Adrian?' I asked, although not certain I wanted the question answering.

'All that I can tell you is that we'll be doing everything within our power to prevent any of you doing any serious time,'

'You still don't sound too confident though and why the fuck was Prey so happy if you'd just told him all of this.'

'I've no idea why Keiran was so happy Billy,' he shook his head. 'He just kept saying no worries and smiling at me.'

'So it's still all coming down to their witness who's willing to testify against us – Even though he's a fucked up crack head,' I sighed.

'I've already been told that,' he smiled turning slightly so the guard couldn't hear the conversation. 'That might just work in our favour though,' he winked at me.

I began smiling at him. 'So when will I see you next now then?'

'Monday morning Billy,' he smiled at me rising from the table.

'See you then Adrian,' I shook his hand again.

The three of them had been travelling around Altrincham's vicinity until early evening before heading back towards the block of flats for eight o'clock. They'd covered the quickest routes available to them out of both there and the area. They'd been plotted up for almost an hour with no sight of anything but lights.

'I can see someone,' Sleeper finally said, his eyes were and had been locked to the binoculars for almost their entire duration there.

'Is it him?' Steve asked.

'No, it must be the officer on guard,' he answered.

'Let's have a look mate,' Steve said taking the binoculars and watching the figure walk around what appeared to be the kitchen.

'Isn't that somebody else?' Eazy asked looking in the direction of the block.

Steve moved the over to the right. 'Got him,' he smiled as he observed Scotty opening what appeared to be the fridge door from the ray of light produced.

'What's he doing?' Sleeper enquired curiously.

'Here,' Steve passed the binoculars to him, content in knowledge that they now knew for certain the location of Scotty.

Although now came the second part of sorting out their problem and he knew that they'd been given no time whatsoever to make the arrangements. The three of them hadn't even spoken about what the full intentions actually were.

361

'What's he saying?' Eazy asked.

'I don't know Eazy,' Sleeper laughed quietly. 'My lip readings a bit rusty these days you daft cunt.'

Steve laughed also. 'Who's that?' he was suddenly pointing to the dark Ford Orion easing itself into the parking lot.

'They both look familiar,' Sleeper said passing Steve the binoculars.

'Walsh and Stevenson,' Steve sneered. 'Come to visit with their little star witness. They've sure got him stashed away safely though – haven't they?'

'We need to time this visit – alright?' Sleeper said nodding at Steve who automatically looked at his watch, as he then looked at Eazy who concurred his understanding to Sleeper as he also glanced at his watch and winked.

Then the three of them fell silent as they watched the two detectives disappear into the fifth block, both looked to be in good spirits as they made their way up to the second floor unaware of the three pairs of eyes keeping watch.

'Evening Scotty,' Stevenson said as he walked through into the bedroom where Scotty lay drinking a fresh can of beer.

'Fuck me – Mr. Stevenson himself.' It had been the first time that Stevenson had visited Scotty since he'd been sent there as Walsh had dropped his gear off every night. 'I am truly honoured.'

'Cut the crap son,' Stevenson told him.

'Alright Walshy,' Scotty said as they both nodded at one another.

'Thought that we'd let you know what's going on and so forth,' Stevenson said sitting on the bed.

'Whatever,' Scotty sniffed ignoring him. 'You got my shit?' he looked at Walsh as he tossed the small sealed plastic bag to him and Stevenson stared coldly back at him.

'In there,' Walsh nodded to the bathroom.

'I know – I'll be back in a minute,' he said disappearing quickly out of sight.

Stevenson immediately turned on Walsh. 'Just what the fuck was that about?'

'No offensive Mike, but I'm the one who's been here all week with him,' Walsh pulled the packet of cigarettes from his pocket taking one and tossing the pack to Stevenson. 'And he's a whole lot calmer on it.'

'We've just got to be careful Martin,' he said lighting up. 'Especially now, at this stage, with Sunday's meeting with the prosecution coming up.'

'Everything's going to be fine Mike,' he smiled sitting back in the chair.

'I know it is,' he grinned. 'Fuck whether or not they've given us shit all week.'

'Jeez, they've really pissed me off though you know,' Walsh sighed.

'Arrogant as fuck about every question,' Stevenson laughed slightly. 'But you've got to respect the way they've operated over the years.'

'I know you have,' Walsh agreed. 'But it's still not stopped us bringing them down.'

Stevenson laughed out loud, just as Scotty appeared again.

'You two enjoying yourselves, are you?' he asked, both eyes glazed from the hit of the drug he'd just done.

'Right Scotty, listen to us now,' Walsh said as Scotty sat back down.

'What,' he smiled.

'All day Sunday you'll have both of us and the prosecution here with you,' Stevenson said.

'We need for you to be a complete star for us Scotty,' Walsh winked. 'We also need for you to be straight headed. You think that you can manage that for us?'

'No problem as long as you see me right tomorrow night Walsh,' he smirked.

'I'll be here earlier on,' Walsh said blowing his smoke out. 'But I've got to shoot straight off as I've promised the missus I'd take her out to the theatre or some bollocks that I've got to pick tickets up for tomorrow. She thinks that I've got something going on the side with you Scotty as I've been here all the time,' he laughed.

'Fuck you Walshy,' Scotty said shaking his head.

'The prosecution has waited to see if we could get anything more before seeing you,' Stevenson informed him.

'And I take it you got fuck all Stevenson,' Scotty smirked.

'That won't matter once we've sat the prosecution here with you all day to cover everything,' Walsh smiled. 'And if you do a good job for us than we'll treat you good and proper on Sunday night.'

'Oh Walshy, how could I turn down an offer like that,' he smiled mockingly.

'Anyway Scotty after that, you'll be working closely with the prosecution to make sure we get the convictions that we're looking for,' Stevenson said.

'Sunday will just be to make sure that we get them remanded to Walton until the trial,' Walsh added. 'Then Tuesday we'll shut down all operations on the estate.'

'You reckon that they'll get remanded?' Scotty asked looking a little concerned.

'They haven't got a hope in hell Scotty of getting bail,' Stevenson smirked back at him.

'We right then?' Walsh asked looking at Stevenson.

'Yeah,' he answered rising from the bed looking at Scotty. 'And you take it easy with that shite.'

Scotty merely grinned back at them. 'Always.'

'So how's this to go down then?' Steve asked as the three of them sat around the living room at Steve's, after returning from the block of flats where they'd been sat all night observing.

'Just how do want it to go down?' Sleeper smiled.

'He's a dead man,' Steve replied, showing no emotion whatsoever. 'There is no two ways about it. If he lives then he'll bring the whole of the crew down with him.'

'There's going to be a lot heat after this though,' Eazy said as he began to remove the lid to his Kentucky Fried Chicken family sized bucket he'd bought for just himself.

Steve looked at Sleeper. 'That's why I figure we use your disposal service,' he grinned knowingly at him.

'I already had that in mind,' he told him coldly.

'I want to have a little fun with him first though, after we take him,' Steve smiled.

Both Sleeper and Eazy looked at one another then to Steve and laughed. 'What do you mean *we*?' Sleeper asked.

'After we take him from the flat,' he looked at them quizzically. 'We're not going to pop him with the copper there, are we?'

'You're not going to be there,' Eazy announced as he began munching on a chicken drumstick.

'You what?' Steve blurted.

'The brother's right Steve,' Sleeper told him. 'Just Eazy and I are on this job.'

'That's not right though,' Steve protested. 'Especially after what you all did for me last Saturday night in the Lakes.'

'It's not happening brother,' Sleeper smiled at him. 'We need for you to get down to Dry Bar or some other place that's busy with all the girls. Flash some cash about, buy punters champagne and shit like that. Basically get yourself fuckin' noticed.'

'That way they'll all remember you being there Steve,' Eazy smiled as the second piece of fried chicken was already being dipped into the gravy.

'But...' Steve trailed off as they both looked at him.

'You know that it makes sense Steve,' Sleeper said. 'You'll be the first person whose door they're coming knocking at.' Steve stared at them both. 'Fuck him up good for me then. Won't you?'

'Oh I've got a better idea than that,' he smiled as he grabbed a piece of chicken from the bucket.

'What's that then?' Steve asked.

Sleeper stared at the piece of chicken he held onto. 'I figure that we take him back alive.'

'You what?' Eazy exclaimed staring at Sleeper.

'We dispose of him whilst he's still alive,' he laughed. 'Have ourselves a little bar-b-scott so to speak eh.'

'Nice,' said Steve smiling as he did so. 'You make sure that the twat sees your face and you tell him just what's going to happen to him before you cremate his grassing little arse.'

'Don't worry Steve,' he smiled. 'By doing what he's done, he's hurt us just as badly mate. You know just how far back me and Prey go now,' he stopped and then stared at Eazy who'd fallen quiet. 'What's up with you Eazy?'

Eazy stared at his piece of half-eaten chicken then smiled also. 'Shit Sleeper... You almost put me off my food then.'

'It'd take a hell of a lot more than that to put you off your food big man,' Sleeper laughed as they all did.

'That's everything covered now Martin, isn't it?' Stevenson asked as the two of them sat in the office and was beginning to clear away for the evening.

'Sure is,' he smiled at his partner. 'I'll go and see Scotty once I've left here, then it's just a case of working with the prosecution tomorrow with him.'

'You might as well get off now mate,' Stevenson smiled triumphantly, then as an after thought. 'You still making sure that you use a different motor at night when you travel over there?'

'Of course I am,' Walsh nodded. 'You staying put for a while Mike?' he then asked, as his partner had practically spent day and night locked away there since they'd arrested them all.

'I reckon so,' he yawned. 'I'm going to make sure 100% all of the files are in complete order for tomorrow.'

'I'll be off then,' Walsh yawned also, as if it was contagious.

'You still off out tonight?'

Walsh nodded wearily. 'Yeah, I picked up the tickets for some show at the Royal Exchange later on tonight. The missus says that if I don't make it tonight, that she's going to find herself a new fella,' he then laughed.

Stevenson laughed also. 'They like to try and use that one don't they?'

'Only thing is Mike – I reckon she means it this time.'

'Have a good evening then,' Stevenson nodded as he watched his partner disappear out of the door.

'Will do,' Walsh shouted back to him as he made his way down the corridor.

'Don't forget bright and early tomorrow,' he just about heard Stevenson shout out to him as he merely nodded, thinking I know bright and fucking early.

'That must be the change over Officer Sleeper. We got almost seven o'clock now,' Eazy said glancing at his watch, as the two of them were and had been well hidden away in the woodland located at the rear of the blocks of retirement flats for the last couple of hours, observing the activities surrounding them.

'Let's take a look,' Sleeper said taking the binoculars. 'You know this whole thing is way too rushed for my liking Eazy.'

'I know mate,' Eazy shook his head. 'But like Steve said, they are to be charged Monday morning then we've no other choice but to hit tonight.'

'Still don't like it,' Sleeper replied as he observed the second officer knock a sequenced knock of four, one, and three onto the flat door. 'No sign yet either of the other two.'

'How do you know that they'll even show up?'

'I don't,' he shook his head as the first officer opened the door smiling and handing a can of beer to the second one. 'That's why we could have done with at least a week of surveillance for an operation like this.'

'What they doing now?' Eazy asked as he strained his own eyes to see.

'Both of them are drinking beer in the kitchen, Saturday night ain't it? Plus it's all paid for by the tax payer anyway,' smiled Sleeper. 'Also looks like the one who was already there is getting ready to leave,' he answered without looking away.

'What time do you want this to go down?' Eazy asked looking at him. 'You've covered everything but the time yet mate.'

'I know I have,' he replied, now looking at him. 'But like I said already, this whole thing is rushed, so we have to be double careful with it.'

'Alright,' Eazy nodded then looked over to the car park as he heard a car engine. 'Who's that there? Is that them two?'

'Different motor... Looks like a Rover,' Sleeper said as he watched the car ease into the space. 'Only one occupant also,' he turned back to observing the flat.

'Has the other left yet?'

'No – Scotty's in the kitchen now, also drinking a can of beer,' he told him. 'That's it, the first ones heading for the front door now, from what I can tell.'

'Who's that entering the building?'

'Shit...' Sleeper exclaimed as he menovered the binoculars to a new position.

'Who is it?'

'It's Walsh from last night,' he told him. 'That must have been him who arrived in the Rover. Must have come on his own tonight.'

'Looks like the doors opening.'

Sleeper observed then let out a little laugh as he watched the first officer almost jump out of his skin as he walked into the corridor and almost straight into Walsh himself. 'First ones leaving now.'

The three were all laughing and joking in the doorway as Scotty appeared and suddenly the mood changed, with Walsh pushing him back through into the flat.

'I don't think that they were too pleased that he showed his face then.'

'The others leaving the building now,' Eazy said as he watched the officer make his way over to his Ford Escort on the far side of the car park.

'Right then, let's wait and see just how long Walsh decides to stay,' he shook his head. 'Hopefully he's not here for the night as it will create us a whole other problem altogether.'

'Just what the fuck did you think you were doing then Scotty?' Walsh snapped as he pushed him back into the bedroom.

'I just heard you all laughing – that's all,' he shrugged nonchalantly.

'You can't be seen,' Walsh shook his head.

'Just who the fuck is going to see me all the way out here Walshy,' he sighed. 'This place is beginning to feel like an asylum.'

Walsh's eye's suddenly angered. 'Do you realise just what it fucking was last week that we had to do to get you fucking off with that armed robbery – you – you......' he shook his head in anger and began to calm himself down, as Scotty merely grinned at him. 'Well, it's a whole lot fucking better than a prison cell you little jerk,' he snapped, as he then began to remove his jacket.

'Fuck you Walshy and just give...' Scotty began to say as Walsh suddenly flipped. 'You little fucking shit – You – You little fuckin...' he was ranting as he tore his jacket away, only as Scotty jumped to the floor and went to cover himself protectively – he saw something fall from the detectives inside pocket.

'Leave me be Walsh,' Scotty said as he huddled into a ball on the floor.

'Come here – you little prick...' Walsh yelled as he went straight at Scotty. Just then the door flew open and the second officer grabbed hold of him.

'Easy guv' – Come on now – He's not worth it,' he told him, yanking him back.

Scotty climbed from the ball on the floor kicking the small envelope beneath the bed as he did so. 'You just watch how you treat me,' he said smugly as he stood before him.

'Let me go,' Walsh said shrugging the officer away.

'You two going to play nicely now,' the officer said mockingly.

'Get out of here,' Walsh snarled at the young officer half-laughing before turning to leave.

'You shouldn't get so wound up Walshy,' Scotty said sitting down.

'You shouldn't fucking wind me up then Scotty,' he sighed deeply. 'It's been one hell of a long week already and tomorrow is going to be a killer of day going over it all once again,' he shook his head as he made his way over to bedside chair and sat down.

'I've told you, I'll come through for you,' Scotty smiled. 'Just like I promised I would.'

'It just seems that now we are relying on you now more so than ever,' he shook his head once again.

'I take it they gave you fuck all then,' Scotty grinned. 'I knew they wouldn't,' he added as he watched Walsh shake his head.

'They've stuck with no fucking comment all week,' he sighed deeply.

'That's why you've got me,' Scotty sniggered then held his hand out. 'In'it now.'

Walsh half laughed. 'You're a little prick at times... Here.' He tossed the bag of crack cocaine to him.

'I'll be seeing you tomorrow then Walshy,' Scotty answered – as all in one fluid motion he caught the bag and rose from the bed.

'Bright and early Scotty,' Walsh said as he rose from the seat.

'Laters then,' Scotty stood there smirking. 'Don't mind if I don't see you out detective, but I've got a date in the bathroom,' he laughed at his own joke as he then disappeared through the door; leaving Walsh stood there shaking his head.

'You seem in a good mood tonight Steve?' Claire said as both of them, plus Donna, Kathy, Sharon and Michelle headed into Dry Bar.

'I didn't really feel like coming out tonight,' Kathy said in an aloof tone.

'So what if you didn't,' Steve said staring at her. 'Stop acting like a distraught widow – He's not dead,' he snapped then shook his head apologetically. 'Sorry that was out of order Kathy... Come here,' he added, putting his arm around her.

'I just miss him so much though,' she said half smiling.

'We miss them all,' Steve smiled. 'But let's just wait and see what happens Monday.'

'What's that supposed to mean?' Donna asked.

'It means that the last thing that they'll all be wanting is for all of us to be sat moping around after them,' he then smiled as they arrived at the bar.

'Do you know something that we don't Steve,' Sharon asked poking his ribs.

'Now whatever gives you that impression,' he laughed as they all made their way past the two burly doormen into the warmth of the bar that was alight with a vibrant music and good crowd that had gathered. 'Three bottles of Bollinger in the buckets of ice,' he shouted to the barman who was only more than pleased to serve him.

'So what are we celebrating exactly?' asked Claire.

'We're not celebrating anything,' Steve shook his head at her.

'So what's with the champagne?' Michelle added.

371

'Just thought I'd take all of you girls out for the night,' he smirked mischievously giving off the impression of a naughty school boy. 'Plus it does one hell of a lot of good for my ego to have all you beautiful girls to myself for the night,' he laughed.

'Cheeky sod,' Kathy told him smiling as she did.

'And I don't fulfil that ego already?' Claire smiled kissing him.

'Always,' he responded by kissing her back.

'I'll bring the drinks over to you,' the barman announced with a hint of jealousy as he watched the old man gallivant around with all of these girls in tow, he then smiled and shook his head to himself.

'Over here then,' Steve announced loudly as he led them all off to a free table located central to the bar itself.

'Don't take this the wrong way but he's sure acting a little strange tonight Claire,' Donna said as they headed over to the table.

'He's been like this since this morning,' she announced.

'Do you have any idea what's up?' Donna asked as they all began to sit down.

'No idea,' she shrugged. 'All that I know is that last night him, Sleeper and the big guy – whatisname – Eazy all came in well late, and were all laughing and joking until the early hours of this morning.'

'Where are them two now?' Donna asked.

'They went back to London this afternoon,' she answered.

'Are you sure about that?'

'That's what they told me anyway,' Claire replied. 'Have you still not seen Chopper yet?' she asked, changing the subject.

'No,' Donna sighed. 'None of us have seen any of them this week. It's been really hard.'

'I bet it has,' Claire said as she put her arm around Donna.

'Adrian told us that he thought it best if there was no interference's until we had this week out of the way,' Donna half smiled. 'To be honest it's not sounding at all hopeful for any of them.'

'Don't say that girl,' Steve smiled, just as the champagne arrived at the table.

'Here we go pal,' announced the bar man, who still couldn't stop grinning at Steve knowingly.

'Cheers son,' Steve reached into his pocket then smiled. 'I tell you what – Why don't you take this extra bit of money and go and buy another bottle of this gear, so all of you bar staff can enjoy a drink also.'

'Sorry... What was that?' The barman asked with a shocked impression upon his face.

'You heard me the first time son,' Steve informed him winking as he did. 'Now go on, enjoy yourselves.'

'Thank you – Thanks a lot mate - Honestly – Cheers,' he couldn't seem to find enough possible ways to thank Steve as he made his way back over to the brightly lit bar – calling out to the other staff as he did.

Steve began filling the glasses on the table and handed them out to the girls. 'To the lads,' he said as he raised his glass the girls doing the same although not seeming to share his same enthusiasm.

'I sure hope that they get bail on Monday,' Kathy declared.

'I know,' Sharon sighed. 'I miss Jonah so much.'

'Likewise for all of us,' Donna added.

Just then the barman called over to reach Steve's attention as the entire bar staff held up the bottle of Moet thanking him. 'To our guests.' They all laughed as they popped open the bottle; its contents over flowing.

Dry Bar's occupants all turned their attention to Steve as he raised his glass to them and smiled back the girls – as he merely sat back and sipped his champagne whilst he thought about what was to happen as the evening progressed.

He's leaving already,' Sleeper stated as he watched Walsh walk through the open door, turning and saying a few words to the officer before descending down the stairs towards the exit.

'What time have we got?' Eazy asked out loud as he glanced at his watch. 'It's just turned 7:21 now.'

'He's heading for the car.'

They both silently watched as the detective started up the engine and reversed out of the parking spot – before changing gear and heading straight for the exit.

'We going straight in or what Sleeper?'

'Give it until seven thirty five precisely,' Sleeper glanced at his watch then looked at the big man who'd been with him on many jobs like this before – but just not as rushed as this one was that they were about to do. He sighed deeply as he thought of this then added, 'That way we'll know that's he's well and truly out of the area for sure.'

'I'll check the tools once more then,' Eazy nodded as he reached for the bag.

'This has to run smoothly Eazy,' Sleeper told him what he already was fully aware of.

'It will do,' Sleeper grinned. 'Is that him leaving now,' he nodded his head towards the car leaving.

'That's him,' Sleeper nodded as he watched through the binoculars then turned his attention back to the flat. 'He's going and getting more beer.'

'Shit,' Eazy laughed, 'If we had more time we could just wait for this guy to drink enough to just pass out.'

'Look... Look at that,' Sleeper pointed to the small window at the side of the building. 'Up there,' he passed the binoculars to Eazy.

Eazy sniggered as he looked through them to the window. 'Is that smoke coming from the window?'

'Sure is.'

'Looks like our little Scotty's just had some supply dropped off for him,' he grinned knowingly.

'Doesn't it just,' Sleeper agreed. 'You finished checking the bag Eazy.'

'Everything's sweet,' he grinned flashing his white teeth in the night's darkness. 'The cars in place – All the tools required are there – Just tell me when brother.'

Sleeper merely nodded his response with a grave expression upon his face as he did so.

As Scotty walked back through into the bedroom his eyes glazed and his whole body rushed in a thousand directions from the hit of powerful drug that he had just consumed – he held out his arms wide and closed his eyes.

His body was filled with the drug that he'd come to depend so heavily on. It controlled both his life – and more than likely his destiny he thought to himself – as the bizarre images that always taunted him in these situations flashed through his mind.

As Scotty's head rolled from side to side he wore a permanent grin. The images becoming more intensified - more violent – more sexual – more twisted – as voices called out to him clear as day... But then came Chopper's face and then he heard Chopper call out his name – as he quickly opened his eyes and shook his head to free himself from both the voice and the image.

It was all too late for him now. He was past any sort of redemption that he could possibly be given. And after tomorrow he'd hammer those final nails into the coffin that would start the entire process in sealing the fates of both his friends and crew for whom he owed so much to.

Most of all, he had betrayed the one person in his life who he had ever cared about. His friend, his best friend... in fact the only person he truly considered to be his brother. They'd always been as close as brothers had – Only now he was helping them to send that brother away for the rest of his life, whilst he walked free from all of it.

He wished now that he could turn back time – Back to all those months ago when Stevenson and Walsh had backed him into a corner and had used and abused him ever since. He used them too, he knew that – But they'd spotted his weakness and exploited it to their advantage and had continued exploiting it to this very night.

Scotty fell forward onto the bed, crashing into it and lay on his front half hanging over the bed and floor as his mind raced – Tomorrow was when the reality of it all would hit him deeply – Sunday when he no longer would be passing bits of information to Stevenson or Walsh, but to the executioners themselves – that being the prosecution itself.

They were the ones who were to be the darkness that the crew feared at this precise moment. The ones who would stand there before a jury and would twist their crimes into new levels of horror, to make both the judge and the jury feel nothing but hate towards the men stood before them.

They would make them believe that these men were the ones, who had helped and succeeded in corrupting and twisting the new generation, as they liked to think of them, into the whole new world of drugs. The new designer drugs, as they liked to refer to them, like Ecstasy and Crack Cocaine. The drugs that had turned the new generation of followers into drug crazed clubbers.

Not that any of this was true, but not that the truth would matter anyway. The way the prosecution would come across to these undefiled people, from that world, would be nothing but its dark side that they'd let them in to witness. They'd make the crew out to be nothing but the lowest scum of all – of course that's what they'd do. That's what they always did... After all that what they were paid to do – day in – day out.

Scotty half grinned as he stared at the floor... Then he realised that he'd been staring at the envelope for the last few minutes that Walsh had dropped whilst he'd been lay there in a world of his own.

He reached out grabbing the envelope... Hoping – *no praying* – that Walsh had dropped his supply for the following night off... But as he picked it up and climbed to his feet, he realised that it was way too light and thin to contain what he really desired.

As he tore open the back of the envelope pulling the contents out... He then began laughing as he realised that he was holding Walsh's tickets for that evening at the theatre. He dropped them when he'd flown into his rage.

'Fuck you Walshy – Fuck you – You twat,' he then fell back onto the bed and roared with malicious laughter.

As he lay there, he started to become all hot and horny as he closed his eyes and the twisted sexual images once again began to fill his mind... The sick sexual images flashed through his mind like a bad – totally sick porn movie. But as fucked up as the images were, the hotter they were making him. He found his hand slipping further down towards himself. The rocks had a bad habit of doing this to him. But it also one of the things he enjoyed most about them.

Sleeper, donned in full black wearing a ski mask had cut both the lights to the hallways and the alarm to the fire exit once he sneaked through the front door, clandestined by the nights darkness.

The fire exit doors were found hidden below the stairwell and led through out of the back of the building short distance from the woodland where Eazy lay in wait for his signal.

As Sleeper quietly eased the doors open, he stopped momentarily and listened out for any sign of reaction. None came, only the muffled sound of the elderly's television screens as they sat watching Blind Date or some other crap program they put on to bore the shit out of you on a Saturday evening.

Whistling as quietly as he possibly could, he watched Eazy's large blackened bulk climb from the woodland carrying with him a black holdall, staying low – well as low as it possibly was for someone his size – as he made his way over to fire doors.

The two merely nodded their complete and utter understanding to one another silently as they then headed up the stairs with the prowess of a couple of panthers towards their prey, who waited in his own world of darkness completely unaware.

As Walsh headed back towards the M56 he smiled to himself. Fucking little Scotty he thought then half laughed.

He shouldn't have lost it with him tonight – But he just couldn't help it sometimes. Scotty could be such an irritating cocksucker at times. He'd always been cocky, but since they'd got him off with the armed blag the pervious week he'd acted like he was almost sacred. Maybe that was just the gear though he thought to himself as he eased the car through the quiet roads.

After all, they'd never really witnessed him on them before. Sure he'd been high on Crack when he'd met with them from time to time. But that didn't come close to the look it gave him as he walked back through those bathroom doors to him.

It was almost like now it was normality to him. If he wasn't smoking them he was a complete fuck up – But you give him his medicine, so to speak and he was alright.

Oh well, he thought as he sighed. There was nothing that they could do about it now. They needed Scotty more so now then they ever needed him before – No matter what the situation at hand was. Scotty was the only one who'd worked close enough to them to be able to get the convictions that they were looking for – Besides if they got onto the fact he was smoking that shit then they'd just have one of their own medical examiners pass him with flying colours no problem.

Ah fuck it anyway, he thought just as approached the roundabout leading onto the M56 – just stop the hell thinking about him tonight.

Tonight, for the first time in weeks he was actually taking his wife out for the night – Even if going to the theatre was hardly his idea of a good night out, although it certainly kept her quiet. He laughed out loudly as he padded his jacket pocket where the tickets were... But there was nothing there... He screeched the car to a halt at the side of the curb as cars behind all began beeping their horns at him shouting obscenities as they did.

'Shit... Shit... *Shit*... Where the fuck *are* they,' he asked himself out loud as he searched his pockets.

'Fuck... *Bastard*... Where the fuck are you?' he was out of the car searching the floor when he suddenly realised what had happened.

'Bastard,' he screamed out loud, as he climbed back into the car and slammed the gears into reverse to turn around.

Sleeper and Eazy had arrived at flat fifty three's front door. Sleeper held his ear to the door, and then nodded as he began to examine the door.

As he searched around the frame Eazy moved over to the door facing and also listened through, he heard a cheer come from both the television and the elderly couple. They must have picked the right contestant he thought to himself, as he smiled and looked over to Sleeper who was giving the signal using his fingers and thumbs in a swiping motion to signal that the door was wired.

Eazy nodded and pulled a small black silk wrap over bag from beneath his top. As he unravelled the wrap he smiled at the sight of his array of small carefully crafted tools before him that belonged to good friend of his who was currently on a six stretch in Parkhurst for a series of robberies spanning over the last five years. And who luckily for Eazy had used one of Eazy's apartments in Lewisham as a safe house and the police had never gotten near it. As an added bonus had also spent time showing Eazy just how to master using the picks and going over different techniques of just how to disable an array of different alarm systems out there.

Sleeper pointed to the small electrical box to the left of the door and the sensor to the top right hand side, and then he left Eazy to it. Whilst Eazy went to work on the door Sleeper descended back down the stairs and out of the fire exit, moving with silent speed around the building checking once again that all was safe.

Once satisfied he returned to Eazy who was sat at the top of the stairs looking at his watch in a bored manor as Sleeper grinned through the ski mask at his friend. He then nodded as Eazy carefully slid the two pieces of the masterfully crafted steel into the first lock, twisting and turning momentarily before smiling and almost instantaneously beginning work on the second one.

Then the second smile came from him, as he eased the flat door through into its own hallway. Just enough though, so that Sleeper could fit his small angled mirror like that used at a dentist through the door.

As Sleeper took his position at the base of the doorway he slipped the mirror through. He could see what appeared to be the living room door to be slightly a jar as the light penetrated through into the hallway. The only sound that could be heard was the television set, as it also blared away.

Just then a figure passed the living room doorway, belching loudly as he did. Banging sounds from the kitchen could be heard as the officer just as suddenly passed back through into the living, belching once again.

Sleeper nodded to Eazy as he made way for the big man to take his place in the doorway. Eazy smiled, and then from the

379

holdall he'd brought with him he produced two sawn-off shotguns, passing one to his friend. He then produced a plastic bag containing a wet handkerchief and tossed it to Sleeper who smiled at the bag then nodded his signal for them to make a move.

Eazy eased open the door and with deadly silence they both found themselves crouched in hallway. Eazy then looked at Sleeper and grinned as his mountain frame straightened to its full height, then simply nodded as he walked calmly towards the living room door.

Sleeper placed his ear against what he thought to be the bedroom room and could hear moaning sounds coming from them. He listened again and heard the same moaning sounds as before... What the fuck was he doing in there he thought just before looking at Eazy who was now standing before the door.

With sheer calmness Eazy pushed the door open.

'Scotty... Scotty?' The voice called out as Eazy walked into the living room; his shotgun aimed right at the officer's head.

'Evening there,' Eazy smiled through the mask.

'What... What the... You... What...' He was picture of pure confusion as he leapt out of his chair.

'You stay calm now and fuck all will happen to you,' Eazy informed him nodding just as calmly as he saw the officer glance at the coffee table where both a handgun and radio lay.

Eazy laughed. 'Now that would be complete stupidity of you wouldn't it son? Now come here very slowly and place your hands behind your back removing those cuffs attached to the back of you.'

'Alright – But do you know just who you're fucking wi...' he began as Eazy eyes turned cold.

He cut him off. 'We know exactly who we're fuckin' with son.'

Sleeper observed Eazy from the hallway then placed his left hand onto the door handle pushing it down both slowly and quietly.

He could still hear the moans becoming louder as he pushed open to door to find Scotty with his jeans around his ankles stood in front of the mirror masturbating frantically as he watched himself. Sleeper grinned broadly then let out a laugh startling Scotty from his activities as he did so. And then he

380

startled him even more so as he pointed the shotgun at his head.

'What... No please... Noooo... Pleaseeee,' Scotty cried out as he struggled to pull his jeans up, spots of semen already dribbling down his hand.

Sleeper walked into bedroom whilst still pointing the gun at Scotty's head, not saying a word as he watched the fear take control of Scotty's eyes. 'Please... Don't kill me... Please... Leave me alone... Go away,' he pleaded as Sleeper placed the shotgun into his forehead.

'Please... I won't say a word... Please... I promise,' he began sobbing.

'And let you put everybody away Scotty? I don't think so,' Sleeper said as Scotty's recognition of him kicked in.

'Sleeper – don't...' was the last thing he said as Sleeper held the handkerchief from the plastic bag and that was filled with chloroform to his tear filled face.

He watched Scotty's eyes begin to roll, he knew that Scotty knew that this was the end and he smirked maliciously, nodding at him as he did so, as he lost complete consciousness collapsing onto the floor before him. Sleeper then went to work with the duct tape, wrapping it around Scotty's face, hands and ankles.

As he dragged Scotty into the hallway, dumping his deadened weight to the ground he walked through into the living room where Eazy was just finishing locking the officer to the radiator with his own handcuffs.

'Everything sweet?' Sleeper asked.

'You won't get away with this,' the officer screamed.

Eazy grinned as Sleeper threw him the duct tape. He turned and faced the officer smiled then began to wrap the tape around his head. 'We just have son,' He laughed.

'Let's go,' Sleeper said nodding to the door.

'Where is he?'

'Hallway – c'mon,' he nodded smiling as he did.

'Just give me a minute,' Eazy grinned, as he began taping the officer's feet together.

'I bet that little prick saw them fall out of my pocket,' Walsh grumbled to himself as he climbed out of his car.

Fucking little cunt – I'll show him, he was thinking to himself. I've been way too nice for too long with the little prick.

Yeah... yeah I know what I'll do to teach him a lesson, he kept thinking as he made his way over towards the block of flats. I'll take his gear back – see who's laughing then eh – the little prick – I'll show him.

That's weird he suddenly thought as he walked into the hallway. What's happened to the lights? He was sure that they were on before when he was here... weren't they?

He quietly looked up to the flat door. Nothing appeared out of place as he carefully made his way towards it.

But just as he reached it he could see that it was very slightly a jar... Had they forgotten to shut it? No, they couldn't of – Surely not?

As he peered through the door he could see light from the living room – He could still hear the television blaring away.

What was that? What is it? He thought as he could see a large darkened mound slumped in the hallway – What the fuck? He thought as he began to ease the door open carefully.

Just as Sleeper walked through into hallway the front door opened fully. 'What the fuck... What's going...' was all that Walsh managed before Sleeper with the speed of a hunting cheetah has crossed the length of the hallway and had his shotgun pressed firmly into Walsh's face.

'Fuck... Fuck...' Eazy exclaimed, just out of Walsh's view. 'Just what the fuck do we do now?'

Walsh smiled weakly to try and hide his fear. 'You're both fucked now... My partners on his way up the stairs now,' he lied.

But Sleeper only smiled confidently back at him. 'Don't try to blag me Detective?   Come on in and join the party,' Sleeper said as he heaved Walsh through the door.

'We going to pop him?' Eazy asked, still out of Walsh's view.

'No... Please... No,' Walsh blurted out as he suddenly realised the position he was in.

'We're not here for you,' Sleeper said as he directed Walsh through into the bedroom with the gun constantly pointed at his head.

'But you can't take him... You can't...' Walsh trailed off as he caught a slight glimpse of the larger of the two haul Scotty's body up onto shoulder with complete ease.

'Turn around,' Sleeper instructed him.

'This isn't right… You just can't… How did you know? This isn't…' Walsh was a mass of confusion as Sleeper nodded at him to do as he'd been instructed.

As Walsh began to turn to his left, Sleeper grinned at him. 'No… the other way and I want to you to go all the way round for me.'

'What?' Walsh exclaimed confused.

'Just do it now… Before I lose my patience with you,' Sleeper snapped as Walsh began to move round to the right.

Just as Walsh's left side came into view, Sleeper smashed his shotgun with all of his force into Walsh face. He felt his cheekbones crumble as the metal crushed through into the flesh.

A slight cry came from Walsh as he then slumped limply to the bedroom floor.

Sleeper went to work on taping and cuffing Walsh to the toilet, so that as he came too it would be the first thing he'd see.

Just then Eazy appeared in the doorway. 'Are we right? We got to make a move.'

Sleeper stood up and looked at the sight of Walsh taped to the toilet bowl and laughed. 'Yeah – We're right mate.'

'Best place for him,' Eazy grinned as the two of them quickly left the scene closing the door behind them as they left.

'How's the kid doing?' asked Macca, as he walked over to the kitchen table and handed his boss the cup of tea he'd just made. Macca had been with Dominic O'Leary since they were teenagers growing up in Salford. 'Is he gonna be okay?'

'You sure they don't know what the fuck happened that night?' he snapped ignoring the question.

'We can't find anybody,' replied Macca. 'All we know is that Alex's firm is kicking off about this as well. They are convinced at this moment in time that we have something to do with his disappearance.'

'How the fuck would we have anything to do with that,' sneered O'Leary. 'Do they know what has happened to my son for fucks sake? He's barely alive. You saw those fuckin' burns?'

'I know,' he sighed. 'Don't worry Dom, we'll find out what the fuck has gone on. Has Vinnie still not said anything?'

'They're pumping full of so much shit he hasn't got a clue where he is right now. The kid ain't talking any sense. Just keeps babbling shit to be perfectly honest about who he knows.'

'Who knows?'

'That's it,' he let his breath out rubbing his eyes. 'He really ain't making any sense. All I know is that when we find who did this then we are gonna kill the fucker. That is the only certainty in this lif...'

Before he fished his words they both clearly heard the front door being smashed in – and not only the front door but the

kitchen door where they were sat went through as the large –
familiar – figure waltzed through the door.

'Morning Dom,' smiled the character before him.

'Anderson,' sighed O'Leary shaking his head. 'What the
fuc...'

'Shut the fuck up Dom,' he snapped. 'You must have heard
that I was back in town? No... well what a fuckin' pity.'

'What the hell is going on Anderson?'

'We've got unfinished business,' he replied as the armed
police burst through the doors grabbing hold of both of them.

'Are you fuckin' serious?' shouted O'Leary.

'Of course I fuckin am,' smiled Anderson.

'You won't find shit on me you prick,' sneered O'Leary.

'Are you sure about that?' smiled Anderson taking O'Leary
by the arm and leading him upstairs.

SEVENTY SEVEN

'How's your face feeling Martin?' asked Stevenson walking through the doors into the room where the nurse had just allowed him in to see his partner.

Stevenson, along with the prosecution had turned up Sunday morning in Altrincham to spend the day with Scotty in complete darkness of what had happened.

They had found both the officer still handcuffed to the radiator, close to sheer exhaustion from the heat and Walsh still stuck in that embarrassing position, his head had been taped with the duct tape so that he was unable to move his face from the basin itself. His left cheek was badly bruised and swollen to the size of a watermelon.

He was in complete agony as Stevenson had helped him free, full of anger, frustration and intense pain.

At first Stevenson had flown completely off the handle at the both of them, before Walsh had shared his same anger and frustration also.

They'd lost the one chance that they'd had at bringing down the crew and they had no idea whatsoever as to just how it had happened.

Scotty was gone – And deep down they both knew they'd never see him alive again.

'How the fuck do you think it feels Mike?' Walsh snapped, as he then winced with the pain.

'I'm sorry – I didn't mean it to sound the way it did do,' Stevenson began.

'It's alright,' Walsh said as he brought his hand to the plaster and bandage that now covered half his face. 'We've lost him –

386

Just how the fuck did anybody find him in protective custody Mike?' he shook his head at his own disbelief.

'There's got to be a full investigation into this,' Stevenson announced as he walked to the window and stared outside.

'I need to get the fuck out of here,' Walsh said as he climbed out of the bed. 'You phoned my missus.'

'Yes,' Stevenson looked at him. 'There was nobody at home mate,' he watched as his partner's face changed.

'Where the fuck is she?' he asked out loud then suddenly remembering her threat and falling silent.

'She's just probably round at her mothers or something,' Stevenson tried.

'Her mother's dead,' Walsh said shaking his head, and then completely changing the subject. 'So what do we do now?'

'You tell me,' Stevenson sat down and put his head into his hands. 'I mean just what have we got left now.'

'Surely we've still got something of a case,' Walsh said, knowing that he was only trying to convince himself more than anything.

'You don't honestly believe that do you?' Stevenson looked directly at him, as he shook his head. 'No – I didn't think so.'

'So what do we do then?' Walsh asked as he began to change back into the previous night's garments. 'We can't just set them all free.'

'You got any other suggestions?' he asked sighing deeply.

'Alright then... What about the murder of the security guard then?' Walsh was clutching, not wanting to believe that they were to get away with it.

'What about him?' he shrugged. 'There is nowhere near enough forensic evidence to take it to court. And all we had was Scotty's testimony that it was actually Chorlton who killed the guard. Both Chorlton and Kulshaw have denied any knowledge.'

'But we just can't... We'll look like complete fools Mike,' Walsh was shaking his head.

'If we take this all the way to trial without Scotty, then it'll all blow up in our own faces even more.' He dropped his head into his hands again like a man who was well and truly defeated.

'What about last night then?'

'What about it?' Stevenson shrugged. 'We've got all of our suspects locked up. I've already checked with our team on the surveillance of the estate and they say that everybody was accounted for.'

'The old guy – It must have been the old guy,' Walsh tried another angle.

'Well, he'll just have to be part of our new investigation as to just how the fuck we managed to lose our star witness. The star witness who just also happened to be in our custody at the time, locked away in a God damn safe house for fucks sake,' he was at the brink of losing it.

'But...' Walsh merely trailed off.

'But fuck all,' Stevenson snapped. 'They walk... That's it. Plain and fucking simple.'

'What about? We've got...' Walsh just couldn't get his head around any of this.

'Tell me... What have we got? What have we got?' Stevenson had risen from seat heading for the door then stopping and staring hard at Walsh, madness racing through his eyes. 'Nothing – That's what... That's all we've got... A big fat nowt pal. That's what we got for trusting a no good fucking crack addict. The same rock head that went on to commit fucking armed robbery, and we like fucking little muggy cunts went and got him the fuck off with,' he yelled at Walsh as he slammed the hospital door shut, both nurse's and patient's watching his display of frustrated anger as he made his way off down the corridor.

'Thanks again for everything Adrian,' Prey said as we all stood there outside of the station late Sunday night. It was the maddest imaginable situation as one minute we were all expecting the worst case scenario and then the next thing we all knew they were merely setting us all free.

I held my own suspicions as to what had actually happened and as to why Prey had seemed in such good spirits the other day... However nothing had been said yet.

'I'm not entirely sure as to what you're thanking me for Kieran,' he replied. 'I was hoping that perhaps you could possible shed a little more light onto the subject for me.'

'Do you actually want him to do that Adrian?' I smiled knowingly at him, although I wasn't entirely sure as too what had actually happened myself.

Adrian laughed. 'Perhaps you're right Billy. It's better that I don't know,' he smiled as he shook our hands. 'We don't wish to go tempting fate now, do we?'

'Really,' Prey smiled. 'Just how the fuck am I supposed to know what happened when we've been locked away all week.'

'So I reckon that there is only one place left for us to head to now then,' I laughed.

'I hope you're talking about going for a drink?' Parksey added.

'In'it,' Jonah said gleefully.

'Does Steve or the girls know that we're out yet?' I asked.

'Not that I know of,' Adrian smiled.

'Might as well let that bit be a surprise then,' Prey said, as he said it both Stevenson and Walsh who were looking worse for wear pulled up outside the station.

'Evening there orifices,' I said as they climbed from their car, smiling smugly as everybody began laughing.

'We'll have you all yet,' Stevenson snapped, as he came to a stand still before us all. 'You've not got away with anything Chorlton... You hear me.'

'Perhaps because there wasn't anything for my clients to get away with,' Adrian smiled. 'Besides what it was that you dreamt up in that fictitious mind of yours Mr. Stevenson.'

'What happened to your face Walshy?' Prey grinned.

'As if you don't know,' Walsh sneered, grimacing as he did so.

'Now just how the fuck is it that I am supposed to know what happened to your face now?' He smiled broadly. 'After all, you boys have had us locked away in 'ere all week.'

'This isn't the end of it,' said Stevenson angrily again pushing through our group as they both made there way through the front doors

'It is for today though,' I smiled, as Walsh threw one hell of a filthy – well half a look anyway – back at all of us.

We'd all headed straight to Dry Bar from the station for a well-needed drink. Steve had been sat beside the phone at Prey's awaiting our call and had been waiting to bring all of the girls with him to see us.

Our faces and names had been all over the papers that week, so as we'd walked through into Dry Bar, we all received warm welcomes from everyone in there who knew us.

Just before we knew the girls were to make an appearance, Prey had taken me to one side and informed me very briefly as to what had happened, obviously not having the entire story himself.

However there was one thing that I was certain of, and that was that Scotty was no longer in the picture. In fact deep down I knew that Scotty was no longer... end of message.

The girls had been ecstatic as they rushed through the doors to greet us, although I had to admit it felt fantastic to see Donna. Before that week we had never been separated like that before.

We'd stayed until closing before all going our separate ways, both Prey and myself receiving scowling looks from Donna and Kathy as we arranged to meet with Steve for the entire duration of the following day. But that's the way it had to be... Things needed to be discussed following the week's events.

Although for now though we could at least spend the night lay in our own decent beds instead of the cold hard plastic ones with which we had become acquainted to over the previous week.

'I've missed you so much Chopper,' Donna said, as she cuddled up to me after we'd just finished enjoying one another sexually.

'That's like wise,' I smiled kissing her again.

'Why've they just released you?' she suddenly asked as she pushed herself up onto me, staring directly into my eyes.

'I don't know,' I answered shaking my head.

'What's happened to Scotty?' she then asked.

'How am I supposed to know?' I said sighing.

'Come on Chopper,' she said. 'You were all looking to go to prison because of him – Then all of a sudden they just decide to let you all go.'

'So you'd prefer it if I was still locked away then?'

'No... You know that's not what I meant,' she snapped. 'But I want to know something that's been bothering me.'

'Want to know what for fucks sake?' I said back at her with anger, irritated at her apparent attitude. 'Even I don't want to know what the fuck happened for Christ sake – Just leave it be, will you.'

'Did you kill that man?' she suddenly asked. 'That security officer they said you did?'

I pushed her away, wondering just why she was being like this. 'Why the fuck are you dragging all of this shit up?' I moved over to the side of the bed.

'Please tell me,' she begged stroking my back.

'Tell you what?' I asked, as all of this was beginning to irritate the fuck out of me.

'Whether or not you killed him?' she pushed, as I was moving further away from her.

'It's not enough that I have gone through this all week, without you now having a pop at me also,' I sighed, climbing from the bed naked and walking to the window staring out into the night's star lit sky that shone brightly over our estate.

'Please Chopper.' She was suddenly stood behind me naked, her arms around me. 'I just want to know whether or not you'd be capable of doing such a thing.'

'Yes I am – And yes I did kill that fuckin' security guard,' I replied angrily at her, breaking free from her embrace. 'But what... by telling you that I did, it's somehow brought us closer to together has it?' I sat back down on the bed and looked at her... I knew right there and then from her eyes that something in that precise moment had changed between us. Something that would never quite be the same again, something had gone. I wasn't quite sure what it was, but the one thing that I did know was it was something that would never return.

She smiled weakly. 'It's alright,' she replied, as she then climbed onto me and began kissing me. 'I understand,' she said very unconvincingly.

Although I knew deep down that Donna would never be able to comprehend that I'd been able to take another's life... No matter what her suspicions to the disappearance of Paddy may have previously been.

I awoke in the dead of night – I'd been dreaming – Only it had been of Scotty – His face was from the past, from our early days together growing up.

I climbed from the bed and Donna's grasp; I wandered to the window again and gazed out over Hulme Estate that was now in the era of change. Despite it being the estate with which the two of us had roamed all of our lives.

Part of me already missed him, despite what he had done to us. I smiled at the thought of some of the things we got up together... Then the smile faded as I then thought of how the past had obscured into the present.

Closing my eyes, I then thought about just what had happened to him for us to be released – But the truth was that I already knew of that answer.

Opening my eyes once again staring again at the estate below me – Our estate – Hulme – We'd ruled for so long now, but after recent events, changes would need to be made. Drastic changes, the ones that no doubt we'd be speaking of tomorrow daytime.

I suddenly felt Donna's arms slip around my waist, startling me as she kissed my back.

'You alright?'

'I will be once you return to bed,' she said as she wrapped her left leg around me.

'Is that a fact,' I laughed out loud slightly, before turning and gathering her into my arms, then carrying her to bed.

So Sleeper said to say that everything has been taken care of,' Steve added as he finished relaying the story of Saturday night's events. The three of us had decided that it was best to conduct this meeting out of Manchester and travelled to The Kings Table, over Steve's way in Congleton.

'Shit...' I exclaimed, shaking my head. 'Did he have to do that shit whilst he was still alive?'

'He fuckin' deserved it,' Prey snapped.

'I know... But...'

'We know that you two went back along way Chopper,' Steve half smiled. 'But let's face it. Out of all of you, you're the one who would have been hit worse, especially with that security guard shit he'd thrown in there.'

'I know,' I sighed deeply dropping my head. 'So where do we go from 'ere then?' 'You know that I didn't want to get Anderson involved,' Steve stated. 'I just couldn't think of any alternative though.'

'Doesn't sound like Chan's keen on him either,' Prey grinned.

'He's warned us that Anderson will be nothing but trouble in the long run,' Steve added.

'Well I suggest that we pay off Anderson with a six month instalment,' Prey declared.

'You what?' I asked astounded.

'I'm suggesting that we break away from our activities for the time being,' Prey told us. 'We concentrate on setting up Macreedy's down in London.'

'But there is no way that Anderson is going to just let any of this drop,' Steve sighed.

'That's right,' I added. 'Plus what the fuck is going to happen to the business if we leave it? I mean what about the crew?'

'Look,' Prey said firmly, staring at the two of us. 'Stevenson and Walsh are going to be bang on it at trying to come after us again. What I'm suggesting, is that we take a break away from it all. It's best that we don't even give them the opportunity. I mean we can always come back to it after the six months or so, once things have calmed the fuck down.'

'But we can't just expect the rest of the crew to just give everything up,' I stated, shaking my head. 'Fair enough, the three of us have got more than enough cash to stay set up nicely, even after what they managed to pull. We still had a hell of a lot still on the street making money, plus we've got Macreedy's as well. But the rest of the crew haven't got anywhere near what we've got.'

'Prey's right though Chopper,' Steve added. 'Besides which some of the crew still has their bonus money coming from Chan's job, so they ain't going to be too bad... Are they?'

'So that's it then,' I said. 'We're just going to throw it all away.'

'Not at all,' Prey shook his head at me. 'The crew can do whatever they want to do. If they want to stay active until we decide that the time is right to return, then that's their own decision to do so. We won't stand in their way, but if when we do decide the time is right, well I'm sure they'll come back on board with us later on.'

I sighed deeply, for I knew what Prey was saying made complete and utter sense. Only for as mad as it sounded, and if truth be known then I knew that I was going to miss it all. The fact that we ruled the way we did only made it seem so much more right. But I also knew that there wasn't any argument. 'Alright then – agreed,' I finally nodded.

'Good,' Prey smiled.

'Also after what has happened, I've been thinking about something else,' Steve added.

'What's that then?' I asked, looking at him.

'Well, if anything like this or otherwise was to happen again then we should go and see Adrian about having papers drawn up to the effect of Macreedy's falling into the girl's authority whilst... and hopefully this situation would never arise. But

394

until our return, that way they would still have financial backing themselves. I mean you've got little Sean to think about now Prey,' he said, and then looked at me. 'And you've got Donna and I've got Claire to think about. I just want to know that they'd be all right.'

'You're right Steve,' Prey said as he sipped his bottle of Budweiser, I was merely nodding my agreement. 'Also with Macreedy's, if we decide to do the London venture then I think that we should also look at setting ourselves a small warehouse for the stock,' he suddenly added.

'You're not thinking of starting warehouse parties again Prey, are you?' I sniggered at him

'Fuck off you little twat,' he laughed back. 'No, I'm serious. Plus I'm sure we can write it off as a tax loss somewhere.'

'Alright – sweet,' I smiled. 'But let's see about setting this shop up down there first.'

'So what's the next step then?' Steve asked.

'We set up a meeting and sort out the cash for Anderson,' Prey said sombrely.

'What about the crew?' I enquired.

'Them too,' Prey said. 'We'll set up a meeting for this week to let them know what our plans are going to be. Whether they like it or not is another matter. But the thing that's most important is that we look out for one another from now on. We've only just managed to scrape out of this one and them two fuckers, Stevenson and Walsh will be busting their balls to do what they can to come after us again.'

'Ain't that the truth,' I sighed once again.

'Are you having a laugh or what?' Anderson sneered from across the kitchen's work surface in the back of Chan's. We'd arranged the meeting for Wednesday night along with the rest of the crew also.

'No,' Prey shook his head. 'There's six months worth of pay off dough right there,' he said, throwing the large padded envelope down.

'You ain't just going to pay me off like this,' he sneered viciously once again.

'It's the smart thing to do, considering the circumstances,' Prey stated firmly.

'You do realise that in six months time payments are to commence again?' Anderson stared with cold eyes at the three of us as he produced a folded A4 envelope from his jacket throwing it down.

'What the fuck is that?' I asked.

'Let's just say that's it's kind of like my little insurance plan that you lads won't try to fuck me over,' he smiled smugly as Steve began to tear open the envelope.

'What is it?' Prey asked not taking his eyes from Anderson.

'You really are a dirty piece of work – Aren't you Anderson?' Steve announced as he passed the photos to Prey.

'What are they?' I asked looking over Prey's shoulder at the photographs.

'I think I know some people that would be more than interested in those shots,' Anderson smiled smugly at the three of us.

'Oh shit!' I sighed, staring at the photos of Sleeper and Eazy, although completely masked, it obviously from their size and builds as being them from Saturday night whilst taking Scotty from the safe house.

'You should show a little trust Anderson,' Prey said coldly as he stared hard into his eyes.

'I've come to believe that you can't trust no fucker these days,' he said leaning further over the work surface, glaring at us.

'We'll have things up and running again, just not yet,' Prey told him. 'Then we'll make the necessary arrangements for your payments – Maybe even another six months worth. Besides what's it matter to you whether we pay you six months at a time or on a weekly basis? You'll still get your dough one way or the other.'

'True – very true Prey,' he then stared coldly at Prey. 'You lads better just hope that there's a big enough piece of Manchester left for your return,' he smiled smugly as he turned to leave. 'Oh, you can keep those photos – I've still got the originals and the negatives anyway,' he smirked knowingly at the three of us and then disappeared through the back door.

'I see why Chan doesn't like him,' I announced.

'What was that?' Chan asked as he suddenly appeared behind us. 'Has he gone?' he added shaking his head.

'I said that I see why you're not keen on Anderson,' I told the old man.

'He's nothing but trouble,' Chan sighed.

'Tell me about it,' Prey said as he returned the photos back into their envelope.

'Are you boys finished now in kitchen?' Chan asked. 'My cooks are waiting to prepare your meals,' he then smiled.

'In that case, we're definitely out of here then,' Steve said half laughing.

'The rest of your boys are outside having a drink, they arrived a short while back.'

'Thanks again Chan,' Prey shook the old man's hand. 'I mean for everything,' he added.

'No worry,' he smiled warmly. 'Now go sit down whilst we get your food ready.'

As the three of us walked out into the restaurant we were faced with the entire crew. Everybody from the lieutenant's to foot soldiers to lookouts was seated around the large table that Chan had put together for us.

'Evening,' Prey announced as the three of us seated ourselves at the head of the table. Everybody fell silent; their faces were mixed with an array of mixed anxieties as to what the night's meeting was to entail.

'I know that you're all a little concerned as to what future plans are to be,' Prey told them as he looked around the table.

'You could say that,' Jonah sighed.

'We've discussed what is to happen with our imminent business plans after recent events,' I said looking at Jonah.

'Now I think that you'll agree that we only just scraped out of this one,' said Steve – who it was fair to say the crew now realised he was more involved than just the shop we owned – as everybody began nodding.

'We truly believe that even though it was, let's say the higher management that had been nicked – the rest of you would have fallen too if their plan had worked and it almost did,' Prey added.

'Just how much did they have?' Dougsy asked.

'Just about everything,' I declared.

'Some of the things we were questioned on and some of the surveillance shots that they had would have been fatal if they'd been able to use their witness,' Prey sighed deeply at the mere thought of what had happened

'And just what did happen to that witness?' Kezlo asked a little quietly.

'I'm fucked if I know,' Prey shrugged.

397

'Who gives a fuck anyway,' Steve added.

'So what are we to do next then?' Diamond enquired.

'Basically Stevenson and Walsh are going to be fuming after all of this has gone to pot for them,' Prey said as he sipped his champagne. 'They are gonna have major fucking boners for us at the moment... Therefore... So...' He paused, dropping his head, then sighed deeply before looking up at everyone again. 'So, we're knocking things on the head.'

There were gasps and whispers arising from around the table as they all looked at us with astonished glares.

'It'll only be around six month period though,' I quickly told them.

'And just what the fuck are we supposed to do?' Parksey asked angrily.

'Whatever the fuck you want to do,' Prey smiled at him.

'So you're saying that we can go it alone?' Knieldy asked shaking his head at us.

'I'm saying, that if you honestly feel that to jump straight back into it after recent events then, sure, go right ahead,' Prey told him. 'That goes for all of you. But just remember that we will return and we will take control once again – But I do seriously recommend that you use your noodle ere' lads,' he began tapping his forehead, 'and think about what you're going to do. Always remember this, you can't make any real bees whilst you're on the inside of a prison cell,' he glared at everybody shaking his head as he did as if to make his point.

'Six months is a long time,' Jonah grumbled.

'It ain't that long mate,' I said smiling at him. 'Be smart about this.'

'You do realise that town will be up for grabs now,' Kezlo added shaking his head in disbelief at what we had planned. 'Them Salford lads will want control of the action if we're out of the way.'

'Then that is something that we'll have to deal with when the time arrives,' Prey said firmly. 'And by that, I mean that we will use any necessary force to retrieve what is rightfully ar's.'

Everybody began smiling and nodding, as they knew what Prey was more than capable of.

'So everybody is at an understanding then?' Steve enquired.

'Like I said before if you want to go it alone until we decide that the time is right to return, then do so,' Prey added.

'Just be careful with what you do,' I said looking mainly at Jonah and Kezlo. 'You all know just how careful we always were... And look what still happened to us.'

'Chopper's right,' Prey nodded. 'Be wise in any decisions that you make.'

'But for tonight, let's merely enjoy each other's company before we say goodbye,' I said grinning. 'For the time being that is anyway.'

Everybody began clapping, as the three of us smiled at one another. We all knew that it was correct decision had been made.

EIGHTY

'That was a cracking bust Anderson,' said the Chief of police. 'How the hell did you find out that O'Leary would have so much gear at his house at that time?'

'C'mon on now Gov,' he smirked. 'You know I can't go revealing those kinds of details to you.'

'Hey Mike,' shouted Chief. 'You hear about Bob here bringing down O'Leary. And only back in town how many months eh? And what about you...'

'Fuck off,' he sneered as he watched Anderson winking at him.

'Hey what the hell's wrong with you Mike?' asked Anderson as though he cared. 'Not getting those numbers in you require? What about those Hulme lads you've been obsessed with for so long?'

'I said fuc...'

'Enough,' sneered the Chief. 'I want to see you in my office Mike.'

'Whatever,' he shrugged changing his direction.

'See you around,' smiled Anderson as Stevenson passed him by.

'These are good fuckin' shots if I may say so myself,' said Anderson – albeit he was talking to himself as processed the latest film from his camera in the dark room that was located at the rear bedroom of his five bedroom house in Wilmslow, developing the photos he had not had chance to look at with being so busy over the last few days.

They were part of his latest collection he liked so much to keep. They were what he used to his advantage with those around him. He had dirt on everybody... and he meant everybody.

From all the criminals right to the chief of police himself, Anderson liked to make sure he was always holding all of the cards.

That was especially so now, with these Hulme lads who were the latest catch now in the picture. But he was kind of glad they had decided to step away for a period of time. Not that he had showed it at the Chink's restaurant. He made out he was pissed – but if truth be told... it worked in his favour.

Also added to the fact he had now rid Manchester of Dominic O'Leary... albeit it was pretty much a fit up. He knew that the charges would stick and that his son would be too scared to take any action following what had taken place with him earlier. After all he was still hospitalised for the time being.

As he held of the photos of his next venture he smiled to himself. Yes he thought – time to pay a little family visit once again.

'**Y**es lads,' Sleeper said grinning, as he opened the front door to his apartment. 'How's it going?'

It was the following Saturday and the three of us had travelled down to Marylebone in London as guests of Sleeper's. The trip was both business and pleasure – of course. Obviously as far as the girls were concerned, it was pure business though. Whilst we were down here, Lisa was to help us with locating the ideal location for our London branch of Macreedy's.

And Sleeper's job was to help us with finding as many quality nights out in the capitol as possible.

'Come 'ere brother,' Prey said dropping his bag and grabbing hold of his old friend. 'I owe...' He paused, glancing at us both. 'No we owe you big time mate.'

'It's like I've always said though,' Sleeper smiled holding Prey at arm's length. 'I know that if I ever needed the same doing for me you lads would be there in a shot.'

'Ain't that the truth,' I added hugging him also. 'That certainly was a class job that you did for us though.'

'You alright old man?' asked Sleeper as he winked at Steve.

'Couldn't be better pal,' he replied.

'Come on in,' Sleeper said, as we all made our way into his hallway. 'Just dump your bags there for now.'

'I hope that doesn't mean I've got to move them then.' It was Lisa walking through from the kitchen, looking as gorgeous as ever.

'Come 'ere and give us a kiss,' Prey scooped her up.

'Oi... less of that,' Sleeper laughed.

'How's little Sean?' asked Lisa.

'He's double sweet,' Prey replied. 'Although I didn't think that I'd be seeing him for a while.'

'None of us thought we'd see you lot for a while,' she smiled warmly, as he placed her back down. 'Funny how things work out sometimes.'

'Cheeky cow,' Sleeper laughed.

'We going to head straight into the centre?' she enquired.

'Why not,' Sleeper smiled.

'Fuck – We've only just got 'ere,' I declared.

'May as well make an early start,' Sleeper grabbed for his jacket.

I began laughing. 'Always said that you southern fucks would end up having heart attacks. You never sit still for one minute.'

Everybody laughed as we made our way straight back out of the door that we'd just set foot through.

'What the fuck is this place?' Prey enquired pulling his face, as we were all seated at our table.

Sleeper and Lisa had taken us to this Chinese Restaurant just off Leicester Square called The Golden Gates. The place looked like a complete dive from the outside, with its old and filthy Perspex sign. Through the windows hung freshly cooked ducks that were openly being chopped as you entered the place. Some of the seats had been taped up with silver duct tape. But, the most apparent thing was that the place was full of Chinese themselves, and all of them were enjoying their meals.

'This gaff is almost better than old Chan's,' Sleeper told us proudly.

'Just look at it though,' Prey said quietly as he fumbled with some silver duct tape holding his seat together.

'Take a look around you though,' I stated.

'Yeah and…' Prey shrugged.

'It's not about the presentation of the place Prey,' Lisa smiled. 'This place is about the food itself.'

'Great then,' Steve said as a small, all smiling waitresses handed him a menu. ''Cause I'm bleedin' starving.'

We all laughed, as I don't think there was ever a time when Steve, as skinny as he was, wasn't hungry.

'What do you recommend then?' Prey asked looking at Sleeper.

'I would suggest the banquets, but that's really for the tourists,' he laughed. 'Why not let Lisa order for us.'

Just then Lisa began talking in Chinese tongue, as the three of us all sat there gob smacked. Sleeper was obviously enjoying the sight of our gaping mouths as to how we were astounded by Lisa, even though none of us had a fucking clue what she'd just ordered for us. The Chinese waitress smiled proudly at Lisa as she took the order down then scuttled away.

'Where the fuck did that come from?' Prey half laughed.

'I didn't know that you could speak Chinese Lisa,' I added.

'If only I'd had a camera then,' Sleeper laughed. 'Your three faces were a right sight.'

'It's from my mother's side of the family,' Lisa smiled at us. 'Her mother, my grandmother was Chinese. I just sort of picked it up as a kid.'

'Well it was mind blowing,' Steve replied. 'But would you now would mind telling just what the fuck you ordered for us?'

The food seemed to just keep arriving from the moment the starters arrived to the moment the desserts arrived. It was as they had both said; the food was fantastic, although loyalty still lay with Chan – of course.

We spent the rest of the afternoon walking – or at least struggling to walk around the streets of London – we hadn't made any particular plans until the following week to actually set our sights on visiting estate agents with Lisa in order to possibly locate a unit for ourselves.

But Lisa had suggested that we might just want to have a walk around the city centre to get a feel for the place itself. Although like I've said before, walking isn't the easiest of agenda's in London. It had been the first time since all them years back that I'd visited the place again, it was still the same though, busy as fuck.

As we wandered around the usual places like Covent Garden, Leicester Square, Regent Street, Carnaby Street and so forth, Lisa then took off into Soho.

Now this was a mad fucking place, what a bunch of characters you had wandering around, everything from blatant gays to crazy looking punks to obvious business types. The amount of homeless was so vast, I mean Manchester was bad, but London was a different story altogether. It almost seemed that every free doorway or street corner was condemned with them. All ages, all sizes, all colours, I honestly couldn't get over just how many there were. It was a sorry sight to have to witness.

But the thing that was apparent with Soho, was that is wasn't anywhere near as commercial, also as Lisa walked us through there we ended up at the other end of Covent Garden, within an area known as Neal Street.

Now the shops that resided within this area were of a more independent nature in comparison to the more commercial shops that resided within say Regent Street. I had to admit that this was the one area that I took a liking to. The whole atmosphere of this area was more like Manchester than any other area that we'd been to. I suddenly found myself stopping at the corner of Neal Street that came to a small square outside of a small Victorian style pub.

'This is where it should be,' I said out loud smiling to myself.

'What's that Chopper?' Prey asked me.

'Macreedy's,' I answered, still smiling and looking at all of them.

'It's nice around here? Isn't it Chopper?' Lisa returned the smile.

'Yeah – it sure is.'

'Why here though Chopper?' Steve asked.

'Because it's about the only place where we've been today that I feel has the right feel to it,' I confirmed, still looking around.

'It's a very up and coming area also,' Lisa added.

'Is it busy now though?' Prey asked.

'Just look around,' Sleeper said. 'Can't you see what it is that Chopper sees mate.'

'No,' Steve said, before Prey had chance to even answer.

'Don't you reckon one of the busier streets would be more ideal,' Prey then added.

'Look – I may not know that much about London Prey,' I smiled at him. 'But the one thing that I have noticed is that everything is very commercial in those areas. Also that everything seems to cost a lot more dough than usual, which if you think about it, will most definitely include the cost of renting any property.'

'Chopper's right there brother,' Sleeper laughed at Prey. 'Do you actually know just how much it's going to cost you set up down here?'

'Yes... well actually no,' Prey then laughed also.

'We've got the dough to do it though,' Steve declared positively.

'I'm sure you have,' Sleeper grinned and winked at the same time.

'It's not just that though,' I said. 'Macreedy's isn't a commercial enough gaff for those other places that we've been to, Macreedy's has been doing extremely well for us back in Manchester. Macreedy's offers something that little bit different from your usual fuckin' Top Man or Top Shop. Were not commercial and this place seems sweet to me.'

Prey and Steve both began laughing. 'You forgetting what the initial plan for down 'ere was though,' Prey smiled at me shaking his head.

'We can't stay scally's forever,' I replied half smiling at the thought.

'You've done a pretty good job so far,' Sleeper smirked.

'Easy son... Do I look one of these little urchins Sleeper,' Steve then smiled.

'A sophisticated one,' Lisa smiled back.

'Alright Chop – I see your point,' Prey informed me. 'Maybe it is time for a career change permanently.'

'I don't mean just yet,' I blurted out, worried that he'd gotten the wrong end of the stick by what I had said.

'We know what you mean,' Steve said, smiling as he did.

'First things first though,' Lisa said, bringing us back down to reality. 'Hadn't we better find out just what's available first in this area,' she laughed. 'You lot really are a bunch of scally Northerners aren't you. You all think that when you go ahead and make a decision, that that is it and you'll immediately get it.'

'Or just take it,' I added with a wink.

'Well it doesn't quite work like that down here,' she added firmly. 'But I tell you what, I know a couple of the daughter's whose fathers own a lot of commercial property down here. So I'll have a word with them for you if you would like.'

'I think after Chopper's carry on. Yes we would like,' Prey looked at me and nodded his approval.

'Alright then,' she replied. 'Come Monday I'll see if I can find anything out for you all. But until then, will the three of you just stop thinking bleedin' business and enjoy yourselves. This little break is on the two of us,' she then winked at Sleeper.

'Is it now,' he half laughed frowning at her.

'Well it is now,' she laughed, then smiled cheekily at him.

We'd all had a blinding few days with our hosts. Both Sleeper and Lisa had taken us all over the place. Saturday night had been spent at one of London's major clubs known as Ministry of Sound; I had to admit the club itself was alright – But the place just wasn't my scene at all.

Everything had started to become way too dressy for my liking with the entire clubbing scene. When it had all begun, the one thing that I had liked so much about it was that it wasn't about dressing up in shirt and ties with a nice pair of trousers. It was that you could wear what the fuck you wanted to wear and it was sweet.

But now – even in Manchester itself with the way that it had exploded into the new era of things. It had attracted a lot of people from out of the area to town. It was even was apparent that the dress sense was changing, although not with the lads we knew. For us it was simply to dress smart but comfortable in whatever you donned. At the end of the day lads would always just be lads... well the lads from Manchester that is eh.

Sunday had been spent with Eazy over on his estate in Brixton, which I had to say was a lot more like back home. We had a top day doing some of the shady boozers that Eazy was obviously more comfortable in.

Eazy had later on taken us to a fantastic little Caribbean food gaff; which I had to admit that the chicken, rice and peas with fried dumpling were even better than Sampson's itself. He had then taken us onto some little dodgy after-hours gambling gaff set in the basement of a large block of council flats. I loved every minute of it, Eazy's taste in things were so much like my own that I fully understood why Kezlo, despite only the love of music, got on so well with him.

Lisa had been gone most of Monday whilst the three of us spent the day with Sleeper merely travelling around checking on some of his shadier deals that he made money from.

We'd spent the day meeting with people in a variety of different establishments in Lewisham and Hackney whilst he collected money owed and negotiated new transactions.

And I can tell you that from the amount of bees that we saw change hands that Sleeper lived more than comfortably. We'd even found ourselves over in Bromley, Kent, with deals involving everything from moody money – to deals consisting of stolen truck loads of computers due to be taken later that week.

By the time we'd returned back to Marylebone, my head was spinning and I hadn't actually been involved with any of it.

As the four of us walked through the front door to Sleeper's, we were hit with delightful aroma of food being cooked.

'Now that smells pure quality,' I declared as we walked into the flat.

'In'it,' Prey added smirking at me.

The four of us made our way through to the kitchen where we found Lisa kneading fresh dough, whilst pans sizzled and warmed around her. You could the see light effulgent from within the depths of the oven, where obviously there was something also cooking from within there.

'What you up to then?' Sleeper asked as he slipped his arms around Lisa's waist making her jump.

'Jesus…' she jumped startled. 'I didn't hear you come in.'

'Sorry,' Sleeper grinned she kissed her.

'That smells familiar,' Steve pursed his lips at the delicious aroma.

Lisa smiled. 'It's the recipe that Chopper gave me for that Indian meal.'

'Seriously,' I asked as making my over to the hobs.

'Probably won't taste anything like yours though Chopper,' she smiled as Sleeper nibbled her neck.

As I dipped my teaspoon into the hot butter sauce and tasted it, I began smiling. 'I think that I've just been put to shame.'

'Give over,' she half laughed, looking slightly embarrassed. 'Why don't you lads get yourselves a beer from the fridge? The bread will be a while yet.'

'We not off out tonight then?' Sleeper asked as Prey had opened the oven door and smelled the contents of the chicken cooking within its realm.

'I picked up some material on some units today,' Lisa informed us. 'I thought that tonight we'd just stay in, eat some home cooking and just have a bit of a smoke for a change.'

'Now that definitely sounds like a top idea to me,' Steve agreed.

'What does,' I laughed. 'The food or getting wasted part.'

'Both, you cheeky sod,' he replied, as we all laughed.

'Now that was fantastic Lisa,' I declared licking my lips. 'I can honestly say that I couldn't have done a better job myself. It was absolutely delicious.'

'Behave Chopper,' she smiled. 'You know it tasted nothing like what you cooked for us that time.'

'Well I thought it tasted pretty fuckin' fantastic to me,' Steve told her.

'In'it,' Prey continued munching on a piece of chicken. 'Probably even better than Chopper's... no offensive brother.'

I shook my head and smiled at him.

'So what did you manage to find out for us today Lisa?' Steve asked he wiped his mouth with a napkin.

'Well first off, I went to see a couple friends who manage shops within that area of London.' She reached down from the table to her bag removing some A4 manila folders. 'They put me onto a couple of estate agents they knew of.'

'Anything that may be worthwhile checking out?' Sleeper asked as he casually began rolling a joint.

'A little... but,' she smiled proudly. 'Carol from one of shops knew of a unit free just down from where she worked.'

'And?' I asked anxiously.

'Well she knows the actual landlord for the unit. It's one of her old man's associates – I think is how she put it. Apparently he's got quite a bit of property around town.'

'What's the unit like itself?' Prey enquired.

'About double the size of your shop.'

'Fuck me,' Steve exclaimed, as he'd already opened the folder Lisa had placed on the table. 'If it's double the size of our shop now and this one here is about half the size, yet the rent is already four times more than we're paying in Manchester.'

'Are you serious?' Prey gasped taking the folder from Steve.

'It's obvious that it's going to cost more down 'ere,' I told them, as you could see Sleeper grinning as he lit the freshly rolled joint.

'Typical bleedin' Northerners,' he laughed. 'Right bunch of cheap fucks aren't you?'

'Will you let me finish,' Lisa injected sharply.

'Sorry,' Steve apologised.

'Like I said, Carol knows the landlord,' she smiled knowingly. 'She reckons if she gets her old man to have a word in his ear for you and you're talking cash, which I presume you lot are,' she then laughed.

'You presume right,' I grinned back at her.

'She reckons that possibly and only possibly, but he may do you a good a deal on the unit.'

'Where about is it?' Prey asked.

'Just down on the right hand side from where Chopper stopped on Saturday. You know by that boozer on the corner in the middle of the square,' she told him.

'It sounds perfect,' I instantly confirmed.

'Well, let's just wait and see what Carol can sort out first. She's going to give me a ring tomorrow afternoon,' Lisa smiled as Sleeper passed her the smouldering spliff.

'E'are Prey,' Sleeper said tossing a small plastic bag filled with solid lumps of charley – cocaine – freshly chopped from the block to him. 'Make yourself useful and chalk some of that out will you.'

'Always a pleasure with this gear pal,' replied Prey with a little smirk, as he then got busy.

Anderson was waiting at Manchester Airport in departures. He'd been here for the last two hours as it was, but who the hell noticed anybody in departures right? It was a cesspool of everybody doing their best to get the fuck out of the country... and who could blame them really.

He needed confirmation that the only other person that he knew could create any problems for him was definitely going to be out of the country. He didn't even realise that he was here in the first place. It had been by chance that he discovered that he had returned originally just to attend Prey's kid's christening until that had been rudely intruded by Stevenson and Walsh of course. But he had just found out that he had stuck around – the only reason he hadn't known was that the person in question had been up in Nottingham seeing his sister who attended University up there.

The guy he was waiting for had probably inadvertently over the years become one of Manchester's main characters. He was not only clever in the ways he went around things – he was also someone not to go messing with as he was one of the most ruthless of them out there... and Anderson knew this better than most.

He took another sip of his rancid luke warm coffee and cringed as somebody suddenly caught his eye as he smile to himself. There he was now. He spotted him. It's not like he would have been a major problem in any way – he was just so well concerned that if he'd stayed in town, he knew that out of everybody this was the one you had to be concerned about.

411

For the simple fact of the matter was that Tony Henessy was known for just what it was he was capable of.

His plan was coming together now. Manchester was full of players – or at least lads who thought they were players. But there was a handful he had to make sure he had control of. Some of them he knew that he couldn't. In fact Prey and his crew had been on his list of people to take care of. However, as circumstances would have it – they walked straight into his hands... so to speak of course. But they were... in their own way dealt with. Well at least for the time being that was anyway.

The O'Leary's had started to make plays within the industry he now felt was going to be the one thing in as many years that had finally arrived that was going to finally give him the kind of pay days he had always dreamt of. He had known the old man from the good old days when he was part of the QSB – as in the Quality Street Boys. He knew that Dom didn't bend for the law and so he had seen to it that he was taken care of.

But above all of that, he knew that this guy here checking in for his flight to Tenerife was, and very much still is – one of Manchester's main players. He had been for years, but had somehow had the foresight to see other areas where he could excerpt money from. Especially ventures like the timeshare operations out in Spain which had made him his millions many times over.

Fair play he thought to himself. But he was also glad to finally be seeing the back of him as he now followed him through to departures area towards the passport control. Tony was probably the one lad in this city whom he could never have any control over. The simple fact being that he had half the country working for him in some capacity was a major factor he didn't want to go fucking around with.

As Anderson watched him hand his passport over he let out a sigh of relief. That was what he had wanted to see.

Come Thursday afternoon we'd arranged to meet with both the landlord to see the unit, then if it was to our liking we were to go on for a meal to discuss negotiations to take the unit on.

'Looks well big,' I said pressing my face against the filthy windows to the disused unit.

'Top location though,' Sleeper said looking around.

'You've got stairs leading from the underground over there and there,' Lisa pointed in both directions for us to see. 'Foot flow seems to work its way in both directions leading straight past here.'

'It's certainly a lot busier than Manchester,' Steve nodded.

'That's the truth in'it,' Prey said. 'There are so many people you wonder where the fuck they all come from.'

'And they don't sit still for one moment,' I shook my head.

'Aw'right there,' I suddenly heard a typical cockney accent from behind us. 'You must be the party that Carol's old man asked me to see,' he seemed chirpy enough and obviously was well wedged up as he was dripping in gold from everywhere. 'I'm Mr. Tucker but just call me Tuck, all my mates do.' He then shook all of our hands whilst Lisa made the introductions.

'Right then... let's take a little look around inside.' He was so full of himself that I was finding myself struck with a permanent grin.

The unit was a lot bigger than our other store. The only disadvantage was the stock room wasn't very big at all, but saying that, Prey had already suggested us getting a warehouse so stock could always be bought in bulk then delivered.

As we walked around we all discussed what possibilities lay within the unit itself. What could go where, expanding the footwear section and so fourth.

'So then,' Tuck said with his permanent smile of polished teeth. 'What do you reckon boys?'

'I got to admit it's alright,' I smiled back with ease. 'Although we were offered two very good deals this morning on similar properties,' I lied.

'Just how good a deal are we talking my son?' he asked as the others all stared at me, although Prey was smirking at me.

'Well, why don't we all go for some scran and see just how good a deal your going to offer us – eh Tuck?' I smiled back at him, shaking his hand again.

'I think me and you son are going to get along just fine,' he announced, putting his arm around my shoulder as he led me out of the shop. 'Come on then you lot,' he called out to the others, on whom glancing back were all biting their lips to control themselves.

The six of us went to this small Italian Pizza & Pasta Restaurant around the corner from the unit. It also just happened that Tuck knew the manager so got us a nice little deal as he put it.

After talking through our plans as to what we exactly were aiming to do with the unit and letting him know all about just how successful our other store actually was. I think that Tuck could smell the colour of the money; he especially liked the part about cash investments, honestly believing if I'd carried on the way I was with him any longer he would have been begging for us to let him invest.

But all in all he did actually make us a fair offer on the basis that we signed for a minimum of a five-year lease on the property. By the end of the meal we obviously told him that we needed to discuss the matter further between ourselves and if he'd give us until the end of the week we'd be most grateful.

He tried the old blag of having other interested parties, so I merely grinned and winked knowingly at him. I informed him that we'd have a definite answer one way or another by Monday morning.

'What you like Chopper?' Lisa laughed as we made our way to the small Victorian pub on the corner of Neal Street.

'True fuckin' blag artist if ever I met one,' Sleeper then added.

'If you never try it on then you'll never know,' I smiled back at him. 'What does everybody want to drink?' I asked taking orders whilst the others seated themselves at a quiet table near the rear of the establishment.

The place had begun to steadily fill with workers from the area; once again you had a real mixture of people thrown together. The others were already talking amongst themselves as bringing the tray of drinks over to the table.

'Everybody sweet?'

'What do you reckon then Chopper?' Prey asked me.

'I think that we're onto a winner,' I smiled confidently at him. 'The only problem is it'll take a shit load of dough to do it.'

'Ain't that the truth,' Steve responded.

'We've got more than enough to do it,' I confirmed, looking at them all. 'But if we're to stop other activities for at least six months, then financially it'll hit us hard.'

'Maybe I could make a suggestion,' Sleeper announced.

'What's that then Sleeper?' Prey asked as he swigged his bottle of Budweiser.

'Well if I can be honest with the three of you,' he sighed, then tutted at the three of us. 'You all kind of pissed me off a little when you never asked me in on Macreedy's in the first place.'

'We didn't know whether it would even work out the way it has done though,' I told him honestly.

'No... Hang on a minute Chopper,' Prey said looking at Sleeper. 'Just what have you got in mind?'

'A four way partnership,' he smiled knowingly at us. 'I'll invest dough into the up and running Macreedy's which will help you three out. Then I'll invest straight into a four way partnership straight into this one.'

'Plus, you'll need someone down here to run it,' Lisa smiled.

'I take it that the two of have spoke about this,' stated Steve.

'Also that you've already got somebody in mind for the job of manageress,' I added looking at Lisa knowingly.

'Well it would make a lot of sense – Wouldn't it?' she smiled at us all. 'Plus I need something do with myself. I've seen the way Donna enjoys what she does and year's back now, I used to manage a store myself.'

'And it will be an equal partnership between the four of us,' Prey looked at Sleeper.

'It'll be good for all of us,' he then smiled.

'I like it,' I announced. 'If the two of you want us to discuss it, that's fair enough. But I feel that with Sleeper on board, we'll be laughing all the way to the bank... well more like, our back pockets eh.'

'You know it's sweet with me,' Prey confirmed.

'Sweet as,' Steve said, in mocking Mancunian accent. 'As you lads like to put it,' as we all began to laugh.

'Fuck me Chris,' exclaimed Westy, as Chris Walker and three of his lads entered the hotel room at The Ravenswood Guesthouse in Handforth where a deal was set to go down involving the sale of two kilos of heroin and a kilo of cocaine.

It had been the first time since Chopper had rearranged Chris's features that Westy had seen him. 'Sorry mate I didn't mean to...' he continued.

Chris cut him off abruptly. 'Look – We're here to do some business, not to look at how pretty I am – this ain't no fuckin' beauty contest... right?'

'Sweet mate,' replied Westy as he tried his best to smile, although at the same time, taking offence to Chris's tone with him. The two had known each other from way back before Westy was forced to leave Manchester many years earlier after his old man had been sent to prison for shooting a rival from the Jackson's family member dead. The family had fallen apart thereafter, Westy deciding that he could make a better go of things away from the town centre itself.

Although he still kept his contacts within town itself. But he hadn't been able to hide his shock at Chris's appearance. It was a lot worse than he'd heard. Well either that or as Chris's reputation was beginning to grow larger for his violent outbursts and take-overs of certain groups activities in and around town, basically no one was going to say a bad word against him. 'Your lads want to test the gear first?'

'No Westy... we're just going to trust you,' Chris said sarcastically. 'Of course they're going to test the gear,' he responded, sneering the last part at him.

417

'You and me are old school Chris,' Westy suddenly snapped, rising from the bed as his two lads stood in the background slipped their hands to their pieces in their jackets. 'But reputation or no reputation around town mate – do not take that tone or attitude with me son.'

He sensed the trouble brewing already, so Chris smiled. 'C'mon... let's just get this thing done with Westy,' he winked to try and relax the situation as his lads were already stood waiting for the first move to be taken.

'Jacko, Dave – Go in the bathroom and test the gear. Mark, you stay put,' Chris instructed without even looking at them. 'If that's all right with you of course Westy?'

'Of course it is,' he smiled. 'As long as Matty goes in there with them,' he then nodded at the large bulk of a man stood behind him. 'Plus it will give us chance to count the dough Chris.'

After ten minutes the bathroom door opened and both Jason and Dave nodded with glazed looks to their faces.

'That's all that was needed to know,' Chris grinned knowingly.

'We smiling?' Westy asked his other lad counting the money.

'Everything is sweet on this side boss,' he answered as he placed the last of the money back into the rucksack.

'We'll be seeing...' Westy began to say, just as the door suddenly crashed open, his first reaction was that they were being ambushed, everybody had their shooters pulled, that was until he saw the same appearance of shocked reactions appeared on both Chris's and his lads face's also.

'Evening all...' The huge figure that stood within the now open doorway smiled confidently, all guns pointed directly at him as he stood there casually smirking back at them all.

'Now I don't think it's going to be too wise of you lot to go shooting a Detective now... is it lads?' he asked and smirked menacingly at the same time. Then he began staring at Chris – whose face now held nothing but contempt towards him stared back.

Everybody was at a loss, not knowing what the fuck was actually going on. The figure with the same casual yet confident manner waltzed into the room with complete ignorance to the array of handguns still pointed at him. He then smiled at the sight of both the drugs and money.

'You can all fuck off now,' he instructed sharply, glaring at all of them with his cold eyes. 'Well with the exception of young Mr. Walker here that is.'

'What the fuck is this?' Westy snarled. 'Just who the fuck are you?' he added staring from Chris to the figure.

'Westy... Just – you'd best...' Chris looked at him shaking his head.

'Are you trying to fuck me over Chris,' Westy said viciously, but before he knew what was happening, the figure had dragged him violently from the bed and had pinned him against the wall, with his own Smith and Wesson revolver pressed firmly against his chin.

Westy's eyes were frantic as his two men pointed their guns at the figure. Unsure as to what it was to do.

'Enough,' Chris simply said. 'Just do as the man says,' he nodded to his lads also, who wasted no time in turning and scampering out of the door as fast as they could.

'You going to leave quietly Mr. West? The Mr. West of I think it could possibly be Biddulph near Congleton right?' said the figure knowingly as he saw the recognition suddenly hit home.

'Yes – We're gone...' He knew they had no other option as he realised just who the figure actually was pinning him to the wall.

'Call your fucking dogs off then,' he sneered so close to Westy's face that he could feel the hot, stale breath against his skin making him twitch. The gun still hadn't been removed from his chin.

Westy began nodding frantically at his men who lowered their guns, the fear that this man before him instilled in you was like nothing he'd experienced before and all that he wanted to do was get the fuck out of there.

'I'll be seeing you,' Westy said, as he tried to stare hard at Chris, but he wasn't able to hold the glare as the figure began smiling at him.

'No you won't Mr. West – Also they'll be no mention of tonight's little events if you're a clever boy,' he nodded his instructions. 'Or we may just have to pay you a little visit... Whether you're out of town or not. Funny how nowadays they can pull you over and find a shit load of gear in the back of your car... Or how with all of the current drug feuds going on that you could easily end shot dead like your old man was.' He smirked then added. 'Isn't it lads?'

419

The three disgruntled men made their way quickly out of the door shaking their heads at the events that had just taken place. You could clearly see that Westy was visibly shaking from the fear that he still felt.

'Make sure you close the door lads,' the figure laughed maliciously as the door slammed shut, he then turned and stared coldly at Chris. 'Alright nephew,' he said smugly.

'What the fuck is going down 'ere Anderson?' Chris asked angrily. 'You realise what you've just gone and done?'

'I know exactly what I've just done,' he replied casually smiling; however the smile couldn't hide his evil side though, no matter how casual he tried to make it. He removed the pack of cigarettes from his jacket and sat down in the chair opposite Chris who remained on the bed. 'And now I'm going to explain just what's going to happen.'

'You set me up,' Chris snapped. 'Just like you did with my old ma...'

Anderson cut him off. 'Just shut the fuck up and listen.' He shook his head impatiently. 'I've been keeping track of your activities since those Hulme lads seem to have dropped out of the picture around town.'

'And?' Chris said staring at Anderson.

'And...' He paused. 'Well to be quite honest you seem to be doing all right for yourselves. You and your entire band of merry scallies,' he smiled at his own humour.

'So what do you want? How much is it going to cost me?' Chris said presuming to know just what it was his corrupt uncle was after.

'Partnership my dear boy,' he smiled broadly as he blew his smoke out.

'You are kidding right,' Chris blurted in astonishment at the mere suggestion. 'This is some kind of a joke right?'

'Do you see me laughing,' he replied sternly.

Chris stared at him shaking his head in disbelief. 'Is this like some kind of trippy fuckin' bad nightmare,' he said with his head seemingly shaking from side to side unconsciously.

'Look Chris,' Anderson sighed. 'I've seen for myself just how much money you lads are making. Especially since that O'Prey and Chorlton have been out of town for the last few months.'

'I hear that they plan on resuming business later this year,' Chris said sombrely.

'And does that bother you?' Anderson asked.

420

'Of course it fuckin' well bothers me,' he snapped. 'Have you seen just what that little prick Chopper gone and done to my face?'

'That's why you'll need a partner like me,' he smiled confidently. 'You just let me worry about the likes of O'Prey and Chorlton. Besides they owe me a favour,' he watched Chris's reaction who nodded.

'So you'll stop them from doing any business?' Chris asked enthusiastically.

'No – They are worth more to me if they still can have some of the action,' he rolled his neck from side to side. 'Plus... They sure are a bunch of smart arse bastards. Remember how your mate has never been found Chris... Paddy wasn't it?' Anderson wasn't even sure that they had anything to do with his disappearance, but realised just how much Paddy had meant to his nephew. He knew that by using his name against them, Chris would appreciate it.

Chris dropped his head at the thought. 'I knew it was them all along...' he looked at him as he said it, watching the smirk spread across his face. 'But you're a high ranking fuckin' officer. You can't become my partner.'

'I'll be your silent one,' he announced knowingly. 'You see I can rid all of your competition around Manchester.'

'And become a fuckin' hero at the same time,' Chris declared lifting his head, he know knew where this was leading.

'Precisely son' he smirked. 'You see – you needn't worry about yourselves. I'll make sure that no one gets near you and with the information you'll supply me with we'll be onto a winner all round.'

'I ain't no grass!' Chris snapped.

'Do you realise just how much gear I can get you and just how much more money we'll be talking about?' he shook his head in contempt at Chris.

'But you're still old bill,' Chris couldn't get his head around this whole conversation.

'If I'm bringing crews down all over Salford and Manchester, what do you think they are going to be thinking?' he smiled as he saw Chris shake his head again. 'I'll be a fucking God damn hero who, with your help – will be a rich fucking hero in the bargain.'

'I don't know,' Chris sighed out loud, still shaking his head.

'What don't you know you little prick,' Anderson stepped up out of the chair and picked up a kilo of the heroin. 'Are you forgetting just where you're sat and what you're sat in the possession of.'

Chris's face suddenly dropped as he realised that he was sat there with not only the gear but all of the buy money also. 'Shit... You really are scum, aren't you Anderson?'

'Come on son,' he crackled a vicious laugh. 'You can call me Uncle Bob from now on if you like.'

'Fuck you!' Chris snarled back at him.

'So I take it we've got a deal then nephew?' he asked as he grinned, then stared at the back of Chris's head held within his hands, as it slowly nodded the answer he had really wanted to hear.

'You sure that we need this Prey?' I asked as we walked into
the empty warehouse on the small industrial estate, over in
Old Trafford that Prey had picked the keys up for that
afternoon.

'Course,' he smiled. 'We've had the London site open for
almost eight months now and with the amount of business that
the store is doing its wiping out our stock a lot quicker than
Macreedy's in town is.'

'So why not have the warehouse down there then?' Steve
enquired.

'Two reasons... And they both come down to money,' he told
us. 'Basically labour costs up 'ere will be a lot less, not to
mention reason number two.'

'The rent,' I said cutting him off.

'Exactly,' he smiled again. 'Besides which it's an ideal little
site this.'

I had to admit it was a nice position for the warehouse with
its quiet location with only a handful of other warehouses on
the estate. With only a single road giving you access to estate
keeping it secluded from any built up areas and it also had
easy access through Sale to the motorway.

'I had known that London was going to be a lot busier, but I
had never expected for it to have quite taken off the way it has
done,' I said, as I then began to check out the security system
the building was using.

'We've only filtered a small amount of our money through
there yet as well,' Steve said lighting a cigarette.

'I know,' added Prey. 'It's colossal, ain't it?'

'So is it time to return then?' I asked not taking my attention away from the system before me.

Prey looked at Steve. 'I reckon so,' he confirmed, as he watched the old man nod slowly.

'Good,' I replied, still fiddling with the system. 'I've really missed Manchester and the estate.'

We'd spent almost the entire time down in London, working with the shop and with Sleeper and Lisa. The six-month break away from business had been put back even further. I'd really become home sick and because Donna managed our other store I'd missed her like crazy, however since our arrest she somehow seemed a little more distant. I knew that the problem stemmed from the murder of the security guard that she was now fully aware of.

Although just lately we didn't seem anywhere near as close as we'd been before – I don't know, maybe it was just me being paranoid. But, I also felt as much as I hated to admit it out loud – the relationship was doomed. It's one thing suspecting something – however the reality of truth can be a real burden. As much as I hated the thought of life without Donna, I knew deep down that was possibly how the cards were going to be dealt.

'You're not too keen on London are you Chopper?' Steve laughed, breaking my thoughts... thankfully.

'There's just way too much going on Steve,' I shrugged. 'Although I have to admit that the money side of things down there makes it somehow more worthwhile,' I replied, grinning at the two of them.

'Knieldy and Diamond said things have really changed around town,' Prey suddenly added.

'Jonah and Kezlo too,' I informed them both, and then continued. 'There – piece of piss system. That's the first thing we've got to get sorted out,' I said, half laughing at how easy it was to bypass the system and began to clamber up the disused crates to give my attention to the security of the windows.

'What have the lads said then?' Steve asked.

'They said that over the last few months things have been becoming really heavy on both sides,' Prey said. 'With both the law – and the personal wars to take over each other's territory around town.'

'Also that Anderson's name has cropped up a lot as well,' I added.

'He received his payment off of us didn't he?' Steve asked.

'Paid another six months off,' Prey said shaking his head. 'Bastard.'

'Well we can't keep doing that if we're not making anything from the street,' I declared, walking back over to them. 'That's where the real money is.'

'How long before we can set the manufacturing side up again?' Prey asked, looking at Steve.

'The lads are just waiting for the word,' he said just a little too apprehensively, making me stare down at him quizzically.

'I think that everybody has missed our little spell away,' I was smirking at him, although closely watching his reaction – No, it was nothing I told myself. 'I reckon that the lads are all itching to get back to work.'

'Did any of them stay at it?' Steve asked curiously.

'None of the lieutenant's did,' Prey told him. 'But a lot of the street grafters only managed to stay away for around a month before trying to make a go of it themselves.'

'Can't blame them really,' I told them. 'But it wasn't with a lot of success,' I then added.

'Why's that?' Steve wanted to know.

'A lot of them either were nicked by Stevenson and Walsh or Anderson more recently. But there has been a lot of fights for territory and from what Jonah said a lot of blood was spilt,' I shook my head at the news.

'We've just missed it all with not being in the area for any great amounts of time,' Prey confirmed.

'We're just going to have to be prepared for whatever is going to happen,' I smiled down at them both knowingly. 'Like we said before... We'll take back what is rightfully ar's anyway. I mean if it hadn't been for us, then a lot of what's happening in Manchester wouldn't even be happening today.'

'Ain't that the truth,' Prey smiled back up to me on the crates. 'But y'know – one day it still would be nice to...' he trailed off at this point.

'To what?' I quickly added. 'Stop altogether? Go completely straight?' I asked jumping back down to floor level, astounded at what Prey had just implied without actually saying it.

'You said it yourself in London Chopper. We can't keep scallying about all of our lives,' Prey replied.

'We don't want an all out war going on though, do we Chopper?' Steve said a little apprehensively once again.

'And neither do we want any fucker walking all over us,' I added sternly.

'Chopper's right Steve... in one sense,' Prey nodded although noticing the slight hesitation as he did so. 'All we want is what is rightfully ours,' he added, although I still had the feeling it was more for my benefit than Steve's.

'Whatever,' Steve said shaking his head.

This was a little confusing, I wasn't at all sure whether either one of them were eager to resume business.

'Don't worry about it old man,' I smiled, putting my hand on his shoulder, trying to lighten the air of uncertainty that had presented itself unannounced. 'Besides which, you're getting too old to be fighting anyway,' I laughed as Prey did.

Steve punched me in my solar plexus, winding me slightly. 'Any day... you little whipper snapper.'

Then thankfully on my behalf anyway, the three of us laughed; breaking through that moment's doubt as we began to make our way out of the warehouse.

Although I had to admit for a couple of moments there, somehow there was a different mood that hung heavily if only briefly over the three of us. I'd been a little shocked at Prey and Steve. The thought of ending business altogether, seriously that is, hadn't really crossed my mind before those moments there.

I knew that legally, we were achieving a lot more than any of us had ever anticipated – But we would never had achieved any of it without our roots through the business we were involved within – Whether it was good or bad, without it we would never have achieved anything that we have on a legal scale.

I suddenly found myself remembering back that one time when Prey had, it seemed at the time gone on with himself about what we were doing was like a fairytale of some kind – What was it now? Once upon a time in Manchester down in ar' back yard – that's what he'd called it. He'd told me back then that we couldn't continue forever in the business that we were involved in.

Was now the time to get out? Could we even get out? What about Anderson? All these questions were coming at me.

'Chop – Chopper,' Steve suddenly broke my train of thought as Prey bolted the warehouse doors together.

'What?' I asked a little vaguely.

426

'Nothing...' he grinned. 'Just lost you there for a couple of minutes.'

'Just thinking,' I replied then added. 'Just thinking about my stomach... Anybody for Chan's?'

We'd arranged a meeting at Chan's with the lads for the following Saturday.

'So how have my boys been?' Chan smiled as he sat down to join us whilst we waited.

'Sweet Chan... In fact double sweet mate,' I smiled.

'The London shop is making a killing that we set up and we weren't even known down there,' Prey told him.

'Good – very good,' Chan replied as he sipped his tea. 'I'm glad things worked out for you boys.' He paused and looked at us. 'How is our mutual acquaintance?'

'We paid him off for another six months,' Steve sighed.

'You know that there is going to be no winning with the likes of him,' Chan sighed. 'I always like you boys and I want for you to succeed like you are my own boys – But the business that we in is changing – Not like it used to be.'

'What's wrong Chan?' Prey asked, looking at the old man somewhat concerned.

'Nothing... well not really,' he smiled. 'All I want is for you boys to be successful without hassles of certain people. The word is out that he going on a one man mission bringing down crews from all over Manchester.'

'We have to get back in though Chan,' I declared, wondering just what had got into everybody this previous week. 'I mean we can't keep bunging bees at someone if we're not making those bee's to give away,'

What I was saying was the truth, although what had happened a week ago at the warehouse, as brief as it been, was playing on my mind, in fact it had been all week

'I know Chopper,' he smiled again just as all the lads walked into the restaurant. 'Chan might have a good deal for you boys... Not quite yet though.'

'What's that then?' I asked suddenly curious.

'Not now – in the future,' he winked. 'We talk later,' he smiled as he then began greeting all the lads, as the three of us merely looked at one another confused.

'Alright Chopper,' Jonah smiled warmly as he shook my hand.

'Yes mate,' I nodded then greeted the others.

'I can't believe that it's all gone so pear shaped,' I exclaimed, listening to the stories being told around the table.

'You better believe it,' Kezlo sighed, as he picked his teeth with a toothpick. 'It's been proper fuckin' nightmares watching everything that we've helped build up turn to pot.'

'And you say that Chris Walker seems to have a big influence over a lot of it?' Prey asked bemused.

'That's right,' Knieldy said.

'Just how the fuck did he get so much backing behind him,' Prey added.

'It's all of them young Salford lads,' Jonah told us. 'I mean I know we've done so mad things before. But we always seemed to do it for a reason.'

'And these kids don't?' Steve asked as he sat back in his chair.

'Exactly,' Diamond added.

'It's like all they want to do is get a name for themselves like the lads from the old days,' Parksey grumbled.

'Yeah, but them lads from back then were the lads,' Prey confirmed.

'Still are,' I added smiling.

'I just can't see how the fuck Walker has got himself so much power though,' Prey said shaking his head at the information.

'You can forget about The Hac now as well,' Kezlo shrugged.

'We don't even go in there anymore,' Jonah added.

'Why's that?' Steve asked.

'Same thing,' Jonah told him.

'They stabbed Dougsy three months back because he was carrying someone else's gear and not theirs,' Kezlo stated. 'He's alright now... But that's just the way it's gone.'

'And this Anderson character? Y'know the one,' Parksey said looking at the three of us knowingly. 'The one who was involved in that warehouse job that went down.'

'We know who he is,' Steve said a little too abruptly.

'Well his name has been cropping up a hell of a lot lately,' Parksey added.

'That's the truth,' I half laughed. 'I think in just the last few days I've not stopped hearing it.'

Prey stared at me. 'Well we'll just have to set things up differently from now on.'

428

'How though?' Diamond asked.

'We'll stick to the estate for now on,' Prey said rubbing the back of his head as if thinking to himself, although leaving myself wondering just what he was actually thinking about.

'Some of Chris's crew has moved in there also,' Jonah added.

'You're joking,' I blurted out, my thoughts broken.

'No he's not,' Parksey added.

'And funny enough they weren't the ones who got nicked when some of the street lads were picked up,' Kezlo said, still picking his teeth.

'We're not standing for that,' Prey declared firmly, the old anger suddenly returning and building from within. 'Just what the fuck are they knocking out?'

'You name it,' Parksey casually said.

'Everything!' I exclaimed, shocked at this latest revelation. 'Just how the fuck has this happened?'

'We stopped,' Jonah responded casually.

'No business, remember,' Kezlo added. 'I mean we've been alright money wise – But...'

'But it's all gone well tits up hasn't it,' Steve said shaking his head.

'You said it,' Jonah smiled.

'Basically it's a buyer's market out there – Alright lads, we've got to ease our way back in,' Prey told everybody, with more enthusiasm. 'But either way, the first situation we take care of is these lads of Chris's on the estate.'

'They'll be an all out war at this rate,' Parksey announced. 'Not that I'm bothered – But...' he trailed off.

'Not if we do it right and merely counter attack the ones, who are trying to fuck us up,' I smiled knowingly. 'There will be no need for an all out war.' My smile turned to a grin as I thought about it. 'Well maybe just a small scale one with Mr. Walker that is,' I laughed as everybody else also did so.

429

'So we're square right?' asked Anderson. 'You know just what it is that I am expecting from you and just what it is that I am offering right?'

'Yeah,' sighed Chris. 'Basically I become your personal little grass and...'

'And you'll eventually get to take over all... well a good 80 percent anyway – of Manchester's drug trade for yourself. So fuck being a shitty little grass you dumb prick. I am going to make you one of town's main boys. Something that you would never have achieved by yourself you cocksucker.'

'I know,' he shrugged. 'But...'

'Stop being a little girl and listen to me.'

'Okay,' he replied looking at the one guy that frightened the shit out of him, yet no matter how much he scared him – he had always in some perverse way wanted to please the cunt. No matter what had happened with his old man. He held his own thoughts on that score – but fact of the matter was that Anderson was a character that he not only loathed and truth be told... feared... but in that perverse way still felt a real connection to and still couldn't put his finger on to what it was.

'Okay so you ready for the next move?' asked Anderson.

'What is that you need?'

'Batty's crew in Wythenshawe,' he replied lighting a cigarette.

'He's hooked up with Prey though,' sighed Chris. 'And I thought that he was off limits to even me?'

'That is true,' he smiled. 'But he has been using someone else since Prey and the rest of them have been out of the picture.'

'Who?'

'That's what I need you to find out for me,' he replied drawing deeply on his cigarette and exhaling the smoke.

'I really don't know shit about the lad,' sighed Chris. 'Apart from the fact Paddy and him had beef that went way back. Something to do with Hennessy,' he watched as his uncle flinched.

'This has fuck all to do with him,' he responded viciously.

'I didn't say it had anything to do with him,' he smiled to himself seeing for the first time his uncle become unnerved at the mere mention of another's name.

He knew – as did everybody else for that matter, just who Tony Henessy was. This was the guy that even Paddy feared. And that was saying something. For apart from Prey – he didn't believe that Paddy feared people. The difference was, that Prey had done what he had done to Paddy to instil that fear – whereas Tony had never needed to even come near Paddy for that fear to be placed so predominately so.

Then again, anybody who knew of Tony either feared him or respected him immensely (possibly a little of both thinking about it) But whichever way you looked at it – Chris realised for the first time in his life that whatever it was that Tony had, had literally crossed over from their world to even the other side...

No matter what is uncle said – he clearly witnessed that something about Tony bothered his uncle. For now though he kept his mouth shut and put it aside for another day.

'So okay,' smiled Chris thinking to himself that all of this really could work in his favour after all, 'tell me who else it is that you are after... Uncle.'

431

EIGHTY SEVEN

We had begun slowly trying to rebuild the business over the months; however things were proving more difficult than we had expected. It's amazing how in just a short period of time things can change so dramatically.

It had been so true what the lads had told us about town, although we'd rid the estate of Chris's lads immediately, with over half of them spending a few nights in the hospital I hasten to add.

I think that both Prey and myself enjoying the violence a little too much. It was more than justified as far as we were concerned. Also it sent back the message, not only to Chris whose response we were awaiting, but also to the rest of Manchester that we were well and truly back.

But still, there was no getting away with it, things had changed dramatically. It seemed that even though there was still alot of business being run through the city of Manchester, Salford was definitely now playing a major factor to this. Also it was like we'd been told; it appeared that somehow Chris was indeed controlling an immense division of this.

More importantly it appeared that anybody that was competition was getting fucked over from the police or from Chris's lads themselves.

With this all in mind we'd stuck completely to the estate for the time being. Things were slowly starting to come together again, although it somehow just wasn't the same anymore... It was... quite simply, appeared that too much had been lost.

Maybe if we could work our way back into Manchester, it would be different but there was no use taking any chances at this early stage. Well not until we'd sussed things out more clearly anyway.

Again my thoughts began to run wild... It had been since that first day in the warehouse, ever since that day I'd began thinking more and more about what it would like to pull out of business altogether.

I was unsure as to what Prey or Steve's thoughts were on this, but deep down thinking that just maybe they were also having those same thoughts – *Damn it* – It was down to them friggin' two that I was thinking the way I was now – I wasn't entirely sure about anything about anymore.

I mean the London store, along with Macreedy's back here in Manchester was actually pulling in some excellent profit margins. Through the money being made we'd all purchased homes and several other assets away from the estate, of course we'd put everything all in the girl's names.

The money that we'd made and were still making from the street was being laundered through several sources and also through the London store. It made no sense living on an estate with the money we had. Therefore we'd all moved well away from there. However that sentimental side of me still missed it – still missed the buzz of Hulme. Saying that though the period of *"squat now whilst stocks last"* had well gone and now the estate was changing... for better or worse was anybody's guess at this stage in the game.

What if we were to get out for good? Could we manage? Sure we could I thought to myself.

What about the buzz though? Although that was beginning to take on a different feel these days.

What about – And this was the big what about... Anderson? There was just no way of getting away from that one. Chan had told us that there would be no winning with the likes of him.

Oh fuck it – I'd just taken too much time off. We'd just taken too much time off – Things would begin to change... Surely... But there it was again... Doubt.

'We just ain't making that sort of money we used to,' Prey stated fact as the three of us sat at Steve's new house in Congleton.

433

Claire had just disappeared into the kitchen along with Donna and Kathy; little Sean was tugging at his father for attention as he just wandered over from the settee from where he'd been dozing. Prey scooped up his son making him laugh out loud; it was amazing to see just how much he'd grown.

'None of us expected things to have turned the way that they have done,' I sighed deeply.

'That's true,' Steve added lighting a cigarette. 'With all that's going out each month from that side of things, I'm wondering whether or not it's actually worth it,' he shook his head.

'For fucks sake,' I blurted out. 'It ain't that bad yet... Is it?' I found that once again, I was questioning myself, I'd known it to be true that we were only making a small amount of the money that we been before but it was still substantial.

'The kids right in one sense Steve and we sure need it at the moment as we've got yet another payment due soon to y'know who,' Prey said whilst he tickled Sean making him giggle out loud as he did so.

'He's one of the reasons I'm questioning this,' Steve added. 'We did what we had to do back then... There's no two ways about it. But there's also no getting around the fact that it's now crippling us financially.'

'He's not going to shift now though, is he?' Prey sighed.

'Fuck – I almost forgot. You both just reminded me,' I said bending down to my record bag that I don't think had ever had any records stored in there. 'Have either of you seen today's Manchester Evening News, I picked it up on my way 'ere after noticing this headline,' I tossed the paper onto the table.

The headline read, 'Anderson's One Man War on Drugs Hits the Streets of Manchester.'

'Shit – You see what I'm talking about,' Steve answered taking the newspaper from me.

'It's actually worse than any of us thought y'know,' I informed them. 'He's taking down everybody big style, including Batty and all of his crew yesterday. That's what's prompted this article y'know.'

'Batty!' Prey shook his head sombrely. 'What else does it say?' he asked coldly.

'It seems that people from all over are being taken down too easily,' I told them as Steve began reading through the article. 'I'm not kidding, even some of the old time crews are beginning to drop.'

434

'And the Salford lot?' Prey asked.

'Two of the main families that we know of and a few other names here that even I recognise,' Steve sighed as he continued reading. 'Jesus... He's going at everyone full on it seems.'

'Ain't that the truth,' I nodded, as I just finished rolling the spliff I'd been building, lit it and began to draw heavily on it. 'Y'know, I not at all sure if there is any possibility – But I reckon that we got to try and fathom out some way of breaking free from this twat. Y'know that Chan always warned us that this wanker would be trouble.'

'I hear you Chopper,' Prey confirmed what I think three of us felt at that precise moment.

'But just how the fuck are we going to manage that then?' Steve asked as he took the smouldering spliff from me.

'Besides which, it seems that every fucker at the moment in time is dropping around us,' Prey added. 'True... But it's like Steve said – it comes down to the money.'

'What about Chris?' Prey asked still playing with his son. 'Does he or any of his croonies get themselves a mention in the paper?'

'Nada,' I shook my head.

'Well at least our names aren't in here,' Steve confirmed.

'Yeah – but both Chris and his lot – or ar's for that matter,' Prey shook his head. 'I mean if they're talking of Manchester's so called underworld... Then especially with what went off with us last year and the way the press had a field day with us they might be snooping around again. And as for Chris not being mentioned, especially with the amount of town that he's controlling. Just what the fuck does that tell you?'

'You reckon that Chris's paying him off also?' Steve questioned himself almost.

'I thought of that as I read it and I think that there is a good possibility of it. I mean it's like you said Prey, neither of us has got a mention. Now we know that on our behalf it's more than likely down to the fact that we been giving this fucker his dough – I mean he's not going to want that to stop that? Is he?' I shook my head. 'But even if Chris is doing that, it don't explain just how the fuck Anderson is managing to bring down all of these crews around Manchester and its surrounding boroughs.'

'Unless he's helping him do so,' Steve added.

'Wouldn't have put grassing down to even Chris's style though,' Prey said shaking his head. 'Besides we don't know that these two have anything to do with one another.'

'I know,' I answered. 'I wouldn't have thought that Chris would have been able to get through to Anderson in anyway.'

'Yeah – but you wouldn't have thought this time last year that Chris would have achieved as much as he has done,' Prey added.

'We only got onto him through Chan though,' Steve said as he drew deeply on the spliff.

'You reckon that somehow they're connected Prey?' I asked.

'Not too sure to be honest,' he answered as he playfully tickled Sean. 'One thing that I am sure of though is that I reckon it's about time that we paid Chris a little visit.'

'Sounds good to me,' I grinned. 'I've not seen him since that last encounter at The Hac.'

'You're last encounter... Is that what you call it nowadays?' Prey laughed. 'Neither of us was there. Come to think of it though, I've not seen your last piece of handy work Chopper.'

'Can't wait,' Steve added sarcastically.

'You sure that he's going to be in there Prey?' asked Jonah from the back seat of Prey's new Mercedes at the forefront of the three car loads that made our way through Cheetham hill towards The Greyhound in Crumpsall. I'd travelled with Prey, Jonah and Kezlo and was positioned in the passenger seat staring out of the window.

'Apparently, it's like his base now,' Prey confirmed nodding. 'Even heard that he's got some dough invested in the boozer itself.'

'I ain't been here for years,' I smiled knowingly. 'Not since I was a kid and all that trouble you had with Paddy.'

'In'it,' Prey smiled stroking the scar that ran the length of his face.

Everybody grinned knowingly; although neither Jonah nor Kezlo were there, the story was a well-known one – I thought briefly of Scotty then instantly shook the thought away.

'You got the bag with you?' Prey asked glancing at Kezlo.

'Nah,' Kezlo said glancing behind him at the VW Golf, Parksey was driving. 'Parksey's got it stashed in that false panelling that he's had fitted beneath his motor. Thought it would be safer there.'

'Ain't that the truth,' I added, thinking to the contents of the bag.

'You reckon we'll head into any trouble tonight?' Jonah asked.

'You never know... Better to be safe than sorry, eh?' Prey announced as he eased the car through the back streets.

437

We then continued the journey in silence, each of us carrying with them their own thoughts, whatever they maybe.

'We'd best pull in over there,' I said pointing to a vacant side street not thirty seconds away from The Greyhound.

'You want someone to go check whether or not he's in there?' Kezlo enquired as we pulled up.

'Fuck that!' Prey laughed. 'Don't want to fuck up any surprise we've got,' he said, sounding like his old self.

'Besides,' I added. 'If at all possible we best try and keep this as business like as we possibly can.'

'Yeah right!' Jonah laughed.

Prey cut him off. 'Chopper's right Jonah,' he told him, looking directly at him. 'For today we just want to confront Chris about his recent activities. Always remember that knowledge is the key to running and also taking over any successful businesses.'

'Some things just ain't adding up,' I added noticing the others approaching from the other cars.

'Yeah... Let's just say that today we need to try and find out just how it is that this fuckers gained as much power as he has done,' Prey said, opening the car door as we all followed suit.

'Everybody ready?' Steve asked apprehensively as we began shutting the car doors.

'Sweet mate,' I smirked at him, then glancing at Parksey who was carrying the large weighty holdall. 'Just like old days eh mate?'

'In'it,' Parksey laughed back at me as he distributed the arsenal in the bag to all of us. I took for myself a familiar looking Beretta 9mm pistol from the bag. After all it was my favoured choice of handgun. There was a whole array of different arsenal from sawn off shotguns to pistols and even a machete, which I noticed Knieldy take for himself with a huge grin as he did so.

We quietly set off down the road toward the entrance of the car park of The Greyhound as memories from the fight that Prey and Paddy's crew had been involved with that came flashing back to me.

As we approached the Pub, we could see seven, possibly eight of the younger runners, no more than thirteen or at the oldest, fifteen years old. A steady flow of customers continually was passing their money over in swift yet obvious transactions.

438

As all nine of us approached the old worn out shell of The Greyhound, we were apparently approaching unnoticed. But then just as suddenly as I thought that, I noticed that one of the young runners had blatantly noticed us and darted out of sight, before appearing briefly as he darted through the front doors.

'There it goes now,' Prey suddenly confirmed, as we were upon the car park, noticing another of the runners scurrying inside through a side door.

'Go now – Quickly,' I told them and with that we swiftly made our way through the front doors into the smoke filled bar, the thick heavy scent was a mixture of good weed and even better quality crack-cocaine, that could be smelt before you were actually through the door.

Almost as suddenly as we waltzed through the door we noticed the young runners from outside over to the left corner of the bar, talking frantically into Chris's ear. Even from where we was standing you could see just how bad Chris's features around his left side of his face were scarred, as I quietly smiled to myself, I caught his sudden glare.

I noticed at first glance that surrounding Chris was a table of around six lads, although the whole establishment was in total apprehension at the mere sight of us standing there. Suddenly everybody rose from their seat's hands darting to inside pockets and jackets.

'Wait,' Prey called out, looking directly to Chris. 'Let's talk.'

Chris looked around without saying a word, and then merely nodded at Prey. As Prey, Steve and I made our way forward towards him, he nodded once again and everybody sat down – Jesus, just where the fuck had he gained so much stature from? The fucking prick was acting like Brando from The Godfather.

'Sit down,' he instructed us.

I glanced cautiously back towards the door; our lads had all kept their same positions around the front entrance. Their eyes keeping a check on all our surroundings each and every one of us could feel the tension in the air. I slowly took a seat, not taking my eyes from Chris's glare, who was also was holding my stare.

As we seated ourselves across from Chris he grinned at me. 'Fucked me up good and proper, didn't you Chopper?' his hand briefly stroking his face.

I couldn't help but smile knowingly at him. 'I tried my best,' I replied casually, as if I'd merely given him a black eye, and not scarred him for life.

'Your day will come boy,' he sneered, adding the last bit as of to intimidate me.

'And I'll be fuckin' your bird on the same day,' I smiled back at him. 'I heard that she's a bit of a slapper... But then you've only got to take a look at your face eh!'

'Fuck this shit you two,' Prey snapped, all of Chris's lads had looks of pure apprehension pasted across their faces. 'We ain't 'ere to talk about how much you two fancy one another.'

'Well just what the fuck are you 'ere to talk about then Prey?' he asked casually lighting a pre-rolled spliff that lay before him, there were several openly laid out before him. The strong sweet scent from the smoke indicated it was charley, maybe even rock – I took a slight sniff at the air – yes, it was defiantly a crack-cocaine spliff he chugged greedily on.

'Look,' Prey sighed as Chris eyeballed me, his face really was a mess to look at.   'You think we're stupid or what Chris. First you send your lads into Hulme – Then...'

'Yeah – That's right,' Chris cut him off, 'and the two of you fucked them up as well.'

'Don't that tell you something then dickhead,' I snarled at him, catching Prey's cold stare at me.

'I didn't appreciate my lads being put in hospital,' Chris grinned. 'But I suppose business is business eh.'

'Well that's exactly right Chris,' Steve finally spoke up. 'You see what you gone and done was to try and move into our side of things. And I'm not just talking about the estate.'

He kept grinning through the thick powerful smoke. 'I got told by an important source that you lads retired or some shit,' he laughed. 'I told everyone that it was bollocks – But guess what though?'

The look on Prey's face was displeasing; just who was his important source. 'What?' he asked holding his glare.

'You retired just long enough for me to take over the rest of town nicely,' he laughed out loud and his lads followed suit.

'Well that's what we're 'ere for,' Prey said simply as a matter of fact. 'We want back what's rightfully ours.'

'Oh okay then,' his laughing abruptly stopping. 'Just take it back.'

'That's just what we plan to do.'

'Yeah right Chopper,' he smirked at me. 'You lads have had your day.'

Prey leaned closer to him. 'Says who?'

'Listen Prey,' he leaned closer to him. 'If you want your business then we go to war over it.'

'Nobody wants a war,' Steve said sighing deeply. 'Going to war over this will be just what every other fucker will want. No money will be made in the long run.'

'Speak for yourself old man,' he glanced at Steve. 'Believe me. No matter what happens I'll still be making bees.'

'C'mon, amuse me Chris,' Prey said his face still close to Chris's. 'Just how the fuck did you manage to get so much business together?'

'What's wrong,' he smiled. 'You think Paddy was the brains?'

'No,' I laughed at him. 'I figured neither of you had any fuckin' brains.'

'You're treading on very thin ice... boy,' he said coldly looking at me.

'Fuck you,' I half laughed at him.

He looked back at Prey. 'Just what the fuck, are you suggesting? Don't you realise just how stupid you sound,' he laughed once again. 'You think that you're just gonna come in 'ere and I'm just gonna to say, "Okay Prey – You lads are back – We just kept things on the boil for your sorry arses. How could we have so fuckin' stupid to think that the great Hulme lads would let us get away with this" He was laughing out loud as his lad's followed suit. 'In fact... 'ere while we're at it,' he reached into his pocket tossing a set BMW keys onto the table and continued. 'Take my fuckin' car as well.'

'You want to tell me why so many lads around town are getting pulled and you're not Chris?' Prey casually asked as if he hadn't heard the last bit that Chris had said.

Chris shot him a worried look that turned almost to anger in the same instant, he snarled. 'Maybe I should ask the same of you?'

I was studying his face for some kind of recognition that he just maybe; possibly he knew Anderson but I couldn't find a trace.

'Maybe we're just careful,' I smiled at him knowingly.

He casually grinned back at me. 'Maybe I am Chopper.'

'You kidding me or what,' I laughed in his face. 'You seen the way you're running things around 'ere – It's like fuckin' Cheetham hill market on a Sunday.'

'Listen,' he sighed and leaned back into his chair. 'You lads ain't taking shit back without a fight.'

'That can be arranged,' I smiled, feeling for my shooter.

'But...' He paused and looked at the three of us leaning closer. 'Like the old boy said, nobody really wants that... Besides you've taken your estate back.'

'We want back what was there before,' Prey stated.

'It ain't happening... Alright,' he was becoming agitated slightly, although not able to tell whether it was the coke filled spliff he'd smoked – or whether it was something else.

'So you want an all out war then?' I asked him. 'Or maybe you just want for me to go do your bird a favour... and show her what a real fuck is.'

That was it; you saw the flash of anger, intensified with the drug that was mixed into his system, dangerous but a little more predictable for me.

'Chopper – you fuckin' little prick... We are at fuckin' war already you little fuckin' runt,' he screamed at me whilst grabbing onto the scarred side of his face. My eyes were darting all in all directions at the scene around me, looking for my slot.

I'd heard just about enough and it wasn't anything that we wanted to hear. So before anybody, Chris included knew what had happened I'd grabbed the Beretta 9mm pistol from with my jacket swiftly and was forcing myself slickly over the table, grabbing onto Chris's face and pushing the cold steel into it all in one fluid motion.

'Let's finish it now then you fuckin' cocksucker,' I screamed at him, yanking his hair back and repositioning the pistol under his chin.

As I was doing so, all around me had pulled their weapons, whatever they may have been; they were loyal to their current so called master. Sensing Prey and Steve's presence from behind me, I knew that they would have me covered.

'Chopper... Chopper...' Prey called calmly. 'This ain't the place ar'kid.'

I was staring into Chris's eyes, which to my amazement were remarkably calm and controlled; everybody was waiting for the first move to be made.

'You want this to end now?' I sneered at him.

He brought his face closer to mine smirking. 'One... None of you would make it out of 'ere alive... son. And two...' he stared at me with cold eyes even more than before.

'Yeah and *two* you fuckin' prick,' I sneered at him, pushing the steel harder into his chin and feeling the heaviness of everything around me.

'Two,' he replied gleefully, this fucker was actually smiling at me – I mean I've got a 9mm automatic pistol stuck in his face and the twat is fucking smirking. His words were only just audible enough for me to hear.

'It'll piss our mutual acquaintance off no end,' he said, as I immediately began backing off with the pistol still aimed at his head.

He had to have meant Anderson? Surely he had.

'Enough - NOW,' he called out, his lads easing just slightly off but reluctantly not dropping their guns.

'We're out of 'ere,' I said backing away, although still pointing the gun at Chris, and observing the bemused faces around me wondering just what the fuck had gone off.

Everybody followed my moves as we continued out of the Pub backwards, I'd heard what I'd needed to hear from this cunt, only now I didn't have a clue what we were going to do about it.

As we backed out, I caught a glimpse of Jonah who grinned then casually said. 'That's what I call as business like as possible, Chopper.'

Nothing at all,' I shook my head at Chan. 'I can't believe that Chris doesn't have anything to do with Anderson.'

A couple of weeks had passed since our encounter with Chris, and we were still none the wiser than we'd been then. I'd been convinced that the mutual acquaintance as he had put it had meant Anderson for sure. However – we couldn't find anything that was now substantiating this theory.

But whom else could he have meant? As we never had any contact with Anderson apart from payment day and Prey took care of that as neither – Steve or I wanted any contact with him at all. Not that Prey did for that matter... only he understood and took sympathy on the two us. We'd discussed contacting him and arranging a meeting, but if our theory wasn't correct then that would merely arouse suspicions if any further action on our behalf were to be taken.

'Not from what my sources tell me anyway,' Chan answered.

'You had any contact with him recently?' Steve asked as he drew deeply on his cigarette.

'Not since last month,' Chan told him. 'He seemed completely full of himself as you can imagine with all the arrests he's making he considers himself some kind of a super-fucking-star. He always in the paper or on the television. Even his past is being brought up; you know – like how they try and kill him years ago – how that failed. It seems to have given him even more prestige. He's nothing but trouble,' he said the last bit almost to himself.

'Any of your lads ran into trouble?' I asked sipping from my bottle of Stella.

'Only the ones who aren't on his books,' Chan half laughed. 'Although I imagine the ones who made bail are now though.'

'We were sure that Chris's reference to mutual acquaintance was him,' Prey declared sombrely.

'From what I hear about Chris,' Chan sighed deeply and looked at the three of us. 'Is that it's far from that. From what a couple of my other sources say is that Anderson was apparently pulling his hair out over Chris not giving him anything. Apparently Anderson pulled him in a few times recently but wasn't able to touch him as the kids that were with him held up his hands to the possession with intent charges,' Chan shook his head in disbelief.

'Who got pulled with him?' I asked.

'Just some young lads…' Chan thought for a moment. 'The thing is that Anderson's pulling everybody else down, well it's got to be Chris's turn soon.'

'I wouldn't be too sure of that,' I replied. 'If you saw the way that he's operating things down there. It's like an open fuckin' cattle market. They're being so obvious it's untrue.'

'It's like he's becoming almost untouchable then,' Chan shrugged. 'They are saying that he has gained so much respect from not only that side of town but also from many of the younger ones around this end as well… who are also now all looking up to him like he's the new Manchester gangster they all want to be.'

'Fuckin' kids though,' Prey half snarled. 'That's all it is. He's got kids backing and worshipping him.'

'He's using fear against them like Paddy did,' I told them.

'That maybe true lads but it's the next the generation breaking through into our world Prey,' Chan told us half-smiling. 'Whether we like it, or not.'

'We're not fuckin' bowing down to a load of fuckin' kids though.'

'You forgetting just how eager you were at that age Chopper,' Chan smiled knowingly at me.

It was more than true, I had literally all my life being worked the wrong side of the law until recent years when we combined both. I had to smile at Chan's comment. 'All right, yeah – Quite true mate.'

'Shit!' Steve started to laugh. 'I hope that there aren't too many up and coming Chopper's out there… Or we're going to be completely fucked for sure.'

445

Everybody began laughing as I broke their moment of humour. 'C'mon this ain't getting us anywhere,' I told them all. 'Just what the fuck are we going to do about this fucker? I mean we can't just leave things as they stand,' I sighed rubbing the back of my head. 'I'm still waiting for some kind of retaliation from a couple of weeks ago.'

'Chopper's right y'know,' Prey announced, looking thoughtful. 'We got to do something about this situation. It's just a question of what's the right choice to make.'

'So you want to go head to head with this cunt? Do you?' Steve shook his head. 'I mean if that's what we got to do... Then... It's...' He was finding all of this harder than either of us.

I studied his face then cut in. 'Look – I don't see what other option we've got if it's the business that we want back,' I looked around the table. 'But also... the way I see it, is that we got ar'selves a couple of options 'ere,' I had to clear some of the thoughts that had been troubling me recently. 'Whether or not you two holding the same thoughts I don't know.'

Prey was staring intently at me. 'Go on Chopper.'

I looked at the three of them. 'Alright – listen...' This was harder than I thought it would be. 'I don't want you lads thinking that I being some of soft twat 'ere – But – Well to be honest it's down to you two that I been thinking this way. Ever since that day at the warehouse months ago... it's been bugging me,' I sighed, and then stared at Steve, then Prey in turn.

'Go on Chopper,' pushed Prey.

'It's just for a moment back there at the warehouse I seen a flicker of doubt with both of you when we discussed setting up business again,' I watched for their reactions.

'Fair play,' Prey spoke first. 'I'll admit it.'

'Me too,' Steve added.

'Well I'd never really, seriously that is, considered dropping out all together,' I sighed deeply, as it was the truth. 'Well, that is until that day. Ever since then I keep drifting off into deep thoughts about – I ain't going soft but...'

'But fuck all,' Prey exclaimed. 'I got to admit it. I enjoyed all those things that we were doing down in London with the store.'

'So did I to be honest as well,' Steve added, Chan was just quietly listening intently.

So what now I thought. 'Well I don't know if I want out yet.'

'I told you a long time ago Chopper that we couldn't last forever in this business,' Prey said looking directly at me. 'Shit man... just look at how old you are how much you've already achieved in life.'

'Prey's right... Jesus!' Steve looked at me. 'Looking back on it if I'd achieved as much as you had at your age I don't think that I would still be in the game.' He shook his head. 'To be perfectly honest I'm growing a little too appre...'

I cut him off before he could finish. 'So what the fuck are you suggesting then,' I snapped.

I'd known deep down that they were having second thoughts about what to do, but hearing it so openly from both them which why I'd just said what I had. Because I had to hear it outright form their mouths. And with that – well I wasn't quite sure what to think.

'We quit – just drop out of the game just like that? Then what? Sure we got Macreedy's... But what about the lads for starters? Besides I don't think I want out,' I was beginning to feel a little confused.

'Either that or we go to war with Chris,' Prey stated. 'One or two situations Chopper.'

'You just said it yourself,' Steve added.

'What's wrong with fighting for what was ar's anyway,' I told them, noticing Chan shaking his head slightly. 'What's your opinion Chan?'

He smiled at me. 'I'm an old man Chopper... What do I know?'

'A hell of a lot more than I do,' I laughed.

'You're so wrong Chopper,' he grinned. 'You've been having these thoughts recently not because you're going soft as you put it... Merely becoming wiser yourself.'

'So you're saying we should just let Chris take what was ar's then?' I asked the question directing it at Chan.

'It's not my decision to make,' he told me. 'You have to ask yourselves that question.' He then looked at all of us.

'I'm getting too old for this shit,' Steve shook his head in bewilderment.

I looked to Prey. 'Listen Chopper,' he smiled. 'Y'know that time we spent down in London... Well it was the first time since I can remember when I wasn't worried about either the door being kicked in, being arrested again or being shot at or any other fuckin' thing that seems happen at the moment in Manchester,' he shook his head at me seriously. 'It just ain't

447

like it used to be ar'kid – I can't quite explain it properly to you.'

'It's different down there,' Steve said.

'That's bollocks,' I blurted. 'It don't matter where you go in the country, there's the same going on there nowadays.'

'Very true indeed,' Chan nodded.

'But 'ere in town is where we're known for it and the main reason when we weren't doing shit other than the shop down there I liked it – Shit – Maybe it's me turning soft,' Prey now laughed. 'I'm telling you now Chopper if we are going to go to war with Chris... Then fuck it brother! But we'll have to go full out with him,' he sighed out loud.

'That'll be a lot of bloodshed on both sides with no guarantee of the outcome,' Chan told us. 'Plus I don't think that Anderson would be too appreciative of you all going to war on the streets of Manchester. Especially as he's looking like a true golden boy at the moment.'

'Maybe... somehow Chris knows about our involvement with him,' I said thinking about it. 'Just maybe that's what he was referring to that day. Maybe he knows that if we go to war then Anderson will come down on all of us hard.'

'Could be? Or maybe Anderson's warned him off of us in some way,' Prey added.

Steve butted in. 'He's not as daft as we thought he was.'

'What the fuck does that mean?' I asked. 'You think just cause he's put together what he has that he's got brains all of a sudden,' I said trying to answer my own question, just the mere thought of that wanker irritated me.

'That's not what Steve meant,' Prey told me.

Chan stopped him there. 'He's had you rattling your noodle for the last couple of weeks hasn't he?'

'Yeah – But...' I trailed off in defeat, yet still irritated at the thought of Chris.

There was no getting away it; he most defiantly had got me thinking intensely to his reference. There wasn't any other fucker that I could associate knowing that would be pissed if it had gone off that day.

Prey had even spoken to the older heads over that way to try and fathom out if it been in reference to one of them, although we didn't deal with any of them as such, the thought had been there as to whether or somehow we'd be upsetting them.

They told Prey that they'd kept their business away from Chris as they considered him a loose cannon.

'Alright then – Just what the fuck are we going to do about Anderson then?' I asked them. 'I mean it's all good and well you going on about pulling out of business, but what you both seemingly have gone and forgotten is that we still got to make our payments to that twat. We can't afford to do that if we're not working the street... Just think about how it's crippling us now.'

'We got another payment three months from now,' Prey sighed deeply at the mere thought of it.

'I told you that he was trouble to begin with boys,' Chan butted in.

'You think that there is maybe some way that we could pay him off all together Chan?' Steve asked as we all looked in Chan's direction.

'You could put him in a box,' Chan grinned as we shook our heads at him. 'I know – I know...' he laughed. 'Wishful thinking on all our behalves, eh.'

The thought of taking out a copper, especially Anderson who with as much pull in the force as he had at the moment – wasn't really clear thinking of sound mind, merely wishful thinking as Chan had put it.

'What about paying him off in one go Chan?' Prey enquired. 'You reckon that he'll go for that?'

'I wouldn't have thought so,' Chan told us. 'At least not without a major payoff to him.'

Steve rubbed his chin. 'How major?'

'No use asking me,' Chan said shaking his head as he did so. 'I am not the one taking the money from you.'

Prey sighed. 'We ain't going to be able to break free from the fucker are we?'

I thought about this for a few moments then spoke up. 'Alright – What about if we get something that we can use against him.'

I watched their reactions as they all looked at me. 'But still go ahead and make a one off payment to him just to keep him sweet. But use what we've got on him so that if he comes back at us he knows that we're holding something on him.'

Everybody fell silent and was all deep in thought when Chan broke our concentration. 'Alright then boys,' he smiled at us. 'I think that Chopper could be onto something here and we could possibly tie it into something that I've got in mind for you... my boys anyway. But if you go ahead with this then I want a promise me that you'll leave the business for good. Just you boy's, I'm not talking about the rest of the lads.'

I think that Chan had us well and truly confused. 'You now want to make a little sense of that now Chan,' I laughed as did the other two.

Chan smiled at us. 'You remember a few months back I mentioned that possibly I'd have something lined up that would benefit us all.'

I thought back and recalled Chan throwing us a bone, making us all curious then telling us fuck all, I grinned at him.

'Well let me tell you boys about it,' Chan sat back and smiled at us.

Chan had our full attention. 'First of all it goes without saying that this goes no further than the four of us.' He looked around to check that there weren't any waiters or any other loose ears floating around and continued.

'I have many contacts as you obviously know,' he grinned knowingly at us. 'My problem is though that all my other business goes through my origin, I don't need to explain that to you, you know who it's in reference to,' he shook his head. 'Don't get me wrong I'm well looked after. But every once in a while, I have other propositions that come along. Very prosperous offers... Only unless I involve my other connections then there isn't a lot that I can do about them.'

'Why not?' I asked.

'Because my people only deal with certain people they know,' he sighed. 'Many a deal that I know of could have made much money but they no want any involvement.'

'And you've got one of these prosperous offers in the pipeline I presume,' Prey grinned at him.

'Yes,' Chan answered.

'So just what is it that you're asking us to do Chan?' I asked blatantly. 'It's not another warehouse job is it?' I remembered back to just how prosperous... yet fucking dangerous that deal had been.

Chan smiled at me. 'Not as much action Chopper,' he looked at the other two. 'But we're talking a lot more money involved with this one.'

Prey's attention was well and truly caught. 'Please Chan, do tell more.'

'Listen,' Chan looked around again. 'Basically in two months time I have a close – Very close diplomatic friend from Iran who just happens to be coming over with a vast

450

amount of very good... No that's wrong, it's excellent, truly pure untouched heroin. Not the brown shite, but the pure uncut, undiluted gear.' He sat back and watched for our reactions, which were of a nodding nature as we absorbed the information.

'So what you're saying is that we do this deal between the four of us so that there isn't any involvement from your side,' Prey looked at Chan.

He smiled. 'Like I say... very prosperous.'

I was thinking over what Chan had said. 'What's the initial layout from ar' side?'

'Divided four ways once I know the exact amount,' he simply stated.

'Any prior layout?' Steve asked.

'Of course there is,' Chan looked at us. 'If you want in on this then it is forty percent up front first before shipment leaves Iran.' He watched our reaction. 'Then the rest upon delivery.'

Prey coughed. 'What sort of amount we talking Chan. I mean you boys are bringing ship loads over and we ain't in that league.'

'No – No, you not understand me,' he laughed. 'This will be two of those large Samsonite suitcases. That's why at the moment I'm not exactly sure of amount.'

'What sort of profit margins we looking at, on average of course?' I asked.

'Depends just how we go about it... Anything from one to five hundred percent,' Chan smiled.

Prey smiled also. 'I take it that it'll be down to us to shift it all.'

'Of course,' he nodded more serious. 'But it's my source and I'm bringing you in on it, so it's only fair that I take an equal cut of the profits.'

'Fair play Chan,' Prey answered.

I looked at Prey. 'If it's as pure as he says it is will we be able to shift it.'

'Of course,' he smiled at Steve. 'You think the lab rats will be able to sort it out to street level.'

'No problem there,' he nodded. 'But if it is as pure as Chan is saying I think that our friend at the other end will maybe get us a better price as it stands.' Both Prey and I knew he was referring to Sleeper. 'Maybe it would be better not to touch it at all.'

451

'I think that you find that Steve is correct,' Chan nodded. 'Also it may be better if a majority of it stays out of Manchester... more for my behalf than yours of course.'

I laughed. 'Maybe keep a little for the lads though, eh.'

I could see Prey thinking again. 'Just how does any of this tie in with Anderson though?'

'Or us taking a step back afterwards?' I added.

Chan glanced over his shoulder again before beginning. 'Basically you boys have got the stores now. It's like I have the restaurant. Only I have others to answer too, where as you boys have got only yourselves to answer to.'

'I don't follow,' I said.

'He's saying that we can pull out when we want to,' Prey told me. 'Where as Chan can't ever walk away... Right Old Man?' he said, looking directly at Chan who nodded his answer.

'Why do you want us to walk away though?' I asked curiously.

'Simply because I like you boys,' he smiled warmly at us. 'You're good boy's with good hearts. You give respect and honour to people that you should. You're decent boy's living on the wrong side, a side that you have played very well... Very well indeed,' he nodded to himself. 'I don't want to see any of you get hurt either through this trouble with Chris or through Anderson,' he told us.

I looked at Chan then the other two. 'So how with what I said earlier does this all tie in?'

'One,' Chan began. 'The bit about having something on him,' he smirked at us then winked tapping his forehead. 'Chan knows more about him than you think. Also...' he chuckled. 'He's not as clever as he thinks he is.'

I was intrigued and so was Prey who asked. 'Just what is it, you've got on him old timer?'

'Three very compromising video tapes of him, not only taking money from people in London... But also giving the orders for the killing of, let's say a less than savoury character that wasn't compromising with him.'

'Are you for fuckin' real?' I blurted out. 'Why the fuck haven't you used this for yourself Chan?'

'Let's say that I was keeping it for a rainy day in case I ever needed it.' He winked at us. 'The information on the tape would finish him. But Mr. Anderson is very slippery character

452

that if I used it as all out black mail then I would more than likely vanish from face of earth.'

'This is some heavy shit you're telling us Chan,' Prey said looking intensely at the old man. 'Interesting... But very heavy.'

'I still don't see why we just don't use this against him,' Steve said. 'Buy the tapes from Chan.'

'Because they're not for sale Steve,' Chan said as a matter of fact. 'If we go ahead and do this then we do it my way or not at all.'

'Alright,' Steve gave way, 'whatever.'

'If you come in on this deal, like I said you'll make a lot of money...' He paused, looking at each of us. 'I imagine more than you have done so before... Enough to let's say to pay off Anderson and do whatever else you wish. Retire with your shops.'

'If we do this,' I looked at the other two. 'I want us to be able to set up the lads on the estate.'

I could see Prey nodding. 'You're right Chopper.'

'So what you're saying is that we pull out but give a load of it back to the estate first?' Steve asked with a look of astonishment.

'Think of it this way,' I said looking at all of them. 'If it hadn't been for us pulling out for all that time the lads would still be making the top dollar that they were before.'

'That's right Steve,' Prey added. 'Also if it wasn't for the estate I – No that's wrong. None of us would have achieved the things that we have done.'

'And from what Chan's saying from this one off, we could pull ourselves right out of it,' I stared at him.

'For Christ sake mate... it's what you've been going on about.'

'Yeah,' Prey laughed. 'Think of it as a company gold watch as they retire for services provided to the company, only it'll be us retiring.'

We all laughed at Prey's humour.

'After that it'll be down to them to do what they want with the business,' I smiled. 'Shit – They know more than enough to go forward with it. We basically do fuck all as it is, besides act as the money,' I added.

'Oh and of course – sometimes the odd bit of enforcing when it's needed.'

We all laughed again then Steve nodded at me. 'I never thought of it that way you know,' he said, shaking his head. 'Fuck – You've gone and made me feel all guilty now.'

We all smiled at him. I thought again about the deal. 'So the next couple of months it's business as usual then after this deal we're out for good.'

'Yeah,' Prey said as he nodded, his face holding a certain glow to it. 'But the way we do this, is that it stays within these four heads of knowledge. The last thing we want is for word to go out that we're retiring or suspicious minds might start snooping... That includes the lads. We wait until everything is a done deal.'

'So you're in then,' Chan asked eagerly.

'Without a doubt,' Prey answered.

'Just one problem left now then,' I confirmed, as they looked at me. 'When the time comes it'll be convincing Anderson to let us break free.'

Chan laughed. 'With the tapes I've got, that shouldn't be too much of a problem.'

Once again we all laughed at the mere thoughts to the contents to those tapes.

NINETY

The court calls Dominic O'Leary to the stand,' said the Courts clerk as everybody rose to their feet – which Anderson thought was fucking stupid considering who the man was.

He glanced round at the others in the large dark oak panel covered room at Knutsford Crown Court. It was one of original Georgian Court Houses dating back to 1815 – 1818 and was located on the main road in the small town centre. It was an imposing building to say the least, with its sandstone columns and cobblestone forecourt. There were 2 large court rooms in use, both with the oak panelling, high decorated ceilings and large windows. It was an imposing room compared to the many modern Crown Courts out there in this day and age. Anderson liked it – it was dark and atmospheric and reminded him of just how things used to be.

He noticed Vinnie, not for the first time that day, stood there and gave the lad a little wink which made him cringe at Anderson. Oh well, fuck that little prick. He was now well and truly on the pay roll and would do as he was told to do.

'The charges that the jury was asked to make a decision on are the possession with intent to supply of four kilograms of heroin along with a kilogram of cocaine and ten-thousand ecstasy tablets. Has the jury made a decision?' Judge Reynolds asked who was known to the area as a judge who did everything by the book with accordance to the evidence. He was a large over-weight individual who reminded Anderson a little of the fat version you may find of the actor who played Inspector Morse... what was his name – that was it, John Thaw. Good actor – of course, he was a crap character

455

to a real life detective thought Anderson as he turned his attention now towards the jury and smiled at them.

'We have your honour,' said the appointed jury member who was a middle aged gentleman wearing a tweed blazer with those stupid leather patches on the elbows, he had thin greying hair and he looked as though this was the proudest day of his life stood up there like that. It was almost as if he had waited an entire nonexistent life time just for this day to arrive. Anderson was smiling to himself.

'And?' asked Judge Reynolds, obviously a little irritated at the pause as everybody waited to hear the verdict.

'Guilty on all accounts your honour,' he announced as his chest protruded.

'This is bollocks,' screamed Vinnie as his entourage, both young and old, erupted around him.

'Silence... I said silence in the courtroom,' shouted the judge trying to be heard over the racket as he banged his wooden hammer. 'Now,' he screamed, banging louder until the noise subsided. 'Before I have you all thrown out for...' He wasn't able to complete the sentence.

'Please your honour,' said Dominic. 'If I may say something.'

'Mr. O'Leary,' replied the judge. 'You realise that the decision has been made.'

'Yes your honour,' replied Dominic smiling at him.

'And do you have you anything to say?'

'Actually thinking about it... What's the point your honour,' he replied. 'You and I both know this is a fit up. You know me your honour. Yes we may be working different sides of the fence your honour... But we go way back now. And you know that the charges are nonsense. You know that I don't play that game.'

'I am afraid the evidence outweighs what I may or may not think Mr. O' Leary,' he replied smiling from Anderson to O'Leary.

'So it does,' responded O'Leary as he bowed his head and thought about the many different ways he could take revenge against that bastard, Anderson, who after all these years had come back to haunt him. 'What will be... I suppose will be then judge.'

And with that Vinnie stared his hatred at the detective who merely grinned back and then winked before bobbing out of sight. His job here was done. Now what was next on his list of things to get done?

The three of us were making our across Manchester down The Parkway, in Steve's BMW. Almost a month had past since our meeting in Chan's and after receiving his call the previous night that's exactly where we were heading for now.

I could hear Prey and Steve both conversing from the front seats, although once again dispossessed in my own thoughts, their voices barely audible to me in the back seat.

We'd kept our business affairs completely to the estate, much to annoyance and ever growing impatience of our crew. They were beginning to complain as we'd promised them that we'd resume business as usual on our return months ago now.

I'd tried my best with Jonah and Kezlo, as Prey had done so with the others. Yet you could feel that they were feeling a little more than pissed at the apparent lack of action we'd promised on our return. We'd managed to keep them at bay with promises of an explanation for our secluded reactions to what had happened with Chris and with what was continually happening around town.

We'd began to hear all of the stories filtering their way across the city, eventually finding their way back to us of how we were being out done by Chris and his crew. How they had also outsmarted us, over powering us that day in The Greyhound. Although I knew the truth to this matter, I had to admit for myself, finding this the hardest part of all, just to hear the mere mention of his name got my back up.

But we had to let things lay the way that they were at the moment or we would endanger our future plans that lay before us.

458

We'd stuck close to one another lately, much to the annoyance of our spouses, who were also becoming more than a little pissed off with us.

Donna and I merely seemed to pass one another throughout the day and night. Although I still loved her more than anything, the distance between us at the present time felt as so great that it was hard to see things ever returning to how they'd originally been before. I didn't blame her in any way here though. I knew that the blame pretty much lay at my doorstep. But I was who I was and there was no going back. Possibly once everything was done and dusted and we found our way onto a different path in life as we had planned – then – maybe then things would go back to the way they were. Only thing was – I wasn't holding my breath.

I kept telling myself over and over that all would change once we sorted out our final deal, yet I didn't know whether or not I was merely trying my best to convince myself. I just hoped that I wasn't doing so, as she was one of the best things that had happened to me. I don't know it just seemed so different these days. Maybe it was just down to the simple fact that my mind in the last few months had worked itself into overtime.

I found that lately, no matter how much weed I smoked in the evening, sleep wasn't so easily forth coming. I imagined that this was more than likely also part of the problem that had been slowly arising within our relationship as I was so distant all the time – even to myself.

My mind was drifting through a vast ocean of continuous thoughts, thoughts from the past, and thoughts as to the present and what we had planned before us, which obviously led to thoughts of what the future held for us.

Were we going to be able to make it away from within this world from which we had lived for so long? We weren't entirely sure that we could break away from it.

With that in mind it obviously led to my some of my darkest thoughts of Anderson – I found myself having nightmares about what this guy had on us. Not just us but those around us, including our friends London, who, through helping us had endangered themselves and become part of Anderson's intrepid web that he held us all within. Last we had heard was that he had somehow managed to take down old man O'Leary, who to be fair was a nasty piece of work, but not only that he had somehow managed to have the entire case fast tracked to Crown Court. It appeared that this son of bitch was exactly what the newspapers were saying he was.

Although Chan had told us what it was that he held over Anderson, I still couldn't help but feel uneasy about confronting him over our departure. We'd discussed several different amounts that we thought might satisfy his greed; although I held a sickening feeling that hung itself heavily over me that enough would never be enough for him.

It went without saying, that Anderson was by far the most crooked out of all of us, using his authority over others to connive and manipulate those around him to his advantage. At least with us we'd always been who we'd been, it's important to always be who you are and always be proud of it – No matter what it may be, we all control of own destinies.

Prey had told us how he'd half expected for us to turn informant on his behalf but dismissing it altogether after meeting Prey face to face, telling him that he knew that it wasn't our style to do so. Now he simply took our money from us, arranged on a six-month basis, so not for any need to too much contact. It was more on our behalf than his; he was nothing other than scum as far as I was concerned.

Also the sickening feeling I was battling to control at the moment was the one that lay with Chris and his crew. In some ways I'd have preferred an all out battle with him, as I'd have dealt with Chris personally without a moment's hesitation.

For the previous month Anderson had continued his one-man wave of depletion of crews around Manchester, Salford and both of their surrounding boroughs, even going out as far as Cheshire, whilst Chris, we ourselves included, went untouched. Yet with each of his busts, Chris seemed to gain more and more control... and at the dismay of our own crew as we sat back and allowed for it to happen.

Although it appeared that our competition was dropping around us, it wasn't us that were gaining anything from it. Although I was uncertain to just how much Chris was dealing with these days, there was no getting away from it, it was a hell of a lot more than we were handling.

I still didn't want to believe that he had gained the power that he had done. Oh well, if things worked out the way that we hoped for, I'd be able to put aside these annoying, sickening, irritating fuckers that hung so heavily over me at the moment.

That was because we had our own game plan, the plan that lay before us as we travelled to China town today.

The million-dollar question, as the Yank's put it, that wasn't even guaranteed though – was – were we capable of pulling off this one final deal? Not only did we have to pull off the deal but also then we had to go through with it and come up breathing fresh air at the end of it all.

'You alright Chopper? Chopper? *Chopper*,' Prey called out, bringing me forth from my trance.

'Who the fuck you shouting at,' I snapped at him.

'I called you three times then... What the fucks up with you?' he asked as Steve eased the car behind Chan's Restaurant.

I hadn't even noticed that we had already arrived in Manchester's city centre. 'Just day dreaming I guess,' I smiled at him. 'Sorry for snapping – I just feel a little strung out at the moment with everything that's going on... Or that's not going on so much.'

'Well if all goes well today,' Steve grinned at us both. 'Then we might have fuck all to worry about.'

'You spoken to Sleeper?' I asked Prey, whilst returning Steve's grin.

'Yeah – But I didn't want to say fuck all over the phone,' he looked at the two of us. 'I figured that we'd see just what Chan has on offer first.'

'Sweet,' I answered.

Prey then smiled knowingly. 'I figured that if we hear what we want to today – Then...' He paused and looked from Steve then to me in the back seat. 'That we travel straight down there afterwards. I don't know about the two of you like... But I sure could do with fuckin' Manchester off for a few days.'

'I guess that Kathy is doing your fruit in as well,' I laughed.

'Tell me about it,' he replied shaking his head. 'I just need to get away for a few days and I reckon that this is the ideal opportunity to do so.'

'Double sweet with me,' I informed him. 'You in or what old man,' I punched his shoulder lightly. 'Or you gonna to just stay pussy whipped and stick it out with the missus.' Both Prey and I laughed.

'Nah fuck that shit for a game of cards,' he smiled at us. 'From what you have just said I figure that it must be something in the water or they're just having their usual three weeks on and one week off... I thought it was just me and I was just the poor old bastard suffering.'

461

We all laughed as we then proceeded to exit the car. 'Fuck it...' I exclaimed, closing the door. 'I say that no matter what Chan has on offer today we go see Sleeper and Lisa anyhow.'

'Yeah,' Prey responded buoyantly. 'Besides I think we'd better check just how Macreedy's is doing down there.'

'Quite right,' Steve nodded all serious like, as the three of began laughing, making our way towards Chan's.

As Chan let us through the locked door we could see that restaurant was still deserted as he silently led us through the empty restaurant into the kitchen area. 'We're on,' he said to us, and then smiled mischievously.

'When and how much are we talking?' Prey enquired.

'What price we talking?' I asked, my brain locking into compute mode.

'Fifty on the key, with around fifty keys being delivered,' he was still nodding. 'I told you that this was an excellent offer.'

Prey looked curiously at me, then to Steve. 'That's two and a half mill,' I said as he merely smiled at me.

'But do you realise just what sort of money we're talking in profits?' Chan said defensively.

'That's one mill' front money though Chan,' I confirmed. 'And we don't even know what guarantee's we're getting 'ere.'

'Like I said Chopper,' he shook his head chuckling, 'my friend is a diplomat... You know what that means?'

'Diplomatic immunity,' Steve stated to no one in particular, as we all knew just what it meant.

'That only guarantee's your friend though Chan,' Prey added.

Chan sighed. 'Look – If you boys are not interested... If it's too much money – then...' He looked at us one by one.

It wasn't that we couldn't afford it, although saying that it would be very tight to pull in the whole amount. 'We just want something more than the fact this guy can walk free from this – Shit Chan...' I half laughed. 'We don't even know who this cat is.'

Chan smiled once again. 'Okay then... Here's what I'll do for you lads then.' Once again he looked at us. 'I'll guarantee the layout money.'

'You might as well pay it then,' I counter attacked straight away.

Chan shook his head at me. 'Don't get us wrong Chan,' Prey intervened. 'We've known each other for time now, so it's not a lack of distrust... But when it comes down to business then...' he trailed off.

'Friends and business don't always mix,' Chan quickly added then grinned again.

My brain was in overdrive with figures. 'If we wholesale this then it will merely be one hundred percent profit,' I half laughed, as by saying merely it was still two and half million pounds four ways. 'There's no way we can get more than one hundred a key... No matter how fuckin' pure this is.'

'But we could turn the fifty into two hundred and fifty and it'll still be bashable,' Prey said.

'I make that roughly one and half mill on top,' I shook my head. 'Is it going to be worth it? Plus we'd be cut out for a lot more work and time.'

'We need a better price Chan,' Steve said sternly.

'Not possible,' Chan shook his head. 'You have any idea just how good a deal this is?'

'What about if we bring in a fifth partner?' Prey suggested as we all looked at him. 'Look we all know just how much more can be made from this deal at street level –   The only thing is Chan 'ere can't shift any of it and there's no way that we'll be able to shift all of it once it's broken down so I say we bring in somebody that can shift at the other end of the scales.'

'You obviously mean our friend we spoke of recently?' I looked at him.

'Who else?' he asked me. 'He's got the contacts at that end. We'll just have to get out there ourselves and push this deal. This isn't going to be easy with Anderson pulling every fucker in. Still it's not unachievable for sure. Plus I reckon that just off the top of my head I can think of several sources out of town that I've not spoken to for a while who I'm sure will be interested if this is as good as Chan says it is.'

'You reckon that our friend will go for that?' Steve asked.

'You know what he's like,' he replied.

I cut him off. 'Yeah – he'd be more pissed off if we didn't include him.'

'Less money for us,' Chan simply said.

'Not in the long run Chan,' Prey told him. 'Just think about it.'

Chan nodded his head. 'Okay – you're right.'

'What about the layout money Chan?' I asked again. 'It's still a lot to lay out in one job lot. Even with your guarantee,' I opened my eyes wide and bent my head slightly shaking it. 'I mean we don't even know just how good this gear actually is.'

At this Chan smiled, and then chuckled. He said nothing and walked out of the kitchen leaving us all bemused looking at each other.

'What the fuck...' was all I said as we simply shook our heads at each other.

Then just as quickly as he disappeared – Chan reappeared holding a brown paper bag. 'You think old Chan would expect any of you boys to part with your money if I wasn't going to be given a taster first,' he passed the bag to Prey who opened it to reveal a clear square snappy bag that he produced. Judging from the size of it there was around a quarter of a kilo in the bag of the whitest powder that I'd ever seen before. It resembled little Sean's talcum powder rather than the lethal drug that it actually was.

Prey face beamed as he opened the bag smelling its contents then taking a little taste then a smile of pure content took over.

'You got yourself a deal Chan,' Prey smiled. 'When do you need the money?'

Both Steve and I just looked at each other, we knew from Prey's expression that we were onto a good thing.

'You sure that's the gear we'll receive?' I asked suddenly.

'My friend he is here in the country at the moment. Here for this week then he'll return to Iran for two weeks before returning with the full consignment,' Chan smiled. 'That's from the latest crop of Opium from Afghanistan and the first batch that they've produced.'

'But will this be the same batch as the full consignment Chan?' Prey asked a little apprehensively.

'Also I presume by the fact the he's 'ere now he wants the layout cash to return home with,' I stared at Chan in disbelief.

'Of course,' he simply answered. 'On both scores.'

'That's bullshit,' I blurted out. 'We pay this guy a mill' just to hand over this little sample bag and the fucker will never return... And we ain't in the business of flying out to fuckin' Iran chasing this fucker down Chan.'

Chan began to laugh enthusiastically. 'Come on now Chopper.' He paused to try and control his laughter. 'How silly an old fool do you take me for? You think that old Chan is senile or something.'

'It is a lot of trust to put into someone though Chan,' Steve said looking at Chan with uncertainty.

'No... No – You boys no understand,' he controlled his laugher. 'Just how do you think old Chan does business? First you think it's on mere trust that the heroin we'll receive will be on my friend's word? Of course I wanted a sample from him – Then...' he began laughing again.

Prey stared at him. 'Then what? What guarantee's that he'll return Chan?' he asked a little impatience in his voice as he did so.

Chan looked at each and every one of us then shook his head again. 'He'll return because his eldest son is my guest for the next three weeks whilst he visits prospective universities in England,' he chuckled again. 'And believe me.'

He stared hard at each and every one of us. 'Wherever he goes – I shall go with him.   As you said yourselves friends and business just don't mix. Well sometimes they do eh,' he laughed out loud, his laugh so infectious that we all joined in

'You crafty old bastard,' I told him.

Chan smiled. 'Not really Chopper – I needed obvious guarantees and he wants for his son to be educated here in England. I'm pulling in a few favours to see just what I can do for him here in the country.'

He tapped his nose and winked at me knowingly. 'I've already guaranteed him places at four universities already so I guess the rest of the time we'll just have you enjoy ourselves... Won't we?'

Prey was shaking his head at Chan's way of thinking. 'How long we got then Chan?'

'Five days to get it tested and have the money to me.' He stared hard at Prey. 'Are you sure that you want to bring someone else in on this deal?'

'It'll take a little longer than doing a one off deal Chan – But the profit margin will be so much better,' Prey held the bag before his face and smiled. 'Plus with the samples from this I should be able to guarantee a good few orders for within the first few days of its arrival into the country.'

'Okay good... Very good,' he smiled. 'Now... If I've got the money by Thursday then I know that I got myself some partners.' Again he paused and looked at us then smiled knowingly. 'If I haven't then I know that I haven't,' he chuckled again like a child who just been told a dirty joke he was too young to fully comprehend, making us all laugh out loud at him.

NINETY
TWO

Sleeper had practically bitten our hands off once he'd had the gear tested. Sleeper had used his own lab guy to test the gear, he informed us that it was without a doubt the purest gear that he'd ever come in contact with.

His guy down there, a student of chemistry, who it was fair to say, enjoyed one or two of the favoured chemicals out there himself. It had been how Sleeper had met him; a friend had told him about this kid who was buying a vast amount of pills and speed each week for his university pals for the weekend.

Only this lad the following week would give a weekly report to the contents of what he'd taken the previous week. When his friend had asked just how he knew so fucking much, he told him just what it was he was studying for a degree in. So being almost certain that Sleeper would have a use for this guy, he introduced them to one another. Sleeper merely introduced him as the kid, which was fine by us.

The kid was unreal; he mixed together a combination of things that he told us the names and purposes for, although we didn't have a clue as to what he going on about. Yet when he proceeded to add droplet's of his formula to samples of heroin it began to turn from a pale into a deep blue, much to the delight of this kid, who shook his head in disbelief at what he saw before him.

Without a single word he smiled knowingly at the four of us and with that smile came the answer we had wanted. Apparently he'd tested numerous batches of different kinds of gear for Sleeper, who said the kid was always spot on, and

466

that he'd never come across gear as pure as this before in England.

'The kid predicts that it could easily be banged twenty even possibly thirty ways before coming close to street gear,' Sleeper had informed us with one of the largest smiles I'd ever seen produced from his face.

That had been almost three weeks ago now when we had travelled straight down to London that Saturday afternoon, without informing Sleeper that we were on way down. Although he was more than delighted to see the three of us, even more so once we told him all about the deal in the pipeline with Chan and especially after he'd had his student test the gear for us.

However – I must admit that when we informed Sleeper of our long-term plans he'd held mixed feeling - 'In one way I can understand what you're all saying... Yes things have even changed down here. Things are changing the length and breadth of the country...' he told us then added, 'but there was still so much money out there to be made.'

I knew that he understood and that it wasn't like we'd be breaking any ties with him personally, as there was still Macreedy's and of course our friendship. But he also knew the stranglehold that we were feeling with Anderson, even to the point of offering that he took care of him for us. Which I have to say was a very nice thought indeed; I can still see the smiles on each of our faces when he made the offer.

Although the three of us knew that the risks involved were way too great. Whenever any copper was killed there was always pure uproar up and down the country, the police working flat out to catch those responsible. I don't think that I would ever be able to relax with something like that hanging over me, over any of us for that matter. No things had to be done our way, whether or not they'd work was a completely different matter altogether.

But either way we were soon to find out what was to be the final outcome.

Chan's guy was expected in from Iran this Friday, only two days away now. We'd managed to get the money together for his guy before he left. No matter what reassurances Chan gave me I'd still spent the previous weeks twisted full of aggressive apprehension. If I'd thought that I was having trouble sleeping the weeks prior to even organising his deal, it had been nothing compared to what I'd gone through the last couple of weeks, staying awake for two, three days at a time. It was safe to say that I felt not only exhausted, but also completely drained of energy.

The money was a major part of it, as since we'd put most of our spare cash into the new store in London, the cash levels were lower than we'd expected. We'd just about to be able to fund this deal, but that was it, if... And God forbid anything did – but if anything were to go wrong, then financially at street level we'd be fucked.

The three of us had spent the days, right up until our final day that we had to pay Chan working through figures. Getting together the cash for the front money was the first hurdle as there would still be the weeks in between where we'd need cash flow on the street the finance our continued operation at that level.

Once we'd pulled that in, we'd then had to spend the next two weeks pulling in old and late debts personally, to make sure that we had the cash. Our manufacturing side of things had been put into overdrive also, with some of the best bargains our wholesale customers had ever received. I'm sure that none of them were complaining and we'd needed that capitol so badly.

We'd pushed everybody to push and try to sell much harder then ever before, leaving everybody confused as to just what was going on. Once again – we were trying to delay any explanation for our actions.

But all said and done with only two days to go, we'd managed to pull the cash together for the deal that was going to be our deals of deals. The one deal that everybody in our line of business, sometimes waits a lifetime for. Even though it sounded like the money and amounts involved were of a vast nature, they were nothing compared to what we knew of being imported into the country.

It always made me laugh when I heard of news reports saying that they broke this smuggling ring or busted this manufacturing facility and this was the best bit it had 'a street value of X's amount and value,' what complete crap it all was.

If the government actually produced genuine figures as to what actually made it through and what didn't, the public would see that it was the slightest percentage –And as for the street value, well what a crock of shite that was.

All that they did there was take the amount, no matter how big or small and break it down fragments say a mere kilo, then transform it into – say £10 bags of smack or sixteenth deals. Then they go and bang the highest price that no fucker in the right mind would have paid for it and bingo... They had a figure that the general public perceived as very impressive... It was complete bollocks, I can tell you.

We'd also made the decision to keep as much of it out of Manchester as possible, as we didn't want anybody getting wind of its source. Luckily Sleeper was to take and shift the largest percentage down in London, although we'd made the decision also not to go and over-step on it whilst breaking it down. No matter what his kid had said we were going step on it just enough so that there was still more than enough room to work with for everybody else.

Luckily the samples that Prey had distributed had been with some of his old suppliers from out of town – from Yorkshire – all the way up to Scotland, who just happened to be paying us the best price of all.

So all in all if everything went ahead as planned this time next week we'd be very well off indeed.

Presuming – And this was the mother of presumptions that Anderson played ball with us, and then we could finally put this business behind us once and for all.

Although I still have to admit that I was still having very mixed feelings on that score. I know that this may sound very sad to some people, but the truth was that apart from the scores that I used to pull down years ago, the drugs business was all that I'd known. I wasn't sure what I would do with myself to be totally honest. I got the feeling that to put down ex-crack and heroin dealer on my C.V. really wasn't going to do me any favours was it?

Sure we had the shops. But in all fairness we merely reaped the benefits from this without any real hands on action with the day to day running of them. Donna ran the Manchester branch, whilst Lisa took care of our London branch; they took care of the staff and worked along side of the buying department. So it wasn't like we really did fuck all – I know, I really shouldn't be complaining, should I?

Oh well, I thought smiling to myself, sat there all alone...

Just two days to go.

'Look Batty if you're not interested, just give the word and I'll call the deal off no problems,' said Tony whilst he stood on his balcony overlooking the Mediterranean Sea. It was just one of his many Villas that he owned in Spain, The Balearic Islands and all of the Canary Islands. The view was something else, he still loved and owned many properties back in Manchester and Salford, but you really couldn't beat this.

'You know I am interested Tony,' replied Batty, smiling at the other end of the line, stood in his backyard overlooking the dismal Wythenshawe estate as the rain started to tumble and thought about the two very scenarios taking place right now. He was in the yard with one of his sons playing football as he talked to Tony.

'So we're on then,' laughed Tony.

'Yeah we're on Tony,' smiled Batty.

'What about your little problem with Anderson?' he then asked.

'We got bailed Tony,' replied Batty. 'The thing won't see court for a long time... hopefully. Besides which it ain't exactly stopped me before has it?' he laughed.

'True,' replied Tony as a young beautiful girl in her early twenties walked out onto the balcony wearing only her bikini bottoms. Her tanned breasts were pert and Tony felt himself getting aroused as she handed him a cold bottle of Heineken beer as he smiled and winked at her, as she turned and made her way back inside as he playfully slapped her backside making her giggle.

'You still there, Tony?' asked Batty.

'Yeah, yeah... Sorry Batty got a little side tracked there,' he replied taking a swig of his beer. 'Okay, so you've got all the details. I'm not going to go through it all again. Especially talking on these damn things. I just don't trust them.'

'I know what you mean,' laughed Batty as he kicked the football back across the backyard to one of his sons. 'You heard about old Dom, right?'

'Yeah – word came through the usual channels.'

'This Anderson fucker really needs dealing with,' Batty sighed.

'I'm feeling what you are saying brother,' he replied. 'But what you gonna do? Go wasting a copper? A high fuckin' ranking Detective to boot?'

'I know it is just wishful thinking on my behalf,' he said.

'You sure all is good Batty?'

'Like I said... no problems, Tony.'

'You know there can't be any fuck ups especially with this character on the war path at the moment.'

'Trust me Tony,' he replied scooping his son into his arms. 'Everything is in place no matter what happens to me. Fuck Anderson and any other fucker who wants to take a piece of me, I've got this thing wired.'

'That's all I needed to hear Batty,' he replied closing the phone and making his way inside to deal with girl who had just got him so aroused.

Jesus - talk about a long fuckin' couple of days,' I laughed to Prey and Steve as we found ourselves making our way across Manchester in Prey's motor towards Piccadilly train station, where we were to pick up Sleeper and his lab rat – as we'd renamed him – who was to do the tests on the gear.

Although he'd be kept well out of sight from the whole consignment, apart from Chan's guy and the five of us, nobody knew exactly when or how much was actually coming in.

'Couple of days,' Steve shook his head. 'Try three fuckin' weeks more like.'

Prey laughed. 'Is that what the fuck been up with the two of you for the last few weeks.' He looked at us both shaking his head as he did so. 'Shit – I just figured that your birds were giving you a hard time again.'

'Always on that score ar'kid,' I laughed. 'But you can't tell me that you've not been apprehensive as fuck about what the fuck happens if this all goes to pot.'

'Nah,' he casually said, then grinned knowingly as Steve punched him laughing as he did so. 'Alright... maybe just a little then.'

'We all set for this to go down later?' Steve asked. 'Chan phoned with the necessary arrangements right.'

Prey nodded as he eased the car up the hill leading into the train station. 'He says that his guy lands at eight-twenty-six tonight.'

'He still wants for this to go down at his gaff?' I asked.

Prey nodded again as he eased the car nicely into a parking space. 'Yeah,' Prey looked at the two of us. 'Reckons that it's the best plan of action as that's where the kids at,' he laughed. 'Says that the kids choose the Uni' 'ere in town... Apparently loves it 'ere.'

'Shit...' I laughed. 'If only the poor fucker knew what really went on.'

We all laughed as we climbed from the car. 'You're right there Chopper,' Steve smiled at me. 'I bet even you could make some of the trouble they have over there seem tame.'

'Yeah right,' I replied. 'I don't think so Steve.'

We all laughed again in good spirits, as we headed for the entrance and made our way through the main doors at Piccadilly train station.

Chan had himself an old Victorian looking place over in Worsley; it was a fantastic sight to perceive. The place was deceiving from the large gravel driveway as we approached, it looked quite large but once you were inside it was breath taking. It was enormous.

'You like Chopper?' Chan asked with much enthusiasm as he saw our looks.

'It's colossal Chan,' I replied.

The place had at least five bedrooms, all of them en-suite. When he explained the purpose and names to the rooms on the lower level, it merely left me even more baffled.

But I have to say that the one thing that did it for me was the garden, it was truly amazing. Chan told that his wife, who happened to be away for the week, cared for it. She'd obviously gone for a very traditional Oriental garden with bonsai trees and the most intricate to elaborate statues. The flowers that filled the garden where of exotic and the most wonderfully coloured flowers that I've ever seen.

'We all set?' Sleeper asked as we made our way back through into the house.

'No problem,' he smiled. 'I'll take Chopper with me to the airport to pick our mutual friend up – then we'll travel straight back here.'

'I'll take you,' Prey quickly announced.

Chan looked at Prey then chuckled. 'My good friend,' he shook his head. 'I've nothing against you coming but do you think that it would wise – I mean you're not the friendliest looking of characters are you.'

We all laughed at this, as it was true with that scar that ran the length of his face he was quite a shady looking character if I say so myself.

'What the fuck's the matter with the way I look,' he snarled, then began to laugh along also.

We'd left the rest of them at Chan's house with his friend's son who Chan merely introduced as Mo, which was obviously an abbreviation of the kid's name.

'We going to meet him directly through arrivals Chan?' I asked, easing Prey's Mercedes into the arrivals car park at the airport.

'No... No Chopper,' he shook his head at me. 'We'll go through to the balcony and just watch for him to pass through. I've already made necessary arrangements with him that as soon as he passes through customs; he's to make his way through to departures.'

Seeing a parking space, I manoeuvred the car into it, turning to look at Chan. 'Then what?'

'Once we know that he's through safely then you return to the car and head off for departures. We'll pick him up outside of there, it's a lot quicker to get out of there than arrivals,' he smiled as he told me this. 'I'll follow him through, just to make sure that he not being tailed by customs... Although by that time I would very much doubt that he is.'

'What makes you so sure?' I asked as we exited the car and headed for the terminal.

Chan winked knowingly at me. 'Old man must keep a couple of secrets to himself Chopper,' he laughed knowingly. 'I mean after all Chopper, do you think that I'd not have this end covered if I was to guarantee your money,' he winked again.

That sly old sod I thought looking at him. 'You've got somebody this end working for you? Haven't you?'

'Always good to keep a couple of keep safe backup plans in ones pocket,' he chuckled again. 'To be honest if there would have been any trouble it would more than likely come from his end, not ours.'

'So why follow him through the airport?' I asked curiously.

'Merely to keep oneself amused,' he chuckled. 'To be honest I just want to check how careful he is being Chopper.'

I began smiling at the old man; he truly was a character.

We'd arrived with plenty of time to spare, so we'd bought a couple of coffees, and then made our way through to the balcony area. The flight in which we were waiting for was on schedule, so by all accounts we shouldn't be waiting too long now.

'That's him now,' Chan said casually as I immediately noticed the two dark grey identical Samsonite cases before even looking up to the very stern looking business man casually walking through arrivals with our fifty kilo's of pure heroin.

'See you soon,' I said to Chan as I turned making my way towards the exit.

Manoeuvring the car to the front of departures, I could see Chan already waiting for me. Just as I was about to ease the car over to the pavement, a black Granada with blacked out windows suddenly cut me off.

'You fuckin' cunt,' I screamed at the car that screeched to the side of the curb.

I had a sudden urge to jump out and grab the perpetrator, but then suddenly thought about just what it was that we were actually doing there. The last thing that we wanted was to start some confrontation over nothing really, therefore causing unnecessary attention to us.

'Cheeky bastards,' Chan chuckled as he jumped into the front seat, obviously reading my thoughts; yet full of exuberance as he did so.

I merely shook my head and laughed. 'We sweet Chan?' I asked still smiling, any moment now and we were almost there, the first hurdle was tackled.

'Sure are Chopper,' he patted my arm, overflowing with affluence.

I found myself still staring at the Black Granada – strangely nobody had exited the car, I shook the thought away. It was none of my business I thought to myself and brought my attention back to the present situation at hand.

'Here he comes now,' Chan smiled, as our guy waltzed through the automatic doors without a care in the world.

That's when it suddenly happened; the movements were swift and so rapid that we barely noticed them. The black Granada's rear doors flew open with two white middle aged men, each dressed casually in dark jeans and jackets made a move for our guy. The guy to right was the thicker set of the two; he looked like he may have worked out, body builder type of guy. The other was nothing but skin and bone, yet he was well over six feet tall, with a more than menacing look about his nature.

'Shit... What the fuck...' I gasped, grabbing for the door handle.

'Wait!' Chan grabbed my arm; his voice took on a sudden edge that I hadn't heard before.

Then suddenly, another man appeared as if almost from nowhere directly behind our Iranian guy, dressed in similar fashion to the two that had appeared from the car, he grabbed our guy from behind.

Although this one looked to be older than the other two, his hair was either grey or was streaked with blonde highlights to cover the growing grey area.

Blondie, as I'd suddenly named him seized our Iranian guys left arm from behind, you could see the panic and shock that took control of his face. There was a sudden jolt to his back as if something had been pressed into it, his stomach protruding.

The two from the car, Body Builder and Skinny grabbed the suitcases and flung them into the boot of the car, Blondie pushed our guy down into the rear of the car with the first two.

All of this was done with swift precision that nobody other than us had even noticed.

'What the fuck is going on?' I snapped edges of panic in creeping into my voice.

'Follow them Chopper,' Chan simply stated. 'Now,' he commanded me; as I put the car into gear and took off after the Granada.

'What the hell is happening?' I looked at Chan, who appeared just as confused. 'Who the fuck were they?' My eyes were darting from Chan to car in front of me.

'I don't know,' Chan said, his voice was cold as he did so. 'But whoever the fuck they are... Don't fucking lose them.'

This was complete and utter fucking madness, what the hell going on? And just who the fuck had just abducted our guy? Not only our guy, but all of our fucking gear.

I was trying my best to concentrate on both the road and the car; Chan had ordered me to stay back, which was fine. Although I was now beginning to fear that if they got too far ahead I'd lose them altogether.

Fuck... This was a whole new kind of nightmare all together – What the fuck had gone wrong? My mind was screaming at me from all directions.

'You reckon it customs or the old bill that's got him Chan?' I asked, my eyes not leaving those of the car up ahead.

'It's not their style,' he said, his eyes also not moving from the car up ahead. 'Something's not right though,' he then added.

'What the fuck are we going to do Chan?' I asked my voice filled with apprehension.

'Stick with the car... That's all we can do.'

The car turned left into a country lane at Style, as we followed it I noticed a Toyota garage to my right hand side. 'Shit!'

'What's wrong?' Chan asked briefly looking at me.

I'd recognised the road. 'This road leads off in all directions – Prestbury – Macclesfield – Fuckin' Wilmslow – Adlington – And God only knows where the fuck else,' I told him. 'If we lose them on this road they could head anywhere.'

'Make sure we don't lose them then Chopper,' he said quite simply.

Oh yeah, quite all right for him just sat there, I thought to myself. We stuck with the car as it worked its way through the back end of Wilmslow and headed once again off into deep country territory. It was becoming more difficult as the roads were winding all over the place.

'Where the fuck are they Chan?' I asked as we suddenly came out of a large winding bend into a long thin straight again – Fuck – They seemed to have disappeared into thin air.

Suddenly Chan's head twisted round to the right. 'The road back there Chopper – I saw car lights.'

'Shit Chan – That ain't enough,' I sighed. 'What if it ain't them and they're further up ahead.'

'Turn around now Chopper,' he snapped.

'You better be fuckin' right old man,' I sneered back at him, slamming the brakes and sliding the gears into reverse.

By the time we got back to the road, there was nothing to see. 'What now?' I asked impatiently, this was all turning pear shaped big time.

'Head down that road,' Chan demanded.

Sliding the gears into first, we made my way down the pitched blackness of this country lane... Going on an old man's fucking hunch for Christ sake.

Suddenly Chan pointed. 'There Chopper – Look,' he pointed off to the left, where stood a large secluded farmhouse of about average size compared to some of the homes and farms I'd seen in this area during daylight.

Sure enough, the old man was right; I could see what appeared to be the black Granada in the driveway, although all occupants appeared to have vacated.

'You reckon that's the same motor Chan?'

'Just keep driving past,' he shook his head. 'We need to work this out.'

I drove for about a quarter of a mile up the road. The farmhouse appeared to be the only property so far on this road; I'd eased the car into a lay by and switched off the engine.

I turned and stared at Chan, you could see the look of concentration on his face. 'What the fuck has just happened Chan?' I asked, still not able to get my head what had just gone off.

'Somebody has tried to fuck us,' Chan confirmed.

'Who the fuck else knew about this though?' I was taken aback by what he'd said.

Chan shook his head slowly. 'Well it ain't me or you is it?'

'Who then?' I was staring at him intently. 'Surely you can't be thinking anybody back at the house.'

He looked at me, and then shook his head. 'The only person that I can think of is my guy at the airport,' he sighed deeply.

'You mean customs got him?'

'That look like the work of custom officers Chopper?' he shook his head at me. 'No... No... No... This greedy little mother fucker at the airport set this up.'

'You fuckin' what!' I snapped, the words pouring from me. 'You serious?'

'He didn't know that I'd be there,' Chan announced. 'He thought that this guy was going to get into a taxi from the airport... That's probably why the car pulled up so hastily outside, they weren't expecting him to be at departures.'

'What the fuck are we going to do now?' I enquired, leaning back in my chair blowing out in what felt like pure exhaustion.

'You got your mobile phone?' he asked me.

I'd never had a mobile and for the first time ever I wished more than anything, that I did actually own one. I looked helplessly to Chan then shook my answer at him.

'Great!' Chan sighed.

'We can't let them out of our sight Chan,' I looked at him. 'You take the car and drive to find a phone – then call Prey…' He was shaking his head at me, frantically like a frightened child.

It suddenly dawned on me. 'You don't fuckin' drive do you Chan?' He merely shrugged his response

'Great!' I now sighed out loud, what a fucking pair we made. 'Well I can't leave you 'ere… What if they decide to leave?'

'What then?' he asked, as he suddenly watched me bend down under the front dashboard of Prey's car.

'What the fuck you doing Chopper?' he asked in bemusement.

'There,' I suddenly said as my hand found what it was looking for. Grasping the cold polymer from it hiding place below the dashboard produced the cool blue Glock 9mm pistol before Chan; I then grinned at him. 'Well it looks like we ain't got any option but to go and get ar' gear back myself.'

Chan shook his head at me. 'Chopper that's suicide you fool. This ain't some fucking Stallone movie… You don't know how many are in there or how heavily armed they are.'

'You're right Chan,' I shook my head then cocked the gun. 'I also know that if we lose this whole consignment then we're finished – So the way I figure it, I ain't got much option 'ere anyway,' I smiled as best as possible at him.

I knew what he was saying was right, but I also knew that my only option was to go in there whilst I still had the cover of nightfall to hold what little protection I had over myself.

I stared at Chan in the darkness and nodded 'You just sit tight… This may take a while.'

And with that I was gone, into the obscurity of night and all the while wondering to myself just what the fuck I'd let myself in for.

'That's this week's bees for you,' Chris told his uncle as he passed over the padded Nike holdall stuffed to its limit with used untraceable bank notes.

The two met weekly at a disused warehouse in Salford. Anderson collected his money and also gave over what he'd been able to take for himself before they destroyed the evidence at the furnace. He had a scam going with the officer that was used in destroying all the evidence once it had been submitted and used as evidence in a court of law.

Anderson smirked broadly as he felt the size and weight of the bag that he held before him. 'Business is good I take it.'

'Double sweet,' Chris smirked cockily. 'In fact we've just moved into some of Batty's action in Wythenshawe this week.'

His uncle looked at him then to the envelope again. 'I hope that I got my cut,' he snapped.

'It'll be next week before we start to see any real dough from that way,' Chris declared, taking a slurp from his bottle of Budweiser as he did so. 'Beside which the cunt got bailed this week.'

'You what?' he asked looking startled.

'Yeah,' said Chris. 'You not hear?'

'No I fucking didn't,' he sneered. 'How the fuck did that happen? What the fuck is he up to?'

'Nowt,' answered Chris. 'That's why we've started to move in on some of his business. He's keeping his head down since they bailed him.'

481

'Fuck it,' smiled Anderson coldly. 'Getting bail will make no difference to that cocksucker with what we've got against him. Let him have his freedom for the time being as long as he keeps out of our shit eh nephew.'

'Too fuckin' right,' he replied. 'Should be a nice little earner with those Wythenshawe lads. Who'd have thought it...? Salford and Wythenshawe in business together?'

Anderson merely nodded, staring coldly at him. 'You just make sure that I see plenty of the action. Well this kind of action anyway,' he patted the bulging bag.

'What you got for me this week?' Chris enquired.

It wasn't as though he relied on the gear that his uncle supplied him with on a weekly basis, but it sure was a bonus to him. As much as he disliked his uncle, there was no escaping the fact that he was certainly reaping all the benefits that his uncle was throwing his way.

The business that he now controlled was so vast that he had lad's working all over Salford, Manchester and even Cheshire for him. Where as he'd only, before his uncle had come along been able to stick to Salford, and only a small part of that as well. Now he was using the younger lads that were more than eager to both impress him, but also bend over backwards to make him even more money each week.

The young scally's that were running around these days had come through the new chemical generation of clubs and drugs, each and everyone of them wanting a piece of it. Work or at least real work wasn't an option to these lads... What the fuck do they have on offer anyway? Some shitty YTS or some bollocks like that. Work all week just to earn a poxy amount that couldn't get you anywhere – or work the streets and make anything from five times to twenty times that amount in a day's work rather than a week's work.

Plus they loved this so called gangster shit and were more then willing to go out there fully armed. Chris loved the control that he held over these lads; it made him feel so much more powerful than he'd ever felt before.

Basically he had anything and everything that he ever wanted – and all because of his crooked uncle. That was also the best bit about it all, as no one would ever believe that his law abiding uncle would ever be involved in anything at all shady when he was bringing down crews all over the city the way he was.

482

'I've got a nice bag full for you in the boot,' his uncle answered. 'I've accounted for what's in the holdall as well,' Anderson then stared hard at Chris. 'So don't go getting any funny ideas about shorting me on any of the money from that lot.'

'As if,' Chris simply said, knowing that it would be fatal to ever try and cross his uncle.

'So tell me,' Anderson stared harder into Chris's eyes. 'Just what the fuck went off the other week with O'Prey and Chorlton?'

'How the fuck do you know about that?' Chris exclaimed, completely shocked at his knowledge.

Anderson tapped his nose. 'Never believe for a single second that you can hide anything from me young nephew.'

He hated it when he called him that. 'It was nothing,' he sighed. 'Just Prey and Chopper snooping about... That's all it was.'

'What was it they were after?' he asked curiously.

'Their business back,' Chris laughed out loudly.

'You didn't tell them anything as stupid as that the two of us were involved in any way? Did you nephew?' he glared at him as he asked.

Chris looked away. 'Nah – Nowt like that.'

'You sure about that nephew,' he suddenly grabbed Chris's chin hard, pulling his face to his. 'The last thing that I need is for anybody to know what our involvement is with each other.'

'Do I look stupid or something?' Chris tried shrugging his face free from Anderson's grip to no avail.

'Don't ask me to answer that,' he smiled menacingly.

'Look with that dodgy batch of spiked gear you supplied for them to test a few months back we disposed of the lads that were at the guest house that time with Westy – Y'know that was a clear case of overdose,' he cackled at what they'd done, 'Also after those blags where you pulled me in and we got those kid's to hold up their hands up to the gear,' Chris grinned smugly at his uncle. 'Well since then, word went around. Especially after all the ranting and raving that you did in each interview, grilling me for hours and me giving you shit that I wasn't no grass.'

'I wasn't too hard on you were I?' Anderson sniffed his arrogance. 'Eh nephew?'

'Well it worked anyway - 'Cause word made it through to the street just how much I seemingly wound you up by giving you fuck all,' he laughed again ignoring the last the question. 'Worked like a treat.'

'Funny really ain't it,' Anderson said staring at him. 'But who would have thought that this would work out as well as it was doing eh? You're doing alright nephew. Not bad work son,' Anderson told his nephew the words he wanted to hear as he suddenly smiled almost warmly at Chris, as he thought to himself... Dumb little prick.

He was merely using his nephew for his own devices – nothing more – nothing less – although he had to admit that he'd never expected the amount of business that he was coming forward with. 'You keep up the good work, eh,' he smiled now almost proudly, he knew that his nephew ate up these compliments that he threw his way every now and then.

'I sure will.'

'So you got any other problems?'

'Just Chopper... The fuck head.'

'I told you before though,' Anderson shot him a stern look. 'I don't want you going causing any trouble with them lot.'

'I don't see why the fuck not though,' Chris shook his head. 'I mean it's not like you don't make enough through my crew... Plus you'd make even more if I took care of his patch.'

'I said no... Alright,' his voice took on a harsher edge to it. 'Look just leave them be. They're worth more to me in the long run left that way. Although – since you've taken control of so much from town – I ain't too sure just how they're managing it at the moment.'

He thought about the three of them. It was true that since their release they couldn't be making anywhere near enough money as before. But that wasn't his worry. Besides they always paid on time. No, fuck his nephew he thought, these were worth more to him alive on the street. He didn't want his dumb little fuck of a nephew trying to cause any problems for him.

Besides which he didn't fully trust those three, because unlike his daft nephew sat beside him, these three actually used their heads with what they were doing. They were a lot smarter than the average dealers that he continually came across week in, week out.

There was something different about them; they'd proved that by out smarting Stevenson and Walsh who recently had both been moved to separate assignments away from Manchester as they'd succeeded in achieving fuck all from their persisted case against O'Prey and Chorlton.

Even though he'd given them a helping hand, he'd felt at the time that even if Scotty had made it to court and they were all up before him, then somehow they'd of come up smelling of roses.

He supposed if he admitted it, that it was true that he almost admired the way they handled themselves – although he would certainly be keeping that one to himself.

'I've heard something about them you may be interested in,' Chris suddenly said, breaking his concentration.

'What's that then?' he asked, all of his attention on his nephew sat there grinning.

'Word is, that they may have a big deal coming together shortly,' he smiled proudly as he gave the information. 'Big smack deal of some kind.'

'How the fuck do you know this then?' he snapped, he'd not heard fuck all about from any of his numerous grasses he held in his pocket.

Chris smiled then nodded at his uncle knowingly. 'I just heard from a pal of mine in Leeds.'

'Stop fucking around then and tell me what you know,' he snarled.

Chris began tutting his impatienaince. 'All that I heard is that Prey was over that way distributing some first class – I mean like pure quality – samples of some shit that will be coming his way.'

'When?' Anderson demanded.

Chris shook his head honestly. 'Couldn't tell you to be honest.'

'So what the fuck you tell me anything for then,' he said angrily, his patience wearing thin.

'Just thought you'd be interested... That's all,' Chris defended.

'You're friend going to buy from him?' Anderson asked, wondering whilst he did, as to why Prey would be taking his business out of town. Not that it mattered to him as he took a fixed amount from them. But still, if they had something big coming off, then surely they could give him the little bonus he deserved of course he thought to himself.

'I reckon so,' Chris replied. 'He said that the gear was like no other that he'd ever come across,'

Chris's angle here was that he wanted for his uncle to try and take the smack for himself – for he knew that if this gear was as pure as Joey from Leeds had made out – then it sure was going to be worth a small fortune to him on the street.

'Find out when.'

'He says that Prey was more than a little vague about when it would arrive,' Chris told him. 'Said all that Prey told him was that when he contacted him he was either to want in that same day or he'd lose out altogether on it.'

'Alright then,' Anderson stared with his hard cold lifeless eyes at him. 'I want to know as soon as this deal goes down.'

'You going to nick them?' Chris asked eagerly.

'That ain't any of your business,' he told him harshly. 'Just let me know once the deals gone down then it'll be in my court and I'll decide what the fuck to do about it. Alright young nephew,' he snarled the last bit at him.

Chris smiled, as he believed that he'd somehow end up with some of that gear.

'We through?' he asked.

'Go,' Anderson commanded. 'And don't forget the bag – I'll see you next week,' he added as Chris was already out of the car.

'Oh you needn't worry about the bag,' Chris winked at his uncle with an air of cockiness, 'I wouldn't forget that – would I now?'

Making my way back along the road through the complete blackness of night – and believe me when I say blackness – I mean I honestly couldn't see a foot in front of me at a time.

So it was more than fair to say that I was finding it both hard to judge exactly where I was walking and just how far I'd travelled. It seemed that I'd been walking for a while and still I was not able to see the house that we had passed earlier. Was it even out here? Had we somehow gotten lost ourselves?

With each step my mind raced as to just what the fuck it was that I going to do. Chan had been so right with what he'd said before leaving the car. Only I wasn't able to find any other solutions to our problem at hand. If they had double crossed us and taxed our gear then everybody should be here backing me.

But as it stood, here I was on my own in the middle of fucking nowhere trying to find a house that both Chan and I at present were presuming, the keyword here being *presuming*, had our gear in, along with our Iranian guy whom had been abducted from outside Manchester Airport.

However the one thing that I did know for sure was that we couldn't let them out of our sight, even if it meant taking off after them again in pursuit. Although I wasn't too keen on that idea as we'd almost lost them once already this time around.

Just what the fuck was I going to do anyway, like Chan told me with his words of encouragement, "This ain't a Stallone movie."

Yeah right... Cheers for that one Chan.

With no idea just to how many were in there, that is –
presuming that they were in there at all, I also had no idea just
how heavily armed they were – or how well trained they were
for that matter.

Basically I was walking in there completely blind of
knowledge; my only advantage was the pitch-black sky that
curtained itself over me. And even with that... I wasn't at all
certain, that that was even an advantage at this moment in
time.

Shit! I was thinking to myself, the first thing I've got to do if
I managed to walk away from this alive... with or without the
gear is get a fucking mobile phone... oh and teach fucking
Chan how the fuck to drive as well.

Just then – the lights up ahead from the house came into
view. I suddenly came upon a large cattle gate to my right
hand side. From my judgement it looked to be around fifty
yards or so from the house. It obviously belonged to it – or at
least I was presuming so. There I was presuming once again –
and what was they said about presumption being the mother
all...

As I pulled the sleeves of my jacket over my hands, so not to
leave any prints, I then hitched myself up and over the gate
hiking toward the house taking in the surroundings as best as I
possibly could, all the while closing in on the house.

You could see only one light on from the top half of the
house, although the lower half was brightly lit, the light cast
out onto the gardens surrounding the property. I thought that
possibly that may help in someway – and also thought that I
wasn't at all sure, as I didn't have a clue just what the fuck I
was going to do.

The car was a lot clearer in my vision as I was almost upon it
now; I was positive that it was the same car that we'd
followed. Jumping over a small fence that surrounded the
house, I crouched down low to the gravel below my feet and
leaned against the car as lightly as possibly. Arching my body
so to get a much better view of the house, I judged it to be a
lot smaller than I'd first anticipated.

A small family looking home was before me, my guess was
no more than four bedrooms, a little harder to judge the lower
level as there was a garage close to me and also a
conservatory on the far side of the house.

Laughter could be heard from within the house, as I stayed
crouched in the same position, wondering just what the fuck

488

to do. I then made the decision that by staying where I was wasn't achieving anything, so looking around again, I then darting toward the back of the house.

Once I was there, I made my way as low as possible towards the rear window. Peeking up through the window was what appeared to be a study of some kind or maybe an office as I noticed files spread across a large desk. Although the room was empty – you could see shadows flickering through the open door – I presumed them to be another room or a hallway.

I decided once again that my position was of no use, so headed around to the left-hand side of the house arriving near to the conservatory I'd observed from beyond the car.

I figured that to be my best possible option, dragging myself as swiftly as possible along the lawn, the voices becoming more audible to me was their laughter. It was obvious that celebrations were taking place from their recent haul.

I lay just to the right hand side of the window, easing my body weight up, peering through the window, yet remaining as low as possible.

There he was in the dining room; I could see our Iranian guy strapped with duct tape to dining room chair. His mouth, hands and legs all bound tightly. His face looked swollen and bruised – the bastards had beaten him up. He looked to be barely conscious. Fuck knows what their plans were for him.

Moving further round to get myself a better view, then positioning myself below what looked to be a living room window. Arching myself up to the window to get the view I'd been looking for.

There sat in the living were four men, three of which I instantly recognised from the airport, the other, I presumed to be the driver who was a small guy, who looked to be the youngest of the four, maybe no older than myself. Before them on the living room floor was the suitcase's that belonged to us.

Arching a little further, and being as careful as I possibly could be, I made out two handguns placed on the coffee tables to the side of them. But that could mean anything; all four could and more than likely were armed. This wasn't a good situation, I wished more than anything that Prey was here with me.

Each and every one of them were in high spirits, however I did not recognise any of them from around Manchester and judging by their accents I presumed that they were from the Midlands area.

Just look at them I thought whilst spying on them, sat there celebrating, each and every one of them gloating and elaborating their tales to one another.

Moving back down into the garden, I tried to figure out just what the hell I was going to do... If I was going to do anything at all that was. From what I could make out, this was as Chan had put it – pure suicide.

As I moved around the house with little ease, I did my best to work things out whilst scoping out the house. As I arrived back around to the front of the house I noticed the light that was on up stairs, was someone up there? I tried to fathom out the light, judging it to be more than likely the toilet or a bathroom as the window was open and they were frosted glass used commonly with toilets and bathrooms.

I scanned the garage and realised that if it was possible to pull myself up onto the garage, I could possibly reach the window. However – once again I was completely unsure what to do once inside.

Although saying that I figured that to be my only option. So heading for the side of the garage, and taking a few steps back, then lightly jogging forward as silently as I possibly could, I threw myself up at the wall. My fingers barely reached the roof; I was struggling to hold on, trying with all my strength and thanking God as I managed to pull myself up onto the garage.

I pushed all of my weight forward with a sigh of relief – when suddenly my foot caught the drainpipe – snapping it loudly – I suddenly found myself then cursing the same God that I'd recently just thanked. So scrambling my body frantically towards the shadows, I then lay as flat and silently as possible.

I could hear the shouting from inside, knowing for certain that they'd heard me. The front door suddenly flung open with all four men rushing outside into the night. All of them ran out into the driveway, I observed them from where I lay, my heart pumping like a speed train that had no intention of stopping or slowing down – I was done for – I had to be.

'What the fuck was that?' Blondie screamed to the others, who were scanning the area to see just where the noise had come from.

'You heard it didn't you?' The driver said, his head flying in every direction as he spoke, he had a very uncertain nature about him. He had a panicked, stricken look of this being the first time that he'd been involved with something like this before.

I was certain that I could be seen lying there on the roof – the other two, Body Builder and Skinny were running around the house, their guns pulled and ready. I found my right hand groping at the back of my jeans for my pistol, once finding it; I then clicked the safety off, certain that it could be heard in the still of night.

I continued the observation of these men running about, my heart still refusing to slow any as I was outnumbered and out gunned for sure.

From what I could tell the driver was the only one who wasn't armed, although that meant shit as he looked none too bright and could have left it inside.

'Must have just been some kind of animal.' I heard one of the first two that I'd seen exit the car shout out. Although I was unsure as to which of the two shouted, from the gruffness of the voice, I guessed it to be the Body Builder.

'Fuck it... Let's get back inside.' Another voice called out.

'Keep looking,' Blondie shouted. He seemed to hold authority over the others as they said nothing and continued half heartily searching. I then consciously made a note of that.

Just then the driver turned and looked straight at me – This was it – It had to be – His eyes darting this way and that like a mouse sniffing out a loose piece of cheese – He'd seen me for sure.

I began squeezing the trigger gently – Then what the fuck was going on – Nothing! I was positive that he was staring at me, but for some unknown reason to me he wasn't acknowledging my presence as to being there. So easing my pistol forward so that it was aimed directly at him, he merely shrugged then turned and completely ignored me.

He had to have seen me – hadn't he? There was no explaining it, but somehow the shadows within which I lay must have acted as my camouflage... Well either that or the little fucker had seen me and he was smarter than I'd thought he was.

Suddenly Blondie called out. 'Fuck it – It must have been fuck all,' he shrugged. 'Man – You hear all kinds of freaky shit out here,' he then laughed, as did the others who began following him back through to the house.

I was still lay there, not believing what had just happened, merely lying there in the same position, still not able to move. The shadow cast down from the side of the house must have saved me, yet it made me realise just how stupid I actually was being there in the first place. I let out my breath, that felt had been held for eternity, finally release itself.

I suddenly thought that I should just get the fuck out of there as fast as I could do... Then realising the position that I'd got myself into.

I figured that for me now to descend back down the garage was just as much a risk as it was going ahead through the window that was positioned above my head.

Fuck it – I'd come this far – May as well go through the fucking thing now. Although thinking back to the sight of those two suitcases in the living room, must have been the final nail in the coffin – Just do it – I told myself reaching up without a second thought to the open window above me.

Placing both hands through the gap, I then hauled my weight up until level with the open window. I'd been right; looking through into the bathroom, which looked to be recently decorated holding a new paint smell within its four walls.

The door was ajar and you could see the landing a light from the bathroom. I was listening intently and you could hear that they'd resumed their celebrations downstairs, their voices and laughter was distant – yet at the same time it was very clear.

Easing the window away from its latch, I hauled my weight through the window and carefully crawled through with much ease, besides it wasn't the first time in doing this kind of thing – Was it?

'I won't be a minute.' A voice suddenly called out, a lot more audible. 'Just going for a piss!' I recognised the voice of Blondie, and was panic-struck instantly.

Fuck, was he coming up here? I darted for the door, hearing the footsteps on the stairs along with seeing his blackened shadow growing larger as he descended upon my hiding place.

I swiftly manoeuvred my body flat behind the door, then clicking open my lock knife into my left hand that I never left home without whilst the right hand held tightly to the semi-automatic pistol.

The door swung into me as Blondie waltzed through the door, already un-buttoning his fly, flopping his cock into his hand without a care in the world. I was observing him silently like a panther watches his prey; I noticed the handgun stuffed into the back of his trousers. It looked to be Walther PPK pistol.

So replacing my own handgun down the front waistband of my jeans, I continued watching like a ghost, as he was totally oblivious to the fact that anybody was stood there. So without any hesitation or a plan for that fucking matter, I swiftly and slickly took three steps behind him.

He was still oblivious, so swiftly moving my left arm around his lower waist with such speed that the shock halted his constant stream of hot piss. I then placed the knife directly under his scrotum, hearing the simple sound of a short sharp gasp.

Grabbing his pistol from the back of his jeans, I then noticed that I'd judged the gun correctly and pressed the cold steel to the back of his head.

'Not a fuckin' word,' I whispered menacingly to him, 'and I may just let you keep that cock of yours. Understand... then you nod very slowly.'

His head bowed forward a couple of time slowly as he began trembling, easing a little more pressure into the knife that was lodged below his cock, and hearing a small whimper.

I then snarled my whisper into his ear. 'How many downstairs? And don't even think about shouting or your shout will turn to a squeal as I'll disconnect your balls and cock from the rest of you.'

'Three,' came a whisper.

'How many guns?' I snarled again at the back of his head. 'Don't lie to me... It will be fatal to do so.'

'Only two now,' came the hushed reply, then. 'Please – Don't – Please!'

'Who the fuck put you onto this job?' I asked hitting the back of his head with the steel of the gun.

'I don't know,' he lied, so I added the pressure of the knife and felt a trickle of blood run through my fingers.

'Gordon,' he sobbed slightly; I hit his head in disgust.

'Gordon – Gordon – Who the fuck is that?' I asked, realising I didn't have a clue who the fuck Chan's guy was at the airport.

'Gordon Mansfield – Customs – Airport' he whimpered.

'You customs?' I snarled.

'No – No – Honestly – No,' he pleaded.

'Why you lot then?'

'He pulled us in to do this job – We've done other jobs for him before – Smaller ones – Not like this. He said he'd pay us big for it,' he definitely had tears in his eyes, even though I couldn't see them.

'Where is he now?'

'We've already spoken with him and confirmed that we've got the gear and the guy at his house awaiting his return. He'll be back here after his shift finishes about seven-thirty in the morning,' I suddenly realised that I didn't even know what fucking time it was with all that had been going on.

'What time is it now?' I asked – then realised the guy was in no position to look at his watch. 'Roughly – what time is it?' I added.

'About Eleven thirty,' he informed me, seeming to relax a little, so then adding the pressure to the knife once again so that the tension returned.

'We're going to take a walk downstairs,' I told him. 'Now I want for you to slowly and I mean fuckin' very slowly put your hands behind your head and turn around to face the door... All right? Nod if you understand me.'

His head bowed as he methodically raised his arms and placed the hands locked behind his head. As he slowly began to turn – I manoeuvred myself with each of his steps around to the back of him. So quickly sliding the knife away, I saw him suddenly cringe at the movement as I'd surely taken more than a nice clean slice out of his balls as I'd done so.

I was grinning to myself as I put the wiped the knife on the back of his top then placed it into the back of my jeans replacing it with my own handgun, now pointing both the Glock and the Walther to the back of his head. 'Move – And any sudden movements and I will no hesitate in taking you out.'

He began to exit the bathroom onto the landing and slowly began descending down the stairs. Following him, I could hear the voices and laughter growing louder as we approached the living room door.

'Go slowly through it,' I whispered. 'Just remember where I'm pointing these shooters you fuck.'

He nodded his understanding and stepped through the door with me directly behind him, using him as my cover.

As soon as they looked up all three were up and out of their seated positions. 'What – What the fucks – Going...' Body

494

Builder darted from the single armchair that matched the three-piece suite; he'd already drawn fourth his pistol.

Skinny leaped from the settee with the driver following suit, although the driver was unarmed as he'd told me.

'Nobody move or I'll blow his fuckin' head off,' I snarled at them, dodging from side to side to to try and find my barings and to see just what the two who were armed were doing.

'Fuck you!' Body Builder to my right snarled back at me.

Skinny, the other to the left of me with the gun pointed shouted. 'Who the fuck are you? How the fuck did you find us?'

'Fuck you all!' I snarled back at Body Builder. I then turned my attention to Skinny. 'The way I see this – Is put your guns down and I'll let you all live,' I stated, with all the cockiness that I could possibly muster.

'Who the fuck are you?' The driver was real jumpy, I was real glad that he didn't have any kind of weapon.

'I'm the person whose gear you've taxed,' I announced, dodging to my left not removing my guns from the back of Blondie's head, the other guy holding the gun was twitching, making me nervous. 'Drop the fuckin' guns,' I screamed at them.

'Fuck off... There is only one of you,' Skinny screamed back at me.

'Make your fuckin' move then lads,' I sneered, yet at the same time praying that they weren't going to comply.

Out-fucking-gunned – Out-fucking-numbered – Just what sort of a situation had I let myself in for.

'Do as he says,' the whimper came feebly from Blondie, who up until now hadn't made a sound. I was still holding him before me as my cover, as I was continuing to move from side to side – my odds here certainly weren't on favourite.

'Fuck you too,' Body Builder to the right hand side of us screamed.

I noticed that all their eyes kept darting down to his groin area as blood was seeping everywhere by now as he stood there with his bleeding cock hanging out.

'Do it – Please...' he cried out, fear taking control of his voice. 'For me – Please...' his voice trailed off.

'You'd better listen to him,' I warned them.

Then without any warning whatsoever I suddenly saw the flash, followed by the thunderous shot as it rang out from my right hand side.

My left hand squeezed without a second thought, blowing the top half of Blondie's head away in front of me away. His thick – hot blood violently stuck my face and chest, blinding me momentarily.

I had shot him at such close range his body was thrown forward from the force of the blast that had exploded from my pistol. He crushed into the driver who screamed like a little girl as his so-called friend collapsed into a heap onto him.

Shot's rang out from all directions either side of me. So squeezing both hands together, I began shooting at the other two as the recoil from the pistols tore at the muscles in my arms as I struggled to control the power of both the guns exploding their sheer voracity.

I instantaneously hit Body Builder in his right shoulder, throwing him backwards, his gun thrown from his grip. Although just as suddenly as he had been thrown backwards, I cried out myself, as his shot tore through my left side, throwing me off balance.

A succession of shots rang out from my left hand side as I threw myself towards the settee, crying out in sheer agony as I then fell onto my wound. I could see that this guy had probably never even fired a gun before as the shakes took control of him with each shot he fired. The panic and confusion that stretched across his face made all of this clear to me.

I dropped the Walther PPK, and then quickly rolled out from behind the settee using both my hands to steady the recoil of the Glock that was a monster of a gun – as I shot the deadly pistol three times at him. At least two bullets struck the target viciously, his screams became deafening along with the drivers whom was still trapped beneath the Blondie's dead body.

Leaping to my feet, I swiftly crossed the room grabbing Body Builder's gun from the floor. He was groaning in agony at the bullet hole in his left shoulder that had torn its flesh apart. Without a second thought, I placed the gun to his forehead and squeezed the trigger, his fiery viscous blood covering me.

I then moved to the screaming driver whose eyes pleaded with me, but merely squeezed the trigger once again – without any emotion whatsoever. I began making my way over to Skinny – but he was already gone; half his face had been torn away with the force of the blast with which I'd killed him.

I turned my attention to the suitcases; I glanced at the scene before me – Shit! I hadn't wanted any of this to happen... Just how the fuck had it all turned so pear shaped?

This was a blood bath and what made it worse was that I didn't have a clue to just how close anybody was to where we were. I hadn't seen any other property, but you just couldn't tell with the darkness of night... Had anybody heard us? The noise must have been deafening.

I grabbed the suitcases and hauled them through to the hallway leaving them there. I found Chan's guy in the dining room, fully conscious with nothing but fear and panic pasted across his face as he stared and struggling whilst trying move away from myself.

'I'm with Chan,' I told him, pulling the tape from his mouth. 'Can you move once I free you?'

He was nodding frantically at me as I began to free him. 'Can you drive?' He looked bemused at the question.

'Can you fuckin' drive?' I snapped at him.

He nodded again at me.

'Listen to me,' I said as he stood up. 'Chan's in a car down the road from 'ere. I need to sort things out 'ere. Go to the end of the drive and run down to the left hand side until you come to Chan.'

I was staring hard at him, realising the sight I must have been, covered in blood – but hey – this was no time for getting sentimental was it?

'Bring the car back 'ere – Wait at the end of the drive for me – *Go now*,' I yelled as he quickly ran from me in sheer horror.

As I stood there all alone, the silence suddenly engulfed me... *Fuck – Fuck – Fuck* – Just what the fuck had gone and happened? My mind was racing as I tried my best to figure out just what the fuck I was going to do.

I suddenly realised that forensics would have a field day with this crime scene – I mean shit – I hadn't even worn gloves as none of this was planned – Destroy everything – A voice suddenly called out to me – Yes that was it – I mean what the fuck else could I possibly do eh?

I dashed through to the kitchen, and began turning all the gas appliances on. Then frantically, I began yanking the old radiators away from the walls with all of my force I could muster, screaming out in agony like a crazed mad man from my bullet wound.   The gas began pouring out with the maddening hiss of a deranged trapped snake, screaming out to break free.

Running through to the living room, I then grabbed all of the discharged guns, dashing through to the hallway and shoving them into one of the cases.

I hauled them with all my might down the gravel path as a car approached, I suddenly panicked before realising that it was Chan and his guy, both leaping from the car running towards me. 'The cases – Take the fuckin' cases,' I screamed at the two of them.

'Chopper... Let's get fuck out of here,' Chan yelled at me.

'I ain't finished inside yet,' I replied through gritted teeth, turning back towards the house.

'Come back,' Chan screamed at me again, as I ran back towards the house, my side in complete anguish where I had been shot with each step that I took.

I was running from room to room, but not finding what I'd was looking for. Yanking doors open, tearing cupboards apart – It just wasn't anywhere to be found. There wasn't any more time left, so I made my way for the front door and there it was – It had to be in the cupboard by the front door. I tore it open and saw the central heating timer; the house stank of the odour that they added to gas.

Luckily the timer was electronic and the time showed eleven-fifty-six. I quickly set it for twelve-o'clock, then punched the operate button and darted for the front door, slamming it shut behind me.

Making my way down the drive in severe crippling pain, I didn't know what it was that was driving me to keep going as I fell through the rear doors that were open onto the back seat, screaming out loud as the shock rippled throughout my entire body.

'Go – Go - Now,' Chan screamed at the Iranian guy who shoved the car into gear as we screeched away.

'What the fuck happened?' Chan screamed at me. 'Chopper – Chopper...' I could hear his voice but I was beginning to drift in and out of consciousness.

'I got it back Chan – I got it...' I was in real bad shape and seemingly for the first time since the bullet had torn its way throughout my body I was fully aware of it.

I could feel the car gliding round the country lanes for what seemed like an eternity, I was struggling to stay conscious as everything began to drift and float in an almost space like way.

We must have travelled at least a couple of miles when we heard an almighty explosion, the explosions exploding into series of explosions as I saw both Chan and the Iranian guy jump unwittingly then stare at one another as they realised what had just taken place.

It had worked – Or had it? I thought as I began to drift – The house would nothing but a fireball – Destroy the evidence – Destroy – Drifting – Drift...

'Just what the fuck did you do Chopper?' Chan asked as he placed his hand on my barley conscious head.

'Destroy – the evi... It was your guy, your guy at the air... porrr... Cha...' I cried out in pure agony as complete darkness engulfed me, and I slipped totally into a state of unconsciousness.

'How's the kid?' Prey asked anxiously, as Chan and Steve arrived back at Chan's house Sunday morning.

'He's in bad shape,' Chan sighed shaking his head.

'Is he alive?' Sleeper snapped.

'He lost a lot of blood, internally as well,' Steve was nodding as he was telling them this.

Once they'd dropped both the gear and the Iranian guy off at Chan's in Worsley, they'd taken Chopper straight over to a doctor Chan knew, who ran a private hospital in Bolton.

Chan had contacted the doctor at his home from Steve's mobile, whilst Chopper remained unconscious in the rear of the car, no matter what they'd done to try and stem the continuous flow of blood that was soaking the seats below him. He'd told the doctor to be waiting at the hospital ready, informing him as to what he knew of Chopper's injuries.

Both Chan and Steve feared the worst, as Chopper appeared to be losing a lot of blood that was clearly decreasing his colour to the kind of greyness related with death.

Chan had used the doctor, an old friend, several times before and the doctor knew just how well paid he was for his services provided and was therefore more than discreet. He knew that if Chan were to visit him, rather than the local emergency room that he would have to provide his services unofficially.

That wasn't a problem at all, as he could easily lose or falsify paperwork when it was a necessity. Although again not a problem as the authority that he held over others at the hospital, questions would go unasked or unanswered without raising too many eyebrows.

Besides which, as soon as any patient of Chan's was stable enough to be moved, that is exactly what Chan did. He moved them as far away as possible so that it was almost as though they had never existed. There had been one time when the doctor had been unable to do anything for one kid that Chan had brought to his attention. As soon as the doctor announced this to Chan, the patient in question was quickly retrieved, and was never to be seen or heard of again.

'He's alive though – Right?' Prey snapped grabbing hold of Chan.

Steve nodded slowly as Chan began to explain. 'They've only just brought him out of surgery after he was in there for hours; it was more than close this time. The doc says that he almost didn't make it through surgery,' Chan sighed heavily as he was completely drained from the night's events, and then continued. 'The doc said basically the bullet wound was a clean shot, probably shot at close range as it went straight through his lower left abdomen.'

'Doc says that it only just missed his liver luckily as he explained that the liver had over five hundred functions and he'd have been fucked for sure if it had hit him there,' Steve added. 'Although it has torn its way through his large and small intestines causing a lot of internal bleeding.'

'Jesus,' Sleeper said shaking his head at the news.

'Also as the bullet exited through the lower part of his back it took out part of his pelvic bone,' Chan added.

'You speak to him?' Prey asked.

Steve shook his head. 'They've kept him there for now. He's still heavily sedated when we left.'

'What the fuck did you leave for then?' Prey asked angrily – more out of concern than anger though.

'The car needs destroying. It's a complete mess from all of his blood. The doctor says that we only just made it to the hospital in time as the amount of blood that Chopper lost – he was on the verge of death. We just couldn't seem to stop the bleeding, no matter what we tried,' Chan told him, shaking his head at the image of Chopper in the rear of the car. 'Also anything else from last night that could connect us to being at that house last night needs destroying fully.'

Prey nodded. 'I'll make the arrangements now,' he said, knowing that it made perfect sense – even though the car was registered in a false name that couldn't be traced back to him. 'Chan just what the fuck happened last night?' he then asked.

'Your guy told us his side of things,' Sleeper added. 'Although he's unclear as to what actually happened as he say's that they had him strapped to a chair in the dining room.'

'But he's told us something about Chopper saying it was your guy at the airport or at least that's what he thought he meant just before passing out.'

'It's been taken care of,' Chan simply said, shaking his head at the thought of the customs guy he'd used. 'He never made it home this morning from work... Let's just leave it at that.'

Chan had made the necessary arrangements that were needed as they travelled with Chopper to Bolton from Steve's mobile phone. He knew who it had been who had double-crossed him and made the arrangements for him to be intercepted and dealt with as he'd travelled home that very morning.

He'd received confirmation that the problem had been dealt with as he'd instructed as they'd travelled back to his house. Although Chan knew that now – along with the aftermath of what went down at the house – the police would tie the two things together as more than mere coincidence.

The guy that Chan had used was someone that he kept for his own services for times like this, his own connections didn't even know of his existence. The hit would have been very cleanly done. The police investigating this would know for certain that it would have been a professional hit for sure.

So with that it mind they had to take all the necessary arrangements to cover themselves, which included the destruction of Prey's motor as it could lead them back to the scene.

Prey nodded at Chan, knowing exactly what he'd meant. 'When can we move the kid?'

'We'll travel back there this evening,' Chan simply said. 'Just Steve and I will check on him. However – the next twenty-four hours will be critical to him.'

Steve sighed through exhaustion. 'Doc says he'll contact us if there's any change, although he reckons that Chopper's stable for the moment. He says that the damage to the intestines could have been a lot worse. He says that it had of been any worse, that they may have had to remove some of his actual intestines. But as it stands they seem to have stemmed the flow of the internal bleeding'

'We can hopefully remove him in two or three day's time,' Chan added. 'But we'll have to be very careful as he'll still be

502

in a very bad way – It'll take a while if he comes through this one alive to recover fully,' Chan smiled. 'He's a good kid – He's got a strong will about his nature... It will be alright... I think.'

Prey let out a deep sigh and dropped to his knees as Steve placed his hand on the back of his head knowing exactly what he felt at that precise moment.

Chan then looked at them all. 'If it wasn't for Chopper last night then...' He trailed off shaking his head as he did so.

'We'll need to get him as far away as possible,' Steve told them. 'Chan told me that from what he can tell Chopper shot all four men,' he shook his head in disbelief. 'Chan says that if that didn't do the trick...' he looked at the two of them as they both nodded.

'I know,' Prey grinned. 'The guy in there told us that he thinks that Chopper blew the fuckin' house away.'

'It looks that way,' Chan smiled as he said this. 'Well at least it sounded like that as we drove away.'

'Shit!' Sleeper said letting half a laugh. 'The kid doesn't fuck about... Look, if he's stable enough then we'll move him down to my manor.'

'What about our goods?' Chan suddenly asked changing the subject.

'Double sweet Chan,' Prey told him. 'Sleepers guy gave it the A' Okay.'

'Good – Very good,' he then smiled. 'How long to shift it?'

'We've been talking about that Chan,' Prey told him. 'We figure with what's gone down last night we're better shifting it all completely out of town.'

Chan looked at Sleeper. 'You are capable of this?'

'I can shift it – It'll just take a little longer, but I can do it. Besides which I'll try and sort out some of your bees as soon as I can as I know that you've got plans for it,' Sleeper told Chan as he looked at Prey and Steve. 'Just as soon as Steve's guys sort it out and we can move it down there.'

'How long will that take?' Chan wanted to know.

'We can transport it about mid week to London,' Steve confirmed with Chan. 'Can you take care of that end of things,' he looked at Sleeper who merely nodded back at him.

'I've already made the arrangements at my end,' he told him. 'I'll just have to arrange for some better equipped transportation.'

'If it wasn't for the kid then we wouldn't be transporting anything,' Prey added.

'In'it,' Steve said smiling. 'Chopper better be alright.'

'We'd better keep it to ar'selves about Chopper,' Prey told them. 'That includes Donna.'

'She'll be pulling her hair out if we don't tell her shit though,' Steve exclaimed, shaking his head at Prey.

'It's the way it's going to have to be for now,' he simply replied with no emotion.

'I agree,' Chan added.

'He'll be sweet down at my gaff,' Sleeper told them. 'We'll keep him there until we know just what the fuck is going on after last night. Just tell Donna that he had to leave the country for a few weeks on business or something.' He looked to Prey. 'You'll think of something to keep her calm for the time being... Won't you?' he added.

Prey simply nodded at Sleeper.

'We don't know just how much damage the kids caused,' Steve announced. 'Has anything been on the news?'

'Nothing yet,' Prey told him.

'Well it will be for sure,' Chan added. 'We're just going to have to keep a low profile for the time being. There will be a lot of heat after what went down last night.'

'Ain't that the truth,' Prey added, then shook his head. 'Chopper sure knows how to create a shit storm when ones not needed.'

They all laughed as best as they could under the circumstances.

NINETY EIGHT

'What we got then Martin?' asked Stevenson as he looked around at the mass destruction of the property before him. They had been called in Sunday morning to go over to an address where there had been an explosion the night before. It wasn't really the sort of thing that they investigated. However the firemen had discovered four deceased bodies – and obviously badly burnt remains in the house.

Again – nothing so strange about that... apart from the fact they all appeared to be full of bullet holes.

'Fuck all,' sighed Walsh dusting off the blue overalls he wore, as the black smoke drifted around him. 'The place is pretty much burnt to the ground. Come take a look for yourself. Here put these on first though.' He handed him the same blue overalls he was wearing along with the forensics officers that were now there.

'Jeez,' sighed Stevenson holding a handkerchief to his mouth and nose as he changed and they made their way through the burnt out house. 'You sure that this is safe?'

'The fire guys have got everything under control as much possible,' he replied looking back over his shoulder. 'There's Lucy now.'

'Morning Lucy,' said Stevenson. 'How's it going?'

'I'm doing a hell of lot better than these guys are,' she replied. 'They were shot a number of times from different angles. This one in particular seems to have caught it at close range to the back of the head.'

'And the rest?' asked Stevenson.

505

'All random bullet holes apart from the ones that appear to have been shot at close range through their faces,' she was pointing at the three other bodies. 'Looks like whoever did this finished them off at close range just to be sure they were dead.'

'And if that failed they went and blew the house up,' he sighed shaking his head. 'Is any of them the owner?'

'Very unlikely,' replied Walsh. 'All we know is that the house is owned by a Gordon Mansfield. Works for customs at the airport.'

'They get hold of him?'

'By the time they discovered that information he had already left this morning,' said Walsh.

'And...'

'And obviously he ain't home,' replied Walsh. 'Unless of course... he's one of the four crispies here. But we're doubting that, based on the time the airport is saying he left work.'

'Right then,' said Stevenson straightening up and looking around again. 'That's the first thing we need to worry about is finding this Mans...'

'Neither of you have fuck all to worry about,' said the voice from the darkness of the smoke as he walked through into the crime scene not wearing the blue overalls like everybody else though. The figure was dressed casually in jeans and a dark blue Ralph Lauren jacket. 'Because this is no longer your case lads,' smiled Anderson revealing himself.

'What the fuck you mean it's not our ca...' began Stevenson barging up to Anderson. 'Exactly what I said you Muppet,' sneered Anderson holding out his hand to stop Stevenson in his tracks.

'But you can't just stroll in her and do this,' argued Walsh, also now by his side.

'The chief reckons there is more of good chance this shit will get solved with me on the case rather than you two Muppets,' he smirked at Walsh.

'This is fucking outrageous,' barked Stevenson.

'No use crying to me about it,' laughed Anderson. 'Now if you wouldn't mind clearing the fuck off my crime scene before one of you amateurs goes and contaminates it I would be most grateful.'

'You're a fucking...' Stevenson began as Walsh grabbed his arm.

'Easy Mike,' he told him. 'Let it go.'

506

'Fuck that,' he spat the words and threw a punch straight at Anderson who was expecting it and easily side stepped it watching as the detective tumbled to the ground and he merely stepped over him.

'Now what have we got so far, Lucy?' he asked watching her shaking her head at him, as he glanced over his shoulder observing Walsh help Stevenson to his feet as he turned his attention back to Lucy. 'Now where were we again?'

They still showing this shit?' I called out to Sleeper who was preparing food in the kitchen, whilst I was laid up watching the television in his guestroom where I'd been for over a week now.

I was still in a lot of pain from the bullet wound. My pelvic bone had been hit also making it hard for me to move properly. Also since leaving the hospital, I'd only just stopped passing blood every time I went for a piss.

The stitches holding my stomach together were a little unnerving as it felt as though they could open up at any given time, with my envisaged intestines ravelling out in continuous streams onto my lap. The doc had tried convincing me that this wouldn't happen unless I managed to receive a severe kick to the area. Although I'll admit that I'd had more than one or two nightmares on that score, awakening from my already restless slumber in cold sweats.

They'd operated within my intestines to stem the flow of blood I'd been losing rapidly; the doctor had told me that if the bullet had entered a couple of millimetres to the upper abdomen, it would have damaged my liver for sure. So I suppose in that respect I'd been lucky, although not feeling it so much at this agonising moment in time.

My real problem was the lack of sleep being achieved. The doctor had wanted to keep me in the hospital to keep a check on me, but things were really beginning to heat up around Manchester whilst the police ran around like headless chickens trying to piece together just what had happened that Saturday night.

508

Besides which, Sleeper had contacted his own discreet doctor who was at present keeping a daily check on my well being.

Everybody had thought it best that I was moved well out of the area as we weren't certain to just how much the police had from that night, other than the regular news reports that we were seeing daily on the television or reading in the papers.

As far as we could tell though they weren't to clear as to what had actually happened anyway. Luckily for me though – the house turned out to be in the middle of nowhere without any other property within a mile radius. Although the explosion had been heard and reported, it had taken the fire services and police way too long to discover the house. By the time that they did so, it had been completely gutted, even to the stage where surrounding trees and fences were alight. Also they'd been unable to discover just whom the house had belonged to, until it was too late for them to do anything about it anyway.

The newspapers were having a field day though with the customs guy as they had completely dragged him through the dirt for the last couple of days. At first there had been a lot of sympathy for him – but then after someone we knew – leaked some dirt to the press on what he'd been actually up to, they'd gone to town on him.

Then to top it all, someone from customs themselves – then went and let it leak that he'd been under an internal investigation also, which did us no harm whatsoever.

News stories were running away with their own theories as to what went down that night, claiming that a very good source had informed them. Stories from a drug deal that turned sour to Mafia involvement all the way through to the Colombian Cartel... that apparently were being investigated recently into shipments that they were bringing into the country at the present time.

'You should have seen it the first couple of days,' Sleeper laughed as he walked into the room with a tray of food for us. 'You were out cold for the first two days.'

'I bet it was mayhem,' I said smiling as I took the plate of fried chicken and dumplings from him. 'Your doctor, what is name? Barker – is he coming to see me again today?'

'He'll be here after he finishes at the surgery,' he told me whilst watching the end of the news.

'I take it he's done work for you before?'

Sleeper looked at me then grinned as he put his plate down, lifting his shirt. 'He's the one who sorted these out.' He pointed to three obvious bullet wounds across his chest.

'Shit,' I shook my head at him. 'I thought that I'd taken a bad hit.'

'Somebody that I'd had trouble with – tried taking me out whilst I was in my car... Fuckin' chicken shit bastard,' he told me whilst returning his top.

'I won't ask what happened to them after,' I laughed as he winked at me.

'Took a while though,' Sleeper told me as he resumed eating his soup. 'I was laid up for months. Didn't even come round for almost two weeks,' he sighed, and then shook his head. 'Almost didn't make it,' he simply added.

'How old were you?'

'Only nineteen. Shit happens though in our world right,' he half laughed. 'As you well know.'

'In'it,' I tried to laugh, but it hurt in doing so. 'You spoken to Prey?'

'This morning,' he told me. 'Says he'll contact you tonight. I didn't want to wake you as I heard you crying out in pain throughout the night. I checked on you but you were asleep.'

'It's just whenever I move around,' I stated. 'It's so fuckin' hard trying to sleep. Can't lie on my back, as it's too fuckin' painful or my front for that matter. About the only side that isn't too painful is my right side and even that hurts like a mother fucker.'

'Prey says that Donna's pure stressing out Chopper,' he told me, looking directly at me. 'She's even called Lisa you know.'

'She told me,' I said. 'The thing is... There's fuck all that she can do, is there? Well apart from worry herself rotten.'

'You should tell her though,' Sleeper told me. 'I mean Lisa felt well bad about lying to her.'

'Don't worry – I'll smooth things over once I return.'

I knew that Donna would be going mad, but I also knew that if she discovered that I'd been shot she'd go right into one.

Also more importantly – was that I didn't want her coming to any conclusions over what had happened, especially with all this mess over the news. Donna was far from stupid and would somehow connect the two events together.

Ever since she found out I'd killed that security guard we'd not been the same. She held her own suspicions as to what happened to Paddy, although that one went unquestioned. On her behalf I knew that she was finding it hard to come to terms with the fact that I'd taken somebody's life.

God knows what she'd think if she suspected that I was guilty of taking a further four lives. There just wouldn't be any understanding of that one... Even if there hadn't been any other option as far as I was concerned. No – I'd just have to come up with the blag of all blags when explaining this one to her.

Besides which, I'd got our gear back, which was in the process of being sold. Sleeper said that things were operating a lot better than he'd anticipated seeing as he'd taken on a lot more than originally had been agreed.

'How are things going with sales?' I suddenly enquired, as I thought about it. 'How soon do you reckon we'll pull everything in?'

'A few more weeks, possibly three or four at the most,' he smiled knowingly. 'Everybody is going mad for this gear. It's just that two of my sources who have heard about this shit are already are out of London for a while. And I've already promised them a bulk of the gear.'

'Prey has got to see Anderson this week though,' I told him.

'I know,' he nodded. 'I've already arranged that side of things for him. He'll have the money to give him at the meeting. Well that's presuming that he plays ball with you lot.'

'Ain't that the truth,' I shook my head. 'I'm still not convinced he's going to let us break free from him.'

'I don't know Chopper,' Sleeper half laughed. 'Prey can be quite persuasive when he wants to be.'

We both laughed as we thought of our friend. 'You reckon that we'll be able to make it away from the business?'

'I reckon that you'll all be alright Chopper,' he smiled at me. 'No matter what you all decide to do.'

'I'm still unsure if I want out altogether.'

He stared at me. 'After what happened to you Chopper I would have thought that you'd be wanting out for good now.'

'I just did what I had to,' I responded. 'Besides you'd have done the same.'

'I ain't too sure about that kid,' he laughed at me. 'Although saying that... I'm sure glad that you did
go and get our gear back or we'd all have been fucked for sure.'

'Ain't that the truth eh?'

'Well, well if it isn't Steve,' Anderson announced as Prey led him through into the office at the warehouse in Old Trafford which they used for storing Macreedy's clothing. 'I am truly honoured Steve. I usually only get to meet with O'Prey here,' he smirked knowingly at the two of them, staring directly at Steve as he took a seat opposite Steve in the office without it being offered.

They'd arranged the meeting for late Friday night. They'd picked up the copied tapes from Chan before arriving at the warehouse; Prey had already set up the television and video recorder ready for the meeting. This was it. This was the day of reckoning – The only question remaining was whether or not Anderson was to go for it.

'No Chorlton?' Anderson sneered as he glanced around.

'No,' Prey simply said as he sat opposite Anderson.

'So then,' he sniffed at the two of them. 'You got my money?'

'We need to talk first,' Prey told him, holding his glare as he did so.

'Don't bullshit me,' Anderson suddenly snapped sitting forward. 'We ain't in the business of talking crap to one another... Well, that is unless you've got some information for me.' His eyes were alight for a second at the thought of another bust.

'No,' Steve spoke up. 'We've got a proposition for you.'

'We want out of the business for good,' Prey announced.

Anderson stared at them both then began to laugh maliciously at them. 'Shit! You had me going for a second there.' He controlled his laughter abruptly. 'For a second I thought that you said that you wanted out.'

'You heard right,' Steve said calmly. 'For good.'

'It just ain't happening,' he smirked at them, shaking his arrogance. 'You're signed up for life now lads.'

'How much?' Prey asked.

'How much? You should know that O'Prey, it's another six months,' he smiled knowingly.

'How much for us to get out for good?' Steve added.

'What's got into you lads for fuck's sake?' he stared at them with his lifeless cold eyes. 'Why the fuck do you want out? You ain't turning soft on me now... Are you?'

'No... We've just had enough,' Prey stared hard at Anderson.

'It ain't got anything to do with the major smack deal that you lads have got in the pipeline... Has it?' Anderson saw the looks of shock on both their faces; it looked as though Chris may have been correct. 'I heard that you lads are going to come into something big. But all has been a little quiet since I heard that.'

Prey's mind raced... Just how the fuck had this twat heard about that? But he'd said in the pipeline. He didn't know that it had already gone down and was in the process of being sold. Thank God they didn't keep any of it in Manchester.

'What major deal?' Prey then casually asked.

'The deal that was just written all over your two faces,' he announced flatly.

'No – you are wrong Mr. Anderson,' Steve told him. 'There is no major smack deal as you put it and we are out for good.'

'No you're fucking not,' Anderson shot back at him viciously, spittle trickling from his bottom lip. 'And I want a nice little bonus from the smack deal,' he grinned at them. 'I mean come on now – I've always looked after you three.'

'There ain't no smack deal and the reason that you let us be is that we pay your sorry arse to do so,' Prey told him.

'Now you'd better listen to us,' Steve said leaning slightly over the table. 'We are going to get out and you are going to let us,' his voice took on a slight menace to it.

'Or fucking what!' he casually shook his head at Steve as he leaned closer still.

'Listen... This ain't getting us anywhere,' Prey sighed. 'The way I see it is that we give you a one off payment that will not only cover us but the lads from the estate also.'

'Bullshit... Nothing but bullshit,' Anderson snarled back, as he then suddenly looked at them both curiously. 'How much are we talking?' he added, obviously a little curious to the amount on offer.

'One hundred and fifty grand,' Prey simply told him.

'Now I know that you're full of shit,' he laughed his response. 'That's worth shit in the long run.'

'How much then?' Steve enquired.

Anderson thought for a moment then smirked licking his lips. 'Five hundred grand.'

'How much?' Prey spluttered.

'Half a fuckin' mill,' Steve added, astonished at the amount he'd demanded.

'Well after your big deal goes down, then you can pay me,' he smiled.

'I already told you,' Prey snapped. 'There ain't no deal, so we can't pay you that much.'

'Looks like you're still in then,' he then chuckled as he sat back in his seat. 'Makes no difference to me. Besides which, I'll eventually take that amount from you anyway so what difference does it make.'

Prey nodded at Steve then turned his attention back to Anderson as Steve rose to the video. 'No Mr. Anderson – Only one hundred and fifty is what is on offer, and you will accept it Mr. Anderson as you'll realise that we are being more than generous with you.'

Now it was Prey's turn to grin as Steve placed one of the three tapes into the machine. 'I think that once you've seen this you'll agree with us anyway.'

'Watch your fucking tone with me O'Prey you cunt!' He suddenly glanced at Steve. 'What the fuck you got there?' Anderson snapped back at Prey, although a little uneasy as he did so.

'Watch and learn Anderson,' Steve said over his shoulder.

'You'll see that we don't really have to give you shit Anderson,' Prey laughed as the video sparked to life. 'Merely a good will gesture on ar'behalf, so that you leave us the fuck alone and the rest of ar' crew once we're out of the picture.'

Anderson's face dropped into a look of compete trauma as he recognised his own face on the television screen as he stood in the back of a Chinese restaurant that he recognised immediately. He could clearly hear himself as he chatted openly about the killing he wanted taking care of with a young

Chinese acquaintance he'd known in London. Although he'd killed the Chinese lad in the video shortly after he'd completed the job being requested before him on the television screen – he'd never anticipated that there was anything else to tie him to either of the murders... How wrong he'd been.

He stared from the screen to the other two, who were enjoying his discomfort immensely.

'Where the fuck did you get that from?' he snarled, pure anger taking control of his face as his coloured deepened with the rage building from within.

'We've another two similar tapes there as well,' Steve said pointing to the tapes.

'Give them to me,' he snapped, flying out of his seat straight at the desk. 'Now – Give me the fucking tapes... Now I said,' he screamed at them both as he pulled his fully loaded Smith and Wesson revolver out, shoving it in their direction. 'Now you cocksuckers – I want those tapes.' Their apparent lack of fear confused Anderson slightly as they merely sat there grinning at him.

'Fuck you Anderson,' Prey casually told him, ignoring the gun. 'You forgetting something or what you dick?'

'What... What the fuck are you two on about now – I should just kill the two of you where you stand – You – You...,' he screamed at them, his cool totally blown, as his face looked ready to pop a valve.

'Who's not here?' Steve grinned at him as he saw the flicker of recognition on Anderson's face.

'Chorlton,' he simply said, knowing he was defeated, his calm slowly returned and the colour began to fade in his reddened face.

'So then,' Prey smiled knowingly. 'I take it we have a deal Mr. Anderson.'

Anderson shook his bowed head. 'I want the tapes first.' He knew that they had him by the balls and hated them more than anything for it.

'Take them,' Steve said smiling. 'They're only copies of the originals that we've got anyway.'

His face flared slightly again. 'When do I get my money?' he snapped.

Prey opened the safe behind the desk removing the carrier bag containing the pre-counted money, tossing it to Anderson.

'Like we said, this is merely a gesture as we don't want to see or hear from you again.'

'And if we find out that you're pulling the estate apart like you've been doing the rest of town then we'll see that the tapes find their way to not only the press and the police. But to some very unsavoury characters within the underworld who would be even more interested than the police would be in them.' Steve told him as Prey smirked back at him.

'There's no need to count it,' he shook his head. 'It's all there.'

'Where did you get the tapes from?' Anderson enquired shaking his head still in disbelief as he glanced into the bag.

'That isn't any of your fuckin' business... Is it now son?' Prey continued smirking. 'All you need to know is that we've got both them and you by the balls.'

'If they come to light,' Anderson snarled as he bent his bulk down over the desk.

'They won't,' Steve told him. 'Just as long as you play ball and leave us and the crew the fuck alone. And those photos of our friends never see the light of day either.'

Anderson glared at the two of them with pure hatred in his eyes. 'Doesn't look as though I got any choice in the matter – Does it?' he told them as he ejected the tape, that was still in motion from the video player, grabbing the other two tapes from the side, God knows just what the fuck was on those ones he thought as he did do.

'No – you haven't Mr. Anderson,' Prey beamed at him.

'That's that then,' Anderson snarled at them.

'Suppose it is,' Steve said smiling.

'I'd like to say that it's been a pleasure,' Prey half laughed. 'But I'd be lying if I did so,' as he said this, both he and Steve laughed at Anderson stood before them as a defeated man.

'Fuck the two of you,' he growled his hatred towards them as he turned, walking straight out of the office, leaving Prey and Steve sat there.

'It was a pleasure... Oh what the fuck am I saying – Fuck you too Anderson...' Steve shouted after him as they heard the large steel doors of the warehouse slam shut.

They both sat there silently then looked to one another, both smiling joyously. 'Yes –   'Yes – Yes – We did it...' Prey screamed with utter joy, as the two of them   grabbed hold of each other lifting one another into the air.

Both of them had never felt as free as they did at that precise moment, the weight and   burden that had been slowly draining them in the form of Anderson had finally been elevated.

'I really wish that I could have been there,' I laughed, as Prey and Steve relayed the story once again – only I couldn't ever grow tired of hearing it. Chan laughed along, as the four of us sat waiting for the lads to arrive at Chan's restaurant where we'd arranged to meet them.

I'd only been back in town a few days as I'd stayed down at Sleeper's until business was completed, after over almost two months. Then I'd travelled back with our money by train. I'd never seen so much money at one time; we made a fortune from the gear, even after we split the money between us and paid off Anderson his amount.

Also we figured that we'd leave the lads and the estate one-hundred grand on top of the money already working the street to resume business. That's what we were doing at Chan's. It was finally time to explain our recent actions and our evasiveness.

I still found it a little difficult to move freely, although the wounds had healed somewhat from the original state, thank God.

Donna had gone ballistic on my return; although I'd known that she would do so. After she found out that I'd been shot, her anger subsided into pure anxiety for the state of my health. I had explained to her that things were too on top around Manchester, it had been important for me leave town. Without anybody, herself included knowing anything about it.

She'd flared up again, when on telling her that I'd been in London. Once again though she gave way – when I informed

her that it all been part of what was going on. Our final deal –
as I'd told her.

Overjoyed at the news that we were finally going to leave the
business for good had been what had won her over completely
as she leapt onto me, only through her joy came my agonising
pain as I cried out. I was still in a lot of pain, knowing that I
should really have been rested up some more.

However – as soon as possible, I'd been back on my feet
wanting – no that was wrong – I'd needed to regain my own
independence. I've never been one to be laid up, it had done
my head right in, although I'd appreciated the time given to
rest at Sleeper's. It had been critical for my health. I was still
not able to fully comprehend the extent of what had actually
happened to me – You know just how close to death I'd
actually been.

I was also glad to be finally back home, plus the money we'd
made was helping immensely. All that was left to do now was
get it laundered so it was clean enough for us to use.

It still felt a little weird to me that we weren't going to be
involved with the business anymore, but also I also felt relief
at the prospect of not having to be constantly worried about
that side of things.

'Alright Pops?' It was Lee as he suddenly appeared as if
from nowhere. 'Alright Prey,' he added as he grabbed his
father's shoulder.

'Lee – Lee – Why you not call me?' Chan was overjoyed as
he rose taking his son into his arms.

'I've only just arrived in town Pop's,' he smiled at his father.

'You've met Chopper and Steve,' Chan announced proudly.

'Of course – All right,' he nodded at the two of us. 'And how
wouldn't I know of Chopper Pop? You constantly tell me of
him in your letters,' he smiled warmly at me.
I hadn't known that Chan spoke of me and I was a little taken
back as Chan grinned at me. 'Like I said Chopper... You're
like one of my own. All you boys are,' he laughed.

'How's the studying going Lee?' Prey asked as the two
seated themselves.

'Just finished my finals,' he announced proudly. 'Still got to
take the Bar exam. But I just had to get away from there for a
while. I don't know how I've done yet – but...' he smiled at
us. 'Hopefully everything will be all right.'

'Of course it wills my son,' Chan looked at his son with the
utter most pride I'd seen in a father looking at his son.

'You've got even bigger than the last time that I saw you,' Prey told Lee.

'In'it,' I added, looking at him. 'You look in good shape,' I told him noticing that we were of a much more of a similar build to one other than before.

'I've taken up boxing lessons,' he smiled. 'So you won't have to jump in to my rescue again Prey,' he laughed as we all did.

'Here are your guests now,' Chan announced as the lads all walked onto the top floor of the restaurant that Chan had kept free for only us.

'Listen Lee... We must go out while you're 'ere,' Prey declared.

'Sounds good to me,' He smiled.

'All of us,' Steve said looking to Chan.

'Okay then,' Chan smiled. 'We all go out this Saturday... Yes?'

'Sweet,' I added. 'Let's just go somewhere out of the city centre if possible eh,' I added as I still felt uneasy about being in town as we were still unsure just how the investigation into that Saturday night was going.

We thought that all was safe but still being cautious we'd decided that I was going to leave the country, taking Donna on a long holiday whilst we found out for sure.

Both Prey and Steve had agreed with me, without any objection to Donna taking the time off also. My head needed straightening out slightly whilst finding my feet so speak with life once again. Besides, what better way to do it than a holiday away in the sun?

'Alright lads,' Prey smiled as everybody walked up to the table.

'See you Saturday,' I said to Lee as he left with Chan, he smiled warmly at me again.

It was safe to say that I really like Lee – despite the fact I barely know the lad.

'Definitely, Chopper,' he replied as he walked towards the kitchen doors with his father.

After relaying the whole story to the lads, they sat there speechless. We told them everything from just how it was that we'd managed to get not only ourselves out of the trouble the previous year, but them also. Although I think that they'd already worked that one out for themselves. Only they hadn't known the finer details, as they were merely relieved at the time to be free.

I didn't think that they'd realised that we'd had to keep up with the payments to Anderson afterwards. The three of us explained just how hard it had been, not only since our return but with the payments that we'd had to make between times also.

There were sombre looks around the table as we then went onto to tell them of our plans to end business all together.

'What about what you said about resuming business?' Knieldy asked.

'Yeah!' Parksey added. 'Take back what was right fully ar's to begin with.'

'Why?' Kezlo asked me.

'Because we can't continue with things the way that they are,' I told him.

'Where does that leave us then?' Jonah simply asked.

'Yeah... What the fuck are we supposed to do now?' Diamond asked.

Prey laughed. 'Listen to all of you.'

'Well without you three we will be finished,' Johnny butted in.

'You've not even let us finish,' Steve said a little irritated.

'There's what? About seventy grand working the street at the moment,' I looked at everybody. 'Right... Yes?' I asked as they all nodded.

Prey smiled at them. 'Well... look along with that seventy gee's you've got working the street we've decided to add another hundred to it.'

We watched for their reactions as they all looked to one another.

'You're just going to give it to us?' Parksey asked in amazement.

'Simple as that,' I smiled.

'You what!' Jonah exclaimed in pure disbelief. 'You mean that you're just going to walk away yet leave us enough to continue ar'selves.'

Kezlo shook his head. 'And you don't want shit from it?'

'Nope,' I shook my head smiling. 'Not a penny.'

'Look, it's like this,' Prey told them. 'If it hadn't been for you lads then we wouldn't be able to break away from the business so it's only fair that we leave the business to you.'

'Besides which, you know the operation like the back of your hands,' Steve added. 'Jonah knows how the manufacturing side of things is set up,' he nodded at Jonah who smiled in exchange.

'You'll be your own bosses... All seven of you,' I confirmed.

'And we can run things the way we want to?' Knieldy asked.

'Take on our own workers?' Diamond added.

'Do what the fuck you want to,' I told them. 'Just use it wisely between you.'

'This is your chance to make a go of it for yourselves,' Prey added.

'I can't believe it,' Jonah smiled. 'Shit – and we just started to give you grief,' he half laughed.

'Listen,' I told them. 'You lads can do it your way, without the hassles of Anderson. It's down to you just how you want to control things where Chris's concerned.'

'Although I'd be careful just what you're going to do where that fuckers concerned,' Steve added.

'Ain't that the truth,' I sighed; I still couldn't help but feel wound up by the mere mention of his name. 'My reckoning... No matter what anybody says. Is that he's somehow hooked up with Anderson so I'd tread carefully there.'

'We can make enough if it's just us from the estate,' Parksey announced.

'Plus I got a few contacts out of town that don't even know Chris,' Jonah added.

'Plus if we set things up like they used to be,' Knieldy grinned.

'Then things should be double sweet once again,' Johnny added.

'Exactly,' I announced to them, watching them with a certain pride as they all began to warm to the idea of branching out on their own without the three of us.

'To all of you then!' Prey beamed as he shook the bottle of Bollinger, cracking the cork open, the white froth spraying everybody at the table.

Everybody began to cheer, as this would be the one final time that we'd be sat here in this given situation.

Saturday night arrived and we had arranged for a night out with Chan and his son Lee, although there was much arguing as to where to go until Chan suggested a night out at the Dog's, as in the greyhound race track in Belle Vue.

He told us that he often went there and Lee told us that his father just loved to gamble, so the excuse to go there was merely an excuse for him to do so.

I'd never been to the dogs before and wondered just what it was going to be like. Chan had booked us a table by the window over looking the race-course itself, I hadn't even known that you were able to dine there. As it turned out the evening was turning out to be a good one.

'This scran's quality,' I commented, between mouthfuls of a roasted rack of lamb with fresh garlic and rosemary served with crushed roasted new potatoes. 'When's the next race Chan?'

'Couple of minutes Chopper,' he replied eagerly, as he checked his tickets again.

'How much have you lost already Pops?' Lee laughed, as he watched his father eagerly looking for the race to start.

'Stop fussing,' he laughed, 'I can afford it.'

'What are your plans on your return to the States?' Steve asked Lee, changing the subject.

'I'm not too sure yet,' he said tossing a potato into his mouth. 'I'm thinking of taking time out and maybe travelling about for a while.'

'Where?' Prey asked through mouthfuls of his chicken smothered in tarragon sauce.

524

'I might go backpacking around the world,' he announced.

'Really?' I asked interested.

'Well after all the studying that I've been doing then I just feel that I need to get away for a while,' he smiled.

'The Far East?' Steve enquired.

'Reckon so,' he looked at his father, who hadn't taken his attention away from the window before him. 'I've got enough relatives and friends over that way and I'd like to see where my roots come from.'

'That sounds colossal,' I declared. 'I'd love to do something like that.'

'Why don't you Chopper?' Chan suddenly asked briefly glancing at me, then quickly to the racecourse once again. 'Come on baby – come on...' he suddenly screamed as the race sprung into action.

All of us were hanging over the table, each one shouting for the dog that we'd choose to bet on. Although I didn't have a clue just what the fuck I was betting on like Chan did who seemed to know everything from their trainers to their previous performances.

'Yes – yes – yes – *Oh yes*,' Chan screamed like an excited child at Christmas time – well either that or he'd just shot his load – as his dog shot through across the final line in triumph.

We all laughed at his excitement. 'I take it you won Chan,' Prey laughed.

He smiled at us all; his face was alight with his win. 'No seriously Chopper,' Chan then looked at me again. 'Why don't you go travelling for a while?'

I'd never really thought about it before. 'I don't know – I mean, I don't suppose that I've really got any excuse not to now.'

'You're still so young Chopper. You should get out there and see the world,' Chan smiled. 'I have many friends and relatives that would make you more than welcome.'

'You could come with me,' Lee suddenly announced.

I looked at him shocked. 'You serious?' I asked him, instantly warming to the idea.

'Sure,' he smiled. 'I'm not going for at least a couple of months, but it'll be a right good crack if we were to go together.'

I thought for a moment about this, what about Donna? Then thinking... I was taking her away next week for a long break anyway, so I would be able to use that as a sweetener to getting her to agree to let me go away with Lee for a while.

'Sure – Why the fuck not,' I smiled.

'It's a hard fuckin' life eh kid?' Prey laughed out loud as Steve did also. 'Don't you worry about the two of us stuck 'ere with the missus and kids,' he laughed again at me.

As I sat there thinking to myself, I found that I was becoming more than excited about taking a trip to the Far East with Lee. It sounded great, maybe pulling out of business wasn't going to be so bad after all – No in fact thinking about it now, we had done the right thing.

We'd put our past finally behind us as we all sat there. Things were going to be different from now on – they were going to be so much better than they'd ever been before.

I rejoined the celebrations with all of my closest friends sat there along with me – no that was wrong, they were more than friends... They were my true family.

For the first time since we'd broken away, I was feeling the euphoria of it all... And it felt too good to be put into words.

As we all left the race track, each and every one of us were in good spirits, laughing and joking with each other.

Making our way over to Steve and Lee's cars I noticed that a large, dark in colour, possibly blue or even black, Bedford transit van had blocked Steve's car in.

'What the fuck!' Steve exclaimed, as he too noticed that he was jammed into the parking space. 'Ahhh fuck,' Steve cried out as he also noticed his tyres had been slashed.

'Fuckin' wankers,' I added noticing the slashed tyres also.

'Makes no difference,' Prey shrugged. 'You couldn't have got yourself out from where that van has parked itself.'

'What sort of parking is that anyway?' Lee laughed, trying his best to lighten the mood.

'We all can fit into Lee's car until we get back into town,' Chan announced, as we'd decided that we'd make our way back to Chan's restaurant, where, still full of his gambling bug he'd convinced us to go there for some after hour's card games.

'Still a bunch of fuckin' wankers,' Steve half laughed now, what was done was done. 'Fuck it. We'll just come and pick it up in the morning,' he declared, shaking his head.

'Just buy yourself a new one old man,' Prey told him. 'You certainly can afford it now.' We all laughed, as we each knew just how much we'd made from our final deal. Not only that but we had money put into other assets and all in all, we were more than comfortable. Not to mention the continued success of Macreedy's, that we were now in, talks of expanding even further still.

As we neared Lee's VW Golf, which Chan had recently purchased for him, I suddenly noticed a movement from within the van – Was somebody in there? I was positive that I'd seen something moving, so I began to make my way towards the van. Maybe it was the fuckers who had slashed Steve's tyres that were in there.

I was almost within a few feet of the van, when suddenly the side doors slid open quickly making me jump as they did so.

But that was nothing in comparison to what we were now faced with stood there, as stood before us were four fully balaclarved men. Each and every one of them was carrying sawn off shotguns pointed directly at us.

'Fuck... Fuck...' I gasped, grabbing for the back of my jeans forgetting that I hadn't brought my piece with me.

Just then the nearest one to me swung the shotgun into my jaw. As I fell to the floor I cried out in agony, as I'd fallen onto my wounded side. The pain from my healing bullet wound rippling through my body in sheer anguish as it did so.

'Enough,' a voice called out as Prey helped me to my feet.

I recognised the voice as unmistakably belonging to Chris. 'You're a dead man,' I snarled viciously at him.

'Into the van now,' he simply demanded, as all the shot guns were pointed in our direction. 'Just the three of you,' he pointed his gun to behind us at Steve. 'Now,' he screamed.

'Move Chopper,' Prey said into my ear.

'Fuck that!' I told him.

'We ain't got any choice in this matter kid,' he stated, pushing me forward. 'We're outnumbered with them hand cannons they're carrying – Plus they only want us... This ain't the old man's trouble.'

I simply nodded my response, understanding fully that he was right it the words he spoke and then climbed into the rear of the van.

'Sit there now.' One of the other masked men snarled at us pointing his gun to behind the front seats.

Just as the side doors were being closed I caught Lee's astonished look as Chan pulled him away.

Was that to be the last time I'd see the two of them? What the fuck was going to happen? I'd known that there had to be some kind of retaliation from what had gone down at The Greyhound amongst all the other shit that was still unfinished between the two of us. All these thoughts raced through my mind as the van screeched its way out of the car park.

We all control our own destinies I thought as the van sped away. Only if this was to all of ours destinies. Then we sure as hell weren't in control of them right now.

I looked to Prey then Steve, merely shaking my head in disbelief. We'd come so far and so close, yet it now seemed to be falling to pieces around us as we sat there. My back was pressed hard against the front seats of the van, four shotguns pointed at our heads as we made our way across the now deadened night of Manchester.

ONE HUNDRED AND THREE

Finally, after what appeared to be an eternity, the van came to a sudden, jolting halt. As we'd been so low down in rear of the van, it had been impossible to judge just how far we'd travelled or just where it was we'd finally arrived at.

'Out of the van,' Chris called, without looking at the three of us as he jumped down from the side door. I knew that it was him; there wasn't a single doubt in my mind to whose voice it had been.

Nobody had spoken the whole time we'd travelled to our destination. Each of us lost within a world of our own thoughts as to the outcome of what we faced before us. The vibes I was feeling weren't good ones – could this be it? Could this possibly be the final curtain? No doubt really.

It was obvious that this event had been planned in advance. My mind had raced as to just how we could get away somehow, only nothing of real help came as we'd sat there under armed guard.

As all three of us complied with leaving the van, I recognised instantly exactly where we were as soon as we clambered down from the side door. We stood directly outside of our own warehouse – Macreedy's Warehouse in Old Trafford.

We all looked at each other in disbelief. Just what the fuck was going on? Just how the fuck had Chris known where our warehouse was? It hadn't been as though we'd ever advertised its whereabouts or that there been even a sign outside advertising the fact we were situated there.

'Inside... Now,' Chris snarled at us menacingly, as I felt one of the shot guns shoved into my back, making me wince with the pain that struck through my all ready wounded body.

Just how the fuck had he bypassed my security system I asked myself as the three of us walked sombrely through the open doors into the brightly lit warehouse, the doors slamming shut behind us.

'What the fuck is going on Chris?' I asked as we were led through into the middle of the warehouse, where the three chairs from the office had been placed next to one another.

'I know it's you Chris,' I confirmed as we were shoved heavily into the chairs. Our arms pulled behind our backs whilst one of each of the men began to tape our legs and arms to the seats themselves as Chris and who presuming to be the driver stood before us holding their shotguns.

'Lost your tongue Chris?' I smirked, as my guy just finished taping me up.

Still he didn't answer me, as he merely glared at me with his cold eyes. We could hear a lot of noise from within the office, so my attention was drawn to there. Somebody was in there; whoever they were they were doing a good job of tearing it apart.

'Who the fuck's in there?' Prey spoke up as he too could hear the noise.

'What is it you want?' Steve asked, yet still Chris refused to answer us.

'What's up Chris?' I sniggered at him defiantly. 'You don't want to go out in public with that ugly fucked up mug of yours.'

'Fuck you Chopper,' he screamed, as I finally got a rise out of him.

'You can remove that ridiculous mask now,' someone suddenly called out, distracting us from Chris's outburst.

Our attention immediately turned towards the office. It was Anderson stood there smiling maliciously at the three of us.

'All right there lads,' he grinned as he waved three videotapes from within our safe at us.

'Fuck you Anderson!' Prey snarled at him.

'They're only copies,' Steve added.

'Whatever!' Anderson laughed. 'Maybe they are... Maybe they aren't.'

'I knew that you two were involved with one another,' I looked at Chris as Anderson waltzed over taking the balaclava from Chris's head, rubbing his hair as he did so.

'Oh – Chorlton or is it Chopper? If only you knew son,' he laughed wickedly. 'If only you knew the whole picture... Involved – Involved?' he roared with laughter, so much so that he appeared to be on the verge of insanity as he stared at the three of us sat there helplessly, four shotguns pointed at our heads.

'He's my nephew...' The two of them then began to laugh along with one another, although you could see the look of bewilderment behind the masked eyes of the four men stood before us, their shotguns momentarily dropping slightly.

Even they were shocked at this latest revelation. Shit – we hadn't expected that one as I glanced to the other two seated either side of me, witnessing their expressions of amazement. This was by far a lot worse than we had ever anticipated.

'Fuck both of you,' I snarled. 'Like Steve told you. They're only copies you prick.'

'I think not,' Anderson simply told me. 'They're not the same tapes that I took all those weeks back for myself. So that only leaves these tapes in circulation and I'll see personally that they are destroyed.'

The truth was that they were copies as Chan held onto the originals, although we were hardly going to tell him that.

'You see what you've gone and done,' Anderson walked over to Prey taking out a lock knife as he did so. 'You had to go and get all smart arsed about things. Didn't you?' he screamed the last bit at him.

'Fuck you Anderson!' Prey replied as Anderson put a blade to his face. 'Haven't you ever taken a good look at me Anderson you prick?'

He smiled as Anderson applied the pressure of the knife above Prey's left eye. Blood instantly appeared, streams beginning to flow. 'You can't scare me that way you dickhead,' he laughed at Anderson as he then proceeded to drag the knife from his left eye across his cheek then continuing all the way back up into the right side of his face in one continuous movement. He severed the flesh away with utter ease as he did so.

You could see the agonising pain Prey felt as he performed this horrific act upon him, although he didn't give Anderson the satisfaction of crying out. Chris laughed as his uncle made

531

his performance; Prey kept his head up as the blood began to pour from the torn flesh.

His face became a continuous stream of blood, pouring out endlessly, his face was awash with its crimson tide. He looked in a bad way as I looked away, turning my attention back to Chris and Anderson.

'What's wrong Chopper?' he smirked at me. 'Can't you stomach that?' he threw his shotgun to the floor grabbing a handgun from the back of his jeans.

'How about this then?' He smirked knowingly as he made his way over to Steve.

I witnessed the sheer panic take control of Steve's eyes, looking frantically from the two of us to Chris pleadingly so as he did. Chris casually pointed the large SIG Sauer P226 pistol to his head, then turning to grin at me, panic-taking control of me as we watched helplessly.

I began screaming at him, the fear showing through my voice. 'No... Don't... No Chris, this is between you and...'

The gun exploded before I could finish, Steve's face exploding with the virtuosity of the blast as we sat there helpless. His whole face was ripped from itself as the bullet tore through his skull, exiting at the rear of his head. His body was thrown with such force backwards, as if it was merely nothing but a brown paper bag blown through a breeze.

The image of Steve's face as he glanced at me one final time, the gun pointed at his head as he realised that the inevitable was about to happen, bore its final, panic stricken, pleading imagine deep within the depths of my mind.

'You fuckin cunt – You fuckin'...' I screamed at him as he walked casually past me, stained from streaks and splashes of Steve's blood.

Standing before Prey, his bloodied face to his, as if he was examining the damage, he smirked at him. 'Do it you prick,' Prey spat the words at him, blood-making contact with his scarred face, as he seemed to enjoy the drama.

Prey knew that our time had come, it was inevitable as we sat there helpless, so Prey smirked at Chris. 'Always said that you were nothing more than a little girl Chris,' he laughed as my eyes darted from him to Chris and back to Steve who lay dead behind me.

'Paddy told us just before we killed him that you were his little girl,' he laughed again.

'Fuck you Prey,' Chris screamed. 'I knew that you were the ones behind his disappearance you cocksuckers. Where's his body? Where is he? He deserves a proper burial you cunt.' Only Prey merely began to chuckle at him.

'You'll never find him,' he laughed one last time. 'Let's just say that we gave ar' own kind of sending off,' Chris forced the gun into Prey grinning mouth as Prey looked at me, trying to smile through what little space he had.

There was no way Prey was going to show his fear, giving Chris any satisfaction as he pushed the gun further into his mouth making him gag.

I looked to Anderson who appeared to love all of this – although the same couldn't be said for Chris's men who obviously had never experienced anything like it previously – and they looked sick to their stomachs.

'Stop him,' I pleaded with Anderson.

'Whose got the originals if these aren't them Chorlton?' he asked, as he produced his own handgun pointing it at me.

Glancing to Prey, he shook his head at me. 'That's them.' I lied to him.

'I knew they were after breaking into your safe,' he stared at me emotionlessly, then merely nodded at Chris, who in turn grinned at me as I turned my head away from the scene.

'Either way I couldn't give a shit though,' he sneered at me. 'Because with everything that I've gathered together in the last few months from all of you lads,' he smiled knowingly at Chris. 'Well let's just say that if it were a necessity to suddenly have to disappear myself. Then I wouldn't have too many difficulties.'

He stared at Chris coldly nodding his head. 'Finish him now...'

I couldn't watch for a second time. But before I knew it, Anderson was suddenly upon me forcing my head towards Chris and Prey as Chris suddenly squeezed the trigger. The back of Prey's head was torn away from the sheer virtuosity of the blast, covering us with pieces of his flesh and bone, along with his fiery glutinous blood.

I couldn't believe it. They'd killed the two people who meant more than anything to me. They'd killed my family before my very own eyes without hesitating for a single second.

'No – Nnnnoooo – *You bastards*,' I screamed at them as they laughed at their two accomplishments.

Anderson then suddenly without warning pointed his Smith and Wesson revolver at the one of the other four men.

Panic suddenly took control of him as he cried out. 'No – Hey no man – this wasn't part of... Chris – Chris – C'mon for fucks sake Chris...' His shots tore through the first of them as he then proceeded to shoot each and every one of them, emptying his revolver into them, before they realised just what was happening.

Their screams tore through the warehouse into the dead of night. I bore no feelings for these lads, they'd signed on with Chris and that was their own destinies that they'd controlled.

You could see the look of sheer shock on Chris's face though; even he hadn't expected that one. 'What the fuck did you go and do that for?' Chris screamed at his deranged uncle. 'They were my best fuckin' lads,' he added.

'You've got plenty more haven't you,' Anderson casually commented as he wandered over to the bodies, reloading his revolver and pumped four more bullets into them just to make sure that they were dead. 'Besides they're part of my plan young nephew.'

'What fuckin' plan you lunatic?' Chris screamed back at him. 'The plan was to take these fuckers and get back your fuckin' video tapes you were so anxious for... Kill these three and get the fuck out of 'ere. That was the fuckin' plan.'

'Don't worry yourself with my plan of action,' Anderson said without looking back as he headed once again for the office. 'Just have some fun with your boy there – Oh and make sure that you un-tape them from the chairs once you've finished,' he added before finally disappearing into the office.

Chris was suddenly before me. 'You think that you can trust that fucker?' I snarled at him. 'You not think that he's going to double cross you as soon as he can do so.'

He shook his head at me. 'Shut the fuck up Chopper you little twat,' he sneered at me. 'You like what he did to Prey?' he laughed viciously before producing a solid looking lock knife.

He began taunting me with the steel blade that he stroked my face with, smiling at him. 'Go on then you prick.'

The blades lethal steel quickly sliced through the right side of my face making me wince as the flesh tore itself open, I bit down on my lip as hard as I could so not to cry out.

'Just kill me you fuck,' I snarled, as he gloated at me. By now, I just wanted the nightmare to end – I'd lost the two people I'd cared most for. I knew for sure that I was to be joining them on whatever journey they now had taken.

'Oh don't worry Chopper,' he spat the words at me. 'I will do.'

'Are you not finished yet?' Anderson called out as he appeared carrying a large wooden box.

'What the fuck is that?' Chris asked.

'A full case of assorted arsenal that they were obviously about to do a deal with. I've got everything from Kalashnikov assault rifles to Glocks, all the way through to an assortment of used sawn-off shotguns,' he laughed as did Chris at his uncle's way of thinking. 'Plus I've got just enough C4 to blow them all and this warehouse to smithereens. It'll take them weeks to merely shift through it all, but when they do they'll find trace of what's here in the box and begin piecing everything together themselves.'

'You're a smart fucker aren't you,' Chris told his uncle almost proudly. 'What about the C4 though?' he enquired. 'Surely they can trace that shit.'

'It was obviously part of their arms deal... Wasn't it? Besides the timer and detonator are from a mate of mine in bomb disposal. It's untraceable afterwards.'

He laughed at Chris who was shaking his head at him in disbelief. 'It won't make any difference as I'll make the affair work in my favour by telling them that I'd followed the suspects here from a tip off I'd got.' He looked directly at me, taped helplessly in agonising pain from the deep gash to the side of my face. 'Turns out that you lot had moved into the arms business Chorlton.'

Chris laughed again. 'And don't tell me – The deal turned sore on them.'

'Not as daft as you look nephew,' he smiled at him. 'I'll have already borne witness them all entering the warehouse but whilst calling for back up something happened and the warehouse turned into a fireball.' Once again he laughed at both of us.

'You're a sick fuck,' I sneered as best as I could at Anderson. 'You're dumber than I originally thought you were Anderson if you think that you'll be able to pull this one off.'

'Watch your fuckin' mouth,' Chris said, as he backhanded the right side of my face. The pain was becoming unbearable as I sat there losing blood freely from the open wound across my face.

535

'We'll see,' Anderson laughed joyously at me, so full of himself at what he'd achieved so far with the help of Chris before me. It had been the first time that I'd seen Anderson appear to be happy – and all that I could think was what a fucking time to have witnessed his happiness.

'I'll finish up 'ere then,' Chris grinned as he turned his attention back towards my bloodied face.

'I'm just going to go and set the timer up with the C4,' Anderson called out as he disappeared from view once again.

'Just you and me now Chopper,' Chris sneered very close to face.

With one last effort, draining me of what little energy that I had left, I thrust my bloodied face at Chris with such speed that he didn't see it coming. My mouth was open and snarling like a crazed wild dog as my teeth sunk into his nose.

With all of my force I could muster, I began biting down viciously, as hard as possible, Chris began squealing as he tried to push me away.

His squeals tearing through night, in agonising pain, as I began tearing away part of his nose in my mouth.

'*AAArrraaaggghhh…*' He was jumping around clutching to the torn piece of flesh, as I spat what little piece that I'd managed to tear away to the floor. 'You fuckin' wanker – you fuckin' – Chopper you fuckin' cunt you just bit my fuckin' nose off – You – You…,' I merely grinned back at him, his blood poured from my mouth as I enjoyed the sight before me.

'What the fuck is going on out here?' Anderson yelled as he darted back into view.

'My Fuckin' nose – My nose – He bit my fuckin' nose off the cunt…' Chris screamed with the sheer agony, no matter what happened now I was taking the final image of Chris hopping around with his nose missing to my grave.

As I glanced at Anderson, I could see a slight grin as he watched his nephew hopping around. 'Calm the fuck down,' he simply told him as he passed him a handkerchief. I knew instantly from that look on Anderson's face that he didn't give a fuck for his nephew, the thought only pleased me more, as I now knew for certain that Chris's day's would be numbered once Anderson had decided that he'd achieved everything that he wished for, from him.

'You wanker Chopper,' Chris thrust his gun into my face where he now stood holding the bloodied handkerchief to his nose. 'It's time to die right 'ere and now you fuck.'

He squeezed the trigger – But nothing happened – He squeezed once again and the same thing happened – Nothing that is – The appearance of pure shock was pasted across both of our faces.

'Fuck – Fuck – Fuck has happened?'

The same words repeating themselves through my own mind – Surely I couldn't be that lucky that the gun hadn't gone off again – I was experiencing pure déjà vu from the one time that Paddy had attempted to kill me.

'It's just stoppage you dick,' Anderson merely commented to Chris. 'Here,' he announced tossing his gun to Chris as my eyes darted from one to the other.

'You should always use a nice trusty reliable Smith and Wesson revolver,' he laughed as Chris grabbed the gun in mid flight, tossing his automatic to the floor.

Chris moved to the left hand of me, although I could still make out his smirk as he stood there aiming the gun at me.

It was finally time and I found myself grinning at Anderson who stood before me shaking his head. 'I've made my peace you dick,' I said closing my eyes.

'I actually liked the three of you Chorlton,' Anderson smirked at me as my eyes opened to his words. 'Believe or not I actually admired the way you worked – But you just had to go and get all cocky and smart arsed, didn't you,' he looked to Chris, still stood to my left; the gun aimed right for my face.

All was said and done though, as my mind was as clear as it been in a long time. This was it, the final curtain. So I opened my eyes, and I stared coldly at Anderson before me, ignoring Chris as though he didn't even exist. My eyes suddenly envisioned not Anderson, but a series of image's that began to flash before me – My past was there for me to see one last time – Donna – Prey – Steve – Sean – Sleeper and Eazy – The crew – The estate – Even Scotty was there – And all of them flashing instantaneously before my eyes.

I realised right there and then that this was my final moment – Anderson and Chris's voices weren't even audible whatsoever as they stood there.

That's when the thunderous explosion happened – briefly – momentarily I saw the white flash from my left side as it blinded my images – Then the burning sensation as the bullet tore its way through my flesh into the left side of my face, numbing it instantaneously – I seemed to fall in what appeared to be slow motion as my body began to pound hard into the concrete floor – My time had arrived – The final curtain was drawn – Lights out...

'Bang bang you're dead mother fucker,' Chris screamed as his uncle abruptly called out.

'What was that?' Anderson exclaimed, his eyes scanning the bloodbath of a warehouse and all of its windows.

'What?' Chris listened as the echo from the shot that had just killed Chopper stopped ringing in his ears.

'You not hear that crash from outside?' Anderson asked him, panic in his voice. 'There was a big bang from outside – I'm almost certain of it.'

'That was just the sound of this thing popping this little fucker 'ere. It was just an echo. The same thing happened when you shot the gun before.' He stood triumphantly over Chopper's bloodied body, as it lay motionless below him, still strapped to the chair.

'No – It was something else,' Anderson snarled at him. 'I'm sure it was.'

'It was nothing – You're just being paranoid,' Chris laughed as he looked at Chopper then Prey, 'Always did hate those fuckers,' he sneered.

Anderson shook his head, glancing around once more. 'Come on Chris – Get them the fuck unstrapped from them chairs. Then let's get the fuck out of here,' Anderson called out. 'We've got fifteen minutes or so before this place goes up in smoke.'

'Let me just pop them a couple more times first,' Chris grinned at his uncle, still holding the bloodied handkerchief to his nose. 'Just to make sure like.'

'Fuck that shit,' Anderson scowled at him. 'There has been more than enough noise made here tonight... No matter how fucking deserted it is around here. Besides, are you stupid or what? Look at them – They're as dead as they possibly can be – Just let's get the fuck out of here.'

Chris looked at each of the dead bodies that surrounded him and smiled to himself. 'You're right,' he laughed out loudly as they both made their way to the steel doors and out into the cool night air.

Anderson watched as Chris struggled, through his bleeding remains of his nose to change his blood stained clothing in the rear of the Bedford transit.

538

'You take the van and get the fuck out of here,' Anderson told him.

'What about you?' he enquired as he climbed into the driver's seat, blood still pouring from the damage Chopper had caused.

'It's almost time,' he smiled as he looked at his watch. 'I'll put the call in just before it's time to blow.'

'I'll see you this week,' Chris told him as he turned the key in the ignition. 'And thanks for tonight. Even if that little fucker did this to me.' He pointed to his face then laughed. 'Killing them was more than worth it,' he grinned as his uncle merely shook his head at his stupidity.

'Go on – Get the fuck out of here,' he sighed. 'This place will be swarming with police in the next ten minutes.'

'Laters,' Chris said as his shoved the gears into first, taking off into the night.

As Anderson watched the van disappear from view he made his way to the public phone box, on the outskirts of the industrial estate where Macreedy's warehouse was situated.

He was thinking about the night's events – As far as he was concerned the three of them had brought all of this upon themselves with their bright ideas to wanting out of the business. Then there was the matter of the videotapes, he suspected that Chan had supplied them the tapes, although he was certain that these were the originals he had with him now.

Besides if Chan had never used them against him before then he probably had no intention of doing so... Even if he did make a threat of some kind, he'd deal with Chan personally.

He no longer considered any of them a threat anymore. And as for his daft nephew – Well he'd be good for a couple more years then he'd dispose of him also. It maybe even sooner than he thought, if he became a liability to him.

Pulling open the door to the telephone box – he threw the coins into the phone, smiling as he did so, then he punched the number for head quarters into the phone.

Just as he made the connection, there was an almighty explosion that tore its way through the stillness of Manchester's nightline – the aftershock even shattering the glass surroundings of the phone box that Anderson was stood within. He merely smiled again as the voice screamed down the phone line at him.

'Jesus Christ – What the fuck was that?' The desk sergeant screamed down the line as Anderson merely smiled knowingly to himself.

Why the fuck do you want me there with you to see the Chink?' Chris asked as he sat in his uncle's brand new Range Rover, attending his regular weekly meeting. 'It's been well over a year since we rid ourselves of them three. Things couldn't have worked out better if we'd tried. Killing those fuckers paid off in more ways than one – I reckon another couple of months and I can start to pull Hulme apart good and proper,' he smiled to himself at the thought.

Anderson merely sat there listening quietly to his daft nephew. Chris had begun to irritate him more and more on each of these occasions. The thing was though, he was making a fortune from the street for him, but with that in mind he had began working with another source that Chris didn't know about... Just give it time he thought as he turned staring hard into Chris's more than cocky eyes.

'It's got fuck all to do with what happened that night,' he then laughed abruptly. 'Besides which nephew, that case has been well and truly closed.' He now roared with laughter even louder as he looked at Chris. 'Well – It was solved more than good enough for me. Plus there didn't seem to be any arguments as to the evidence that I provided along with the remains from that damage that was caused.'

'So why the fuck, do you want me there then?' he asked again.

'Because I don't fully trust the Chinky fuck. Also I know he was upset about the death of his three friends.' He shook his head. 'Chan has never called me for a meeting before. Usually just has an envelope ready and waiting once a month for me.'

'It's about those fuckin' tapes again... Isn't it?' Chris said looking directly at him. 'Just what the fuck was on those things anyway?' he asked as an after thought.

'Nothing that concerns you,' he simply told him.

Nobody could ever find out what was on those tapes that they had held over him, although they'd been well and truly destroyed in the furnace soon after that night in question.

'Look... It's just that I reckon that it was Chan who'd supplied them with the tapes.'

'So?' Chris shook his head. 'You must have got rid of them by now? So what the fuck does it matter?'

'Maybe the Chinks got more copies that he now wants to use.'

Chris stared at him whilst absorbing the information. 'You reckon he's going to try and blackmail you with them?' He panicked slightly as he saw his meal ticket threatened.

'I just don't know,' Anderson sighed. 'All I know is that he's never called a meeting before like this and he also says that it's within my own interest to attend... Business wise that is.'

'Maybe he's got a good job that needs covering,' Chris smiled. 'Or maybe he's onto a good deal that we can pull off.' His greed was now blatantly on view.

'Could be,' he smiled also with his equivalent greed. 'I need you there for me as back up nephew.'

Chris liked the sound of that – back up eh. 'Alright then... sweet,' he winked at his uncle. 'I'll be your back up. If this Chinky fuck has got any bright ideas then we'll soon put a stop to them.'

'Good – that's good my son. I'm glad you're in with me,' he smiled proudly, loving the way he ate up the praise. Besides which it wasn't as though he could take anybody from the office to the meeting with him.

'When we got to go and see the Chink?' Chris sneered, trying to show face.

'Friday night after he's closed,' he told him without even looking in his direction.

'You think that's wise or what?' Chris exclaimed, panicking slightly at the thought of a meeting after hours. 'Not that it makes any difference to me,' he added, again trying to show that nothing bothered him.

'Not really,' Anderson shook his head. 'I reckon we change the meeting at the last minute. That way if the fuckers got any smart arsed plans it'll have to be in front of a restaurant full of customers.'

'Nice plan,' Chris complemented him. The truth was though that he much preferred that the meeting was held whilst there were civilians around as they weren't too sure just what it was they were walking into.

'What time then?'

'He wants to see us at midnight,' he stared at Chris. 'I say we change it to more like nine o'clock right in the middle of service... If this fucker doesn't like it, then he can lump it.'

'Sweet,' Chris smiled. 'Now what the fuck you got for me this week?' he added, after all business was business.

What the fuck did the Chink say?' Chris asked
as Anderson walked from the phone box where he'd just
called Chan. Friday night was upon them and like planned
they'd changed the meeting at the last minute as it almost nine
o'clock now.

'He sounded a little edgy at first when I told him that we'd
be there at nine,' he grinned. 'But he says for us to head
straight over there.'

'Good – I bet the fuck doesn't realise that we're only round
the corner. I seen that he's pretty full already,' Chris smirked.
'I popped my head round the corner as you was in the phone
box. Let's hope that he's got something good for us,' he added
as an afterthought.

As the two walked the short journey to the restaurant,
Anderson wondered just what the fuck it was that Chan had
wanted to see him for. Hopefully it was a business
arrangement that needed sorting. He hoped that Chan hadn't
gone getting himself any smart arsed ideas like Prey, Steve
and Chopper had done. In a way he missed those three, he'd
liked their style, the way they worked.

If only, they hadn't gone and tried to get so fucking smart
arsed. He thought that they'd even been as fair as to give him
one last pay off, he would have preferred it if they'd stayed in
the game altogether.

Even though the three were dead, he'd let the rest of their
crew go about business as he'd agreed, even though he wasn't
quite sure as to why he'd not taken them down, it's what his
nephew had wanted for him to do.

Chris was even planning to try and take control of the estate by force; he'd merely listened to his plans to do so. He knew that those lads weren't any given force without the other three backing them and with them dead and buried; from what he could tell they'd kept themselves to themselves and the estate.

He knew that Chan had held a soft spot for the three of them. He had sensed Chan's sadness as to the deaths of them after he'd visited him shortly after all the news reports that were aired and printed on a daily basis until they bored themselves of it, finding something new to report on.

Anderson had played that one so well though, he thought as they neared the restaurant. He had gone ahead with the original plan to say that he'd followed the seven men to the warehouse from the tip off he'd received about an arm's deal due to go down that evening.

He'd said that the suspects were known to him to be involved in the drugs business heavily, that's why he'd followed up the lead thinking that possibly the informant had got it wrong about the arms. Although from the explosion at the warehouse from the C4 he'd obviously been correct.

Once forensics had sifted through the debris and chaos surrounding the industrial estate they'd found traces of all kinds of arsenal that had obviously been intended for the deal. Although Anderson had used a little too much of the C4, it was the first time he'd used it though. The whole area had needed to be closed down whilst forensics combed the area, although Anderson had given the police the names of all seven as he'd known exactly who they were.

The press had praised him for once again putting a stop to the ever-increasing crime levels in Manchester. They'd reported how he'd been lucky to escape the blast itself when he'd put the call through for back up.

He'd loved every minute of it, he thought to himself as they arrived outside Chan's restaurant.

'You ready?' he asked his nephew who merely grinned and nodded at him, as he patted his jacket where his gun was concealed.

'Hopefully they'll be no need for any of that malarkey at this time of night,' he laughed as he pushed open the door.

Chris noticed the sign as they entered and laughed as it said, 'Booking's only tonight'. 'I take it you made our reservations for the evening,' he chuckled.

Anderson glanced at the sign and laughed also at his nephew's little joke. As they walked through into Chan's they noticed the restaurant was full of Chinese couples dining around the restaurant. Just what they had anticipated as Chan noticed the two of them and walked over all smiles.

'How are you Mr. Anderson?' he took hold of his hand shaking it firmly, and then glancing to Chris.

'Sorry Chan... Let me introduce Chris Walker,' he smiled. 'You may have heard of him.'

'No... no... not at all,' Chan said warmly as he took hold of Chris's hand. 'How are you both – Please – Come, come we'll dine upstairs as you are my guests.'

Chris not saying a word glanced at his uncle, whilst at the same time thinking how stupid the old man was. He didn't have a clue that it had been him that night that they taken Chopper, Prey and the other old fool by armed force, the thought amused him as he brought his attention back to the present.

'What wrong with down here?' Anderson asked suspiciously.

'Nothing – Nothing at all,' Chan smiled at him. 'If you prefer to sit down here than we can do so. I just thought that you'd like a little privacy.'

''Ere's fine,' Chris added abruptly.

'Over there is quiet enough,' Anderson told Chan pointing to the far side of the restaurant.

'Whatever you wish,' Chan beamed at them.

As the three of them began making their way through the crowded restaurant, Anderson noticed that it was all couples dining, nothing too strange about that as it was Friday night after all and the restaurant was of a usual Friday night atmosphere. Everybody appeared to be in good spirits as he smiled to the couples, a couple of them with looks of recognition in their eyes as they dined. It was then clear that he was recognised as he was always in the newspapers or discussing latest busts on the television, the thought amused him as Chan led the two of them to the free table that faced the kitchen.

'Drinks?' Chan asked as they both were seated, then clicked his fingers to a waiter who was waiting to be summoned.

'Beer,' Chris said with an air of cockiness.

'Whiskey for me,' Anderson added as Chan clicked his fingers at the waiter who quickly disappeared.

'So how are things?' Chan asked as he sat opposite Anderson and Chris.

'Cut the bullshit Chan,' Anderson snapped, then controlled himself as the waiter returned almost instantly with their drinks.

'What the fuck is this meeting about?' Chris asked as his uncle shot him a cold look that told him to shut the fuck up.

'Business,' Chan confirmed, looking to Anderson.

'What kind of business Chan?' he asked sternly. 'The only business we ever do with one another usually is the monthly business that keeps me within the styles I've become accustomed to,' he grinned knowingly as Chris let out a little laugh.

'We need to talk about some unfinished business Mr. Anderson,' Chan said, his voice taking a serious edge to it as he began staring coldly at him, then turning his glare to Chris.

'With you also Mr. Walker... Mr. Anderson's good little nephew here.' He watched the slight changes of recognition within their faces.

Suddenly Anderson heard chairs scraping from the dining area, as he began to turn he saw all the women suddenly leaving the restaurant, panic suddenly took hold of him for a second.

'What the fuck's going on?' he growled at Chan who clicked his fingers.

Before either of them could do anything, all of the male clientele had surrounded them, each holding a handgun of assortments, pointed directly at the two of them.

'Fuck this... Fuck this... Get the fuck off...' Chris went for the inside of his jacket pocket as Anderson grabbed his arm.

The young Chinese man that stood closest to Chris removed his gun for him, smiling as he did so. The one closest to Anderson repeated the same act, removing Anderson's revolver although this time patting him down to check for any other firearms that may have been concealed. Anderson stared his hatred at Chan as this was carried out, only the old man sat there emotionlessly.

Chan sat there silently as he then observed all the blinds that hung heavily over the windows drop, leaving them all alone from any prying eyes outside. Next Chan clicked his fingers as two more Chinese appeared holding in their hands, several sets of handcuffs.

'You know what the fuck you're doing Chan?' Anderson asked as coolly as he could have done. He was trying his best to fathom this situation out as he hadn't expected for any of this to happen.

His mind began racing, how the fuck had Chan known he'd change the meeting time? How the fuck had he let himself walk so openly into this blatant trap? The sign – that fucking sign in the window – the fucking Chink had expected for him to change the time.

The biggest question of all was just what the fuck did Chan have planned for them? Surely he must know that even he couldn't kill him – The heat that would surround the case would never stop until those responsible were brought to justice.

'Get these fuckin' things off me,' Chris squealed as the handcuffs were forced around his wrists to the chair, along with his ankles. 'You can't do this to us... You know just who the fuck you're dealing with,' he yelled out, although Chan merely sat there smiling silently.

'Come on Chan,' Anderson said calmly, as the one responsible for his captivity finished locking the last pair of handcuffs. 'You want to tell me what this is all about?'

'A story,' Chan simply replied.

'A Fuckin' Story – You Fuckin'...' Chris screamed as the one closest to him struck him heavily with his piece, splitting his mouth open.

'What fucking story Chan?' Anderson sneered, not even looking to Chris's bloodied mouth.

'I just wanted to make sure that I had your full attention Mr. Anderson,' Chan smiled.

'Well you've fucking well got it,' Anderson confirmed, shaking his head as he did so. 'Although do you think that it was necessary to go to all this trouble?'

'Oh – I think that it was,' he grinned. 'Let me begin,' he sighed deeply, dropping his head.

'Go on then Chink,' Chris snapped as his nose made contact with the same gun once again, crushing it from the blow.

Chan shook his head at him. 'Fucking idiot... No fucking manners have you Chris?'

'Fuck you!' he snapped as the gun struck his right eye, the wound opening itself instantly.

548

'What the fuck is this story about and just how the fuck has it got to do business Chan?' Anderson snarled, his patience wearing thin by now.

'It's a story of my son,' Chan began, ignoring Chris's suffering. 'I have several sons Mr. Anderson, but this one was the youngest.' He smiled proudly.

'Yeah... And?' Anderson asked as Chris sat there silently.

'You see this son is very special to me,' he continued. 'He is special to me like three others I could mention... Three others I hasten to add that you both took part in the killing of.'

'It wasn't personal Chan,' Anderson told him as a simple matter of fact, he knew the three he was referring to and figured it would be to his advantage if he didn't try bullshitting the old man with having no knowledge of it. 'I actually liked them myself.' He then added smiling slightly.

'So why kill them?'

'Because they had something on me,' he stated, looking to see if there was any recognition in Chan's eyes to knowledge of the tapes.

Chan clicked his fingers, as a young Chinese lad appeared holding three videotapes. 'You mean these I think Mr. Anderson.'

'So it was you, who gave them the tapes,' Anderson suddenly flared up. 'I knew it was you... You Chink Fuck,' he screamed his rage at the old man before him, as his nose encountered the same damage Chris's had as the gun he didn't see coming smashed it cleanly from his left hand side.

'Fuck this bully boy shit,' Chris snapped. 'What the fuck is it that you are going to do with those tapes anyway?'

'Nothing... That's what Chan,' Anderson snarled viciously. 'Because if you were going to, then you would have already. Wouldn't you old man?' The anger was rising from within him.

'Well trying to black mail you with them won't work? Will it Mr. Anderson?' Chan casually said as he stared from the tapes to him.

'No,' Anderson replied. 'Not unless you want to meet the same fate that...'

Chris cut him off. 'Those three fuckers met,' he screamed at Chan as the gun hit him hard once again.

'Obviously,' Chan sighed deeply, as he stared at the two of them. 'Let me continue,' he shook his head. 'You know what. The three that you kill were like my family. They were

549

considered by me to be my family just like my own blood related sons they were also my sons.'

'They stepped over the line,' Anderson casually informed him, his lower half of his face covered in blood. 'I had no option.'

'They gave you an option,' Chan suddenly lost his cool, then breathing deeply to calm himself. 'They not only gave you money as a gesture but they also approached you in a businesslike manner to resolve the problem they had. They wanted out of the shitty business that we work in. They only kept the tapes so that you wouldn't hassle them further,' he screamed the last bit at the two of them.

He glanced at the state of Chris, sat there covered with his own blood. 'You Mr. Walker was one of the reasons they wanted out,' Chris looked at him through bloodied eyes.

'Fuck them!' he sneered viciously.

Not taking his attention from Chris. 'They knew that they would have to kill you if they stayed in the business. They had no need to go around killing more people with what they had achieved,' Chan spat at Chris, his spittle making contact with his face, trickling down his face with the blood from his open wounds.

'I pity you Chris...' Chan shook his head at him. 'You are nothing but the shit from my shoes I stepped in earlier tonight.'

'Fuck you too!' Chris wheezed and tensed instantly as the gun struck the left side of his face.

'You wouldn't have got anywhere without this crooked no good uncle of yours,' Chan looked at Anderson, who actually appeared to be enjoying all of this. 'I mean for fucks sake Christopher...' He said the name mockingly. 'This scum set your own father up with those armed robbery charges. You know that your old man carried out those robberies on the information that was supplied to him by this piece of shit that calls himself an uncle of yours. You know that he then went and used that very same information against him when he wanted too. Just so that like always Mr. Fuckin Anderson here looks like some sort of golden fucking boy. You know this... But the fucking idiot that you are ignored it...' Chan paused, staring directly at Chris. 'As you can tell we've been doing a lot of research into both you and your uncle before calling this meeting. Look at me when I address you boy,' Chan suddenly screamed at Chris who then had his face forcibly lifted towards him.

'And now you work for this very same piece of shit that set you father up.' He shook his head pitifully, as Chris dropped his head at his own disgust for what he had done.

Chris knew that Chan's words spoke the truth. Just what the fuck had he gone and got himself involved with... His uncle was everything that Chan was telling him... But he'd wanted the power – The money – The stature – But just what was the price going to be for the want of those things?

Anderson sneered at Chan who eyes bore their darkness into his own. 'So what now old timer?'

Chan, once again clicking his fingers, the same lad that fetched the tapes handed a newspaper to Chan as he merely tossed it onto the table in front of Anderson. He recognised the headline straight away.

'Anderson Stops Manchester's Major Arms Deal From Taking Place.'

'It was a good piece that one,' Anderson smirked confidently at Chan who showed no emotion whatsoever.

'It says that everything was destroyed at the warehouse,' Chan said looking from one to the other.

'That's right,' Anderson nodded. 'Although I'd already witnessed the suspects entering the warehouse... Therefore I knew before hand just who the suspects had been Chan.' He said with such confidence in his own bullshit that Chan thought that daft cunt actually believed it himself.

'Being taken by armed force you mean,' Chan yelled at him. 'They were taken there to be executed before you planted the guns and blew the warehouse sky high with the C4 that you planted. You knew that what little forensics they'd find could be explained as an arms deal that turned sour. You could explain how they must of shot each other involved in the deal before somehow igniting the C4 blowing them all to pieces.'

'Bravo Chan – Bra-fucking-vo,' Anderson smirked through his blood filled mouth, as his nose wouldn't stop bleeding. At the same time he wondered how it was that Chan did seem to know a little more than he should have done... But then, he simply dismissed it as down to the fact that Chan had merely come to his own conclusions.

'You also then took control of the case so as to hide any evidence that you wished to.'

'What's done is done Chan,' Anderson told him shrugging nonchalantly. 'We can't bring back what you've already lost. They are gone Chan... Dead and fucking buried where they deserve to be old man.'

'I know they are,' Chan said coldly.

'Listen why don't we make a deal Chan,' Anderson suddenly announced, he was almost certain that he could win over this situation before him. 'You're not really going to do anything stupid are you Chan? I mean like killing either of us over three people that you was fond of for Christ sake old man. Just think of the fucking consequences you fool?'

'I was there,' Chan dropped the bombshell.

'What?' Anderson's mouth gaped.

'What the fuck you on about old man?' Chris added wincing from an expected blow that never came.

'I was at the warehouse when you shot my three friends.' He clicked his fingers again; the kitchen doors opened and in walked two characters that Anderson recognised immediately... There was no mistaking the larger one.

'I think that you know both Sleeper and Eazy Mr. Anderson,' he smiled knowingly at him. 'You see these lads weren't too happy about what happened that night either.'

'What the fuck are you going to do?' Anderson began panicking as he struggled in his chair as he felt the fear presented before him.

'Who the fuck are you two?' Chris snapped, as he didn't recognise either of them.

'I believe that you also tried to hold onto these as to blackmail my two friends here,' Chan held out his hand without looking back at Sleeper who handed the file to him.

'I believe that you took these pictures.' He tossed the photographs along with their negatives onto the table before them. They were of Sleeper and Eazy taking Scotty from the safe house in Altringham.

The shock on Anderson's face was frightening to observe; it was the look of pure horror that somebody had discovered that one secret you held that you never wanted discovering.

'Where the fuck did you get those from?' he snarled viscously.

'Where do you think Mr. Anderson?' Chan laughed. 'From the floor safe that you keep in that lovely garage of yours in Wilmslow.'

Anderson couldn't believe it; they would have discovered everything that he kept hidden there, including the bulk of his money that he kept stashed there for emergency if anything was to ever go wrong.

'How the fuck did you find it? How the fuck did you know where I lived?' he screamed at Chan.

'It's amazing the information that you can purchase from officers where you work. It seems that not only you take money for services provided,' Chan laughed as they all did.

'Although,' Chan continued. 'You were more than careful with the hiding of the floor safe I must admit. We almost over looked it... Only the cement that you forgot to remove from the garage gave you little hiding place away. Not bad though,' he smiled gleefully at him.

Then looking to Chris he said, 'You remember what I was just telling you Chris? You know, about how your uncle likes to keep hold of certain information.' Chan began to laugh menacingly then abruptly stopped and stared at Chris coldly. 'You'd be amazed at the stuff he had on you in there Chris.'

'You what – You fuckin' what?' he screamed at his uncle, who shook his head.

Eazy passed another file to Chan that he tossed to the table. 'It's all in there Chris,' he laughed out loud. 'Everything that if need be, could send you away for a very, very, very long time... Just like your old man,' he added with a wink.

'You fuckin' bastard Anderson,' he screamed at Anderson who looked back to Chan, ignoring his nephews ranting.

'How much do you want Chan?' he tried. 'I'll leave you be for good.' He looked at everybody. 'All of you,' he stated, but they all merely laughed at him.

As the silence dawned over everybody again the old man smiled. 'My son was also with me,' Chan suddenly announced, as everybody fell silent.

The silences hung heavily in the air – Anderson looked confused. Just what was it with this son business that he kept going on about?

'So,' Anderson sneered at Chan. 'You're alive aren't you? You're lucky we didn't find you that night or we would have killed the two of you also.'

'Oh but you are missing the point Mr. Anderson,' he stared at him then looked to Chris. 'You are both missing the point I am making.'

'Stop talking in fucking riddles old man,' Anderson snapped.

553

'My son, he just finished studying in America to become a lawyer.' Chan smiled at the mere thought of Lee. 'He also a very brave – very courageous individual. Always going out of his way to help others around him,' he shook his head. Chan stared coldly and directly at Anderson with sheer hatred controlling of his eyes. 'I suppose that it was his courage and willing to help others that led to what happened to him.'

Anderson's mind raced as he tried fathoming out just what it was that Chan was telling him. 'Is there a point to all of this?' he sighed, all this was becoming too much for him to take in.

Chan simply nodded to his man stood by Anderson who struck the left side of his face with such force that the chair with which he was held captive toppled. The same man then grabbed the chair back into seating position.

'You killed my son that night,' Chan told him coldly, holding his glare.

'How the fuck did I kill your son Chan?' Anderson's mind was all over the place from the blow he'd just received and also the statement that Chan had just made.

'At the warehouse that night you cock-sucking-mother-fucker,' Chan rage began to build from deep within him.

'You killed my son – and the people who I thought of as my family…' he screamed at Anderson as he produced a silenced 9mm Beretta pistol from the beneath the table.

'This is for my son…' He casually shot Anderson twice through both of his shoulder blades. 'This is for my Lee.'

The gun merely made a slight popping sound through its silenced cylinder that muffled the explosion. Only Anderson's tortured screams were to be heard, as he tried to compose himself again he stared at Chan.

'You're just signed your own death warrant Chan,' he sneered at him through gritted teeth; the pain from the bullet wounds were agonising, as blood oozed from there gaping holes.

Still he couldn't work out what Chan was going on about… His son's body was never found at the warehouse. Only seven accounted bodies were discovered there. What was left of the warehouse or those who inhabited it anyway.

Chan smiled knowingly at Anderson as though reading his thoughts. 'You know something though Mr. Anderson,' he looked to Chris, who face and body was shaking uncontrollably, 'and you too Chris.'

'Two things actually. The first is about a promise that I made a few years ago now,' they all stared at him. 'I made a promise that one day I could return a favour for which a job was achieved for me. One day I would be able to repay that favour and help those people who helped me – It looks as though that day has arrived,' he smiled wickedly at the two of them. 'But listen... Because there's more... Number two... They also say that when someone leaves this world then another will enter it.'

He sighed as Anderson and Chris looked from one another totally bemused by Chan's apparent gibberish then to all of those stood before them, each and every one of them smiling knowingly at them both.

'Now I don't know whether or not I believe that I received something new back into the world when I lost my son that night,' he smiled as he lifted his right hand signalling Sleeper behind him, stood directly by the kitchen door.

'But I did get to keep hold of something that already existed within this world before that night... Would you like to see Mr. Anderson?' he stared at Anderson's confused look, and then turned to Chris whose both scared shitless and confused stare was returned to Chan.

Sleeper pushed the kitchen door open as a large figure casually walked through into the dining room. At that precise moment everybody enjoyed immensely the look of nothing that can be described a less than unbelievable shock that took control of Anderson and Chris's faces.

'This can't be... You're dead,' Anderson blurted out he looked at the figure – It couldn't be true – No it wasn't possible he thought – Not even a scar on his face – This had to be a nightmare that he was having.

'I saw you take the bullet... You're dead... Speak to me... What the fuck's going on?' he cried out, his voice losing control of itself as tears began to roll down his face.
Anderson closed his eyes and shook his head, opening his eyes again – He was still there.

Chris's mouth was moving but no words were fourth coming. His head shaking from left to right more and more rapidly as he tried to shake the smirking image away... Only it wouldn't disappear.

Finally Anderson's mouth gaped open, the name tumbling from it – The name that everybody knew him by.

'Chopper.'

'Thank you Mr. Young. You'll check in at Gate Fourteen,' said the check in hostess at Heathrow Airport who smiled warmly as she passed the tickets back over the counter. 'I hope you enjoy your flight to Hong Kong.'

'It's Lee,' I replied, returning the smile, again warmly then half laughed. 'Mr. Young sounds so formal Samantha,' I added, flirting a little, looking to her name badge, although still doing this more for my benefit, as I was still becoming used to the name.

Her large brown eyes lit up slightly as she flirted back with me. 'In that case. I hope you enjoy both your flight and your stay in Hong Kong Lee. Please if I'm to call you Lee, please call me Sam – Samantha also sounds so formal,' she giggled.

'Thanks a lot Sam,' I smiled warmly. 'I'm sure that I will do.'

'Is it business or pleasure?' she enquired trying to keep the conversation alive; her eyes still had a certain glow to them. 'Lee,' she added a little coyly bowing her head.

'Pure pleasure I hope,' I winked. 'Who knows...? Maybe it's the beginning of something new and unknown,' I grinned, as Sam blushed slightly before turning her attention to the next customer behind me, turning from the check in desk at Heathrow airport I walked away smiling.

I made my way through to the bar area after passing through customs, seeing as there was still plenty of time to spare. Sleeper and Eazy had wanted to see me off, but with the thought of things maybe becoming a little sentimental, I'd said my goodbyes leaving them both at Eazy's in Brixton this morning.

Both Chan and I had said our goodbyes earlier in the week; it was down to Chan that this trip had been made possible. As I sat there all alone I began thinking back to everything that had happened and the reason why it was that I was still here, unknown to almost everybody... Donna included.

It was true in a sense that I had been buried along with Prey and Steve almost a year ago now. Part of my soul had also been buried that day along with the two people that had meant more to me in this world than anything else. As the thoughts returned to the family I'd lost, I was suddenly overwhelmed with their sadness immensely – I missed the two of them so much. They had meant so much to me, I had always considered Steve to be like a father to me, with Prey like the older brother I'd never had.

Then I began thinking of the good times that we had had together over all them years spent together. The really good times and their sadness subsided into happier times.

The funeral had apparently made all the headlines as we were given a huge send off. The police had to close down several roads on the day of the precession. Lads from all over Manchester and Salford had attended the funeral, along with people travelling down from as far as Scotland. Respects had run highly with the three of us, a lot of anger had been felt as to our demise. Everybody, who had known us, had known that this so-called arms deal was nothing but a load of shite.

However – As I sat there sipping my cold beer thinking to myself about the funeral that I'd missed in more ways than one. My mind began to wander as I stared out of the window, thinking back to all the events from that time. Sleeper had shown me the newspaper cuttings and video's he'd taped from the news on television. Apparently, a well-known magazine had contacted the girls and friends to try and put together a piece about us, it was as though we were celebrities. It was crazy thinking about it. We'd been far from anything like that, although well over a thousand people had attended our final send off.

Thus being part of the reason for my departure from the country at the present time. It had been Chan and Lee who'd saved me from the warehouse that night, even though I had believed that I had died from the bullet wound shot by Chris.

Thinking back, I remembered how my life had literally flashed before me, although by the time it had done I was past caring anymore as they'd killed two of the closest people to me, right before my very eyes.

Chan and Lee had arrived at the warehouse itself, and Lee had climbed up the side of the warehouse to the windows along the roof of the building. He'd witnessed first hand the shooting of me, before falling from the warehouse at the sheer sight and shock of the sickened incident.

Both he and Chan were convinced that Lee had to have been heard as he'd crashed to the through the loading crates on the floor. So the two of them had hidden out of sight, observing both Anderson and Chris both leaving the crime scene totally unaware that the two had been waiting outside for them to leave. They'd rushed into the warehouse without a second thought, oblivious to the fact that Anderson had planted the C4, along with the case full of arsenal.

Apparently from what Chan tells me, Lee had felt what he said was the faintest trace of a pulse from my neck, as I lay there apparently stone cold dead to the bare eye. Half of my face had been blown away from the blast of the gun, with the other side hanging open from the gash that ran the length of it.

Chan says that he'd never seen anything as horrific as the scene before him. He could have sworn that we were all dead, if not for Lee checking my pulse I certainly would have been. Carrying my lifeless body back to his car that he'd parked just on the edge of the industrial estate after they'd followed the Bedford transit, when we'd been abducted at gun point outside of the Dog Races in Belle Vue that Saturday night.

They'd obviously not known that Lee's car had been there that evening as they'd only slashed the tyres on Steve's motor. Lee had informed his father that he was going back to the warehouse to check Prey and Steve against Chan's protests.

But Lee had insisted that he return as he might have... Just might have missed one of their pulses. He just had to be certain that he wasn't leaving anyone else alive back there. No matter how close to the verge of death they may have been.

Watching Lee run back into the industrial estate had been the final time he'd seen his son alive.

The explosion had followed shortly after his departure back down the road. Chan had waited and prayed for the return of his son... Only he never did do. Chan knowing that police would be swarming all over the area soon, had somehow, although even to this day not quite sure how he managed it. But he had manoeuvred a car for his first time in his entire life in order to get us to a safe distance before calling for help to retrieve us safely out of Old Trafford for good.

All of this was unknown to me; I still have no recollection of the night's events preceding Chris's gun exploding that is. However – the memory of that is still as clear as day to me, right here and now as I sat alone thinking back to the incident.

Apparently as doctors have explained to me now, was that the bullet that Chris had fired into me had entered two inches below my left temple. It had left a small hole without any exit hole to my right side of my face. The shot was of a low velocity, causing minimal shock waves even from the distance which he had fired the gun, therefore causing minimal tissue damage.

The bullet had penetrated the maxillary sinus, shattering several bones through my facial skeleton. God... If there was such a thing, my beliefs on favourite after that night's events must have been looking down on me for sure that night. There had been no vital structures in the path of the slug that had torn its way through into the side of my face.

The doctor had removed the bullet from my maxillary sinus; it's amazing to think that I'd survived with a bullet lodged into to my face. They'd had to rebuild my face over several months with plastic surgery.

Chan had booked me into his private hospital in Bolton, through his friend as Lee Yung, his son. Although from what I can tell all paperwork relating to my existence there has been destroyed.

Chan had expected that when they sifted through the debris from the warehouse that forensics would discover that it wasn't me in there at all. He'd said that, that bridge he would have crossed when the time was necessary. However it never came to light. Chan suspected that if there had been any indication of it not being myself, then almost certainly Anderson would have covered it up.

Although he also believed that Anderson would have just passed over the information as being me from witnessing the fact he'd been there, although putting it into his own words as he did so.

So with all that in mind we'd started to put together our plan of revenge. It was believed that I was dead. So therefore we'd used this strength against him. Only Sleeper and Eazy had

559

been contacted after the funeral. I began smiling to myself sat there; I can see the looks on their faces when Chan brought them to the hospital. Although still undergoing surgery for my inflictions, they'd known exactly who it had been.

Once we'd explained the whole story to them, they had agreed immediately to help us with avenging our lost ones. We'd agreed to keep everything from everybody else. The only possibility of pulling this off was for everybody to continue to believe that I had died, that was to be indefinitely.

For if the police were to discover that I was still alive, either now or in the future they'd do everything that they could to bring me down.

All the evidence that we had on Anderson would find its way to the police shortly after his disappearance, although that would remain a mystery of its own. He'd become another Lord Lugan or Shergah.

The police could draw their own conclusions, although none would ever be close, as only five of us, including Sleeper's crematorium guy knew the final outcome from that one.

I thought back to the looks on their scared shitless faces as they lay helplessly in the open coffins we'd prepared for them will always stay with me. Only its image will never haunt me, far from it. The image is my only comfort to hold onto after the loss of everything suffered.

I still can see the coffins as Sleeper's friend fed them through into his furnace at the crematorium, their screams deadened from the duct tape although more than visible in their eyes. From their greed's and desires had demised everything that we had built, but in that exact moment at the crematorium we'd taken back a little of what they managed to tarnish.

No remorse should be felt for scum like that. They'd played the game, only it wasn't a game they'd won in the long run.

Chan had made all the necessary arrangements for the paperwork for me, although we'd changed Yung to Young without any hassles. We felt that the name Yung would raise too many suspicions. Therefore I became his lost son, his son whom was it not for; I would not even be here right now. I became the person that I would be eternally indebted to for the rest of my life. We'd avenged Lee, Prey and Steve's deaths the only way we'd known how to do so. By using ar'own kind of street law that we'd lived all of lives under.

The girls had been looked after I thought to myself. Although I missed Donna like crazy, the pain of not being with her hurt me more than I ever thought imaginable. I never knew that somebody was capable of hurting someone as emotionally as she had done... It's like they say, *"you don't know what you've lost, until you've lost it."*

Only it had to be this way – Who knows, maybe one day she could learn the truth – Would she ever believe it or forgive me for my deceptions.

It wasn't fair to her to think like this, for it was I that had created the deception, although not being left too many options as to any other choice to make.

The three of us had left all of our interests in Macreedy's to each of them in the case of anything happening to us. They had now become full partners along with Sleeper and the stores, which were growing each day from strength to strength. The news surrounding our deaths had created news surrounding our stores, trying to show another side to us, as good hard working citizens – and in the process had done the stores no harm with their free publicity provided.

It was safe to say that the girls and little Sean would be all right financially.

And for me... Well that's why this trip was a necessity. I was to leave the country for at least a few years, in doing so, the plan was seeing a little more of the world than Manchester, which had been all I'd never known throughout my life.

Hong Kong was to merely a stop over for a short while as I had visa's allowing me to visit several more countries and that's exactly what the plan to do was.

Chan told me before I left his home that we'd made our peace with those around us. He'd made the necessary arrangements for me to leave the country. I was to visit with several of his friends and relatives on my visit to the Far East.

Travelling into the unknown I thought to myself... Just what did they future hold for me now? Could I make a go of things? Sure that I could – Besides I didn't have to worry about money for a long while.

Everybody had said that it was right that both Prey and Steve would want for me to have their share in the money we had made from the final deal. Although I'd made sure that little Sean was left a bulk of Prey's money with Sleeper who would invest it until he was twenty-one years of age.

Then he'd become a very well off individual indeed. The thought of little Sean growing up without a father was saddening – but he had all of the girls around him. They'd look after him; he would never go without the love that he deserved.

As for me... who knows?

I was suddenly brought out of my thoughts as the call for my flight was announced over the speaker, calling for me to make my way through to Gate Fourteen. Gathering up my hand luggage, I took one last look around smiling to myself as I made my way forward.

The past is and always will be in the past – what can I say lads? Everything grew beyond all of our beliefs and for that I will always be thankful to all the people of Manchester and Salford. For without you guys and the fucked up crazy times spent back then, then this story would never have been told. And for that I will always be grateful to those people.

After all what do I have to look forward to now? It will be discovering what the future holds for me and seeing which path I will choose to follow, and whether or not it is the right or wrong one.

And who knows, maybe... just maybe... one day I'll return to my hometown of Manchester.

www.ingramcontent.com/pod-product-compliance
Lightning Source LLC
Chambersburg PA
CBHW030742030726
47497CB00001B/100

* 9 781907 461675 *